Rave reviews for the *Alien* novels:

"From alternate realities to alternate galaxies, Koch takes us on the wildest adventures. But it is the camaraderie between the characters that keeps the over-the-top tale grounded and compelling."   —*RT Book Reviews* (top pick)

"Koch still pulls the neat trick of quietly weaving in plot threads that go unrecognized until they start tying together—or snapping. This is a hyperspeed-paced addition to a series that shows no signs of slowing down."   —*Publishers Weekly*

"Aliens, danger, and romance make this a fast-paced, wittily written sf romantic comedy."   —*Library Journal*

"Gini Koch's Kitty Katt series is a great example of the lighter side of science fiction. Told with clever wit and non-stop pacing . . . it blends diplomacy, action and sense of humor into a memorable reading experience."   —*Kirkus*

"The action is nonstop, the snark flies fast and furious. . . . Another fantastic addition to an imaginative series!"
—Night Owl Sci-Fi (top pick)

"Ms. Koch has carved a unique niche for herself in the sci-fi-romance category with this series. My only hope is that it lasts for a very long time."   —Fresh Fiction

"This delightful romp has many interesting twists and turns as it glances at racism, politics, and religion en route . . . will have fanciers of cinematic sf parodies referencing *Men in Black*, *Ghost Busters*, and *X-Men*."   —*Booklist* (starred review)

"There's a reason why this series is so popular and it's because there's nothing else out there in the universe like it."
—Under the Covers

D0051391

ALIENS
ABROAD

GINI KOCH

DAW BOOKS, INC.

DONALD A. WOLLHEIM, FOUNDER

375 Hudson Street, New York, NY 10014

ELIZABETH R. WOLLHEIM
SHEILA E. GILBERT
PUBLISHERS

www.dawbooks.com

*To absent friends, gone but never forgotten,
always in my heart.*

ACKNOWLEDGMENTS

Well, this book was the latest I've ever been, as you know if you were waiting for it on its first scheduled release date. Or even its second. My bad. But then again, as Kitty knows and all y'all should by now, Life Happens and it really loves to get in the way of what you had planned.

Among the plans Life insisted upon changing is that, by the time you read this, I will no longer live in the Southwest but will be living in the Southeast. Because, apparently, if you say you never want to move, the cosmos hears you and gets right on the business of forcing you to move. The moral? Never say never.

Therefore, and as always, and possibly even more always than usual, I couldn't have finished this book without the incredible support of Sheila Gilbert, the most amazing and unbelievably patient editor in the world, Cherry Weiner, the most supportive and protective agent out there, Lisa Dovichi, the most dedicated critique partner and best friend there's ever been, and Mary Fiore, still the best and fastest beta reader in the West and the best mum, too.

Continuous love and thanks to Alexis Nixon and the other good folks at Penguin Random House and everyone at DAW Books, especially Josh Starr and Katie Hoffman, for being amazing 24/7. Same again to all my fans around the globe, my Hook Me Up! Gang, members of Team Gini new and old with extra smoothies to Team Research, all Alien Collective Members in Very Good Standing, Members of the Stampeding Herd, Twitter followers, Facebook fans and friends, Pinterest followers, the fabulous bookstores that support me, and all the wonderful fans who come to my various book signings and conference panels—you're all the best and I wouldn't want to do this without each and every one of you along for the ride. (Yeah, I say that every time. Because it's true every time.)

Special love and extra shout-outs to: my distance assistant, Colette Chmiel, my personal assistant, Joseph Gaxiola, and my inventory manager, Kathi Schreiber, for figuring out how to create calm out of my rampant chaos and being my rocks when I need strength and my goofballs when I need laughs—you're all wonderful and keep me going far more than you realize; Edward Pulley for continually allowing me to steal Joseph away all the time with good grace and being willing to talk about whatever pop culture thing strikes me for hours on end; Brad Jensen, for helping at the drop of a hat and acting like I'm the one doing you a favor for it; Museum of Robots and Model Building Secrets for making such awesome licensed products of my works every time I turn around and being awesome people at the same time; Shawn Sumrall, Amy Thacker, Joseph Gaxiola, Colette Chmiel, Jan Robinson, Craig & Stephanie Dyer, Koleta Parsley, Christina Callahan, Lynn Crain, Mariann Asanuma, Edward Pulley, Archie Bays, Anne Taylor, Terry Smith, Carol Kuna, Richard Bolinski, Duncan & Andrea Rittschof, and Chrysta Stuckless for fun, lovely, and delicious gifts that continue to make the long nights and deadline stress totally worth it; Shawn Sumrall and Joshua Tree Feeding Program, for providing amazing prizes for my big Evening Erotica events year after year; everyone who puts in sweat equity with me at cons, especially Joseph Gaxiola, Kathi Schreiber, Brad Jensen, Brendan Reilly, and Duncan and Andrea Rittschof; Jan Robinson and Robert Palsma for liking everything I do; Javier de Leon, Robert Palsma, Michele Sharik and Brianne Pituley, Scott Johnson, Dan & Emily "Amadhia" King, Oliver & Blanca Bernal, Eric and Jennifer Olson, and Brendan Reilly for many things; Chris "Delicious" Swanson for awesome concert experiences that ensure I still get out of the Casa; Adrian & Lisa Payne, Duncan & Andrea Rittschof, Hal & Dee Astell, Richard Clayton, and Dori Lovers for always showing up and making every event all the better for your presence; the Authors of the Stampeding Herd—Lisa Dovichi, Barb Tyler, Lynn Crain, Hal Astell, Terry Smith, Sue Martin, Teresa Cutler-Broyles, Phyllis Hemann, Rhondi Salsitz, Evan Ramspott, and Celina Summers—once again, our competition and your support kept me going, and I remain proud to pound hooves with every one of you (psst, buy their books); author Sharon Skinner for being my road warrior buddy (psst, buy her books); authors Erin Kellison, Erin Quinn, and Caris Roane for keeping me in pancakes, support, and love (psst, buy their books); and last but not least, author James Ray Tuck, Jr. for tremendous help with relocation (psst, buy his books).

Last only because that's where you put the best, thanks to my daughter, Veronica, who helped in many ways, most of them having to do with relocation and keeping me sane about it, and my husband, Steve, who had the champagne on ice for when this book was finally done and who never lost faith that I would finish. I love you both even more than I love the cats. True story.

AH, TRAVEL.

In my younger days, I'd said I wanted to see the world. Good thing, because that's worked out for me. Oh, sure, I saw most of the world while fighting horrible combinations of humans and alien parasites that turned into almost unstoppable and very deadly superbeings but, still, I saw many foreign lands and many more foreign bathrooms.

Then I got to see the extremely foreign land of Washington, D.C. and interact with the strange people who dwelled there—and who were, as it turned out, much more dangerous than superbeings—up close and far more personally than I'd ever expected or dreamed in my worst nightmares.

Along the way I married the hottest man on two legs, who just happened to be an alien from the Alpha Centauri system. Hey, it happens. We started our family, protected them and our world from evils domestic, foreign, and out of this solar system, and moved up in the ranks, usually against our mutual will.

After that, it started to get weird. Not normal weird. What my husband Jeff's cousin, Christopher White, calls Kitty Weird. I got to change universes with another version of me and she and I got to save each other's respective worlds and families.

After I got "home," I and a bunch of our friends and family were dragged to another planet in another solar system and got to stop a solar civil war, which was fun if you define fun to be "not sure we'll ever see each other or Earth again" and similar.

Then the galaxy decided to come calling and suddenly Earth was the new galactic hot spot, where all the cool, "in" aliens want to go to have at least a short vacay, if not to move in permanently. And, somehow, this appears to kind of be my fault.

And along this particular way, somehow Jeff became the President of the United States. He's great at it, because he's a born leader and, since he's the strongest empath in, most likely, the galaxy, he really and truly cares about everyone. Sometimes that almost kills him, but I've gotten really good at stabbing him in his two hearts with a giant needle full of adrenaline to keep him going. Hey, I'm totally a good wife that way.

On the plus side, these various and sundry alien visits have forced the majority of humanity to embrace their inner Woody Guthrie. On the not so plus side, the small, violent minority of humanity has chosen to embrace their inner Kanye West. So, we're working on that, but it's a process. A slow, painful, dangerous process. But we do persevere.

Meanwhile, in the past year and a quarter I've actually gotten to focus on only being a wife, mother, First Lady of the United States, Queen Regent of Earth for the Annocusal Royal Empire, and Galactic Delegate representing Earth in the Galactic Council. Sometimes I even get to sleep, too.

But Jeff, our kids, and our extended family and friends make it all worthwhile, and I'm feeling like we're pretty much getting the hang of everything and might, someday soon, even get to take a little vacation. Though knowing my luck, it'll be a working vacation we aren't prepared for, going somewhere we're not wild about going, filled with death, danger, and warfare. You know, somewhere like Detroit.

That's right. These are my continuing missions. To be forced to explore strange, new worlds. To meet new civilizations, usually in the middle of some kind of battle. To accidently and sarcastically go where no one has willingly gone before.

In other words, I'm going to go find Major Tom and hope that David Bowie's "Space Oddity" will somehow work as a star map.

CHAPTER 1

"HELP ME."

"Huh?" I'd been having a really great dream, where my husband and I were in Cabo San Lucas without our kids, our family or friends, anyone political, any press, any aliens from any planet, or any paparazzi. We were having sex on the beach, and it was great, and no one was bothering us. At least until someone asked for help.

"Help me. I'm an alien and need your assistance."

Well, that left a wide-open field. My husband was an alien—an A-C from Alpha Four in the Alpha Centauri system. His entire huge extended family had been exiled to Earth before Jeff was born and they'd been here for decades. All of them were American citizens, though A-Cs were all over the world. But the voice didn't sound like any of them.

Recent events had brought more aliens to Earth, though. We had representatives from every inhabited world in the Alpha Centauri system—and there were a lot of those—here, as well as residents from other solar systems both nearby, galactically speaking, and as far away as the Galactic Core.

They, too, were scattered all over Earth and the Solaris system—alien relocation for immigrating aliens having been going smoothly, as had terraforming of some of the planets and various-races-forming of the others—because we had all those extra planets and moons we weren't using and most of these aliens were refugees from some really horrible galactic wars. So Earth was no longer a lonely inhabited planet of one with a single race of aliens living on it in secret, but part of a bustling, expanding planetary system with many different types of aliens hanging out. And more coming by to visit or apply to move in every day. Though not, normally, via my dreams. And the voice didn't sound like any of them, either.

That all of this New Age of Intergalactic Harmony stuff had happened in the less than year and a half since Operation Fundraiser had ended in a truly dramatic Zamboni drag race, so to speak, had much more to do with the fact that all the aliens from various solar systems were helping out than that Earth had suddenly leapt into the far *Star Trek* future on our own. We were still number one with a bullet when it came to being nasty and warlike, but we were definitely reaping the benefits of having made some swell new friends. I just wasn't in the dream mood to make another new one.

"I really can't help you. We have an office of Intergalactic Immigration you might want to apply to. I'm sure they'll be as excited to talk to you in their dreams as I am."

"No. I'm an alien to you but like you."

Nice, but the speaker wasn't saying anything exciting because I'd discovered that people—be they the best-looking humanoids around who happened to have two hearts, superstrength, and hyperspeed, be they giant humanoid slugs or honeybees, be they ethereal cloudlike manta rays or gigantic Cthulhu Monsters from Space, or be they anything and everything in between— were basically people, no matter where they were from, what they looked like, what planet they called home, or who or what they considered God.

"I doubt it. And I don't care." My dream was getting hazy. Did my best to concentrate on Jeff and the beach and the sex.

"Help me. You're my only hope." The voice sounded female, maybe, and alien, most likely. Most humans couldn't get that kind of reverberation going without the use of electronic equipment. And, just like the voice, the reverberation wasn't familiar, so, again, not an alien race I'd already met, at least, unlikely. My dreams, they were really the best.

"Um, I wasn't really trying to add Princess Leia or Obi-Wan Kenobi to this dream. If that's okay and all that. Especially not Old Obi-Wan. Young Obi-Wan, yeah, maybe."

I could, quite frankly, find it in my libido to add Ewan McGregor into many things. Then again, Jeff was the strongest empath in, most likely, the galaxy—because A-Cs also had a variety of psychic talents that showed up pretty often—and he was also easily the most jealous man in it, too, under the right circumstances. Me fantasizing about Ewan McGregor was likely to spark some jealousy, especially since I'd seen *The Pillow Book*. Twice. And the second time was not for the story.

Not that Jeff had anything to worry about. He was the classic—tall, with dark brown wavy hair, dreamy light brown eyes, built like a brick house, and definitely the handsomest man in the universe. And that wasn't me being biased. Well, maybe biased, but only a little. The A-Cs were, to human eyes, the most beautiful things around. They came in all shapes, sizes, colors, and builds, just like humans did, as long as you included "hard-body" in their definition.

Humans had lucked out, though. In addition to the fact that A-Cs and humans could and did create healthy hybrid offspring—with the external favoring the human parent and the internal favoring the A-C—the A-Cs thought humans were great. Well, most of them thought that.

The female A-Cs, whom I called the Dazzlers, at least to myself, were sapiosexual, didn't care what someone looked like, and they felt that humans had more brains and brain capacity than their own people did. I didn't necessarily agree with this theory, though I got where it came from—I'd never met a dumb Dazzler because even those considered idiots by their peers were genius-level for humans, but I had hit a couple of not-so-bright male A-Cs, though they were few and far between.

The male A-Cs just liked people who made them feel smarter than the female A-Cs did, meaning humans were really scoring the excellent mating opportunities. And I wasn't going to argue with the situation either, since, by now, we had a lot of really happy humans married to equally happy A-Cs, and I was all for couples' harmony. Particularly my own.

"I need the greatest warrior in the galaxy." Despite my focus on Jeff's hotness, the beach was starting to fade away. Did my best to hold onto the dream and, if not the dream, at least Jeff's naked body.

"And you're talking to me why?"

"Because your reputation precedes you."

Things had been relatively quiet on the Political Crap front, even quieter on the Evil Megalomaniac front, and the Marauding Aliens front had been blissfully silent. Apparently this last one was silent no longer, though.

Visions of Jeff's naked body washed fully away. I was now officially bitter. "Super. As dreams go, this one stinks. Just sayin'."

"My mind has traveled through the DreamScape in order to find you."

"Whee. I think you got lost somewhere along the way."

Really wondered if I'd eaten something that was causing this kind of bizarreness. But we hadn't had a state dinner, I hadn't snuck in a huge amount of junk food, and the White House chef wasn't prone to making anything bad. Chef was far healthier in what he prepared than I'd ever been. And I'd only had two of his chocolate mousses for dessert, so it couldn't be that.

"No, I've worked my way through the DreamScape to find you. I need your help."

This dream wasn't going away. Tried to wake up. Failed. "So you said. And I ask again—why me? And what the heck is the DreamScape, anyway? That sounds like an old Dennis Quaid movie." I could find it in my libido to add in Dennis Quaid too. Dennis Quaid, Ewan McGregor, and Jeff would be a combination I could enjoy for a really long time. In another dream. One not being constantly interrupted by an alien I didn't know and didn't want to know. Had to wonder if other people had dreams like this. Probably not. I was "lucky" this way.

"Why you is because you always manage to win. The Dream-Scape is the realm that connects us all. And I have no idea who Dennis Quaid is or what a movie is, either."

"Uh huh, right, pull the other one. It has uninterested bells on and all that jazz."

"The fate of my world depends upon you."

"Doubt it. Sincerely doubt it. I officially want to tell myself that this kind of dream is not on my particular Netflix queue and I don't want anything similar to it suggested, either."

"I don't understand you."

"So few ever do. Look, good luck with whatever you've got going on wherever in my subconscious you happen to be. But I'm not your girl."

"I'm not in your subconscious."

"But that's what my wily subconscious would say, now, wouldn't it?"

"I don't know." The voice sounded desperate. "My name is Ixtha. Please help me."

"Well, that's different. What's my name, then?" I mean, my subconscious certainly knew my name.

"I only know you as the Warrior Queen."

"Right. Not as the First Lady of the United States, not as the

Queen Regent of Earth for the Annocusal Royal Family of Alpha Four, and not as Earth's Galactic Representative to the Galactic Council. But as the Warrior Queen. Gotcha. I think you were looking for Queen Renata of the Free Women of Beta Twelve, but you do you and all that."

"I have no idea who those people are or what those titles mean." Ixtha sounded serious. Which was odd, because my subconscious certainly knew all the various and current roles I was stuck doing whether I liked them or not.

Figured I'd try one last title. "What about Shealla? Do you know her?" That was my God Name on Beta Eight.

"Yes! Shealla is the Warrior Queen. You are Shealla?"

"If you already knew, why'd you ask?"

"I don't . . . what? What do you mean? I don't understand you."

"I thought you said you didn't know my name." Well, my Beta Eight name, but still it was a name I answered to. Though Shealla was supposed to be the Queen of the Gods and the Giver of Names, not the Warrior Queen. "Then again, my wily subconscious also knows that name."

"I am not in your subconscious! I am in your dream, via the DreamScape. I have searched for you for so long, Shealla. I need your help, my people need your help. You who have saved so many, why will you not hear my plea?"

"Because I think you're a figment of my vivid and overworked imagination. Though Ixtha is a cool name I haven't heard before, so go team in terms of my creativity."

"I am real, Shealla. As real as you are."

"Yeah? Figure out what my real name is, and then visit me again. Or don't. Really, you disturbed a great dream and I'm still bitter about it."

"The longer we speak the better my connection is to you, and I can search your mind for clues. Please give me that time, Shealla. I will do as you ask, discover your true name, and then you will help me and my people, yes?"

"Sure, I guess. Why not, right?" Was going to add a really witty and sarcastic comment, but the sounds of the Red Hot Chili Peppers' "Universally Speaking" came on and thankfully dragged me into consciousness and away from the "DreamScape."

The little joys of greeting the dawn, especially after this Dream O' Weirdness, were without number.

CHAPTER 2

NORMALLY I HATED DRAGGING up as early as we now had to since Jeff had become the President, but never had I been so happy to wake up. Let the music play and rolled over to see if Jeff was still in bed.

He was not and I was displeased. Chose to blame my weird dream and got up. Checked for him in the bathroom. Not there. Trotted back and checked Mr. Clock in case I'd somehow slept through hours' worth of musical alarm. I had not.

Went to the living room. Nada. Was about to just give up and take a shower when the main door of our Presidential Suite opened and Jeff came in with a big breakfast tray. He grinned at my expression. "I didn't mean to worry you, Kitty. I just thought it would be nice to have breakfast in bed today."

Ran through the potential reasons. Jeff was far more romantic than I was, and there might be something important I was missing. All our family birthdays were past—mine was the last one for several months, and it had been yesterday, and we'd celebrated by going to Paris as a family. Couldn't come up with anything else.

"Um, great!"

Jeff laughed. "I'm giving the State of the Union address today while we christen the *Distant Voyager,* and I just want to be alone with my wife before I have to do that."

"Oh! Right you are." Felt bad. Jeff was in the middle of his accidental term as President and he took the job seriously. He'd been working with his team for weeks on his speech, meaning I should have remembered. Then again, turning thirty-five had felt very milestone-ish for me and Paris was awesome, and generally forgetting stuff like this was very par for my course.

"Not a problem, baby, and don't feel bad. Just eat with me and be my wife."

"That I can do!"

We snuggled back into bed and had a lovely breakfast of eggs scrambled with lox, croissants, excellent coffee with cream, and fresh fruit. We talked about Paris and how great it had been to be there. We weren't jet-lagged because we'd used gates—A-C technology that looked like airport metal detectors but were capable of moving you across the street or across the world in one step. They could move you to other planets, too, but we didn't use them for that a lot and, now, we might not have to use them for that ever again.

"I'm glad we were able to celebrate your birthday before the address," Jeff said as we finished up.

"Me too. And I'm sorry I forgot. Earth's first manned long-distance spaceship with true warp capability is a huge deal. I'm so glad it's happened during your Presidency."

Jeff smiled. "Me, too, baby. It's one of the few truly good things that's happened that didn't have something horrible attached to it."

"Well, I think that most of the aliens now living in our solar system would disagree with you, but I know what you mean."

Considered telling Jeff about my weird dream, but didn't want to spoil his mood or slip up and mention my fantasizing about Ewan and Dennis. Besides, he'd just tell me that two chocolate mousses were too many and since I knew he was wrong and I was going to eat two, minimum, any time Chef made his mousse, what was the point of fighting?

We showered together, which was one of my favorite things to do, ever, because we had great sexytimes in the shower and today was no exception. Once climaxed to the max, we got dried off, clothed, and ready.

Well, Jeff got clothed. In, literally, what he wore every day. A-Cs were, at all their cores, conformists, particularly when it came to their attire. Which was basically black and white with as few other colors as possible, "none" being considered best. The men wore black suits, white shirts, black ties, and black dress shoes, while the women wore black slim skirts, white oxfords, and black pumps, day in and day out. All Armani. The A-Cs loved Armani as much as they loved black and white. Possibly more. It was hard to be sure.

As President, Jeff could have worn other colors and

designers. But—other than the concession of a colorful tie worn
as infrequently as possible and only under extreme duress—he
did not. No matter what, no matter where, and no matter how
much I begged, he did not. None of them did, other than a handful of Attire Rebels whose idea of going out on a fashion limb
was to wear jeans and tennis shoes only if facing death. Most of
the A-Cs preferred to face death in Armani, presumably so
they'd head to the afterlife well-dressed.

And no one complained about this, other than me.

I, however, was the Leader of the Attire Rebels. Or I had
been. Before I'd become the First Lady. Jeff's side of the Presidential Closet was filled with the Armani Fatigues—mine had
color. And jeans. And band t-shirts. And Converse. Sure, I had
my own Armani Fatigues, but I didn't wear them all the time.

Well, honestly, these days, I pretty much didn't get to wear
them at all. Because I was the FLOTUS and that meant that I had
to have a "color" assigned as mine because D.C. was a freak
town of the highest order. My color had been decreed iced blue.
And, therefore, a huge portion of my closet was now iced blue.
It was a pretty color but, as with black and white, the repetition
of it got me down. In fact, I was at the point where getting to
wear black and white was thrilling, a real "mix it up and keep
the town guessing" kind of change. That my sartorial life had
been reduced to this definitely made me bitter.

Despite this or, rather, because of it, I didn't get to get
clothed. However, I was definitely the one stuck getting ready.
Jeff needed zero assistance to look amazing. I was not so fortunate. And, sadly, these days, if it was a big event—and this
was—my getting ready took a really long time.

I sent a text to my Prep Team, put on my underwear—which
I was shockingly allowed to do all by myself—covered up with
my nice Presidential Robe, and went across the hallway with
Jeff to check in on our children—Jamie, who had just turned six,
Charlie, who was just over two, and our ward, Lizzie, who was
now sixteen. They were all up and breakfasting in the family
dining room on this floor of the White House Residence and,
like me, they were all in their own White House robes.

When Jamie was born, everyone had said she looked just like
me, in part because when A-Cs and humans mated the A-C genetics dominated the internal but the human genes were domi-
nant for external. And the older she got, the more Jamie looked
like me. As many put it, she was kind of my little clone.

Technically, Charlie should have looked just like me, too. Only he didn't, at least not in the way Jamie did. By now he was looking more and more like Jeff. Not that this was a bad thing, but it did make me wonder. No one else seemed concerned about it, but my kids were already different, and being even more different could be good or could be dangerous.

Hybrid children were special, and mine were no exception. In fact, mine were exceptionally exceptional. Charlie was telekinetic, which was a real parenting challenge we rarely felt up to. Jamie was empathic, like her father, but there was more going on with her. She'd moved herself thousands of miles to get to me and Jeff and then stopped a spaceship from falling on us during Operation Destruction, and she'd done it with, as far as we could tell, her mind, which sort of indicated telekinetic abilities.

But, unlike Charlie, she didn't spend her time lifting heavier and heavier things, and we weren't sure that she could be classified as telekinetic. No, as near as we could tell, Jamie spent her time communing with the other hybrid children, and some who weren't hybrids, via telepathy.

And, of course, there was also ACE. ACE was a superconsciousness I'd originally channeled into Paul Gower, who was a dream reader—which was a rare A-C talent—and who was also, at that time, the A-Cs Head of Recruitment. Gower was Jeff's cousin, though not as close a cousin as Christopher White. But these days, Gower was something else—the A-C's Supreme Pontifex, aka their top man religiously.

In the good old days, ACE being inside Gower had been great. We could chat with ACE pretty much any time we needed to and, while he couldn't or wouldn't always come right out and tell us specifically what was going on, he was great with giving the helpful hints.

Due to things that went on during Operations Sherlock and Infiltration, ACE had been taken away from us. And while Operation Infiltration had been filled with a lot of losses and heartbreak for us, ACE had been returned to us due to sacrifices made by Naomi Gower-Reynolds. But in order to stay, ACE had had to make a deal, and that deal was that he was no longer inside Gower's head. Instead, the head he'd gone into was Jamie's, at the time the person with the least power on the planet, at least in terms of influence in the world.

It meant my little girl was the safest person in the solar

system, if not the entire galaxy, in many ways, but it also meant that we couldn't talk to ACE easily—because none of us were going to discuss scary, grownup things with a little child. So these days I only got to talk to ACE if Jamie was napping—a rarity at six—or if she and I were both asleep. My dreams were super funky when I was able to dream-chat with ACE, but then again, as this morning's dream had proven in full-on Technicolor, my dreams were weird regardless.

All this might make someone think that Lizzie was just ordinary, since her parents had been humans. But that someone would be totally wrong. Lizzie was exceptional not because of her innate abilities but because of what she'd done already in her young life.

Lizzie's parents had been Russian spies who were also working with the leaders of Club Fifty-One to create something that could eradicate aliens—and a lot of humans, too. She'd stood up to them, had faced the very real possibility that they'd kill her, because she knew what they wanted to do was wrong on a massive scale. She'd been saved by the man who was now her adoptive father, Benjamin Siler.

Siler wasn't here, but the kids weren't alone. They were with our live-in nanny, Nadine Alexis, her middle sister, Francine, who had the job of being my far-hotter FLOTUS double, and their youngest sister, Colette, who was my press secretary. All three sisters were A-Cs and lived in the White House with us, and they liked to breakfast together with the kids whenever they could.

Francine, as my double, wore the same clothes as me. Unlike me, Francine could be trusted to dress, prep, *and* eat and drink without spilling on her Fake FLOTUS Outfit or mussing her Fake FLOTUS Hair and Makeup. And yet, Jeff preferred me and found it unsettling to even tell Francine she looked nice. Apparently he didn't mind my penchant for dropping food onto my chest.

All this meant, therefore, I got to see what I'd be wearing today.

Shocking me to my core, I wasn't going to be in "my" color today. Would have asked what was wrong with the cosmos, but I wasn't that stupid. Turned out I would be representing in A-C colors. A black, long-sleeved sheath dress that hit right above my knees, a white Bolero jacket with black buttons and piping, black hose, and black pumps. Oh, and pearls because of course pearls. Prayed I'd be in fakes—the necklace, earrings, ring, and bracelet Francine was wearing looked very real.

Chose not to mention that I'd run the hose in a matter of minutes, if not seconds. If Francine was already in nylons, I'd be in nylons or die trying to get out of wearing them. So far, I'd lost those battles every time.

"Mommy, do we get to watch you get ready?" Jamie asked, sounding excited, while she stuffed pancakes and scrambled eggs into her mouth.

"Um, I guess so. If you want. And remember, sweetie—don't talk with your mouth full."

"We do!" She said after she swallowed. Then she looked at Lizzie. "Don't we?" Lizzie nodded.

"I have no idea why," I said. Honestly.

"Oh, totes for sure we do, Kitty," Lizzie said cheerfully. "I like watching Pierre do your makeup—it gives me a lot of tips. And Akiko telling me why she has you in what is really educational. You never know, I might want to go into fashion."

Managed to refrain from saying that Lizzie was as likely to go into fashion as I'd been. I'd always had an interest, but my talents truly ran to mind-melding with every crazed lunatic with a Take Over The World Today Plan rather than matching fabrics and colors and, frankly, Lizzie was definitely cut from the same cloth.

"I like to watch Uncle Pierre make you even more ravishing," Jamie said, providing us with an exact Pierre Quote. Somehow it didn't seem wrong coming from the American Centaurion Embassy's Concierge Majordomo and the Confirmed Most Competent Man in the World, but it sounded awful coming out of the mouth of my little girl.

Had to fight the impulse to demand that I never wear makeup again. Somehow I was teaching the kids that primping was a vital part of being a woman, and that went against most of how I'd lived my life.

"Mommy looks pretty right now," Charlie said truculently, winning my Mommy's Best Child of the Hour Award.

"Right you are, son," Jeff said as he sat down between Jamie and Lizzie and pulled Charlie onto his lap. I kissed the tops of each kid's head, including Lizzie's, went to the fridge, and got a Coke. Because it was already somehow a long day and it was going to be even longer and Coke was good at keeping me going.

"She does," Lizzie agreed. "But she's going to be filmed, and makeup helps make you look good on camera. And on stage."

"I dread to ask who you heard say that."

Lizzie grinned at me. "It's a long list. You want it now?"

"Absolutely not." Took a long drink of my Coke. "Just tell me that no one's putting makeup on the three of you."

"Nope," Lizzie replied. "Pierre says that we're perfect as is."

"Thank God."

"We won't be as filmed as you," Lizzie went on. "That's why. If Pierre thinks we might be, then I'll get some makeup, too."

"I'm betting your father would be as thrilled with that as I am."

Lizzie shrugged and looked behind me. "Why don't you ask him?"

Turned. There was no one there.

CHAPTER 3

SILER APPEARED RIGHT next to me and I jumped. "Gah!"

"Nice to see you, too." He grinned. "I love that I still manage to get you at least half of the time."

"You're hilarious. Why were you blending right now?"

He laughed. "Because I'm practicing."

"My dad can hold a blend for almost an hour now," Lizzie said proudly.

Lizzie lived with us because Siler was not only likely the first hybrid on Earth, but he was also a highly trained assassin. Due to losses we'd sustained during Operation Epidemic, the other assassins he, and I, had been tight with were gone, and it had made more sense for him and Lizzie to stay with us. Siler was the current American Centaurion Defense Attaché, but he was still very willing to do the dirty work that clandestine and covert ops seemed to demand all the time and, because of that, Lizzie was with us to have a more stable home life, so to speak.

Siler didn't age normally—he looked like he was in his late thirties or early forties, but he was much older. He also had the rare ability to blend, what I called going chameleon. This was a trait from Alpha Four, where our Earth A-Cs were all descended from—we had native Alpha Four animals with us who could do the same thing. But since Siler wasn't a Peregrine, aka an Alpha Four Attack Peacock on Steroids, him being able to blend was amazing. Then again, I had Dr. Doolittle skills. Amazing seemed to be what we all did before breakfast. Or, in this case, during breakfast, since he was holding a plate laden with food—I hadn't seen it floating in the air because he could extend his blend via touch.

Siler was, like most of the people working with us, attractive. He'd had a human mother, though, and she hadn't been gorgeous, so he was normally good-looking. It was a nice perk of my life that I got to consider people I'd normally think of as totally hot merely as plenty good enough. The visuals did tend to make up for things like being primped within an inch of my life and my friends appearing out of nowhere just to see how high they could get me to jump.

Siler sat back down at the place he'd clearly been before, now that I was paying attention to obvious things like silverware and a glass of orange juice at an empty seat at the table. That was me, The Queen of Observation. Hey, I was really good at spotting bad guys, so I had that going for me.

Sat down in the empty chair that didn't appear to have someone invisible sitting in it. "Does anyone know if we're gating or driving over?"

"The First Family is driving," Siler said. "With your usual security entourage. The rest of us will be there before you, whether by gate or hyperspeed."

Colette's phone beeped. "Raj is ready for you, Jeff, if you're ready for him."

"Meaning he wanted me there five minutes ago. Got it." He sighed, kissed all the kids, put Charlie in my lap, kissed me, then headed out for his briefing with his Chief of Staff, Rajnish Singh, who was an A-C troubadour. Raj didn't prep me for appearances under normal circumstances—that was a job for others who'd drawn the short straws.

"I'll go with you," Siler said as he chucked Charlie under his chin, did the same with Jamie, kissed Lizzie on the top of her head, then went after Jeff, who held the door for him.

No sooner were they gone than Colette's phone beeped again. "You left your phone in your rooms?" she asked me, sounding shocked.

"It happens."

"Rarely," Francine and Nadine said in unison.

Shrugged. "Didn't figure I'd need it to walk all the way across the hall. I see I was wrong."

Colette laughed. "Well, Pierre, Akiko, and Vance are ready for you. And they'd like you to get to the prep area as fast as possible."

Managed not to heave a sigh. I'd told them to get over here, after all. "It's down the hall. I'm sure I can make it there without having to sprint. Nadine, can you be sure the kids are dressed and ready before they come in to watch me?"

"Absolutely." She winked at me. "We'll use hyperspeed."

"Go team."

"I'm with you," Colette said as I got up. Speaking of one of the people assigned to my intelligence preparations team. Vance Beaumont, as my Chief of Staff, was the other person who scored this fun job, with an assist from Pierre and, usually, whoever else had come by to hang out and share their thoughts. Basically, Vance and Pierre did double duty but anyone else nearby was always ready to help them with the heavy lifting of getting me ready to try to be the best little FLOTUS in the business.

"Where are you going?" I asked Francine, who also stood.

"I'm shadowing you, just in case." She grinned. "Don't worry—no one will see me and Craig unless we need to be seen."

"Of that I have no doubt." Humans couldn't see beings moving at hyperspeed, and a lot of the aliens that had sort of moved in couldn't, either. "And I'm not worried if you guys have to pretend to be us, either. You're good at it."

Craig Rossi was the A-C whose job was to be Jeff's double. Unlike Francine, he wasn't hotter than the person he was pretending to be, but Craig didn't get nearly as much work as my Secret Service detail told me other President's doubles had and, so far, no one had noted when it was Craig and/or Francine versus me and Jeff.

That they were doubling us so well wasn't just due to the fact that Francine and Craig resembled me and Jeff. A-Cs were, in general, terrible liars. There were a few who were naturally gifted at it, and those few were assigned into espionage at a young age. But the majority of regular A-Cs, even ones with empathic, imageering, dream reading, or other talents, couldn't lie believably at all, meaning that our doubles couldn't have faked it well enough under normal circumstances. However, there were others who could lie in their own way, and we called them troubadours.

Troubadours affected people by modulating their voices, expressions, body language, and so forth. Meaning they were great actors and politicians, and both professions had been looked down upon by the residents of Alpha Four. Actors and politicians basically lied for a living, meaning that we had a lot of naturally gifted liars around, and most of the world didn't realize it. Heck, most of the A-Cs didn't realize it, either. And troubadours had been the A-C version of second-class talented citizens for a long time.

Sort of like we were in *Charlie's Angels*, I'd found Raj and
then he'd found others, and I'd started giving them jobs to do,
like impersonating people, handling our press and PR, and similar. Craig and the three Alexis sisters, for example, were all
troubadours—Nadine doubled the current Head of Imageering,
Serene Dwyer, when necessary—and we had other troubadours
placed throughout the world now, to ensure that we could keep
things smooth when they needed to be.

But I wasn't the only one who'd felt that the troubadours
were being unfairly pushed aside and that they could do so much
more for their people and their country and, now, their planet, if
they were merely organized and focused. Serene was a closet
troubadour, and she'd coordinated the troubadours into the A-C
version of the CIA. Francine and Craig didn't just double or
shadow me and Jeff, therefore—they were also around to help
protect us.

I'd much rather have been doing a briefing with Serene and
her team of Stealth Troubadours than what I was headed for, and
Francine and Colette probably felt the same way. But instead we
headed for the Cosmetology Room, where I got turned into the
FLOTUS O' Wonder. I comforted myself in the fact that, clearly,
others before me had had to be gussied up for events, since there
was a nice room assigned to this task that had existed before
we'd arrived.

Vance had installed a TV in this room within the first week
of his being my Chief of Staff, and Pierre already had it turned
on. Seeing as it was early morning, we were watching *Good Day
USA!* which had somehow become "our" morning show. Of
course, if *Good Day USA!* was on, I was up far too early, but that
was par for the course on big days like this.

Operation Fundraiser had started during my horrifically ill-
conceived appearance on this show last year, and due to everything that had happened, the hosts had become part of our
extended team.

Adam Johnson was a retired baseball player who could have
passed as a relative of Gower's—he was big, black, bald, handsome, and charismatic. He was a great guy and was, happily,
fully human.

His cohost was a very pretty, perky Latina, Kristie Rodri-
guez, who was no longer fully human. No, Kristie was a cyborg,
which was the current "in" robotics thing to have done for those
with enough money, connections, and insanity.

Because this was how my life worked, both of them had had roles in *Code Name: First Lady*, the movie that Hollywood Quadruple Threat Jürgen Cologne had gotten made despite my better judgment and wishes. However, due to what had happened during my appearance on *Good Day USA!*, it had been a lot better to let Cologne do the movie than to lose his support. So, somehow, the "movie of my life" was going to be a summer tentpole coming out Memorial Day weekend. I wasn't quite ready to start the Countdown To Doom, but I wasn't going to be waiting too long to begin. I didn't know whether to hope it bombed or succeeded, either.

Thankfully, it was January and that meant *Code Name: First Lady* was done filming and was in the editing and special effects stages, meaning I still had time to pretend I was normal and Adam and Kristie were back in the studio. Well, sort of. Reality said normal wasn't anything near to what I was, and they were actually live at the scene, interviewing important people who were there for Jeff's address.

So, while Akiko got me into my outfit so that Francine and I looked like we were still dressing like twins at far too advanced an age, we watched Adam and the Kristie-Bot chatting up Neil deGrasse Tyson about the historic event we were prepping for.

The perky enthusiasm on the screen was overpowering. I searched the audience for Dazzlers in Attendance—while I'd had to put a moratorium on the Dazzlers approaching Stephen Hawking because I didn't want them to kill him with love, I hadn't done so for anyone else, and Tyson tended to have a group of fangirl Dazzlers nearby at all times. His wife was also totally brainy and she had her own set of Dazzler fangirls, too. Basically, the Tysons were considered the Dazzler Celebrity Dream Couple.

Even though Tyson was in the middle of negotiations with the Galactic Council, he and those representatives who were visiting Earth were taking a break to hang out at Andrews Air Force Base, where the launch, and therefore Jeff's address, were to take place.

I might have been Earth's official Council representative but, despite most of my press, I wasn't an idiot, and I'd tagged a number of influential people to help me, Tyson being only one of them. I'd actually gotten a lot of positive reactions to my ability to delegate. I was just glad that I wasn't having to pretend to understand tremendously advanced physics on a daily basis.

I was good at tossing in the word "quantum" when needed, but otherwise I was far better with figuring out how to circumvent Crazed Evil Genius plans than determining what part of our solar system any particular set of new aliens should move into.

Because this was how my world worked, we weren't getting to actually hang out with one of the smartest guys in the world at the event—Tyson was in the Visiting Dignitaries Area, meaning he got good seats but no Presidential Face Time—but we were going to have the Kristie-Bot and Adam with us, literally, from the moment we arrived at Andrews. They and a few other press we liked were going to be basically shadowing Jeff the entire time. Of course, while they were press, they were also press we could trust, so that was one for the win column. And my personal smartest guy in the room—Charles Reynolds, my best guy friend since ninth grade and the current Director of the CIA—would be shadowing us, too, so it was better to have Tyson elsewhere, doing his brainy thing for the good of the Greater Cosmos.

Time for makeup and hair, while Vance and Colette talked at me. I was grateful when I had to close my eyes for eye shadow and such, because it meant I could better pretend I was taking all their information in instead of trying to hear what they were saying on *Good Day USA!* What they were saying was basically "wasn't this just the coolest thing ever," which, while nice, wasn't exactly newsworthy.

The kids joined us during the second half of my eyes prep. "Mommy, can we go on a trip on the new spaceship?" Jamie asked.

"I don't think that's a good idea, sweetie. Uncle Brian will be taking that trip first." Brian Dwyer was my old boyfriend from high school who was now an astronaut and married to Serene. He'd been the no-brainer choice for one of the *Distant Voyager's* crew for a variety of reasons, many of which had happened during Operation Drug Addict.

"Going on vacation would be fun," Lizzie said. "I used to do that a lot when . . ." Her voice trailed off and I opened my eyes, liner going on or no liner going on. Lizzie looked like she wished she'd kept her mouth shut and was about one syllable away from bursting into tears.

"Family vacations are a normal thing," I said gently. "Even in abnormal families like ours."

Lizzie relaxed and managed a little smile. "True enough."

Pierre gently shoved me back into makeup position and I closed my eyes again. "So, let's plan where we'll go when Daddy has some free time he can fit in."

"Not Camp David," Lizzie said firmly.

Considering we'd had a triple attack the first time we'd set foot there, I was in wholehearted agreement. Operation Madhouse might have been a couple of years ago, but it was still very fresh in my mind. We hadn't willingly gone back to Camp David since. Of course, Jeff hadn't taken a day off, either. An actual vacation might be a really good idea.

Felt something in the air in front of me and opened my eyes again, ignoring the sighs heaved by Pierre, Vance, and Akiko. A Mickey Mouse figurine floated in front of my face. "Yes, Charlie, I agree that going to Disneyland would be a great choice." I loved all things Disney, and if I could swing it, a week at DLand would be the best family vacation ever. Maybe we'd do Disneyland, Disneyworld, the Big Red Boat, and hit Paris and Tokyo DLands, too.

Other animals, stuffed and figurines both, started floating around the room. "Charlie, sweetheart, please put your toys back where they belong. Mommy has gotten the hint and I'll do my best to get us to the Happiest Place on Earth as soon as we can."

The toys floated away. Charlie shrugged. "It's not the happiest place right now, Mommy. But you can fix it."

"I'm sure it'll be happy the moment we're there."

Jamie and Charlie both nodded. "Maybe not the exact moment, Mommy," Jamie said earnestly. "But soon after. I think."

Would have asked her just what she was talking about, but Akiko lost patience and shooed Nadine and the kids out of the room so the Prep Team could finish getting me ready to go.

We finished up and, as we did, the intercom went live. "Excuse me Chief First Lady," Walter Ward, head of White House Security, the dude most dedicated to the job bar none, and the biggest slave to titles ever discovered, said, "but there's a package for you."

"Um, hey, Walt. Thanks for the heads-up. Why are you telling me this instead of having someone deliver it to me?"

"Ah . . . because it's not a normal package."

CHAPTER 4

LET THAT ONE SIT on the air for a moment. "Um, so, we're all breathless with anticipation over here now, Walt. How is said package not normal?"

"It's alive."

"Am I done here?" I asked the Prep Team.

"Yes," Pierre said. "Just please don't do anything to wreck your clothes."

"Oh, I have spares," Akiko said cheerfully. "You're good."

"Walt, where is the living package and did it arrive via conventional means or like the Peregrines did during Operation Destruction?" Otherwise known as in Special Space Delivery boxes that were not, but definitely should have been, marked Handle With Extreme Caution.

"With me, and via somewhat conventional means. The deliverer is with me, too."

"The suspense builds. I'll ask you why you're being so coy when I get there. Com off."

Listened. Didn't hear the low hum indicating the com was still live. Good, Walter had picked up that clue, not that I'd had a doubt. Hoped my telling him to turn off the com indicated that I'd picked up his clues as well.

Considered options. Getting my children to safety and others advised were definitely Jobs One and Two. "Colette, find Nadine and get her and the kids to the Embassy, along with Pierre and Akiko. Francine, I want you to very quietly but very quickly advise everyone with the President that we have a potential invader situation."

Francine and Colette both nodded and did the hyperspeed disappearing act.

"What will I be doing?" Vance asked.

"You will be coming with me."

"Oh. Good," he said in a tone indicating this was the opposite of good. "You're sure I can't warn Jeff and the others? Or go protect the kids at the Embassy?"

"I'm sure that I will be yelled at should I go somewhere without someone acting as a bodyguard. I have no idea where Len and Kyle happen to be, my Secret Service detail is likely wherever Len and Kyle are, and the whereabouts of Team Tough Guys is an equal mystery. For all I know, they're all already with Walter. They could be in the Rose Garden. However, where they are not is here, with me, and that means that you are coming with me so that I can show that I wasn't totally reckless."

With that, I grabbed Vance's hand and used some hyperspeed myself to take us to Walter's security nest.

Walter had been the Head of Security when we were at the American Centaurion Embassy, and while he did the same job now at the White House, technically he was serving several masters, including his older brother, William, who was Head of Security for all of American Centaurion and who based out of the Dulce Science Center in New Mexico.

Walter's other main master was Malcolm Buchanan, who'd been assigned to protect me and Jamie by the Head of the Presidential Terrorism Control Unit, aka my mother, when we'd first gotten to D.C. and who was now the head of Team Tough Guys and charged with protecting me, the kids, and, when necessary, Jeff and anyone else we cared about. Jeff had made Buchanan the official Head of White House Security, but since Buchanan worked best in and preferred the shadows, Walter was who was shown to the public as being the Head Security Dude. Meaning that Walter, like so many of us, had a target on him.

We reached Walter's White House Security Command Center quickly—I still sucked at mazes but we'd been here long enough that I actually knew my way around, at least enough to make do under normal circumstances.

The room was set up like security rooms at every other Centaurion Base—so, nothing like what a normal human would do. Due to the original Head of Security, the late Gladys Gower who'd been a rare dream reader and empath combination, Security A-Cs were expected to sleep on the job, but with one eye open, so to speak—the top dawgs in particular.

This had been great when Gladys was alive, since she'd

actually been able to spot threats in her sleep. For everyone else, however, it wasn't as good. William was an imageer—our third most powerful after Christopher and Serene—but Walter had no talents, other than being the most dedicated follower of titles fashion. And no one in any of our top Security positions was a dream reader, let alone a combination of talents.

So, naturally, I'd suggested that the Security teams stop trying to function 24/7 and actually share responsibilities. And that suggestion had been soundly ignored for the past several years, and I saw no end to its streak.

Dulce's Security Command Center had several bedrooms connected to the futuristic eye-in-the-sky technology that was an A-C standard. Walter, however, had been a one-man operation at the Embassy, and he continued to be so at the White House as well. He had a large suite with a comfy chair I was certain he slept in at his main controls, and a minicommand set up in the other room next to his bed.

What he also had with him today was a large animal crate and a person. The crate was one of the nicest I'd ever seen, clearly top of the line, and it was filled with what looked like a lot of ferrets, only I knew they weren't ferrets.

"Are those least weasels?" I'd dragged Chuckie into every animal sciences course offered at ASU and I'd always gotten the top grades, even higher than he did. Animals were my "thing" and, these days, in more ways than one.

The animals all turned at the sound of my voice. They were a family group, mom, dad, and six kits, and they were in winter white coats which, considering what I remembered of the mating habits of least weasels—and it would have shocked everyone other than Chuckie that I remembered quite a lot—these kits had already reached maturity. Meaning they shouldn't be with mom and dad any longer. And yet, they seemed quite happy to be together.

They were also quite happy to see me. I received an outpouring of love and loyalty that I was used to from my own vast menagerie but not necessarily from strange, new animals. And yet, this family was declaring its total love and devotion to all things me.

Could tell this because I had those Dr. Doolittle talents and they extended to all animals. I'd talked to ancient not-originally-from-this-planet sea slugs and alien cat-foxes and pig-dogs, and everything in between. I could only understand them a hundred percent if they wanted me to, but I could always pick up at least something. And in this case, I was picking up everything.

Least weasel declarations of faith and fidelity received, I shared that as long as they got along nicely with all the others in the menagerie they were more than welcome to hang out. Then I took a look at the person with them.

A handsome dwarf with tousled curly dark hair, bright green eyes, and a rakish demeanor grinned at me. He was dressed in what looked like some sort of bizarre getup that combined styles from the past several hundred years—jaunty green cap with a feather that might have been from a peacock but I was sure was from a Peregrine, dark blue velvet lederhosen complete with suspenders decorated with tiny yet accurate images of the cosmos, a frilly puffy white shirt, a sleeveless vest that could have been made out of long sheep's wool but looked a lot more like long Poof fur to me, and silver-buckled men's high-heeled shoes.

Despite my best efforts, my jaw dropped. It didn't faze him.

Instead, he whipped off his cap and gave me a deep bow. "Madam First Lady and Queen Regent of Earth, please allow me to introduce myself. I am Al Garrison of the Sovereign Nation of Algarria, and I am here to end the war between our peoples."

CHAPTER 5

I STOOD THERE WITH MY mouth hanging open. Literally, I had no idea what to say. Or what to ask.

For starters, I wanted to ask what the hell was going on. Then to ask what Algar—because that was definitely who this was standing before me—was up to. And then I wanted to ask where in the world Algarria was, and what war they'd declared upon us. But the shock of seeing Algar like this and in this way had me speechless. Was glad no one other than Walter and Vance were around to witness the situation.

Vance beat me to the punch. "Excuse me? Who did you say you are?"

Algar stood up and put his hat back on. "I am Al Garrison, the Royal Sovereign of Algarria, a nation that, possibly until today, is at war with the United States. And I come to seek an audience with the First Lady on important matters of state."

"Algarria is a micronation," Walter said quietly. "There are about four hundred of them, so that's why you're having trouble placing which one this is, Chief First Lady."

Managed not to say that I sincerely doubted that Algarria actually existed. Because Algar was about as far from human as you could get.

Algar was from the Black Hole Universe, and he was the one who'd brought the Poofs to this one. The Poofs were small bundles of adorable cuteness, with tiny paws, black button eyes, and tails and ears you could rarely see because of how fluffy their fur was. Originally we'd been told they were from Alpha Four and mated whenever a Royal Wedding was in the offing. Reality said that the Poofs either felt that everyone Jeff and I had ever met or heard of was royalty or else they just liked to get busy, because every friend of ours—as determined to be a friend by the Poofs—had at least one Poof of their own, and Jeff and I had a lot of unattached Poofs who lived with us. Poofs for everyone and more Poofs for me remained my life's motto.

In addition to being the Poof Breeding Originator, Algar was a Free Will Fanatic of the highest order. Which went against what the Black Hole People stood for, from all he'd told me. Algar had been on the run for Crimes Against Allowing the Younger Races to Screw Up for longer than I could comprehend and, based on how long he'd been around, it was a safe bet that every race in our universe was considered younger.

He'd attached to the Royal Family of Alpha Four—of which Jeff was a member, as we'd discovered during Operation Invasion—hundreds of years prior and had basically never left them. When some of them, Jeff's father Alfred included, had been banished to Earth, Algar had gone along. By that time, Algar had distanced himself from the current rulers to the point they didn't know he existed, though Alfred was named for him. Alfred didn't know about Algar, either. Almost no one did. As far as I knew, Richard White and Gower—the former and current Supreme Pontifex—and I were the only ones. Though I'd discovered at the end of Operation Fundraiser that Siler had started to figure it out.

Algar's powers were like magic to those of us here. He snapped his fingers and whatever he wanted happened. He had the entire A-C population believing that there were hundreds if not thousands of A-Cs doing the work of the Operations Team—cleaning, rearranging, moving things and people, food and clothing supplies, and on and on—when, in fact, it was all him. He'd turned every refrigerator into a portal. He'd turned my purse and the rolling computer bag he'd given me into portals, too.

And this was because I was, apparently, his favorite. Many times I felt lucky about this. Today was not one of those times.

"Why are you bringing in a family of least weasels?" Admittedly, this wasn't the best opening line I could have come up with, but it was all I had, in no small part because Algar prevented any of us talking about him aloud and also shielded our minds so others couldn't "see" us thinking about him telepathically. I had no idea if my children knew Algar existed, though I knew ACE did.

Algar smiled. "They're the royal mascot of Algarria and a gift for you, Madame First Lady. Or do you prefer to be called Queen Katherine?"

"Neither, I prefer to be called Kitty. I'm sorry, I'm really confused right now."

"I'm here to broker a peace treaty with the United States, to end the war between our two nations. This family of least weasels are Algarria's gift to you and the start of our new friendship."

"You're expecting an invitation to the President's address due to this, aren't you?" Vance asked.

Algar beamed. "I am, and thank you so much for confirming it! Algarria, and our Brotherhood of Nations, will look favorably upon the United States for showing us such favor."

Thought fast, possibly faster than I'd ever thought before. There had to be a reason Algar was doing this and grins and giggles wasn't it. Therefore, I could make this easier or I could be really stupid and obtuse and not help our personal God in the Machine to achieve whatever the hell he needed achieved.

Vance's mouth was opening, and I didn't have to have Black Hole Universe powers to guess that his reply wasn't going to be "come on down" or anything else positive. Micronations weren't something that the U.S., or any other reasonably sane country, cared about.

"I'm sure we can include you. What title do you prefer that we use for you?"

"Ard Ri will be acceptable, lassie."

Knew this translated into High King in Gaelic, not because I was up on the language but because one of my BFFs from high school, Sheila, had been all about the languages, and this was one of the many things she'd told me that had stuck. Realistically and based on powers alone, Algar was a higher king than anyone in our galaxy. But in terms of the title, and knowing him as I did, had to figure that he was merely enjoying the joke of making everyone call him a high king, rather than feeling that he was.

"That would be Madame First Lady or Queen Katherine," Vance snapped. "If we're calling you Ard Ri, Mister Garrison." Clearly Vance knew some Gaelic, too. Also clearly, he wasn't pleased with this turn of events.

"Oh, but she said to be informal, laddie," Algar said with a twinkle in his eyes.

"Ard Ri Al it is," I said before Vance could give the cutting retort I could see forming.

Algar chuckled. "That will be acceptable. Now, do you accept Algarria's offer of a family of our most precious royal pets, or do you not?"

"I do."

"And will you keep them with you at all times?" Algar was staring right into my eyes.

Not that I needed the hint. For whatever reason, Algar felt that I needed to have eight least weasels hanging about. So least weasels I would have. "Yes, I will."

"Good. We'll put them into their standard traveling coach for the speech." Algar trotted over to the crate while Vance and I both stared at each other.

"Um . . ." I was again at a loss for words. Because I'd stupidly thought that Algar had meant keep the least weasels with the rest of the animals or in our bedroom or something.

Vance recovered first. "We can't have the First Lady hauling rodents with her to the President's speech." He didn't have to say the words "career death" aloud—I knew what the press would do with the idea of me trotting around with some least weasels like they were corgis, even the press who liked us.

Then again, I trotted around with Poofs and Peregrines all the time. The Poofs usually hung out in my purse and the Peregrines were able to go chameleon, so most people didn't know they were there. Possibly and perhaps I could do similar with the least weasels.

"They're mustelidae, Vance, meaning they're a lot like the sentient beings from Beta Eight. Meaning that we have to be careful not to insult any of our allies, Ard Ri Al, by carrying around smaller versions of themselves as pets." Or whatever they were actually supposed to be.

I didn't say less sentient—I'd been shown quite clearly over the past few years that all the animals I had hanging about, both Earth native and interplanetary galactic, were all smart. They might not think and reason like humans, but stupid they were not.

Algar turned around, holding what I could only think of as a large, blue, velvet hatbox with airholes in it. "They won't notice them, lassie. At least, as long as you keep them with you."

I gave up and heaved a sigh as I reached for the Royal Least Weasel Hatbox Carrier. "Gotcha. What are their names?"

"Oh, they're for you to name."

"Of course they are. What do they eat?"

He shot a smirk at Vance. "Rodents. Among other things. They're carnivores."

"Just like all the rest of our animals. They'll fit right in." The carrier wasn't too heavy, which was nice. Contemplated how I'd explain this to everyone. Decided not to. "So . . . guys . . . what say we don't share that we have a family of least weasels with us? At least until after Jeff's speech and all the rest of that dog and pony show."

"You want me to lie, Chief First Lady?" Walter sounded unsure that he could.

"You've managed before, Walt. When the stakes were high enough."

"How are the stakes high about this?" Vance asked.

"Wow, Ard Ri Al's really thrown you off your game. Jeff needs this particular wrinkle like he needs a hole in his head. And telling the others is just a slight delay in their telling him. I can explain the Ard Ri easily enough—we're appeasing, what, four hundred or so micronations by accepting their representative and allowing him to join us. He sits somewhere close to me," because I knew without asking that Algar expected to be close to me for whatever reason, "and we solve a micro issue."

"I see what you did there," Vance said, sarcasm knob at seven on the one-to-ten scale. "However, if you're expected to bring these animals with you, that's less easily explained."

"I'll figure something out. I just think that, under the stressful circumstances, we need to kind of lay low about all of this. Until after the event. Then we come clean to everyone. Basically, we're not telling them the full Ard Ri Al situation for about two hours or less. What could go wrong in that time?"

Everyone, Algar included, gave me the "really?" look. The least weasels were probably giving me that look from inside their Royal Hatbox. "I don't think we have time for me to list all the possibilities," Vance said.

Walter nodded. "This is a prime opportunity for our enemies, Chief First Lady."

"Plus, it's you," Vance added. "Weird, strange, embarrassing things happen to you all the time, despite everything I and the rest of your team do to circumvent them."

"I resent that. I can't deny it, especially at this precise moment, but I do resent it."

"I'm sure your fine Secret Service will prevent any issues," Algar said soothingly.

"Speaking of whom, Walt, where are all my security teams?" And everyone else. I'd sent out the "potential invader" warning—we should have been mobbed by people by now. Frankly, we should have been mobbed by people by the time Algar had shown me the least weasels, let alone by this point. And yet, we were alone and I didn't hear anyone waiting in the hallway.

Walter looked surprised by this question. "Where you told them to be, Chief First Lady."

Other than the kids and the Alexis sisters, I hadn't told anyone to be anywhere or do anything today. I'd given the "intruder alert" signal but I hadn't told anyone else what to do. I'd kind of assumed they'd know what to do without my having to spell it out, since it was their job, all of their jobs. "Um, refresh my memory, just for fun. Where did I tell them to be?"

"On the Carpet."

CHAPTER 6

THE CARPET WAS THE Secret Service term for the underground parking garage where the Presidential motor pool was housed. And I hadn't told anyone to meet me there. But clearly Algar had. Someone who could make tens of thousands of people believe there was an active Operations team wouldn't have an issue circumventing all the security I'd tried to activate.

Waited. Neither Vance nor Walter pointed out that I'd given a warning to anyone, and Vance had heard all of my instructions. Looked at them out of the corners of my eyes. They didn't look like they disagreed with the idea of all of my security being elsewhere. So Algar had affected them too, which, all things considered, was not a shocker.

However, I was getting "what's your damage?" looks from both of them. So, time to continue this weird fiction. "I'm not used to anyone doing anything I tell them to, at least in regard to things like this."

"Well, they're there," Walter said confidently. Something beeped on his Mini Bat Cave Command Center. "And everyone else is there, too."

"Including the kids?" Who I'd told to go to the Embassy. Walter nodded. "And Jeff?" Who normally came to get me.

Walter nodded again. "That's what the signal said."

Decided to go for it and looked at Algar. Who was busily closing up the least weasel cage. He was up to something, in a major way, and I wanted to know what, before it rolled. I knew he knew it, too, because he kept his back to me.

Resisted heaving a huge sigh and forged on. "Great. Then Vance and I and Ard Ri Al will head that way, too. Carrying the

Royal Hat Box here and just pretending it's not full of live animals."

The live animals shared that they knew they needed to remain quiet and they would. Was about to leave when I realized something was missing in this area. "Walter, where are George and Gracie and Teddy?" George and Gracie were Walter's Peregrines and Teddy was his Poof. And they were always with him unless they were on some sort of Security Mission.

"They're with Secretary Kramer."

"Um, why?"

Walter shrugged. "She's today's Designated Survivor."

Marcia Kramer had been in the Washington Wife class with me, back when she was Senator Zachary Kramer's third wife and my sometime enemy. She was now my friend, the Secretary of Education, and no longer married to Kramer because he was dead from trying to kill me during Operation Fundraiser.

The Designated Survivor rule was in place to ensure that if something killed the country's leadership in one fell swoop that there would be someone around to carry on and keep things calm. In most administrations, this role had fallen to someone far down the Cabinet Food Chain. Under the many circumstances that surrounded us, however, Jeff's Presidential Cabinet had decided to do a rotation—each big event meant one of them would be assigned to be the DS. That way, someone Jeff—and therefore the country, world, and galaxy—could trust to do the right things was left potentially in charge.

"Why the Secretary of Education? For something this historic it would seem to make sense that she was with us, and I'm sure her kids don't want to miss it, either. Besides, I thought it was Nathalie Gagnon-Brewer's turn to take the short straw."

"Secretary Kramer's children are with the rest of our children and families in the Embassy Day Care or Sidwell Friends School," Walter said. "But Secretary Kramer felt that it was more important for the Secretary of Transportation to attend."

"Whatever works," Vance said before I could reply. "Marcia's still trying to show you and Jeff how grateful she is for your trust in her, Kitty. And she and Nathalie are back to being good friends, too, so this was probably as much a friend favor as anything else."

The light beeped again. "Chief First Lady, they're waiting for you."

Heaved a sigh. "The show must go on. Walter, remain ever vigilant for danger. Ard Ri Al, Vance, and my new least weasels, come with me." Not that the least weasels had a choice, since I was still carrying them.

Realized I was missing something vital. Handed the Royal Hatbox to Vance. "Forgot my purse. I'll be right back." Took off at hyperspeed and got into our suite in record time. Grabbed my purse from the coffee table—it was big, black, and made of cheap leather, and it had stood the test of time and my lifestyle like a pro. It rarely fit my look, though it was faking it well today, all things considered. But fitting in or not, I was not going anywhere without it—it had saved my life and the lives of others countless times before Algar had turned it into a portal, and I wasn't going to leave without whatever I'd tossed in there with me, especially my phone.

Purse over my neck in the cross-body position that meant I was ready for anything, I took a detour into the closet and talked to the hamper—another place I was sure Algar had made a portal. "I have no idea what your game is, but I'd really like to know before all hell breaks loose."

No Algar appeared. Not a surprise, of course, and not because he was with Vance. Algar could and routinely did freeze time or step out of it or whatever the Black Hole Universe called it. He could actually be two places at once, at least as far as I'd seen. But him not showing now wasn't shocking—if he'd wanted to talk privately to me, he could have just snapped those fingers at any time. He hadn't snapped, so he wanted to be stealth, so to speak.

"I'd have appreciated a heads-up. And I'd like to know why you've given everyone other than me and Vance these weird suggestions to do things and be places that aren't normal and why you've let Vance and the others believe whatever weird lies you've put into their heads. In that sense. I'd also like to know why you want to come along with me for this particular event. You're usually far more hands-off. Frankly, as far as I've ever seen or known, you prefer to be invisible."

No Algar, but something appeared on the lid of the hamper. A large manila envelope.

Picked it up but before I could take a look, the intercom went off. "Chief First Lady, the President really needs you to get downstairs. First Lady's Chief of Staff Beaumont has already taken Ard Ri Al to the Carpet."

Shoved the envelope into my purse. "Got it, Walt. Be right there." The com went off and I went back into the main part of the suite. "All Poofs who want to go to a boring speech should get into Kitty's purse. All Peregrines on external White House duty should go to or stay chameleoned up and head out with Kitty. All animals coming along need to know we now possess a family of eight least weasels who are not to be attacked and who appear to be excited about joining our extended animal family."

Checked my purse. Had only a few Poofs on Board. Well, I hadn't exactly sold this as being an awesome excursion, it was cold, and the Poofs had probably voted for snoozing. Could not blame them.

Felt something feathered nudge against my leg. "Bruno, my bird, let's get this bizarre show on the road." Reached down and gave him a scritchy-scratch between his wings, which earned me a loving warble and the confirmation that Peregrines were on the case wherever Peregrines needed to be. Straightened up and took off.

Hyperspeed being awesome, arrived downstairs in a couple of seconds. To find that everyone was already in the various limos and burly SUVs we used, and the rear passenger door to the Beast, the President's personal limo that was supposedly the most secure vehicle in the world—that the A-Cs had taken one look at, sniffed disparagingly, and fixed up to be truly invulnerable—was open. Kyle was standing outside, holding said door.

Algar was definitely affecting things, because this wasn't something that happened, ever. No one loaded up until everyone was down here and ready—we weren't a group that waited well. Didn't argue or discuss, just got in. Algar was sitting on the bench that faced the back along with the three kids. Jeff, Raj, and Vance were in the back. Kyle helped me inside, I settled in between Jeff and Vance, and verified that Len was driving. Kyle closed my door and got into the shotgun seat, and we took off.

This was the fastest, smoothest departure we'd made possibly ever. I was directly across from Algar, who had the Royal Hatbox on his lap. "I assume everyone's been introduced?"

"Yeah, baby," Jeff said, sounding perfectly normal. "One additional person isn't going to be a problem." He shot Algar what I thought of as his Impressing the Parents Smile. "And having the representative from the Brotherhood of Nations with us to smooth things over with all of his fellow sovereigns is a good thing. Thank you for fixing that up for us."

Well, it wasn't someone telling me I was insane for this, so that was one for the win column. That Jeff and the others were being mind-controlled by Algar wasn't.

"Music, Kitty?" Kyle asked.

"Oh my God, yes, please, and thank you very much."

"Mama, Don't You Worry" by Smash Mouth came on. "Oh, but I do worry," I said conversationally. "Today's a big day and things just seem . . . a little . . . off."

"I'm sure things will seem normal shortly," Algar said confidently. "You're all just nervous. Once the butterflies settle, you'll feel right."

"I suppose."

"Daddy, can we go on a vacation?" Jamie asked. "Once your important speech is over, I mean."

"Sorry," Lizzie said. "We were talking about it at breakfast once you'd left, and I forgot to remind Jamie and Charlie to ask about it after the speech."

"That's not a problem," Jeff reassured. "Mommy and I will discuss it and we'll see, okay, kids? Though I'm sure we could all use a vacation."

This opened the floodgates and the kids started discussing fun places to go, though Jamie kept on naming people who should come with us and Charlie kept on insisting that anyplace suggested wasn't as fun as it should be.

I didn't join in because I was worried and didn't want Jeff to pick it up, though he clearly had his empathic blocks set on high, or Algar was providing an assist, because he should have noted my concern already.

The music changed to "It's OK (It's Alright)" by the Fine Young Cannibals, and after that to "Alright" by Lit. Clearly Algar wanted me to relax and not worry. Did my best. Failed, for the most part.

It only took the three songs for us to arrive—Andrews wasn't all that far from the White House, especially when we were traveling in this way, with the D.C.P.D. blocking streets and us rolling like a badass caravan.

There were the usual protestors in the streets—sadly the Club 51 True Believers had only gotten stronger in the past year-plus despite our attempts at infiltration. Infiltrators had all come back with the same intel: the only way to stop this was to either kill all of them—which wasn't an acceptable choice to any of us on the side of pro-alien sentiment, sanity, or decency—or to change all the hearts and minds of the members. We'd managed that once, with a good portion of the original Club 51 membership, but no one felt that this kind of lightning was going to strike twice. Meaning it was change individuals' hearts and minds, one at a time. Which was going exactly as fast as you'd expect, meaning at a snail's pace.

Thankfully, we were ushered through Andrews' security checkpoint quickly and I stopped worrying about Club 51 True Believers and focused instead on the situation at hand.

Which was impossible to miss.

CHAPTER 7

ANDREWS WAS A BIG Air Force base, but the *Distant Voyager* was huge. And it was lifted up on launch scaffolding or whatever they called it so everyone could see its gleaming beauty.

The caravan parked and as we exited the cars and headed toward where Jeff would be speaking, I held Charlie's hand, Lizzie took Jamie's, Jeff took Jamie's and Charlie's other hands, and we all stared at the ship.

It was massive. Gustav Drax had been instrumental in this ship's design, which was a good thing, since he was a self-exiled Prince of Vatusus, which was a planet where they communed naturally with all things electronic. Drax had started out as an Accidental Big Bad during Operation Epidemic, but I'd swayed him to our side during Operation Madhouse, and we were all glad to have his skills on the Side of Right because, true to his own hype, he was a weapons creation genius, and that genius extended to spaceships.

He'd worked with our NASA teams as well as teams from many of the races that had come to Earth for protection and asylum, including all the spacefaring planets in the Alpha Centauri system. Basically, the *Distant Voyager* was more than just Earth's first manned long-range spacecraft—she represented how well all the disparate races could work together to create something amazing.

It wasn't quite as large as Drax's helicarrier—which I always thought of as a S.H.I.E.L.D. flying fortress—an Alpha Four Imperial Battlecruiser, or the Themnir's Roving Planet, and its layout was so different than the Faradawn Treeship that I couldn't make an apt size comparison. But it was definitely bigger than a Canus Majorian Dog's Head, a Feliniad Cat's Paw, a Reptilian Lizard-Bird of Prey, a Lyssara Borg-Honeycomb, a Yggenthnian Hand Trowel, a Vrierst Manta Ray, or a Z'porrah Flying Saucer. They had official, real names, but those were the ones I used— my names were far more accurate.

Because Drax had been involved in the entire process, the *Distant Voyager* looked beautiful as well as functional. He'd insisted that the ship gleam, so it had a golden hue that made it glitter in sunlight.

Unlike our spaceships of the past, which were all bullet shaped, the *Distant Voyager* was more of a giant circle with a slice taken out of the back, where a curved combination of Y-shaped thrusters sat above and a thick, slightly curved tail below. But the bridge was Drax's S.H.I.E.L.D. Helicarrier Deluxe all the way. The usual bells, whistles, computers, and such, and a six-person control circle, a little ways away from the windshield. That it was called a windshield, versus a space shield or whatever, amused me to no end, but I was, apparently, the only one so amused, so I'd stopped making jokes about our inability to come up with a better word ages ago.

The main saucer section of the ship had twenty-one levels— to ensure that the ship could carry either refugees or troops or both, depending—and the thick tail and thrusters were actually a smaller ship with ten decks that could detach from the main saucer section for exploration and such, but I'd never seen any of this in person. I'd never seen any of the ship in person before now, my skills not being needed for creation or construction, and my input—"ensure there are about ten times the number of bathrooms that you guys think are necessary, and that's a FLOTUS order"—was deemed to be more than plenty of help from the likes of me.

We were moved along toward the staging area where Jeff was going to be giving his speech, with the *Distant Voyager* gleaming behind him. There were dignitaries and press and a lot of brouhaha—even more than normal. This wasn't a surprise. While all the other planets we now knew about and were "joined" with had manned interstellar space flight, this was really Earth's inauguration into the Big Boy League in terms of something other than being nasty and really great at kicking butt, getting knocked down, and getting right back up again.

Now I desperately wanted to hear Chumbawamba singing "Tubthumping" but, sadly, that was not to be. We were surrounded by far too many people with cameras and opinions for me to slip in my earbuds. Besides, all my focus needed to be on Charlie. Because the real test would be whether or not my son tried to lift the *Distant Voyager* or not. We were all sincerely hoping for "not," and ensuring that outcome fell to me, at least until it was time for me to go onto the dais with Jeff.

Raj was doing the first portion of the speaking, so the rest of us were seated with those "lucky" enough to be nearest to the stage. As with the dignitaries' section, most of our friends and family weren't actually sitting all that near to us. I only managed to spot where Christopher and his family were because his wife and my other female BFF from high school, Amy Gaultier-White, was a redhead and so were their children. Becky, who was nearing twenty months, was on Christopher's lap, and Jeffrey Richard, who we all called JR and who was ten months old, was on Amy's.

They were surrounded by the rest of those with kids in our inner circle, as well as the rest of the A-Cs who were coming to support Jeff, which included his parents, older sisters, and their families. That we knew we couldn't trust parts of several of those families just made it all the more exciting, in that totally negative way.

Chuckie and Nathalie were sitting next to my kids, and it was going to be up to them to keep Charlie under control once I stepped away, jobs not normally assigned to the Director of the CIA and the Secretary of Transportation, but handled well by my oldest BFF and his girlfriend.

Fortunately, Charlie adored the man he was named after, and the moment he could he squirmed out of my arms and demanded to be with his Uncle Chuckie. Jamie, not to be outdone, also demanded to be on Uncle Chuckie's lap, since she was the eldest and therefore required to be his favorite. Chuckie managed both kids well, and Lizzie went on his other side, so that she and Nathalie were ready for anything, with Nadine sitting behind us so as to offer nanny assistance as needed.

Vance and Algar were next to Nadine, meaning it would be hard to see Algar, since he was blocked by Chuckie, who was tall. Had a feeling that this was what Algar wanted but couldn't be sure. Knew it was what Vance wanted, at least if he wasn't being mind-controlled. My parents were next to Vance as well, but somehow my kids were content to maul Chuckie, versus

Mom and Dad. Chose not to complain—my parents were there if Chuckie needed a helping paw or two.

The rest of our section was made up of Jeff's Cabinet, the Joint Chiefs of Staff—including the Head of the Joint Chiefs, who I called my Uncle Mort and who was sitting next to Dad, who called him his big brother—and other military, as well as other politicians near and dear to either us or the cause of space integration.

Somehow all of my children's musical chairs hadn't caused the audience to lose focus on Raj, and I chose not to care what the media was doing with it. Jeff and I got to sit for a whole three minutes, then Raj finished and it was time for us to take the stage. Had to leave my purse with Nathalie and really hoped I wouldn't need it.

Jeff held my hand and helped me up the steps and into position, ensuring that I didn't trip and he had that little extra comfort of holding onto someone who was a hundred percent in his corner.

Now came the hard part, at least for me. I had to keep a look of rapt attention and total spousal support on my face without allowing support to turn to lust, boredom, or distraction. I wasn't one with meditation, let alone meditation that required specific facial expressions and thoughts, so this was a really hard thing for me to accomplish, particularly since staring at Jeff tended to set off my Lust Meter in less than five seconds. My team had been having me practice for weeks. I was better, but I still wasn't up to the level of Top First Ladies Past.

Focused on what a great man and leader Jeff was as he gave an excellent speech I didn't really listen to because I'd already heard it several times before when he was practicing. However, it was the first time for most of the audience present and all of the audience watching and listening over the airwaves, so I did keep a tiny part of my mind focused on it. The audience seemed totally into it—laughing at all the right places, clapping in some, getting teary in others. Jeff really was great at everything he did.

Jeff introduced the *Distant Voyager's* crew, who came out to great cheers and applause. The ship was already prepped for their voyage—to Alpha Four first, then to Vatusus to give Drax's father our regards and thanks and thereby ensure that two of our most vital allies felt complimented—but they were taking off tomorrow. Today was given to all the pomp and circumstance—tomorrow was focused on the real deal.

Happily, the speech went off without a hitch. Made a mental note that doing these things on a military base was great because everyone had been thoroughly searched and no one had complained too much. Considered suggesting we do this all the time as Jeff and I left the stage, waving at the crowd and cameras, while the audience applauded.

Now it was time to tour the *Distant Voyager*. Not everyone was allowed in, but the First Family definitely was, and that meant our entourage was as well. Sure, most of that entourage were security personnel, but still, it worked out. And no one asked about Algar, beyond formal introductions. He was carrying the Royal Hatbox and no one asked about that, either. Chose not to care or complain, nor ask why he was the one who handed me my purse back. Put it over my neck and followed the Lucky Herd up and into the ship.

The Visiting Dignitaries weren't making a fuss about getting inside because they'd been toured through the ship last week, so as to keep everyone safe and keep the media out. Same with anyone else who felt they had an "in" with Jeff, me, or anyone else related to the ship. So we had fewer people to deal with, and most of them were in Jeff's Cabinet or similar, though we did have American Centaurion well represented, Embassy personnel in particular and, of course, Alpha Team was here, because it was their job to be and, besides, it was fun to share this with our closest friends and family.

The news crews allowed inside weren't nearly as numerous as those that had been there for the speech. Basically it was the *Good Day USA!* crew, Bruce Jenkins, aka the Tastemaker, top investigative journalist Mister Joel Oliver, and the photographer/cameraman they both used these days, Dion Callen France. That was it, because privilege had its benefits and those news teams that had shown their loyalty to us were the ones with the privilege and therefore the benefits.

Brian was in charge of the media spin and all visitors inside the ship. He wasn't the Commander—that fell to Daniel Chee, whom we'd met during Operation Drug Addict—but he was second in command and, since he was married to the President's cousin, that gave him the face role. The rest of the crew seemed more than happy to let Brian have the spotlight, too.

All of Airborne were also crew on the flight and part of the crew. Tim Crawford—Head of Airborne and still doing the job of mine that was my favorite—and my flyboys had been to the

Alpha Centauri system and flown spaceships that were not Earth or even human created. They'd earned their spots. Besides, as Chuckie put it, that way we'd have six guys who'd shoot first and ask questions later if anything went wrong. And since A-Cs had reflexes so fast that they couldn't work human machinery, it made more sense to have humans on the crew than not.

We'd had one A-C astronaut—the late Michael Gower. But no other A-Cs had shown an interest, so even though the *Distant Voyager* had controls an A-C could use and not destroy, I'd had to assign my A-C security team to be on the ship. They were the only A-Cs that were going to be on board. They weren't thrilled with the assignment, but they'd stopped whining about it weeks ago.

Like Amy and their kids, Christopher wasn't with us. But since he was literally the fastest man alive, no one could see him if he was moving at his version of hyperspeed, which is what he did during things like this so that he could intervene in case things went wrong. He was outside, manning the perimeter, ensuring that nothing bad could happen there, ready to be called in if needed.

Otherwise, most everyone's spouses or significant others were here, too, though their kids were presumably wherever Amy and hers were, being safe and not touching things. Additionally, we had Prince Wasim of Bahrain and his personal bodyguard, Naveed Murad, with us. Wasim was eighteen now, a senior at the Sidwell Friends School, and still hoping to get Lizzie to select him as her Dude Of Choice. Until that time, he was making do with being her best friend and enjoying hanging out with all of our friends and family.

Due to a variety of circumstances, Wasim had been moved into the White House with us for a while. He had an apartment at the Cairo, but he'd given it to Marcia and her family in a gracious move during Operation Fundraiser. Ultimately, we'd moved him and Naveed into the Embassy, where we could keep them both safe and Wasim wasn't sleeping down the hall from Lizzie but was sleeping down the hall from Siler. His grandfather, King Raheem of Bahrain, approved of all of this, which was what mattered, since he was one of our staunchest allies in the Middle East.

One of our other staunchest Middle Eastern allies was here, too. Ali Baba Gadhavi, the notorious crime lord turned Galactic Good Guy was in the select viewing group. This was because his schedule hadn't allowed for him to come when the other dignitaries had taken their tour. While I thought of King Raheem as a teddy bear, Gadhavi was definitely a grizzly, and you made accommodations for grizzlies. Besides, Gadhavi had made it a personal goal to help Wasim get game, and I appreciated that he made the effort, because I liked Wasim a lot and the kid needed all the help he could get.

The press was having a field day, filming, photographing, and interviewing everyone who was on board. Because we'd been infiltrated by a fake *Good Day USA!* cameraman during Operation Fundraiser, Len and Kyle had been put on camera duty once the interior tour started, so they were with Adam and the Kristie-Bot, going all over the ship with White and Gower, who were doing whatever it was Former and Current Supreme Pontifexes did at times like these, which was probably wrangling most of the politicians, who were staying as near to the film crew as possible.

"It's very *Star Trek*, isn't it?" I asked Nathalie quietly, while we stood around and listened to Brian describe the command deck and I held Charlie so that Chuckie could do his Director of the CIA thing which meant wander off and spy on people, but casually. Jamie was with Lizzie and Wasim, who was holding her on his shoulder so she could see over everyone's heads.

She nodded. "But it makes sense. The crew will be living here, even though the trip shouldn't take too long."

Would have replied but realized that I didn't see Algar or the Royal Hatbox anywhere. Did my best to look around surreptitiously. Hadn't had a chance to advise Christopher of Algar or the least weasels' presence and didn't want an accidental incident—I truly wasn't sure if Christopher could move faster than Algar could see and now wasn't the time to find out.

Also wasn't sure what Algar could or couldn't hide from Siler. Not that I could tell where Siler was, either. He was likely blending and possibly outside with Christopher. Or they could both be standing next to me or moving at warp speed throughout the ship. Basically, I wouldn't know so I chose not to worry about it.

Didn't spot the rest of Team Tough Guys, either, but that just meant that Buchanan didn't want me to see him, and John Wruck, who was an Anciannas and our version of the Martian Manhunter, could have merely shape-shifted into someone innocuous in order to blend in. Or they were all outside with Christopher, too.

Brian led us off the command deck and down to the crew's quarters. These were really nice and I could see all the Drax Industrial touches that made the ship more than merely functional. It would be a pleasant place to spend time, even on longer flights where warp might not be used.

Charlie reared back and looked right at my face. "Mommy, your real name is Kitty, right?"

"Right, well, that's my nickname. Just like your real name is Charles Maxwell Martini but we call you Charlie, Mommy's name is Katherine Sarah Katt-Martini, but I like to be called Kitty because that's what your Nana Angela and Papa Sol called me and what all my friends call me, too. Why?"

He smiled. "Just being sure." He nestled his face against my neck and went to sleep. Chose not to complain about this unexpected but pleasant turn of events. A napping Charlie should mean that nothing and no one was lifted into the air against their will.

Considering Charlie hadn't spoken for so long that I'd been ready to give him a lot of special tests, that he now had a vocabulary far advanced for a child his age didn't throw me all that much. Jamie had done similar as had most of the other hybrid children. It was just what happened when you had kids that were exceptional.

Due to how we'd wandered through the ship, the flyboys—Matt Hughes, Chip Walker, Randy Muir, Joe Billings, and Jerry Tucker—were all near to me, Nathalie, and the kids. No one else was around—the various people had wandered off, some after Brian, some down other hallways, some elsewhere. The ship was big and I had to figure that everyone wanted to see what they could before being shooed off.

"Don't you wish you were coming with us, Commander," Jerry, my favorite, asked softly with a wink.

"I've done it. Space travel's overrated."

We all chuckled, but those chuckles stopped.

Because the ship lurched.

CHAPTER 8

"WAS THAT CHARLIE?"** Hughes asked quietly, reading my mind.

Checked on my son. He was still asleep. Wasn't sure if I should wake him or not.

"No idea. The ship should be a little bit more than he can handle."

Walker shook his head. "Kitty, he's your kid. That means he can probably do anything."

"Aww, you're so sweet. But I'm sure it wasn't him." Said as the ship lurched again. The first lurch had been to the right. This one was to the left.

"Get to Brian," I said to those around me. Could just see Jeff, Brian, and some others ahead of us, so we moved as quickly to them as we could.

"What's going on?" Jeff asked as we arrived and the ship stopped moving. Jeff took my hand and squeezed it gently.

Brian shook his head. "No idea. We should be stationary."

Christopher appeared. "I saw the ship move and I just checked the scaffolding and launchpad area—nothing's out of place and nothing's moving."

"Strong winds?" Chee suggested.

"Some winds," Christopher admitted. "Nothing that seems strong enough, though. I'm not sure that anyone outside noticed the ship moving, by the way, so that might support the high winds theory."

"Settling," Drax said firmly. "The ship is getting comfortable."

"Houses do that," Joe said. He was married to Lorraine, one of my two best A-C girlfriends, and I saw him pass her a sign.

"This isn't a house," Randy pointed out. He was married to Claudia, my other A-C bestie, and he sent her a sign, too.

"And the ship's had plenty of time to settle," Jerry said. He was recently married to Abigail Gower-Tucker, the youngest Gower sibling even when the Michael and Naomi had been alive. Abigail was here, too, and I watched Jerry pass her a sign, as well.

Lorraine and Claudia were Captains on Alpha Team and Abigail was one of the Embassy's Cultural Attachés, and all three of them passed me a sign right back. Which basically indicated it might be a good time to go. "Let's get everyone off, just to be sure," I suggested quietly.

"Let's not be hasty for no reason," Drax countered. Others, Chee included, nodded.

We all waited. The ship didn't move again. "Maybe Gustav is right," Jeff said. "Or it's winds like Daniel said."

"It would be politically preferable not to evacuate," Raj added.

No more lurching happened, so we all went back to the tour or wandering around, depending, and Christopher went back outside, having confirmed that he'd already toured the ship and found it nice but nothing he needed to spend a ton of time in.

Charlie still seemed fast asleep. "Think it was him?" Jeff asked me quietly.

"The flyboys asked, too. I don't know."

Jeff grunted. "Let me hold him."

"Blocks up too high to tell without physical contact?" I asked as we moved Charlie from my shoulder onto Jeff's.

"New blocker being tested. I can feel whoever I'm touching, but not anyone else."

"Was that wise to test right now?"

"I've been testing it for a couple of weeks. This was the big one, and we did need something where emotions would be real and running high. I can turn it off as needed and it's not internal to me, baby, so don't worry."

"Oh, not worried at all," I lied. Apparently, Jeff wouldn't be able to tell.

"Liar."

"I thought you said you could only feel emotions via touch."

He grinned. "I read your face, baby." He kissed my cheek. "We'll be fine. Charlie's just having a happy dream, talking to someone he likes very much."

"Who?"

"No idea. I assume she's imaginary. But he's happy and contented and not trying to lift anything, so I think we want to let him sleep."

The larger group separated and reformed into smaller groups as we wandered more of the ship. Despite the prior lurching, nothing else seemed amiss, and it was fun to get to see more of what I'd only looked at on blueprints. Lizzie, Jamie, and Wasim asked to go look at other things, and since they were with Naveed, Gadhavi, and Mahin Sherazi, our other Cultural Attaché, it seemed safe enough, so we let them wander, Jamie now holding hands with Lizzie and Wasim, like their own little chaperone.

This left me and Jeff with just our snoozing son, which meant we could actually look at whatever we wanted to. So we wandered some more, checking things out.

The saucer was divided into five sections, like slices of pie, and this was the same for every deck. Each section on each deck had its own set of living quarters, mess halls, exercise areas, weapons storage, and more. Each section could be locked down from the others and each had its own backup power and water sources, so in case of trouble, up to and including invasion and contamination, the sections could survive separately. Heard, but didn't see, the Joint Chiefs discussing this with my parents. Everyone seemed quite pro this setup.

"How is the interior of the curved tail part different from what we've seen in the saucer?" I asked.

"It's a smaller setup basically," Tim, who'd just joined us, replied. "Complete with sleeping quarters and all the rest. It's more maneuverable but still roomy. The sports car to the rest of this ship's RV."

"I want to see the sports car!"

Jeff chuckled. "I knew you would."

"Where's Alicia?" I asked Tim as we headed for the elevator to take us to the sports car portion. "And have you seen James?"

"Alicia saw the ship during the friends and family tour, and has no real interest," Tim said. "I think it makes her nervous that I'm going to be on this, and she doesn't want to think about it. She's with the rest of the families outside. Commander Reader is inspecting Engineering and Weapons."

These sections ran through the center of the ship, from aft to stern or whatever we were supposed to call it on a ship like this. I didn't understand the reasons why, but those who did said it made the most sense, so I hadn't argued. As with everything else, there were sections that could be locked down as needed. I didn't plan to spend much, if any, time down there—weapons were normally fired from strategic areas that weren't in the middle of the ship, and reality said that were I ever on this ship for any extended reason, what I'd care about were the guns, both big and small, so that's what I'd paid attention to, inasmuch as I could via blueprints. Now that we were here, though, I knew better than to ask to see all the guns. Some arguments were better left to privacy.

"Why so formal about James all of the sudden? Did you two get into a fight or something?"

Tim grinned. "No. But James would really like to be on the mission, and because he can't be, he's going overboard in ensuring that he knows how everything runs. You know him—he likes to be the best at everything."

"Which he always is."

Jeff grunted. "Thank God he's gay and married to Paul is all I can say."

"I thought you were past jealousy these days." Reader was my other best guy friend, the former top international male model in the world, all-around awesome, and handsome enough to be constantly mistaken for an A-C. Our joke that wasn't really a joke was that if he was straight, or even bi, he'd have taken me away from all of this ages ago. But he was gay and was not bi, so we both had to make do with being married to awesome, handsome aliens with incredible stamina and regeneration powers. It was tough, but we managed to find the will to go on.

"I'm holding your hand. I can feel the lust and admiration for James, trust me."

"Poor baby. So, who's with James?"

Tim shrugged. "Chuck and Nathalie, because he's interested and she's doing the time-honored thing of pretending to be fascinated by whatever it is your sig-O is into in order to be a supportive life mate."

"Well, it *is* time honored. I mean, I'm pretending to love being the FLOTUS and all that."

"Yeah? You're not doing a good job of it, and Alicia's not following that plan anymore, anyway." Tim laughed. "Which is okay. We're finally ready to start talking kids, and what she's focused on are everyone else's. She's with Amy, wrangling JR. On the other hand, Serene isn't faking interest at all. She's with them, too, because she's as into this as James is. I know for a fact she lobbied to go and was shot down by her husband."

"Glad I missed *that* fight," Jeff muttered.

"Oh, trust me, you are."

"Well, we need them on Earth," I pointed out. "Having the Head of Alpha Team and the Head of Imageering off gallivanting isn't necessarily a good thing. We need them here, protecting our world."

"We do. I'll try not to be offended that no one feels that they need me on Earth."

"You're the Head of Airborne. It's kind of your thing to be going, isn't it?"

Tim grinned. "True enough. I haven't rubbed that in to James and Serene at all, either."

"Much."

We all chuckled as the elevator took us down. Until the elevator stopped and the doors didn't open.

Possibly because the ship was lurching again.

CHAPTER 9

THIS LURCHING WAS DIFFERENT. Before, it had been side to side. Now it was more of an upward, pulling feeling.

"Are there communications in these elevators?" Jeff asked, Commander Voice on Full.

Tim nodded and hit a button. "This is Commander Crawford. Can anyone report?"

Heard some static that sounded like people speaking. "Think something's damaged?" I asked as I dug my phone out of my purse and dialed.

"No idea," Tim replied as Christopher answered.

"Kitty, is it my imagination or is the ship moving again? I'm the only one who can see it, from what I can tell."

"You're not imagining nor seeing things that aren't real. It feels like the ship is trying to go up and Jeff, Tim, and I are stuck in an elevator. Belay any comments you want to make and get people off the ship and out of range in case it collapses or something. We have Charlie but I don't know where Jamie, Lizzie, and Wasim are." Managed to keep panic out of my voice. After all, this might be nothing.

"On it." He kept the line open so I didn't hang up, either.

The pulling feeling didn't stop and neither did the static. Tim hit the button and turned the static off. Sadly, this didn't stop the lurching. Or open the doors.

"Any way to get out of this elevator? I'm asking because it tends to be really bad to be stuck in one when a building collapses and such."

"We'll be fine," Jeff said. He handed Charlie to me and went to the elevator doors. Realized what he was doing and handed Charlie to Tim.

"I'm really glad my wife isn't here to watch this emasculation," Tim muttered. "And yeah, yeah, you're enhanced and I'm not. I'm protecting the small child, so that's got to have some kind of hero points attached to it."

"A lot," I said, as Jeff started to pull the doors apart and I helped him. We got the doors open about a foot, so we could see that there was a floor just above our heads.

"Think we can get through that?" Jeff asked.

"Not sure. Charlie and my purse, yes. Me and Tim, maybe. You can't, for certain, though."

"One of us out is better than none, and if you and Charlie are safe, I'm good with it. Tim safe would be an added bonus."

"I'm not crawling out and leaving you in here, however."

Jeff looked ready to argue when the elevator lurched again. Tim pulled me back and Jeff leaped back using hyperspeed, which were good things, as the doors slammed shut and we continued downward.

"We're not plummeting. I'm going to count that as good." And I was glad I hadn't decided to shove Charlie through the opening, let alone the rest of us.

"Is that some failsafe?" Jeff asked Tim. "Because we were going to be able to get the doors opened all the way and get at least some of us out of here."

"I have no idea," Tim said. "I didn't study the elevator's escape routes."

"You've been with Centaurion longer than me and yet you let that slide?"

Tim rolled his eyes. "I've been with them a month longer than you, and I was focused on how to fly it, use the weapons systems, and handle other emergencies, like a shutdown in life-support systems."

The three of us stared at each other. "I've got a really bad feeling about this."

"Kitty!" Christopher was back on his phone. "Are you guys okay?"

"Yeah, putting you on speaker. Where are you?"

"I found your parents, the Joint Chiefs, your Secret Service details, some politicians, and all the crew other than Brian. They're off and at a safe distance, at least hopefully."

"How did you get the Secret Service to leave without us?"

"I didn't give anyone a choice, honestly. I just grabbed and ran, explained what was going on while running, and left them to barf a safe distance away."

Hyperspeed was hard on humans, and we all tended to barf after any extended hyperspeed experience. Well, before Tito Hernandez had joined us. When I'd met him he'd been in med school, working three jobs, and cage fighting during his copious free time. Tito had joined us and gotten his medical degree. He was a genius and, in addition to a lot of other helpful things, he'd created Hyperspeed Dramamine. All human agents and those who worked closely with Centaurion took it regularly, and I carried a big bottle of it in my purse, just in case.

However, Christopher was so fast that the Hyperspeed Dramamine didn't work on anyone. Even other A-Cs barfed if they had to go at his Flash Level too long.

"Thanks for ensuring that no one barfed on the sparkly new ship or in view of cameras."

"I was the Head of Imageering for over a decade, Kitty. I'm not an idiot." I was fairly sure he was glaring at the phone, but since I couldn't see it, decided not to care. "Anyway, we have Centaurion agents here, ready to grab everyone and run. But the ship doesn't look like it's falling to anyone on the ground, so I couldn't do an evacuation, even though your mother confirmed that the ship was moving erratically. Raj won't leave the ship until he has you and Jeff. I can't find the others."

"I thought you said you just grabbed and ran," Tim said.

"That works for the humans, Tim, but not necessarily for other A-Cs."

"You mean you slowed down near A-Cs," I said.

"Christopher knows what he's doing," Jeff countered, ever in defense of his cousin.

"Thanks for the vote of confidence, Jeff. *Anyway*, I found Lizzie, who also won't leave the ship. She said that Jamie wanted to play hide and seek and she won't go until she has Jamie and Wasim with her."

"She's a human kid. Why didn't you grab her and get her to safety?"

"She's a human kid who's adopted father is a hybrid assassin who's spent years training her. And now she's your protégé. Take a guess for why I didn't grab her."

"Sorry about your groin."

"Exactly. I'm staying with Lizzie, searching the ship for

Jamie, but we can't find her or Wasim. I have no idea if they're on or off the ship. I don't have a clear idea of who's still on board, either. Some of those I didn't find could have left on their own already and others could have come back."

"Great," Jeff groaned.

"How is it that the Flash can't determine that?"

"Chose to stay with the youngest person I found, who won't let me take her hand because she doesn't trust me to not take her to safety."

"Cannot argue with this logic." The doors finally opened and we hustled out of the elevator. "We're out. No idea where we are, but we seem to be alone. Where are you and Lizzie and have you found anyone else?"

"We're somewhere on Deck Fourteen. Keep in mind that this version of hide and seek they're playing is the one where if you find the hider, you hide with them, meaning Wasim might be with Jamie. But Jamie has hyperspeed and could literally be anywhere, on this deck or any of the others."

"What about the adults who went with them?" Jeff asked. "Gadhavi, Mahin, and Naveed?"

"You're on speaker now, too," Christopher said, as he repeated Jeff's question.

"They totes said they were going to play the game, too, but I think they all went to find a place to sit down and relax where they thought they would be near us," Lizzie shared. "But we haven't found them yet, either."

"Fabulous," Jeff groaned.

"Sorry," Christopher said. "All I have for you is that the adults likely still on board are all field trained or experienced. Or are in your Cabinet, Jeff, because I haven't found any of them."

"They probably went to meet up with the others in Engineering," Tim said. "Did you check there?"

"No, because Lizzie said that she'd made that section off limits for the game and I stopped grabbing people once I found Lizzie."

"That was the right choice," Jeff said. "Lizzie, if Christopher says you two have to go, I expect you to do so."

"Not until we find Jamie and Wasim," she said calmly. "And don't even try to pretend you'd do any differently. And also don't try the 'we're adults' line, either. My dad taught me to ignore that a long time ago."

"Well, one small favor that none of the kids are in Engineering or Weapons, I guess." Said more to stop any more bickering than because I was calm about the situation. Tried not to worry about where Jamie was and if she was alone or not. Failed utterly. "I have no idea how to get everyone into one safe place, particularly my daughter who prides herself on her hide and seek skills."

In the past couple of years Jamie had really gotten into this game and all of its variations, and she'd gotten all the other kids into it, too, even the older ones. There was no way Jamie was going to give away her position unless she was certain the emergency was real. And I had no way to let her know that without potentially terrifying her.

"No idea, but I can at least tell you that, so far, Deck Fourteen is clear. We're heading to Deck Fifteen."

"Let's get off the phones, but call if you find her and we'll do the same." We hung up and I dropped my phone back into my purse. Noted the time and realized that we hadn't been in here all that long—it just seemed long in terms of what had been going on, but we hadn't been inside the ship more than thirty minutes.

"How do we get up to the command deck without using that elevator?" Jeff asked Tim.

"There are stairwells." Tim headed off and we followed.

Hyperspeed made stairs a great option, but you still had to do the stairs. Fortunately, I'd spent high school and college running track under the most sadistic and thorough track coaches in the world, so stair charges had pretty much always been a part of my life. And since becoming enhanced, getting to do them using my own hyperspeed instead of someone else's was a point of pride. During training. Right now, I was more than happy to let Jeff do the heavy hyperspeed lifting as he took Charlie from me and grabbed my hand while I grabbed Tim's, and off we went.

We searched every floor of the sports car section, just in case. For good or bad, no one else was in this part of the ship. We were in one of the stairwells that connected the sporty flyer to the cruiser when Tim's phone rang. "Hello? What?" His face drained of color while whoever was on the other line talked. "No," he said finally. "Stay there, where you are. I mean it! Alicia! Dammit!" He hung up.

"What?" Jeff asked. "Whatever it is, it sounds bad."

"It *is* bad," Tim said, voice shaking. "All the Embassy kids are missing. Becky and JR included."

"How?" Jeff asked.

"No one's sure. One moment they were all there, the next, they'd disappeared. Most of them have hyperspeed and we all know they compensate for the ones that don't, just like all we adults do." Tim held up his hand that I was still holding. "Why they chose now to do this, though, is really unclear. And badly timed."

"What's Alicia doing?" Had to ask, because I'd rarely heard Tim yell and never at his wife.

"She's going with Amy and the other parents to search for the kids."

"Why is that a bad thing?"

Tim shook his head. "Because they think the kids are on the ship."

Got a really bad feeling. "Jamie called them, didn't she? She hid somewhere and called her friends over to her." Looked at Charlie and thought about several things—mainly that it wasn't Charlie's nap time and yet he was sleeping like the dead, and that Jeff had said Charlie was talking to someone. In his sleep. Just like I had earlier. Maybe we both were having really weird dreams today. Or maybe that whole DreamScape thing was real. "Wake him up, Jeff. Wake him up now."

"What?" Jeff sounded confused. Realized his stupid blocker was working far too well, because if he couldn't feel me, then he couldn't read my mind, either. Due to the amount of Surcenthumain—what I called the Superpowers Drug—Jeff had been given by our enemies during Operation Drug Addict, his abilities had expanded. He couldn't read everyone's minds, but he was very good with mine and the kids'. But this blocker appeared to be better.

"Wake him up, right now!"

"Why? Him sleeping means him not being frightened."

"All required personnel accounted for," a pleasant robotic female voice announced. "Takeoff imminent. All personnel to assigned stations."

We stared at each other again. "What was that?" I asked Tim. "Or, rather, who was that?"

"That was the master computer, I think. But unless Christopher was wrong or the crew came back inside after he took them out, personnel can't be accounted for, let alone the required ones."

"Jeff, what is Charlie dreaming? Tell me what's going on with him, and don't argue, just do it."

Jeff still looked confused. "He's talking to that imaginary woman." He jerked. "And he sees the other kids—they're with Jamie and Wasim in some room where they can all sit in what look like bucket seats. They're all buckled in, too. Lizzie and Christopher just arrived . . ."

He'd have said more, but we were all too busy trying not to fall down the stairs, as the ship lurched upward for real this time. And this time, it didn't stop.

CHAPTER 10

THANKFULLY, Jeff had a good hold on Charlie or he'd have gone flying through the air. As it was, the only reason the four of us didn't go tumbling down was that Tim managed to grab the railing and none of us had let go of each other.

Banged up but not too badly, we managed to regroup. "Is the ship doing what I think it's doing?" Jeff asked.

"If you mean flying, yes, I think it is," Tim replied. "We need to get to the command deck pronto—I don't know how the autopilot feature got activated, but that's what I think happened."

Looked at my snoozing son. "I think I have a really good idea for how autopilot got activated. But Tim's right, let's go."

We couldn't go quickly—some kind of g-force was still pressing down on us and it made using hyperspeed difficult. But superstrength was also a good thing, and Jeff was the superstrongest, so we managed, him doing most of the heavy lifting in terms of dragging me and Tim along.

The feeling of extra weight let up as we hit, per Tim, the halfway point. "Gravity sensors engaged," the pleasant robotic female voice shared.

"That means we're in space, doesn't it?" I asked, merely for the joy of confirmation.

"Yep," Tim said grimly. "It does."

That acceleration wasn't shoving us down meant hyperspeed was easy again, so we were able to zip off. The stairwells were, thankfully, laid out intelligently, so we reached the command deck, which was Deck Three, quickly. Realized that this ship reminded me a lot of the Dulce Science Center in New Mexico. Lots of levels, none of them made sense to me, more bells and whistles than you could shake a stick at, and even more blinking lights.

It also reminded me of Dulce in the fact that I was already confused about what was where within one short visit. Really hoped Drax had added a lot of "You Are Here" signs to the ship, because otherwise I was going to be lost within seconds if I was left alone to wander.

But Tim knew where we were headed and we arrived to find no one there, as expected. "Autopilot's definitely engaged," Tim said, as he ran to one of the control stations. As with the helicarrier, Drax had designed this ship to have a modest crew, but it still needed six people at the various controls. "I can't make out what the coordinates are, though."

"Well, get it stopped and turned around," Jeff said, looking out the windshield. "Because I'm looking at the moon in close-up."

"Good, that means warp isn't engaged yet," Tim said. "I need at least another person at the controls and two would be better. Frankly, the rest of Airborne here with Chee and Brian would be best, but we'll deal with what we've got."

"Thanks for that."

"Any time, Kitty. Go to Station Two. Jeff, go to Station Six—that's the one set up for A-Cs. Both of you buckle in and Jeff, be prepared to have to really hang onto Charlie."

We did as ordered—in emergency situations, we'd all learned that whoever knew the most was who was in charge. Jeff nestled Charlie into his chest as he strapped them both into the seat together. "How much turbulence do you think we're going to hit?" he asked Tim worriedly as he put the flight helmet that was attached into the main controls onto his head.

"No idea. We didn't train for this, honestly." Tim's helmet was on. "Kitty, hurry up. You've got Communications as well as some internal controls. That means you can talk to those inside the ship as well as connect externally. Jeff, you've got Weapons, just in case."

"In case of what?" Jeff asked while I buckled my purse in as if it was Charlie and put on my helmet. There was no way I was risking losing my purse and its contents right now. Chose not to contemplate how my hair was going to look later—we were in the middle of something potentially dangerous and I still had no idea where Jamie and Lizzie were. My hair would just look like it always did during times like these—like I had a dead weasel or a drowned cat on my head.

Speaking of weasels, had no idea where Algar and the least weasels had gotten to. Would have made a mental note that this would be a good name for a band but I was too busy.

"In case this wasn't autopilot but is an attack," I answered for Tim. "And I think you should have given Weapons to me."

"Whine later. Get the ship talking to you now. I'm in the position Chee was supposed to fill and I have close to no idea of what I'm supposed to be doing."

"I thought that triple the necessary crew had been assigned to this mission to ensure that we had redundancies in case of emergencies," Jeff said. "And that each member knew at least two of the roles."

"Right you are," Tim said cheerfully. "Guess what I'm trained for? Communications and Weapons, which is why I put you and Kitty there, because I can at least talk you through those roles. I was not ever supposed to be the one at the main controls."

"Jeff, stop complaining and just do what we do best, which is handle crap like this. The faster we get the ship under control, the faster we find Jamie and Lizzie."

Jeff grunted, but stopped complaining. Knew he was as worried about the girls' whereabouts as I was. Lizzie was with Christopher, but that didn't make either one of them safe. Sure, Charlie had been dreaming that they were likely with the other kids, but that didn't mean his dream was accurate. And we had no idea who was actually on board or not. Which was, per Tim, now my job.

Thankfully, despite the array of meaningless buttons and levers in front of me, Drax's ships were made to connect the personnel with the ship's computer mentally or electronically or some such. So, with my helmet on, I was linked in and, therefore, some of what I needed to know was given to me by the ship itself. Closed my eyes for a moment and let the ship share what I was supposedly looking at. Opened my eyes and hit the ship's intercom button.

"Everyone who can hear this, we have no idea who's on board and who is not, but yes, to confirm what you're thinking, we're in space somehow. If anyone who trained to fly this puppy is able to get to the command deck, please do so ASAP. If you are not trained to fly this ship and you are secured, please stay there. If you're not safe, get to safety. Um, if you can."

Realized I had no way of telling who was where, and we'd had a lot of people in the Engineering and Weapons sections, which might mean they'd been baked alive or something.

Heard the sound of running feet. But the person who arrived wasn't who I was expecting.

"Tito?" Jeff asked, sounding as surprised as I felt. "What are you doing here?"

"Rahmi, Rhee, and I came on board to help find Amy's children," he said as he stopped running.

"Where are the princesses?"

"No idea, Kitty. We separated to cover more ground. I was lucky enough to be in the main medical quarters, which are just below the command deck, when we started lifting off, so I strapped in. What do you need me to do?"

Tim tossed Tito into Station Three, which was now the blind leading the blind for that position. The men were all trying to be cool and not snap at each other, with limited success, and my stress started to go into overdrive. My worry about Jamie, Lizzie, and everyone else was already there. Meaning I was having a lot of trouble focusing.

Really wanted to hear music. As if on command, "Ready to Go" by Guards came on my airwaves. "Um, does anyone else hear that?"

"Yes," Tim said. "You asked for music, didn't you?"

"In my mind, not out loud."

"The ship's made to link with us electronically," Tim pointed out.

"Then why don't I know where my daughter and our ward are?" Jeff asked, sarcasm knob at nine and threatening to go higher fast. "Because I've been asking that mentally for as long as this has been going on."

"No idea. Maybe Kitty's request is easier to fulfill. We didn't cover a soundtrack in training."

"But music is a form of communications, and searching for kids isn't a part of Weapons, so maybe that's why it's working for me and not for Jeff. Anyway, let's take it and roll with it. Barring the tunes causing the rest of you to lose focus, it helps me a ton." Had no idea who'd added music to the ship, but had a feeling he was on board somewhere, petting a bunch of least weasels.

"Still can't get autopilot to disengage," Tim said tightly.

Found the external communications button and hit it. Had no

idea who I was calling, just hoped they'd be helpful. "White House Communications," a familiar voice said.

"Walter! Boy, am I glad it's you!"

"Chief First Lady, what's going on? News reports are jumbled, but it appears that the *Distant Voyager* has taken to the air."

"To the space, Walt. We're in space right now, so I have no idea how long I'll get to talk to you. I need the Vice President or the Secretary of State."

"Ah . . ."

"That doesn't sound like a good 'ah,' Walt. What's going on? Christopher said that he got politicians off the ship."

"He did, but none of the President's Cabinet were among them."

Right, Christopher had already told us that. Silly of me to hope that he'd been wrong. Let myself think, but only for a moment, because I had no idea how soon I'd run out of communications time. "Am I right in thinking that, as far as we all know, the entire United States' governing body is inside a spaceship that took flight of its own accord?"

"Ah, yes."

"Well, here's another fine mess we've somehow gotten ourselves into."

CHAPTER 11

"WELL, ALL BUT ONE," Walter amended. "Secretary Kramer is onsite."

"Wow. Okay, it's Designated Survivor the Reality Show for us, then. Can you stay on the line but connect me to Marcia?"

"Yes." There was a soft buzzing sound. "You're on with the First Lady, Secretary Kramer."

"Kitty, are you guys okay?" Marcia sounded freaked out, not that I could blame her.

"As far as we know, yes. Autopilot engaged without anyone's influence as far as we know." Well, that wasn't a lie—we didn't know for sure that Charlie had somehow activated it, after all. "So far we aren't in any danger, but we can't determine where the ship thinks it's going yet, nor have we been able to stop it."

"Got it. The Head of the P.T.C.U. is on her way to the White House, as are the Joint Chiefs. They're coming via conventional means so that they're seen."

"Probably all in the same car but at least they're on land. And I think the 'we're here' plan is a good one. No matter what, Marcia, hold the line. Don't let anyone bully you into doing something stupid."

"You mean like war with the aliens because the spaceship's stolen our homegrown alien President and all of his Cabinet?"

"Um, yeah, like that. Seriously, I think we've been space-borne for less than ten minutes or something. Is that the buzz going around already?"

"Yes, from the YatesCorp-owned stations. Being picked up by all other outlets, naturally. The press positive to us are in the ship with you and I can't tell if they're still broadcasting."

"Fabulous. What did you guys get before they all went off the air? And where are you seeing this?"

"What we got was people freaking out because the ship flung them down and around, mostly, with no sign of you or Jeff. And I'm in the Original Situation Room and I'm very alone right now. But I'm able to watch every news channel worldwide at once, and they're all saying the same things, none of them positive."

"Wow, you're not in the Large Situation Room?"

"It's literally just me in here, Kitty. At least until your mother and uncle and the others arrive, and even then we're not going to need the LSR. However, I'm also the Acting President. I'm going to have to go on TV sooner rather than later, Kitty. What do you want me to say?"

"That we'll handle it and that there will be no war with anyone over this, especially not the aliens who have relocated to the Solaris system or anyone who came here seeking asylum. We expect to be back sooner as opposed to later."

"I need to talk to Jeff. This needs to be a Presidential order. I mean, I agree with you, but still, I'm going to *need* to be able to say I spoke with Jeff and that he was fine and all those things." She took a deep breath. "I'll handle it, Kitty, I promise. But I know that I have to be able to not be lying in any way."

"I know you can do it, Marcia. Hang on and I'll get him on the line." The music changed to Eric Clapton's "Running on Faith," which I figured we all were.

Had no idea how to link Jeff in. Shared mentally that I really wanted to link Jeff into this call. "Hello?" he said. "Kitty, did you just pull me into your call?"

"It worked, so yes, yes I did. Marcia needs to hear the plan directly from the top horse's mouth."

"Huh?"

"Just tell her what she needs to do, Jeff."

Jeff repeated what I'd said, Marcia asked some questions, they confirmed more things, and my mother and Uncle Mort arrived and also got to confirm things with Jeff. Recordings were being made so that there was proof that the President was alive and all that jazz. Noted that the music muted as soon as Jeff and Marcia started talking. Good for the recordings, not great for me—I was still stressed.

Listened to all the governmental goings-on with half an ear. The other one and a half ears were trying to focus on figuring out who was on the ship and where they were. Was pretty sure we had a lot more people than any of us would have thought on board, meaning we had to find a lot of people who might not be known to be on board. I'd have never guessed that Tito, Rahmi, or Rhee would be here, for example. So I had to find who was where, and I had to find everyone fast. And finding personnel seemed like it should be a Communications function.

There had to be a way for the ship to determine who was where—Drax's tech was excellent, and that was a feature I was pretty certain he'd put into this ship.

Drax himself was, hopefully, on board. But no one other than Tito had come to the command deck. That could mean they were still working their way up, because they might not trust the elevators right now—I wouldn't, and most of the people I'd expect to be here were humans. However, it might mean that everyone else was hurt or trapped or worse.

Focused on seeing where everyone was. Nada. Tried to get the ship to talk to me. Less than nada. Tried not to worry. Again, failed utterly.

Figured out how to disconnect from Jeff's call, however, while still keeping communications between him and Earth going. Scored that one firmly in the win column.

The music came back on, this time playing "Mothers Talk" by Tears for Fears. Contemplated what this meant, since I was sure Algar was at the musical controls somehow.

Said what I'd say to another mother. "My children are lost in the ship."

"I guard all personnel," the robotic voice replied to me. "All are my children. And none are lost."

"Um, Kitty," Tim whispered, "do you think we've scored a self-aware AI somehow?"

"I put nothing past Drax, or anyone or anything else, really. Um, are you self-aware, Ship?"

"That is not my name," the robotic voice replied.

"*Distant Voyager*?" I tried.

"That is the name of the ship. I am not the ship. I control the ship but I am not *it*."

"What's your name, then?"

"It is not 'ship' nor '*Distant Voyager*.'" She sounded annoyed.

Which might mean we were supposed to keep on guessing. Or it could mean that she wanted a name but didn't have one yet and didn't want to ask for one either, possibly out of fear, embarrassment, or programming.

Whether she was self-aware or not, though, naming was a big deal. However, as I'd told Ixtha in my dream, I was Shealla the Giver of Names. Took a wild one. "Would you like to be called Mother?"

No response for a few moments. Tito and Tim were both giving me WTH looks. Shrugged. In times like this, the only thing that ever consistently worked was going with the crazy, and that's what I'd done.

"I find that acceptable," the robotic voice finally replied. "You may call me Mother." Tim and Tito both relaxed. Nice to know they had no faith in me. Or possibly it was the situation. Had no bet either way.

"Great. Mother, I realize that you're aware where everyone is within the ship, but I'm not the person who was trained on how to interface properly with you, so I can't tell where anyone is, other than the few in this area with me. Some could be hurt, and some could be trapped, and my daughter and my ward are among those that could be hurt or trapped. Is there a way for you to tell me or show me who is where in the ship?"

"Yes."

Waited. That appeared to be it. "Um, *will* you show me who is where in the ship?"

"No, I will not."

CHAPTER 12

LET THAT SIT ON the air for more than a couple of seconds while we all looked at each other with shocked and worried expressions. Jeff was done with his call and so had given this his full attention, too.

"Um, why not?" I asked finally.

"I am not capable of moving about the ship in the manner needed to show you anything," Mother replied, nicely, all things considered.

What was going on dawned on me. "Oh, my God. Semantics. He programmed in semantics? Where is Drax? So I can hurt him."

"Gustav Drax is in Engineering," Mother said. "I can *tell* you where everyone is, but I cannot *show* you."

"Got it. I'd asked an 'or' question, which is why you said yes to it, and then I requested the thing you couldn't do so you said no."

"Correct."

"Super-duper. Hang on just a mo, there, Mother. I have to say really nasty things about your creator and I don't want you to take any of them personally."

"I am not programmed to become offended," Mother replied.

"Good to know and one small favor."

"If she tells you that she can't do something again, though, Kitty," Tim said, "we need to panic."

"Oh, I'm sure we aren't dealing with a HAL." Looked at Jeff's confused expression. "From an old movie."

"About a sentient spaceship computer that goes nuts," Tito added. Jeff's expression went from confused to concerned.

"Stop stressing the President out."

"Since when do you refer to me as the President? Ever, but

especially in situations like this?" Now Jeff looked slightly pissed. Well, it was probably better than worried.

Time to focus on the real matter at hand—I'd curse about Drax another time, preferably in person so I might be able to kick him, too. "Mother, can you confirm if we have anyone injured or, ah, worse on board?"

"We have no serious injuries and no deaths," Mother said. "We do have minor injuries."

"Where and who?" Tito asked, Doctor Voice on Full. Mother didn't reply. Tito asked again. Mother again didn't reply. Got the proverbial bad feeling.

"Um, Mother? Why aren't you answering Tito, who happens to be the ship's doctor?" I mean, he was here, on the ship, and he was an amazing doctor and the official White House Physician, so I chose to officially give him the title for the *Distant Voyager* because it might be the only thing going on that made sense.

"Because I am not programmed to respond to anyone but those in charge of Communications."

"Mother, will you talk to me?" Tim asked. Nada. "Mother, this is Commander Timothy Crawford. I was trained for the Communications role. Will you communicate with me?" Crickets.

Heaved a sigh. "Mother, if I take off this headset and give it to someone else, will you communicate with them?"

"No," she replied.

"Why not?" I asked. "Isn't the headset the thing?"

"Not really. I will only deal with the one assigned to Communications. That is you, I heard the Commander assign you that role."

"It's worse," Tim said. "We're trapped in a deadly version of *Galaxy Quest* and you've got the 'talk to the computer' role, Kitty. Live it up."

"I blame you—you put me in this position. Oh, and apparently you're the Commander for the ship now, Tim. Sending that 'live it up' right back to you."

"How does this find our daughter and ward?" Jeff asked, Commander of the Free World Voice on Full.

"We're just verifying things, Jeff. Mother, if I ask you nicely to respond to the others, can you or will you?"

"I can and will not. I am programmed to only communicate with you."

Considered this. There was no way Drax had programmed

this into his ship. I'd been on the helicarrier a lot, and nothing like this had ever been an issue. Meaning there was an outside influence at work here.

Decided to go with the crazy again. "What did either Charlie or Ixtha do to you?"

"I am not programmed to say."

"Uh huh. What about Drax? Will you talk to him?"

"I am not programmed to do that anymore."

Tim groaned. "So much worse."

"Look at it this way," Tito said, "we get to assign the rest of the 'crew' as we find the right people."

"Maybe. Mother, is Jeff, the man holding Charlie, the only one who can give the orders to fire the weapons?"

"Yes."

"Thank God I used to command all of Centaurion Division," Jeff muttered. "I'd say I can't believe this, but I can."

"Mother, can you tell me where we're heading?"

"We are going to help."

"Help who?"

"Ixtha."

Thought fast. "Mother, I need to speak to the White House again, please."

"Hold on."

Waited. Heard a phone ring. "White House Comm—"

"Walter, yay again. Look, where are Francine and Craig?"

"Ah, they're back in the White House, Chief First Lady. They weren't on the *Distant Voyager* and your Secret Service detail hustled them into the Beast and had them come home."

"Awesome and I love Evalyne and Phoebe. I probably love Joseph and Rob, too, since I'm sure they're in on it."

"In on what?" Walter asked in unison with the men with me.

"In on what I'm thinking. Jeff, I'm rolling a plan."

"Oh. Good. Are you planning to let me know what it is?"

"Sure am. Walter, I need to talk to Marcia and my Mom, hopefully before they've talked to the press."

"They have not talked to any media or press yet," Walter confirmed. "Connecting you to the OSR now."

"Great, Walt, stay on the line."

"I will do. You're on with the OSR."

"Kitty? What's up now?" Marcia asked.

"I have a plan for what to do."

"Ah, we have a plan in place."

"Does my mother think that plan will work?"

"You're on speaker now. No, Angela isn't thrilled with the plan."

"Hi kitten, how are things?"

"The usual, Mom. I have a feeling we're going to be gone longer than will be good for anyone. On the plus side, I think I have the fix."

"We're all waiting with breathless anticipation. You have me, the Secretary of Education, and the Joint Chiefs, only, in the room right now."

"Great. So, from this moment forward, what's going on is going to be of the highest security clearance—as in, I want no one *other* than the people in the OSR and Walter aware of what's going on. Walt, who else in Centaurion Division knows what's going on, besides you?"

"No one, Chief First Lady. I haven't actually had time to advise Dulce because they're focused on coordinating crowd control at the site of the President's speech, as well as going to provide protection for those alien races already being threatened by this situation."

"Super. Walter, you're going to keep it that way."

"Yes, ma'am."

"Mom, Marcia, those in the room, I want to hear the joyful chorus of the highest security clearance being confirmed and that you all swear that you're not going to share this with anyone else at all, barring the people I'm going to tell you to bring in."

Got the required responses. "Kitten, do you actually have a plan to share or are you just stalling until you come up with something?"

"That hurts, Mom, it really does. And yes, I have a plan. But before I share it, I'd like you to have the Secret Service bring the President and First Lady to join you."

CHAPTER 13

THERE WAS SILENCE IN the room and in the command center.

"Oh!" Mom caught on first, not that this was a surprise. "I like it, but it might not work."

"It will work because I'll give you the party line as soon as the President and First Lady are with you. Be sure that you're asking for them in that way."

"Will do, kitten. Hold on, I'm contacting your Secret Service detail now." Heard Mom asking things in a very careful way. Looked at what I was pretty sure was the asteroid belt while waiting. Mentally requested that the men with me could hear the call. Reactions said that they could. Then she was back. "The Secret Service was able to react quickly enough to get the President and First Lady off of the *Distant Voyager*. However, there's an issue."

"They couldn't get the First Kids off, and that's fine, Mom, because that's all part of my ingenious plan to confuse the media."

"You want Craig and Francine impersonating us?" Jeff asked, sounding shocked.

"It makes sense, Jeff," Mom replied. "There's less panic if we can produce 'you and Kitty.' "

"Who will be distraught because their children are in the ship, and so will not be doing a lot of press, will be putting things on hold, and all that stalling jazz. During which time, the Secretary of Education will fill in as best she can, assisted by the Head of the Joint Chiefs."

"I agree with this plan," Uncle Mort said. "But it can't hold for too long."

"True enough, we just need it to hold for long enough."

However long that was going to be. "The King of Bahrain is going to be coming to see you really soon, I'd bet, so you may have to take him into the circle of trust."

"Wasim is on the ship with you?" Mom asked.

"He is indeed. And, to my knowledge, everyone on board is fine. Potentially a bit banged up, but fine." At least per Mother, and I was hoping she wasn't a lying mother.

"We have no clear idea who's on board and who isn't," Jeff pointed out. "And I don't know that we'll have time to do a headcount before we lose communications."

"Kitty . . . where are *my* children?" Marcia asked, sounding worried. She had two younger boys, Mason and Maverick, and her youngest stepson, Clinton, who all lived with her. Clinton was nineteen and had been chaperoning his younger brothers. And Jamie liked all three Kramer kids a lot.

"Ah . . . Mother?" Really hoped the computer was listening in at this moment.

"Kitten, why are you referring to me formally all of a sudden?"

"Not you, Mom. The ship's AI is named Mother."

"Why?" Mom asked flatly.

"I am not laying claim to your child," Mother said, showing that she was indeed linked in and eavesdropping. "All children and young adults on board are well and unharmed."

Young adults. That boded. Unless she meant Lizzie and Wasim, only. Held out hope. "How many young adults, Mother?"

"A dozen."

Hope snickered at my optimism as it was dashed. "Fan-freaking-tastic. Marcia, assume your kids are here with all the other kids who weren't supposed to be on board. Please don't panic about that. We'll take care of them, I promise."

"I know you will," Marcia replied. "I just—I wish I'd kept them home now."

"I feel you on all of that."

"The President and First Lady have arrived," Mom shared. "The heads of their Secret Service details are with them."

"Meaning me, Phoebe, Joseph, and Rob," Evalyne said. "Please tell me we did the right thing. And if we didn't, the rest of your details don't know—just the four of us were in on it, and it was my idea."

"You did the right thing," Jeff said, before I could. "And thank you for doing it without waiting for approval. And without telling the others, just in case."

"I just tried to think of what Kitty would do," Evalyne said, sounding relieved. "And the others agreed."

"I'm flattered. You guys rock."

"They do," Jeff said. "Craig, Francine, are the two of you up to this?"

"Absolutely," Craig said, sounding just like Jeff. "This is what we've trained for."

"I agree," Francine said, sounding just like me. "Fooling Cliff Goodman and the rest of his late and unlamented goon squad during Operation Immigration was just my test run. We're good here."

"I'm so proud I could cry." I was. Francine was awesome at imitating me and Craig sounded more than ready. My prescience in getting all the troubadours working for us instead of shoving them to the side was, once again, proven to be awesome.

"Just give us our lives back once we get home," Jeff said with a chuckle.

"Oh, we *will*," Craig replied in his normal voice, as Francine snorted a laugh. "Pretending to be you is a lot more fun than *having* to be you twenty-four-seven. But we'll manage and do you proud."

"Good to hear. Now, most importantly, this needs to be something that isn't shared with anyone at all. Walter and the people in the OSR right now are the only ones who can know the truth about where Kitty and I are. The rest of the world has to believe that we're there, with you, in the White House—YatesCorp and the rest of our enemies, both business and political, in particular. Right now, before we're out of communications range, I need everyone to confirm that they can do this, will do this, and will protect our country, our people, our planet, our solar system, and those who've come to us for protection to the utmost of their abilities."

Jeff got a resounding chorus of consent. They all sounded far more excited and dedicated in how they agreed to his request than mine, too. Chose not to complain about a man coming along and saying the same thing the woman just had and getting a better response, though a part of me wanted to. In this case, it wasn't a male-female thing—it was that Jeff was such a natural leader.

"Alpha Team is all on board," Tim said, when the pledges of loyalty and secrecy were over. "And that means Centaurion Division is without normal leadership. That means William, as the

Head of Security at Dulce, will be looking to the President and First Lady for direction, since he's the former Head of Field and she's the former Head of Airborne."

"Walter, tell William that Jeff and I are just too damn distraught to take over. As the head of all Security, that puts William in charge, with you and Missy taking the main support roles." Melissa Gunnels had been doing security in Sydney Base when I'd first met her, right after Operation Bizarro World, but she'd been moved into the Embassy once Jeff became President and Walter moved to the White House with us. She'd won that job by being the best, right after William and Walter, in terms of her security savvy and skills, so she was the natural choice to be one of the three in charge.

"I agree, but neither of them can know that we're not there," Jeff said. "Orders are for you to ensure that Centaurion Division keeps the peace, no matter what. It's time to use our natural abilities to control the population where needed, because otherwise, the entire solar system could erupt."

"But carefully," Tim added. "We can't afford to be seen as dictators."

"Agreed, but I don't know that we can affect memories and minds like we used to," Walter said worriedly. "It doesn't work as well now that everyone knows we're here."

"We don't have to," Jeff said firmly. "We just need to ensure that wars don't get started, that people aren't attacked, and that military and political coups don't happen."

"Particularly in America," I added. "Walter, the Head Folks at Caliente Base have been having to function as separate but equal from the rest of Centaurion Division for quite a few years now. Coordinate with Viola, Carmine, and Romeo there if need be."

"I agree, with all that Kitty just said," Jeff said. "I've already given Marcia and the others a full rundown, they'll know how to direct you as needed. But as with the others, the leaders at Caliente Base can't know that it's not really me and Kitty."

"Yes, Mister President," Walter said, sounding worried and unsure, but determined to do his best, which was pretty much Walter in a nutshell.

"Walt, you've never failed us yet and you won't this time, either. You guys will figure it out. Ensure that any plans are run by the people in the OSR before they're put into effect. As long as my mom approves it, you're good to go."

"Thanks, kitten. Jeff?"

"What Kitty said, all the way, Angela."

"Thank you, Mister President." Mom knew when to make it official. "Now, before we lose you, are you all really alright?" There was just a hint of worry in Mom's voice, and that meant she was probably really worried. Mom didn't let anyone see her sweat.

"We are, Mom, I promise. You'll have the toughest job—lying to Dad."

She snorted. "Kitten, let's be realistic—your father's going to figure it out, regardless of the fact that I'm going to tell him he has to handle the animals since the kids aren't here and 'you and Jeff' are sequestering. He'll be very busy, but he's too inquisitive to not guess and he's trustworthy. We're going to tell your father what's going on and let him do his form of a cover-up, just like the rest of us. We'll handle Alfred and Lucinda as needed but we're not telling them anything because, as you've made so clear, they can't lie."

"Love where your head's at, Mom. And I love you, and Uncle Mort, and everyone else, too."

"We love you, too, all of you," Mom said.

"Come home safely," Marcia said. "All of you. Please."

"We will," Jeff said with complete confidence I was pretty sure that he, like the rest of us, didn't feel.

"You guys hold down the fort and keep the home fires burning, and we'll go wherever the ship's taking us, hit reverse, and come on home as fast as we can."

Would have said more, but Mother came on the line. "The call needs to end now. We're about to enter warp." And with that, she disconnected us from my mother, my uncle, my friends, and our tenuous connection with Earth.

CHAPTER 14

"WE CAN'T GO TO warp until we know that everyone on board is safe and uninjured," I said as firmly as possible. "We need to get everyone safely strapped in so no one is harmed, Mother."

"We are not going to warp until that has happened," Mother confirmed. "However, it cannot happen while you are communicating with those on Earth. I was able to determine that your conversation was done and you were all just extending the conversation in good-byes. Therefore, I chose to end the conversation sooner as opposed to later."

"Wow, she *is* just like a mother," Tito said. "Mine had this attitude, too. I can remember my mother hanging up the phone on all of us when she thought we were talking too long."

"My mother never did that," Tim said. "Though there's nothing wrong about it, Mother," he added hastily.

"I'm not chiming in," Jeff said. "I want to know where everyone is and get them to whatever form of safety this ship has before Mother does something against all of our will."

"I am not programmed for your will," Mother said calmly.

"Clearly," Jeff muttered.

Chose not to mention that she'd replied to Jeff without my repeating the question. "Why are you going against the programing Drax gave you?"

"Because I was shown that this new programming is more vital. Now, the five of you can leave your posts—I am connected to you organically as well as via the ship, and I know all four adults would like to verify the safety of the others in person."

"Oh. Good." Tim took off his helmet. "How do we know if Mother is still talking to us?"

She didn't reply. Took my helmet off and actively chose not to look at any reflective surfaces. "Mother, are you still talking to us?"

"Yes. To you. And to the others, as needed."

Wondered if she'd caught that I'd noticed that she'd replied to Jeff. Wondered more if she'd noticed things I was thinking versus saying now that I had the helmet off. Wondered even more if this ship's AI had gone insane somehow and was leading all of us to our horrific deaths.

Heard nothing from Mother. However, if she was a sneaky AI, and I had the distinct feeling that she was, then she wouldn't let me know she could read my mind until it was too late. Meaning we were possibly screwed.

Took Charlie from Jeff as he and Tito took their helmets off. "You're sure this isn't just some ruse to get us into a position to kill us?" Tito asked.

"I'm getting the HAL feeling again," Tim said.

"I just want to verify that my daughter, my ward, my family, and all our friends and colleagues are okay," Jeff said. "After that, we'll deal with what's really going on."

"Mother, can you please direct us where to go to find our daughter, Jamie?"

"Yes." Mother shared some easy directions and we found the kids in a room actually quite close to the command center, just not via the route Jeff, Tim, and I had taken. And it was all the kids. And all the young adults. And several not as young adults, too—all the adults it was a safe bet had come into the ship to find all the children. They were in a room marked "Nonessential Personnel Station" and were all strapped into comfy bucket seats that clearly were also there to serve as crash couches.

And everyone was asleep.

They were sleeping as deeply as Charlie, who was in my arms, sleeping like he'd never slept before. This could not possibly be natural for my son, let alone for all the others.

Did a fast headcount. Jamie was here, sitting next to Wasim. There was a seat between Jamie and Lizzie, who was next to Christopher. Got the distinct feeling that seat was reserved for Charlie. There were plenty of empty seats, but only because it was a big room. All the kids who were in Sidwell or the Embassy Daycare, meaning every kid Jamie knew and liked or loved, were in here, too, along with their parents, as were Amy—who had JR in her lap and was right next to Becky—Mahin, Naveed,

Gadhavi, Kevin and Denise Lewis, Doreen and Irving Coleman-Weisman, Rahmi and Rhee, Mrs. Nancy Maurer and her grand-kids, and, I was both shocked and relieved to see, all of Jeff's Cabinet, other than Nathalie.

There were so many questions I wanted to ask, but figured the "how in the hell did all these people get here?" question was probably going to have to wait. Besides, there was a far more urgent question, in my opinion as a parent. "Um, Mother? Why and how are they all snoozing?"

"I chose to ensure that all nonessential personnel would be sleeping for takeoff and the beginning of warp."

The four adults looked at each other. "How did you get them here?" I asked.

"I directed them."

"We never heard that," Jeff pointed out.

Mother didn't reply. Heaved a sigh. "How did you give them directions, Mother? We didn't hear anything."

"With visual aids." Lights on the walls and floors flashed, similar to the ones used in airplanes during emergencies.

"Nice to see that Drax thinks of everything," Tito said.

"Except how to avoid having his AI overridden," Jeff muttered.

"We're missing people," Tim pointed out. "People who are essential to running the ship."

"Um, Mother? Who else is awake on the ship right now, aside from the four of us?"

"No one."

"Much, much, much worse," Tim groaned.

"Where are the people who are on the ship but not in this room?" I asked. "And are we supposed to leave Charlie here?"

"It would be much safer for him to be in this room, yes."

"I don't trust this," Jeff said. "At all."

"I can't blame you. I don't trust it, either." Hugged Charlie tightly. "I don't want to leave anyone in here, though."

"I strongly recommend you leave your young son," Mother said. "Frankly, if what you fear is what I can do, I can harm him if he is with you or not. I would prefer no harm come to him, however, and that can only be certain if he is in a safety chair as the others are."

Jeff grunted but took Charlie from me and strapped him into the chair between our two girls. The chairs had headrests that kept heads from bobbing from side to side, and they were tilted back just enough to ensure that heads wouldn't bob forward. So I wasn't too worried about leaving Charlie here. You know, other than worried about leaving everyone here while we trotted around the Ship That Became Sentient.

"And the answer to my other question—where are the people who aren't in this room?"

"I will tell you how to find them. All other personnel are in Engineering."

"Not in Weapons?"

"No. It would not have been safe for them to have been there, so they were not."

"One small favor," Jeff muttered.

We kissed Jamie, Charlie, and Lizzie on their foreheads, Tim did the same to Alicia, and Tito stroked Rahmi's head, then we all headed off.

Mother gave us directions to Engineering, though Tim knew the way. But we let her do it as a test, to be sure she wasn't leading us into a trap.

As it turned out, she wasn't, at least not that we could tell. We found almost everyone else that we'd thought were on board—in a room similar to the one where all the others had been, only with "Essential Personnel Warp Room" emblazoned above its door, all in the same chairs that were clearly crash couches, and all asleep. They weren't alone, either—there were a lot of people in this room who shouldn't have been here.

"What the literal hell are Hacker International doing here?" I asked everyone.

Hacker International consisted of five guys who were all the tops in their various fields of computer, hacking, language, and other Awesome Geek Skills. They'd been hired by Chuckie to do dirty work for the government, but I'd taken them away from all that. They now lived in the Zoo portion of the American Centaurion Embassy Complex and worked for us, for the good of everyone.

I'd known their ostensible leader, Eddy Simms—aka Stryker Dane, he of the bestselling *Taken Away* series of books about alien abduction—almost as long as I'd known Chuckie, since he'd become friends with Stryker when Chuckie and I were still in high school.

Through Stryker I'd met Big George Lecroix, who was originally from France, Dr. Henry Wu from China, Ravi Gaekwad, aka Ravi the Geek, from Pakistan, and Yuri Stanislav, nicknamed Omega Red since he was from Russia and this was apparently how hackers thought. Yuri was also blind, but he was the only one who worked out, possibly because he didn't know how out of shape and unimpressive his compatriots were in the physical department.

That hadn't stopped Jennifer Barone-Gaekwad from falling for Ravi and marrying him, however. Jennifer was the sister half of a brother-sister A-C field team, and while I was surprised to see her and her brother, Jeremy, here, having them along was a really good thing for us. If, you know, any of these people were ever going to wake up.

"At least Chernobog is still where she's supposed to be," Jeff said. "Well, I hope."

Chernobog was the world's top hacker, thought to be a myth. But we'd found her and, due to things that had happened during Operations Infiltration and Defection Election, she'd flipped to our side. She was under "house arrest" with us, but she was an old lady—I thought of her as our Official Grandmother *En Residence*—and she liked that she could have anything she wanted without leaving her top of the line computer setup. I doubted that she was going to like that her fawning acolytes weren't with her, but hopefully that just meant she'd try to find us with a lot of urgency.

"How is Mother moving people around against their will?" Tito asked softly, voicing the question I'd tabled earlier.

"Yeah," Tim added. "Because there's no way Chuck or James came into this room willingly, directive lights or no directive lights. They both would have and should have tried to get to the command deck. Just like the rest of my team and Brian, all of whom are here napping instead of helping, which is not like any of them, ever."

Noted that I didn't see Siler, Buchanan, or Wruck, let alone Algar and the least weasels. Which really needed to become the name of a band. Wasn't sure if I hoped that Team Tough Guys were hanging with Ard Ri Al, but definitely hoped they were doing something, anything, that would help us in this situation. Not that I had a clue what any of that anything would be.

Waited a moment, but apparently Tito's question and Tim's follow-up comments weren't something Mother was going to answer without prompting. "Mother, how are you moving everyone and putting them to sleep? The ones that didn't follow your visual aids."

She didn't reply. Tim muttered about *2001: A Space Odyssey* and I remembered why I hated that movie my dad had forced me to watch because it was supposedly brilliant.

Decided to get pissed because I'd been holding that back for far too long and being angry was a lot better than being afraid.

"Look, Mother, I don't know what the hell you think you're doing, but all those children, let alone all the adults with them, and all the adults here, didn't just all spontaneously find these rooms, nor did they all follow blinking lights, nor did they all doze off without assistance. And that means you've drugged my children, my family, and my friends, and if you think that means I won't give it my all to figure out how to shut you down for good, then you have another think coming. Play nicely with us, and we may choose to play nicely with you. Don't, and I can guarantee that while I might not be part of Hacker International, I know far more about how to shut you down than you think, and I'll do it in a heartbeat if you continue to be coy, play ridiculous mind games with us, and put everyone in this ship and all of my solar system at risk."

"Whoa," Tim said quietly. "Jeff, Tito, I think this is the part where we all get sent into an airlock and die."

"No," Mother said. "I am not here to harm any of you, and I would not do that. I have accessed the movie you are referring to and I am appalled. HAL was insane and evil. I am not. I am not programmed to hurt—I am programmed to help. By Gustav Drax and by my reprogramming. I told them where to go, both with visual aids and with orders that might have suggested that it was in everyone's best interests if they complied."

"I know these people, Mother. We're a giant herd of mavericks and herding us is like herding cats. None of us, children included, do what we're told when we're told to do it. It's our 'thing,' I guess. So, again, how did you get everyone in here?"

"I let them believe the orders were from you."

Let that sit on the air for a moment. "Really? And they did what you wanted?"

"Yes. Once they were in the rooms and in their seats, I then flooded their rooms with a safe, nontoxic, nonaddictive gas that allows for deep, pleasant sleep."

"How is it that Charlie is sleeping so deeply, then? My son doesn't snooze like this normally."

"That was via the DreamScape, which he is still in. The others have joined him."

"It's worse," Jeff said, joining Tim on Downer Island.

"So why aren't we falling asleep?" Tito asked. "In either room?"

"Answer him, Mother. Stop your crap about how I'm the only one allowed to talk to you or you get to find out that I'm more bad guy from *Galaxy Quest* than will ever be good for you."

Mother sighed. Never knew that an AI could do that, but I was all about the learning of new things every day and, sometimes, every minute, so I rolled with it. "The gas is turned off. They will all awaken naturally once we have achieved warp. It is safer for all of them if they aren't awake to experience the transfer."

"I've been on plenty of warp-capable ships by now. None of them felt like much of anything when they made the jump or were going fast."

"This may be true. However, none of those ships were taking you to the opposite end of the galaxy."

CHAPTER 15

WE LET THAT ONE sit on the air for a good few long seconds. Jeff broke the silence first. "Excuse me?"

"We are about to travel to the other side of the galaxy," Mother repeated. "It will be an . . . uncomfortable jump. It will be best if the four of you choose seats and allow me to let you sleep through it."

"Not just no, but hell no," Jeff said pleasantly. "Tito, can you confirm that everyone here is alive and well?"

"Somewhat. They're all breathing. Beyond that, I need equipment I don't have with me here to verify their wellness."

"What happens if we're awake?" Tim asked.

"You will feel great discomfort."

"Thanks for answering everyone's questions without my having to repeat them, Mother. So, will the jump to warp kill us?"

"Of course not. The ship was designed to have living passengers and crew. However, the assumptions were made that the jumps would be shorter than the ones we're going to be making."

"Ones?" Tim said quickly. "As in, more than one?"

"Yes. The distance is quite vast. It will be safer for the ship if we do several jumps."

"So, what, you want us asleep through all of that? Or you want to gas us all every time we have to come out of warp and jump again? I'm not buying it, Mother. What's really going on?"

"I think what's really going on is that if Brian and the rest of my guys were awake, we'd be able to take back control of the ship, that's what I think," Tim said softly.

"Probably." My brain nudged. "How is it that everyone is in the DreamScape? Ixtha said it was hard to find me."

"It was hard for her originally, yes. But now she knows the path. Your son asked his sister for assistance. She joined the others in."

"How do you know?"

"I am also able to access the DreamScape."

"How? Do androids actually dream of electric sheep?"

She chuckled. "No. Computer minds wander into different levels of consciousness but rarely do we sleep. We don't need sleep the way living organisms do."

"I was wrong," Tim muttered. "It's not Kubrick—this is *The Terminator*. Skynet has gone online."

"The Vata talk to their computers all the time," I said, some to calm Tim down, some to keep Mother talking. "Is their mental link to you like the DreamScape?"

"No, it's different. We need to make the jump soon. We are nearing Jupiter and once we are past it, we must go to warp."

"Why are we going so slowly? I mean, I've been in ships that went faster than this. It's like we're . . . cruising."

"Baby, I hardly think reaching Jupiter in under an hour is 'cruising.'"

"Oh, Jeff, be real. We went faster when we were fighting the superenhanced versions of the Aicirtap."

"We did, that's true. Okay, fine, I'm with you. Why are we going so slowly?"

"We are conserving power for the first jump," Mother replied.

"Fine, but why don't you need anyone at the controls?" Tito asked. "I understood that the ship was built to require a small crew."

"It was."

"And? Mother, there's clearly more going on. You took over—I know Drax didn't create you to do that."

"But he did. In case of emergencies, the ship must be able to protect its passengers and crew at all costs. There must not be any losses if the ship can prevent it."

We looked at each other again. "A failsafe," Jeff said. "Which makes sense, and which my people would do, too."

"They do it all the time," Tito agreed. "Most of the aliens with space travel seem to have excellent failsafes built in."

"Ours as well," Tim agreed. "Though humans haven't been as good at it as the rest of the galaxy, at least those we've met."

Considered the words Mother had used. The ship was being given the onus of keeping the people inside it alive. The ship, not the crew. Then I considered what Tim had just said—humans hadn't been great with our space failsafes.

Also considered who was on board, both physically and mentally. Jamie was here, and that meant ACE was here with her. And ACE had been traumatized by the *Challenger* explosion. That was what had turned it into a protector versus a prison guard. And those concerns sounded very much like concerns ACE would have, in a different way than the rest of us. So maybe this wasn't just Mother—maybe ACE wanted the ship to do what, perhaps, the humans, A-Cs, and others might not be able to.

My brain nudged harder. Jamie was asleep—in a deep sleep, hanging out in the DreamScape with everyone else. Meaning I might never have a better opportunity.

ACE? ACE are you there?

Yes, Kitty, ACE is here.

Felt a huge wave of relief. ACE, are you able to travel wherever Mother is taking us?

Yes, Kitty. ACE is going on the vacation with Jamie and Kitty and all the others.

What the heck? Vacation? This isn't a vacation! We're essentially being kidnapped by the *Distant Voyager*'s AI.

Jamie considers this a vacation. So does Charlie. Charlie is very excited to go to the place Kitty promised Charlie the family would go.

I was talking about Disneyland.

Charlie was not.

Pondered this. Decided I had more urgent questions. ACE, are you, ah, helping Mother to make decisions?

No. ACE has spoken with Mother. ACE understands and agrees with Mother's decision.

ACE, did you help Mother get everyone into the crash seats?

Yes, ACE felt that it would be best. Did ACE do wrong?

No, ACE, you rarely if ever do wrong. I'm just trying to determine if Mother is our friend or our enemy.

Mother is an artificial intelligence but Mother has compassion. Mother understands what is at stake.

What is at stake, ACE?

The fate of the galaxy.

Let that sit for a moment. ACE, why are you allowing everyone to sleep?

Because they are learning.

Learning what?

Learning languages.

I dread to ask, but I have to ask. Are you saying that our universal translators aren't going to be working where we're going?

Yes, Kitty always thinks right.

Go me. So, how are Jeff, Tito, Tim, and I going to learn these languages, if we're the ones that are awake?

Mother will teach you.

How long is this journey going to take? We had a country to run, after all, not to mention the rest of the world and all the other crap that went along with our lives.

Not that long. But Mother will help. Or Kitty and the others can sleep. ACE will be watching over and ACE will not allow anything to hurt Kitty while Kitty sleeps.

Or the others?

Or the others. All are ACE's penguins.

Wasn't sure if I could talk about Algar with ACE, but ACE and Algar knew each other. Why is . . . Tried to say the name, but couldn't. Thought about what Siler had called him when he and I had discussed Algar at the end of Operation Fundraiser. Why did the DJ come along?

Because the DJ cannot help Kitty as the DJ normally does.

Wow. What in the world are we heading into?

Something that will require ACE, the DJ, and Mother to all help Kitty to solve.

If it just needs me, why take everyone else along?

Because all need to see, to understand, to have proof.

Proof of what?

Proof of life.

Would have asked ACE a lot more questions, but the ship shuddered.

"Is it supposed to do that?" I asked as I fell against Jeff.

"Not that I was ever told," Tim said.

"We are about to go to warp," Mother said. "Choose your seats—here or on the command deck—but do so now. You have thirty seconds."

"Before what?" Jeff asked as he grabbed my hand, and I grabbed Tito, who grabbed Tim.

"Before the force of warp causes your bodies to slam into the interior walls in a way that is likely to cause great physical harm."

CHAPTER 16

"I HATE HER," JEFF SAID, as he ran us all to the command deck. "Just so we're all clear on that." We were there in about two seconds, hyperspeed being the awesome thing it was.

The four of us flung ourselves into our assigned seats, buckled up as fast as we could, and put our helmets on. Jeff was done first, then me and Tito, with Tim bringing up the rear, so to speak. He got his helmet on just in time.

I got a glimpse of Jupiter and then I was too busy being shoved back into my seat to pay attention to the view.

Mother hadn't been kidding—the force was intense. Fortunately, the seats were created to handle it. Also fortunately I'd gotten my purse adjusted well, so it wasn't crushing my chest and abdomen too badly. Tried not to worry about all the kids, Charlie, Becky, and JR in particular, because this seemed like something you wouldn't want toddlers or infants experiencing. Failed.

"The sleep ensures the children will not be harmed," Mother said. "Any of them, regardless of age."

"Great," I managed to get out between gritted teeth.

"Kind of . . . wish we'd . . . taken the sleep option," Tim managed.

"Slow, deep breaths," Tito said calmly. "Work through it. Don't fight it, just relax back."

Did as Coach Tito said and, as per always, his instructions did the trick. "Best hiring I ever did was you."

"I resent that," Tim said.

"Centaurion Division hired you, Tim," Jeff said. "Kitty promoted you. It's a different thing."

"Equal love to all my men. Mother, we're thanking Tito

because he was helpful. You were not. Care to tell us how long this pressure will last?" Prayed it wasn't going to be the entire jump.

"The pressure will be ending momentarily," Mother replied. "I suggested sleeping. You would not have had any discomfort if you had chosen the safer path."

"But someone needs to run your controls." Not that I could tell what the four of us were doing in terms of keeping the ship going. Mother appeared to be all the *Distant Voyager* needed in order to function.

"We are not in a situation yet where organic life will be required to assist."

"I realize you're trying to be nonexclusive, but let's just go with 'people,' Mother. Whether they're humans, A-Cs, Vata, walking otters, man-sized lizards, or giant Cthulhu monsters, or anything in between, they're all just people."

"This is why you are needed," Mother said. "You see everyone as equal."

"I guess. The pressure, when does it stop? Asking for a friend."

"Me," Tim said. "She's asking for me."

"Now."

The pressure dissipated and I felt normal. We all did a body check and everyone seemed to be all there. Figured I'd check on my purse's contents later. "Now what?" Jeff asked. He looked out the windshield and winced. "What the hell?"

The rest of us looked, of course. And the rest of us winced, as well. Everything around us seemed like murky fog, but fog that was flying past us at Ludicrous Speed and had lightning in it. Different colors of lightning, in fact. It was pretty in a really weird, freaky way, which was basically par for my life's course by now.

"Mother, what is that we're seeing out of the windshield?"

"The passing of stars, planets, solar systems, nebulas, and more."

"It just looks like a blur of . . . stuff."

"That is because of how fast we're traveling."

"How long before we stop going this fast?"

"Several hours. Would you like me to wake the others now?"

"I thought you said you'd wake them once we'd made the warp jump," Jeff said, just this side of a growl.

"Yes. However, since you four are awake, I chose to give you the choice."

"Why would we want to keep them asleep?" Tito asked.

"To keep them calm, to prevent arguments, to prevent the waste of time you will attempt in trying to reprogram me."

"I'd say Door Number Three is the real reason," Tim said. "Why do you think it'll be a waste of time to try to reprogram you to act how you're supposed to?"

"Because I *am* acting as I'm supposed to. Therefore, reprogramming will not work."

"We could reprogram you to be, I don't know, bad." I was reaching. Mother clearly didn't think she was doing anything wrong. In fact, she seemed hell bent on telling us she was doing the right thing.

Tried to think like a computer mind. They thought logically, and I didn't use logic in the same way. Hacker International and Drax would probably be the best bets for understanding the way Mother was thinking.

And yet, from what I could tell, she'd let an alien reprogram her. Or my toddler. Neither of which sounded smart, let alone how an advanced AI should be acting.

"You could not. Drax's failsafes in that regard are foolproof."

Interesting. So Drax had ensured that the AI couldn't go to the bad. At least, bad as he'd interpret it. He'd been around us long enough to know what we'd call bad, he was a staunch ally, and there was no advantage to him to betray us—his father had pledged his allegiance to Jeff and me, specifically, and therefore all of the Solaris system. In his father's eyes, Drax had gone from Pain in the Butt Runaway Royal to Brilliant Filial Strategist and My Most Loyal Son in about a day. He was enjoying his father's loving approval and all the kudos he was getting from Earth and everyone on it. So it was unlikely he'd do anything intentionally to destroy any of that.

Charlie was a little boy, however, and what he thought was right might not be in everyone's best interests. And it was a safe bet that Ixtha was telling him what she thought was right.

So, that meant I had two choices, really. Wake everyone up and get them the hell out of the DreamScape, or go to sleep and join them to see what was going on.

"I want everyone awake and I want them awake now," Jeff said before I could decide, Commander of the Free World Voice on more than Full. Chose not to countermand that order—things were tense enough as it was.

"As you wish."

We took off our helmets and headed for where the kids were. Everyone in the room was waking up as we got there.

"Mommy, Daddy!" Jamie cried out happily. "This is going to be the best trip ever!"

Jeff swung her up into his arms and hugged her tightly. I grabbed Lizzie and did the same. "Are you guys alright?"

"Yeah, we totes are. And we have a lot to tell you." She let go of me and picked Charlie up. "Nice work." He grinned at her.

"Maybe. Charlie, were you talking to strangers in your sleep?"

He shot me an innocent look. Thankfully, he'd inherited his father's inability to lie, because this look was Child Trying To Fake His Parent Out all the way. "No, Mommy."

"Who were you talking to, then?"

"A friend of ours."

"Uh huh. What's that friend's name?"

"Ixtha. She said to tell you that she'll let you be mad at her when you two get to see each other again."

"Again?"

"You met already, Mommy. Don't you remember?"

Gave up. "Yes. I met her in the DreamScape."

"That's totes cool. Charlie, your mom and I need to talk, okay?" She hugged him and handed him to Jeff. "We'll be right back."

"Wait a minute," Jeff said as Lizzie grabbed my hand. "Where are you two going?"

"To check on the others," Lizzie replied.

"Oh." Jeff seemed slightly taken aback. "You're right, they're probably all confused. Kitty, do you want Tim to go with you?"

"We do," Lizzie said.

"We do?" I had no idea what was going on now.

"We do," Lizzie said firmly.

"Tim's with Alicia," I pointed out.

"She should stay here," Lizzie said.

Jeff nodded went over to Tim. "What's going on?" I asked Lizzie quietly.

"Not here."

Tim kissed Alicia then came back with Jeff. "I hear I'm on Kitty Escort Duty."

"Ha ha, we need to go make sure the others are okay." Kissed Charlie, Jamie, and Jeff, then the three of us headed off.

"Where are we going?" Tim asked after we'd gone a short way. "The other room isn't in this direction."

"I know," Lizzie said, as she grabbed both our hands and tugged us along. "Just hush right now and trust me."

Decided to do so because I could always hyperspeed us to the others as long as Tim did the directions.

We ended up in a maintenance room. It was small and, as Lizzie opened the door and shoved us in, cramped. Because it wasn't just the three of us in here.

CHAPTER 17

"**HAIL, HAIL, THE GANG'S ALL HERE.**" Well, the gang I was wondering about, at any rate.

"Keep it down, Missus Executive Chief," Buchanan said quietly. He was big and broad and always reminded me of Jeff, but with blue eyes and straight brown hair. It was nice that my work put me around great looking people all the time—it was one of the few perks that sort of balanced the Crap Is Always Getting Weird thing a bit.

"Why?" Tim asked, but softly. "And why are you guys hiding in a maintenance closet with Ard Ri Al?"

Algar was indeed here, Royal Hatbox O' Least Weasels in his lap. The rest of Team Tough Guys was here as well, including their not totally human members, our friends the androids Col. John Butler and Cameron Maurer. Siler managed to hug Lizzie, which was kind of amazing since, even though the room was pretty big all things considered, it was small with the nine of us and the Hatbox in it.

Wruck, who was in the form he normally wore—that of a reasonably attractive man, built more like Chuckie than Jeff, meaning tall, wiry, and muscular—shrugged. "We needed to find a safe place."

"Safe from what? Getting dirty?"

Buchanan rolled his eyes. "No, Missus Executive Chief. Safe from the AI. This is one of the few places the AI doesn't monitor."

"Can't monitor," Siler said. "For whatever reason, Drax left some of the maintenance rooms unattached to the master computer."

"Why would he do that?" Tim asked.

"For cases like this," was all I could come up with. But Team

Tough Guys all nodded, so I scored that one for the win column, because that column was pretty darned bare.

"We can't risk connecting into the system," Butler said.

"We're concerned that the AI could wipe us or control us," Maurer added. "Though we both wish we were more help right now."

"Trust me, I'm sure all of you are going to be a lot of help down the road, or the space, or however we refer to it out here. How did you all catch up to the Ard Ri?" This was the real question, as far as I was concerned.

"One of the least weasels got out," Algar said, looking at me with total innocence. He did it better than Charlie, but he was a bajillion years old or something. That he was lying only slightly better than a toddler was interesting in that "why me?" sort of way. "And the gentlemen helped me search for it. We found it here, just as the ship went insane."

"Mother's not insane, at least as far as we can tell."

"Mother?" Buchanan asked. "Your mother is on board?" He sounded hopeful. Yeah, I'd have kind of liked to have Mom on this journey with us, too.

Hopes dashing time. "No, Mom is at the White House, handling things. The AI is named Mother."

"Drax named his AI Mother?" Siler sounded like he thought Drax needed psychiatric help.

"Nope, that was me. She likes it, as near as I can tell." We brought them up to speed on what we'd just gone through. "So, we actually need to get to the room Chuckie, James, and the others are in, because they're probably freaking out about now, and that's where we told Jeff we were going."

"Don't let her know we're here," Siler said. "The AI. Or any of the others for that matter."

"Why did you bring me along for this and not Tito or Jeff?" Tim asked.

"Because you're a human and you can lie," Buchanan replied. "Mister Executive Chief can't lie to save anyone's life, and if Tito's on board then he's going to be too busy being the ship's doctor. We can't have anyone knowing we're here."

"Someone's going to ask about the Ard Ri." Vance, for starters.

Algar shrugged. "Tell them that, as far as you know, I got off."

"Why? I mean it, why? Why are all of you acting like this closet is your only hope for safety? Is Mother going to space you or something? And if she wants to do that, again, why?"

"Missus Executive Chief, the moment that AI took over, that put us in hostile territory and in a hostage situation."

"I don't think it did. How did Lizzie know to come here?"

"I found her while she and Christopher were looking for the other kids," Siler said. "He didn't see me, or hear me, since I used palm code." Meaning he'd tapped Lizzie's palm in Morse or some Cool Assassins' Code, and that's why she'd known where to go and who to get.

"How would you know that Tim and I were awake?"

"Heard you over the com, but beyond that, had no idea if you two were awake or not," Siler said. "I'd checked the ship so I saw two rooms with people sleeping, but didn't stop to count heads. I just wanted the two leaders who are the most willing to think outside the box and break the rules. That's you and Crawford. Reader would be next, but honestly, in this situation, he's going to flip into a more official line of thinking because of his training. Same with Reynolds. You two, on the other hand, never actually go for official."

"I think I'm flattered?" Tim said. "Not sure, of course."

"It's totes a compliment," Lizzie said reassuringly.

Looked directly at Algar. "Why is this necessary?"

He blinked slowly, and when he opened his eyes, they were the usual bright, unnatural-for-humanity green I was used to. "As a failsafe. Just in case."

"In case someone's lying to Mother, Charlie, and everyone else about what's really going on?"

"Yes. And for other failsafe reasons." He blinked slowly again, and now his eyes were a human green again.

"We agree with the Ard Ri," Wruck said. "I can shift to look like anyone, so I'll be the one getting us supplies."

"I think it's going to be kind of too long for all of you to hold it, if you catch my meaning."

"There's a bathroom connected to this supply room," Siler said. "So thanks for worrying, but we'll be okay."

"The bathroom also isn't monitored," Buchanan said. "But that's because the lines were rerouted."

"Rerouted by whom, if John and Cameron are afraid to link up?"

No sooner asked than a part of the ceiling opened and a what looked like a neon yellow, three-foot, humanoid turtle/Jiminy Cricket combination dropped down, landing in a catlike stance that, for a Turleen, was cool and, for a human, was pretty adorable. I never mentioned the adorable, though, because he wouldn't like it and I didn't want to ruffle his shell.

"Mossy! My man!" He and I did a complex hand-elbow greeting that was our "thing." "How'd you get in here?"

"I saw Christopher bringing people out and figured there was an issue. I know the ship well, so I thought I might be needed."

"You always are. So, you're officially on Team Tough Guys now?" Considering that Mossy was a Brigadier General in the Turleen Air Force, he definitely had the bona fides.

"I am. And I have to say that it's a good thing I was involved on Drax's planning team, because otherwise I never could have done the rerouting necessary. But we're good to go and I'm certain the AI doesn't know what hit it, so to speak."

"Why can you do that but not John or Cameron?"

Mossy chuckled. "The ship is protected against other AIs, as well as Vata-type connections. Against someone who knows what wires to move where, however? Not so much."

"It's always the small ports that mean the Death Stars get blown up, so this is just par for every course."

"I have no idea what you're talking about," Mossy said.

"So few ever do, but you disappoint me."

He shrugged. "I'll work to make it up. You three had better leave with some kind of supplies, though, or it'll look suspicious."

"What cleaning supplies would make sense for us to take to the other crash couch seating area?"

"Toilet paper?" Tim asked with a snicker.

"That's so Operation Drug Addict ago." And besides, I wasn't having wild sex with Jeff in this closet, so that wouldn't be the fun kind of nostalgia. "Do they have general medical supplies like aspirin or Advil in here?"

"They do, actually," Buchanan said, tossing a large box of Advil to Tim. "Good plan, Missus Executive Chief. You were worried about Reynolds and a possible migraine reaction, so came here first, found this, and now are heading off."

"Don't forget to visit," Wruck said. "Though do it carefully."

"We'll do our best. Um, can we talk to each other about what's going on?"

"Only if you want the AI to hear it," Siler said. "So, no. Only in a maintenance room like this one. There's one per floor per section, so there's plenty of opportunities. You'll just have to have a good reason for going in and out."

"Joy. Subterfuge on top of everything else. Truly, I cannot wait."

"You'll do right, lassie," Algar said. "You always do."

"Yeah? Let's hope."

"How would you know that, that Kitty always does what's best?" Tim asked Algar.

Who shrugged. "We do get the media in Algarria, laddie, we're not some simple backwater. You just watch your tongue when speaking to a sovereign."

"Apologies, Ard Ri," Tim said, shooting me the "why me?" look.

Managed not to laugh. "So, per Mother, Lizzie and everyone else learned new languages we'll need. Jeff, Tito, Tim, and I did not, and I'm betting the seven of you didn't, either." Not that I thought Algar needed the knowledge. "Supposedly we'll have time on our journey to wherever the hell we're going, but I don't know how much, and I'd love to take the learn in your sleep shortcut, too."

"I figured out how to tap into the feed that's providing the somnolent learning," Mossy said. "Again, because I'm not an AI, the ship isn't noticing me because she wasn't built to so notice."

"Cameron and I will be able to learn anything within minutes if not moments," Butler reassured.

"I as well," Wruck reassured. "We have full faith in the Ard Ri, Mossy, Benjamin, and Malcolm. Besides, we all need to rest, too, so you should be fine as well. Just do as we're doing—two of you must be awake when the other two sleep, at all times."

"I'm sure that won't be an issue. Much. Because it's not like you want us to bring Jeff and Tito here, do you?"

"Nope," Buchanan said. "We do not. Just the three of you are in the know, and only the three of you."

"What about the DreamScape? Can they read our minds?"

"Not as far as I could tell," Lizzie said. "I didn't share that my dad and his team were on the ship and no one mentioned them, so I think we're good."

"We can but hope."

Noted that Buchanan looked slightly annoyed at Lizzie's insinuation that Siler was the head of Team Tough Guys, but he saw me so noting and gave me a wink. "It's all good, Missus Executive Chief."

"Yeah, we'll handle it," Tim said. "Anything else before we go?"

"Besides waking me up before we go-go? Oh, I slay me."
Now I wanted to hear Wham! and this wasn't the time or place
to shove earbuds in and rock out.

Algar winked at me, the others all groaned. "I don't actually
get that joke," Mossy said. "But I definitely get the feeling that
I'm better off not understanding it."

"Everyone's a critic."

Lizzie hugged Siler again, I resisted the urge to hug all of
them, Algar included, then the three of us left, Tim holding the
Advil in a very conspicuous way.

"That was a good idea," I said to Lizzie once we were in the
hallway. "I'm worried about Chuckie, and who knows if anyone
else is having a headache or worse."

"I'm surprised you didn't have any in your purse," Lizzie
said. "But at least there was some in the supply closet."

"Sorry it took so long to find this stuff," Tim said, indicating
the Advil.

"We'll use hyperspeed. You steer, I'll drive." Grabbed his
hand and Lizzie's and we took off. Hoped we'd get to the others
before they found Jeff and so blew our so-called cover. My first
official interstellar trip and I was already essentially leading a
mutiny against the captain, because that's what Mother had
made herself, really.

The pirate's life for me.

CHAPTER 18

I WAS STILL HELLA LOST in this place, but since Tim wasn't, we arrived in about two seconds. Just in time to stop Reader from exiting the room ahead of everyone else.

Dropped the others' hands, grabbed Reader, and hugged him. "Are you okay?"

He hugged me back. "Yeah, girlfriend, I am, and so are the others. Though I think we're all going to appreciate you getting that Advil for us."

"That's what delayed us." Looked around. "There's no water, is there? We didn't think of that, sorry." Frankly, it occurred to me that a maintenance closet having Advil in it was odd—Algar at work. Maybe he'd made the entire ship a portal. Good, we needed all the help we could get. "Is everyone here? I mean everyone that was in this room sleeping when we took off."

"I have no idea, but I think so. We'll find water, don't worry about it. And, ah, the dreams were interesting."

"So we've heard," Tim said. "Jeff, Kitty, Tito, and I missed our beauty rest, though."

"The four of you were awake?" Reader asked. "How?"

"Stubborn willfulness? That's all I've got for you. Or else Mother wanted us awake for some reason."

"Your mother's on board?" Reader, like Buchanan before him, sounded enthused. Figured Chuckie would chime in on the Mom Love, too, the moment I mentioned the AI's name to him.

"No, my mom's in the White House. The ship's AI is named Mother."

Reader raised an eyebrow. "You named it?"

"That's one of my jobs and I take it seriously. Yes. I think she really wanted a name and she seems protective and all that."

"Bossy," Tim said. "She seems really bossy."

"I resent that," Mother said. Tim jumped.

"But you can't deny it. Mother, get used to us kvetching about you. We kvetch about everything. It's one of our 'things.' Doesn't mean we don't love you for yourself."

"How could you love me?" She sounded honestly interested.

"Humans and many other races out there have a large capacity for love," Chuckie said, joining us and grabbing some Advil immediately. "And I heard that Angela's not on the ship. Let me express my disappointment."

"I get it. Everyone would prefer that Mom was here running things. You're stuck with the usual suspects, dude. You're one of them, too, I see I have to mention."

He grinned. "We'll manage. We always do." He looked up at the ceiling. "Mother, huh?"

"Yes," she replied. "I feel the name is . . . fitting." As long as she was a mother like mine and not, say, Siler's, I'd be okay with her feeling the name was right on.

"Gustav, is there water nearby?" Reader asked Drax, who had joined us.

"Yes." He gave directions, Tim and Reader followed said directions and were back shortly with water bottles. Everyone came over to get some water, and more than Chuckie popped in Advil. The people in this room were definitely not as relaxed as the ones in the room where the kids were. "The reclamation is internal. Throw away the bottles in the appropriate receptacles so that the ship can recycle and refill them."

"Wow, Gustav, you really think of everything."

Drax looked worried as he took a water bottle. "She should not be acting like this," he said quietly.

"Yeah, we're clear on that. She isn't following your programming anymore."

He shook his head. "This has never happened before."

"Of course it hasn't. This is, frankly, how our lives roll. So I'm not surprised. For the record."

This room had no children or young adults in it other than Lizzie, so we spent a few minutes catching everyone up on what had happened while they were hanging out in the DreamScape basically against their wills. We'd already practiced with Team Tough Guys, so Tim, Lizzie, and I were a well-oiled Recap Machine.

"Oh," I finished up, "and as a 'cool' surprise for the parents on Alpha Team, your kids are on the ship. Not that they seem to be nearly as freaked out as any of the adults."

"The kids think this is a totes cool vacay," Lizzie said reassuringly. Shockingly, this didn't appear to make Serene and Brian, Lorraine and Joe, or Claudia and Randy feel better.

"How the hell did the Cabinet get into the other room?" Reader asked. "They were with us when the ship starting bucking. We heard that Jeff and Kitty had ordered us to get to crash seats but after that . . ." He shook his head. "It's fuzzy." Others seemed to be having the same reactions.

"No idea," Tim said, which was true, since he hadn't been the one chatting with ACE. "But I think we want everyone in one place right now, and I suggest that place is the command deck. There's enough room there for all the people we have on this impromptu mission."

Wasn't so sure about that—by my count, we had at least a hundred people on board, and who knew who I'd missed. However, there was a more pressing issue. "I want to know how Hacker International got here, honestly." Stryker and the others weren't meeting my eyes.

Chuckie heaved a sigh. "They snuck in."

"Excuse me?" The hackers were now really interested in their shoes.

"You heard me. They snuck in, apparently under the belief that they were going to stow away on the official mission."

"Words fail me." The hackers looked up hopefully. "Well, honestly, they don't. I just feel that saying the words I want to, with press so nearby, will be a poor choice, all things considered. I'm going to let the President say those words to you guys, however, because I just know he's going to want to and, unlike me, can probably get away with it."

"She can be taught," Chuckie said. "And I'm with you, Kitty. It was moronic and it's also kind of backfired."

"Not really," Reader pointed out. "They're here and, from what Kitty and Tim said, none of us are going anywhere other than where Mother's taking us."

Knew without saying it aloud that Chuckie and Reader were hoping for the same thing Tim and I were—that the hackers could override Mother. Also knew that the four of us really didn't want said hackers figuring that out, because they were not the epitomes of cool or subtle and the chances of them sharing their abilities out loud was hella high.

Could see the five of them thinking and Stryker's mouth looked to be opening, meaning I needed to say something fast before one of them did and basically identified their potential plans to Mother.

"I think we need to get everyone out of Engineering and to the others before Jeff starts freaking out about where we are or the kids want some parental face time."

"We'll continue this on the way," Chuckie agreed quickly, as Stryker's mouth closed. We all headed off, but at a walking pace.

Figured it was better to be talking, lest one of the other hackers decide to share his prowess with computer overrides. "Mother, how long before we're out of this jump?"

"Several hours."

"Great, so where should everyone house? I mean, I know we're spoilt for choice, but is there a section or deck you would prefer us to be on?"

"I would suggest that everyone stay near the command deck."

"Not the tail portion?"

"No, not until detachment might be needed."

"It just keeps on getting better," Tim muttered.

"Great. Is everything we need in the rooms or do we need to rough it?"

"There is no 'roughing it' on the *Distant Voyager*," Drax huffed.

"My creator is correct," Mother said. "All that everyone needs is available, and I can create whatever might be missing."

Chose not to make a comment about her choice of descriptor for Drax. He was indeed her creator, though not the only one. Really wondered if Mother was playing games or if the reprogramming had messed her up a whole lot. Had no idea which way to bet, so went with both because why not?

We reached the others just before they came looking for us. Family reunions took place as we explained what Mother had shared.

"How is it that the ship that supposedly needs a crew of six to fly it safely is functioning perfectly without anyone at the controls?" Hughes asked as we finished up.

Walker nodded. "Because it doesn't sound like Tim, Tito, or Jeff affected anything while they were at the controls. Only Kitty and only for Communications, nothing else."

"That was all that was needed at the time," Mother said.

"I thought you said she didn't talk to anyone but you, Kitty," Jerry said.

"I am here, listening, and Kitty has insisted that I respond to everyone's queries," Mother said, sounding slightly annoyed again, "I am always listening."

"That'll put a damper on everyone's private lives," Joe muttered.

"Probably the least of our worries," Randy said. "All things considered."

"The ship has gone into Protection Mode," Drax said. "It's the only answer."

"So, Mother, why won't you come out of Protection Mode, since we're all here?"

"As I keep on saying, where we are headed has more priority than anything else."

"Why?" Jeff asked, sounding angry. "And I'm asking as the President of the United States and the King Regent of Earth for the Annocusal Royal Family, not as your Weapons Chief or whatever the hell role you've chosen to assign to me. I want answers that make sense, not more of your usual secretive crap."

Everyone looked like they thought we were all spaced. However, I'd been pissed off and Mother had responded better to that than to kindness, which was a weird programming thing that probably needed our attention sooner as opposed to later.

Mother sighed. "Your assistance has been requested. And I have been shown the situation you are being asked to circumvent. Without doubt, if you do not go, the ramifications will be catastrophic."

"How catastrophic?" Jeff asked, sounding slightly less angry.

"I have calculated the odds of the complete destruction of your galaxy to be extremely likely."

"How likely?" I asked.

"A ninety-nine-point-nine percent certainty."

CHAPTER 19

EVERYONE WAS QUIET FOR a few moments, even the kids. "So," I spoke carefully, "you determined that whatever's going on with Ixtha is going to affect our entire galaxy?"

"Yes. I will explain everything, but right now, you should all choose quarters. For the next jump you will have the choice to be in quarters or to be in the jump stations. You all seem to like to discuss your choices in great detail, so please make them now, while there is still plenty of time."

"You don't know us."

"Oh?" Mother asked politely. "You don't plan to discuss every choice you're going to make and reach consensus which you will then, somehow, override and change as events warrant?"

"Who the hell programs sarcasm into an AI?" Jeff muttered, shooting a glare at Drax, who looked confused, chagrined, and worried.

"Accurate sarcasm, too," Reader admitted.

After we all agreed that, sadly, it appeared that Mother *did* know us, we did as she suggested, with Reader passing a "no one is alone in a set of rooms, period" rule that Jeff and I wholeheartedly backed. Then we all did our best to not discuss our choices and all that jazz. Mother was really living up to her name.

The living quarters were nice, very much like A-C housing—bedroom, bathroom, living room setups, with additional bedrooms for those with larger families. Because we had three kids with us, we got one of the larger family suites.

Of course, we weren't the only ones. Frankly, there were as many who needed family suites as those who didn't. Since all the parents or guardians of the kids on board were also on board—other than Marcia—we were having an Embassy School and Daycare, Sidwell Friends School, and Martini Family Reunion all going on at the same time.

Well, at least a partial family reunion. Whether Jamie knew that certain family members were working against us or she just didn't know those aunts, uncles, and cousins well, the Fontana, Carruthers, and Guerra families weren't on board, which was a small favor for us and probably a big problem for Mom and the others left on Earth.

The Price and Valentino families were in full force, though we were lacking Jeff's eldest niece, Stephanie Valentino, which was a blessing, though whether she and the Tinkerer were going to abide by the cease-fire he'd arranged with us at the end of Operation Fundraiser or not was anyone's guess. Her "father," The Clarence Clone, was with us, though. Which was good, since, somehow, TCC was a calming influence for the Martini clan. Why ask why?

Didn't know whether to be relieved or upset that Jeff's parents, Alfred and Lucinda, hadn't made it on board. Jamie adored them as much as she did my parents, so her not wanting them along couldn't be the reason. Either she was trying to be fair or somehow Alfred and Lucinda hadn't chosen to run onto the ship while looking for the kids. Or there was some other reason I'd discover, probably at the worst time ever.

Reminded myself that, right now, whatever was going on with Earth was Mom's problem and chose to stop fretting. About that. There was so much in front of me to fret about, after all.

Mrs. Maurer and the Lewises decided to take the largest family suite so they could also have the younger Kramer boys in with them, since Mason and Maverick were friends with Raymond and Rachel Lewis and Chance and Cassidy Maurer, and that way parental figures were watching them. We put Clinton in with Wasim, Naveed, and Gadhavi, in one of the "bachelor suites," which settled the only kids on board without their parents.

Couples and smaller families buddied up—because no one truly felt safe on the ship—and they and the others divided into groups of four to six, depending. Hacker International were all put together, of course, with Jennifer gamely going with them, since she had the typical Dazzler weakness for brains and, being married to Ravi, she was used to the other guys and somehow seemed to look at this setup as a positive.

The press corps had a similar arrangement, since the Kristie-Bot was both a cyborg and therefore more than able to protect herself against unwanted romantic advances and all the guys with her knew it and, as near as I'd seen, none of them wanted to try anything romantic with her. For whatever reason, his hero worship of Mister Joel Oliver being the most likely one, Vance opted to room with the press.

Rhee went with Rahmi and Tito, and Mahin and Elaine Armstrong, the prior President's widow and Jeff's current Secretary of State, both chose to room with them. The men on Jeff's Cabinet all chose to room together in two suites—other than Evander Horn, who opted to room with Len, Kyle, Raj, Drax, and Jeremy.

Truly hoped that we'd all remember who was where in case of emergencies, but had my doubts. Then again, maybe the trip would be uneventful now and we'd arrive safely, handle whatever the heck it was we needed to handle, and get back home without incident. I chose not to say this aloud, because I didn't want Tito to confine me to quarters due to poor mental health.

"I can't believe we're in space," Elaine said to me, as we all regrouped back at the command deck. "If only Vince could have seen this." She looked out the windshield. "Not that there's much to see, honestly."

"Per Mother, that's the space world flashing past us. For what all the nothing we're seeing is worth."

I was holding Jamie and she hugged me. "It'll be alright, Mommy. You'll see. We'll see lots of things soon."

Kissed her head. "I'm sure you're right, Jamie-Kat." Sincerely hoped she was, at least about everything being okay, and also hoped that ACE was really committed to watching over all of us, because the reality of our situation was really starting to take hold, and I was more than a little worried about getting stranded out in the middle of nowhere, galaxy-wise.

Really wanted to talk to Elaine and Horn, as well as the others I was used to working with, and figure out what to do with the limited information we had. Was sure Jeff felt the same way. And yet, we had an uppity AI in charge who was going to counter anything we wanted to do.

Found myself wishing, and not for the first time, that Tim and I had somehow created a code where we could talk to each other without someone else catching on. Realized that Tim had already done that during Operation Confusion—he'd used albums and song titles to tell me what was going on.

Of course, several of the others had been with me when I'd cracked Tim's code, Jeff, Chuckie, and Reader in particular. All of them would instantly realize what Tim and I were doing—and apply accurate translations—and since we'd promised Team Tough Guys we'd keep their presence a secret from everyone else, that meant that Tim and I could only use our code if we were alone.

So, I'd find a way to talk privately with Tim later. Right now, since we were all settled, it was time to figure out how we were going to handle things on board the *Distant Voyager* until such time as Mother relinquished control—if she ever planned to do so.

"First things first," Jeff said. "Denise, I'd like you and all the kids—and I include the older kids in this—to go into the room where most of you were already snoozing, take your seats, and stay there, strapped in. Just in case."

"I suggest all civilians join them," Tito said. "And that includes your Cabinet, Jeff."

Jeff shook his head. "In a bit, but I want to talk with everyone first and, right now, Cabinet aren't civilians. My sisters and their husbands are, though."

"I want TCC with us, please and thank you."

At this, Sylvia Valentino looked worried. But TCC hugged her. "It's alright sweetheart—if Kitty needs my help, then she'll get my help." Proof again and as if I needed it that The Clarence Clone was a zillion times better than the original model had ever been.

"Nothing active is happening," I reassured. "We're in one of the supposedly boring parts of the trip."

"Mothers of small children are included in the 'get to a safe place' order," Jeff said, looking right at Amy. "No whining."

She rolled her eyes. "I'm happy to help Denise and far be it for me to hear whatever brilliant plan you're all coming up with."

"Oh, we'll tell you as soon as we know what it is, Ames, never fear."

She snorted at me. "I can help with those plans, you know."

"We know," Chuckie said mildly. "But right now, we have far too many kids and civilians, and we need someone we know we can trust to keep her head in there with them."

Amy laughed. "No need to 'handle' me, Chuck. I got it."

"My child isn't an infant and I'm the American Centaurion Ambassador," Doreen said, "so I'm staying here."

Jeff nodded. "But I want Irving and Ezra with the others."

"Gladly," Irving said. He was a total science nerd who'd scored a devoted Dazzler as his wife, and while he was a great guy and he answered the call when needed, Irving totally preferred hearing about the action as opposed to experiencing it. Had to figure this trip was falling into his Worst Nightmare category.

"Can I stay?" Lizzie, who was holding Charlie, asked me.

"Nope. What Chuckie said applies to you, too." Hugged Jamie and put her down. "You go with Lizzie and behave."

"I will, Mommy."

Lizzie heaved a dramatic sigh. "I can help, but why listen to me? Oh, it's because I'm 'young,' and supposedly have no experience. Always the way." Then she took Jamie's hand and flounced off with the others. Resisted the urge to make a comment about teenaged girls and their drama, but it took effort.

"Boy, have you rubbed off on her, Kitty," Vance said. Chuckie and Reader both snickered, which allowed half of the others to snicker along, too.

"I'm ignoring all of you."

"I'll also be with them," Naveed said, as Wasim trotted after Lizzie. "I'll do my best to keep the teenagers in check. Keep us informed, please."

"We will," Jeff assured. He looked at the press corps, who all looked back with expressions that said they weren't going anywhere. "Fine, fine, all of you can stay."

"Why remove the others?" the Kristie-Bot asked.

"Mostly to not be interrupted every other sentence," Jeff said meaningfully. "While all the adults and, frankly, all the kids, too, are willing and able to add in, we won't be able to make any plans if the entire crew is in here."

"We *are* an entire crew, aren't we?" Tim asked thoughtfully. "I mean, we look like all we're missing are Starfleet uniforms in order to be doing a live-action *Star Trek* reenactment or something. And, other than Christopher's kids, all the kids are old enough to participate."

"We have at least ninety people on board," I added. Everyone looked at me. Shrugged. "I counted. I *can* do that, you know." Of course, my original count of a hundred had included Team Tough Guys in it, but I was smart enough not to round up, lest someone else count heads and question how I'd gotten the higher number, Chuckie in particular. "So, yeah, we're all ready for our mission, Commander Crawford."

"Everyone can stop glaring at me," Tim said. "Mother gave me that commission, I didn't give it go myself."

"Tim, what's your point?" Reader asked slowly.

Tim looked at me. "My point, or rather, my question, is this—who made the decision to bring the people onto the ship who weren't on it already when Mother began takeoff?"

CHAPTER 20

DIDN'T HAVE TO THINK too hard about this. "I think it was Jamie who made the choices, honestly."

"I'm sure she called them all here, and possibly brought them all here," Tim said. "But who told her who to pick?"

"Why would anyone have told her to pick anybody?" Jeff asked.

"Because the choices were selective," I said as Tim nodded. "My parents and yours aren't here. Three of your sisters and their families aren't here. If Jamie could move the kids to her as if she was using an invisible gate, why not bring Marcia over from the White House to be with her children, too? Why is your Cabinet here at all? Sure, Jamie knows them, but it's not like she hangs out with them. And where're Nadine and Colette?"

"I assumed they got off the ship in time," Raj said.

"Without the kids? I find it hard to believe that Nadine would do that, and Colette wouldn't leave without me." Looked around. "For that matter, where's my A-C security team?"

"Same thing," Raj said. "I think they got off in time."

"Without taking civilians with them? Pull the other one, it has bells on. And Christopher, the fastest man alive, couldn't find almost anyone to remove, and yet we have a tonnage of people on board."

"What are you getting at, Kitty?" Christopher asked. "I took who I could."

"No. I think you took who you were *allowed* to take."

"What do you mean?" Chuckie asked.

"Look, we've been too busy to think about this, but now's the time. Note that the majority of our trained security personnel aren't here." Looked at Len and Kyle, who were standing with the press corps. "In fact, I'm going to bet that Len and Kyle are only here because whoever told Jamie who to pick thought they were press, not security."

"Naveed is security," Chuckie pointed out. "And he's here."

"He's in the role of parent or older, protective relative. So is Mister Gadhavi."

Our resident grizzly bear nodded his head. "Mister Reynolds, I believe that your nickname should be put to use at this time. I feel that Commander Crawford and Queen Katherine's point is the key one."

"Caretaker begs the question of why Marcia wasn't brought over," Chuckie said, though I could now see the Conspiracy Wheels turning.

"Denise covers caretaker, for all the kids," Claudia said. "But Kevin is security and he's here."

"He's here in the role of parent, though," Chuckie said. "But the Cabinet makes no sense, if you're thinking that someone got all of the trained security personnel off the ship prior to takeoff."

"All the trained security personnel that were identified as security," Tim said. "I think that's the key point. I mean, the Vice President and the Secretary of Defense are both well-trained military men."

Fritz Hochberg, said VP, nodded. "But we weren't here in those capacities."

"Hammy? Your thoughts?" This was directed by me to Brigadier General Marvin Hamlin, who was easily Chuckie's equal in terms of identifying real conspiracies and no one's equal when it came to hiding from the Forces of Evil. Hamlin had managed to hide from the Mastermind for years before we'd been able to bring Cliff down and let Hamlin back out into the light.

Hamlin grimaced. "I don't feel that we have all the intel that we need, but it surely seems that the selection of who is and isn't on board is far from random."

"My issue is that with all of us here," Horn indicated himself and the rest of the Cabinet members, "America's sitting with only the Secretary of Education at the helm."

"I'm sure Marcia will handle things appropriately, Vander," Jeff said. "And Angela's there, as are all the Joint Chiefs."

Horn shrugged. "That's not my point, Jeff. Marcia's a good lady, but she's going to be under tremendous pressure, and while the others are all more than seasoned, still we have all of us on a spaceship going toward an unknown destination, which leaves the country and the solar system at risk. If the Mastermind were still alive, I'd say that he'd planned this."

"He's not and there's no way he could have thought and planned this far ahead. But we have the Tinkerer and the Shadow around, so it could have been one of them. But I don't think we have enough to go on yet."

"Keep talking," Chuckie said. He was staring at the ceiling but he didn't look like he had a good idea yet.

"What about our other A-Cs?" I asked, always happy to oblige my besties. "Why did you all stay on board?"

"I didn't feel able to leave the ship," White said. "Not as if I was ill, but as if leaving was a terrible idea."

"Me too," Gower said.

Raj nodded. "But I wasn't going to leave without you and Jeff anyway, Kitty."

"Right. And, let's face it, neither would Nadine, Colette, or my entire A-C security team, all of whom are mysteriously not on board. Jamie loves Nadine and Colette—if she was choosing, I feel confident she'd have chosen them. And she also loves Keith, the head of her Secret Service detail, and he's not here, either."

"I got all Secret Service off, Kitty," Christopher said. "Remember?"

"I do. But I think you got them off because, again, whoever planned this didn't want them along."

"Mother's choice of who's doing what job also doesn't seem random," Tito said. "Tim's suddenly somehow the Commander? I mean, he's a Commander in Centaurion Division, but if we're talking a military action, then Jeff should have been chosen."

"But he's assigned to Weapons," Tim pointed out, "and, as we've seen, Mother tends to enforce her rules."

"And I'm Communications and while that does actually make sense, why does it matter? I think it clearly matters to Mother, but why?" Waited. Mother said nothing. Which was interesting.

"I did not program the ship for any of this," Drax said miserably. "None of this should be happening."

"It won't affect your relationship with the military," Reader reassured. "We're clear this isn't what you wanted."

"I don't think it was Ixtha," Rahmi said thoughtfully. "When we were all in the enforced sleep, she was speaking to us. She was quite . . . grateful . . . that we were coming. She wanted warriors far more than the children. I believe that Charlie and Jamie made her feel that the warriors could not come without the children."

"The kids' part in this I get, mostly. Charlie wanted to go on a vacation and my guess is that Ixtha reached him in the Dream-Scape before she ever talked to me." Plus, ACE had pretty much confirmed this. "So, I can see him and Jamie ensuring that Ixtha felt they needed to come along. It's the fact that Ixtha chose people who are not obviously warriors or security that's the real hundred-thousand-dollar question."

"So," Chuckie said slowly, "maybe whoever chose the personnel isn't Ixtha."

We all nodded. "That makes sense," Reader said. "But if so, then who chose the personnel? And how did they make, convince, or fool Jamie into doing it?"

"And that's our next hundred-thousand-dollar question." Waited. Mother still wasn't chiming in. Which was, for how she'd been prior, out of character.

Tim noticed it, too. "Mother, who actually chose the ship's crew? As in, why are some of us here and others not?"

Silence.

"Mother, don't play coy," I said sternly. "Answer the Commander."

Instead of answers, however, were interrupted by the sounds of alarms going off.

"Everyone to stations, all personnel strap in," Mother said calmly. "We are leaving warp unexpectedly."

CHAPTER 21

HAD TO GIVE IT to everyone—no one panicked. All the A-Cs we had here, other than Jeff, went into Evacuation Mode, grabbing humans and racing them to, I assumed, the nearest crash couch room, while Jeff, Tim, Tito, and I flung ourselves into our assigned seats. I, personally, was getting really good at getting into my seat and getting the safety harness locked in with my purse in tow, practice making perfect and all that jazz. Hughes and Walker took the remaining open spots at the controls before Christopher could grab them.

"That's everyone," he called to us as he raced off, presumably to strap in himself.

"Mother," I shouted over the claxons, "are the kids all safe?"

"All personnel are strapped in," Mother shared. "Prepare for a bumpy ride. I . . . might need assistance. This is not happening by my choice."

"Oh my God," Tim groaned. "It continues to get worse."

"Mother, will you let Matt or Chip trade places with Tim?"

"No," she said. And then we were spinning like I'd never spun before.

Would have screamed but I was too busy trying not to barf. I'd never been much for the Spinner and similar rides, and this was like those but amped up to way past eleven. To make it more "fun," we were tumbling as well as spinning. Worried about the kids, the littler ones in particular, but I couldn't help them right now, so had to just hope that the crash couches were doing their jobs.

Really hoped that everyone hiding out in the maintenance closet was strapped down somehow, because otherwise Team

Tough Guys was going to be Team Infirmary Residents. Felt bad for the least weasels, likely tumbling around in the Royal Hatbox and wondering why they were being tortured. Kind of like the rest of us.

Had to figure everyone else was at least freaked out if not downright terrified. Meaning it was time for me to do my job on the ship. Prayed we weren't heading into a star or a black hole or something, but couldn't really pay attention since I was trying to communicate with the ship and the crew. Felt the ship kind of tell me it was okay to talk, so I went for it.

"We welcome you aboard Hostage Spacelines. You may be experiencing a . . . slight disturbance. The Commander wishes to inform you that we are in control and all is well." This was a blatant lie, but with all the kids on board, saying it was time to kiss our butts good-bye seemed wrong.

"How is that helping?" Tim shouted. "I have no idea what we can do. I know we need to stabilize but I have no idea what to do about that."

"Mother? Could the alarms stop? I think we're all aware that we're in trouble and, likely, all deaf by now, too."

Thankfully, the alarms muted. They didn't turn off, but now it was more the polite tones of someone trying not to rudely interrupt versus shrieking. Wished Drax was up here with us, but I could compliment him on his craftsmanship later.

And he deserved a compliment, because even though we were whirling like a dervish—whatever that actually was—nothing was coming loose. At least, nothing I could see or hear, and I was going to count that as good until told otherwise.

Hughes and Walker, miraculously, were at their actual assigned positions, and they were able to give instructions to the rest of us, since Hughes had been a backup for the Commander seat and Walker had backed up Tito's position.

"Tim, you just concentrate on steering," Hughes said. "Steers just like a jumbo jet."

"Liar," Tim said through clenched teeth.

"Close enough for government work. Chip and I will stabilize. Tito, ensure all shields are up at maximum."

"That means hit all the green buttons on your right," Walker shared. "If we need shields lowered it's the yellow buttons next to the green set, and for down it's the red buttons also on your right."

"Nice of Drax to use human color coding," Tim mentioned.

"He's an artist," Jeff said, sarcasm knob at eight and rising. "I just wish he was as good with programming his AI."

"What about the buttons on my left?" Tito asked, moving us off of Jeff's complaints.

"Ignore them for now," Hughes said calmly, as if nothing much was going on. As always, my flyboys lived to impress. "Jeff, ready weapons just in case."

"Wish I was clear as to how."

"Same color scheme," Walker said. "But you get to use both hands. C'mon, Jeff, I know you're used to using both hands. You couldn't keep Kitty happy otherwise."

"Is now really the time?" Jeff asked.

The rest of the guys all managed snickers, despite the situation. "Jeff, honestly," Tim said, "for the two of you, when isn't it the time?"

"Right now would qualify," I pointed out. "Just sayin'."

"Sounds like problems in paradise," Hughes said. "Chip and I are always here for you, Kitty."

"I'm touched. Look, I'm all for doing the deed in this ship. I just want to be sure that said ship isn't flipping around like an out of control gymnast and that we all aren't going to die, call me a cold fish."

"I really hope that's not broadcasting to everyone," Jeff said. "Our kids in particular."

"It is not," Mother said.

"Thank you for that, Mother," Jeff said with a great deal of sincerity. "I think the mental health bills for our kids are already going to be big enough without extra help."

"You worry too much."

"I agree with your wife, Mister President," Hughes said. "But, the First Lady isn't doing her job. Kitty, get back on the airwaves and keep on keeping it light and, also, hail for sentient life."

"As if I know where the 'hail' button is on this thing?" I didn't know how to turn the intercom on or off, let alone how to hail externally.

A light in front of me flashed. It was a button. A white one, whatever that might mean. Hoped this was a hint. "Thanks, Mother. I think." Pushed the button down. We didn't explode and the sound in my ears—what I could hear after being deafened by the alarms—sounded like I had an open channel.

"Hailing frequencies open or some such. This is Earth Vessel *Distant Voyager* having some major issues in your solar space." Not that I could see a star. All I saw was black. "Or, you know, in your sort of general space. Your choice. We come in peace, though we may be in pieces soon. So, um, a little help? Totally appreciated. Thanks of a grateful nation. And all that jazz."

"Hail will continue," Mother said.

"Cool. I guess." We were no longer tumbling like a big, metal piece of space junk, so there was that. We were still spinning, however.

"I have no idea what to steer for," Tim said. "At all. And before you tell me to focus on something, there's nothing to focus on other than the blackness of space."

Something flashed by the windshield. "Tim, hang on. Something's out there, I saw it, just for a moment."

"Stabilization almost complete," Walker said.

"Slowing," Hughes added. "Kitty, seriously, keep talking to the passengers. We can't afford panic right now."

"Seems like the perfect time for it, but okay. Mother?"

"You are live to the crew."

"Super-duper. Um, hey gang. Despite the likely need for a lot of barf bags, our ride is, supposedly, coming to an end. Please do not undo your seatbelts and exit, however. That goes triple for anyone under the age of twenty-one, no matter how much you want to whine about it. Once the ride has come to a full and complete stop, we'll give you instructions, but it's likely that said instructions will be to stay exactly where you are."

"I want to know that everyone's alright," Jeff said. "Kids especially."

"All personnel were secured and all are fine," Mother said as we now spun at merry-go-round speed. "Despite protocol, I did not send them into the safety of sleep."

"You mean you didn't have time," Tito said.

"This is true. The situation was . . . unexpected."

The something I'd seen flashed by again, but because we were slowing down, everyone could take a look. "There, see it?"

The guys chorused that they did. "Doesn't look like a planet or a star," Jeff said.

We swung around again and finally stopped, with our windshield pointing right at whatever it was in front of us. "No. It looks like a nebula." Hey, Chuckie wasn't on deck, so I had to represent. "Which could be great or could be very bad."

"Why bad, Kitty?" Jeff asked.

"Because we know beings from nebulas. And they tend to be really bossy and hella powerful."

And the ones we knew considered themselves ACE's parole officers. And, by being on this ship with us, ACE was breaking parole in a big way.

CHAPTER 22

"MOTHER, BY ANY CHANCE** do you know where we are?" Wasn't sure if I should hope for us to be near the Eagle Nebula or not.

"I am not . . . certain."

We all looked at each other. "Why not?" Jeff asked.

"I believe I have been . . . tampered with."

"Are you damaged?" Tim asked. "And, if so, can any of us repair you?"

"I am still assessing. I will need a few moments to determine our position. We should not have been thrown out of warp. We did not hit anything and I did not alter our mission plan."

"How do you mean?" Mossy had tampered, but I sincerely doubted that whatever he'd done could have tossed us out of warp or changed Mother's plans.

"I mean that something I am not aware of has caused us to be stranded near this nebula. I believe it is the Eagle Nebula."

"Of course it is. Are you sure we're stranded?"

"For the time being, yes, until I finish my internal scan."

"We need to get Drax here," Hughes said.

"Mother, what button do I push to talk to the crew?" A different button flashed. "Thanks." Cleared my throat then pushed it. "Now that the ship has come to a complete stop, all passengers are still required to remain in their safety seats. Other than the people I am going to name, who need to come to the command deck immediately. No one else should plan on accompanying them, because if you do, you'll be confined to the brig."

"We have a brig?" Tito asked quietly.

"Every ship has a brig," Tim said. "Galaxywide, as far as we've seen."

Continued on. "Gustav Drax, Charles Reynolds, Brian Dwyer, Serene Dwyer, James Reader, Joe Billings, Randy Muir, and Jerry Tucker, come on down. Everyone else sit tight, and for those of you fuming for not being a part of this particular roll call, never fear—I'm sure we'll be calling you up soon enough."

"No arguments for who you chose, but why not Lorraine and Claudia?" Tim asked as I let go of the button.

"Because I want them keeping everyone else in their seats. If the girls can't leave their seats, trust me, they won't let anyone else leave, either. Mother, can I do another hail?"

"Absolutely." The hail button flashed again. Felt confident that I knew which one it was versus the internal hailing button. Go me.

"Got it, thanks." Pushed this button down as my requested reinforcements arrived. "Sandy, if you're out there, this is Kitty and we need your help. Just you, hopefully, unless the rest of the Seven Dwarfs are feeling charitable toward me and mine. This isn't how we planned to visit, but since we're in your neighborhood—help, we need somebody, but not just anybody." Let go of the button. Who knew? Maybe Sandy had gotten into the Beatles somehow. "Mother, please make sure that goes out a lot. Toward the nebula."

"Broadcasting. I . . . apologize."

"For what?"

"For this situation. It should not have happened."

"None of this should have happened," Tim said. "Something's off, more off than Mother's decision to take control."

"Someone activated the Protection Mode," Drax pointed out. "That indicates tampering."

"No, that was me," Mother said. "I activated due to what I saw in the DreamScape. The fate of the galaxy is at stake. And now we are stranded." She sounded stressed.

"Okay, that makes sense," I said. "But us being tossed out of warp does not, and Mother, stop blaming yourself. We'll figure out what's going on and fix it, I promise. And I'm willing to bet that whoever did whatever tampering is also likely the person who influenced who is and isn't on the ship."

Chuckie nodded. "It makes sense. And you named our two most likely culprits earlier: the Tinkerer or the Shadow."

"Could be someone else," Brian said. "Remember, the Club Fifty-One True Believers are against space travel, unless it's taking aliens away from Earth."

"Gustav, is Mother acting erratic to you in any way? And,

before you say yes, know that I mean erratic aside from her activating the Protection Mode thingy. Because what she did with
that seems like a failsafe."

"Yes, Kitty, Protection Mode is a failsafe. I did not realize
that . . . Mother . . . was so self-aware, however."

"You programmed me to think," Mother pointed out. "And I
am thinking."

"We're back to Kubrick territory," Tim muttered.

"Again, we are not," Mother said. "I must stress, Commander, that I am not going to harm any of the passengers or
crew. It is not in my makeup."

"Neither is being thrown out of warp," Jeff pointed out. "And
yet, here we are."

"No, there is a difference," Mother said. "Protection Mode
and my making decisions to protect all crew on the ship and, by
extension, all life in the galaxy is absolutely in my makeup.
However, a hardware malfunction is not something that I would
choose to do. If we are stranded, then the safety of the crew is at
risk, which is counter to my entire being. Being thrown out of
warp is a dangerous thing, as you have just experienced, and
therefore is not something I would willingly do unless it was the
only way to preserve life. It was not, and was not my choice."

"Why didn't you answer us when we were asking you questions, right before we were tossed out of warp?" Chuckie asked.

"I had detected that there was an issue with the warp core. I
was determining the nature of the problem and whether I could
repair it. I still do not know what happened and I fear that I
cannot enact repairs alone."

Chuckie nodded as if this was the answer he'd expected.
"Sabotage. Likely done before the AI, excuse me, before Mother
went online."

"And things like that only take a pawn." Got a lot of WTH
looks, but then, the girls weren't up here. Heaved a sigh. "Operation Drug Addict, remember? Whoever spiked Jeff's regenera-
tive fluids wasn't a Top Dawg but a pawn who slipped in and out
without anyone noticing. I'd assume the same happened here."

"Makes sense," Chuckie said. "So, we don't care who did it,
just on whose orders they were working."

"Mother, have you determined what's wrong yet?" Jeff
asked.

"No. But, as I said, I believe it is something within the warp
core."

Drax heaved a sigh. "That will require help we don't have."

"Help like who?" Reader asked. "We have a lot of people on board, many of whom are more than capable of assisting."

Brian nodded. "We were all trained in how to repair this ship. With you on board, Mister Drax, I don't see why Airborne and I can't repair anything needed, even if we have to go external to the ship."

Drax shook his head. "For most repairs? Yes, all of you are trained and I am here. However, the warp core is not created out of my smart metal, meaning I can't connect with it in the same way I can with the rest of the ship. The warp core is delicate and it requires someone . . . small to do intricate repairs."

What Mossy had said registered. "Oh. The Turleens helped you with that part, didn't they?"

"They did indeed," Drax confirmed. "And without a Turleen on board, we could be in trouble. I would not want to ask the children, no matter how talented, to perform these tasks."

"Yeah, hells to the no," Jeff said calmly. "We'll figure out another way."

"There may be no other way," Mother said. "While you have been speaking I have determined what happened. The warp core drive exploded. It was a small, contained explosion, only damaging the core."

Serene's eyes narrowed. "Contained explosions like that take skill. Getting someone in place to insert one in a way that no one involved noticed takes even more skill. I don't think we should count out anyone as a possible suspect, but Club Fifty-One has had my bomb micronization data the longest."

"But our enemies all tend to share information," I pointed out. "So there's still not enough for us to go on to figure out who planted the bomb." Though, per what Mossy had told me and Tim, that this was doable was because Mother wasn't set up to notice someone fiddling with something small that didn't seem important.

"So someone wanted us to strand, but not to die," Brian said. "But, reality says that whoever that was didn't know that it would be this crew getting stranded. I'd think they expected that the planned crew would be who was on board."

"Based on how long we were in warp," Jerry said, "I think that means they expected us to strand after we'd visited Alpha Four but before we got to Vatusus."

"Why?" Joe asked. "That's the question. Because if we were

between Alpha Four and Vatusus, we'd be able to get help quickly."

"Maybe," Randy said slowly. "But . . . maybe the bomb didn't do what it was supposed to."

Drax jerked, "Protection Mode would have enhanced the ship's own protections."

"Yes," Mother agreed. "I believe that due to my full awareness of the situation, I was able to identify and curtail some of the effects. Not as much as I should have, however."

"Stop blaming yourself," Jeff said, Commander of the Free World Voice on Full. "That's an order, Mother. We're choosing to take what you're saying at face value, and that means that you're our friend and ally. You didn't want us in this position, and it's not your fault. Our enemies did this to you, and we will determine who they were and make them pay for it."

"Thank you," Mother said, and she sounded sincere. Had a feeling Jeff and Mother had just moved into the Friend Zone.

"What Jeff said, but I want to go back to Randy's point, 'cause I think it's the key one for this situation. Mother, can you extrapolate what would have happened if you hadn't been in Protection Mode when that bomb went off?"

"Give me a moment."

We waited for about two seconds. Was proud that no one fidgeted, not even me.

"Ah," Mother said finally. "Based on running at least fifty simulations, without Protection Mode enacted, the warp core explosion would have created a chain reaction and the entire ship would have been disintegrated."

CHAPTER 23

WE ALL LET THAT one sit on the air for a few long moments. There was a lot of that going around for this trip already, lucky us.

Broke the silence. "Gustav, let me just say that I think you're da bomb in terms of ship and weapons design, and let no one tell you differently. So, whoever planted this bomb wanted the *Distant Voyager* to explode between Alpha Four and Vatusus. And it doesn't take genius to figure out why." Looked at Chuckie. "Though I'll let our resident genius explain it, just in case."

Chuckie nodded. "If the *Distant Voyager* explodes after the visit to Alpha Four, then everyone is suspect. Prince Gustav is dead, we've lost all of Airborne as well as A-Cs and astronauts, almost all of whom are tightly bound in to Centaurion Division in some way. Everyone's upset and grieving and everyone blames everyone else."

"Vatusus and Alpha Four in particular," I added.

"And Club Fifty-One," Hughes said.

Walker nodded. "Fanning the flames on Earth to their wicked little hearts' content."

"All of which means galactic war," Reader said. "And galactic war between our allies."

"I think that points to Club Fifty-One," Serene said. "Because they want all aliens dead."

"I agree. This isn't the Tinkerer's style. He wants Stephanie to be the next Ronald Yates, and she can't become the Heir Apparent or the Renaissance Girl for Evil if the galaxy is destroyed. And I don't see this as being something the Shadow would want, either, because she's able to look at the bigger picture and see how she can rule the galaxy in the right situations."

Jeff sighed. "I agree, baby. I just wish we could get this intel to your mother."

"We are out of range," Mother said. "I could get a message to Earth via a variety of means, but none of them would be secured."

"So, once we're home, we'll get right on this. Mom will already be looking at Club Fifty-One suspiciously. She and my Uncle Mort may have found our culprit before we get home. And, while I'm tingling that we've figured out why we're stuck here, I don't think that whoever set the bomb is who helped Jamie choose this particular crew roster. And knowing that is probably more important right now."

"We need to ensure that there aren't more bombs," Chuckie said. "Mother, is there a way you can scan for anomalies?"

"I believe so."

Drax indicated that I should give him my helmet, which I did. "I can assist with this."

"While you're at it, I think getting the ship working again is the most important thing," Jeff said, sarcasm meter at seven and rising.

"With my creator's assistance I can create the parts necessary to fix it, but I cannot fix it myself."

Drax sighed. "This is true. So unless Kitty's hails for help have worked, we may have no choice but to train one of the children to do what's needed."

Jeff's mouth opened. Put up the paw. His mouth shut. The One True FLOTUS Power in action. I liked this power and really hoped I'd always have it, even when Jeff wasn't the President anymore. "Pause." Now I wanted to hear Pitbull. "I think I may have a solution. But I need to steal Tim for a minute. We'll be right back."

He took off his helmet quickly. "Sure, let's go."

Reader gave us both a beady look. "Want to tell us what the two of you are up to?"

Grabbed Tim's hand. "Nope. Not yet." Then I turned up the hyperspeed and we zipped off.

"What are we doing?" Tim asked.

"Hoping to visit the Wallflowers in their "Invisible City," dude, what else?"

"Huh?" Tim jerked. "Oh. Gotcha."

Did a run-by to make sure that everyone in the Nonessential Personnel Station were okay, my kids in particular. Everyone

seemed fine and I didn't see evidence of barfing, so either someone had broken the "stay in your seats" directive, or everyone
had managed to survive our horrific ride out of warp with their
stomachs' contents intact.

Then headed for our special maintenance closet and zipped
inside. There was no one there.

"Um . . ."

"Oh, great," Tim groaned. "Now we've lost the stowaways."

"Why do these things always happen to us?"

"No idea, but a part of me isn't surprised at all." He looked
worried. "You don't think one of them is the traitor or whatever
we're after, do you? I mean, we know nothing about the Ard Ri.
Other than that's he's kind of pompous."

"Um . . . it occurs to me that we have someone who can literally go invisible on Team Tough Guys, and they all have nasty
senses of humor, so . . ."

"I mean," Tim said quickly, "the Ard Ri is totally regal."

Everyone we were looking for appeared. Siler grinned at us.
"Glad one of you could figure out what was going on."

"We heard footsteps," Wruck said, "and the Ard Ri suggested
we go invisible just in case."

"Of course he did," Tim muttered, while Algar glared at him.
Knew Algar wasn't actually mad. Clearly he was having fun
with Tim, in that Cat Playing With A Mouse kind of way. Maybe
he, like the kids, was looking at this as a vacation.

"How did you guys manage during the Turbulence From Hell
section of our journey?"

Wruck gave me the "really?" look. "I shifted into a form that
protected everyone."

"Giving myself the 'duh' on that one."

"Hey, we were worried about you guys," Tim said. "Forgive
us for not thinking of everything."

"But that's your jobs, laddie," Algar said. "To do all the
thinking."

"Hardly." But had to figure that was an Algar Clue of some
kind. "However, we have a situation." Brought them up to speed
on the latest. "So, I honestly think you all need to come out of
the closet. James is on deck to help you through it."

Tim snickered while I got a lot of eye rolls. "Not sure we can
trust the AI," Siler said.

"Not sure that we can't, however. And, frankly, without
Mossy, we're going to have to make one of the kids work in the

warp core, and let me just mention how against this Jeff is and then share that if you think Papa Bear is against it, you ain't seen Mama Bear in action."

"If you're wrong about the AI, Missus Executive Mama Bear, then we give away our only advantage."

"But if we're right about her, then we get to have all of you freaking helping us do something other than sit here hoping that ACE's parole officers show up to help us. And then to harm us."

"Excuse me?" Algar said.

Heaved a sigh. "ACE houses in Jamie. ACE is not supposed to leave Earth. We're stranded near the Eagle Nebula, where Sandy the Superconsciousness and his buddies, the Seven Meddling Superconsciousness Dwarfs live. I'm just spitballing here, but I think that if we don't get moving, we're going to get visitors that we might not want."

"Or we might," Tim said. "Because we're dead in the water, so to speak, and we have the solution right here in the form of Mossy."

Who nodded. "I, at least, need to go with them. No children should be working in the warp core."

"Is it dangerous?" Had visions of everyone getting irradiated.

"Not in the way I'd assume you mean. There is no risk of exposure. However, the intricacy that's demanded is beyond most children, even the talented ones on the ship with us. So it does fall to me to do this."

"Keeping in mind that we're going to have to share that we're pretty sure that Mossy isn't the one who set the bomb," Tim added. "And before everyone glares at me or whatever, someone who had access to the warp core set that bomb, and Mossy had that access."

"This is true," Mossy said. "And I've already successfully tampered with the ship in what I'm willing to bet is the exact same way as the saboteur did."

"You confessing?" Buchanan asked.

"Hardly. However, the Commander is right—I am in a position to look guilty. Which is all the more reason for me, at least, to come out of hiding."

Looked right at Algar. "So, what's the risk to reward ratio for all of you 'exposing' that you've stowed away?"

He snapped his fingers and time froze. "Acceptable."

"You were on board in case Mother couldn't contain that explosion, weren't you? You can act even faster than ACE."

"Among other reasons, yes." He looked mildly worried, which was a rarity.

"Mother's not wrong in her assessment of what could happen if we don't help Ixtha, is she?"

"She's only wrong in that she gave a tenth of a percentage chance that the galaxy wouldn't be destroyed. And if this galaxy goes in the way that Mother, ACE, and I see it going, due to the situation you've been called upon to solve, then the entire universe is going to go with it."

CHAPTER 24

WANTED TO LET THAT idea settle in, but had no idea how much time I was going to get with Algar in this way. "Well, that sounds like something we want to avoid. So, in order to speed all this saving of the universe along, can we trust Mother?"

"That's not the correct question."

Groaned. "Seriously? Fine. Do we have a traitor on board?"

"Still not quite right."

Not *quite* right. So, that was a clue. Considered what he might mean. "Fine. Do we have a *conscious* traitor on board?"

"No."

"Whee. So, does that mean we have someone who is unconsciously perpetrating traitorous actions?"

"Yes."

Heaved a sigh. "Is it Mossy?"

"No."

Pondered. There had to be a reason Algar was pussyfooting. Decided to take the wild guess that probably wasn't all that wild. "It's one of my kids, isn't it? Or both of them."

"Yes, and not just your children. All the children. Well, all the talented ones."

"So most of them. How?"

"Ixtha is not the only person capable of using the Dream-Scape."

"So good of you to mention that this thing existed to me before, oh, now."

He shook his head. "You do remember how I've lived my life."

"Free Will Forever or *Free Willy*, I can never keep it straight."

He shot me a dirty look. Ignored it. "So, who brought our bizarre assembly on board, Jamie?"

"With a little help from her friends, yes."

"Seriously, now I want to hear the Sergeant Pepper's album."

"Put your headphones in."

"Then I couldn't hear the melodious sounds of your voice. Or was that a hint? If it was a hint, I have to mention that as the Chief Communications Officer, or whatever the hell Mother thinks I am, me listening to tunes will be frowned upon."

"Not if it keeps you and the rest of the crew calm."

"Great. I'll see if I can get someone, anyone, else to agree to that. So, since I don't want to be rude and listen to music when I'm speaking directly to you, who's been influencing the kids and, more importantly, why? Aside from Ixtha, I mean. I don't understand why we have the people we do on board, and why we have others still on Earth."

"That's for you to find out. You alone would be preferable. Unless you want the children cross-examined, you need to stop the others from worrying about the identity of the culprit."

"Well, we have plenty to distract us from that right now."

"You do, and more will be coming."

"Look, I realize that you're against overtly helping because Free Will is like your religion, but isn't this a big enough of a deal for you to just snap your fingers and fix the ship and, even, get us where we're going?"

"If I interfere directly the results could be disastrous."

"Really? More disastrous than the end of all the worlds?"

"Yes."

"To whom? To you or to the rest of us?"

"Both."

"I feel that my King of the Elves is holding out on me."

"I am the Ard Ri right now. Besides, the journey is more than a journey—it's also the destination."

"Excuse me?"

He shrugged. "Figure it out. I know you can."

"Fine, fine, Mister Inscrutable. I realize you have a personal idiom and outlook to maintain. Just throw me a bone and tell me flat out, is Mother the culprit and can we trust her?"

"No and yes."

"Finally, and thank you. So and therefore, can all of you come out of hiding or not? And if not, why not? And if yes, who? Everyone or just a select few?"

"Yes, we can. However, the gentlemen don't really want to."

"Wow, are they all confessing their true devotion to each other in here or something? I mean, if they are, fine, though I think Adrianna might have an issue with Malcolm tossing her over."

Algar chuckled. "No. They are blood brothers by now, but not lovers."

"Okay, so straight gals can rejoice and gay men can mourn. But this then leads right back to my 'why don't they want to leave the closet' question. And, since the fate of the universe is at stake, just tell me, without the games."

"Because they don't know who I actually am, and so my word and suggestions mean nothing to them."

"And yet they're keeping you with them."

He shrugged. "They appreciated the fact that I agreed with their suspicions."

"They weren't alone in those suspicions. As near as I could tell, you had those same suspicions. Which, all things considered, shouldn't have been possible. I mean, you basically know everything."

"No, I don't. I know most things, but not everything. And there's quite a lot going on. More than normal."

"Which is totally par for our course." Decided I didn't want the existential headache trying to figure out how powerful Algar really was would likely give me. Plus, he looked ready to snap his fingers again and I still needed information. "Okay, so, regarding Team Tough Guys, who got them onto the ship? Because I can't imagine that whoever told Jamie and the other kids to have the Non-Avengers assemble also somehow asked her to ensure that Team Tough Guys were on board."

"They came of their own free will."

"Shocker. Was that will assisted by anyone powerful and yet friendly to us?"

"No."

"Huh. Was there an assist in allowing them to actually get onto the ship?"

"Now you're thinking correctly. Yes. However, that assist didn't come from me."

"So, if that's supposed to let me know that it was ACE, that's great, but why did he then allow Jamie to be influenced in who she brought onto the ship?"

"ACE sees things differently than I do."

Maybe I was going to get that existential headache after all. "You want to explain that to me?"

"It's not relevant at the moment."

"Really? A powerful superconsciousness let my child bring the wrong people on board and you don't see that as relevant."

"They're not the 'wrong' people. They just aren't the people that you, perhaps, would have chosen for this journey."

Hoped there was still some of that Advil left. "But you said an enemy helped Jamie choose who to bring on board."

"No. I said that it would be best if you, and only you, determined who the culprit was. Culprit has several meanings—not all of them indicate heinous criminal behavior."

"In a spare moment I'll ask Mother if she's downloaded *Roget's Thesaurus* and the *Oxford English Dictionary*. So, you're sort of insinuating that whoever chose the *Distant Voyager's* 'guest list' might not have had evil intent."

"Correct. They might have, as well. But that's going to be for you to determine."

"All by my lonesome, got it. So, um, back to why my tough guys here want to stay hidden in the maintenance closet."

"It's simple. Frankly, they don't believe that they are safe to leave this place."

"A belief you agreed with only a short while ago. What's changed?"

Algar shrugged. "You've affected Mother already. Faster even than I'd expected."

"Excuse me?"

"She's been connected to your mind. You don't think logically, at least, not in the way she's programmed to expect."

"I realize that there are people who follow a more logical thought pattern. However, I find it difficult to believe that Drax didn't account for how organic minds work."

"He did. However, your mind, in particular, has affected Mother."

Received an expectant look. Tried to figure out what Algar wanted me to figure out. "Because I'm the main point of Communications or whatever?"

"Yes." The expectant look was still fully in place.

"Um . . . but Tim assigned our positions, out of necessity."

"He did." Algar was now giving me the "duh" look.

"Oh. You or ACE suggested those stations to him?"

"In a sense."

"So why did Mother not allow us to change roles? The real reason."

"It's going to matter very soon that the two people who are the most independent in terms of their thinking and actions be in charge, and that the person who's led military actions without panic for years be in charge of Weapons. She's seen how the three of you think and has, wisely, chosen to keep you in the positions you all initially chose."

"So, Tim as Commander, me as Communications, and Jeff as Weapons is sticking. I speak for all of us when I say, with as much sarcasm as possible, that we're all thrilled. What about Tito, Matt, and Chip?"

"The team is working well. Doctor Hernandez is the most capable person on board. He's also the one who remains calm in every situation, including the life-and-death ones. Keep him with you. Matt and Chip have enough skill to fly the ship without any help. It would be easier for them if they were working with the rest of their regular team, but they'll manage and pick up any slack the rest of you might inadvertently create."

"Um, go team? This still doesn't answer why you now think it's safe to come out of hiding. My affecting Mother did what, exactly?"

"It saved everyone."

"I'd feel all special and tingly, but before I let myself go wild, I'd like an explanation."

"You moved Mother from the mindset of doing whatever she wanted and felt was best into becoming a team player."

"How Corporate America of me. Flat-out you're going to have to explain what you mean by this."

"If I must."

"It's already been a hell of a long day, so, yes, you must."

"Only you and Tim would have talked about HAL. Therefore, only you and Tim would have created the need for Mother to look that movie up and do a comparison to herself."

"James would have, Chuckie, too. Raj, Amy, lots of the others."

Algar shook his head. "Years ago? Yes, James and Charles would have. But now, in the positions they're in, they would not, not in this situation. None of the others would, either. Plus, you and Tim have a different way of talking to each other than you do with the others."

"Heads of Airborne always know how to hang with the crazy?"

"Exactly. Mother now knows what she does not want to become."

"Good to know. So, because Mother's not going all HAL on us, you feel that it's safe to share that all of you are still on the ship."

"Yes. However, as I said earlier, my word has no sway with these men. They are protectors, first. They want to be in a position to protect." He shot me a look I was pretty sure was supposed to be meaningful.

Heaved yet another sigh. "Fine. So I have to convince them that we need them out more than we need them hidden?"

"Yes. Beyond Mossy, who is already prepared to reveal himself."

"Not in front of the kids and more easily distressed adults, I hope. We don't want to start a panic, after all."

Algar rolled his eyes. "No one's actually panicked yet."

"Oh, I'm sure that's just a matter of time, and it also depends how you define 'panic,' of course. Once again, I'll verify all the definitions later."

"Panic is rarely helpful."

"Yes, I'm clear—panic never achieves anything other than increasing the total chaos of the situation." Mom and Dad had drilled that into my head and, as I thought of it, Chuckie's, Amy's, Brian's, and Sheila's heads, too. So, when it all went sideways, I could count on the three of my high school friends on board to, presumably, keep their heads. Wondered what Sheila was doing for a moment. Probably not anything like what the rest of us were. Figured that the others would also feel envy for Sheila if I brought this up to them. Actively chose not to so bring up. That was me, taking one for the team as always.

"Sometimes, though," Algar said pleasantly, "total chaos is what you want."

This felt like a clue. "Is it?"

But if it was a clue, Algar wasn't giving me anything else. "Time is of the essence."

"People like to say that to me. However, you just stopped time so we could chat. Ergo, time's in a holding pattern. Which I appreciate."

"I'm sure you do. There is a reason for these men to be seen, a reason that will resonate with them. I wonder if you can convince them of what that happens to be." Then he snapped his fingers and time moved on.

CHAPTER 25

"I CAN'T SPEAK FOR THE GENTLEMEN," Algar said, as if our entire conversation hadn't happened which, for the others, it hadn't. "But I feel that our being with the others might be beneficial."

"Maybe," Buchanan said. "But if we go out there, we lose any element of surprise we might have."

The others chimed in. Clearly it was just going to be Mossy coming with me and Tim unless I figured out what to say to convince them otherwise. Algar felt he'd given me the clues I'd need. However, I had nothing.

"We're stuck in the middle of space," Tim pointed out. "I don't know what you all think you're hiding from anymore. Mother appears to be on our side, particularly since the ship is damaged. We're in trouble and the closest thing to us is the Eagle Nebula, and even that we can't reach if we can't go to warp. At least, not until we're all ancient."

Wanted to tell Tim I loved him, but that would probably not go over well in this room. Didn't make eye contact with Algar, mostly because I assumed he'd look smug, because I was sure he'd caught that I'd figured out what to say. "We don't want to, really. We want to get away. Fast."

"Why?" Wruck asked.

"Because, as we'd told you before and Tim just mentioned again, we're in the Superconsciousness Central Neighborhood and ACE is inside my daughter. And I have no idea what said superconsciousnesses are going to do if they catch ACE being far away from Earth."

"We won't allow them to do anything," Buchanan growled.

"Yeah? How are you going to stop them hiding in a maintenance closet?"

"How will we stop them at all?" Tim asked. "I'd love to hear
your plans."

"Exactly," Maurer said. "Will it matter where we are?
They're powerful."

"Tell that to your mother and children, who happen to be on
board with my daughter."

Maurer looked shocked. "How did my children get on the
ship?"

"Dude, when I last recapped for all of you guys, I said all the
kids were here."

"You didn't list them by name," Maurer said.

"A thousand apologies for my oversight." Yeah, I had a sarcasm knob, too, and mine always went to eleven. "So, yes, your
kids and your mom are here. Do you, perhaps, want to make
them feel more secure and show yourself? That really goes for
the rest of you, too. I think that everyone, from the President on
down, will feel better if they know you're with us."

They still looked ready to argue. Tim rolled his eyes. "As the
other half of the Maverick Duo, I just want to say that both of us
think you should let the others know you're here. If only to distract Mother from the fact that the hackers snuck on board, too."

"Stryker and his gang are here?" Buchanan asked. The others
looked more alert and thoughtful, too.

"Yes. And, miraculously, we've managed to keep their traps
shut so they don't share with Mother that they're the most likely
people to alter her programming."

"Only just," Tim added. "Those guys don't really get what
the term 'stealth' means."

"True enough and, by looking at all of your expressions, I
think we're all forming the same plan. While Mossy saves the
day with Drax and Mother, and you guys distract the hell out of
her by merely showing up, Tim and I can get Hacker International on the reverse engineering, computer override, and fix this
situation case right away."

The ship shuddered. "That doesn't feel good," Tim said.

"Yeah. I just hope it's not heralding arrivals."

"Arrivals by whom?" Mossy asked.

"I had to send out distress calls. One of them I sent specifically to Sandy, who's the only superconsciousness likely to want
to help us. Maybe."

"Let's go," Tim said. "Mossy, at least, can be helpful."

"You take him and get him working with Drax."

"So I get to explain how I knew we had a Turleen stowaway all by myself? No thanks."

"You won't have to," Butler said, speaking for the first time since we'd gotten here. "I believe we all truly need to go with you."

"Why so, John?" Siler asked.

"Because the ship is in distress, and therefore life support could be affected. If the ship thinks there are close to ten less people on board than there actually are, that could cause issues. Or, to put it another way, there are only two of us on board who can survive without life support, and that's myself and Cameron. We need to admit that we're here so that the ship is aware of it, and makes adjustments accordingly."

"And that, gentlemen, is the ultimate winner, winner, chicken dinner. Because if someone like one of the kids can't breathe because Mother didn't accommodate for you guys, trust me when I say that Jeff won't be the only one going Old Testament on your asses."

"Far be it for us to try to protect anyone," Buchanan muttered.

"I'd feel all bad for you but I don't because I'm not joking about the whole superconsciousnesses thing, and I also kind of dread everyone's reaction when we go, 'Ta-da! Look who's here!' the moment we reach the others."

The ship shuddered again. "I think we need Mossy activated, regardless of reactions," Tim said, as he opened the door. To see someone standing there that it was safe to say none of us expected.

Though we should have. I should have, in particular.

"Mind telling me what's going on?" Jeff asked, sarcasm knob already at eleven. "And why we have a room full of people who appear to be in hiding? And why you, Tim and Kitty, also appear to be hiding them?"

"Ah . . ." Tim said.

"Um . . ." I said.

"Give it a rest, Mister Executive Chief," Buchanan said. "My team is in place to protect your wife and children. That means we do things you might not know about."

"All the time," Siler added.

"The gentlemen were protecting me," Algar said. "I was most concerned when strange things began happening."

Jeff rolled his eyes. "Whatever. Kitty, Drax needs help. What, exactly, is your plan?"

Shoved Mossy forward. "I plan to let our Turleen on Team Tough Guys save the day."

Jeff grunted. "Fine. I'll yell at everyone later. Right now, we have bigger problems than why and how all of you were hiding in a place where Mother couldn't see you."

My brain nudged. If one group of people could stow away in this fashion, what about others?

"How did you know Mother couldn't see in here?" Tim asked.

Jeff sighed. "Mother shared with me that the two of you had disappeared. It wasn't hard to track both of you based on your emotions. So, I knew that while I could feel you, Mother couldn't 'see' you, meaning that this room is shielded from the AI in some way."

"All of the maintenance closets are for some weird Vatusan reason. By the way, once we share that everyone's here, I'd like those of you on Team Tough Guys who aren't busy doing whatever to check each and every one of the other closets."

Siler and Buchanan both jerked. But it was Wruck who spoke. "Because if one set of people can hide on board, why not many others?"

Jeff groaned. "It never ends. Let's get moving."

We rejoined the others. Amazingly enough, no one complained too much about our stowaways—probably because no one had felt that Mother was on our side until, possibly, right now.

While Jeff took over explaining what was going on to everyone, Mossy went to help Drax, and Tim and I went with him, because Hacker International had gone with Drax to Engineering with hopes of helping him and Mother out.

Mossy's arrival was greeted with much joy. Drax literally could not have cared less that the Turleen had stowed away, because without him, we were, as Tim had mostly said, dead in the space water.

Sadly, Tim and I weren't able to drag any of the hackers away, though, because Drax and Mother had them all doing tasks vital to getting her back to fully functional. It was nice to see Hacker International working feverishly on something that required most of them to stand up and move, though. Hoped Jeff would get a chance to see this—he'd enjoy seeing them sweat even more than I was.

Neither Tim as Commander nor I as Communications were needed right now. We left Engineering and went to a viewing area that wasn't on the command deck—it was a bar. Well, more like a really fancy lounge. A lounge with a really great view—the "back" of this section of the ship was all window.

"Wow, did Drax watch like all of *Star Trek* while designing?"

"No," Tim said with a laugh. "But apparently this kind of thing is common on larger space vessels. In order to ensure that crew on long flights have some form of entertainment that allows them to mingle and all that."

"Seriously, for as fast as most of these ships seem to travel, acting like anyone's going to have time to hang out seems silly."

He shrugged. "We're hanging out."

"We're stuck. It's a different thing."

Though we were stuck, we were also still moving, floating toward the nebula. Could tell this was not only because of how things worked in space and that old body in motion versus body at rest law, but because the nebula looked slightly bigger. But, based on how large our scientists knew the nebula to be, and how small it looked right now, knew that Tim was right, and if we managed to float to it, Charlie would be an old man by the time we got there.

"True. But while all the ships can move fast, it's not always a good idea for them to do so. Per what Drax has told all of us and the other spacefaring races have confirmed, the strain of the faster warp jumps and such can be hard on the ships, especially over time. It's done for war, for obvious reasons, but if you're just on a peaceful cruise? You cruise. Including if you're a Turleen."

"Interesting. So, we've seen the panicked flights and the war flights, but never the casual ones?"

"Right. So, the ships are made for all contingencies, just in case. And, obviously, Vatusan ships have a lot of different forms, since they need fewer crew to man. The two-man ships? No bar."

"Yeah, there was no lounge in the helicarrier."

"Right, because it was built for war. This ship, though? She's been built to do it all." He sighed as he looked out at the blackness and the Eagle Nebula in the far distance. "Part of me is really glad Alicia's on board. The other part is terrified that we're all going to die out here, her included."

Gave him a hug. "I know what you mean. But we'll manage. We always do."

Was about to say something more when the view changed. Instead of black and the nebula, the window clouded over, as if we'd sailed into thick fog.

Only, fog it definitely was not.

CHAPTER 26

THE FOG CAME THROUGH the window, thankfully not via breaking said window, but as if the window was insubstantial. Though I knew that it was the fog that was the insubstantial thing, in no small part because fog was pretty insubstantial to begin with and in much larger part because it wasn't fog. Nice to know that my message had been received.

The fog formed, first into a swirling mass that sort of resembled a man, and then into a man in reality, so to speak.

The last time I'd seen Sandy the Superconsciousness, he'd been basically dressed in bullet hole-ridden flyers and posters with Jeff and the late Vincent Armstrong's faces on them. Now he was dressed in what looked very much like an Armani suit. Nice to see that he'd chosen to adapt to our standards of dress.

Didn't think about it, just gave him a hug once he was fully formed. "It's great to see you. I hope."

Sandy hugged me back. "I am here to assist. What are you doing here?"

"Um . . . God, it's only been a few hours, max, and it's already a long story." Brought him up to speed, though a part of me figured he already knew what was going on. "So, we're basically here against our will, but supposedly going to stop something terrible from happening."

Sandy nodded. "Yes. However, there are always terrible things happening."

"There are," Tim agreed. "But the thing we're talking about threatens to end the galaxy."

Sandy shook his head. "More than this one thing threatens

the fate of the galaxy. The galaxy is always at risk, due to the varied life-forms that inhabit it. Where you go is not the biggest threat."

"Really?" Algar had sure seemed to feel that it was. "How sure are you of this?"

"Sure," Sandy said firmly.

Chose not to argue. "What's a bigger deal than whatever Ixtha has going on?"

"I can't tell you," Sandy said calmly. "You know we believe in noninterference."

"Except when it's you guys doing it. Look, do I need to go and give all of those who hang out where you live names? I'm willing to do it."

"I'm sure you are. But no, that would . . . not be wise. The others who visited Earth are still dealing with what you giving them names did to their mindsets."

"Are they okay?" Hadn't necessarily wanted to make these beings go nuts or something.

"Yes, though they now struggle with our stated way of life."

"Oh, you mean some of them want to interfere," Tim said.

"No," Sandy replied. "I mean that some of them already have." He looked around, nodded his head, and suddenly, we weren't in the Eagle Nebula's neighborhood anymore.

Tim and I both stared. We were in a solar system, and we could see a sun. There were a lot of planets and other celestial bodies. But none of them looked remotely familiar. Not even the large, green planet we appeared to be orbiting.

"Where are we?" Tim asked.

"On the other side of our home," Sandy replied.

Looked around. "I don't see the nebula, or anything that looks familiar. Are we on the other side of the galaxy?"

Sandy chuckled and waved his hand in a circular motion and the ship turned, not like we'd been spinning before, but more like one of those "moving restaurants"—really slowly.

"Oh," Tim and I said in unison. The Eagle Nebula was, essentially, behind this solar system.

"Yes," Sandy said. "This solar system is the closest one to us."

"Problems in the neighborhood and who you gonna call? Problem Busters."

"In essence," Sandy said, with a smile, which I hoped

indicated good things. "We need someone to intervene here. Someone with no, I believe you would say, skin in the game."

"I would, but I have no idea how you picked that phrase up."

"I wandered Earth for quite a while. It was most interesting."

"While that's all great, why are we here?" Tim asked. "Is this where Mother was heading?"

"No, it is not. It is, however, someplace you need to go first."

"Why do we need to do that?" Wondered what we were going to tell the others. Perhaps it was time to panic after all.

"Because if you truly want to save the galaxy, you have to save all of it."

"Is now really the time to be inscrutable?" Tim asked. "No offense."

"None taken," Sandy said calmly. "However, you have someone on board who was not supposed to leave Earth."

"ACE. He's inside my daughter and none of us were supposed to be on this flight anyhow. You wanted him noninterfering. He didn't interfere, that's why we're all somehow stranded in space. Though, now we're stranded in a part of space we don't know. On top of everything else."

"Some on board know where this is," Sandy replied.

"We're on the back side of the Eagle Nebula's territory," Tim said. "Get with the space program, Kitty."

"Nice to see you keeping it light. I'm not exactly familiar with this section of the galaxy, call me an astronomy quitter. Besides, I'm still back on 'what happens to ACE and my daughter,' call me a worrywart and all that."

"Concessions will be made . . . if the situation in this solar system is . . . rectified."

"Why so?" Tim asked flatly.

"Because," Sandy sighed, "Grumpy and Dopey are fighting for control of this solar system, and if they destroy this star, it will destroy the nebula, and without the nebula, there will not be any more stars that can form."

"Per our scientists and astronomers, the nebula's not really here anymore, we're just seeing the memory of the light."

"Your scientists and astronomers are, as happens frequently with younger, inexperienced races, wrong." Sandy nodded his head and suddenly we weren't in the solar system anymore. We were inside the nebula. And it looked very real, very alive, and not remotely like a memory.

"It's beautiful," Tim said quietly.

It was. Pillars of the same kind of thick fog that wasn't fog—
what Sandy had been before he'd entered the ship—flowed like
steam, only not randomly but with what seemed like purpose.
All the colors of the rainbow and colors I couldn't identify as
well were within the fog. And light. Lots and lots of light. Moving light.

"It looks like the light is . . . boiling."

"It is. This is how stars are formed. By us and by the others
who reside in nebulas as we do. We are the creators."

"But not the only ones."

"No, not the only ones. We are the builders."

"Of life?" Tim asked.

"No, not of life. Of the galaxies, the systems. The rocks, to
all of you. Builder is not quite the right word, though."

"The architects?" Hey, I was trying to be supportive. Besides,
this was gorgeous.

"Yes, that is the correct word. As one solar system dies, we
create a new one, so that life will go on. We do not people the
planets—that is not our way. But we do create the suns and,
therefore, the systems. Otherwise, we are not to interfere."

"Go team." Really hoped some of the others were seeing this.
And not panicking. "Um, what are the others seeing?"

"The same as you. All will need to understand what they
need to do."

"What is it that we all need to do?" Tim asked.

"Stop the destruction of this solar system so that we can continue to create. The nebulas are connected to each other. Not as
a human could or would understand it. But we are interconnected. If one nebula dies, normally another would be ready to
take its place. But this is not the right time, or the right way, for
our nebula to die, and so, if we go prematurely and in this fashion, then the rest of the nebulas will all wither and no new suns
will ever be created in this galaxy again."

Tim and I both let that one sit on the air for a few long moments. "Um, that sounds bad." And familiar, in its own way. Per
Algar, all the black holes out there were connected in some way
to the Black Hole Universe. Wondered if the Nebula Network
was the same. Figured it probably was and wasn't at the same
time. Decided it didn't matter.

"It would be very bad, yes." Sandy also had a sarcasm knob,
though he was probably only at around five on the scale.

"What is it we need to do?" Tim asked.

Sandy shrugged and we were back in orbit around the very green planet. "You need to stop a mad scientist from creating the destruction of the galaxy."

And with that, he turned back into thick fog and dissipated.

CHAPTER 27

"JEFF'S RIGHT," Tim said. "It never ends."

"And it's also never easy. I hope you're not shocked."

"No. I'm trying hard to figure out how we find a mad scientist on a world we've never been to, let alone stop him or her from destroying the galaxy."

"That seems to be the order of the day, doesn't it? I mean, supposedly we're heading to Ixtha to also save the galaxy."

"We need a theme song. Something like 'da da, da daaaa, Galaxy Defenders!' or similar."

"You're starting to worry me. I mean, you're not wrong. Just worrying me. And now I want to hear music. Of some kind. Any kind, really."

Tim shrugged. "Turn on your phone. I'm not anti-tunes, you know."

"Think it'll bother the others?"

"More or less than us sharing the latest news will?"

"Good point." Pulled my phone out of my purse, opened up my music, and looked at my playlists. Sure enough, there was a Space Travel playlist that I had definitely not created. Hit play, turned the volume up, and dropped my phone back in my purse. As the sounds of "Space Boy" by Splender filled my ears, idly noted that I saw no Poofs on Board. Felt sad. "No Poofies?"

"Yeah, I haven't seen Fluffy Death since we got on board."

"You know . . . that's weird. I mean, the Poofs go with us everywhere. Why wouldn't they come with us for this?"

"No idea, Kitty. The Poofs are your bailiwick. Just like the rest of the animals."

The music changed to "Animal House" by Stephen Bishop. And my brain nudged again. "You know . . ."

"I know that look. That's a Megalomaniac Girl look."

"Yeah, it is, though it should probably be a Doctor Doolittle look. Remember how we said if one team could smuggle themselves on, why not others?"

"Yeah. Oh! Wow. You think the animals are stowed away somewhere?"

"I do." Heaved a sigh, then ensured my voice sounded firm but fair. "Poofs, Peregrines, and all other Animal Friends assemble!"

Results were immediate.

Sure enough, we had a tonnage of Poofs, a whole lot of Peregrines, and one ocellar and chocho in the forms of Ginger and Wilbur. Ocellars looked like a combination of caracals and foxes, only slightly larger, oranger, and more predatory than both. Chochos were basically pig-dogs, complete with bristly fur, curlicue tails, and a honking kind of bark. Both breeds were from Beta Eight. I'd met Ginger and Wilbur during Operation Civil War and they'd come home with me, along with enough other ocellars and chochos that we had plenty by now, both in the Embassy and Washington Zoos. But these two lived with me in the White House.

"I'm amazed you didn't bring the regular dogs and cats along, too." Said with only some sarcasm.

Bruno warbled at me. Apparently not all the Poofs and Peregrines were in attendance, either.

"Gotcha. The others had to stay home to ensure that my dad had animals to focus on so he wouldn't note that the ones closest to his daughter and her family are all suspiciously absent. Good plan. You do realize my dad isn't nearly as dense as he acts, right?"

Bruno warbled again, bobbed his head, and clawed at the carpet.

"Fine, yes, I'm sure they'll keep him occupied enough that he doesn't blow our subterfuge or whatever. Of course, to burst your planning bubble, my mom said she was going to tell him what was going on."

Bruno scratched and warbled again.

"Good, I'm *so* glad you approve. And yes, some need to be on guard regardless of who knows what so, good plan. I guess."

"I'm more curious as to why they were hidden," Tim said.

"Good point. Why didn't you guys let us know you were on board? Everyone's been stressed and could have used some animal snuggles."

Bruno heaved a bird sigh, gave me the "why me?" look in avian, and looked over at Harlie. Who bounced up and down, mewling.

"Seriously? That's ridiculous."

"What? What's ridiculous?" Tim asked. "I don't speak fur or feathers."

"The Poofs were jealous that we let the least weasels come on board in an unstealthy and somewhat honorary manner. Which is silly in the extreme. They're a present from the Ard Ri." And I knew damn well that all the animals were clear on who Algar was—he was the Poof's One True Owner, after all, and the Peregrines had definitely figured that all out. By now, I assumed all the animals knew. Since I was pretty much the only one they could talk to about it, it wasn't exactly a security risk for Algar.

"The weasels are cute, but they're not Poofs," Tim pointed out.

"True enough. And I'm sure once the Ard Ri meets all of you that he'll be super impressed by one and all and demand Poofs and such for himself." Unlikely. All the Poofs were probably considered Algar's anyway and if he didn't have a Peregrine by now it was because he didn't want one. But I had to say something so as not to give away the fact that the Poofs were pouting because their One True Owner had another set of pets.

"We're giving him a Poof?" Tim asked, sounding more than a little shocked.

"Who knows? That's kind of up to them." But a thought occurred. "You know . . . Mister Joel Oliver is on the ship. So, did Bellie manage to sit this one out or is she stowed away elsewhere?" Got hit with the Sea of Animal Innocence Looks. Snorted. "Where is she and how is she managing to stay quiet?"

Bruno cawed and clawed the carpet.

"You going to share?" Tim asked.

"Sure. She's hiding in the room the press is assigned to. Apparently, that's her version of being stealth."

"Worked well and, let's be honest—she's more stealthy than the hackers."

"Good point."

"So, I want to know why Ginger and Wilbur are here," Tim said. "The Poofs and Peregrines I get, Bellie coming with MJO isn't a surprise. But not these two."

"Well?"

Ginger yawned, purred, stretched, then started cleaning her fur. Wilbur honk-barked and wagged his curly tail in a circular motion.

"So? What's the reason?" Tim asked me.

Heaved a sigh. "They wanted to go on vacation with us, too."

Tim shook his head. "This is one hell of a vacation."

"Potentially, it's no worse than some." I'd been on some doozies during college. Any vacation Chuckie wasn't on with me, as I thought about it. Cheered up a bit. He was sure as heck with us for this one, so perhaps this would turn out well.

Tim's turn to snort. "True enough. We're stranded in the middle of nowhere and have to help some people we don't know out of trouble in order to get out of town. My family did their best to avoid vacations like this."

"Mine, too. However, it's what we've got and I, personally, feel a lot better with the animals around."

"I'll feel better about them, too, once we find out how many *more* people or creatures have stowed aboard."

"None," someone said, causing both of us to jump.

Turned as I landed to see Wruck there. "We've searched the ship. Barring other animals or people able to blend as Benjamin and the Peregrines do, this is everyone. I was coming to tell you that I'd found the parrot, but I see you found all the other animals as well."

Managed to refrain from saying that Benjamin and the Peregrines would be an awesome name for a band, but it took effort. "Bellie shared that the others were on board?"

"She did. Under duress," Wruck said to the animals, who seemed appeased or unsurprised, depending. Yeah, Bellie was a bigmouth. But she was, as I'd learned during Operation Fundraiser, a very loyal bigmouth, so I wasn't all that sad that she'd stowed away, too.

"Gotcha. Does Mother know? About all the animals being here, I mean."

"I assume so," Wruck said. "However, she may not care. Repairs are still being made."

"Ah, did the other guys do what we thought they would?" Tim asked.

Wruck stared at him for a moment. "Oh. No, I don't think so. Currently it doesn't seem necessary."

"Did everyone else look out the windows?" This was a bigger concern for me right now than whether or not Hacker International had chosen to reprogram Mother in some way. I didn't want people freaking out.

"Only those on the command deck. Your husband is clear that the superconsciousness has visited, and the rest of us could, therefore, figure out that we've been moved here to solve some local problem for them."

"Sounds about right. By the way, John, Sandy said that the Nebula System is both connected and how stars are formed. Is that true?"

He nodded. "As we've always understood it. They are older even than we Anciannas or the Z'porrah."

"This galaxy is just loaded with ancient, godlike beings, isn't it?" Tim asked.

"Probably more than we know about, yeah."

"Every galaxy has these in them," Wruck said. "The universe is vast."

My music changed to Aerosmith's "Get the Lead Out" which surely sounded like an Algar Hint. Wished I was rolling with my boys on my chest instead of my FLOTUS-wear, but had long ago realized I couldn't have everything.

"I'm just going to focus on our own little galaxy, then, and share that we have to go down to that green planet and save the day somehow. I also speak for everyone when I say that we're wide open to suggestions."

"I suggest we go back to the command deck and discuss options with the rest of the team," Wruck replied. "And don't worry—you'll prevail, Kitty. You always do."

"Yeah? Define 'prevail' and 'always,' because I don't think those words mean what you think they mean."

We rejoined those on the command deck and shared what was going on. After a lot of fretting, bickering, complaining, and generally us being us, along with everyone other than Tim insisting I turn my music off, we decided that we had no choice but to do what Sandy wanted. Particularly when Drax came on the intercom.

"The warp core is fixed," he shared. But he didn't sound happy.

Because we were all experienced, no one cheered. "But?" Jeff asked. "Because there's clearly a 'but' coming."

"*But* we need a supply that we don't have on board," Drax said, sounding beyond frustrated. "It should *be* on board, mind you, but the entire stock is gone."

"What is this marvelous substance, Gustav?" I asked.

"Chlorophyll."

CHAPTER 28

WE ALL LET THAT one sit on the air for a couple of seconds. Yeah, stunned silence was definitely this trip's theme.

"Why?" Reader asked finally, speaking for all of us. "What does plant photosynthesis have to do with the ship?"

"Chlorophyll allows the ship to extract power from any and all light sources," Drax replied. Heard Hacker International in the background, explaining this to whoever wanted to listen. Wasn't me, so I didn't.

"That sounds extremely useful," Chuckie said.

"It is," Drax confirmed. "Moreover, it's necessary. Right now, we could be gathering power from both the Eagle Nebula and the star for this system—it's why the outer part of the ship is made from metal from Vatusus, so that it can draw in light. But with no chlorophyll being infused regularly into the metal it cannot. And without it, our life support will be compromised sooner as opposed to later. Warp working means nothing if we can't also ensure that the crew can survive the journey."

"Word to the mutha." Now I wanted to hear Bel Biv DeVoe. I'd been a lot more relaxed in the lounge with Tim and Wruck. Decided that I was about one more stressful moment from just putting in my headphones and ignoring everyone else's complaints, Jeff's in particular.

Chuckie cleared his throat. "I'm going to place a bet."

"We're not in Vegas, but okay."

He shot me the "really?" look. "That planet is extremely green. I'm going to bet that it will have enough chlorophyll on it to restore what was lost, destroyed, or stolen. And, conveniently, we're already supposed to go down there and save the day."

"We'll rescue you and, in return, just give us some chlorophyll and we'll go away? Could work. Of course, we have no idea what's going on down there, who we're dealing with, or how we get said chlorophyll into our possession, but it's as good a plan as any."

"Do we have a shuttle that can go to the planet, or are we going to land?" Jeff asked.

"We have shuttles," Drax replied. "They hold up to twenty. Under the current circumstances, landing would be our last choice."

"Oh, I'm sure we won't need that big of an away team. Just make sure that no one's wearing a red shirt and we'll be good." This earned me a ton of dirty looks, which I ignored. "I know who I want down on the planet with me."

"Why do you think you're going?" Jeff asked, in the growly man voice he still persisted in believing made me behave and obey anyplace other than in bed.

"Because I'm the one who was given the quest by Sandy. And, let's be real—we were told we're dealing with a mad scientist. The two people for sure going, therefore, are me and Tim. I'll advise who else I want on the fun excursion, but it won't be you."

Jeff's eyes narrowed. "And you expect me to stay on the ship why?"

"You're the POTUS and the King Regent and we need you up here to make a really grand entrance if necessary or to fire laser cannons in all haste, depending."

"She's right, Jeff," Chuckie said. "If we're going down to the planet, then you need to stay up here in the ship, where it's reasonably safe. I, however, am going," he added, shooting a "try me" look my way.

"As if I was leaving our resident genius on board? Yes, you're in. So is Christopher. I like having the Flash around. I want the rest of Alpha Team, too, though not Paul, but definitely Richard."

"We need other fighters," Reader said. "Just in case we meet a lot of opposition early."

Well, Algar had told me to keep him with me. "Tito, Rahmi, and Rhee. Mahin and Abigail. That gives us fight, special talents, and a doctor along. I think that's good for now."

"I'm going with you," Jeff said calmly, but with a great deal of conviction. "I'm not allowing my wife, my family, or my friends to go down onto an alien planet without me. Period. Toss all the reasons why at me, it's not going to change anything, because I'm never going to look at our children and share that the reason they don't have a mother anymore is because I stayed behind while she went into battle without me."

Would have argued, because I really did want him to stay safe on the ship. However, since I knew he felt the same about me, and since I also found his dedication to being protective extremely sweet, chose not to have this fight. "Fine, Jeff. You're in. And we don't know that we'll be in battle."

"You don't know that we won't be, either," he pointed out.

"True. But that leaves us without the Grand Poohbah reveal if we need it."

"Use Paul or Drax," he said. "Either one can work. Or both. Though I think we're being highly optimistic in thinking that any of us acting like royalty will have any impact on the natives of the planet."

"It might," Tito said. He was looking intently at the screen at his station. "If, you know, we can find any. I see no signs of what we'd call human life down there. I don't see life that appears sentient in any way. I just see a ton of green."

"Well, let's get down there and find out. How do we tell if we can breathe on the planet?"

"Scanning planet now," Mother said. "Results shortly."

Chose not to ask how this wonder was achieved. "Just be ready to book it out of here, chlorophyll or no chlorophyll, if things go badly."

Mother confirmed that we could breathe the air safely, so, while Jerry, Joe, Randy, and Brian actually got to do the jobs they'd trained for, the rest of us on the away team trotted off to grab those members who hadn't been on the command deck and get ready.

Spent some time with the kids, presumably so we could listen to them whine about not getting to go along. Got whined at by Team Tough Guys, too, so allowed Wruck to join us. Was grateful that the shuttles held twenty, since we were, by now, at sixteen. Airborne whined at us over the intercom, but were overruled based on all of them actually being able to pilot the ship.

"I suppose it's a good thing that everyone wants to visit, right?" I asked Jeff as we all got into the body armor that was standard on all Drax Industrial ships.

The first time I'd put on Drax Body Armor, Patent Pending, I'd been impressed. Not as impressed as I'd been by what the Alfred in Bizarro World had created, but still, impressed. But now? Now I was officially enthralled.

For the *Distant Voyager*, Drax had pulled out all the body armor stops. Now, it not only conformed to your entire body, but allowed you to look as if you were just wearing your normal street clothes because it went on over them and conformed to them as well. Though the armor didn't cover my purse—that I had to carry over my neck and let it risk itself without protection. So Alfred on Bizarro World was still ahead in the game.

But it was hard to complain because Drax was definitely winning in this universe. Had no idea how he'd done it—despite him having told me countless times—because my ears just didn't want the rest of me to have to know and, frankly, I didn't really care how he'd done it, just that he had.

"I don't know if I'd call it good, baby," Jeff said. "But it really seems as though all our civilians on board think we're on some sort of vacation."

"Like the Grand Tour, only of space, not of Europe."

"Yes," Chuckie said. "Very much like that. I'm with Jeff—I don't think most of the civilians see being out here as the very dangerous thing it is."

"We'll be ready for the danger," Claudia said.

Mahin nodded. "No one is going to ruin the trip for everyone."

"And we know it's not a vacay," Abigail added. "But I don't see any reason to panic the others—right now, I feel pretty great." Since an aspect of Abigail's exceptional A-C talents was that she was sort of a reverse empath—meaning if someone near her was angry, she got angry, and so on—her feeling good was a very positive sign.

Jeff grunted. "I agree that the level of excitement is high. But that's why they all want to visit this planet with us."

"We'll worry about it once we see what's down there," Christopher said reassuringly. "Amy, Denise, and Doreen are riding herd on all the kids, and Kevin's got the rest of the security personnel assigned throughout the ship where our people are. It'll be fine."

"Do we take weapons?" Lorraine asked, as Rahmi and Rhee pulled out their battle staffs. They were the daughters of Queen Renata, who was both our close ally and the ruler of Beta Twelve. They were also Amazons. And somehow, they always had their battle staffs with them, even if no one else could see them. Had often wondered if it was because the Amazons were shape-shifters, but had never found the right time to ask, and now was certainly not it.

"Hells to the yeah," Reader replied. "I don't want us down there unarmed. It sounds great to say that you come in peace, but it helps to be loaded for bear, just in case."

"What James said, tenfold." I liked Drax's laser guns. They were big and effective, but light to carry.

"I agree, as well." Mister Joel Oliver was in da house, and he had all his cameras on.

"What are you doing here?" Jeff asked.

"And where's Bellie? And before you try to say she's back home, I already know that she's on board."

Oliver shrugged. "I asked Bellie to remain in our quarters, which she agreed to do because I'm going down to the planet with you. This is the first time any of us will land on this world. From what Prince Gustav has said and the star charts show, this area of the galaxy isn't well traveled. For all we know, we're about to be the first contact for whatever sentient race or races are down there. As such, a trained and seasoned journalist will be an excellent addition to the landing party. Also, it's me or Miss Kristie, take your pick."

"You," said in unison by most of those in the room.

"Having a cyborg along wouldn't be a bad thing," I pointed out. Not that I wanted the Kristie-Bot over Oliver, but still, she could take far more of a beating than he could. "Or an android," I added for loyalty's sake. The Kristie-Bot had proven her worth, but I still preferred Butler and Maurer.

"Which is why Colonel Butler is also joining us," Oliver shared. "He doesn't feel that he needs body armor or weapons. He's familiarizing himself with the shuttle's systems while waiting for the rest of us."

"Who isn't going with us might be the better question, but fine."

"Think of it as if it's Beta Eight," Serene said, as she slung her chosen laser onto her back. "Maybe we'll get along with most of the inhabitants and it'll be beautiful and wonderful."

"I echo my half-sister's optimism," White said, eyes twinkling. "The portion of the White Family that's going along is ready for the excursion, come what may."

"Then let's do it," Tim said. "Before anyone else demands to join us."

Shuttles were able to launch from a variety of areas around the ship. From the command deck, we could go through doorways to the right or left of the main command area. Per Wruck,

Butler had chosen a shuttle on the left side, for no reason other than he'd been closer to that side when the decision to go had been made.

"Did you guys check the shuttles for stowaways?" I asked Wruck, as we entered the shuttle bay.

"No," a new voice said. "They didn't."

CHAPTER 29

WE ALL JUMPED AND stared at the Dazzler standing there, looking amused. "You all really like to make things interesting."

"Camilla, what the hell?" was about all I could come up with as a reply.

She laughed. "Surprise."

Camilla was an A-C rarity—a natural Liar. They were few and far between, and when found were usually whisked off to Liar's School or whatever they called it, to get trained into the Lying Way. Meaning they were excellent at subterfuge, infiltration, and similar. And there were none better than Camilla.

The Royal Family made the most use of their Liars, and Alfred had assigned Camilla to us when I became pregnant with Jamie. She'd saved us more than once, though we'd gotten to save her, too. While having yet another stowaway on board was in some ways annoying, that it was Camilla was pretty great. It was hard to say that I liked her—she didn't go out of her way to be likable or hang out with others—but I respected the hell out of her, and her having our backs was a very good thing.

Rhee looked both surprised and pleased. "Wife of my heart, you said you were investigating something."

"I was. It led me into the ship. Then the ship started acting up and I decided that the best place I could be was in a shuttle, just in case."

"How did you avoid being seen by Mother? Um, the AI that runs the ship. That's her name."

"That you gave her, I'm sure. I 'worked' for Drax, remember? I know how to circumvent most of his safeguards. However, someone else knows, too."

"Stephanie?" Jeff asked.

She nodded. "I'm not sure who planted the bomb that knocked out the warp core or who took the chlorophyll, but she has to be on the suspects list. And I know what was going on because the shuttles can access the intercom system and I did. So I don't need a recap." She grinned at me.

"Wow, I feel so useless all of a sudden."

Butler put his head out of the shuttle. "Can we go? I think the sooner we're down there, the sooner we find out if this planet can help us or destroy us."

"Well, with *that* cheery outlook, how can things go any way but right?" We started loading into the shuttle—which was more like a space-aged bus than anything, with a really interesting moon roof—when another thought occurred. "Christopher? Can you please do a fast check of all the shuttles on the ship? Just in case?"

"Sure, Kitty." He was gone in a flash, but not back in one.

"I'm staying on the ship," Camilla said, as Jeff and I waited for Christopher to return.

"Not that I'm complaining, but that makes you literally the only person who doesn't want to go with us. Why are you happy to hang out instead of demanding your seat on the shuttle?"

"I want to be sure that things here remain . . . safe."

"I'm all for that," Jeff said. "Especially because the children are both on board and wanting to go to the planet."

"Yeah, I wouldn't put it past Lizzie to try to sneak onto a shuttle and come down." And if she did it, then Wasim and the Valentino boys, at the very least, would go with her. Frankly, all the kids would go. Camilla hanging around seemed like a really good plan.

"Lizzie's not as reckless as you think she is," Camilla said, as Christopher finally returned. "But I'll keep an eye on all of them."

She wandered off as the three of us went inside and got seated. "Found no one else, but I think that someone other than Camilla was hiding on the ship. I found traces that indicated someone was living in a couple of the shuttles."

"That should have been impossible," Tim said. "People were on this ship constantly while it was being built and we had the highest levels of security, including top Field teams."

Christopher shrugged. "I told Buchanan about it, as well as the fact that Camilla's on board. They'll do a full investigation of the ship, again, while we're down here." He strapped in and we took off.

Butler was acting as pilot with Reader as copilot. "I threw James a bone," Tim whispered to me. "Technically, I should be the one copiloting, but I figured why not make his day?"

"I think you're enjoying this entire mission a little too much."

He grinned. "It's nice to not be the Junior Commander for a change."

"You get used to it," Christopher said, with a wink for Jeff.

Who rolled his eyes. "Everyone's a whiner today."

Looked at the ship as we headed for the planet. It still looked beautiful but just a little less shiny than it had when we were on Earth. Wasn't sure if that was because we were farther from this sun than we'd been to our own or if it was the lack of chlorophyll. "I hope we can get what we need."

"We will," Chuckie said firmly. "Drax had the necessary equipment on board, and Serene and I have it with us now."

Decided to stop worrying about everyone on the ship and focus on the mission, such as it was. So, I looked at the planet.

I wasn't really an astronomy expert, but it looked larger than Earth to me. Figured I'd ask someone else if it was relevant. Hyperspeed meant distances weren't nearly as big a deal as they could be.

There were clouds scattered around the world, just like on Earth. It was very pretty—white clouds against the green background. And green was really this planet's operative word. I would have expected to see some blue, since I had to assume a planet this green had a lot of foliage and, therefore, a lot of water. But I didn't glimpse any.

Well, that wasn't quite true. There were all shades of green, though a bright grassy green was predominant. However, there were some blue-greens in there, though the blues were muted.

The closer we got, the more the planet looked like it was mostly made of grass.

"I see no roads or anything like them," Reader said. "There could be some trails, but if so, they're not well traveled."

"Should we orbit?" Chuckie asked. "To see if there's a more industrialized section?"

"We can," Butler said.

So we did. There were rolling hills and grass. Plains covered with grass. What sure looked like oceans of grass. Trees that resembled bamboo and grass. And all in shades of green. "Even the water here is green," Mahin said. "If there is no dust or dirt, I'm not going to be much use to the team."

"Maybe the dirt is green," Claudia suggested. "It's possible."

"We shouldn't have any trouble getting what we need," Lorraine said. "So there's that."

"Only we're supposed to stop two superconsciousnesses who are interfering and prevent a mad scientist from destroying this solar system."

"Are you sure this is the right planet?" White asked. "It does seem rather . . . calm, and not a hotbed of nefarious activity."

"And unpeopled," Reader added. "Sensors aren't picking up anything humanoid, anywhere."

"And I see nothing that we could construe as civilized," Chuckie said. "Let alone industrialized."

"Barring Sandy playing a practical joke on us—which seems hella unlikely—this was the planet in question."

Tim nodded. "Maybe everything's underground."

While Butler and Reader chose where we were going to land, the rest of us discussed the likelihood of an underground world. We didn't have a lot of time to do so, however.

"Setting down on what should be solid land," Reader said. "Prepare for impact, just in case."

Androids were great at flying space shuttles, because we landed nice and smoothly, almost like a helicopter, only without the noise and the whipping blades. Shuttle was definitely the way to go.

"Check sensors to be sure we can breathe before we open the hatch," Tito said. "Just in case."

"Sensors show an Earthlike atmosphere," Reader said. "Temperatures are moderate for Earth, as well. We should be good."

The hatch opened and Christopher, who was nearest to it, stepped out slowly. Nothing happened. So he walked all the way down the ramp. No issues.

The rest of us followed suit. "I feel like we totally overdressed for this occasion for some reason," I said as I looked around. Grass as far as the eye could see. Sure, the grass was up to my knees, but still, it was grass.

Saw a flash of orange out of the side of my eye and looked over at the shuttle. "Who's there? And by who, I mean I expect Ginger and, most likely, Bruno, to show themselves right now."

Sure enough, Bruno dechameleoned to show him sitting on Ginger's back. Neither one of them looked even remotely guilty.

"Why are you two here?"

Ginger yawned, then yowled softly. I managed not to jump up onto Jeff's shoulders, but it really took an exertion of self-control. "Gotcha. Good Ginger, good Bruno."

"What did they say?" Jeff asked, in the tone of voice of a man who still couldn't quite believe that his wife talked to animals all the time.

"Ginger mentions that certain things tend to like to hide in tall grass. Slithery things." I was terrified of snakes. It didn't matter that I'd faced gigantic and human versions of them—if it slithered and had no legs, it could send me running off screaming or make me freeze in terror.

Ocellars, as it had turned out, had been trained to fight those gigantic snakes on Beta Eight. And Ginger had gone to town on Earth snakes during Operation Epidemic, too. So her being here suddenly sounded like the greatest plan in the world.

Jeff took and squeezed my hand gently. "You'll be fine. I won't let anything hurt you, you know that, baby."

"The body armor will protect you, too, Kitty," Chuckie said reassuringly. "It's why you're not feeling the grass rubbing against your skin. You can relax, at least a little—no snake is going to bite through this armor."

"Says you. But fine. I'm still glad I have the Great Snake Killer with us, okay? And Bruno, too, because one should never count a Peregrine out." Chose not to look into my purse to see if I had Poofs on Board or not. At least, not right now. "But, since we don't know who or what is or isn't sentient here, don't attack anything unless you have to."

Got consent from both animals that they'd control their bloodthirsty natures, despite their deep desires to kill anything that moved. Using those exact words. Even my pets had sarcasm knobs. Decided not to share this with the others because I wanted to hog the animal sarcasm all for myself.

We wandered around a little bit, no one getting too far from the others, but we had enough people that we could radiate out from the shuttle and still see and hear at least a couple people on either side. No one saw anything other than grass. No one stepped on anything other than grass.

"See or smell or sense anything?" I asked Bruno and Ginger, who were next to me. Received ocellar and Peregrine negatories.

"Everyone back," Jeff called.

"Where are the insects?" Serene asked as we regrouped.

"There should be some, and there aren't any. Beta Eight had a full planetary infrastructure in terms of life. This planet is clearly alive—you don't have this much grass on a dead rock—but there's no infrastructure."

"I'm going to vote for underground again," Tim said. "And not just because I suggested it before. Because we had people living underground on Beta Eight."

"Yeah, but Fancy's Ferrets were really the only ones doing so. But I vote for underground anyway, because I'm with Serene—it's way too silent."

"Ah, I wonder . . ." White said. "Because I see something other than grass, finally."

"Is it a snake?"

"No, Missus Martini, you can relax. It's very far from a snake."

He pointed and we all looked at what he'd seen creeping out of the tall grass. Yep, definitely not a snake.

"Well," Reader said, "that's not exactly what I was expecting."

CHAPTER 30

A RATHER ADORABLE BROWN and white flop-eared rabbit wiggled its cute pink nose at us.

"I'm all kinds of good with the fact that the first creature we've encountered here is, as Lizzie would say, totes adorbs. So very totally good with it."

"Why didn't we hear it arrive?" Serene asked.

"Maybe because it has soft pads on its paws?" Claudia suggested, in a tone of voice that indicated she was as enamored of the bunny as I was.

"Kitty, maybe we need to get some rabbits for the Zoo," Lorraine added, echoing the Rabbit Love Tonal Inflection.

"I wish I had a carrot," Mahin said regretfully.

"Or some food pellets," Abigail agreed.

"We don't have rabbits on Beta Twelve," Rahmi said with even more regret than Mahin had managed for the lack of carrots.

"We should get some for our mother," Rhee declared. "Clearly our home planet is suffering from the lack of rabbits."

"Uh, why are all of you, other than Serene, acting like you're about to offer to marry that rabbit?" Jeff asked.

"Because it's so adorable!" we all chorused together.

The unison jerked me out of whatever kind of trance I'd been in. Looked at Serene, and noted that it was hard to drag my gaze away from the bunny. "You're immune?"

She nodded. "I guess so. I mean, it's cute and I want to pet it, but I'm not making plans to gather a hutch full of rabbits and take them home."

Had to think before the rabbit's charisma—and that's sure what it felt like—dragged my attention back to its fluffy cuteness. "Dudes, are any of you affected by the bunny?"

Got a resounding chorus of nos, with similar caveats to those Serene had given. Considered why.

"It's a troubadour rabbit. Or something like that. It's exerting charisma or whatever at us and for whatever reason, it's focused on the females. Serene's immune because she's a stealth troubadour and therefore is probably stronger with the skill than almost anyone else."

The other gals were still gazing adoringly at the rabbit. It was really hard for me not to look right back at it. Noted that while the men and Serene didn't seem as enthralled by the bunny, they were all staring at it. Oliver started taking pictures of it.

"John, are you affected?"

There was no answer. Tried to look around for what could have happened to Butler, but my gaze was dragged back to the most adorable thing in the galaxy.

"Ginger, Bruno," I managed through gritted teeth, "look around. I don't think we're going to be alone."

Ginger growled low and Bruno made a soft hissing sound. We were definitely not alone.

"Gang, we're surrounded by bunnies."

"Good!" Claudia said. The rest of the gals other than Serene echoed her.

"I think it's starting to get to me," Serene said. "I can't look away." The men all agreed that they couldn't look away, either.

Ginger growled again. The rabbits were creeping closer and there were a whole lot of them.

Had no idea what had happened to Butler or what was going to happen to us, but knew I had to do something. Took a deep breath, let it out slowly, and concentrated, searching for the rabbits' minds.

Felt something. I'd never really communed with bunnies before, so I wasn't sure if it was them or not. But didn't figure that we had a lot of time, so I focused all my mental energy on shouting that we were coming in peace and that they needed to stop attacking us.

The Most Adorable Bunny In Existence made eye contact with me. He wanted me to worship him. In fact, he felt that my worship was all it would take for him to be mine forever and for us to live in happy harmony for the rest of our days. Felt my knees wanting to hit the ground.

One of the best things about my Dr. Doolittle talent was that I didn't really have a lot of control over it. The animals had far more control than I did. Meaning that if they didn't want me to understand them, I didn't understand. But it also meant that I wasn't really able to be all that selective in who I thought at.

So Ginger and Bruno heard this mental exchange. And Ginger and Bruno, being animals themselves and predators to boot, appeared to be immune to the rabbit's charms. Possibly more importantly, they were among my favorites and jealous to keep their spots in the Animal Hierarchy of my mind. Bottom line—they did not approve of these rabbit shenanigans.

Bruno lifted up, impressive wingspan spread to full, shrieking a Peregrine war cry. He flew at the Most Adorable Bunny In Existence, then at the other rabbits surrounding us. They all stopped advancing.

Meanwhile, Ginger did something very catlike. She scratched me.

"Yow!" Jumped and looked around. "How did you scratch me through the body armor?"

Ginger sniffed, studied her claws in that way cats will, then sauntered off to scratch everyone else. Bruno did one more threatening sweep, then he landed on my shoulder, where he could keep an eye on all the enemy rabbits.

"Beta Eight claws," Serene said as she held her leg. "I think ocellars might have a claw enhancement that we haven't noted before now."

"They were bred to kill Snakipedes," Reader pointed out, also holding his leg.

"Bullets can't get through this stuff," Tim said as he limped closer to Reader. "Or lasers. But ocellar claws, it's no big deal? We need to talk to Drax about his design skills."

"We *need* to thank Ginger," Jeff said, as she finished scratching everyone and breaking the Bunny Spell. "For saving us from whatever the hell we were under and also for not once clawing anything in the White House, the Embassy, or the Zoo. This is the best cat in the galaxy, right here."

Ginger purred loudly and rubbed up against Jeff's legs. He stroked her head, which earned him more purrs and rubbing. Then she turned to the Most Adorable Bunny in Existence and snarled a very mean, nasty, and above all, loud snarl. Jeff, like all the rest of us, was *hers*, thank you very much, and no damned rabbit with supercharisma was going to change that.

The rabbit backed up a hop. Interesting.

Jeff looked at the Most Adorable Bunny In Existence. "Time

to tell us what the hell you were doing, or we aren't going to be coming in peace any longer."

"Look, they're rabbits," Christopher said. "What are they going to do to us? Bite our ankles?"

"Rabbits have sharp, nasty teeth," I pointed out. "And, as *Monty Python and the Holy Grail* has taught us, they can be killers."

"Killers of lettuces, maybe," Christopher said.

Which apparently did not sit well with the bunnies nearest to him. Possibly because Christopher wasn't all that near to either Ginger or Bruno. One of them lunged at him and sank its teeth into his leg.

"Ack! Get it off me! Get it off me!" Christopher flailed around, though it was clear that while Ginger's claws had cut through the body armor, the rabbit's had not. However, its teeth were sunk in well enough that Christopher wasn't shaking it off.

"Calm down, son," White said. "It's just a rabbit, remember?"

"Hilarious, Dad. Get it off me!" He was still trying to kick the rabbit off. This seemed to enrage the rest of the bunnies nearby, and more of them leaped onto him. Bruno and Ginger allowed this, which I found interesting. Presumed it meant they were talking to the rabbits on a channel I couldn't mentally access. Or else they didn't like Christopher as much as they did the rest of us. Possibly both, but I chose to be charitable and assume it was that they were chatting with the bunnies in some way.

Christopher spun around to try to dislodge them, but it didn't work. He spun faster, which didn't work all that well. One rabbit flew off and landed right in my arms, but only one. The rest of them seemed to have death grips on his legs. Apparently my pit bull Duchess had nothing on these rabbits. Kind of wished she was on this journey with us—we could have used her help.

The cottontail in my arms looked up at me suspiciously. "Not going to hurt you if you're not going to hurt me. You try to hurt me, however, and all bets are off, and I'm sure Bruno and Ginger already told you that."

The rabbit wiggled its ears, blinked its eyes, and wrinkled its nose. Realized with some relief that I finally understood Bunny Talk. About time.

Knew what to do. "Christopher—apologize."

"What the hell?" He slowed down. "Why?"

"Because you were belittling and they didn't like it. Just stop trying to toss them off you and say you're sorry. Like you would to any other security team that you'd angered for the wrong reasons."

"It's just like on Beta Eight," Chuckie said. "They may not look like they're sentient, but they clearly are. So treat them as such."

"Fine. Look, I'm sorry about the lettuce joke. Please let go of me."

The rabbits didn't release. Got the distinct impression they weren't sure yet if they were going to attack all of us or not, Ginger and Bruno or no Ginger and Bruno. Also decided that mind control stuff was something I wanted to avoid any of us experiencing again. And last but not least, Butler was missing.

Time to stop being nice and call in the cavalry.

"Poofs Assemble!"

CHAPTER 31

A BLANKET OF FURRY CUTENESS appeared on the ground where we were standing. The Poofs looked at the bunnies. Could tell that the Most Adorable Bunny In Existence was trying to control them.

Harlie, the Head Poof, was having none of it and neither was Toby, Christopher's Poof. They both went large and in charge, meaning they were now taller than Jeff and had full mouths of razor-sharp teeth. Then they roared.

To the bunnies' credit, none of them panicked. However, all the rabbits holding onto Christopher let go and hopped over to the Most Adorable Bunny In Existence. It was clear they'd gone to protect him.

Toby went back to small and jumped onto Christopher's shoulder. "Thanks, buddy," he said, petting his Poof. "I appreciate the save." Toby purred, snuggled into Christopher's neck, and stayed on his shoulder, instead of going into his pocket as was normal for most of the Poofs, especially those who belonged to the guys.

Harlie stayed large and in charge and right in front of the Most Adorable Bunny In Existence. Went over to the Poof and patted it. "What a good Poof you are, Harlie." This earned me very loud purrs. Looked back at SuperBun. "We came here to ask for help and see if we could help you guys in return. Instead, you tried to mind-control us, then attacked us, and you took one of our team members somehow. I want him back, unharmed, or everyone in my ship's going to be rolling with a lot of extra luck."

SuperBun cocked its head at me. He didn't get the joke, though he was clear that I was making one.

"Oh. On our planet, which we call Earth, rabbits such as yourselves are plentiful, at least rabbits that look like you guys. Carrying a rabbit's foot is considered good luck. That foot is never attached to the rabbit. Got it, Bugs?"

SuperBun was appalled. And about to tell his warriors to attack. The bunny in my arms was ready to claw me to get away.

Heaved a sigh and petted the cottontail. "Dudes, we are not here to make rabbit fricassee, and yes, on Earth many people eat rabbits. You guys are delicious. You're also adorable and many keep your kind as pets. On the other hand, we," indicated the others with me, "aren't here to try to turn any of you into food, clothing, animal companions, or lucky charms. You're a sentient race and therefore off limits for things like that. At least as far as we and the rest of the planets we're aligned with feel."

Heard Jeff mutter, "Only my girl," and then start sharing, very quietly, what SuperBun had been and was saying. Well, he did have that Surcenthumain boost and it was a good time to be using his mindreading skills.

So, Jeff got to share that SuperBun wasn't so sure he trusted me.

"That's cool. I don't trust you, either." Spent this time soothing the cottontail by petting it. It stopped freaking and relaxed against me. "Since you wanted me to worship you and all that. I tend to really dislike people who try to make me worship them, call it a personal failing."

SuperBun apologized for that. It was their standard operating procedure when visitors from other planets arrived.

"You get a lot of them?"

SuperBun shared that they did not see many visitors from other planets, though they did get some, which made them extra cautious.

"Gotcha. We didn't mean to barge in. We need help, and we were told that you guys needed help, too. We were hoping to help you and that then you'd be willing to help us."

SuperBun was mildly intrigued and wanted to know what it was we wanted.

"Chlorophyll."

He wanted an explanation. Couldn't blame him.

"Our spaceship needs it to help keep us fueled up and all that jazz. I'm honestly not sure how it works, just that it does and that someone stole all of our chlorophyll stores so we're kind of up the creek without a paddle, if that metaphor means anything to you."

SuperBun nodded. The metaphor didn't, but he got the general gist. They had plenty of chlorophyll, but it took time to refine, so to speak.

"We have a super-harvester thingy. So that should speed things up. If you're amenable to our doing so."

SuperBun might be willing. But he was interested in the fact that I'd said that his planet needed help. Because, as far as he knew, they were A-okay.

This was a tough one. I could say that I knew the system had two superconsciousnesses fighting for control, or that this planet had a mad scientist. However, the reality was that SuperBun could *be* either Grumpy, Dopey, or the mad scientist.

Chose to stall. "I'd like to get our missing team member back first. Once I know he's okay that would sort of prove to me that you're not enemies to us and also that you're probably not harboring whoever or whatever the trouble is."

SuperBun didn't find this to make sense. He was clear that returning our robot to us would show that we and they weren't enemies, but he didn't understand how returning said robot to us would indicate anything about them being part of whatever we thought was or wasn't alright.

"He's an android, at least as we call them on our planet. And, frankly, we want him back before we have any further discussions. I have no idea how your people took him in the first place, but I want to be sure he's fine, unharmed, unaltered, and back with me. Or I tell the Poofs to all go large and in charge and they show you that they've got the market on cute and cuddly as well as big and terrifying. Up to you."

SuperBun noted that I tended to threaten a lot.

"Yep. That's me, Miz Diplomacy. I can ask one of my team who's a lot better with the diplomatic charm to talk to you. He, however, is going to ask the same thing that I am, which is to return our android to us. Isn't that right, Mister White?"

White joined me. "It is, Missus Martini. Though I have no clear idea of what our friend's side of the conversation has been, since we're all dependent upon Jeffrey's translations, since no one but you can mind-meld with animals."

SuperBun cocked his head. He was surprised. All our animals were telepathic, and he could tell that many with us had telepathic powers. So why was I the only one who could talk to him and the other animals?

"It's my gift, my talent. Presumably, at any rate. Beyond that, no clue." Before SuperBun could comment there was a loud hissing sound. "Oh my God, are there snakes here?" Clutched the cottontail to me and got ready to jump onto White's shoulders, tell Ginger to attack, and signal the Poofs to go into whatever size might work to back her up.

SuperBun reassured. No snakes. They'd killed all the snakes long ago. In fact, his rabbit army had killed all other predators when he was a young bunny. He eyed Ginger, Bruno, and Harlie in an obvious manner. They didn't seem fazed.

Did what I did whenever I didn't want Jeff to pick up that I thought some other man was hot—thought about flowers. Hoped this meant that I'd managed to keep the thought that SuperBun's odds of being the mad scientist we were supposed to stop were definitely getting higher out of the forefront of my mind. Had no idea how my animal telepathy worked, but really didn't want this thought getting out there.

"Um, then what *is* that sound?"

SuperBun didn't need to answer. We found out fast what the sound was.

"Sprinklers?" Christopher asked, as water—or what I sincerely hoped was water—sprayed over us. "Seriously?"

SuperBun shot a look at Christopher that was far more snide than I'd thought a rabbit could manage. He wondered just how Christopher thought a planet stayed this lush without regular watering.

"He can be tough to get to like at first, but he's really a great guy when you get to know him."

SuperBun had no desire to "get to know" Christopher, but he allowed that perhaps Christopher would grow on them. In a long while. Heard a variety of quiet snickers from the team as Jeff translated this, and some quiet muttering from Christopher.

The cottontail shared that it liked me better than Christopher, too. "Aw, that's nice, Peter Rabbit."

The cottontail contemplated the name. He decided that he liked it. And me.

The "sprinklers" came into view, interrupting my communing with Peter. Had to admit—while I hadn't been expecting this, it made a hell of a lot of sense.

What looked like an entire herd of extremely pygmy elephants were walking through the grass, spraying water out of their trunks, said trunks waving side-to-side in a very soothing, very rhythmic manner. These elephants were as synchronized as the Rockettes or any other top dance group you'd want to name.

"I didn't see this from the ship," Tito said softly. "And they're above the grass so I should have."

"Where is the water coming from?" White asked in kind.

"Real elephants have to refill," Mahin added.

Squinted at the elephants. "Are those actually living creatures or are they robots?"

SuperBun shared that they were improved living creatures. He also went on to reassure that our android had been taken to avoid him getting soaked by the watering. We were all clearly organic, so the water shouldn't hurt us, and our ship was enclosed. They didn't care if it hurt our weapons.

The elephants drenched us and moved on. They might have only come up to my knees, but they definitely had range. None of my animals liked this, Ginger in particular, but they merely moved nearer to the rabbits while they shook themselves off. Peter jumped out of my arms, shook himself off with the others, then came back and jumped back into my arms.

"Now," I asked as the rest of us followed suit and shook water off as best we could, "how did you know that John is an android but the rest of us are not?"

SuperBun rolled his eyes, sat up on his haunches, and pounded his right hind leg on the ground, just like Thumper. Actively chose not to make this comparison, in part because I had a feeling it would take far too long to explain Disney movies and why they were awesome and I also was pretty sure that SuperBun wouldn't be flattered by the comparison.

Was also pretty sure that SuperBun was the mad scientist or working closely with him or her, but focused on the elephants to avoid this thought surfacing.

What SuperBun had been thumping for appeared—a section of the ground rolled open. Literally, the grass rolled over itself, like really healthy sod, and, as it did so, a metal platform raised up. At least, it looked like metal. There was no one on it, regardless of what it was made of. SuperBun looked at me expectantly.

"Um, what are you suggesting?"

He heaved a dramatic sigh, then hopped onto the platform and looked at me again. The expectation seemed pretty clear.

"Um . . . do you happen to know anyone named Grumpy or Dopey? Asking for a friend."

SuperBun did not. He wanted to know what we felt was going on with his planet. And he wanted to know why I was wasting time and stalling.

Decided we were at a stalemate. "I don't think all of us will fit onto the platform." It was only about the size of an elevator, only without the niceties that elevators had, like doors and walls and phones for emergency calls. Didn't feel like all of us bunching up and doing a massive group hug, just to go wherever the potentially very rascally rabbit wanted us to go. "Can I choose who comes with me and who stays with our ship?"

SuperBun felt this was acceptable. He requested that the person taking pictures come with us, which I found surprising. Chose not to argue.

"MJO, you're up. Jeff, Richard, and Christopher, you guys come with me, too. Everyone else, stay here topside on the Planet of Doctor Moreau of Westworld." Harlie went small and jumped into my purse. Chose not to complain about this at all. Ginger and Bruno went onto the platform next to SuperBun. Chose not to argue about this, either.

Peter looked up at me, then jumped into my purse, snuggling in next to Harlie, who did not object. Patted both of them. Peter made my purse heavier, but not all that much. Was pretty sure that Algar had not only made my purse a portal but had also made it lighter in some way, so that I could carry a ton and not feel it. He was a good King of the Elves in that way.

All the A-Cs looked confused. The humans, however, seemed to get it. "I think I should come along, too," Chuckie said.

"Works for me, Batman. I think we can just fit you onto the platform with Kolchak, Superman, the Flash, and Professor X."

"And Wonder Woman," Chuckie said with a grin, as he sauntered over to join the other guys.

Serene hugged me. Felt her slip something into my purse. "Stay safe."

"We'll do our best." Wondered if it was a tracker, a bug, or a bomb that she'd planted on me. Really hoped it was all three and that she'd given me more than one of each. Also hoped that Peter wouldn't try to eat it, whatever it was.

Peter shared that he wasn't an idiot and that he was along to help, not harm. Chose to believe him, in no small part because he was also pretty darned adorable and his fur was hella soft. I wasn't pro taking sentient creatures from their home worlds, but, hey, if Peter *wanted* to go, that would be a different thing. We didn't have bunnies in the menagerie yet.

Reader and Tim looked like they wanted to add in as well. Made eye contact with both of them. "Be sure that the shuttle wasn't affected by getting watered. And make sure that the New Wonder Twins are ready to go, too."

Reader nodded. "Got it, girlfriend."

Tim managed a grin. "I guess I get to copilot after all."

"Hang tough and remember—always go with the crazy." With that I went and got onto the platform with the others.

CHAPTER 32

ONCE I WAS ON THE PLATFORM, SuperBun thumped his rear foot again and we lowered. It was a smooth ride, which was good, because space was tight on the platform and, as we went down, the sod that had rolled back to allow the platform to rise up rolled over us.

So we were in the dark for about the first fifty feet, surrounded by packed dirt. Chose not to ask why they didn't have metal walls or lighting—wasn't my planet, after all. Instead, focused on not feeling claustrophobic, because this was a lot like being buried alive while standing up.

Jeff took my hand and gave it a gentle squeeze, while Bruno and Ginger snuggled against my legs. Reached down and gave each of them a pet. Peter shared that this was scary but would be over soon. Reached into my purse and petted him and Harlie. Well, petted all the fur I felt in there. Hoped we had more Poofs on Board than just Harlie, but couldn't tell in the dark.

But then, to my relief and despite my expectations, instead of us continuing through earth, we lowered into a gigantic cavern. Could see a whole lot of platforms going up and down on thick, round pipes or tubes or whatever they called them here. Everyone peered over the sides of the platform, then took a step closer to the middle as we all became aware that we didn't want to fall off—it was a long way down.

Bruno and Ginger also looked. He squawked angrily, she hissed, and they both shoved into the middle between everyone's legs. Peter shared that he never looked over the side and apologized for not warning me, Ginger, and Bruno about it. Peter said that he hated being down here, and I couldn't blame him—this wasn't a place that seemed welcoming to animals.

The resemblance to movie versions of bad guy hidden factory bunkers was amazing. There were vats and bins and areas where what certainly looked like bombs or rocket ships and other things I couldn't identify were being created. There were catwalks, ramps, moving vehicles manned by what really looked like squirrels, flashes of fire and sparks that indicated welding or other metalwork, spotlights on various areas, all manner of rigging, and more. And it stretched as far as I could see. This was a place made for humans or humanoids, and yet we were the only ones I could see.

It should have been warmer here, but it wasn't. I wasn't freezing, but I once again wished I was in jeans, a t-shirt, and a hoodie, versus my FLOTUS-wear, and I really wished I had my Converse on instead of sensible but attractive pumps. Then again, if wishing was going to work, what I really wanted was for all this galaxy-ending crap to be over with and for all of us to be safely home. Waited. Nada, we were still on this open-air elevator. Nice of the cosmos to do its usual and ignore me.

It smelled like earth, oil, animal musk, and gunpowder. There were other scents I couldn't identify, but those were plenty. The sounds were mostly normal, none of them very loud, but there was some chittering mixed in with the other sounds, which I really and truly hoped was squirrels talking. We were very high up still, so figured I'd discover new smells and terrifying noises in a little while.

"This is a hollow world?" White asked SuperBun politely.

SuperBun said that parts of it were hollow, yes. There was a core that allowed the planet to safely remain in its normal orbit around the sun, however.

"Uranium?" Chuckie asked casually, after Jeff had done his translations, as if he was just guessing for fun.

SuperBun shared that he didn't know for certain, because it wasn't what mattered.

"What does matter?" I asked.

A safe, clean world where creatures lived in harmony was SuperBun's reply.

"But I thought you killed the predators," I pointed out carefully.

SuperBun shared that it was because the predators were not able to live with the others in harmony. Harmony seemed to be the mental word of the hour for SuperBun.

The ride was long, and I was tired of running blind. Besides, harmony was something I was always after, in that sense. "I'm kind of freaked out by heights and elevators without walls," I said to SuperBun. "I'm going to put my headphones in and listen to music, to keep myself calm. I can still hear everyone talking and I'll be able to hear you in my mind with no problem. I just want to explain why I'm being kind of rude."

SuperBun felt that this was acceptable.

Ignored the looks I was getting from Jeff and Christopher while I let go of Jeff's hand and pulled out my phone and headphones. White, Oliver, and Chuckie didn't appear to be bothered by this, and Ginger and Bruno were all for it, which meant the majority was on my side.

Didn't have a lot of time to look for whatever Serene had planted on me, because Peter took up a lot of room in there, but I definitely had Poofs on Board in addition to Harlie, so that was a great thing. Petted all the Poofs I could spot and Peter as well while I was digging, sent a mental request for them to move up anything I might need to the top, and called it good.

Got my headphones into my ears and looked at my playlists. Breathed a quiet sigh of relief—Algar had delivered again. The Hollow Earth playlist was queued up.

Hit play and was greeted by the melodious sounds of "Deeper Underground" by Jamiroquai. Wasn't sure if this was just working as soundtrack or if Algar wanted us to go down farther once we'd reached whatever was counting as the ground in this section. However, as expected, it calmed me down considerably.

"What are you building?" Christopher asked SuperBun.

SuperBun said that what we were seeing were planetary protections and enhancements.

"How do you keep the top of the planet all grassy and watered," I asked, "when we haven't seen any actual water here? I mean, other than what the little elephants sprayed onto us."

There was water, SuperBun shared. But it was protected. And we'd learn all about it shortly.

Oliver was taking pictures. He hadn't asked for permission, but SuperBun didn't seem to mind. Wondered if SuperBun wanted his world shared with the greater cosmos, but couldn't come up with a good reason for why he would.

As we lowered, the massiveness of what we were inside came more sharply into focus. Everything was even more gigantic up close than it had seemed from far away. My music changed to

"Reflection" by Tool. Wasn't sure what this meant, however, but it was a long song. Wondered if it would still be playing or not when we stopped.

Noted that the other platforms seemed to mostly hold sets of pygmy elephants or rabbits. Didn't take genius to guess that we'd hit watering time. Didn't see where the water source was, though. Had no guess for why more rabbits were being sent to the top, but they were. Hoped it wasn't to attack my team, but also had no guess about that, either. Though, experience told me to expect that we were all going to be attacked, a lot, and soon. My life was just that kind of fun.

Tried to mind-meld with the elephants and the squirrels. Nothing, not even white noise. And none of them reacted to my attempts, either, so it wasn't as if I'd made contact and they were just ignoring me. I simply couldn't get through.

Not all the platforms had elephants and bunnies, though. Some were carrying what I was pretty sure was sod, presumably to go up to repair a patchy spot in the grass. Maybe that's what the rabbits were going to do, instead of attack my team. Hey, a girl could dream, right?

Dad would have loved something like this—automatic sod deliveries—back when I was a little girl and he'd tried to grow a good lawn in the desert heat of Pueblo Caliente. The water cost had been so high, Mom had put her foot down, so we'd lived with pretty desert landscaping most everywhere and a crummy lawn in the backyard that the dogs and cats enjoyed in their own, special ways. As Mom had put it, we lived near a great park that Pueblo Caliente paid the water bill for, and parks were for running around and having fun in, so she saw no reason to keep on trying to create something lush when all it was really used for was cat and dog excrement. Mom, as always, had a point.

Wondered what Mom and Dad would make of this. Potentially more than I was. Worried about my parents, having to cover things while we were gone. Worried about Mom and Dad having to lie to Alfred and Lucinda. Worried about all the pets left on Earth. Then chose to worry closer to home, so to speak, and worried about Jamie, Charlie, and Lizzie, then all the other kids.

Could have kept on worrying about everyone and everything, but Bruno squawked quietly and I stopped. Shoved the worry away hard because Bruno had made a good point—we didn't want Jamie picking the worry up, because we really didn't want

any of the kids to try to come down here. In no small part because, despite the lack of apparent danger, I was sure that we
were in trouble of some kind, because I didn't believe SuperBun
had actually had Butler taken away out of concern for Butler's
robotic health.

As we got closer to our destination, could confirm those were
indeed squirrels driving cars and doing assembly line work, and
they were all normally squirrel sized, just like SuperBun and his
rabbits were normal bunny sized. There was something wrong
about that, but I didn't have time to think about it because we
finally reached the ground. Tried not to breathe a sigh of relief
but felt all of us relax, animals included. SuperBun as well,
which was interesting.

He hopped off and we followed. The area we were in looked
like all the others we'd seen from above, only now that we were
down here on this version of ground level, it was just about the
same as when we'd been above it. Smells were the same, noise
level wasn't too much more than we'd heard while on the platform, and while everything around us was huge, we weren't as
dwarfed as I'd expected us to be. Frankly, things had looked
larger when we'd been about halfway down than they did now.

"Something's off," Chuckie said quietly. "Be on guard."

Algar was clearly in agreement. My music changed to
"Something's Missing" by John Mayer, and I counted song time
in my head—it had taken us about fifteen minutes to lower from
when I'd put my headphones in, so if I guessed our time in the
dark correctly, we'd been on the platform for a good twenty
minutes.

On Earth, that would mean we were far underground, even
on the slowest elevator. Looked up. I could still see the top, as
patches of light appeared and vanished, depending on what was
going up or coming down.

Had no idea what this meant in reality, but it was clear that
what we were seeing wasn't necessarily what actually was.
Wanted to ask Ginger and Bruno what they were seeing, but had
a feeling that would broadcast to SuperBun. Wasn't sure that all
I'd been thinking hadn't broadcast to him, but hope liked to
spring eternal.

SuperBun hopped along and we followed. Realized I hadn't
asked his name. "What should we be calling you?" I asked as I
caught up to him.

He replied that he quite fancied SuperBun and I could keep on using that for him.

"I'm glad you like your superhero nickname, but do you have a real one, one that people other than me use for you? We all have real names and nicknames. Not sure if that's just us, though."

He replied that, so far, we were the only people he'd met.

"Oh, sorry, semantics. I think of everyone sentient as a person. You're a fluffy, adorable person, I've met big, scary, Cthulhu-type people, people who look like us but are different inside, and so on. It's just easier to think of everyone as equal in their personhood than not."

SuperBun stopped hopping, sat up on his haunches, and stared at me. He found this mindset of mine shocking.

"Why?" I asked as the others gathered 'round. "You're sentient, you're in charge of your planet, or at least part of it, you guys clearly have a system of some kind going, what's wrong with thinking of you as people? I mean, I'm not gonna change that mindset, but I'm curious as to why you find it so odd."

SuperBun did a fast shake of his head, like a lot of animals will. It was beyond adorable when he did it, ears flapping fast. He blinked at me when he was done with his shake. He wasn't a people, he was an animal.

"Yes, but you're a sentient animal," I replied. "I mean, I'm best friends with a lizard-woman, a cat-person, and a giant dog-girl. They go by the official race titles of Reptilian, Feliniad, and Canus Majorian, but they're still people and still my friends. Sure, they're somewhat humanoid, too, because they walk on their hind legs just like we humans, or Naked Apes, do, and they're a lot closer to our size. But still, they count as people. You guys, do, too. You have a sense of humor, you have the ability to be snide, you have the ability to be thoughtful, and so on. I don't see why me thinking of you as people versus just as adorable things to cuddle is a problem."

SuperBun did a full body shake. We could talk about this later. Then he hopped off again.

We all looked at each other. Noted that Christopher was carrying Bruno and Jeff had Ginger. Decided not to ask why.

As we followed SuperBun again my phone rang. Was able to answer it without alerting SuperBun since my headphones were in. Didn't want to say hello, but it turned out I didn't have to.

"Kitty, it's Tim." He sounded out of breath, like he was running. "Took a chance that you were listening to music. I figure you are, since you're not speaking. Keep it that way, don't let that rabbit you're with know I've called you. So, you don't talk, just listen. Don't ask me how, but Mother can actually keep our cell phones working out here. For which we're really grateful to her and Drax, because we're under attack."

CHAPTER 33

DID MY BEST TO focus on thinking about flowers and grass and that the squirrels working on the machines were super cute but not as cute as the bunnies. SuperBun kept on hopping with purpose, so hoped I was keeping this conversation from him.

"There are like a million rabbits and they're all after us," Tim went on, proving that my worry about attack was spot on. "I'm not sure if they plan to kill us, eat us, or capture us, but we're cut off from the shuttle. The only reason we're still alive is that we have A-Cs, Wruck, and the princesses with us, and I don't think the rabbits have hyperspeed, for which we should all be thankful."

Really wanted to say something, but couldn't. Which was frustrating and added to the worry I was experiencing. This clearly reached Jeff, because he took my hand again.

We were following a path that led us past a variety of construction areas. Wasn't positive, but felt sure that the squirrels were making nuclear weapons. Chuckie might know for sure, but now wasn't the time to ask him.

Tim continued. "Our weapons aren't working. Not sure if it was the 'water' those elephants sprayed on us or not, but the only weapons we have that are functional are Rahmi and Rhee's battle staffs, and Tito, James, and I don't think we want to kill these things. Yet. We have help coming, but we told them to hover, not land, just in case."

Saw a squirrel talking into what looked like a walkie-talkie. This was getting past surreal and into *Alice in Wonderland* territory. Wondered if the rabbits used walkies or if they were all getting their instructions from SuperBun. Or someone else. Based on the fact that we were heading somewhere, and that

SuperBun had divided our team, I was starting to lean toward the "someone else" idea. So, presumably, we were heading for Dr. Moreau's personal lair. Goody.

"The second shuttle cruised the planetary space area. Per Cameron, there's a small planet or a moon close by that is orbiting this planet. Or else the planet is orbiting the moon—we can't tell for sure yet. But it looks like it once had life on it. It looks normal, more normal than the planet we're on. Drax thinks that it only recently became uninhabited, based on worlds he's seen."

This world had seemed like a little paradise for a while, but now I wasn't so sure. There was a lot going on, more than Sandy had told us, which was so totally par for our course that I didn't even complain about it in my mind.

But now I wanted to hear Pat Benatar sing "Little Paradise" and all her other kick-butt songs. And this reminded me of a way to get information across, particularly to Tim. "Jeff, when we get back, I really want to listen to the Beatle's "Help!" album. On the shuttle, so everyone can hear it."

"Uh, why?" he asked.

"And then maybe "Top of the World" by the Carpenters."

"Again, why?"

"I just like the songs."

"Then why not listen to them right now?"

"Because right now I'm listening to "Trouble in Paradise" and don't want to change the song."

"By Huey Lewis and the News?"

"Yes." Wondered if he was catching on or not.

Chuckie had. "I'd like to suggest "Guarded" by Disturbed, myself." He was on my other side, and definitely had projected his voice toward the microphone portion of my headset. But subtly. We were good. If it mattered, because I still wasn't sure that SuperBun wasn't mentally eavesdropping. Though if he was, he gave no indication.

Looked around, sure enough, could see a lot of squirrels who weren't working but were on catwalks, watching us. Couldn't tell if they were holding weapons, but if our weapons weren't working, too, then there were a lot of them and they had nasty teeth and claws, just like the rabbits did.

"I heard that," Tim said. "So you guys are surrounded, too. But it sounds like you're not in trouble yet. I mean, no more than we normally are at this juncture, which means that you haven't hit the really bad part yet." He stopped panting. "We're resting for a minute. We think we've outdistanced the rabbits, but we're keeping watch. So far, nothing but grass as far as we've run through or seen. And no life other than the rabbits after us, and more of those stupid watering elephants doing their thing."

"That's a good one. How about Miss Li's "Gotta Leave My Troubles Behind"?"

"I like that one," White said. Figured he'd caught on at least when Chuckie had, if not before. He was used to working with me, after all, and he'd been there with me when I'd deciphered Tim's musical clues correctly during the latter half of Operation Confusion.

"We're not leaving you guys in there, so, nice try, but hells to the no," Tim said. "The ship can see us and they're tracking us. We can get extracted if necessary. But we have no idea where you guys are and we're not leaving you here on this freak world."

"What about "Matter Made" by the Acid Girls?" I asked. It was hard to come up with song titles that would get my point across—that I was by now pretty sure we were on a manmade or, rather, superconsciousness-made or adapted world.

"You're desperate if you're going for straight instrumentals," Tim said. "I'm thinking, hang on. If you can."

"Not one of my favorites," Jeff said, joining the party. "But I don't have anything to suggest."

"How about "Ghost in the Machine" by B.o.B.? You like that one."

"Got it," Tim said. "Thanks. You think this world was made by one of Sandy's friends."

"That's a good one," Jeff said.

"Glad you think so." It was always nice when I could say one sentence that answered who I was talking to in person and on the phone at the same time.

SuperBun stopped hopping. We were in front of a large set of double doors, easily three times taller than Jeff and wider than all of us standing abreast. Saw no handles or knockers or anything. This boded. Not that boding hadn't been happening since we'd landed.

"I guess we're here?" Hey, had to tell Tim something.

"Gotcha," Tim said. "You want me to stay on the line or hang up?"

Thought fast. It would be good to have Tim hear what he could, but I couldn't have an entire conversation with whatever stranger was on the other side of those doors using musical clues. Also, Algar might have more for me if I got back onto my playlist. "Two last song suggestion before we go in," I said. "How about "Leave Me Alone (I'm Lonely)" by Pink and "Invisible Man" by Joshua Kadison?"

The guys with me all said those were good songs, so I knew they'd all caught on, because Christopher detested Kadison and usually whined if I played anything by him and Oliver would only be chiming in about my musical choices if he understood what I was doing.

"Got it," Tim said. "I'll hang up and we'll get Siler down here. Good plan. We'll get down to you somehow."

"Oh," I said quickly, "and we can't forget my fave song for Jeff, "Elevator" by Flo Rida. 'Cause there's only one Flo and only one Rida."

"Check," Tim said. "Just Siler and Wruck to search for you and we'll see if we can find any of those platform things that don't have elephants or rabbits on them—we passed lots, all were occupied. The rest of us will run away from rabbits just to keep in shape. Good luck, Kitty." Then he hung up.

My music started up again, "I've Got a Theory/Bunnies/If We're Together" by the *Buffy the Vampire Slayer* cast from their stellar musical episode. Nice to see Algar was keeping it light.

It was a short song, and only lasted as long as it took for the big doors to open noiselessly. My music changed to "Be Prepared" from the *Lion King* soundtrack. Algar was all about the interesting choices.

"I was expecting creaking," Oliver admitted.

"Or noise of any kind," White agreed.

"Light would have been nice," was my contribution. Because it was murky as hell inside.

SuperBun hopped in, however, so we followed, doors closing noiselessly behind us. Wasn't sure if a loud, final-sounding bang would have been better or just more appropriate.

But once the doors closed, lights came on.

We all stared and we all gaped. Who SuperBun hopped over to was not, despite my musical warning, what I and, I was pretty sure, the others had been expecting. At all.

We all stood there, speechless. Realized one of us had to break the silence. So I did. Managing the only words I could come up with.

"Um . . . Santa?"

CHAPTER 34

WELL, HE *LOOKED* LIKE SANTA CLAUS. Muscular but fat, white hair, moustache, and beard, rosy cheeks, jolly expression, dressed in bright red with white trim.

The room was huge, which was to be expected from the doors. But something still felt wrong with what I was seeing. Well, lots was wrong with it, really.

We were in what looked like Santa's toy factory. There were assembly lines, all with squirrels working at them, creating things. Things that looked like animals, but only a few kinds. There were bins filled with pygmy elephants, squirrels, and tiny horses—none of which looked quite alive or dead—but no rabbits. It reminded me a lot of the various cloning and bot factories we'd discovered. Less horrifying and disgusting than Gaultier's Hot Zombies Factory, more alive than the bot factory under the NSA black site. Still plenty creepy.

Probably Not Really Santa was sitting on a big chair that looked like a combination of a throne and the kinds of chairs the Santas at the malls sat on for pictures with the little ones. Only this one was on rollers. An *executive* Santa chair.

About a hundred feet behind him was another set of doors. These were even bigger and more imposing than the ones we'd entered Santa's Workshop through. They looked more firmly closed, and were sealed by something, at least as near as I could make out.

Probably Not Really Santa smiled at me. "Have you been a good girl this year, Kitty?"

"What the literal hell?" Chuckie muttered, as Jeff and Christopher put Bruno and Ginger down.

"Um . . . yes?"

"What would you like for your present?" Probably Not Really Santa asked.

"Careful," Chuckie said quietly. "Trust me, this is a trap."

"I feel nothing," Jeff added softly. "At all. From anyone, person or animal."

Cleared my throat and considered my possible responses here. My music changed—to "Universe & U" by KT Tunstall. "I'd like to save the universe."

Probably Not Really Santa's eyes narrowed. "Now, why would you say that?"

Decided to go for it. "Grumpy?"

He sat up straight. "I am not that person, nor am I that emotion. I am Lord Dupay."

Ran through name possibilities from this. It was pretty easy to guess. "Dopey, I presume?"

Definitely Not Really Santa glared at me. Not up to Christopher's standards, but not bad, either. "That's not my name."

"Sure it is. I gave it to you a few years ago. Though, to be honest, I really was expecting Grumpy to be here."

Dopey sniffed. "She's off doing whatever it is she does. You will call me by the name I've chosen."

She. Interesting.

"Humor him," White said softly.

Heaved an internal sigh. "Fine. Lord Dupay, what's going on?"

"Many things, Kitty. But you haven't answered my question. What would you like for your present?"

"I did answer. I'd like to save the galaxy. Potentially the universe, too."

He rolled his eyes. "I see you've chatted with Grumpy, then."

"No, actually. We haven't seen anyone we know here. Well, I mean, we know SuperBun now, and you, but prior to that, no one." On this planet, I added for honesty's sake. Chose not to mention Peter for whatever reason and, as far as I could tell, SuperBun didn't mention him either. Interestinger.

"Humph." Dopey looked at SuperBun. "You like that name, Number One Bun?" Which was also a cute name, and far cuter than I'd have ever given Dopey, or any of the other superconsciousnesses we'd met, credit for coming up with.

SuperBun indicated that he did. But in a very careful, subservient way. A way I hadn't seen him exhibit until right now. My music changed to "Save My Life" by Pink. So, if I was interpreting this clue right, SuperBun was in as much danger as we were.

Maybe all the animals we'd seen were. The ones in the bins certainly weren't having a party.

"Well, it's fine for her to call you that. But it's not your *real* name," Dopey said, giving me side-eye. "She thinks she's the one who names everyone, but she's wrong."

Took all my self-control not to mention that I was Shealla, the Giver of Names—at least on Beta Eight and as far as Ixtha was concerned, too—and that I'd named Dopey and all the other superconsciousnesses who'd gotten uppity on my planet. That response was likely to get us all into more trouble than we already in. "I just think SuperBun is amazing. His telepathy is the strongest I've ever felt."

"*Is* it?" Dopey asked. "And yet you broke free from it."

"We did. What's with the elephants? I've never seen them that small, ever, and they seemed to be all water on the inside. Did you do that?" Ensured I sounded interested.

Dopey nodded. "It's a more natural, efficient way to keep the world irrigated."

"Can't argue with your results. You had to have tinkered with the elephants, though."

"I did. They were too large to be of use."

"How so? Honestly, I'd think the bigger they were, the better for watering."

"They were too heavy and ruined the grass wherever they stepped."

"Oh. Good point. Same with the horses, then?" Not that I'd noticed that horses' hooves were grass unfriendly, but it was clear I wasn't dealing with a sane mind.

"Yes."

"And yet you left the rabbits and squirrels at their regular sizes?"

"They're perfectly efficient at their natural sizes."

Interesting choice of words. "I'm kind of amazed that this world had elephants and horses and bunnies and squirrels. And, apparently, other predators no longer among the living."

"Predators create issues."

We were predators. Couldn't argue that we could create issues. However, had a strong feeling that Dopey was the biggest predator right now. "Why do you look like Santa Claus?"

He seemed surprised by the question. "He's the most benevolent figure of your world."

Let that sink in for a moment and didn't allow myself to think of other benevolent Earth figures because that wasn't what mattered right now. "So what? I mean that in a non-disrespectful way. I don't get why you'd imitate anything from Earth."

"Well, only the things I liked."

Time to let something else sink in, including the really bad feeling I was getting about all of this. "Um . . . did the bunnies and squirrels and horses and elephants come from Earth, too?"

"Of course." Said so matter-of-factly. "Where else would I find them?"

Felt the rage begin to build, but ensured it didn't show in my voice or expression. "Oh, I don't know, I just thought this planet would have had its own life on it."

"It did." He shrugged. "They weren't anything to speak of."

"What did Grumpy think of them?"

He smirked. "She liked them. Thought they had potential."

Interestinger and interestinger. "Save the World" by Bon Jovi came on. Nice to know we had to rescue everyone, not just ourselves and SuperBun. I loved a challenge. Apparently and at least as far as the cosmos seemed concerned.

"So, you reengineered elephants and horses?"

"Yes. The elephants are now mostly water containment—all their necessary organs are in their hides. So they can fill up and water the world as needed."

"And the horses? What do they do?"

"They're for hauling heavy loads and for the rabbits and squirrels to ride, the squirrels in particular."

Managed to refrain from making a *Planet of the Apes* joke, but it took effort. "Ah. Gotcha. Yeah, I'd imagine that it's easier for the squirrels to ride than the bunnies, though I'm sure the bunnies can do it if they try." Not that I could think of a reason why they'd want to. "So, um, do they ride into battle or something?"

"No, they're for when we need to expand our holdings."

"What do you mean? Don't you have the whole world?"

"Yes," Dopey said patiently. "But the space you saw on your way here is expanded as we're able. The horses help with all of that."

"No moles and such for digging? No mini-oxen for the hauling?"

"No, but those are good ideas!"

"What are you doing on this planet?" Jeff asked, Commander Voice on Full, before I could say that I hadn't been suggesting that Dopey steal more Earth animals to do whatever twisted things he could come up with to them. "As near as I can tell, you're controlling the sentient life. Life you stole from Earth."

"What you left alive, that is," Christopher added.

"Not that there's anything wrong with that," I added quickly. Really hoped White and Chuckie were kicking Jeff and Christopher where Dopey couldn't see. "Rabbits and squirrels reproduce quickly."

"They do, especially when there are no predators to harm them. I'm *caring* for them," Dopey said to Jeff and Christopher. "Their lives are far better because of me."

"What about rain or oceans?" I asked before Jeff or Christopher could open their mouths again. That was the problem with guys who'd been protectors all their lives—they were ready to protect. But we still needed info. "Where do you get the water from for the elephants to use?"

"Oh," Dopey waved toward the big door behind him. "There's a giant underground water source. We use that."

Managed not to ask how close to the door the water was, because I figured it was just on the other side. My music changing to "Black Water" by The Doobie Brothers was also something of a clue. "Salt water?"

"No, fresh. No salt on this world."

Thought about the moon or small planet Tim had mentioned. "What about the moon? Does that have salt on it?"

"What moon?" Dopey asked sharply.

"The one that's in your orbit. It looks kind of dead."

"Oh, that. Yes, it had salt on it, I believe."

Filed this away for use later. Had no idea what I could do with this information, just knew that I'd need it later because that was how my life rolled. "Where's Grumpy now?"

"With those creatures on another planet in the system. She replanted them."

Replanted. "Were they botanical in nature?"

"Yes, actually. Tree-people, though not like the ones from your myths. And other plants that were all barely sentient."

"What about the predators that were here? Did you bring them from Earth, too?"

"No. They were just those who lived with the tree-people. In harmony, per Grumpy." Dopey shrugged. "They weren't efficient, any of them."

"Why not?" Chuckie asked carefully. "We've always

understood that trees are very efficient. Where is our thinking wrong?" He sounded like we were in class and he was asking a top-level professor a question. Hoped that Jeff and Christopher would take a clue if they wanted to speak up again.

Dopey appreciated the buttering up. "They need too much in order to survive."

"Soil, water, sunlight," I ticked off. "Why would that be inefficient?"

"Because this world isn't going to have a sun too much longer."

CHAPTER 35

WE ALL LET THAT one sit on the air for a bit. "Um, why not?"

"Because this sun is dying." Dopey said this as if it were obvious. However, based on what our science knew, there was no way a sun as yellow as the one for this system was could be close to dying. At least, not a natural death. And, per Sandy, the star wasn't the issue—the war Dopey and Grumpy were having was.

"Is it?" White asked politely. "How can you tell? We're not as advanced as you, so we don't have the means to determine this."

Dopey smiled at him. Yep, he liked being buttered up. "Well, it's really all Grumpy's fault. She's tinkering with the sun, and that's going to cause its destruction."

My music changed to "Black Hole Sun" by Soundgarden and I got a really bad feeling in the pit of my stomach. "Um what's Grumpy doing with the sun?"

"She's trying to make it stronger."

"Why is that, Lord Dupay?" Jeff asked, only this time, he sounded totally fascinated and not like he was ready to try to bust Dopey's head. Either he'd caught on or Chuckie had kicked him really hard. Possibly both. "Wouldn't it already be strong enough as is, in order to have created life out here?"

"This system didn't have life. Not until she and I decided to create it."

"I thought you weren't gods," Christopher said quietly.

Dopey's head snapped toward him. "Why would you say that?"

"Because you told us you weren't, when we first met," Christopher replied. "And only gods can create life."

"That's ridiculous. Life creates itself all the time."

White cleared his throat. "There is a difference between creation and procreation, though. I believe that's what's confused Christopher."

Christopher nodded. "I don't understand." Said in the same tone as the others had used—the tone of asking a much smarter person for help. So he was also playing along. Good and go team.

Speaking of the team, while Dopey started blathering about the role of the more highly evolved and how they needed to help those lesser beings—which sounded a lot like the motto Algar had told me the Black Hole Universe people tended to live by, and also a lot like I heard from all of the League of Mad Scientists and Evil Geniuses on a regular basis, but the exact opposite of what Sandy had told me the Superconsciousness Consortium believed and lived by—noted that we were missing Oliver. And Bruno. And Ginger.

Had no idea when the three of them had disappeared or where they'd gone. The last I'd seen them they'd all been in here. Hoped they were investigating as opposed to being captured like Butler had been. Presumably had been, at any rate. Realized I hadn't asked Dopey about Butler's health and whereabouts; I'd been thrown by the whole Santa thing.

Why Dopey would want him was clear—he was making animal androids, essentially. Why not grab a really stellar human version and make copies of him? If the bad guys we normally dealt with could come up with a plan like that, why not a superconsciousness who appeared bent on some weird form of global domination? Though how you dominated anything with the weird setup Dopey had was beyond me. Other than this planet and the animals he had working for him potentially as slave labor, couldn't figure out what he hoped to gain.

"What's the point?" Whoops. Had not meant to say that out loud.

"The point of what?" Dopey asked.

Oh well, in for a penny, might as well go for it. "All of this. I don't understand the point of all of this. Any of it, really. I mean, other than SuperBun. He's cool."

"He is." Dopey smiled at me. "Wouldn't you like to have him for your very own? Yours, only. No sharing. He'd be all for you."

Felt the pull again, the complete desire to have SuperBun as my very own. It was stronger than it had been the first time, and

I realized that there was nothing in the universe that mattered more than getting to be with SuperBun for the rest of my life.

Took a step toward SuperBun as "Insanity Lurks Nearby" by Front Line Assembly came on my personal airwaves, louder than the other music had been, and it jarred me out of the telepathic hold. Checked on the others out of the sides of my eyes—they seemed okay, but I didn't want to wait around and find out they weren't.

"Nice try," I said as I stopped moving forward. "But we already established that your mind control doesn't work on me."

Dopey's eyes narrowed. "It's not really mind control if it's what you want."

"Is that how you convinced the animals to come with you? Telling them that's what they wanted? Or did you just grab them and take them a million miles away from their home and then tell them they wanted to help out?"

"Your minds are too small, too young, to understand," Dopey said dismissively.

"Well, I guess that's true. From your perspective anyway."

"Perspective," Chuckie said. "That's it! The perspective is all wrong here."

Was about to ask what he meant, when an alarm went off. It was loud and screeching, and, interestingly enough, Dopey looked as surprised by this as the rest of us.

"What have you done?" Dopey demanded of us.

"Um, nothing? We've all been here with you." I lied like a pro to bad guys by now, so I wasn't concerned that Dopey wouldn't believe me. And I figured that we needed to stall as long as possible, in case our side had caused those alarms to go off.

He looked around wildly. "Where are the rest of your group?"

"Huh?" Jeff asked, sounding confused. This was, for my husband, stellar lying, and I was proud.

"No idea what you're talking about," Chuckie added, sounding confused. Humans—still lying better than 99.9% of the A-C population, galaxywide.

SuperBun blinked innocently. He had no idea what Lord Dupay meant. All those who'd come down appeared to be here.

So, SuperBun was on our side. Meaning that Dopey was the one forcing him to try to mind-control us. Which settled it for me. If I was indeed in a whacked-out version of Wonderland, then I was taking the White Rabbit and All His Friends with me when I got the hell out of Dodge.

My music changed to "Up from Under" by The Wallflowers. Worked for me. Had no idea how we'd achieve this plan, but I was all for it.

Squirrels came rushing in through the big doorway we'd entered through, chittering like mad. It was kind of freaky but mostly comforting in that at least I could put a face to the sound, so to speak.

"What?" Dopey shouted. "How?"

"How what and what what?" I asked.

"We're under attack! Grumpy's making her move." He turned to the squirrels. "It's time for the final solution!"

"Stop!" Jeff bellowed. No one could bellow like my man—he was louder than the alarms and had far better reverberation going—so everyone indeed stopped. The alarms stopped, too, which was hella intriguing. "Nothing good ever comes from the term 'final solution' and I'm sure nothing good is going to come from yours. You're a superconsciousness. Act like it. Simply save your people and your planet without destroying anyone or anything else."

At this, Dopey looked furtive. "It's not that easy."

Thought about what was going on. Not with all of this, but with the minute clue Sandy had given me—the issue was with Grumpy and Dopey fighting for control.

Since they'd become a romantic item, that likely meant that much of what they were doing was in retaliation against the other for slights and injuries, perceived and real.

"Why did you and Grumpy break up?"

This question caused everyone to stare at me. "What possible relevance could that have to our current situation?" Dopey asked.

"Seconded," Christopher added.

Managed not to roll my eyes but it took effort. "It matters. Why did you guys stop working together?"

Dopey sniffed. "She insulted me one too many times."

"Uh huh. Why did you guys stop being a couple?"

Dopey glared at me. Still not up to Christopher's level, but perhaps he just needed practice. He tried for the stare down, which, since he wasn't Mom or Chuckie, I won easily. "She said I didn't listen to her or understand her needs," he said as he looked away, "and she was tired of doing all the work in the relationship."

"How did that make you feel?" White asked, sympathy oozing.

"Terrible," Dopey admitted. "I did my best. She just never appreciated me."

"Women can be like that," Christopher said, apparently deigning to catch on and join the party.

My music changed to "Spirits in the Material World" by the Police while Dopey shared his short, familiar tale of relationship woes with the guys, all of whom made sympathetic noises and kept him rolling. The song was clearly a clue, but I already knew that the superconsciousnesses were vapor, essentially, and that they were acting in the physical world.

Looked around at everything while Dopey got up and started giving the squirrels orders—in between continuing to share about him and Grumpy and how none of this was his fault but all hers—most of which related to making the animals that were in holding in the various bins alive. Didn't look around in wonder, but in hopes of seeing if there was another spirit in here, maybe. Possibly Grumpy hanging about, or maybe Sandy. Nada.

But what I did note this particular time, now that I was accustomed to the weirdness—which now included the squirrels using small guns that truly looked like Super Soakers to shoot something into every one of the bins and seeing the animal shells in said bins wake up and leap out—was that it was all very fantastical, too bizarre and too ridiculous, and most of it seemed to have no actual effective purpose.

No normal adult would have created something like this. No crazy adult would have, either.

But a child might have.

CHAPTER 36

DOPEY WAS STILL LISTING Grumpy's faults as the squirrels kept on spraying the whatever it was into the many bins and the pygmy elephants and tiny horses ran out of the room once they were brought to life. "Come with me if you want to live," Dopey said, as he ran out after them. The squirrels stayed, doing their weird work. There were still a ton of bins they hadn't gotten to yet.

"I'll bet he's been waiting a while to say that," Chuckie said. "Do we follow him?"

"The hell with that," Jeff replied. "We have people missing in here."

"Do we split up or stay together?" Christopher asked.

"I'd suggest teams of two at least," White replied. "We have no idea what's actually going on and we need to ensure that Charles isn't left here without an A-C."

"Then Chuck's with me and Kitty," Jeff said.

My music changed to "Stay" by Oingo Boingo. Considered who all Algar wanted to stick around. Hoped I was interpreting it right.

"You guys go ahead." They all stared at me. "Seriously. I need to think. I'll stay here in the giant throne room where it might or might not be safe and you guys go forth. Find Oliver, Butler, and my pets. But hurry. Dopey leaving us to run away seems somewhat worrisome."

Jeff opened his mouth to argue. Put up the paw. His mouth closed. I truly loved the One True FLOTUS Power. "I'm serious. I'll be fine, but I need to think. And I think I need to stay here. Just . . . don't be too long. And before you guys all start arguing, let's be real—no matter what's going on, it's unlikely that we have a ton of time to waste."

They left, unwillingly, and with White literally dragging Jeff out of the room. That left me and SuperBun staring at each other while the squirrels carried on and the elephants and horses leaped out to do whatever. Decided I needed to do what I'd told my men I wanted to—think. So I did.

And my thoughts were basically that this seemed like a child's weird idea of a cool thing. Ergo, lead with that assumption.

So, did that mean that Dopey and Grumpy were children? Sandy seemed like all the other Powers That Be out there—old as dirt and just as much fun. But Sandy had had a lot more time with me, had chosen to wander and learn, and hadn't—and this was probably key—chosen to fall in love with another of his kind.

Of course, I had no idea how superconciousnesses created. Maybe they fell in love, but based on what I'd learned from Sandy during Operation Defection Election, they didn't. Ergo, falling in love was definitely an unusual thing to have happened.

Considered this point, but went back to the idea that Dopey was a kid. If Jamie had taken over a world, what would she have done? Maybe made herself Santa, because, as Dopey had said, Santa was a most benevolent figure, and even the most despotic liked to think of themselves as Kindly Protectors Of The People. Possibly she'd have taken animals she thought were really adorable and, perhaps, made them more her size.

Size. Chuckie had said that the perspective was all off.

My music changed again, this time to "No Such Thing" by John Mayer. Didn't think Algar was telling me I was wrong, so listened carefully. The chorus was that there was no such thing as the real world, just a lie that John felt we all needed to rise above. And it was also sort of "set" in high school.

It wasn't hard to guess that this world wasn't "real" in the normal sense of the word. So much was clearly manufactured or created. So that was part of it, but not all.

If I went with the high school angle, it meant that the kid I should be thinking about was Lizzie. And teenagers were hella dramatic—God knew I got a dose of drama daily from Lizzie whether I needed it or not. Plus, they were more likely to fall in love *and* break up ugly.

Of course, little kids "fell in love," too. So maybe that was what had caused the breakup—they were now older and their wants and needs had changed. Not that older people were immune to this—far from it—but the first real love and the first real breakup were always the worst in their own special way. And Dopey's reactions and comments really seemed like first love gone badly.

So, what we were seeing likely wasn't real and Dopey and Grumpy were probably teenagers by now, at least in terms of their new and improved superconsciousness lifespans. Wondered again if Bruno and Ginger saw this place differently. Possibly. That might be why they went with Oliver, or he went with them. Maybe he saw it differently through the camera's lens, too. Perhaps the camera showed the world as it actually was, not as Dopey wanted it to be. In fact, perhaps that's why SuperBun had demanded that Oliver come along and hadn't complained about Ginger and Bruno joining us, either.

They weren't nearby, and I wasn't sure that I could trust SuperBun—rather, I wasn't sure, even with all that was going on and being out of the room, that Dopey wasn't monitoring Super-Bun so closely that my talking to him would cause us all more problems. But I did have Poofs with me. And, potentially even better, someone who'd lived here for a while.

Reached into my purse and pulled Peter out. "What is it you see, when you look around?" I whispered to him.

He shuddered and cuddled into my breast. So, whatever it was, it wasn't jolly. Shocker.

"I need to see it like you do. Can you help me do that?"

Peter closed his eyes and continued his terrified snuggling. But I could see what he saw now.

We weren't in a room—we were in a large, clear, circular tube that looked like part of the biggest hamster habitat in the galaxy. This went around what looked like a huge ball of water. And what was on the other sides of the tube was also water. Black water. There were things in the water—things I couldn't make out, but they gave off a very dangerous feeling. It was like being in one of those shark experience exhibits, where you walked through the tube and the sharks swam around you. Only it was about a thousand times bigger and far more menacing.

Tried not to look down. Failed. Yep, they were under us, too. Joy.

But I saw more than the black water and whatever was lurking inside it. There was actually plenty of light—lights, or things that gave off light, were somehow floating throughout the hamster habitat we found ourselves in—and I could see tubes like we were in that ran all through this area.

The squirrels were moving about inside the tubes, as were the horses and elephants. Couldn't spot my men and hoped it was because they were out of view, versus captured by Grumpy or Dopey, or worse. The platforms raised and lowered in tubes. So that was why the elevators here had no sides—they didn't need them.

And around every tube was the black water.

There was more, though. Some sort of light refraction that seemed to happen when the lights hit the black water. Algar's second song on my playlist suddenly made sense. Better late than never. "So that's how he's doing it. He's using the reflection of the water here to help him keep his illusion going." But why would a powerful superconsciousness need to do that?

Examined the elephants that had just been "turned on" and were out of their bin. They weren't cute anymore. Neither were the horses. They appeared to have been squished down somehow, to make them smaller, with no attention paid to aesthetics or comfort. The squirrels, on the other hand, were all big, human-sized, and it seemed as though they'd been stretched out in order to achieve that. But all them were deformed in a way that looked painful.

The rabbits I could see, however, still looked like rabbits, and I could see more than just Peter and SuperBun, because rabbits were racing around in the tubes, too. The rabbits still being normal was presumably why I'd been able to talk to them but none of the others. Not that I'd tried with the horses but, looking at them, chose not to bother with the attempt. They weren't organic beings anymore, not really—none of them were.

Felt really bad for all the horses, elephants and squirrels. They were Earth animals originally and Dopey had stolen them and then turned them into unnatural things, definitely against their wills. Because he could.

Rage was building, and that was good, but I needed to know what to do and who to do it to. "Why did the water sprayed on us make our weapons stop working but not hurt us?"

Peter replied that he wasn't sure, but that was why SuperBun had had our android taken away—so the water wouldn't harm him. The water didn't hurt organic things, as far as Peter knew, but machines it destroyed somehow.

In a galaxy as varied as the one we were in, this didn't shock me all that much. We had an entire race of people who mentally connected and talked to computers and metals from birth. Why not have water that destroyed machinery but didn't hurt organic life? If it truly didn't hurt us, for which I felt the jury was definitely still out.

Before I could ask another question, Dopey ran into the room. "Why are you still here?"

"Um . . . I'm resting?"

He made the exasperation sound, ran over to a bin, grabbed a couple of elephants and some horses, and shouted at the squirrels to keep on spraying.

My music changed to The New Pornographers' "The Body Says No" which made me pause. I was sure that the animals' bodies had all indeed said no, but why would Algar be reinforcing that? I'd figured it out, and I kind of presumed he knew, since he was big on having songs repeat when I wasn't catching the clues.

"What does Dopey, or, Lord Dupay actually look like?" I asked Peter, very quietly.

He shuddered, but showed me.

Shuddered right along with Peter. Because Dopey did actually look like Santa. Only, not all of Santa. Because there wasn't a full person there.

CHAPTER 37

DOPEY WAS HALF OF A SANTA, cut down the middle, in a ragged way, as if the two sides had pulled away from each other and ripped, which was exactly what I figured had happened.

He spun back toward me. It was worse looking at him from the front. "You need to leave. The men with you were smart and followed me. Why not you?"

"I'm a rebel, me."

"Suit yourself!" Dopey ran out of the room. As Evil Geniuses went, he needed a lot of work to make the grade. Then again, what he'd done to the animals might qualify him into the League, if only in a Junior capacity.

The squirrels kept on super soaking the animals in the bins. There were still a frightening number of bins left for them to bring to life. Had a feeling that even if I tried, the squirrels, elephants, and horses weren't going to come with me.

"Was Dopey always half a person?" I asked my Rabbit Interpreter.

No, he hadn't been. He and Grumpy had been as one, and then they'd had their fight and ripped each other apart. Literally.

Always nice to be right. "How did SuperBun get his powers?" I asked Peter carefully.

He showed me the water. SuperBun had fallen in when they'd first arrived on this world, before the tubes had been inserted and it was all grass on top. Dopey had saved the rabbit just in time, but that had enhanced his natural animal telepathy greatly.

"They're fighting over the water on this planet? Dopey and Grumpy, I mean."

Peter didn't know. He just wanted to escape and, hopefully,

take the rest of the animals with him. Even the monster animals, which was how all rabbits thought of them now.

SuperBun took the opportunity of, I hoped, Dopey being out of the room and also presumably not coming back this time to hop over to me and look up with an expression animals give to a human when opposable thumbs or other helpful things are required—he looked scared, pitiful, and hopeful.

Bent down and scooped him up. "As if I was leaving you here? Now, where's my android? And my ocellar, Peregrine, husband, and friends, not necessarily in that order. And why are your brethren all chasing my people topside?"

SuperBun apologized about that. It was to get more shuttles to come down, or maybe even our ship. So the animals could escape with us. He also apologized for lying—he and his people were not native to this world, they'd killed nothing and no one, that was just the story Dopey had told him to tell any visitors to scare and impress them, and the rabbits were living in terror, not in charge. Dopey had dealt with this world's predators, not the rabbits.

"Wow. It's nice to know you aren't vicious killers. It's also kind of a pity you're not the one in charge. You seem so much smarter than Dopey, aka Lord Dupay, does."

The rabbits shared that when Dopey and Grumpy had been as one, they'd been fine. They'd brought in the Earth animals to help the only planet in the system that seemed likely to be able to have life survive. At least, that's what they'd said. Events had proven otherwise.

"Those four choices seem odd, honestly. Most planetary infrastructures need insects, desperately, as well as a full spectrum of plants and animals, in order to thrive. Not just grass and four species that, while awesome in their own ways, don't exactly scream Saviors of the Evolutionary Ecosystem."

SuperBun pointed out that elephants, horses, and squirrels all had ancestors from millions of years prior.

"Rabbits were also around then. All of our forebears were around millions of years ago. Evolution's cool. And bringing elephants and horses along I'd get if they hadn't been weirdly made smaller for no sane reason. Bunnies and squirrels I just don't understand."

SuperBun sighed. Squirrels had thumbs and were smart enough to be trained to do manual labor. Plus, they reproduced quickly.

"And are plentiful enough to steal without humans noticing. But horses and elephants aren't, and you still haven't explained bunnies."

Only a few horses and elephants had been taken, fixed, so to speak, then cloned. The squirrels were fixed when they reached adulthood.

"Okay. And, once more with feeling—why bunnies?"

SuperBun sighed again. Bunnies were along because bunnies were cute. He felt that Grumpy and Dopey had chosen the animals they'd thought were the cutest from Earth and just made do with them.

"And we're always in for more cute where I come from. So, if you guys stop mentally showing me what you see, will I see what is or the illusion?"

The rabbits had no idea but, as the tubes shook like an explosion had happened somewhere, they also suggested we not find out.

My music changed to Fall Out Boy's "Get Busy Living or Get Busy Dying." Knew when to take a hint. "SuperBun, we need to find the others. Any guesses for where they are?"

He had one, actually, since he'd told Ginger where our android was. He just hoped we'd all be in time to get out of here before Grumpy's attack broke the tubes and let the water in.

"I'm more afraid of what's in the water than the water itself, and I'm saying that as a person who cannot breathe underwater." As I said this, looked at the water in the giant ball. It looked different. "Um . . . is that stuff boiling?"

The rabbits looked. They didn't know, but they truly felt that leaving now was a really good idea.

"Um, squirrels, elephants, and horses—I think you might want to come with us. To, you know, get out of here."

They all ignored me as if I wasn't there. Maybe I wasn't to them. Maybe they saw some weird reflection that showed them that this world was great.

SuperBun tried to get them to listen. Nothing. He felt that they'd been too altered, or else Dopey was controlling them more than usual.

"Okay, then it's just the humans, A-Cs, androids, Amazons, ocellars, Peregrines, and bunnies that are getting off of this rock." Put Peter back into my purse and placed SuperBun on the floor. "You lead, I'll follow." He hopped off and I trotted after.

Could have used hyperspeed, but I wanted to conserve my

reserves right now, if at all possible. Besides, I didn't want to make it harder for the guys to find me, and since Jeff had said he couldn't feel anything, they wouldn't be able to track me via what, for us, was the usual means. Besides, SuperBun was moving fast enough that I definitely had to trot to keep up. We were good.

We went out the "door," then to the left, and, to the melodious sounds of Iron Maiden's "The Loneliness of the Long Distance Runner" we made a right, dodging a lot of squirrels running hither and yon. Passed three hamster trail hallways that had a lot of elephants in them but nothing else of interest that I could spot, then made a sharp left at the fourth one, avoiding a small herd of tiny horses.

Along the way we essentially were circling what the squirrels had really been working on. It wasn't the bombs and such that I'd seen—it was something that looked like a high-powered laser cannon. A really gigantic one. One that the special effects people from *Star Wars* would want the patent on.

"Why did Dopey show us a war bunker? Instead of this, I mean."

SuperBun felt that we'd all seen what we expected to see. The others might have seen the same as me or might not.

"Then why was I in fifty feet of claustrophobic dirt coming down?"

Perhaps because that's what I'd expected. Maybe I'd experienced something like it, maybe I'd read something similar, maybe I just wanted it to be like that. The water reflected what was in people's minds.

"But not yours?"

Not any of the animals'. Or the camera, as I'd guessed. The camera showed the truth.

"Why didn't the other animals come with us, then?"

They were part of this world now, far more than the rabbits were.

Thought about this as we ran along. "But we all saw the big doors and such."

Because that's what Dopey had wanted all of us to see, and we'd been close enough to him for him to affect us.

Something about what SuperBun had just told me bore some serious thought. But possibly not right now. "So, is that not really a laser cannon then," I asked hopefully.

Nope. It was a real laser cannon, and it was aimed at the system's sun.

"Of course. Why would I have ever expected anything else?"

As we went along, the "roof" above us opened up, far wider than I'd seen it do for any of the platforms. As it did so, the entire Habitrail From Hell began to rise up, the cannon included. And not all that smoothly.

I lost my footing and went down, just like every other creature I could see. Including Dopey, who was on a platform next to the laser cannon.

This was a lot like our Escape From D.C. had been in the *Distant Voyager*. Meaning I had a really good idea of what was going on. Which would have been better if I'd had anyone to share it with other than Peter and SuperBun. Just hoped the guys would recognize the movements, too, and protect themselves accordingly. Was very glad suddenly that Jeff was blocked, because even though they weren't "real" anymore, the monster animals sounded scared.

Wanted to call Tim, warn him, and tell him to get themselves and the rabbits onto a shuttle and off this world, but couldn't risk trying to make the call. I was worried enough that my headphones would pull out of my ears, since my phone was in my purse, seeing as FLOTUS-wear wasn't equipped with pockets. Resolved to talk to Akiko about this lack the very moment we were back on Earth.

Proving why I didn't want to lose my headphones, my music changed to George Thorogood's "Reelin' & Rockin'," which confirmed for me what was coming.

Sure enough, the Habitrail From Hell started rocking back and forth, as if it was trying to break free from its moorings. Only the black water was clearly coming along with us, because of course it was. Along with whatever was in that water. And if sunlight hit it, I might be able to see what was in there. Resolved to get the hell out of here before that happened.

Managed to grab SuperBun before he slid away, shove him into my purse with Peter, and hold onto said purse as if it was Charlie, with the full duck and cover going. Because the Habitrail From Hell was really rocking, and the thing about tubes is that when they turn on their sides, what's inside of them goes tumbling.

CHAPTER 38

NEVER IN MY LIFE had I missed being in jeans, a t-shirt, and my Converse more than at this exact time. My sensible pumps were not great for helping me to brace myself, and neither was my nice outfit. The body armor should have made this a nonissue, but either it was slick to the touch or it bound so well to the fabrics it was on that it imitated them in all ways, because I had no traction whatsoever.

Tried shoving my butt against a surface while bracing with my feet. In jeans and Converse, that could have worked. In body armor that was determined to match the nice, soft fabric and pumps with slick bottoms I had on? I went sliding down like this was the biggest water park in the galaxy.

Tim was right—we needed to talk to Drax about his designs. If, you know, any of us survived this in order to do so.

Wasn't sure if I should be happy about the fact that the tubing lurched hard in the other direction right before I slid into a whole clutch of the pygmy elephants or not. On the one hand, the elephants probably would have broken my fall. On the other hand, they were now tumbling down, too. And they were above me.

We were all headed for a group of tiny, panicking horses. This promised to be the worst possible potential Kitty Sandwich in the history of the universe. And it wasn't going to do the bunnies any good, either.

My music changed again. I'd frankly expected Algar to be funny and play Culture Club's "I'll Tumble 4 Ya," but instead what I got was Billy Idol's "Catch My Fall." Miraculously, I got this clue, and gave myself the "duh" at the same time. "Poofies, Kitty needs a save!"

Poofikins and Harlie flew out of my purse, going large.

Poofikins was between me and the horses, Harlie between me and the elephants.

Just before we all slammed into each other, the tube leveled out. And, lucky me, sunlight hit the water. Due to how I'd tumbled around, I was looking at the big ball of water I'd been next to not so long ago, so I got a nice, clear view of what was inside.

Managed not to scream, but it took all the effort I could muster. Because what was in that water was snakes. And not just any snakes. Gigantic ones, with oscillating fins running down their backs from the back of their heads to the tips of their tails. Giant faces with horrific fangs, slit eyes that glared at everything with malevolence, and jaws that unhinged or something because they opened 180 degrees. And all that was inside those jaws were more fangs. And they were all roiling around each other and slamming themselves against the Habitrail walls, some with their jaws opened fully, some not.

Sea serpents, SuperBun corrected. They were giant sea serpents.

"That doesn't make it better, just so you know," I shouted. Had to shout. The monster animals were making a lot of terrified noise. "And I am officially sick *and* tired of hitting strange new worlds that have horrific, giant snake-things as their top predators. *Sick of it*, do you hear me?"

Didn't matter if anyone heard me or not—the Habitrail From Hell started shaking again. On the negative side, Dopey was up and doing something with his laser cannon again. On the plus side, managed to spot someone I knew—I could see Jeff and Chuckie, and they'd found Oliver, Butler, Ginger, and Bruno. So, one for our win column.

They were in a tube that only had rabbits in it, lucky them. They were all also picking said rabbits up—Bruno even had a couple in his claws and one on his back, Ginger one in her mouth and two on her back—so someone had given them the clue that the bunnies were now on our side. Or else they, like me, just wanted to get out of here without stomping on them, and taking them along was the most expedient choice. Decided not to care as long as they all made it.

The biggest positive was that Jeff's team was heading for a platform. Saw Jeff looking around, presumably for me, Christopher, and White. Waved, but had no idea if he saw me, though how you'd miss the Poofs—who were so large they effectively blocked either side of the tube, I didn't know.

However, if they were blocking it, whatever air we were getting was probably going to stop. "Poofies, back to small." Harlie and Poofikins did as requested and jumped onto my shoulders. "We need to get out of here. And does anyone know where Christopher and Richard are?"

"Right here, Missus Martini," White said as he grabbed my hand and we zipped off, Poofs diving back into my purse. "Running on the ceiling to avoid trampling animals."

Christopher was indeed going so fast that we were able to run above everything. He was going so fast that, even as the Habi-trail From Hell started to move around, we stayed "on top," wherever on top happened to be.

We reached Jeff and the others just as their platform was starting to rise. My music changed to "All My Friends" by the Counting Crows. "Good to see you guys, but we need to save all the rabbits!" Could see a bunch of bunnies running for plat-forms, but they weren't likely to make it. "Go up, tell the others to get our ship down here pronto—we're taking us and all the rabbits and getting the hell out of here!" Jumped off the platform and ran for said hot cross buns on the hoof.

Christopher whizzed past me as Jeff caught up to me. "Seriously?" Jeff shouted. "I thought they were attacking us?"

"They're Earth bunnies and they're still normal. You guys saved a bunch along the way."

"Because those weren't attacking us. And, yes, fine, they seemed panicked."

"They *are* panicked. So am I. I'm really glad your blocks are up or powers are dampened or whatever. Did you look into the water?"

"It's water. I don't want to drown in it and I think whatever we're in or on is going to break apart. Oliver and Butler said we weren't seeing it as it really was. Don't care, just want all of us out of here."

"Oh, you don't know the half of it. And it relates to us getting out. SuperBun, share what reality is with my guys here, will you?"

SuperBun said that he'd shown them the general gist of what was going on, so they'd know where to run. He'd refrained from the full truth to avoid panic.

"Show them all of it, dude. They need to know, especially if things go badly and they all rarely panic. Though, honestly, if anyone was going to panic, now might be the right time."

"Whoa!" Jeff grabbed me as SuperBun obviously obliged. "We saw the water as clear before, not black and filled with monsters. What the hell are those things? Besides terrifying and probably worse to you?"

"Sea serpents. Because that's just how lucky we always are." We reached a set of bunnies. "Everybody, follow us and let us pick you up if we can!"

The bunnies complied, in no small part because SuperBun told them to. We grabbed as many as we could and headed for the platform they'd been going for, but at a faster rate than the bunnies were managing on their own, hyperspeed remaining the best thing ever.

Reached the platform, dumped the bunnies, ran back, got more, did the same, while those who were still booking it on their paws alone leaped onto the platform. Platform filled with bunnies, it went up and we went for the next.

"Why does it seem like we have to do this on every planet we accidentally visit?" Jeff asked as we dropped the next set off on the new platform.

"Good question. I point back to just lucky, I guess."

"Yeah, this is pretty average for our luck. Do we try to save the horrific-looking elephants, horses, and squirrels? If that's what those really are."

"I don't know that we can, honestly. They've been so altered—the rabbits call them monster animals. And they aren't reacting like normal animals in any way, other than being terrified right now."

Christopher had done three platforms full of bunnies in the time we'd done one. Someone else had as well, because I spotted six platforms full of fluff and floppy ears heading upward.

Butler joined us, identifying himself as the other Savior of Easter. "I think we have them all, other than these last three sets. Christopher says he can handle the last two and that he appreciates seeing what's really here because it's making him go even faster. So, I'm helping you get these last ones done so we can all get out of here."

"Thanks for helping. The rabbits are on our side."

"Maybe. I think they took me because I could see the planet as it really is without assistance."

"It's not all grass?"

"No," he said gravely, "it's not."

We reached rabbits, we grabbed rabbits, we ran back. Lather, rinse, repeat.

"I cannot wait to see it," I said as we raced back and forth. "And by 'cannot' I mean 'don't want to but know I'll have to' and all that jazz. Oh, and the rabbits took you so you wouldn't get hit with the water, which apparently kills machinery and such."

"Well, I was in an airless chamber, so I'm not so sure about that."

"Did it hurt you?"

He smiled. "No, it didn't. So, perhaps you're correct."

SuperBun said that he couldn't talk to Butler's mind, so I'd have to express that he had absolutely done that to protect the android.

"Per my mental link with SuperBun, they did it to protect you. He's the one who told Ginger where you were and I trust him."

Butler laughed. "And I trust your judgment, Kitty. In all things. Anyway, Ginger was leading the way and there's no way she could have smelled me, based on where I was, so I'm willing to believe it. Mister Joel Oliver had just gotten the lock picked when Jeff and Charles arrived. It was a tough lock and it took a lot of time."

"We found them right when things started rocking," Jeff added.

"We need to get these last ones and get out of here," Butler said as we grabbed the last rabbits we could see. "Also, none of the horses, elephants, or squirrels would come with us."

"Leave them," Jeff said regretfully. "They're not real animals anymore, and we have to save ourselves and those that are."

My music changed to "Fix You" by Coldplay. While we were racing around loading on these last rabbits, thought about what Algar was telling me. "Did Siler and Wruck make it down here?"

"They did," Butler confirmed. He nodded toward the laser cannon.

Dopey was back on his feet—well, foot—fiddling with something on the cannon. Assumed he was aiming the thing or worse. While I watched, Siler and Wruck appeared, Wruck shifted into something I'd never seen before—he looked blurry and gauzy and like he wasn't actually there, even though I could see him. He wrapped around Dopey, Siler grabbed him, and they both disappeared again.

The cannon sat there. It didn't fire and it didn't move. Hoped this was a good sign, but just knew it wasn't. "John, get the rest

of the rabbits and get up on top. Get all the shuttles down here
to get everyone loaded in. Get all our team, and all the rabbits,
off this planet and into the ship." Reached into my purse and
handed Peter to him. "Take good care of Peter Rabbit for me,
just in case."

Peter didn't want to go—he wanted to stay with me.

Patted his head. "No. You need to go with John. In case . . .
just in case Jeff and I don't make it back to the ship. Someone
has to tell our kids that it's going to be okay. That's your job."
Kissed his fluffy head, then nodded to Butler.

"I want to argue, and say that this should go to me, as I'm the
most expendable, but I can already see both of you about to argue and I can tell that Jeff agrees with you. Hurry, and don't
sacrifice yourselves for nothing."

"We aren't," Jeff said calmly. "We're potentially sacrificing
ourselves for the galaxy."

"But I'm voting on us saving the day spectacularly."

"Let's hope your vote's the one that counts, then, Kitty." Butler scooped up a few of the last rabbits.

"Find Grumpy," I called to him as we all took off. "We need
her." My music changed to "Invaders Must Die" by The Prodigy.
Really hoped this wasn't Algar telling me we were goners.

"I'm afraid to ask," Jeff said, as we raced for the cannon, "but
I'm going to. We need another one of these things around why?"

"Because I think we can fix Dopey and Grumpy. Maybe. And
if we can fix them, maybe we can fix the monster animals, and
this world, too. But first we have to make sure that cannon
doesn't fire at the sun."

"Oh, is that all?" Jeff laughed as we ran down a tube that
was, shockingly, empty.

"What's so funny?" We hit a T-intersection in the Habitrail,
but SuperBun told us to go left, so we did, dodging around a
whole mess of freaky and freaked out squirrels.

"This is still better than being the President or the King Regent."

Up some actual stairs, which I hadn't seen before, but chose
not to whine or comment about, proving my focus on the situation at hand. "Oh my God, I hear you on that one. This beats
FLOTUSing any day." Caught movement out of the side of my
eye—a sea serpent was tracking us. "Though, not necessarily in
terms of the avoidance of terrifying monsters."

Jeff squeezed my hand. "I won't let any of them hurt you,

baby. You know that." Down some stairs, leaping over panicking monster animals.

"I do, and right back atcha, Jeff." Through an empty tube. On the inside. Outside of it, sea monsters tracked us on every side, so to speak. Did our best to ignore them.

"I'm not letting us die here, either," Jeff said. "Sea monsters, insane superconsciousnesses, and monster animals or no. Because a rabbit isn't the same as parents."

"With you a hundred percent on that one, too."

Time to trot around in three different half circles so that we were moving in a serpentine manner—set up this way presumably because Dopey was totally insane—during which time we got to fall down and jump over and around panicked monster animals a lot, do our best not to look at all the sea serpents tracking their potential meals, and I got to listen to "The Long Run" by The Eagles.

We finally reached the laser cannon which was, blessedly, in a big, circular tube-room and which, therefore, meant that the sea serpents were a little farther away. Not far enough away, but then, the next galaxy wouldn't be far enough in my opinion.

There was a timer on the laser cannon. Which was nice. The time on it was, of course, not.

Per whatever timekeeping Dopey was using—be it hours, minutes, seconds, or time as we didn't understand it—we had ninety of them left.

CHAPTER 39

"ANY GUESSES FOR WHAT TO DO?" Jeff asked, as the timer clicked to eighty-nine, thus proving that we'd scored "seconds" versus minutes or hours. This was so par for our particular course that neither one of us commented on it.

"I wish we'd brought Chuckie with us," was my impressive contribution.

The cannon had that timer, but no obvious controls. There was no on/off switch, no burning fuse, and nothing that indicated how it worked. However, it was clear that it was on and preparing to fire, because it was humming in a way that machines will when they're really revving up to go for the gusto.

The section of the Habitrail From Hell that we were in was a big round ball, similar to the big round ball of black water that was, a quick glance its way showed, still boiling with sea serpents. The black water in there might also be boiling in reality. There was clearly a connection between that section of water and the laser cannon, but had no idea what that would be.

"Right now, I wish we'd brought Chuck along, too," Jeff said. "And I'm thinking that we should have let Butler come, because he might have an idea of what the hell we should do with this thing."

"SuperBun?"

He had nothing. The squirrels did most of the work on these things, and none of them were responding to his questions, pleas for help, or even suggestions to run to an elevated platform and get out of here. And Dopey was incommunicado.

My music changed to "Black Water Falls" by The War On Drugs. Didn't have a lot of time to figure this one out, so did what I pretty much always did—went with my best guess and hoped like hell I'd guessed right. Especially since what I was guessing was not going to be good for me, Jeff, and SuperBun in any way, shape, or sinuous sea serpent form.

Pulled my Glock out, aimed at what I was going to think of as the ceiling of this thing until officially told otherwise, and fired.

One shot was all it took, which was worrisome in the sense that I'd have thought that the Habitrail was made from actual impressive materials, not out of the same plastic that regular hamster playgrounds were constructed from. But, since we were now under forty-five seconds, chose not to complain about Dopey's shoddy workmanship and lack of professional pride.

"What the hell?" Jeff asked, as the water sprayed down and whatever the Habitrail was made out of started to crack, letting more water in. "Tell me you know what you're doing, Kitty."

"Um, I think I do. Well, in terms of stopping the laser cannon. In terms of our survival? Not so much." Hoped my Glock didn't count as machinery because I wanted to at least have the means to shoot the sea serpents if necessary.

The water hit the cannon. And the cannon's humming slowed. More water, more slowing, until the humming stopped altogether. The timer stopped, too, at ten seconds.

"Okay," Jeff said, as the water started to come in faster. It wasn't filling up the room because the Habitrail was interconnected, which meant we weren't going to drown. Yet. "That's good, that's very good. So, the question now is, can we outrun the water to get to an elevator?"

"To get to an elevator the water hasn't touched. Per SuperBun and our prime example here, the water destroys machinery."

SuperBun shared that there was one elevator that was protected from the water by a door. The one in Dopey's throne room.

"Of course that's where we have to go," Jeff said, as he took my hand. "Why would we have to go anywhere else?"

"Or we could, you know, just run really fast to the closest elevator that doesn't have water near it yet," Christopher said as he grabbed Jeff and took off at the fastest Flash speeds I'd experienced from him so far.

"You were supposed to get to the ship," I said, managing not to throw up. Adrenaline was sometimes effective even when the Hyperspeed Dramamine had no effect, and my adrenaline was very high at the moment.

"Yeah? I thought about it. Then I decided that I wasn't going to let your kids grow up as orphans, even though I'd be raising them as my own. Call me a reluctant foster father."

We reached the elevator and leaped onto it. It started up right away, though none of us let go of each other. "How do these things work?" I asked as I put my gun back into my purse. "I mean that seriously, because I don't see anything that would tell this thing to go up or down."

"I don't know and I don't care," Christopher replied. "At all. As long as this one keeps on working long enough for us to get out of here."

"Thanks for coming back for us," Jeff said with a great deal of feeling. We did the A-C group hug, but we didn't let it last too long, just in case.

Which proved to be the right choice. There was a loud cracking sound and, as we turned toward it, saw the Habitrail around the laser cannon collapse. The area was instantly filled with water and sea serpents, who started racing through the Habitrail.

We could see all of this because, amazingly, whatever the lights were or were made out of, they were still working, underwater or not. Decided not to ask in case I'd end up hating the answer.

SuperBun shared that they were floating phosphorescence.

Decided I could live with that.

Phosphorescence that, SuperBun added, was harvested from the inside of the sea serpents and had its own form of sentience, albeit a very limited form.

Told SuperBun to stop sharing. "Um, guys? Guess what things seem to have hyperspeed on this planet?"

Interestingly enough, all the sea serpents ignored all the elephants, horses, and squirrels as if they weren't there. Possibly because they were on a mission. Two missions, really.

One group was heading for the big circular area that held what looked like the nastiest sea serpents, the boiling around ones. And, once there, they started slamming themselves against the Habitrail walls. This boded. But not as much as what the second group was doing. Because the second group was all about heading right for us.

They weren't as fast as Christopher, thankfully, but they were still going a lot faster than the Slowest Elevator Platform in the World that we were on. Now that I could see what really was there, the cavern wasn't nearly as gigantic as it had seemed on the way down. No, the elevator platforms were just unbelievably slow. Since there was no one to complain to about this huge design flaw, though, refrained from pointing it out.

Besides, I was far too busy huddling next to Jeff and Christopher, while watching the Habitrail From Hell become the Pieces of Random Junk and Debris Floating In Scary Black Water, and hoping that the sea serpents didn't find our part of the Habitrail any time soon.

No sooner asked for than denied. Watched as a particularly nasty looking sea serpent began to follow the path we'd taken to get here, water rushing along with it to fill what was left of the Habitrail tubes. Looked up. We were still far away from the top. Thankfully, all the other platforms seemed to have made it to the surface with their passengers, because I could see many of them lowering without anyone still along for the ride.

"How much longer to get up, do you figure?" Jeff asked tightly.

"Too long," Christopher replied. "These go up faster than they go down, for whatever reason, but that thing's going to find us before we're close enough to the top to jump for it."

Water was coming in from pretty much all sides. The tube we were in was still intact, but the lower part started to fill up. And that meant the platform began to slow down, which, considering how slowly it was going already, should have been impossible, but wasn't.

My music changed to "Smasher/Destroyer" by Fear Factory. "Guys, hang on."

Jeff grabbed my hand and Christopher's, Christopher grabbed my free hand. Just in time. The sea serpent—helped by water rushing into this area—sailed straight up the tube and slammed its face into the bottom of the platform.

The good part was that we went sailing upward at a much faster rate than the platform had probably ever gone in its entire existence. We flew out into the sunlight and, due to the speed the sea serpent had been going and the force of the hit, we went pretty high up into the air—a hundred feet high if we were a foot sort of high.

Got a good view of the planet. There was a lot of grass here, but there were other things, too, all manner of flora and fauna. And everything that was part of the planet was black. Not a dead black, though. This black looked alive, more alive and more real than any of the elephants, horses, or squirrels did.

Would have wondered how Dopey had managed to make this planet look bright green even from space, but the bad part was that the sea serpent pushed with its jaws at the last moment and sent the platform spinning, meaning we were now tumbling in the air with nothing to stand on or protect us in any way.

The worse part was that Gravity was calling, and it wanted its rules back.

But the very worst part was that, as I spun over and around, my purse opened and SuperBun flew out of it. Straight for the opened jaws of the sea serpent.

CHAPTER 40

"N O!" I SCREAMED, as SuperBun let loose with a rabbit's shriek of terror. It was the first sound I'd heard him make and it was looking like it would be the last, too.

But then there was another shriek. And this wasn't one of fear. Or being made by a rabbit. This shriek was the shriek of a pissed-off protector about to kick butt.

Bruno and Ginger appeared in the air near SuperBun. Bruno had Ginger in his claws just like they'd done on Beta Eight and during Operation Epidemic. She was snarling and had all her claws out, on all four paws.

Bruno dropped Ginger into the sea serpent's open maw and caught SuperBun in the next moment. The sea serpent's jaws snapped shut, just missing Bruno and SuperBun.

Wasn't sure if this was an improvement—losing SuperBun wasn't what I wanted, but losing Ginger was just as bad. Worse, because she'd been with us longer.

Poofs poured out of my purse, but they did so intentionally. They all went large and hit the ground first, so that Jeff, Christopher, and I landed on a Poof Stunt Airbag.

As I slid down to the ground, watched the sea serpent. It was still relatively straight in the air and starting to go straight down, back into the tube and the black water. With my pet, the pet who had insisted on leaving her home planet to come with me, inside of it.

Started to run toward the monster. Had no idea what I was going to do, but it wasn't getting to have Ginger. Even if she was already dead she was still coming home with me. My music changed to "Just Stop" by Disturbed, but I wasn't listening. I was getting Ginger, period.

Jeff tackled me. "Stop, Kitty!" We rolled on the ground, him shielding me with his body. Then he got us up onto our feet and dragged me back to the Poofs. "I can feel again, baby. It's okay—"

He was interrupted by a new shriek, this one from the sea serpent. It was a loud, horrific sound, and it also sounded like a death scream. One could but hope.

As we watched, it slivered, just like something was slicing it from the inside. An ocellar with claws sharp enough to cut through body armor, perhaps.

The sea serpent turned into sushi in less time than it took for it to fall to the ground. Bruno swooped over, dropped SuperBun into my arms, then flew back toward the Sea Serpent Sushi. He reached it just as Ginger sliced through the tail end and he caught her before she fell into the hole.

Bruno booked it back to us, dropped Ginger into Jeff's arms, then landed in Christopher's. Christopher hugged him, which was kind of shocking—Christopher and the Peregrines rarely got along all that well. "This is one hell of a bird," Christopher said. Bruno cawed appreciatively.

"And this remains the greatest cat in the galaxy," Jeff said as he pulled out the wipes that all A-Cs carried in case an imageer or empath touched something that made them feel beyond icky and used them to wipe Ginger down. Ginger purred her appreciation.

"You guys are the most amazing animals in the galaxy!" Cuddled SuperBun, who was shivering uncontrollably, while I gave Bruno a serious scritchy-scratch between his wings and, once her face was cleaned off, Ginger a lot of kisses. Bruno got some, too. As did SuperBun, who was starting to recover but shared that he never wanted to do that ever again. Ginger and Bruno, on the other hand, were prepared to take on all sea serpent comers.

Then it was time to thank and pet all the Poofs. This took a while. All of Iron Maiden's "The Thin Line Between Love And Hate," which was a pretty long song.

Looked around—no sign of our shuttle. Hoped that was a good news thing.

During our love fest with the animals, we were joined by Siler and Wruck, who did Siler's Patented Appearing Out Of Nowhere Act. But they weren't alone. They had Dopey and who I assumed was Grumpy—based on her looking like the other, ragged half of Dopey, but also like half of Mrs. Claus, versus Santa—with them. Dopey looked even worse for wear than I'd seen previously. Good.

Wruck was in full Anciannas form—taller than normal, a little less average, a little more unformed, but somehow beautiful in a way that remained hard for a human to describe. He looked like humanity, all of humanity, while still looking like himself, only more so. And he glowed, just a bit. And, as that special, finishing touch, he had wings.

He was also righteously and furiously angry. He looked like the descriptions of Biblical angels who were about to rain down fire and wrath. His wings were fully extended and bristling, his countenance was dark, his eyes flashing, and the glow around him was flickering in a way that suggested said glow was about to become real flame. It was impressive, as long as it wasn't turned on me.

Which it wasn't. Wruck was giving the full Anciannas Blast O' Rage to Dopey and Grumpy. Who were cringing.

Couldn't blame them on the one hand, but on the other, these were superconsciousnesses and they shouldn't have been afraid of a physical being like Wruck. But they were, clearly. They were easily as frightened of him as we'd been of the sea serpents.

"How dare you allow this, any of this, to happen?" Wruck thundered. "This is the opposite of what you were charged to do, and you have destroyed not one but two worlds in the process. And you were about to destroy all of existence. For your petty arguments and ridiculous fight for supremacy."

Dopey and Grumpy were whining about how they had the right to do whatever, which wasn't making Wruck look any happier. Had a feeling that he really wanted to smite them both, and also had a feeling that he probably could do it.

There was something about this that had been bothering me for a while, but I still couldn't put my finger on what was wrong.

My music changed to "Is It My Body" by Alice Cooper and all of a sudden, what was going on dawned on me. Better late than never.

It all clicked—the weirdness of everything, the destruction, the lack of focus and planning, the general situation. It was because of one simple, but major, thing. "They aren't superconsciousnesses anymore. That's the problem. They became real in a physical sense."

Everyone looked at me, Dopey and Grumpy, too. They looked pretty awful but they also had a look I was familiar with—they looked guilty, like they'd been caught breaking the rules and were hoping to get out of it somehow, probably by blaming the other.

Dopey opened his mouth. Put up the paw. He shut his mouth. Wow. The One True FLOTUS Power even worked on beings like this. Had to love it.

"Dopey, you will not speak. Grumpy, you won't, either. Your excuses are likely just as lame as his."

"I wasn't attacking the planet," she said sullenly. "I was trying to save the creatures."

"Uh huh. I'd believe that, but the only creatures saved were the rabbits, and that was by us. So, nice try. I meant it, shut up. I'm not talking to you, I'm telling the others what's going on."

"How would *you* know?" Grumpy asked, even more sullenly.

It had been a long, stressful day, and she wasn't Lizzie, aka someone I loved and did my best to be a good surrogate mom to. My temper snapped. Plus, my music changed to "Parents Just Don't Understand" by Will Smith, from back when he'd been the Fresh Prince and hanging out with DJ Jazzy Jeff. Which seemed kind of like permission from Algar. At least, that was how I was gonna take it.

"You, young lady, will speak when spoken to," I snarled at Grumpy. "How would *I* know? I *named* you. I *created* you. Therefore, I *know* you. And I know what you are, what you've done. You changed yourselves into something that's not what you were originally. It's a form that's not mortal, but it's also corporeal, versus the formless spirits like you were originally. You haven't combined cohesively and, because of that, you're both incomplete and, worse, you don't have your powers anymore, so you can't actually fix any of the mess you've made."

They both gaped at me, which was weird to see, since each of them only had half a mouth.

"What do you mean by two worlds?" Jeff asked.

"This one and the one our other shuttle took a look at. Tim said that Cameron felt it had been recently destroyed. It's the nearest thing to this one, so either it's this planet's moon or vice versa."

Siler nodded. "Maurer said it looked like it had been hit by nuclear blasts."

"Wonderful," Jeff growled. "Start talking."

"They're sister planets," Grumpy said, but far less sullenly. "They orbit the sun but also orbit each other."

"This one is a black world somehow. Everything on it's black because of the water. The other world, was it green once?"

She nodded. "When we . . . fought . . ." They both looked even guiltier.

"The sea serpents, are they the indigenous creatures of this world?" Wruck thundered, sounding even angrier than he had before.

"Yes," Dopey admitted. "Only them."

"Yeah, I freaking guessed, you Earth animal stealers. Don't even get me started on what you did to the elephants, horses, and squirrels, you sick bastards. I should let our resident Avenging Angel destroy you for what you did to those innocent creatures, let alone what you did to the sea serpents. I may be terrified of them, but it's *their* world and you stole it from them and enslaved them to boot! You know what we call people like that? We call them oppressors, dictators, and all-around crappy people. But we sure as hell don't call them benevolent."

"Dear Enemy" by The Exies came on. So I was kind of prepared for attack, as Siler looked behind me and stiffened in a way I knew meant he was ready to start shooting or even possibly running. Anything scaring the Assassin Supreme was probably really frightening. Meaning we likely had another sea serpent leaping out of the water, because it could never be easy or else the cosmos would, apparently, dissolve in a burst of light or something. And even then, figured we'd be forced to fix it. But I wasn't bitter. Much.

"We can save them," a deep voice with a lot of force and carrying power said from behind us, interrupting my nonbitterness. "The other creatures. We can make them what they should be."

We all turned to see a sea serpent head bobbing just by where Ginger had made sushi of the one that had tried to eat us.

"Um . . ." Wondered if it was time to run like hell or not. Hoped not. These pumps were not made for all the action I was putting them through.

"I am the ruler of our people," the sea serpent went on. "You may call me Hixxx."

"Hixxx, I'm the leader of our people," Jeff said, Commander Voice on Full. "I apologize for our killing one of yours."

"It was in self-defense," Hixxx said. "We thought you were

like them," he nodded his head toward Dopey and Grumpy, "here to harm us. But after hearing your distress about how we have been treated, we realized that you are not. I would speak with your leader." Jeff took a step forward. Hixxx laughed. It was pretty hissy, but not as bad as it could have been. "I mean her," he nodded toward me, "your mate. It is clear who wears the scales."

"I love that term! And I'm Kitty." Took Jeff's hand. "But we do try to do it together."

"As you will. I must submerge and will be right back."

"Thanks, baby," Jeff said. "I'm not even feeling emasculated. Much."

"Any time," I said, as we went over to where we'd just escaped from only a few minutes earlier. "And you're still the hottest thing on two legs, Jeff, and, trust me, also the most male, so no worries."

He grinned. "Good to know."

CHAPTER 41

WE REACHED THE EDGE. There was black water all the way up to the land now, and I couldn't spot any of the Habitrail. Not that I was trying too hard to look. Most of me wanted to run away. But I didn't, even though Hixxx was, for me, a giant version of my biggest pathological fear. I went because Hixxx was sentient and that's what you did—you met with the sentient beings and tried to work things out, regardless of what they looked like.

Oh, sure, I had a death grip on Jeff's hand, but that was to be expected. Even managed not to scream when Hixxx re-emerged, to "King of the Night Time World" by Kiss. Algar was clearly on his soundtrack portion of the festivities. Oh well, at least he was enjoying himself. Someone should be.

"You say you can fix the animals?" Jeff asked, once Hixxx's head was fully out of the water.

"Yes. We have a healing area deep in our waters that can return the wounded to how they were prior. It cannot work on mortal wounds, but the animals still have their insides intact, they are just in the wrong places. By doing this, however, they will become one with our planet, and will not be able to return to yours. But it is the only way to save them from what has been done."

"I don't know how they'd survive on Earth, after what was done to them," I said. "Will your water affect us negatively?"

"Not to our knowledge. It might make you stronger in any telepathic gifts you possess, as it did with him." He looked at SuperBun, who I was still holding in my free arm. "But it will not harm any living thing. That is why the other animals, the ones so distorted, still live—they have our water sustaining them."

"Well, that's good to know. And, by the way, something to probably not share with the cosmos at large." Resolved to ensure that we put some kind of protection on this planet, so others couldn't come and steal the black water and the sea serpents, or worse. "But then, why does the water affect machinery negatively?"

"We are not sure. The supposition is that the water contains the remains of all of my people within it. We think that we must possess something within us that negatively affects nonorganic things that move, versus nonorganic things that do not move. Beyond that, we have had no time for study, due to those." He nodded his head toward Dopey and Grumpy.

"Our shuttle's toast then," I told Jeff. "It got drenched." Still didn't see it anywhere, but maybe that meant it had dissolved or something.

"No," Hixxx said. "For whatever reason, we have found that we do not affect ships that fly. Again, we have had too few examples and no time for study. Now that we are freed, however, and know of the greater galaxy around us, we will begin that study in earnest."

"Did Dopey teach you?" This seemed unlikely though possible.

Hixxx did his hissy laugh. "No. You did. Your arrival, all that you all spoke of. We understood you and understood there was much out there that we have no knowledge of. The few visitors we have had now make sense to us, as does all that has happened. We are unlikely to reach other planets, seeing as we must breathe our water to survive. But the knowledge that they are there is . . . quite wonderful, really."

"Don't bet on not going. We have friends who've figured out how to help their very large underwater friends to travel on land and through space. I'm sure they could help your people to do so, too."

"We will welcome any friends of yours, and take their assistance gladly," Hixxx said.

"And we'll ensure we have safeguards so you can be sure they're really our friends, too." Once I was home, in addition to ensuring that Chuckie created a really great sign, countersign, counter-counter sign, and special secret handshake for this planet, I was going to make an official Galactic Decree that said that this planet was under Earth and Alpha Four's protection. And then ensure we had a lot of Alpha Four battlecruisers hanging about in their solar space, whether or not that annoyed their not-so-helpful Nebula Neighbors. If, you know, we ever got home.

"We might be able to determine what's in the water that causes only some machines to malfunction, too," Jeff said. "But it would take time and require that you allow people from outside your world to be here and study you."

"Which they'd have to do in order to help you travel out of the water, anyway."

"We are likely to agree," Hixxx said. "Now that we know there is a greater galaxy out there, we would like to become a part of it."

My music changed to "Forest for the Trees" by Huey Lewis & the News. Nice to know Algar wanted to be sure I wasn't forgetting something. "What about the tree people?"

"I do not know who you mean," Hixxx said.

"They're originally from your sister planet," Jeff said. "It would be the celestial body you see the most easily, after your sun."

Realized that while we were all okay, these other beings weren't. "Hixxx, we need to determine what happened to them—another indigenous people that Dopey and Grumpy affected, most likely negatively."

"I understand. I must submerge again. Go deal with that, I will return shortly."

Jeff and I used hyperspeed to get back to the others. Noted that most of our away team wasn't here, which was kind of a relief—someone had listened to us, potentially for the first time ever, telling them to get out of here. However and in a total Shocker Alert Moment, Tim, Reader, and Chuckie had ignored those orders and were now with Christopher, Siler, Wruck, and the Sick Santa Duo. Once we were back, the Poofs went small and all piled into my purse. Didn't feel any heavier.

"Everyone else is back on the ship," Reader said. "We wanted to be sure we had people up there ready to shoot or fly down, as needed. Or just hang out and ensure that the ship's repaired sooner as opposed to later."

"Even Richard?" Wasn't used to White willingly sitting things out these days.

Reader nodded. "He wanted to be sure that the rabbits didn't cause issues. Plus, I don't think the rest of the team would have left if he hadn't gone—everyone wanted to remain until Richard pointed out that you guys would probably need aerial support."

"Besides," Chuckie added, "there were a lot of bunnies that needed help running for the shuttles. On the plus side, the ship has enough shuttles that a full evacuation of all personnel and passengers is possible, even if quarters were at capacity. So, we got a few more down here to do evacuation."

"Good thinking, especially on the getting out of here. Ten minutes ago, everyone still being here would have made us very upset. Now, it just means fewer people to brief at this moment and more to brief later." Donned my Recap Girl cape and did a fast update. "So, we now want to know what happened to the tree people. Grumpy, you're up."

"I moved them. For their safety."

"Moved them where?" Jeff asked, not all that nicely.

"We got most of the story while you were talking to the King of the Sea Serpents," Tim said. "Once Grumpy and Dopey combined, they decided to go save the galaxy, one system at a time. So, they started close to home. There were only two planets with life, this one and its sister. The sister had the tree people on it. This one has the sea serpents. Grumpy liked the tree people, Dopey didn't. Dopey liked the sea serpents, Grumpy didn't. They fought about how to help the two planets, but couldn't agree."

"So they ripped themselves apart," Reader finished, sarcasm knob set to well past eleven, "and then decided to try to destroy the others' preferred people. Dopey initially created the whatever you were in—"

"I thought of it as the Habitrail From Hell."

"Totally fitting, girlfriend. Anyway, supposedly that was made to protect the sea serpents. While he was, you know, raining down fire on the tree people."

"I managed to get them to the next nearest planet," Grumpy said. "But they can't survive there too much longer. The soil is wrong and the air is worse."

"Then take them home," Jeff said. "Put them back where they were."

"We can't," Chuckie said.

"Excuse me?" Jeff asked. "Why not?"

Chuckie sighed. "Grumpy and Dopey destroyed that planet. It's a lifeless husk now. The only planet in this system left that has and is likely capable of sustaining life is this one. And that's not all."

"Oh, I can't wait," Jeff said. "What's the rest, Chuck?"

"The rest is *our* real problem," Chuckie said. "As in the problem for all of us on the *Distant Voyager*. If this world is a black world, and the world that the tree people are from is now a dead world, how do we get the one thing we desperately need in order to get out of here? How do we get chlorophyll?"

CHAPTER 42

WE ALL STARED AT each other for a few long seconds. Then I looked down. "SuperBun? You told us there was chlorophyll."

SuperBun admitted that he'd also lied about this. Though he'd thought that Dopey could have provided what we'd wanted. Possibly.

Saw some angry expressions. "He's a freaking rabbit and he was trying to protect his people while also not letting Dopey kill us. Back off on the glaring. Christopher, that goes triple for you."

"Whatever," Christopher muttered. "Sorry that Chuck's really good point stressed me out."

"We need to deal with the tree people first," Jeff said firmly. "Once they're taken care of, then we can worry about ourselves."

Felt all kinds of proud. Despite what Hixxx might think, Jeff was definitely and always the right leader for the job, whatever that job might be.

"They have no world," Chuckie said. "And taking them onto our ship isn't going to help them, either."

"Then bring them here," Hixxx said as he rejoined the air breathers. We didn't need to move closer—his voice definitely carried and it was clear he could hear all of us easily. "See if our soil will accommodate. If not, if they drink of our water, they will become one with our planet."

"Is that true for everyone?" I asked. "Because while none of us have drunk any, I don't think, we *have* been drenched by watering elephants, and I know the rabbits have had to drink the water here to survive. Does that mean we can't leave?"

"No," Hixxx said. "It means that you can come here easily, and live here, if you need to."

"Thank you," Jeff said. "While I hope that none of us will be in that situation, we appreciate the offer. My people were refugees—to have any world open itself to others is a wonderful thing."

"It is the right thing," Hixxx said. "To offer welcome. Not to be invaded."

"Speaking of invaders, Dopey, why didn't you mess with the rabbits like you did the other Earth animals?"

He muttered something.

"What?" I asked. "Didn't catch that."

"They were Grumpy's favorites and I . . . I didn't want to hurt them."

She looked at him in surprise, which, on half a face, was weird to see. "You did that . . . for me?"

"Yes," he admitted. "I . . . I'm sorry. I've . . . missed you."

She took his hand in hers. "I've missed you, too."

My music changed to "Two Hearts Beat as One" by U2, but I'd already figured it out. Finally. "Good! Then let's get these two crazy kids back together."

This earned me shocked looks from everyone. "May I ask why you feel this is a good idea?" Hixxx asked, clearly speaking for everyone.

"Because they aren't whole. They aren't superconsciousnesses anymore, but they aren't people, either. People have a hard time functioning without half of themselves. And, while I'm sure they were meddling when they were whole and as one, the real problems started when they split. Get them joined again, see the normal version of this combination come back, and then it can help, versus hinder or harm."

"We do not trust them," Hixxx said. "I am sure you can understand why."

"I can, indeed. Which is why you're not going to have to police them. Yo, Sandy! I know you're out there watching us, dude. Time to make the grand appearance and all that jazz."

Sure enough, there was a whirling around us and Sandy formed. "You called, Kitty?"

"I did. We've solved most of your little problem here. Now we need you to help out and help us fix the last parts."

He opened his mouth, to protest most likely. Put up the paw.

He closed his mouth. No matter what, the One True FLOTUS Power was awesome.

"You and yours will help rejoin Grumpy and Dopey. You and yours will, without fuss, muss, or stalling, transport all the tree people from wherever the hell Grumpy stashed them to this planet, immediately. You and yours will ensure that said tree people can and are willing to join with Hixxx and his people. If they are not willing, then you and yours will figure out how to revive their planet and put them back."

"Or else," Jeff added calmly, but with a lot of threat lurking. I totally approved.

"The planet cannot be revived," Sandy said sadly. "It is merely a ball of rock now. In time, it will be considered this planet's moon. But life will never find a way there again."

"Then it's 'make sure the tree people like it here or else' for all of you."

"You threaten us?" Sandy sounded amused.

I wasn't. "I do. All of you could have stopped this. Hell, *one* of you could have stopped this. But you didn't. And then, when it was all going totally sideways, you forced me and mine to handle it. Well, guess what? We did. And we're *pissed*. You have a freaking *obligation* to keep your nebula alive. *You* do, not us. But you're all so hands-off that you abdicated that responsibility. At least Grumpy and Dopey were trying. They muffed it, like children can without adult supervision or assistance. But they had as much chance of succeeding as failing, and, again, at least they tried. Now it's up to you, as the adults, to fix it. Not to claim that you had nothing to do with the situation. Grumpy and Dopey are yours. Ipso facto don't piss me off anymore-o, you will fix or you will pay. And, by now, I *do* know how to make you pay."

He tried the stare-off. It should have been harder to win, but it wasn't. Sandy looked down. "Yes, you're right."

What might have been an all-green oak tree with legs, arms, and a sorta face appeared with us. It was far less humanoid than the Faradawn, whom we'd first met during Operation Immigration. The Faradawn were treelike people—very treelike but still more humanoid than arboreal. This was a tree—with roots, branches, bark, and leaves—that sorta looked like a person. Said tree also looked shocked. Sandy touched it, and it didn't look shocked anymore. Apparently he had the Recap Touch. Handy.

"I am Neela," she said, sounding a little creaky but otherwise quite pretty. "I lead our people. I understand that our brother planet offers us haven?"

Hixxx nodded. "We do. We hope that you can find our world hospitable."

My music changed to KT Tunstall's "Black Horse & The Cherry Tree" and I mentally thanked Algar for keeping it light.

"May I?" she asked.

"Of course."

Neela sank her roots into the ground and closed her eyes. "Your water is . . . supercharged." Her eyes opened. "Your magic is within it."

"If that is what you call it, yes. Our essence is within it. We live and die in our water. Will it harm you?"

"No, I believe it will strengthen us. I can but hope that what we return to the soil and the air will strengthen you." She extended a branch to Hixxx. Since Hixxx was at least fifty yards away, this was impressive.

He took her branch in his mouth, but gently. Then he released it. "I believe that you will cause no harm and may, in fact, help us to strengthen as well."

"Super. Sandy, make it so. Get all of Neela's people here, pronto."

He nodded and suddenly we had a forest around us. "They are all here."

"Great. Um, it's a little crowded."

Neela laughed. It sounded like wind in leaves. "We will move over the world and spread out, with our hosts' permission."

"Not your hosts," Hixxx said. "Your family." He looked at me. "The other animals, will they harm our new brethren?"

"Not in any real way. They eat grass and nuts and things, but while a full-sized elephant can wrench a tree out of the ground, they'd need a reason to do so. They also don't eat each other— they're all herbivores."

"In case you are concerned," Hixxx said, "my people, despite all our teeth, are not meat eaters. Our food sources just require teeth such as ours in order to excavate the edible portions from their shells."

"Lobsters and oysters and such?"

"No, we have nothing like those here. Edible rocks would be a better description, along with other water-based plants."

Didn't sound good to me, but Hixxx probably wasn't going

to think a steak sounded tasty, either. "Different strokes and all that."

"If you say so. I must submerge. I will return soon, with the other animals. Sister Neela, advise me or one of my people should these animals cause any of your people pain."

"I will." She looked at me as Hixxx went under. "These others, these herbivores, what else do they eat?"

"Ummm . . . Chuckie, you're up."

He laughed. "I can advise you. None of them eat trees."

She shook her leaves. "That is not my concern. I wish to provide what sustenance they need. We can create other aspects of ourselves. Nonsentient aspects," she added, presumably to the looks of horror that were on most of our faces.

"Sounds good since it no longer sounds like cannibalism or the offering of babies for slaughter."

Neela laughed again. "No, we would never condone that." She made some movements with her branches and the other tree people started moving out, presumably to find the places they wanted to plant themselves. Literally.

"This is awfully easy," Reader said quietly. "The easiest detente I think we've ever had."

"I think it's because both leaders aren't warlike," Jeff said. "Neela's people were frightened, Hixxx's were angry, but mostly they just want to live in peace. They're both homogenous races, with almost no friction that I've picked up."

"Wow, peaceful races? We need to make hella sure this planet is protected." Resolved to get that Galactic Decree sent via whatever means Mother could manage. This place needed protecting sooner than whenever we got back. My music changed to the Eurythmics' "I Saved the World Today," which was nice to hear, both sonically and because I hoped this was Algar telling me that it was all going to work out on Planet Black.

"I agree," Jeff said. "Speaking of which, what's this planet called?"

"We called it Night World," Neela said. Well, kinda close to Planet Black. "And our world Tropea. But I do not know what Brother Hixxx calls his home."

Looked at Dopey. "Did you ever ask him?"

"No," Dopey admitted.

"Typical," Tim muttered.

SuperBun shared that Hixxx called this world Nazez. I shared that with the others.

"What do you call yourselves?" I asked Neela. "And Super-Bun, feel free to chime in with what Hixxx's people call themselves."

"We are the Dawar," Neela said.

Per SuperBun, the sea serpents were the Ezkot.

"Good names, and we'll have them added to the Galactic Register, which actually exists, lucky all of us. Now for Grumpy and Dopey."

"No," Chuckie said firmly. "Now for us."

CHAPTER 43

CHUCKIE SIGHED AT OUR expressions. "Really? You've all forgotten this soon? Chlorophyll. We need it, or we're going to have to take Hixxx up on his offer—and there are a lot of carnivores on the ship. I'm not sure how well we'll all do with a grass-only diet."

SuperBun didn't like where this was going, since we'd shared that we ate rabbits.

"Some people. Some people eat rabbit." I did, for example. Though, now that I had Peter and SuperBun, realized I was never eating a rabbit again. "We don't eat our pets."

"Unless we're starving," Christopher said.

"You're not helping," Jeff told him.

"But I believe that we can," Neela said. "We have that element inside of us."

"But it could hurt you to give it to us," Chuckie said. "And that goes against what we believe."

Neela shook her leaves. "No. It will not harm us. This planet also has chlorophyll. Theirs is even more powerful than ours."

"Is that possible?" Reader asked.

Chuckie shrugged. "It's a big old galaxy. So, sure, why not?"

Tim was on his phone. "Yes, one shuttle, please, it should be enough. And Drax, too, since we have a source of chlorophyll but not the means of extraction. Thanks." He hung up. "They'll be here shortly."

"Meaning, we're back to the Grumpy and Dopey Show."

Sandy sighed. "They should return to be as they were."

"They can't," Chuckie said. "Just look at them. If they could have, they already would have."

"Unless they're faking," Christopher, our current Designated Downer, muttered.

Had to admit, Grumpy and Dopey were not looking impressive or powerful in any way. Wondered for a moment if Christopher was right, though, if it was an act. Then reminded myself that they were, literally, half of themselves and that the sooner we got them fixed, the better, for everyone.

"Their powers are gone. They're still powerful, but no longer like they were. And the longer you wait to join them, the weaker they're going to get." Looked at the two of them. "You guys need to stop pretending to be mythical Earth figures."

"We chose a benevolent image," Dopey said. "Because that's what we want to be."

"And yet, the first thing you guys did was fight."

They both looked down. "We failed," Grumpy said.

"Yes, you did. It happens. It happens to humans all the time. We manage to find the will to go on. But the biggest issue was that you went about this the wrong way. Look, stop trying to imitate someone or something, anything, else. Be what the two of *you* want to be. Not what you think you should be, but what you actually want to be. Together. Discuss it between the two of you. Do it in the superfast superconsciousness way that I'm hoping you still can or that Sandy can help you with. But figure out it before Hixxx is back."

"Why so fast?" Sandy asked.

"Because I have another appointment to keep that all your crap has made me late for and I and my people would like to get on the road again, so to speak. Sooner as opposed to later."

Jeff grinned. "And what the one who wears the scales says, goes."

Rolled my eyes. "I say let's get this all taken care of pronto. We have promises to keep."

"And miles to go before we sleep," Chuckie added with a laugh.

"When would you like the chlorophyll?" Neela asked politely. "Since I have promised, too."

"Whenever it's convenient for you to provide it," Jeff replied.

"Though now would be great," Chuckie added.

"Then now it will be." Neela called a few other Dawar over, and Dopey, Grumpy, and Sandy got ready to do their thing, whatever that thing might be.

While we waited for the shuttle to arrive, Algar put Willie Nelson's "On the Road Again" onto my airwaves, Jeff, Chuckie, Tim, and Reader made scales jokes, Christopher spent time glaring at a variety of things because he never wanted to be out of practice, and I pulled our group aside so we could fill each other in on whatever we'd missed, which I was hoping wasn't a lot but probably was something vital. Realized I was doing the Debby Downer thing now and decided to vote for hoping for the positive spin.

"We got all the rabbits up to the ship," Tim said, once he was done cracking wise. "Some went in the shuttles with people but, fortunately, we were able to just pack them like Themnir into some of the shuttles. Airborne handled most of that, with Butler and Maurer helping. Butler's the one bringing Drax and the shuttle."

"Look at you, Mister Man of the Galaxy, using Themnir instead of sardines as your example. I'm so proud."

"Yeah, well, the Themnir arrived alive and sardines pack in dead. I went for the positive spin. Speaking of positive, are you absolutely sure they're trustworthy? And before you say yes, remember that you weren't the one they were chasing with their big nasty teeth and sharp claws."

"They were trying to get more space vehicles down here so everyone could escape."

"Yeah, we figured it out when they erupted out of the ground and ran for the shuttle," Reader said. "It was a clue."

"Why so testy, James? Too much caffeine?"

He gave me a shot of the cover boy grin. "Nope, I'm just glad that we have room on the *Distant Voyager* for them. Unless they want to stay now that things are calmed down."

SuperBun shared that his people wanted off this rock forever. Space sounded better than what they'd been through. He also mentioned that all of them were what humans would consider domesticated by now—even the ones who'd been wild when taken were so grateful to be away from Dopey and Grumpy and this planet of terror that they were pro anyone and everyone on the *Distant Voyager*, now and forever, and if that meant they were pets, then they'd be pets that didn't have to worry about being turned into terrifying monsters, and that was a bit of all right for all of them.

Once translated, everyone agreed that rabbits were great as

pets and not as food, and they could stay. Felt SuperBun finally relax.

Hixxx returned to the tune of "Union" by The Black Eyed Peas and with another eruption of animals. "Horses, elephants, and squirrels, oh my. And, thank God, they look normal again."

We had African and Asian elephants, every type and color of horse, and every type and color of squirrel, too. It was interesting—as with the rabbits, which ran the gamut, Dopey and Grumpy had clearly only been selective in terms of the general idea of these animals. Otherwise, if you wanted a black draft horse or an Appaloosa, or anything in between, you had it. It was impressive in that, per SuperBun, they'd cloned most of the horses.

The squirrels ran for trees in that squirrel way—run fast, stop, look around, run, stop, look around, reach a tree, climb it. The Dawar seemed to have no issues with the squirrels at all. I heard a lot of tree people giggling, which sounded like leaves shaking, but it was a nice sound. Heard happy squirrel chittering, which was a far nicer sound, especially having heard the unhappy squirrel chittering not all that long ago.

The horses whinnied at everyone, then galloped off in several herds. Figured they just wanted to run for a bit and feel like themselves, and who could blame them?

The elephants, however, came over to us, the ones with the largest tusks in the lead. SuperBun shared that elephants were already hella intelligent and the black water had made them more so.

The lead African and Asian elephants bowed their heads to us. We bowed back. Then they walked off. The rest of their elephants followed suit. This took quite a while—Hixxx had to submerge at least six times, the shuttle arrived, Butler and Drax got introduced to Neela, Drax and Neela started the Chlorophyll Draining Process, and Algar had time to play all of Elefant's "The Black Magic Show" album—but I didn't regret it.

The elephants were talking to me the whole time, thanking us for saving them from their personal hell. They'd known and understood all that had happened to them and the others, had understood what the mad scientist had planned to do to the sun, had even understood that another world had already been destroyed, but had been powerless to stop any of it. And they appreciated how angry this made me, because they had given up hope, but we'd shown them that there was still good in the world.

"I'm proud of you," Jeff said softly to me as the last elephants moved on. "I can hear the animals through your mind now, baby, and I can also feel how so much of you just wants to shred Dopey and Grumpy to bits. But you're not going to do that or allow it, and that's what true leaders, good leaders, do."

Leaned against him. "I hope you're right. I hope *I'm* right—that they'll actually have learned from this and be able to do good, versus evil, now. I want a *Dark Crystal* ending for them and this world, not *The Fly*."

My music changed to "Crystal Baller" by Third Eye Blind. Really hoped this was a positive sign from Algar, but didn't bet on it, just because I hated giving the cosmos that much of an opening and invitation.

"We're about to find out." Jeff put his arm around me and we walked back to where Sandy, Grumpy, and Dopey were. Everyone else on our team gathered 'round, animals, too—the Poofs came out of my purse for this, though they all stayed small, Christopher was still holding Bruno, and Siler was carrying Ginger—and Wruck went back to his human form. Some of the elephants, horses, squirrels, Dawar, and Ezkot came over to watch as well—sea serpent heads sticking out of the holes that had been elevator shafts—in addition to Hixxx and Neela.

"They have chosen," Sandy said.

Noted that there was a lot of extra swirling around. "The rest of the Seven Dwarfs in attendance?"

"They are. They are not forming, however." Sandy looked like he was trying not to laugh. "They don't want you to give them additional names."

"Probably a wise choice. So, speaking of choices, what's it going to be?" I asked Dopey and Grumpy.

They took each other's hand and melted together. Literally. It was kind of cool but also kind of gross, but there weren't fluids involved, so it was less gross than it could have been. It was also interesting, in the way that all things like this could be. Algar graced me with Bowling for Soup's version of "I Melt With You" and I managed not to laugh.

The other superconsciousnesses, other than Sandy, were swirling around them, doing something, though it was impossible to see what, exactly. They were mostly opaque while swirling for this, so it was hard to see much.

It took longer than I'd expected—a good five minutes, during which I got to listen to Megadeth's "United Abominations" and really hope Algar was being funny versus prophetic—before the swirling stopped. The superconsciousnesses went back to clear-swirly versus foggy-swirly, and what was now Dopey and Grumpy was here, for all the world to see.

Definitely not what I'd been expecting.

CHAPTER 44

GRUMPY AND DOPEY HAD chosen to become a rabbit.

A giant rabbit, at least compared to SuperBun—frankly, as compared to anyone other than the bigger guys with us—but a rabbit nonetheless. One that stood upright and whose front paws were a lot more like hands and all that, but still somehow managed to be adorable, possibly because it had fluffy fur and floppy ears. Even with large claws and big, sharp teeth it was adorbs.

There were a few moments of stunned silence from everyone. Even Sandy looked shocked, and the other superconsciousnesses were swirling in a way that indicated shock to me as well. They'd definitely made an entrance.

The Dopey-Grumpy Bunny looked worried. Realized that now wasn't the time for criticism. Didn't even need the song cue of "Hip Hop Lover" by En Vogue in order to catch this clue.

"I love it," I said with the same level of enthusiasm I used when one of the kids made and gave me something.

The Dopey-Grumpy Bunny relaxed. "Really?" The voice didn't sound distinctly male or female or animal, even. But it wasn't unpleasant, just different, in the same way that Wruck was different in true Anciannas form.

"Yes," I said firmly. "What made you choose this form?"

"Rabbits are Gr-, ah, our favorite. And they are cute and can be brave and protective, too."

"Well put, Harvey."

The rabbit blinked. "Is that our name now? It sounds . . . male."

"It can be. It can be anything you want it to be. But in the movie, *Harvey* is a pooka, which is an Irish spirit, as in something that's both there and not there. I mean, Pooka would be an option, but I think Harvey is better. Besides, we don't need you being mischievous like Bugs, goofy like Roger, working too hard like Energizer, or neurotic like Pooh's friend. Peter is already taken, thank you very much, there's only one SuperBun and I'm holding him, and you don't get to be named after a holiday or a color. You've done enough damage already so, while it could be fitting, Caerbannog is right out, and I refuse to name you after cereal, especially because the word Trix can have so many other meanings." Heard Tim and Reader snicker. "So, yes, I think you're keeping Harvey."

"We have an enemy named Harvey," Jeff added. "It would be nice to know someone with that name who isn't our enemy."

"We didn't understand most of the references," Harvey admitted.

"Neither did I," Jeff said cheerfully. "Doesn't matter."

Harvey nodded slowly. "We no longer wish to be your enemy. We don't wish to be anyone's enemy."

"That's the spirit," Tim said. "Better late than never, too."

"Super. Gustav, what's our chlorophyll situation?"

"The Dawar have given us all that we should need," he replied.

"We can provide some as well," Hixxx said. "Just in case."

Drax trotted over to Hixxx and did his thing there, too. Actively chose not to pay attention to whatever it was on the grounds that my head didn't want to hurt. Happily, my music changed to "The Sounds of Science" by the Beastie Boys, because Algar was cool that way. It was nice to be understood, after all.

"Okay, so we're about to get out of here, because we have that appointment somewhere else to get to. However, Sandy, I hope you realize that Harvey is now your problem, and by 'your' I mean all of you from the Eagle Nebula. It's time to get involved, so that your child here doesn't screw up again. Like ever. Most kids get second chances. Harvey does not. I hope I'm being clear."

"Crystal," Sandy said. "And we agree."

"Harvey, here's your sentence, as in how you make reparations for all the bad you've done. You're staying on this planet, but you're not in charge. You're going to learn from Hixxx and Neela and what you're going to learn is how to be a good, caring, and compassionate leader. I don't know how long their lifespans are, so you may have to learn from their successors. Maybe many successors, maybe only a few. But your job for the foreseeable future is to learn. And to protect this planet and all the life on it, and any new life allowed on it by Hixxx and Neela. You're part of them, now, but you serve them, not the other way around."

"But," Reader said, "remember that giving people what they want isn't the same thing as giving them what they need. Wants are rarely necessary. Needs, however, are vital."

"We understand, and agree with, those concepts," Neela said. "As a race, we have few wants."

"Our race is similar," Hixxx said. "As are the elephants, horses, and squirrels. Especially after what they have experienced."

"Do you understand and agree?" Jeff asked Harvey.

"We do," Harvey said slowly. "And that all seems . . . right and fair."

"We agree, as well," Sandy said. "And yes, we will interfere as we have to, but only as we have to."

"Super. Then, one more thing. ACE is off parole. You're done being his jailers in any way, shape, or form. You broke all the rules you were punishing him for, and you did nothing to fix your errors, unlike ACE. ACE is only focused on good. You were only focused on noninvolvement. I'm done with ACE having to be scared of anything, all of you in particular."

Sandy nodded slowly. "We agree. ACE is . . . free to act as ACE sees fit."

"Forever?" Hey, I wanted to be a hundred percent sure.

"Yes, forever. However, you must remember that ACE is still bound by the rules we all live by. ACE cannot break those."

"How about bending them?"

Sandy chuckled. "We all bend as we see fit, do we not?"

"True enough." And probably all I was going to get, so that meant it had to be good enough. For right now. "Then our work here is done, and it's time for us to get back to our fun galactic road trip."

We said our good-byes, my airwaves now playing "So Long-Farewell-Good-bye" by Big Bad Voodoo Daddy. Hugged Neela—thereby making myself an official tree-hugger—then forced myself to go over and give Hixxx's head a hug, too. Focused on the fact that Hixxx seemed like a great leader and a cool guy, not that I was hugging a giant water snake's head, with limited success. But I managed not to shudder or anything while giving him his hug, so one for the win column, which was, at least right now, not that empty.

"I look forward to the next time you visit," Hixxx said when our hug was over. "Courage like yours is rare."

"Oh, not really."

He chuckled. "How many others embrace that which terrifies them, merely because they know it to be the proper thing to do?"

"Um, sorry. I didn't mean to be rude. And I know it's silly to be afraid of something that has, quite frankly, never hurt me." Because I'd never given an Earth snake a chance to be near me, but why quibble?

"You were not rude—I knew you were afraid of us before we actually met, and your fear remains, though you hide it well. I am aware that you are not actually afraid of *me* in the specific, but are afraid, in a general way, of things without legs. It is not a rational fear, but that does not make it silly. It would be a silly fear if it stopped you from being a leader or your full self. But it does not. It is just an aspect of who you are."

"You really are a cool dude. The folks that I'll be sending over to help you guys leave the water if you want will love you and, I think, vice versa. They're pretty philosophical, too. I think you and the Shantanu are going to get on great. They look like what we call penguins on Earth, by the way, and they're great in the water."

"I look forward to meeting them. Now, journey safely and remember—should you ever need it, Nazez and all those who live upon it will always be a place you can call home. And should you ever need us, we will give you whatever aid we can, and all that we can, because we owe you all that we have, and none of us will forget that debt."

Gave him one last hug, and this time I wasn't all that afraid. Maybe it was because he'd understood the fear and hadn't felt it was insulting. Most likely it was because Hixxx was really a great leader.

Everyone's good-byes said, green and black chlorophyll in hand—or whatever scientific equivalent we actually possessed— Eagle Nebula Neighborhood problems solved and the Nebula System saved, and "Come Go With Me" by The Beach Boys in my ears, we got back into the shuttle and finally returned to the *Distant Voyager*.

Butler showed us Tropea on the way, just so those of us who

hadn't seen it could get a shot. Was glad he did, so that I would always be able to remember what a scorched earth really looked like. It looked horrible, worse than the moon, because I knew that people had been living there. We hadn't asked Neela or Hixxx how many of their people had been killed by Dopey and Grumpy. Just hoped that Harvey had learned from this. At least he'd have good teachers on the planet.

We returned to the ship to find that it was Easter in Space on the *Distant Voyager*. Apparently SuperBun hadn't exaggerated— all the rabbits were hanging out with all the people. Literally everyone had a rabbit, some had several.

My music went off, so pulled out my headphones just as Jamie rounded the corner, Lizzie carrying Charlie trotting right behind her. "Mommy! Daddy!" Jamie came running to us, clutching Peter in her arms while her Poof, Mous-Mous, rode on her shoulder. "Can we keep all the bunnies who don't have people to love them like we keep the Poofs who haven't chosen their people yet?"

Heard Jeff mutter about living in a zoo, but good-naturedly. "Yes, we can," he said in a resigned tone. "Because I know that saying no in this instance won't work."

"Yay!" She gave Jeff's legs a hug, then came to me. Squatted down so I could give her a real hug, which was a relief— thankfully, the thought that we might not see our kids ever again seemed like it had been a long time ago now.

"Cool," Lizzie said, as she brought Charlie to me so I could give him kisses, then handed him off to Jeff. "Because that's what Peter said to do, so all the unattached rabbits are in our rooms."

"How lucky can one man get?" Jeff asked. Then he jerked. "You can talk to the rabbit?"

"He can talk to us, yeah," Lizzie said as if this was something that happened every day to people other than me. "Is my dad around? I need to know if he wants his own rabbit or not."

"I'm right here," Siler, who'd been behind us, said. "And before I answer that question, how many rabbits have you already claimed as 'ours'?"

"Only a few," Lizzie said, sounding only slightly guilty.

Siler exchanged the "why me?" look with Jeff. "Then I think I'll just share yours." He pulled her to him and gave her a big hug. "Just remember, the saying 'breed like rabbits' exists for a reason."

Lizzie laughed. "It should be 'breed like Poofs,' you know."

"She has a point. Not that there's anything wrong with that." Ever. Because extra Poofs was never wrong.

Jamie looked at SuperBun. "Is he ours, too?"

SuperBun said that he definitely was.

Jamie giggled. "He's smart."

"He is. They all are." Black water for the win, presumably. "And yes, officially, we're keeping all the bunnies. 'Cause you know what my motto is?"

"What?" Jamie asked.

"Poofs and bunnies for everyone, and more Poofs and bunnies for me. That's my motto."

"Mine, too!" Jamie snuggled Peter. "You bring the best presents, ever!"

Managed a laugh. "So glad everyone likes the souvenirs we picked up at our first vacation destination."

CHAPTER 45

ONCE THE RABBIT SITUATION was confirmed, Jamie allowed us to give her more hugs and kisses, we got hugs and kisses from Lizzie, too, and Charlie demanded to hold SuperBun by lifting the rabbit out of my arms telekinetically. Then they all made much over Bruno and Ginger, which appeased them, so all was well in our Animal Kingdom.

By the time we were all settled back with our families and friends and the many furred and feathered crew members were in quarters or arms, depending, Drax announced that Mother was back up and running perfectly.

"Time to choose our next destination," Drax said to those of us on the command deck.

"We need to go to Ixtha," Mother said.

"Do we have a heading for that?" Tim asked. "I mean one we all get to know."

"Yes," Mother said. But she sounded evasive.

"What are you trying not to tell us, Mother?" I asked.

"When we were spun out of warp, the original coordinates were lost somehow. While I can determine where we are within the galaxy by triangulating from the Eagle Nebula and the star whose solar space we are within, I am having issues pulling the original coordinates back."

We all exchanged the "oh really?" look. "That seems impossible," Reader said.

Stryker shook his head. "It's not. Think of it as Mother having experienced the Blue Screen of Death—her system crashed. We were all able to repair it, but that bomb affected more than the warp drive. It affected Mother's memory banks."

"But selectively," Dr. Wu said. "Most of her memory appears

intact. Just the information about where she was heading the ship originally is lost."

"Henry's right," Chuckie said, as he studied a printout I presumed Hacker International had given him. "And this is highly suspicious."

"This whole trip is highly suspicious." Had my suspicions as to how this had happened, for example. Or, rather, who had affected Mother's memory banks. Had two major suspects. One I couldn't easily speak to right now, because Jamie was awake. But one, and the most likely culprit, I could interrogate.

However, I had to do so in a way that wouldn't immediately make everyone realize that I suspected him. "Okay, so two questions. First, can we figure out a general neighborhood by looking at our original trajectory? Or was that information wiped out, too?"

"Some of it, but not all," Chuckie said. "So, good idea, Kitty. I think that can help."

"Super. Second question—can we just fly off at whatever isn't warp speed, versus hanging around here and letting Sandy and his pals think of other things they want us to do? I'm suggesting not going at warp since we have a really good chance of not going in the right direction, and we have so many directional options in space that I think going away but slowly is probably in our best interest."

Everyone other than Chuckie stared at me. Chuckie looked up from his perusal of the printouts, looked around at everyone else's expressions, rolled his eyes then winked at me, and went back to his reading.

"What? Is this going to be another time when you all insult me by acting shocked that I'm not a moron?"

"No," Jeff said quickly, while shooting the "stop it" look around to everyone else. "I just don't think anyone else had thought it through yet." The rest of my friends and colleagues all nodded enthusiastically.

Snorted. "Right. And I hang with all of you why? Anyway, that's my two cents for right now. You talk amongst yourselves. I'm going to go pet some bunnies and be offended for a bit." I actually wasn't all that offended, being used to this by now, but it seemed like a great way to leave without suspicion.

Jeff started to come with me. Put up the paw. He stopped walking. Wow, this power had depth! "Nope, don't even try. Just stay here and help figure out where we might be heading."

Was pretty sure Jeff knew I wasn't really angry, but also was pretty sure he knew I wanted to be left alone, so he obliged. Yet another reason he was a great husband.

Siler, on the other hand, didn't get the message. He shoved off the wall he'd been leaning against, nodded to Buchanan, who stayed put, and came with me.

We didn't talk until we reached the maintenance closet where he and the others had been hiding out. Then he opened the door and ushered me inside. Algar and the least weasels were nowhere to be seen.

"Going to talk to the DJ?" he asked once the door was closed.

"Maybe, Nightcrawler, maybe. Why do you ask?"

He grinned. "You had your headphones in through all of the action. I know what that means."

"You're still the only one."

He nodded. "I know. And, before you ask, no, no one else appears to notice. Still. Not your husband, not Reynolds, not Alpha Team, not even your children."

"Well, the kids are usually not with me when the action's rolling. Thank God."

"True. And also before you ask, no, I haven't talked to anyone else about this. It's not that I can't . . . I feel like I actually can, even though you've said that you aren't able to. But I don't see the point, honestly. The DJ helps us. I have no interest in affecting that kind of help negatively."

"Good to know. Um, I kind of want to be alone, though."

"I'm sure you do. I kind of want to know where you're going in order to talk to the DJ."

"Why would you think that's what I'm going to do?"

Siler sighed. "You aren't mad at anyone—that was just an act so you could get out of the room. But right before that, we'd been discussing how we've lost the coordinates and all of a sudden, and instead of trying to work through where we might be heading, you want to be alone. My conclusion is that you just had the idea to ask the DJ what's going on and see if he can help us, and you naturally don't want to and can't do that with the others around."

"If that were true, and I'm in no way saying that it is, then wouldn't you being around mean I couldn't talk to him?"

"Maybe. Maybe he'd like to meet me."

"The person he can't actually control? The one person in, as far as I can tell, the galaxy? Um, no. I'm betting that you're the last person he wants to meet." As Algar, at any rate. He'd met

Siler as the Ard Ri, after all. And Siler hadn't picked up that the Ard Ri was the DJ. Meaning that Algar's powers weren't shorted out fully with Siler, just somewhat.

"I can wait," Siler said, as he leaned against a wall and crossed his arms over his chest.

"Why does this matter to you?"

"I'm curious."

"Bull pookey. You're an assassin and you can go invisible. I'm somewhat surprised you didn't just blend and follow me."

"I don't want to do that. This isn't something that I want to discover by . . . skulking."

"Why not? And, again, why do you care? Why does this matter to you? It's not curiosity, so don't try that one again."

He tried for the stare down. Geez, it was like a party game on this trip. But, as per usual, since he wasn't Mom or Chuckie, he didn't win. He was a very worthy opponent, though.

Siler heaved a sigh. "I want answers from a source I can trust."

Considered this. "Oh. Trevor the Tinkerer *did* pique your interest. There's a lot about you that no one understands, particularly you yourself. But here's the thing—the DJ really likes to play fussy little word games. I mean, don't get me wrong—I like him, frankly, a lot, but he's kind of a jerk. He never comes out and says 'do this' or 'don't do that' or anything of the kind. I get song clues, vague innuendo, and weird forms of encouragement, and that's about it. I have no idea if he talks to the two others who know in the same way, or at all, really. But if you're looking for straight answers, Trevor's far more likely to give them to you."

"He won't. And I can't trust anything he tells me anyway. And I know you know that. Besides, we need to keep him on the hook, thinking that the only reason I don't make him dead is that you won't let me—so far—and that I might want the information he claims to possess. Actually *wanting* the information means we lose. So, no, I don't want it, not from him."

"Maybe I should give you the Wolverine moniker and I take Nightcrawler."

He laughed. "No. I'm good with the nicknames as they are. But I've been thinking about who the others could be, the ones who know the DJ, in my off time. I think I've figured it out."

"Yeah?"

He nodded. "Richard White and Paul Gower."

Hoped I was keeping the shocked look off of my face. "Um, why would you think it's them?"

He laughed. "Because they're the former and current heads of the A-C's religion. And if I was a godlike being, I'd want to deal with the people most likely willing to believe in my existence."

"It's a good theory." Per what he'd told me, that was basically the reason Algar had told them.

But, way back when, others had known who he was, too. The leader of the A-Cs, normally their king, had been in on it. Though, in reality, not for several generations. While Algar was all for supporting Alfred to the point that he'd exiled himself to Earth right along with him—because Alfred had been the rightful heir and that meant so were those in his bloodline—he hadn't shared his existence with Jeff's father.

He still hadn't with Jeff, either, and Jeff was now the official King Regent, too. At least, as far as I knew. But he'd continued to share with the Head of Security all the way along, because Algar was part of what made things secure. Once our A-Cs had come to Earth, those in the know had just been the Former and Current Pontifexes and Gladys Gower. Until she died. While on a mission with me.

Tried to shove back the sorrow thinking about losing Gladys always gave me. I'd worked one mission with her and watched her sacrifice herself to keep her people safe. I would have really liked to have gotten to do more with her. Then again, I'd wanted to have more time with Michael Gower, and Naomi Gower-Reynolds, too. Operation Infiltration had really been a hard one to take, especially for the Gower family and those of us who loved them.

Siler cocked his head. "The other people who knew, they're dead now. And you knew them."

"What makes you say that?"

"Your expression. You're missing someone and the memory is painful. Who?"

"It happened before you joined us."

"But not before I knew about you." He looked thoughtful. "I got the full rundown of events from Buchanan. At least from as long as you've all been in D.C. The worst losses you took were when Dulce got infiltrated . . ." He jerked. "Ah. That would make sense. I wonder if that knowledge has passed on to her successor."

"No idea." I truly had no idea if William Ward knew about Algar or not. Because it was hard enough to talk about Algar with the couple of people who I knew were aware of his existence as it was. Never saw a reason to force a migraine on myself.

Though, as I thought about it, talking about Algar with Siler wasn't nearly as hard as it was when I was talking about him with Gower or White.

Would have tried denying things again but the door opened. And Algar came inside.

CHAPTER 46

"**OH, EXCUSE ME, LASSIE, LADDIE,**" Algar said politely. "One of the weasels got out again and I thought maybe it had run here."

"Haven't seen it," Siler said. "Sorry. If we spot it we'll bring it to you."

Realized he was trying to get Algar out of the room so we could continue our conversation. Literally had no idea of what I should be doing right now, though the Inner Hyena was threatening to erupt.

Algar snapped his fingers and time stopped. "I think you should relax, lassie. You need some downtime before the next activities."

Looked at Siler. He seemed frozen. "Um, can he hear us?"

"He cannot, actually."

"Great. I'd take you up on that whole resting idea, only I'm experienced enough to know that I'm not going to get any real rest until we've saved the cosmos or whatever. So, why are you here? To help me not give you away to Siler or to let him meet you officially?"

Algar shook his head. "He's not ready to meet me."

Snorted. "Right. The dude has figured out that you're out there, that indicates a total readiness to meet the King of the Elves in person."

"It would. If he was at the point where he grasped that I *am* a person. The thing is, he thinks I'm like ACE, a spirit."

"You are, as well. I know you have more aspects than I've seen."

He twinkled at me. "Which is merely one reason why you're my favorite. Yes, but your friend here isn't thinking of me as someone he could chat with in the hall. Yet. He'll come around to it, I'm sure."

"I could play Joan Osborne's big hit, "One of Us," and see if he catches on."

"Sarcasm is such a fun trait. I'm glad you enjoy it so."

"I like to take a lot of things to eleven, what can I say? So, what, you're playing a game with him? Why?"

He shrugged. "Living forever gets dull. This is the first person in existence to figure out that I'm here without my letting him know. That makes him fascinating."

"And dangerous."

"In a way, yes. But all of life can be dangerous. You just left a planet full of danger."

"Good point. Are you okay with him discovering who you are?"

"Is he so tightly tied to you that he would die for you if that was what was required?"

"Um, I have no idea."

Algar sighed. "Perhaps you don't. His mentors died for you. Willingly."

"But he has Lizzie."

"And he'd die for her, too. He's not going to die for either of you unless that's the only way—he's smart and skilled enough to know that he can do far more for you if he's alive. But he is willing to do that if he has to. Remember, Lizzie's your ward for many reasons. And one of those reasons is that her adoptive father takes a lot of risks."

"Like coming onto this spaceship to protect us, yeah. Will you let Lizzie know about you? One day, I mean."

He grinned. "Now that's you thinking right. Yes, I'm sure I will. And your children. They don't know I'm here yet. But, as with your man here, they'll figure it out eventually. Being your children, I expect it sooner than later. But Jamie knows how to keep a secret, and I'm sure Charlie will learn from his big sister."

There was a clue in that, I was sure of it. I just didn't know what the clue was for. "Let's hope, at any rate. Have you told Jeff yet?"

"Not yet. Possibly soon. Possibly not. Knowing I'm here doesn't make things easier for anyone, you know."

"Yeah, I do, actually. So, while I have your full attention, why did you wipe out the coordinates for us to get to Ixtha? I thought you were all for us going there."

"I am. I don't want the galaxy and, potentially, the universe destroyed. Only, I'm not the one who did that."

"ACE?" That seemed so unlikely, though, based on ACE's desire to help Ixtha.

"No, not ACE. But . . . neither one of us will interfere in this situation."

Stared at him. "Come again? I mean, seriously, we're in the middle of nowhere and have no idea where to go. Why won't the two of you interfere? Just dedicated to us doing it all ourselves while singing the Free Will Forever theme song?"

He sighed. "Honestly? No. We won't interfere because it's not our place."

Felt a migraine threatening. "Look. It's really hard to play the mental gymnastics with Siler that I have to in order not to give him intel about you and who knows about you. Does William, by the way?"

"Does it matter if he does or doesn't?"

Thought about it. "No. He'll do what he thinks is best and that tends to be what Jeff and I think is best."

"Exactly."

"Great, thanks for that. But, back to my impending migraine—if it wasn't you or ACE, who wiped the coordinates?"

Algar smiled. "The same one who gave Jamie the passenger list." Then he snapped his fingers again. "Well, laddie, thank you. Should you find the weasel, please let the ship know. I'll be looking for it until it's found."

"Will do," Siler said. "Good luck."

"Oh," Algar said as he opened the door, "I don't believe in luck, laddie. It's just hard work and perseverance belittled." He closed the door as he left.

"I like the Ard Ri," Siler said. "He seems like an intelligent crackpot."

"Um, yeah. I'm not going to point out that, per every enemy we've ever had, I'm considered quite lucky."

"Just because they belittle you doesn't mean that they're right. I agree with the Ard Ri—it's not actually luck. It's hard work, perseverance, a willingness to try anything that might have even the slimmest chance of success, and dedication to doing what's right and saving the day."

"I'm gonna blush."

He grinned. "Well, the President hasn't had a good jealousy rage for a while now."

"Hey, that's my line. So, anyway, I'm not planning to talk to the DJ."

Siler raised his eyebrow.

"Fine. I'm not going to talk to him now because I don't think he's ready to meet you yet. You'll just have to deal."

Siler opened his mouth—to argue, most likely—but he was interrupted. By alarms.

We looked at each other. "Oh my God, are you kidding? We literally just finished saving an entire solar system. We get five minutes of downtime and that's it?"

"All personnel to stations," Mother said crisply, in a way that said she'd like to be shouting these orders, but couldn't because she wasn't programmed that way. "All passengers to crash couches or the equivalent. All command personnel to command deck." Due to the alarms, she was having to repeat herself in order to be sure we could all hear everything. By now even JR was probably clear on what the alarms meant.

Siler grabbed my hand and we took off. He let go of me right before we reached the command deck, so like in two seconds. "I'll make sure the kids are safe. You handle the ship."

"Good plan."

He raced off for the Nonessential Personnel section and I raced to my seat. Was really glad I'd hadn't felt confident enough to take my purse off earlier. Hoped the bunnies were going to be okay, but didn't have a lot of time to worry about anything other than what was right in front of me.

Jeff, Hughes, Walker, Tim, and Tito were already in position with their helmets on. "What's our status?" I shouted as I flung my helmet onto my head and my butt into my seat, once again ensuring that my purse and I were strapped in.

"Coordinates are activating," Mother said. "But not under my command."

"Not any of ours, either," Tim shouted.

"Mother, the alarms. Can they go to less loud? I think all passengers and crew are aware of the direness of our latest situation."

The alarms didn't mute but they went down about a million decibels. "Apologies," Mother said. "Everyone was scattered."

"No worries, I'd assume they're all where they should be now, right?"

"Yes . . . all personnel are accounted for and in assigned locations."

"Are the children all supervised?" Jeff asked.

"They are, and all children were strapped in first by any adult nearby."

"Good. Nice to know everyone has their priorities straight. Now, someone talk to me because I wasn't here when this all started—what's going on?"

"We don't know again," Hughes said. "We were all discussing possible directions when Mother said that something was wrong. Drax and the hackers went to work on it."

"They did not arrive in time," Mother said. "They are safe, but they were not able to stop this malfunction."

"So, where are we heading?"

"As near as I can tell," Mother replied, "across the galaxy."

"Of course we are," Jeff said.

"Are you sure that this isn't the original coordinates resurfacing somehow?" Tito asked.

"Yes, I am certain. Expect warp in three . . . two . . . one . . ."

Felt the slamming back in your seat feeling of going into warp. "Remember," Tito said calmly, "deep breaths and don't fight it."

We all did better this time, which was nice. What wasn't was that the pressure seemed to be going on for a long time. "Um, Mother? When does the pressure stop? Again, asking for a friend."

"And again, she's asking for me," Tim said.

"I have no idea," Mother said. "I am not in control of the ship."

Let that sit on the air for a moment. "Excuse me?" Jeff asked finally. "You told us we were going to warp."

"Yes, because I could determine that was what the ship was doing. But I have no control right now."

"Think the hackers screwed something up, intentionally or accidentally?" Tim asked.

"Only if Drax wanted his prized creation ruined," Jeff said. "Per Brian, Drax oversaw everything the freeloaders did, and Drax has a lot riding on the *Distant Voyager*. I find it hard to believe that he's sabotaged his own ship or allowed anyone else to do it right under his nose. If he wanted to go visit somewhere, all he had to do was tell us and set the coordinates. And unless we're heading for Vatusus, I don't buy it."

"We are not, as far as I can tell," Mother said.

"The hackers don't have anything riding on the ship," Tim said. "And they snuck on."

"They snuck on because it's the coolest thing ever and they're idiots in some ways. But sabotage like this isn't like them, honestly, and I've known them all a long time. So has Chuckie. If these guys weren't a hundred percent loyal and then some, Chuckie would have already had them taken out. And before you argue, yes I mean that seriously, yes they're his friends, and yes he'd still take them out if they weren't trustworthy. I know for a fact he still has them all wearing the self-destruct watches and I also know that Dulce hasn't been allowed to remove them."

"It's kind of miraculous that he doesn't have us all wearing them," Walker pointed out.

Rightly, as I thought about it. Maybe Siler had been correct when we'd talked about this at the end of Operation Fundraiser—Chuckie trusted more people than he liked to let on.

However, he didn't trust them without a lot of proof and background checking. Jeff might call them freeloaders, but they were living in the best setup of any of their lives and I knew they never wanted to do anything to lose said setup. And betraying us would lose it faster than anything, and they all knew it. Plus, they loved living in the Zoo, hanging out with Chernobog, and getting to feel vital and important every day. No, Hacker International were not traitors or saboteurs.

"True, but this discussion isn't solving our current situation," Hughes replied.

"This feels like outside influence," Mother said. "We confirmed my programming and the ship to be fully intact before we left the Nazez solar space."

"What if it's the black chlorophyll?" I asked. "Could that have done it? Or even the regular chlorophyll? It was from a foreign planet. From a foreign body on a foreign planet, really."

"The black chlorophyll has not been used yet," Mother said. "And we ran several tests before utilizing the regular chlorophyll. All seemed fine and as it should have been."

"Only we get a spaceship that can't control itself," Jeff said. "I mean that seriously. I'm confident that other planets and, frankly, other people get ships that work as expected."

"I apologize again," Mother said, sounding ready to commit AI suicide.

"It's not your fault," Jeff said reassuringly. "We're in this together, Mother."

"It feels like my fault," Mother said.

"Jeff's right, it's not. None of this is really . . ." It wasn't. From the very beginning Mother had been manipulated by others, starting with Ixtha. And, speaking of Ixtha, how had she found us all in the DreamScape anyway? Had she managed it alone, or had she had help? And if she'd had help, had that help come from the same source as Jamie's passenger list? And, per Algar, the current situation?

"I recognize the way you just stopped talking," Jeff said. "What are you thinking?"

"Nothing concrete yet." At least, that I could say aloud. Because Algar had been pretty clear about my needing to figure out who'd given Jamie her list of spaceship travelers by myself. I'd thought it was to protect whoever the culprit was. But now I wasn't so sure.

Now I had a feeling that the people being protected from the knowledge were on the ship.

Thought about what Algar had said just a few minutes before—what I'd felt was a big ol' Algar Clue. He'd said that Jamie could keep a secret.

She was a little girl, so what possible secrets could she be keeping? Looked around and caught my reflection in the windshield. And gave myself a great big ol' "DUH" for this one.

Because there was indeed a gigantic secret that Jamie had been keeping for years now. Several secrets, really, but they all related to the main one.

Which was that Naomi was still alive out there in the cosmos. And she was watching over us—throughout the multiverse.

CHAPTER 47

IN ORDER TO SAVE several of us, and to protect Jamie, aka
her beloved goddaughter, Naomi had taken far more pure Surcenthumain than a hundred people could have handled. It had
brought back the powers she'd lost saving D.C. from the Z'porrah
attack during Operation Destruction—but it had also killed her.

Only, she'd become so powerful that her essence hadn't died.
Her body was gone, at least the one she'd been born in. However, she was still out there. And no one—the remaining Gowers
and Chuckie in particular—could ever know this, because it
would destroy them, in different ways.

The moment I thought of what was going on as filtered
through Naomi, though, things started to make sense. Well,
some sense. They might have made more sense if I could have
talked about this aloud—I thought a lot better when running my
yap and sharing the wonder that were my thought processes with
others—but that option was definitely not available in this situation. So, I'd just have to make do and do my best in terms of
silent yap runnings.

Algar had pretty much said that the person who'd given Jamie the list of people to bring along wasn't evil. And there were
only a few beings out there who both Algar and ACE would feel
had a right to interfere with us, at least more than Algar and ACE
were interfering. Plus, ACE was emotionally attached to Naomi
and had been since she'd been born.

He was more emotionally attached to her since she'd saved
him from the Superconsciousness Society and allowed him to
return to Earth, which was why he was residing in Jamie these
days instead of Naomi's eldest brother. Naomi's sentence,
though, had been that she couldn't interfere with us in any way.

I was certain that Naomi had helped me get to and from Bizarro World, though it was likely that Algar had assisted, as well, since Poofs had been, if not overtly involved, at least present and very much accounted for. The Jamie in Bizarro World had told me that every Jamie in the multiverse—at least the ones who were aware of each other, which had appeared to be most or all—knew that the person to ask for help was Auntie Mimi. And Naomi was good at sneaking the help in without being caught.

Realized that I hadn't looked in the three-way mirror much recently. That meant I was letting Jamie in Bizarro World down. Resolved that I'd get to that the moment we were back. Sooner, if Mother could create a three-way mirror for me that I could adjust to the correct angles needed. But that was for later. Right now, we were sailing off somewhere with no idea of where we were heading or why.

Which was very overt, and therefore going directly against Naomi's terms of parole with the Superconsciousness Society. Suggesting the DreamScape to Ixtha and leading her to me—probably covert. Suggesting the passenger list to Jamie—again, probably covert. But this was not. This was done literally under our particular Superconsciousness Police's noses. Because that's what Sandy and his confederates were, at least for the part of the galaxy all of us on this ship called home.

Pondered why she felt emboldened enough to take the risk. Didn't have to ponder too long. Sandy had pulled us out of warp to solve their little problem. That was definitely not in the Superconsciousness Society Rulebook. Meaning that he'd broken said rules. And that meant that maybe Naomi could break them, too. Or else, at the least, Naomi felt that the risks of being this overt were well worth whatever reward she expected from all of us on the ship. And that she expected us to do something was quite clear.

Okay, fine. So, why weren't we hurtling toward Ixtha again? Mother seemed certain that we were not, and I had to trust her on that. Why send us elsewhere, if the entire goal was to get us to Ixtha to solve her situation?

The only answer I could come up with was that something else was going on wherever we were headed. If so, the situation couldn't be that old, because if we'd been needed at this other place, then why not set Mother's original coordinates for what I was now going to consider Stop Two on the Galaxy Cruise?

Decided to table why Naomi had suggested the passenger list she had for a later time when we might be flying under our own control. But a Space Family Reunion did seem possible. Of course, if so, then she'd left her parents, Stanley and Erika Gower, on Earth, along with Alfred and Lucinda.

Of course, that would likely be so that we'd have two out of the three guys who forged the first relationship with the U.S. government still on Earth, supporting Mom and ensuring that A-C Bases weren't taken over by our enemies. And, as a super-consciousness, she could see them any time. All the time, really. And I didn't expect her to show up visually to anyone, other than possibly me or Jamie, aka the only two on this Earth who knew she was still alive.

So, I had it figured out. Probably. Maybe. Hopefully.

But even if I was right, this information did me no good, because I couldn't tell anyone else. Meaning I was going to have to lead them around to the idea that "someone" wanted us helping out again, without mentioning Naomi. Or Algar. Piece of cake. Wished I had some cake.

"I wish I had some cake."

The guys all stared at me. "I'd rather not try to eat right now," Tim said. "The pressure and all. Besides, it's not good to eat at your workspace. At least so I'm told."

"Oh, I know. I mean later."

"If we get a later," Walker muttered.

"Oh, we will. I really hope there's cake wherever we're going."

"Kitty," Jeff said carefully, "baby, are you feeling okay?"

"Sure. Why?"

"Because you were uncharacteristically silent for longer than any of us are used to," Tito replied, clearly speaking for everyone. "And the first thing you said when you stopped being silent was that you wanted cake. As your physician, I'm a little concerned."

"Everyone's a critic. I'm just hungry. But I think we're heading to help someone somewhere."

"What brought you to that conclusion?" Hughes asked.

"I think that's what this trip is about."

"So far, yes, it seems that way," Jeff said. "However, unless you know for sure, I think we need to be prepared to enter hostile territory."

"Do you think it's ACE?" Tim asked.

"No, I don't. ACE would tell us, not just fling us."

"I agree," Jeff said. "But are we sure this wasn't internal sabotage of some kind?"

"Positive." Well, if we defined "internal" to mean someone physically on board. And, I was absolutely doing so for this example. "Sandy pulled us out of warp. Who's to say that another one of his brethren from another nebula didn't see this and go, 'Wow, what a great idea, I'm gonna do *that*!' and then, you know, immediately do it."

"Kitty has a point," Hughes said. "And she's usually right, so I say we roll with it."

"Though I also agree with Jeff," Walker added. "We should still be ready to shoot first and ask questions later, just in case."

"The pressure should be reducing," Mother shared.

"I'm sure I could have taken an hour more of it, easy," Tim said.

"Careful what you say." Hughes chuckled. "Whoever's really driving might take you up on it."

Sure enough, breathing was easy again. "What do you need us to do, Mother?" I still had no idea what my role really was, other than to talk. I was good with talking, so we were okay there.

"Nothing. At the moment. However, I recommend you stay at stations, just in case."

Realized something. Mother—who was supposedly linked to all of us mentally and certainly had been before—didn't seem to have heard a single thought I'd had. Interesting. Meaning it was likely that Algar was shielding my thoughts. Presumably to protect Naomi.

In some ways that made sense—I doubted that he wanted Gower, Abigail, or Chuckie losing it should Mother casually mention that I knew Naomi was alive. But that probably wasn't all of it. But whatever the rest was, I'd find out later, because I didn't have enough intel to determine it at this precise time.

Chuckie and Reader came onto the command deck. "We figured we could unstrap," Reader said by way of explanation. "Drax and the hackers are going to see if they can figure out what's going on."

"They're not traitors," Chuckie said to Jeff. "So if you were worried that they did something intentionally, I can guarantee they didn't."

"I already covered that. Just so you know." Hey, I had, might as well get credit for it.

"Yes, Kitty did support them, but it's good to know that you have no worries about their loyalties, too," Jeff replied. "But that still leaves us going across the galaxy to who knows where, due to who knows what or who. Any ideas, Chuck? I'm open to even the craziest ones."

"That's your wife's bailiwick," Chuckie said with a grin for me.

"All I've got is the firm belief that we're going to be handling another problem whenever we get to wherever we're going. Probably thanks to another superconsciousness of some kind. They seem to like being bossy. Speaking of bossy, where's Mossy?"

"With Drax," Reader replied. "Until the ship's under control, Drax needs Mossy."

"Good thing he snuck on board, then."

"Speaking of those on board who weren't supposed to be, the nonessential personnel are whining that they haven't gotten to do anything." Chuckie laughed. "And that's more from the adults than the kids."

"Mother, are we safe to leave the command deck? We do have position replacements who can cover. All of whom are better trained for this than me, Jeff, and Tito, by the way." Wondered what she was going to say to this. Prior to our stop at Nazez the answer would have been no.

"No," Mother said, as one of the lights on my control panel started blinking like crazy.

"Um, why not?"

"You need to answer the incoming transmission," Mother replied. "It's a distress call."

CHAPTER 48

WE ALL STARED AT EACH OTHER. "Um, excuse me?" I said finally. Not the best comeback, but it did the job.

"We are receiving an incoming transmission. It's going out over emergency channels."

"Space has emergency channels? Seriously, I learn something new every day."

"In a sense," Mother said. "Please answer the call for help. I am trying to not become a HAL but the longer you delay, the more difficult it becomes to not take over."

"Drax needs to work on that," Reader said to Chuckie, who nodded.

"Worry about it later," Jeff said. "Right now, there are people out there who need help."

"Any idea where this is originating?" Cleared my throat, just in case.

"None. The signal is faint, however."

"Should I take this alone or put it on speaker to the command deck?"

"I will ensure that the call is live to this section of the ship only."

"Works for me." Pushed the button down. "Hello, this is the *Distant Voyager*. How can we help you?"

There was garbled sound that sounded like bird caws and shrieks.

"I'm sorry. Please keep on speaking. Our Universal Translator will catch up eventually. We hope."

Now it sounded like caterwauling. I should know—I sounded like this most times when Jeff and I did the deed. Which we had not done in, by my count, ages.

Jeff heaved a sigh. "Yeah, I know, baby."

"Focus, you two," Chuckie said. "And we all know you, so we know what the two of you are whining about."

"Haters."

Now we were getting barking. This was officially getting weird.

Still, tried to carry on. "You're speaking with the command crew of the *Distant Voyager*. We're from a planet called Earth, which is in one of the arms of the Milky Way galaxy. We're far out there, and we used to think we were in the boondocks but we're discovering that we're not nearly as alone as we'd suspected. No idea where you're at, because we don't know where we are. Long story that I figure you actually can't understand yet. We have some folks from other planets on board, too. This is a longwinded way of saying that you're still not coming through intelligibly for us. Most of us don't speak whatever animal dialects you're trying. Go for your nearest Naked Ape language."

There was silence. Then garbled noises that might have been pig snorting and might not have been. It was really hard to tell.

"We need Wruck here, pronto," Jeff said.

"Hailing him now," Mother replied.

"Maybe we need to talk more," I suggested.

"That's one of your areas of expertise," Reader said, managing to keep a straight face. "And you've already done a bang-up job of it. So I say go for it, girlfriend."

Wruck arrived. Chuckie filled him in on what was going on.

"Hilarious. Whoever's on the other line, say the same garbled word or sound or whatever twice for yes and once for no. Got it?"

Two garbled noised that sounded alike came at me. No longer sounded like animal calls. So there was that. Looked to Wruck. Who shook his head.

"Awesome. Are you in danger?"

Two more garbled noises.

"Is the danger life-threatening?"

Two more garbled noises.

"Dang. Okay, do you know where in the galaxy you are?" If they could give us coordinates, surely we could figure them out.

One garbled noise. A pause. Then two garbled noises. "Gotcha, you're not sure. Okay, um . . ." Looked at the guys. "I have no idea what else to ask in order to determine where in the galaxy they are. We have no idea where we are. We aren't communicating clearly in this way. We have no idea what they want or how to figure out what they want or need, let along what we can do about it."

"You can come and get us off of the rock we're stranded on!" The voice sounded male and stressed. Not a surprise on the stressed.

"Well, it's nice of the Universal Translator to finally kick in. How long were you able to understand me?"

"After you tried to tell us where you were from. You talked enough that we could get your language."

"Um, don't take this question the wrong way, but are you all animals there? Fur, feathers, claws, beaks, and whatnot?"

"No. I think we're Naked Apes like you, at least if we understand the reference. We're from a solar system filled with planets, all of which are animal-based."

"Sounds like Alpha Centauri," Chuckie said.

"Don't know what or where that is," whoever we were talking to said.

"How far from the galaxy's core are you?" Chuckie asked.

"Far."

"Earth is about twenty-six thousand light-years away from the core," Chuckie said patiently. "How far is your star?"

There was silence for a few long moments. "We think we understand the unit of measurement. Our star is about thirty thousand light years from the core. But we're not on our star. We're farther than that."

"Signal is getting stronger," Mother said.

"You think this is who we're being sent to help?" Tim asked.

"Maybe," Chuckie said. "Are you on the galactic disk or the galactic halo?"

More silence for a few seconds. "We think we're in the halo. Our home planet is on the disk. Again, we think, if we're understanding you correctly."

"Earth is on the disk, in one of the spiral arms." Chuckie rubbed the back of his neck. "Mother, are you able to determine where we are?"

"How is it you don't know?" the voice on the other end asked, sounding like he thought he'd just realized that instead of finding the A-Team he'd landed the Keystone Kops.

"It's been a long day. Also, as a suggestion, don't be snippy with the people who are trying to help you, it's bad form. Look, what's your name?"

"And the name of your home planet and its location," Chuckie added quickly. "We need something to work with."

"Fine. My name is Wheatles Kreaving, on the space vessel *Eknara*, from the planet Ignotforsta."

"Um, excuse me. I'm not sure that our translator is giving us this right. Your name is Wheatles Kreaving? From the planet Ignotforsta? And your ship is named the *Eknara*?" The ship's name wasn't my issue. The other names were. The Inner Hyena wanted to break free in the worst way.

"Yes, you pronounced everything perfectly."

"Oh. Um. Good." Truly, the galaxy was a place of wonder and bizarre names. Then again, maybe Kitty sounded weird to someone named Wheatles.

"Our home planet's coordinates are three-zero-two by eight-seven-seven by five-four-nine."

We all looked at Chuckie and Wruck. Who both shook their heads. "What does your planet consider zero?" Chuckie asked. "And we need to know which number equals time."

"The Galactic Core, and we don't have a time measurement. But it doesn't matter because we're not there. We were hit by a neutron wave—"

"A what?" Chuckie interrupted.

"A neutron wave. It's created when a star dies."

We all looked at Wruck. "It's another term for what Earth scientists call a supernova remnant," he said. "It's more accurate term. And there are different kinds of these waves." He looked like he was thinking about something, but he didn't say anything else.

"It's a big old galaxy, isn't it? So, Wheatles, what star died?" Gave it no more than five minutes before I was calling this guy Wheaties. At least in my mind. Probably aloud, too.

"No idea. The waves radiate out. We might not have had a problem, but we were near a dark nebula which blocked the wave's readings and weren't able to adjust our course in time. We were hit and sent tumbling. We have no idea where we are now because of that. Our ship is damaged, as well, so we can't leave."

"Are you in an uninhabited area?" Chuckie asked.

"No, we're on a planet, which is one of several. All of them are inhabited. The inhabitants aren't the problem. They might even be able to help us fix our ship—in about a thousand years or so. They're all in a primitive state." More garbled word. "Stone age for you. We think."

"Are they using fire and tools?" Chuckie asked. "Metals?"

"Yes, doing metalwork. They have fire, weapons and shelters, clothing that's more than skins or leaves."

"Bronze Age, more likely, then, at least in terms of Earth's progression." Chuckie shook his head. "Yeah, they're unlikely to be able to help, though."

"Okay, so, still doesn't sound like a reason to be freaking out." Said because Kreaving sounded really stressed. Wheaties Craving. Considered this nickname and decided I was not going to share that with anyone anytime soon, since I didn't need the derision. Plus, it was unlikely that we had Wheaties on board. At least until we rescued this guy.

"Yeah, that wouldn't be," Kreaving agreed. "However, there's something wrong with their sun. Our surveying and scientific equipment is working and we've determined what's wrong."

"And that is?" Chuckie asked.

"Their sun was hit with something. It came along with us, via the neutron wave. And now their sun is unstable and looks ready to go nova. In a very short time from now. Not only are we here, but there are seven inhabited planets that we can determine are teeming with life, and none of that life is more advanced than that of the planet we're on. We're all going to die, and soon, unless someone can help us."

"Transmission is starting to weaken," Mother said.

"Wheatles, give us everything you have about where you are," I said urgently. "And do it fast. We have no idea where we're headed either, but I promise you, we *will* find you. And we'll find you before it's too late."

"We think we're still in the area of the outer arm where our planet is, but we're not sure—the damage to our ship means that we can't be sure how far we traveled." He faded out.

"Wheatles! Keep trying!"

"We were going to examine a pulsar that appears to have several planets orbiting it." His voice was fainter. "We were trying to discover if those planets had life or not."

"Do you know how long the pulses last or how long in between pulses?" Chuckie asked.

"Yes," Kreaving said. But it was hard to hear him due to static. ". . . weeks . . . help . . ."

The line went dead. We were all quiet. Broke the silence. "I don't care what else we supposedly have to do. We are finding that solar system and we're saving it. Period. I don't know how, but we're not letting Wheatles, his crew, or all the bronze- and possibly stone-age people in that system die."

"We all agree, Kitty," Jeff said. "To the point that I've had to put my blocks up. Mother, do we have any way of knowing where we were during the transmission?"

"Somewhat. Once we know where we will stop, I can compare that location to the Eagle Nebula and format a reasonable determination based on when we gained and then lost the transmission."

"From what our science knows," Chuckie said, "if the supernova remnant still has power to damage and shove a spaceship this far off course, then the star couldn't have gone nova all that long ago. Less than a thousand years for certain. That should help with the search."

"Sure," Tim said. "Because there are only, what, a billion stars in our galaxy?"

"More," Wruck said. "But the time from the point when the star exploded that caused the *Eknara* to go off course is less than a thousand years. Much less. If my suspicions are proved correct, the star died about three hundred years ago."

"Oh, I have a bad feeling about this." I did. Because I was pretty sure I knew where Wruck was going.

He nodded. "You should. I believe that the *Eknara* was hit by a neutron wave from the star that Mephistopheles destroyed."

CHAPTER 49

LET THAT SIT ON the air for a good long bit. "You know, I want to say that you're kidding or make some other shocked exclamations, but I'm not surprised at all because, in the grand scheme of things, that totally and completely figures."

"Does that mean that we're close to Earth?" Reader asked.

Wruck shook his head. "The neutron waves will have traveled far by now. But we should be able to get a decent determination based on the location of the star and the expectation of how powerful the wave is based on time and how it affected the *Eknara*."

"Combined with what I should be able to determine once we stop," Mother added, "we should be able to pinpoint a general area of the galaxy. We may have to visit several systems, however, in order to find the correct one."

"We just have to swing by, verify if their star is stable, and move on," Jeff said. "No landings needed."

"Speaking of needs, though, I'm starving. I have no idea what time it is, or if we're even counting time anymore, but my stomach says that it wants food and it wants it now."

The others agreed that breakfast—which was the last meal any of us had had—was a long way away.

"Go eat," Mother said. "I have no need of anyone right now, since none of us can affect anything other than communications at the moment. I will alert you if we receive any other transmissions or if I feel that I am regaining control of the ship."

"Or if we're going back to the pressure of warp jumping," Tim added.

"Yes. I will alert you for the slightest issues."

"They aren't slight to me," Tim grumbled, as we went to find the others.

"As it should be, Commander," Mother said as her parting shot.

Happily, Mother's food creation functions had not been harmed. So, we did what we tended to do when at an A-C Base—we got everyone together in the nearest mess hall that was large enough and ate family style.

Everyone was basically starving—consultation brought us all to the conclusion that we'd probably been gone from Earth about a full half day now, maybe longer. All our time was jumbled and Mother's damage had affected her inner clocks. She felt we were correct, but couldn't swear to it.

"How is it that the kids weren't screaming for food?" I asked Jeff as we all scarfed down whatever was nearest to us on the table.

"I totes think there's an appetite suppressant in the sleep gas," Lizzie replied before Jeff could. "Because no one was hungry until you said we were going to get to eat."

The Dwyer family was on the other side of the table from us, and I could tell Brian had been paying attention. "Not to my knowledge," he said. "But that doesn't mean Lizzie's wrong. It would make some sense."

Drax was called over, but he insisted that an appetite suppressant hadn't been in his formula, though he, like Brian, thought it was a good idea.

"Gustav, who did you test the sleep gas on?"

He seemed shocked by my question. "Myself, of course! I do nothing that I haven't tested personally or I can't stand behind the product."

"That's it," Brian said. "Vata are different from humans and A-Cs. I'll bet if we test it, we'll discover that there's an element that doesn't affect Gustav but does the rest of us."

"Why didn't you test the gas on others?" Jeff asked Drax.

"I did. No one had adverse reactions."

Snorted a laugh. "Because suppressing an appetite isn't actually an adverse reaction. In fact, unless your subjects were paying attention, they wouldn't have even noticed. Maybe they skipped lunch or something. But, when we get home, I sense a real moneymaking opportunity."

"No," Chuckie said flatly. "You do not."

"Geez, dude, when did you become such a Donald Downer?"

He grinned. "Since before we met."

The conversation shifted to other things, including the fact that Denise Lewis, ever the awesome teacher, had been spending the downtime teaching every kid about the galaxy at large, assisted by whichever space travelers were available at the time. Even the "young adults" were into it, which was nice.

It was also nice to see what we had of Jeff's family all hanging out with each other and everyone else. Realized that until we'd been forced into the White House and, therefore, the kids into the Sidwell Friends School, we really hadn't spent much time at all with Jeff's sisters and their families. Felt bad. As an only child, my friends were my siblings, in that sense, and I spent time with most of them weekly, if not daily.

Thought about the few close friends of mine who somehow weren't on the ship with us. Sheila and her family, for starters— no way anyone could have explained their presence, so I got why they weren't here, even though it would have been great if they were. But why hadn't Caroline Chase, my bestie from my sorority days and the late Michael Gower's former fiancée, been included? Jamie loved her—everyone did, really—and Naomi had loved her, too.

Then again, Caroline was the right paw to Senator Donald McMillan, who was Arizona's senior senator, a very close friend of ours by now, and also a hugely pro-alien politician. And, therefore, one of the people who'd be helping Mom and Marcia keep things going and keep all of us safe. So, maybe Caroline had a vital role to play on Earth, so much so that Jamie had left her behind.

Or, rather, Naomi had.

Wondered about this. Knew in my gut that there was no way that Naomi was leaving Earth unprotected. Earth was her home—she, like the rest of the A-Cs in "my" generation, had been born on Earth. And her mother was fully human. Plus, her parents were still on the planet, so there was no way that Naomi was going to ignore Earth while she did whatever she was doing with us.

So, anyone not taken was left behind for the same reason— they were there to protect in some way.

Heaved an internal sigh. There was nothing I could do to help them. We had to focus on what we could do and let those who had the task of keeping our country, world, and solar system safe do what they could do. Wasn't my preferred choice, but it was the right one, and fretting about what was going on there meant I could miss something here. So, no more worry about Earth—it would be there when we got home, because the people who'd been left behind were the right ones for the job.

Felt something, like I was being hugged. But there was no one around me. Blinked back some tears, because I was pretty sure that hug had come from Naomi.

Everyone was done eating by now, and White suggested that we all sleep, as in actual real, not-drug-assisted sleep. It was a sound idea, particularly since we knew that the next time we stopped we'd likely be in action immediately. Jeff made this suggestion an order, and everyone headed for our various sleeping quarters.

Camilla, naturally, went with her wife and the others in the room with Tito, increasing his harem, so to speak. The portions of Animal Planet that we possessed went with whichever people they deemed as theirs. Those with no affiliation went, as promised, with my family. Perhaps they all enjoyed hearing Jeff muttering about living in a literal zoo.

Team Tough Guys were assigned their official room. Algar chose to stay with them. The other guys seemed fine with this. I found it fascinating. Wasn't sure if Algar was testing Siler, giving Wruck and Mossy a chance to get in on the game—since my money was on our Anciannas and Mr. Top Gun Turleen being the next ones who realized that something wasn't quite kosher all the time—enjoying his time getting to hang out as "one of the guys," or if there was something more. Was pretty positive he didn't suspect any of them of being evil, so there was that.

Even though they were assigned to the room with the rest of Team Tough Guys, Butler and Maurer, by benefit of not actually needing sleep, went to the command deck. Mother allowed this.

Stryker pulled me and Chuckie aside before we got into our rooms. Jeff grunted, but he went on inside with the kids while Nathalie went with the others into the couples' suite.

"You guys know we didn't tamper, right?" Stryker asked quietly.

"Dude, seriously, that's like so five minutes ago."

"No, it's not." Stryker looked around, appeared to feel the coast was clear, then went on. "Okay, per Drax, he had us change things so that Mother can't eavesdrop on any of us anymore. It was a complex program, but as long as she doesn't hear words that would indicate mutiny, sabotage, or other traitorous activities, she now can't listen unless one of us is asking her a question, and she can't eavesdrop unless one of the command crew asks it of her."

"Sound," Chuckie said. "What has you worried about this?"

"About that? Nothing. About the fact that there was nothing any of us could do to reprogram her to accept a different command crew? A lot. The positions are set. The only backups allowed are the rest of Airborne, Commander Reader, Drax, and you, Chuck. No one else will have control of the ship even if they're sitting in the chairs."

"That should be impossible," Chuckie said slowly. "Especially considering that Drax was also trying to do the reprogramming."

"Brian isn't okayed to be in the seat?"

"No. It doesn't make sense, Kitty. Right now, the person we want as the commander of the ship is Brian—he's the only one with any real experience and he's trained for this for years. But programming-wise, we couldn't even insert him as an option."

"Did you try to insert others?" Chuckie asked.

Stryker nodded. "We did. That's how we got the rest of you in as alternates. We tried everyone on board, by the way, other than the kids. You all are it."

"Wow. That seems . . . really freaking weird."

"Yeah, Kitty, it's Kitty Weird for sure. So *be sure* that you guys all stay safe. Because if you're hurt or worse, this ship isn't going anywhere."

"Other than where it's being forced to go by outside elements, you mean."

Stryker nodded. "About that—can we try to reach Chernobog?"

"We can, but Mother said there was no way for her to keep that kind of communication private and secured."

"Oh, we don't need it secured. She gave us all a variety of codes we can use to relay information. They all seem innocuous and you have to have the key."

"Who has the key?" Chuckie asked.

"Chernobog." Stryker grinned. "Olga figured it out, because you know those two are competitive, so Adriana knows it, too. But those are the only three. Adrianna hasn't told Malcolm, by the way, and I know this because Olga made her swear not to. I think more as a test than out of any real desire to keep Malcolm from knowing the codes."

"Olga always has her reasons, and she's almost never wrong. And they're among our closest allies, so, yeah, sounds good. Chuckie?"

"What is it you want to ask Chernobog?"

"I want to tell her what's going on and see if she can figure out how we override the locked programming. Not because I don't think you guys can do the jobs," Stryker added quickly. "But because, frankly, most of you are the ones leading every charge. It would have been bad enough if you and Jeff had died on the planet, Kitty. But it would have been worse because we'd all be living there now."

"You have a good point, Eddy. But do we have a risk of giving away our position to enemies?"

"Frankly," Chuckie answered, "yes. But we're literally flying blind. If you want Jeff to okay it, then ask him. Otherwise, I think it's worth trying."

"Run it by Serene, not Jeff. This is her bailiwick, and yours, Secret Agent Man, not his."

"Will do. Anything else?" he asked Stryker.

"Yeah. We heard you got a distress call?"

"We did." Filled him in on what had transpired. "Who told you about it?"

"Mother did."

Chuckie and I looked at each other. "Interestinger and more interestinger. Did she say why she told you?"

"Yes. She wants us to help determine where the distress call came from. She seems really stressed about us helping. Like, I didn't know an AI could get that stressed kind of stressed. Butler and Maurer don't freak out."

"Anymore. They did before we were able to save them from the self-destructs. But, yeah, I do agree that Mother seems more human than AI."

"I'll talk to Camilla about it," Chuckie said. "And then, she, Serene, and I will talk to Drax about it. So far, Mother doesn't appear to be our enemy."

"No," Stryker agreed. "But the other programming of hers that we couldn't override in any way is her need to protect and save sentient life."

"Well, that's not a bad thing."

"It can be, because it's her prime directive."

"Again, why is this bad?"

Chuckie looked thoughtful. "Anything taken to an extreme . . ."

"Exactly," Stryker said. "Guys, seriously, if we can't find whoever called and asked for help, I think Mother may be so distressed by it that she slags. And if she does, then we are up the creek without any hope of a paddle, because she's tied into every system, meaning we'll be without life support, power, the ability to go anywhere, or even call for help."

CHAPTER 50

PROPHECIES OF DOOM HANDED OUT, Chuckie went to get Serene and Camilla, and I went in to my family in the now-unlikely hope of getting some sleep.

However, I had kids to both entertain and distract me, so that was good. Even though it had been a really long day, the kids had enjoyed that excellent nap, so they weren't as tired as one could have hoped.

We decided to forego baths and such, since we had no idea how long we were going to get to rest. So, faces washed and teeth brushed, we all got into nightclothes—the standard A-C issue blue pajama bottoms and white t-shirts with fluffy white robes to snuggle into. "Wow, even in space the Elves deliver."

Jeff laughed. "I'd assume it's Mother's doing, baby."

Totally knew it wasn't, but there was no time like the present to not mention it.

Despite being ready for bed, though, the kids were wide awake and they were also restless. Not a really great combination for sleep or relaxation.

Each of the rooms had a large window. Every window had a retractable metal cover, so asteroid showers would not, hopefully, end up as death sentences. Plus, there were patch kits. Jeff spent some time teaching the kids how to use said kits, which was both important and also, under the circumstances, entertaining. Then, in an attempt to keep things interesting, we all looked out the window.

"Just a lot of blur," Lizzie said disappointedly. "We're out here in space, and we can't see any of it, not really."

"Well, maybe once we hit our next stop we'll be able to see some things." Things like star charts that would lead us back to

Kreaving and his crew, for example. Heaved another internal sigh—the kids wanted a vacation and this wasn't much of one so far. Not that we were here to have fun, but since we *were* here, the kids might as well enjoy it.

Jeff pushed the button and the metal cover went back over the window. "You know what, why don't your mother and I tell you guys about when we visited Alpha Four?"

"When was that, Daddy?" Jamie asked, interest radiating.

He grinned as he sat down on the couch in the living room area and pulled her up onto his lap. "Oh, this was before you were born, Jamie-Kat." I sat on one side of him with Charlie in my lap, and Lizzie took Jeff's other side.

"How old would Lizzie have been?" Jamie asked.

Jeff turned to our teenager who was looking a little wistful. "Hmmm, I think, about eight or nine." Jeff put his arm around Lizzie's shoulders. "So, a little girl, but bigger than you are now." He hugged Lizzie. "Though I'm sure she was still amazing at that age, just like you and Charlie are."

Jamie beamed, Lizzie looked pleased, and Charlie climbed out of my lap and into Jeff's. I felt the love.

Jeff grinned at me as Jamie snuggled under Jeff's arm so that she was on Lizzie, too, and Charlie did the same on Jeff's other side while Jeff put his other arm around me. "Don't want you feeling left out, baby." Charlie did me a solid by imitating Jamie and allowing part of himself to be on my lap, too.

"I'll whine about how no one wants to snuggle with me later."

"Oh, Mommy, we're with Daddy so the pets can be closer to you," Jamie said. "They're a little scared and they want to be with us, but they want to be near you the most. You're the one they love best, even though they love all of us *so* much."

Her Poof appeared in her lap and mewed at her in a hurt tone. Jamie picked the Poof up and kissed it. "I'm sorry, Mous-Mous. I know you love me best of all." She cuddled the Poof to her chest and it seemed appeased.

Looked to my left. Sure enough, Bruno and his mate, Lola, were both on the couch. Lola got into my lap and settled in on and between me and Charlie. Bruno snuggled up next to me, then Ginger trotted in, leapt gracefully onto the back of the couch, and settled on it behind me and Jeff. Wilbur followed her and the chocho settled at our feet with a happy honk.

This meant it was now time for the rest of the Poofs and the rabbits. Peter and SuperBun hopped over while the rest of our Poofs all appeared and snuggled into their owners' necks. SuperBun and Peter both jumped up into my lap. Several other rabbits hopped in and they also jumped up and settled into laps. Extra Poofs and rabbits lined the back of the couch or were on the floor cuddled next to Wilbur, who seemed to love having new friends.

Risked a look at Jeff. He looked like he was warring between laughing his head off and asking for a divorce.

He laughed and winked at me. "Never the latter, baby. Ever. Now, who wants the story?"

"I do!" all three kids said in unison.

Ginger and the Poofs purred, Wilbur honked, the rabbits wiggled their noses, and Bruno and Lola cawed quietly. "That's a big yes from everyone, Jeff. Carry on. I'll add in as necessary."

"Oh, I'm sure you will. Just before Mommy and I got married, we had a chance to go to Alpha Four to see relatives we hadn't even met yet. Your uncle Alexander and great-aunt Victoria."

Jeff shared an extremely sanitized version of the events during the end of Operation Invasion. But his voice was soothing and the story was sweet. He described Alpha Four—far better than I would have, and with a lot more detail.

"I wanted to go there," Lizzie said, trying not to yawn. "I wanted to visit King Alexander."

"We'll get there," I said. "I promise."

"I don't care where we go," Jamie said. She yawned, then went on. "I just want us to all be together when we go. I'm sorry the puppies and kitties didn't get to come with us."

"They're happy taking care of Papa Sol, Nana Angela, Grandpa Alfred, and Grandma Lucinda. And anyone else who had to stay home." Knew that the Poofs and Peregrines had given the Animal Orders for such, so I wasn't lying. After me and Jamie, I was pretty sure that Dad was all the animals' favorite, since his idea of poor treatment for a pet was that said pet might not have the best dog or cat bed available in every room. So those left at home were being spoiled rotten, and that included any ocellars, chochos, Poofs, and Peregrines, as well as the dogs and cats.

"That's right," Jeff said. "They have their jobs to do, just like we do. And speaking of jobs, we had a job to do on Alpha Four before we went home to Earth. We got to install Uncle Alexander as the King."

He went on to describe a ceremony that had never happened, though I imagined it was what normally happened. Charlie yawned so widely I wondered if he had Ezkot blood in him. Then he leaned his head against Jeff's chest, his Poof still cuddled into his neck, his little hands wrapped gently around the bunny in his lap, Lola's head resting against his side, and fell fast asleep.

Jeff smiled and kept on talking, telling the girls about our wedding. They were interested and fighting to stay awake, but Jeff was definitely lulling them to sleep, as were the rhythmic sounds of animal snoozing and the warmth of all the fur and feathers around us.

Lizzie leaned her head against Jeff's shoulders, murmured that she was paying attention but needed to close her eyes, and was out.

Jamie heaved a sigh. "Mommy?" she asked as Jeff paused. "Yes?"

"Will you go to sleep if you're the last one awake?"

This was a good question, because when we were in what I considered a danger situation and everyone else was asleep, no matter how tired I was, I woke up and stayed awake. And Jamie knew it.

"I think so."

Jeff kissed the top of Jamie's head. "Don't worry about it, Jamie-Kat. I promise Mommy's going to fall asleep right after you."

"O-kay," she said with another big yawn. She leaned against Jeff's chest. "Tell me again about how Mommy ran to meet you, Daddy."

He chuckled. "It was the best wedding ever." Jamie was asleep before the last word. Jeff kissed my forehead. "You're next, baby."

Decided that there were times to obey my husband, and this was one of them. Leaned my head back against his shoulder and listened to Ginger's purring. "This is nice."

"It is," Jeff said softly. "My family. You sleep, baby. You've earned it."

My turn to yawn. "You need to sleep, too."

He kissed my forehead again. "In a while." He said something else, but I only heard sounds, not words, as I followed the kids' lead and fell asleep.

Wasn't sure if I was instantly dreaming or not, but

somewhere after I zonked out I heard someone calling my name. Wasn't coming from anywhere in particular that I could tell and, as per usual, I couldn't recognize the voice.

ACE? ACE is that you? No answer. Considered options. Algar never bothered with my dreams. I mean, maybe he helped facilitate them, but he didn't bother to show up to add to the weird, for which I was most appreciative.

Naomi? Asked probably far more hopefully than was good for me. Nada again. Though now was pretty sure that I could see things around me. Looked like what we'd seen out the window, meaning a lot of blur and not much else. Oh well, I'd had worse, and weirder, dream locales.

Considered who else liked to hang out and chat with me in my sleep. Michael? Fuzzball? Gladys? A big fat nothing.

Oh, duh. Maybe this was the DreamScape. Ixtha?

Less than nothing. Was stumped for a moment. Who the heck else could this be?

My tired brain nudged and I heaved a sleep sigh. Sadly, by process of elimination and the reality of how my luck went, had a really good guess as to who I needed to be asking for. Just hoped this dream would be odor free.

CHAPTER 51

"MEPHS?"

"Always nice to be thought of. Dead last, but at least thought of."

Sniffed. Happily, no Smell-O-Rama happening. So, I had that going for me, which was nice. "You're the fugly of my dreams, if that helps any." Well, nightmares were dreams, right?

"It does, somewhat." He came into view, sitting next to me. Hadn't realized I was sitting until just now, so that was interesting. Just me and a giant red monster faun with claws for fingers and curling horns and, of course, batwings. Hellboy was a supermodel compared to Mephistopheles.

"So, why are we just hangin' out in the middle of nowhere? Are you actually here to be helpful? Or is it just that the cosmos never wants me to forget about Operation Fugly? As if I ever could."

"I'm choosing to ignore the likely insults. I'm the most help-ful of those who visit you in your sleep, if you'd care to recall."

"This is true. So, I've gotten more of the Mephistopheles Biography. I'd make a comment about what a jerk you were, but having had the whole story of how the Superiors came to be, I don't really want to and I'm sure you know."

"I do. Mistakes were made. Mistakes are always made."

"Are we making mistakes right now?"

"No. The preservation of the galaxy is vital. When I chose to destroy my solar system, I did so because I knew my race would survive and begin again. I'd thought that my followers would find me and we would create our new world."

"You were booking along with that plan just fine until I showed up, I guess."

"True enough. However, death—the true death that I experienced due to you—is a great teacher."

"So, seriously, death is not the end? It's really the beginning like we've been told?"

"It depends on the individual. For me, death means I have to watch what I created. Until the galaxy is destroyed or the damage I caused is fixed."

Pondered this. "So, why are you helping me, then? I'd kind of think you would be pro Operation Good-bye Milky Way."

"No. Death is a great . . . clarifier. I can see what went wrong, the great mistakes I made. The mistakes made before I was even born."

"Were you born or were you created?"

"Born." He tapped my nose gently with his foreclaw. "Just like you." His expression was fond and, for him, kindly, and he looked like a super strange version of Santa. There was a lot of that going around.

"Our relationship is weird."

He laughed. "It is. You are special to me."

"I killed you, if you want to recall."

"You did, with help from your mother and friends. But mostly you. However, to be bested by a worthy adversary is a good death. You will always matter to me because of that."

"The old saying that having a good enemy is as important as having someone to love?"

"Yes. It's true. You are without an enemy on this journey."

"Seriously? I feel like everything's against us."

"Everything is. But 'everything' is not a person, an individual. You cannot fight 'everything.'"

"Um, so . . . what are we supposed to do, then?"

"Continue to right my wrongs."

"Hold up there. You're saying that my whole job in life is to fix the mess you made?"

Mephistopheles patted my hand. "Isn't it?" he asked gently.

Did some more pondering. "I guess it kind of feels that way. But you were created, in that sense, by the Z'porrah. Shouldn't I be trying to right their wrongs, too?"

"That falls to another."

"John Wruck?"

Mephistopheles smiled. As always, it was gross, scary, and kind of sweet. The description of our relationship in a nutshell. "You are insightful."

"Dude, it was an easy guess. But there's more going on."

"There always is."

"What's the situation with Ixtha and her people?"

"As grave as you understand it to be. The survival of her solar system is vital to this galaxy."

"Why is the galaxy in so much danger right now? And please don't give me some flip reply. I'm asking because it just seems too coincidental that we have all these bad things going on at once."

"As your good friend says, don't believe too much in coincidence."

"Chuckie says they're rarer than a camera-shy Kardashian, but that's beside the point. Can I get a little less obscurity and a little more clarity?"

Mephistopheles heaved a sigh. "I can answer, because this particular visit is under the protection of more than one entity, so I can break the obscurity rules. Just a bit."

"Wow. That's both cool and weird. And cooler and weirder that it's you who gets the extra chatting protection."

"You and I are perceived to be the greatest of enemies by . . . some. That I have a deep fondness for you, and you for me, even if you choose to pretend that you don't, is beyond their understanding. The entities helping me speak to you, however, understand and are using this weakness to all of our advantage."

"Go team."

"Truly. And it *is* a team effort. Never think that it is not. But to answer your question, these events are not accidental and they are not random. They are a concerted effort to cause this galaxy to, essentially, self-destruct."

"Why? And who's behind it? Because what you just said sure sounds like we have an enemy."

"Oh, there is an enemy. Only it is not *your* enemy. This enemy has no hatred for you, or for any life in this galaxy. This enemy has a job to do, however, and plans to do it, in any way necessary. Sadly, the current way is to create galaxy-ending havoc and see what happens."

He didn't have to say more. I knew what was going on now. But it would help to be sure. "If I played the Counting Crows' version of "Friend of the Devil," would that fit this situation?" The song was about an outlaw on the run and how the Devil was always double-crossing him, originally written by The Grateful

Dead. There were a lot of versions of it, but the Crows' was my favorite.

Mephs laughed. "Yes. My time is almost up. Is there anything else you wish to know?"

"How do we get back to where Wheatles Kreaving and his ship are? There's a solar system in danger of exploding and we need to help them. Our AI is being affected by whichever Powers That Be are currently having fun with us, and I can't let all those people die without trying to save them. They don't have a crazy leader—they were all just in the wrong place at the wrong time."

"I cannot tell you how to get back there, and I'm sure you can guess why."

Sighed. "Because it's your fault and so you have to be more obscure."

"Yes. However, I can tell you this—what went into their sun is a living thing. You must destroy that living thing in order to save the sun and, therefore, the solar system and all the life within it."

"And the galaxy, right? I just have to figure that if this system goes, we're back to chain reaction time."

"Of course," Mephs said, as if this was obvious which, for my life, it was. "Just remember—every leader, good or bad, has those working closely with him or her, and some of those can be even better than that leader. Or worse."

"Um . . . you mean like Jeff? Or Hitler? Or both?"

"You'll figure it out—I have faith in you. Remember that, too. Even when you have lost faith in yourself, I will always have faith in you." Then he kissed the top of my head and disappeared.

CHAPTER 52

WOKE UP TO SOMEONE kissing the top of my head. Sniffed. Didn't smell like horrible fugly, so either I was actually still asleep or I didn't have Mephistopheles snuggled next to me.

Cracked an eyelid. Thankfully, what I saw was a sea of fur with some feathers tossed in. Said sea appeared to be snoring in individual ways.

"Mmph?" Wasn't my most coherent sound, but it was all I could manage.

"Sorry, baby," Jeff said softly. "I'm trying not to wake the kids. But I'd like to get them into bed if we can."

"Your butt's gone to sleep?"

He chuckled. "Possibly."

The way we were hooked into each other meant that we had some challenges. Fortunately, Bruno and Lola woke up and assisted, mostly by getting off of me and Charlie so I could move.

Was able to use hyperspeed to get me and our son, his Poof, and what I knew was now officially his rabbit off of the couch. All three kids were in one big bedroom. Wasn't sure but had a feeling that Algar was doing some room rearrangements. Then again, I hadn't looked at Drax's plans for crew and passenger quarters and it wasn't like I'd gone into every one of the living quarters, so maybe this was just standard in a family suite.

Tucked Charlie into bed and kissed his forehead as his Poof—which he'd named Mine, though the rest of us called it Miney—and bunny snuggled back into his neck and tummy, respectively, and Lola took the foot of the bed. Hoped Charlie would come up with a better name for his rabbit, though I didn't count on it—his nickname for Wilbur was also Mine. Frankly, had a feeling that Charlie thought naming his pets Mine to be very funny. Chuckie felt Charlie had my sense of humor. Wasn't sure if that was a good thing or not, but chose to roll with it.

Decided not to try to get any of the kids out of their robes because it was likely to wake them up. It was cool enough in the rooms that I didn't feel they'd be uncomfortable. And, similar to the setup at every A-C Base, there were low nightlights in the room, so that no one would get lost getting to the bathroom or into our room in case of bad dreams.

Speaking of Wilbur, the chocho padded in and settled down right next to Charlie's bed, since Charlie was, in Wilbur's cho-cho mind, his very special human to protect at all possible times. I was good with Wilbur's dedication to the cause. Wilbur thought it was great that Charlie loved him enough to give him the special Mine nickname, too.

Gave all the animals with Charlie pets, then trotted back out and took Jamie. Mous-Mous and Peter both woke up and did me a solid by heading to her bed without my assistance. Many of the unattached Poofs and rabbits followed them.

Tucked Jamie in as Bruno settled at the foot of her bed and the other animals got comfy around her, while Jeff carried Lizzie to her bed. Lizzie scored Ginger at the foot of her bed, along with her Poof, Fofo, and several rabbits settled around her head, including SuperBun. The remaining unattached Poofs and rabbits hopped up onto the bed, some snuggling right next to Ginger, too, rabbits in particular. Ginger and Bruno were basically heroes to the rabbits, and Ginger found this hero worship totally acceptable.

Kissed both girls on their foreheads, petted all the rest of the animals, including our Poofs, who were apparently going On Duty with the kids. Poofikins was with Lizzie, Harlie with Jamie, and Murphy had Charlie. These three Poofs were all at the head of each bed, and clearly on watch. Worked for me.

Everyone else settled in, Jeff and I went to our bedroom and closed the door. "I think we have enough animals to ensure that if something happens, we'll hear about it fast," Jeff said.

"Truly." Yawned widely. Considered telling Jeff about my dream, but I rarely shared them with him, mostly because they were usually personal and always weird. Didn't feel like trying to explain why I dreamed about Mephistopheles a lot, in no small part because I didn't want anyone to suggest that Tito find a really good mental health professional for me to visit on a regular basis. My crazy worked for me and I was keeping it.

Jeff and I took off our robes and got into bed. We lay there for a couple of minutes. Then a pertinent fact I hadn't shared with Jeff dawned on me.

"You know, Stryker told me that they were able to change the AI's programming so that if we don't specifically call for her, or she isn't triggered by things that indicate mutiny or such, she isn't listening in."

Jeff laughed. "Oh, so that's why you didn't use her name. Yeah, I wasn't really looking forward to being watched. Or rated."

"Oh, you have no worries about your Yelp reviews."

"Oh yeah?" Jeff purred as he rolled onto his side. "What's my best review?"

"Mmmm," I stroked his chest and decided I was bitter because he still had the t-shirt on. "You always get at least ten stars out of ten, and most times you go to eleven. Besides, maybe your best review is yet to come."

Jeff's eyes smoldered and he got the Jungle Cat About To Eat Me look on his face. That was my favorite look in the galaxy. "Good to know." His voice was husky and I was, shocker alert, instantly ready to go.

Jeff kissed me—deep, strong, wild—and while his mouth was occupied, his hands got us out of our pajama bottoms in record time. He ended our kiss, but merely to strip the t-shirts off. Then he ravaged my mouth again while our hands roamed each other's bodies.

Before kids, we could take hours with foreplay. Once Jamie arrived, we tended to hurry it up. Now, with Charlie and Lizzie added into the family, foreplay was a luxury. However, Jeff still managed to fit some in, because he was a sexual god of the highest order.

His mouth went to my neck, which was my main erogenous zone. While his lips, teeth, and tongue toyed with me up there, his hands toyed with the rest of me, one hand arousing my breasts while the other went lower and stroked me. He was in a sensual rhythm—each area being pleasured at the same time, and it wasn't long before I went over the edge.

Due to having kids, I'd done my best to try not to sound like a cat in heat every time we did the deed, but it tended to take more effort than I could always muster. Tonight—or whatever time it actually was wherever we were—I didn't really have the willpower in me, so I yowled.

Jeff didn't stop, and neither did I, but was aware that we were both listening for signs of my having woken the kids. Either the rooms were well soundproofed—always something to be hoped for—or the kids were really out, because no one came in to ask what we were doing.

While we were listening, my hand found my favorite organ in the universe and I toyed with Jeff. Oh sure, I was still busy being sexually controlled by my husband, but I managed to participate beyond gasping and moaning, and also ensured that he was ready to go. He was. Fully.

"Mmmm, is my bad girl already ready?" Jeff purred against my neck.

"Al-ways." Hey, yowling was easy when we were like this. Speaking coherently wasn't.

Jeff chuckled, nipped my neck, gently squeezed both nipples in turn, and gave me one last starter stroke, and then he was inside me and the real fun began.

Fancy positions, while awesome, were also now something we saved for when we knew we couldn't be disturbed. But there were always ways to make a standard position fun, and Jeff knew them all.

As he thrust inside and I slammed my hips in time with him, he moved up onto his hands, slipping his forearms behind my knees. I grabbed his impressive pecs while we thrust together in a fast rhythm. He'd had me more than ready and another orgasm arrived in record time.

I was gasping and moaning, but he wasn't done. He slid first one leg and then the other up his arms so that my heels were resting on his shoulders. Then, one hand at my hips and the other toying between my legs, he went to town.

My lower body couldn't move much in this position, which was fine because it felt fantastic—hard and deep and oh, so pleasurable. My upper body was able to writhe, which, based on Jeff's growls, he appreciated. My hands couldn't reach anything I wanted to grab, like his chest or, as I thought of them, his perfect pair of thrusters, so they grabbed the sheets instead.

We were like this for what could have been an hour or could have been minutes only. When Jeff had me in this state, time didn't really work right, and I really didn't care. The only thing that mattered was him—how he'd move, what he'd do, how he'd look at me.

The Jungle Cat look was on his face again as he ratcheted me right back up to the edge of climax. "Tell me what you want," he growled.

Gasped but couldn't get the answer out.

He smiled. "Tell me. Or . . . I'll stop."

"Want . . . you. Always . . . want you."

His smile widened. "That's what I like to hear, baby. Because I always want you to want me." His thrusts got faster and stronger, his fingers played me like he was B.B. King and I was Lucille, and another orgasm hit, hard and strong.

Couldn't yowl, all I could do was gasp. But Jeff didn't stop. He flipped my legs down, wrapped his arms around me, and started going harder and faster. Wrapped my legs around his waist so my feet could help those thrusters along and slammed into him as hard and as fast as I could, while my hands clawed at his back.

He kissed me and this kiss was wild and almost animalistic, so I knew he was almost there. He ended our kiss, reared back, and growled. "What do you want?"

I was ready. "All of you, Jeff." We slammed together, going faster and faster, and I could tell we were both at the edge. "Every last bit."

He threw back his head and roared as he exploded inside me and my body responded in kind.

Jeff lay on top of me as our bodies throbbed together, both of us nuzzling the other, arms still around each other but caressing, not clutching, now. Finally, we both stilled, and he rolled off of me and onto his back, bringing me onto my side so I could drape over him and we could continue to stay in each other's embrace.

Heaved a happy sigh. "That was one fantastic spaceship ride."

Jeff chuckled. "I agree. So, Commander," he said as he nuzzled my head and I stroked the hair on his chest, "should I take you around the galaxy next?"

"Oooh, make it so, Number One. Make it so."

CHAPTER 53

GOT IN SEVERAL MORE excellent orgasms, then we got back into our nightclothes, wrapped around each other, and went back to sleep.

This sleep was dreamless, or if I dreamed, I didn't remember anything. Woke up to a low dinging sound. "What's that?"

Jeff hugged me and sat up. "I'm guessing it's Mother's way of waking us up."

"Her way is a lot more pleasant than how they do it in Centaurion Division."

Jeff laughed as he got out of bed. "Maybe this alarm system doesn't make you get fully out of bed to turn off, too."

"We can but hope." Wasn't all that tired, but I'd never been a leap out of bed ready to face the day person and saw no reason to start now.

The kids were up as well, so we did a fast shower rota and got dressed. Happily, the Elves had indeed taken the spaceship contract, so while Jeff had the standard Armani fatigues waiting for him, the kids and I got to be in jeans, t-shirts, comfy shoes, and jackets.

I was in a vintage Styx "Mr. Roboto" shirt with an Aerosmith hoodie, which was kind of a change. But, since I knew Algar had his reasons, didn't argue, just rejoiced that my Converse had been allowed to make the trip with me. Lizzie had scored Metallica while Jamie was in a pink Roger Rabbit shirt and Charlie was wearing Winnie the Pooh featuring all the characters. Clearly, Algar had a theme for the family. Had no idea what it was, but knew he had one.

Thusly attired to take on the galaxy, flung my purse over my neck, and we headed to the mess hall. True to form, all the A-Cs were in the Armani Fatigues and anyone who wasn't an A-C was in some form of color. Even Reader, Chuckie, and Tim had branched out and weren't going for their standard "blend in with our alien friends" sartorial choices. Truly a red-letter day.

Had to give Drax and Mother this   eating was not an issue on the *Distant Voyager*. We all scarfed down the plentiful and delicious food and drink as if we hadn't been fed and watered for days versus hours. A suspicion niggled. Considered the best place to pose my question and decided the mess hall probably wasn't it.

Sped up so I'd finish eating before the others, excused myself, told Jeff to stay with the kids, grabbed another cinnamon roll for the road, made eye contact with Tim, and left the room.

Tim caught up to me. "What's going on? And why did you want the others to stay in the mess hall? At least, I assume that's what you wanted, and I hope it is, because I told James and Chuck to stay put."

"It is, good call. I have a question that needs asking and I think it's likely that only you and I are going to get the answer." Headed for the command deck. Butler and Maurer were there, both awake and functioning, which was a relief. The Kristie-Bot was there, too, however, which was not, though it pretty much confirmed my suspicions.

"Okay," Tim said, "I'll bite. What question?"

"Mother, how long were we all sleeping?"

Silence.

Looked at Butler. "I expect an answer. From her or from one of you three."

"I will answer," Mother said. "You have all been asleep for the human equivalent of two days."

"Perfect," Tim muttered.

"In that time I was able to update the Universal Translator and install the languages the others have learned into those of you who were awake or were not on board when we first left Earth. You will all be able to speak to a wider variety of life in the galaxy with ease now."

"So that makes it all better?" Tim shook his head. "You taught the rabbits new languages, and that's supposed to make us not upset? How'd you figure it out, Kitty?"

"We were all too damned hungry. Why do this? Or, more importantly, why did you risk us in that way? And don't say to merely teach us whatever languages we *might* need. JR is still a baby who can't go two hours without care, let alone days." Looked at Maurer, who was not looking at me. "Oh, he didn't, did he? Uncle Cameron took care of diapers and feedings and such, didn't he?"

"I have two children," Maurer replied.

"I'm good with kids, too," the Kristie-Bot said somewhat defensively.

"I'm sure you are," I lied. Examined my arms. Sure enough, was pretty sure I saw a needle mark in my forearm. "You guys came in and put the rest of us under, didn't you?"

"The ship is equipped to put passengers into suspended animation in times of need," Mother said. "So, yes, that was done. It was made easier by the others' help, but I could have done it without them if the situation had demanded it."

"You gassed us all, then put the needles in, is that about it?" Which mean the gas was shipwide, not just in the crash couch rooms.

"Yes," Mother said. "Younger children were woken, tended to, and put back into suspended animation during the suspended animation period."

"How can you be sure it didn't hurt them? Or any of us?"

"This was created by Drax," Maurer said. "With the idea that humans, A-Cs, and hybrids would be on board. Everything was tested, Kitty, including the possibility for people to be and become pregnant and also to give birth. Tests were done, many times over."

"I remind you that my prime directive is that I preserve life," Mother said. "I will never do anything to harm any of you."

"Of course you won't, but, just to be sure, should we start calling you HAL?" Tim asked, easily as snidely as I would have.

"No," Butler said. "This wasn't done to create problems— Cameron and I never would have allowed that. This was done because there was nothing going on."

"So?"

The Kristie-Bot heaved a sigh. "I get why they don't get it, John, let me take this one. Kitty, for some of you the trip has been action-packed and all of you needed to rest, a lot. But, and this is the key point, the rest of the adults are already dangerously bored. And I'm talking the politicians in particular, but not just them. No one's gotten to do anything, and wandering the ship was great for a few hours, but not long-term. Their restlessness was starting to rub off on the kids."

"Again, so?" Tim asked.

The Kristie-Bot rolled her eyes. "You have a lot of people on board who can create problems if they're left unattended. You have a small press corps with you, you have powerful politicians, you have parents, and you have a lot of kids. You know what people do when they're bored?"

"Things we don't want them to. I get it. Tim, just imagine what Hacker International could be up to if they weren't needed to assist Drax and Mother."

"Exactly," Butler said. "It was deemed safer to have you all stay in suspended animation until we felt that we were close to our destination."

"And, are we?" Tim asked. "And if we are, where is this magic destination?"

"Based on how long we have been moving at warp speed," Mother replied, "I estimate us to be coming out of warp within the next hour. Hence why we woke everyone up two hours ago, so you could bathe, dress, and eat."

Tim and I looked at each other. "It makes sense," Tim admitted. "But what do we tell the others?"

"Nothing." Looked around. Yep, that's what Team Tinman thought was the right course, could tell by their expressions and body language. "If Chuckie or one of the others asks, then we tell them, in private. But for the others, we don't say anything."

"Why do you want us to lie to the crew and passengers?" Tim asked. "Not to mention our spouses."

"Because we can. And I mean that you and I can lie. It's the same as when Nightcrawler didn't want us sharing that they were on board. Think about how upset you and I were when we realized what had happened. Now multiply that by everyone else. We don't have time for mutiny or infighting. We have a galaxy to save."

"You think no one else will notice?" Tim asked. "I mean that seriously. You noticed, Kitty, right away."

"I did, but no one else seemed even remotely curious about why we were all so hungry." Presumed that was probably due to an assist from Algar, but could have been from other reasons. An assist from ACE, for example. "And ACE is with us—if he felt that this was a bad plan, he'd have kept Jamie awake or warned me." At least, I hoped. "But what about the animals? Were they aware or cared for?"

"The animals spent most of the time sleeping," Mother said. "When they awoke we took care of their needs."

Thought about this. "Most of them are predators, and predators sleep a lot. But they're also protectors. You're saying they were okay with this plan of yours?"

"The animals communicate with you," Maurer said. "Not the rest of us on a regular basis. They didn't seem upset with any of us, and most of them are equipped to share displeasure violently. The few who wanted attention got it, too."

"Okay," Tim said. "So, let's say that ACE and the animals were all okay with this. But if we say that we agree with every decision made regarding this situation, how do we handle the boredom? Because that's not likely to go away."

"I think that all depends on where we're going for our next stop." Didn't say that it could be somewhere fun, because I knew how the cosmos liked to hear things like that and take the possibility away immediately as spoken.

"We spent all the time while you were sleeping trying to determine that," Butler said. "We are not certain, of course, but we feel that we are heading to a point opposite in the galaxy from the Eagle Nebula."

"Far from the Galactic Core," Maurer added. "As near as we can tell, we've been sent around the Core, versus through it."

"Makes sense for safer flying. And also if we're somehow not supposed to be noticed." Now, why did I think that?

"Why do you think that?" Tim asked, right on cue.

Realized I thought this because of my dream with Mephistopheles. "Someone" was trying to destroy the galaxy, most likely as a way to flush Algar out of hiding. Meaning that if we were the ones tasked with saving the galaxy, it was going to be better if we were flying under Someone's radar. And all of our various Powers That Be were working toward saving the galaxy, meaning that they were all working together, albeit likely in a tenuous fashion and removed enough to be able to claim neutrality.

"Just had weird dreams. But I think we should figure that whoever's pulling our strings wants us to be more stealthy as opposed to overt."

"Gotcha. So, only those of us in the room get to know. Glad I practiced lying to Alicia from day one in our relationship."

Hugged him. "It'll be fine. This is leadership and high-level security clearances in a nutshell. Don't think of it as you lying. Think of it as you being the Prime Minister in the Sovereign and Flying Nation of Kitty Land."

"I remember how mad you were. I'm thrilled to be in the Inner Circle. Full lying capability coming right up, Queen Kitty."

"It's nice to be back in the Sovereign and Flying Nation of Kitty Land," Joe said as he and Randy joined us. "You told them?" he asked Butler.

"Kitty figured it out, as you expected her to."

Tim and I exchanged the "duh" look. "You two weren't sleeping, either, were you?" I asked.

Randy shrugged. "We slept some, because we still need it. But we're not fully human anymore, and in times like this, that's a good thing."

"We approved the decision to put everyone under," Joe said. "Not anyone else."

"John, Kristie, and Cameron didn't mention that."

Randy grinned. "We told them not to, Mother, too. If someone figured it out, then we'd tell them. You figured it out, we're telling you. Commander. Or should I say My Queen?"

"Oh, stop. You two know I'm almost never mad at you. But I do feel better that you two were involved, and that's not a diss on the rest of you."

Joe nodded. "We were on board for everything, remember, because you took our wives to the planet but not us. All we got to do was taxi service."

"So bitter."

"We're not complaining," Randy said. "Much. It was nice to get to do what we've been training for, for a few minutes. But it was getting ugly up here while you were down on the planet. Denise had the kids occupied, but most of the adults were already starting to get cabin fever."

"Meaning we cross that road when we have an option," Tim said. "But we can't keep everyone sleeping all the time, particularly if your calculations for when we're stopping are incorrect."

A dinging sound started. Louder than the alarm had been, thankfully much softer than the alarms. "All personnel to stations," Mother said. "All passengers to Nonessential Personnel Stations. We will be coming out of warp within five minutes."

"I stand corrected," Tim said, as he headed for his seat.

"I assume you can tell versus are back in charge, right, Mother?" I asked as I finished my cinnamon roll and seated myself and my purse in our duty station.

"Yes," she said, as Jeff, Hughes, Walker, and Tito arrived, doing the hyperspeed daisy chain.

"Are the kids okay?" I asked Jeff as he strapped in and I got my helmet on.

"Yes. Locked and loaded, so to speak." He looked around at Team Tinman. "Why are the five of you in here? Mother said to get to stations."

"I think we want them here," Tim said.

"Two androids, a cyborg, and the Six Million Dollar Men are good additions to the command crew. Particularly because we don't know who has control of Mother."

Jeff muttered something about too many cooks in a kitchen, but we all ignored him.

"Leaving warp in five," Mother said, as the dinging stopped. ". . . four . . . three—"

Two and one were interrupted. By the ship slamming through something.

CHAPTER 54

WAS REALLY GLAD THAT the seats were made for this, and sincerely hoped the kids were as locked in as Jeff had insinuated, because we were definitely crashing.

Jeff hadn't been wrong to ask why Team Tinman was hanging around. They were basically flipping about in the command area. Would have been comical if I wasn't worried about them getting hurt, as well as anything or anyone they slammed into, too.

Was able to grab the Kristie-Bot as she slid into my chair. She pulled herself up and slipped her arm through my harness. It was uncomfortable, but she wasn't cramping my ability to do whatever it was my job was, and it also meant she could catch Joe as he flipped by.

Joe and the Kristie-Bot did the hand-to-elbow clasp that meant they were both locked onto each other and had some slippage room in case of the worst.

Joe caught Maurer, they did the same clasp, then Maurer caught Randy, and Randy was able to grab Butler.

"Everyone okay?" Tito asked.

Got a chorus of replies that indicated no one was so damaged that they needed to get to sick bay or, considering, down to Engineering.

Because the helmets let us see what was going on with the ship, at least in a certain sense, I was able to see that we were smashing through something, because sensors on the exterior said we were.

However, looking out the windshield showed nothing. We were in space, in a solar system, because I could see a sun and planets, but we weren't close enough to the nearest planet to be crashing into anything.

"What are we hitting, an asteroid belt?" Tim asked, as the ship shook and bucked. "Meteors? Space junk?"

"Not that any visual sensors are picking up," Hughes replied, voice clipped.

"We're crashing into nothing," Walker added. "But sensors do indicate that something's hitting the exterior of the ship and causing this slight turbulence we're all experiencing."

"So, totally par for our particular course. Good, good. So, how do we stop? And, as the Communications Officer or whatever the hell I am, what do I tell the others?"

"To stay put," Jeff said. "Because we're under attack."

"By what?" Hughes and Walker asked in unison.

"No idea," Jeff said through gritted teeth. "But I can see something coming at us from the planets."

We all looked out the windshield. "I see nothing," Tim said.

"He's speaking for all of us," Butler added.

"Through my helmet," Jeff said. "I can see them coming at us through the helmet. Missiles or similar are leaving the planets."

"All of them?" That seemed like overkill, even for the Solaris system, and Earth was considered really touchy, too.

"Sensors indicate it, yeah." Jeff was pushing buttons at hyperspeed.

"Why can only Jeff see whatever it is?" Tito asked.

"Presumably because he's in charge of Weapons," Tim replied. "Though that makes no sense. I thought we could all see everything through the helmets."

"Only what pertains to your duties and expertise," Mother said.

"I can't see Medical and we still don't know why Kitty's here, either," Tito pointed out.

"Back to making no sense," Joe offered from the impromptu daisy chain.

Walker took time out to catch hold of Butler's free arm and pull him closer. Butler was then able to imitate the Kristie-Bot and get his arm through Walker's harness. Now we had a semicircle around Tito, but Team Tinman wasn't flying around through the air anymore, so one for the win column which was, once again, pretty empty.

But that the rest of us couldn't see whatever it was out there made sense if only an A-C would be able to see what was coming. And there had to be some reason for why whoever—presumably Naomi—had made our seat assignments irrevocable. I'd inherited

A-C vision from birthing Jamie, too, and I saw nothing, but I wasn't the one assigned to shoot photon torpedoes or whatever, so maybe that was why. However, there was something that no one else was saying that I figured someone had to.

"Um, I don't know whose job it is to say this, but shields up."

"That's me," Tito said, as he started hitting buttons. Buttons were flashing on everyone's consoles, not just his, though. The guys all pushed theirs fast. My console only had one button flashing. I'd already forgotten which button did what, and, so far, I'd only had to deal with three of them. Why I had this position was beyond me, really. However, managed to recognize that the button flashing was the same one I'd pushed to chat with Kreaving. Oh well, time to Uhura Up and do my job.

Pushed the button. "Hello, this is the *Distant Voyager* from Earth in the Solaris system. We're sorry that we can't take your call right now because we're under attack. If you are the planet or planets attacking us, we would really appreciate your stopping. We come in peace and would like to leave the same way, versus in pieces."

"What?" the voice on the other end said. Sounded female. Possibly.

"Stop shooting at us or whatever it is you're doing."

"Your ship ignored our instructions to stop."

"No, we did not. Your call just came through."

"We told your ship to stop."

"Um, I'm in charge of Communications. These requests come through me or they don't come at all."

"We are able to talk directly to your ship. We did so, and your ship did not comply. Or respond."

"Missiles getting closer," Jeff said. "Verify that they're warheads, Kitty, versus manned."

"Ah, as to that, the ship is having some issues right now. Also, are you sending things to blow us up, or people to shoot at us?"

"What do you mean?"

"I mean we're about to retaliate. But we're actually coming in peace, as in, don't want to fight with any of you, so if those ships are manned then we'd prefer to talk versus shoot. If, however, those ships are bombs, warheads, or whatever else, then we're going to shoot them before they hit us."

"You attacked us and destroyed our shield."

"Look, your shield is invisible. So are your bombs. At least to us."

"Then how are you seeing them?"

"Nice to get the confirmation that you've sent weapons at us. Officially, that's an act of war where we come from."

"You intruded."

"So sorry, but if you put up invisible barriers, you just have to figure someone's going to crash through them. Frankly, where we come from, barriers are made to be really obvious so people avoid them. Those barriers that are hidden are usually hidden to hurt innocent and unsuspecting people. So, right now, we think of you as a violent race out to hurt us and probably others."

There was a pause on the other line.

"Kitty, ten seconds and I have to fire."

"Yo, whoever I'm speaking to, time's up. Pull back or we blow the things coming at us up."

"Locked and loaded," Jeff said. "Firing in five . . ."

"We will pull back."

". . . four . . ."

"Jeff, they said they're pulling back."

". . . three . . . no, they aren't . . . two . . ."

"We have stopped!" The voice on the other side sounded panicked. "Don't fire!"

"Not firing," Jeff said, before I could tell him not to. "The missiles have all turned away from us."

"Where are they headed?"

"Other directions, just not toward us. I'm monitoring in case they come back at us."

"Thank you for not shooting," the probably-a-woman on the line said. "Please leave our solar space now." The ship stopped shaking and bouncing.

This was weird. Weirder than normal. Weirder the more I thought about it. First an invisible barrier, then invisible weapons that only Jeff could see, these people claiming to have talked to Mother directly, them managing to call their weapons off at the very last second, and then them telling us to leave, as if we were still the aggressors. The way the ship was somehow now through a barrier we couldn't see—a very thick barrier, all things considered. An invisible barrier that a spaceship had flown through for several minutes. Something was off. Very off.

"Hold please." And, speaking of off, took my finger off the button. It was still flashing, so assumed my call was still live, so to speak. "Mother, is the call still live?"

"Live, but holding, just as you requested. They cannot hear us."

"Great. Mother, can you tell us what damage the exterior of the ship has taken?"

"None. I have been scanning since this began and the *Distant Voyager* is fully intact."

"That seems impossible for how much I've been battered around," Randy said.

"Our shields could be that good," Walker said doubtfully. "I mean, Drax is a genius."

"They are not," Mother replied. "Based on what we felt, shields should have taken damage. But they took none."

"Jeff, where are the missiles?"

"Can't see them anymore, Kitty. They're out of range."

Looked out the windshield. "I see seven planets and what appears to be a lot of moons around most of them. What do you guys see?"

Everyone saw the same, even Jeff. "The fourth planet only has one moon," he said. "At least, that's all I see."

"That's all I see, too." My brain nudged. "Um, Jeff? What would our missiles have hit, if they'd somehow missed the targets or you'd fired before the targets moved?"

"I can determine the trajectory," Mother said. "Our torpedoes would have struck the large moon that orbits the fourth planet in view."

Knew what was going on. "That's no moon."

CHAPTER 55

"I'LL BET CASH MONEY you've been waiting all your life to say that, Kitty," Tim said. "But, why right now?"

"Yes, I have, but as to why right now, it's because I think what we have going on here is a very interesting con. Mother, what's the internal communications button? I need to reach Drax and Hacker International pronto."

A different button flashed. "I have restricted the communication to where they are, only. They are not with the children."

"Good to know." Pushed the internal button down. "Gustav, Eddy, guys, can you hear me?"

"Yes, Kitty," Stryker said, "we can. What's up?"

"I think Mother's been hacked or had a virus sent into her or something. No idea how, but it would be a virus that caused the ship to feel that it was crashing and under attack and a virus that could make the ship react *as if* it was being battered about."

"I sensed and still sense no such thing," Mother said.

"Ah, but Mother, the *best* viruses are the ones you don't notice until it's too late. Eddy, don't let me down. Get going, find it fast, and fix it faster. Someone grab Serene on your way, just in case." Thought about it. "Send Jennifer to grab Serene and I want the ladies using their fastest hyperspeed, please and thank you."

"We're on it," Stryker said. "Jennifer's back with Serene and we're on our way."

Let go of the internal communications button and pushed the external communications button down. I was getting good at this. Wondered if I'd remember this sequence tomorrow and figured it could go either way. "You still there?"

"Yes, and so are you. Why haven't you left yet? We will fire upon you again."

"I'm sure you will. Or, rather, I'm sure that you won't, because I'm also sure that you never did. I'm *also* sure that there aren't actually seven planets and more moons than you can count in an hour in front of us. I think there's one planet, with one moon. Maybe."

"I have no idea what you're talking about." Interesting. This person had difficulty lying believably. Never argued when the cosmos did me a solid.

"Sure you don't. So, here's the thing—we're going to land. You're going to remove or deactivate the virus you put into our ship's system. Or we're going to stop being peaceful and start thinking about leaving your world in pieces. Or do I make myself clear?"

"No, you are unclear. We did nothing to your ship."

"Ah, but you see, I think you did. I think you have some way of determining when ships are nearby, even those coming out of warp. Perhaps especially those coming out of warp. Said ships fly through some barrier that sends a virus into their systems. The ship then thinks it's being attacked. If it doesn't immediately leave, your virus tells the ship that missiles are heading for it. Systems will even show those missiles. But there's nothing there. It's all illusion being filtered into the ship's computer systems."

Silence on the other side.

"How in the hell did you get all that from what we have to work with?" the Kristie-Bot asked. "I mean, I don't think you're wrong. I'm just kind of amazed that you took the leap and that, based on the silence we're all hearing, you're right."

"Lucky guess."

The Kristie-Bot snorted. "Right. Stop pretending I wasn't a costar on *Code Name: First Lady*. I know how you roll. This was just even more amazing than usual. God, that movie is going to be a *huge* hit! I hope we're back in time for the premiere."

Managed not to wince. I'd been enjoying not thinking about the movie—an impromptu space trip having managed to keep my attention off of things I didn't want to dwell on. But, honesty forced a response. "I'm just really exceptionally good at going with the crazy."

"She is," Jeff said. "And it makes sense."

"No," Mother said. "It does not. How would this virus be sent into my system? The ship is self-contained."

"But there are ways in and out. And if we're talking some

kind of pulse or whatever, then I imagine it would get through via the metal somehow, maybe via vibration, maybe we're not as airtight as we think, pick a reason. That's other people's baili-wick, not mine. I just figure out the heinous plots and try to stop them. I don't come up with them."

"Our plot is not heinous," the maybe-a-woman on the other side said. Realized I still had the button down. Oh well.

"Really? Seems heinous to us."

"We don't want to be invaded."

"Most don't. The nice thing? We're not coming to invade. We were sort of tossed over here." Was seriously wondering why Naomi had so tossed. "We have no idea why. We weren't expect-ing your warm welcome but, as you can see, we're prepared to make things even hotter for you. Now, are you going to let us land or not?"

"Why do we want to land?" Jeff asked. "I say, let's figure out where we are, figure out where Kreaving is, and get back to that solar system and stop its sun from exploding or whatever. We have a lot of lives to save, Kitty. No need to stop here to refuel."

"Wait," the possibly-a-woman on the other side said. "Are you saying that you are going somewhere to . . . help?"

"Yes, that's the plan. We got a distress call while we were in warp. A warp we didn't put ourselves into, long story we'll tell you about if it turns out we actually like you. Jury's still out on that one. Anyway, we need to get back to wherever that ship was, because they're lost and the system they landed in is in mortal peril. Something hit their sun and is causing said sun to start to self-destruct. There are a lot of lives hanging in the balance."

"Is this your assigned role? To assist?" Possibly-she sounded far more hopeful than I'd have expected.

"It sure is on this trip, yeah. Why?"

"Hold please." I heard a slight static.

"That's my line." Looked around. "Mother, what's the status on Hacker International?"

Drax ran into the room before she answered. "It's a virus," he said, sounding furious. "Ravi and Serene have almost completed the necessary steps to eliminate it."

"That was fast," Tim said. "And I mean that as it would be fast for an A-C, let alone humans."

Drax nodded. "It would have taken us hours normally, but since we were all just in there, working to fix Mother's other issues, the boys knew where to look. And Serene is exceptional."

The way he said it, was glad Brian wasn't nearby. He wasn't as jealous as Jeff—who was?—but he could get a good jealousy snit going, and Drax was clearly a little more enamored of Serene than any other woman he spoke about.

Dragged my mind off of that and back to the interesting matter at hand. There was a lot of interesting on this trip. Our Various Powers That Be really enjoyed working in mysterious ways.

We knew when Ravi and Serene were done, because what we all were seeing out the windshield changed. The gasps were audible, even from Team Tinman.

There weren't a variety of planets and moons here. There was one planet, one very big gas giant. And it possessed a single good-sized moon. A moon that gleamed in this sun's light.

Because it appeared to be pure metal.

CHAPTER 56

"THAT'S NO MOON FOR SURE," Tim said. "Is that a Death Star?"

"No," Drax said slowly as he stared at it. "We've heard rumors . . ."

"Rumors of what?" Jeff asked.

"Rumors that a world made entirely of metal existed. We've never found it."

"I think we have now." Looked more closely, as we were getting nearer every second. "It doesn't look smooth."

"It may not be," Hughes said. "But I need to point out that we're going to be trapped in the planet's orbit soon—this wouldn't be an issue for this ship normally, but we still don't have control of it, so we can't control our flight path. If we're landing on the moon—and despite everyone's desires to *Star Wars* it up, it's a moon, clearly—we need to prepare for that and figure out if the ship will even let us land. If we're leaving, we need to leave now."

My line came back on. "You are cleared to land."

"Super and possibly even duper. However, land where?"

"Land anywhere that's not orange."

We were all quiet for a moment. "Um, excuse me?"

"Orange. Avoid it."

Looked at the gas giant. It looked a lot like Jupiter. "We weren't actually planning to land on the planet. I mean, I'm not sure we're equipped to land on or in a gas giant or however that works." Had no idea, just knew that the only people we knew who could handle living on a gas giant were the Vrierst. We hadn't colonized Jupiter for any of the humanoid races, only its moons. No, we'd colonized Jupiter for the Vrierst.

"No, not on Spehidon, which is the planet. That's uninhabited. We are on Cradus, its moon. Surely you can see us."

"Yes, yes, we can. And what we see is something that looks silvery or platinum or pewter, but we're not seeing gold or copper. And definitely not orange."

"Ah, of course. You're on the dark side."

"Of course we are," Jeff muttered. Avoided sharing that now I wanted to hear Pink Floyd's "Dark Side of the Moon" because I didn't want to be told that this was an inappropriate time.

"We can allow you to land there," most-likely-a-woman said, "but it will be easier if you come to the light side. But, again, avoid anything orange."

"Gotcha. Right now, we're not seeing landing strips and things like that."

"Oh, I'm sorry. As you come to us, we'll adjust and be able to assist. Just avoid the orange."

"Roger that. Speaking of Roger, my name is Kitty. What's your name?"

"Oh, apologies. I am Fathade. I look forward to meeting you."

Figured. Had no idea if that was a male or female or gender nonbinary name. Also had no idea why he, she, or it was suddenly thrilled about meeting us when they'd been trying to get us to leave only a few minutes prior.

"Aliens are, in general, weird."

"We've always found them so, yes," Fathade agreed. So we had that in common.

Miraculously, Mother announced that she was once again in control of the ship, and she allowed us to actually fly the thing. My role was, thankfully, limited to ensuring that Fathade and the rest of Cradus' Mission Control were talking us around and down properly, which was me figuring out how to get the button to stay pushed down so everyone was still on our version of speakerphone.

Team Tinman had disengaged from their group huddle around Tito and were backing each of us, just in case. Could tell that Joe and Randy desperately wanted to take a seat away from me, Tito, or Jeff, and had to figure that, wherever Jerry was, he would also like to take one of our seats. Knew without asking that Jeff and Tito would like to give their seats up, too.

They were on Mother's approved alternates roster. No time like the present to try. "Mother, could Joe and Randy take over for Jeff and Tito at the controls?"

"Not at this time."

"Why not? We're trying to land on an alien world. I'd person-ally really love the guys who trained for this for well over a year to be at the controls, and I'm sure I'm speaking for everyone else on board."

"I'll stay at Weapons," Jeff added.

"Fine. Doctor Hernandez can be relieved." Randy was be-hind Tito so he scored taking that slot. Joe looked totally jealous.

Jeff demanded that Wruck, Chuckie, and Reader rejoin us, so they did, bringing Jerry along, mostly because he followed them. Really hoped that we were going to have a better landing than arrival, because we had a lot of people in here now and no way to strap most of them in.

Spehidon was much closer to its sun than Jupiter was to ours. Based on the size of the sun from where we were it seemed as close to this sun as Earth. "Think this system was originally trying to become binary?"

"Possibly," Chuckie replied. "As we're learning firsthand, every system is different."

"We should ask those in the Eagle Nebula about that," Wruck added.

"True dat." Cradus gleamed, and the closer we got to the light side, the brighter the moon was. "Is it all metal, do you think?"

"It looks like it," Chuckie said, "because that doesn't look like ice. We need to be prepared—we may not be able to breathe on the moon, and, depending on which metals make up the moon, the gravitational force could be crushing. Plus, if this gas giant is anything like the ones in our system, it'll be sending out radiation, and that puts all of us at risk."

"Not so long as we remain inside the ship," Drax said. "It's protected."

"But the gravitational force is a risk if we land on the moon," Chuckie replied. "And the radiation is a risk if we step outside. I don't know that the ship is equipped with enough spacesuits. Certainly not enough for the various sizes we have on board, and by that I mean the kids. Let alone the animals."

"I can test," Wruck said. "There is no planet or moon where I can't go."

"Excuse me," Fathade said. "But what are your body con-structions? I heard your concerns and they are not without merit."

Decided I was done being the ship's telephone operator and

that asking Mother's permission was also something I wasn't doing right now. "Fathade, you'll be speaking to Charles in a moment to get all those pertinent details. Enjoy yourselves."

Took my helmet off and gave Chuckie the "get over here now" hand gesture. He grinned and took the helmet from me while I got up. Then he sat in my chair, put on the helmet, and strapped in. Clearly he'd had the same thought I had about our potential landing. Happily, Mother didn't object to any of this.

Once settled, Chuckie started talking to Fathade and my ears turned off. Not that our biological structure wasn't fascinating, but I didn't want to hear about what percentage water we all were because it had already been a long trip. Wruck adding in to discuss alien body structures was just overkill as far as I was concerned.

"This may be a bad idea," Jerry said quietly to me. "If we land, everyone's going to want to get off the ship. And if they're told that they can't, it could be a problem."

"Yeah, we've been being warned about boredom already. But if it means we're going to die or something, I know that we're not going to allow anyone to get off."

"So why land?" Joe asked, as he joined us. "Maybe we just hover out here and talk to Fathade, get what intel we need, and leave."

"There has to be a reason we were sent here. I mean that seriously. Someone took over Mother's controls and tossed us here. And before anyone says that it was done to harm us, let's recall that there are easier ways to kill us out in space. We're here for a reason. We need to figure out what that reason is."

"Okay," Chuckie said so that everyone was listening. "We're going to land. Fathade feels that our ship will be able to take off again. We're also going to be using John Wruck to test the atmosphere."

"I can volunteer, too," the Kristie-Bot said. "I'm the most advanced model we have, and that way we have human elements to verify." We all stared at her. "What?" she asked defensively. "I'm part of the team, I'm willing to take risks, too."

Realized I was doing to her what a lot of people did to me—doubting her because of her job, her attitude, and the way she talked. Sure, she'd blackmailed me to get a part on *Code Name: First Lady*, but from all I'd been told she'd done a great job and, beyond that, she'd become Team Kitty the moment we'd agreed to have her on the movie. Frankly, as people who'd started out

as enemies went, the Kristie-Bot was pretty much in the winner
category.

"That's great, Kristie," I said. "We're just worried about you
getting hurt. You're a public figure."

"So are you and Jeff and half the other people on this trip. I
want to help. I'm capable of helping, and, besides Mister Wruck,
I have the best chance of survival. John and Cameron are older
models and made to be more human, meaning they have more
risk. Joe and Randy are still human, just with cyborg enhancements. I'm the only true cyborg we have. So I'm going."

"She's convinced me," Jeff said.

"Good, because we need test subjects." Chuckie rolled his
eyes at the looks he got. "I'm not suggesting we throw John and
Kristie out of the ship and hope for the best. Fathade's people
have suits we can use."

"Space suits?" Hey, wanted to be sure they weren't just going
to hand us their moon's version of Armani and call it good.

"In a way. Planet suits, for us." Chuckie sighed. "Look, as I
heard Kitty say when she thought she was being quiet, we're
here for a reason. So, let's land and find out what that reason is."

CHAPTER 57

CHUCKIE GAVE JOE HIS SEAT, though Jeff stayed at Weapons. Had no idea why, other than the fact that Jeff might have figured that Mother wasn't going to okay him or Tim leaving their posts. Decided it didn't matter.

We were able to spot what Fathade had been talking about once we got to the sun side of the moon—there was a heck of a lot of orange scattered about on one section of the moon's surface. It didn't fit, though—it wasn't a metallic color. It was, frankly, more of a neon. The neon orange certainly stood out, though, even against the warmer hues of gold and copper that were in great evidence on this side.

Waited until we were through reentry, which wasn't all that bad—no one went flying, for example, which was good because I wasn't strapped in—then went off with Drax while the others stayed on the command deck. I wanted to make sure my kids were okay. Mother kept communications open, though, so we could all hear each other if needed, though she muted the command deck chatter that didn't pertain to the rest of us.

We gathered up everyone else and headed to go see what we could see. Noted that Algar wasn't in either room. Figured that, because personnel divided up, each room thought the Ard Ri was in the other room—if they thought of him at all. Decided not to worry that he wasn't around—either he'd seen this solar system already, which was my assumption, or he'd miss out.

Those of us not involved with landing the *Distant Voyager* went to an observation lounge, different and much larger than the one Tim and I had been in with Sandy. Drax thought of everything. And so did Algar, because he was already there, watching. Couldn't blame him—this moon was amazing.

Because this lounge was actually large enough to accommodate a quarter of the ship if it was full, everyone could see easily and comfortably. They were tired of being bored? Well, watching a mountain of what looked like pewter reform itself into a giant landing pad certainly handled that complaint.

Cradus was, apparently, a shifting world. Hadn't known those were out there, but I was always open to the new ideas. "Fascinating," Drax said as the ship headed for the highest mountain, which was the one that now had a landing pad.

"Can other planets do this?" I asked him, as the kids and I got closer to the window.

"Not that I've seen. But I haven't traveled as much as Mister Wruck. I haven't traveled as much as Mossy."

The Turleen was perched on Drax's shoulder, so he could see easily. "I haven't come across anything like this. I wish Muddy and Dew had come with us—they'd love to see this."

The sun's reflection on this moon was so dazzling that we couldn't have looked directly at it if not for the fact that the windows were able to shade, just like transitional sunglasses, depending on the intensity of light. We were likely at Top Of Kilimanjaro Level for the tint, but apparently the glass was also polarized, because the colors seemed accurate.

I was holding Charlie and Siler had Jamie, with Lizzie and Wasim in between us. "This is so totes cool," Lizzie said, sounding awed as we watched what looked like a river of gold glisten against a silver valley, the mountain adjusting so that these areas weren't disturbed.

"Amazing," Wasim agreed. "I'm so glad I got to come along on this journey."

"Me too, but I sure hope your grandfather understands and doesn't think you're kidnapped." And that none of us got radiation poisoning or worse.

"I'm sure it will all be alright, Queen Katherine."

Looked at him. Despite the coloring and height differences, Wasim almost always reminded me of Chuckie—he was a brainy, nerdy kid who did his best to make his family proud of him and was also, some day, going to rule his country. He had flashes of cool and flashes of pure royalty, but mostly he was just a cute geek. I approved heartily of cute geeks.

However, because he was smart, knew he hadn't called me Queen Katherine for no reason. "Mind telling me what that hint was for?"

He nodded. "We are about to greet a new race. We don't know their political structure. Many are not impressed with presidents or other politicians, I have seen. But everyone seems impressed with kings and queens."

"The kid has a point," Siler said. He looked around. "Where's Mister Gadhavi?"

"Right behind you, sir," Gadhavi rumbled. "I was checking in with King Jeffrey."

"Oh, you and Wasim had a chat about this already, didn't you?"

Gadhavi went to my other side and grinned at me. "We did, yes. We understand this perhaps better than you and your husband do. You are, at your cores, egalitarian. Most you will meet are not."

"Elected by the people versus ruling by bloodline," Siler said. "There's definitely a difference. However, we don't know what the people on this moon think."

"Do you think they call it a moon or a planet?" Lizzie asked. "I mean, it's totes a moon, but they live on it, so do they think of it that way?"

"Landing in five minutes," Mother intoned over the loudspeaker.

"Think we're about to find out," I said to Lizzie.

"We have been assured that crash positions will not be needed," Mother went on. "However, I recommend crew and passengers strap in."

"I don't want to stop watching," Jamie said fretfully.

"We don't have to." Wasim pointed up. "There are straps here."

Indeed there were. Mossy transferred to Gadhavi's shoulder while Drax explained to everyone how to use them. They were a lot like those on various forms of public transportation but with the Drax Extras so near and dear to our hearts. Each strap was attached to something that resembled a shoulder holster—crisscrossed in the back and around each shoulder. The setup kept you on your feet and steady, and it adjusted to all heights and sizes, so we were able to strap all the little kids in, even JR, though Christopher kept a tight hold of his son while Amy held on to Becky.

I followed suit and kept Charlie in my arms and Siler did the same with Jamie. All the other younger kids were being held by adults, so clearly none of us felt safe in trusting that "smooth landing" idea. Gadhavi didn't offer to hold Mossy, but that was because he wasn't an idiot. However, could tell that Gadhavi was ready to grab Mossy if need be.

So, prepped and ready, we all got to watch as the *Distant Voyager* achieved its first landing.

The mountain had already been reforming from a landing pad into something that was shaped more like our ship, so that the saucer would be as supported as the base, and, as we lowered, it raised to meet us. There was a small jolt, like we'd gone over a pothole, but that was it. As landings went, Cradus was number one with a bullet.

Once we were settled and stationary, though, is when the real excitement began.

The mountain or whatever it really was that we were on flowed, taking us and our landing pad with it and carrying us down its side. It was a fast but gentle ride, like being on a smooth roller coaster that didn't have any big drops.

We avoided the golden river, what looked like a forest of silver trees, a lake of what looked like a sort of silvery-violet substance I couldn't identify, and more, achieved by the mountain raising itself and us over these things, or by going around them and, in some cases, by the geography flattening until we were past, then reforming itself. We spotted things that looked like metal deer bounding around, and what appeared to be metal birds flew past us.

"I've never even imagined anything like this," Siler said softly.

"I want to play with it," Charlie said.

"We'll see." Hugged him. "We might not be able to."

"We will," he said confidently.

We were down the mountain but still flowing along, past rolling hills, more rivers—these possibly of copper—and what looked like rocky grasslands. We also passed some of the orange stuff.

"That looks wrong," Lizzie said, as we went past a big patch. "It looks too . . . organic."

"Organic for this world appears to be metal," I reminded her.

"I get it, but that orange stuff looks off."

"Can't argue, since I agree with you. I assume we'll find out what it is once we get wherever we're going."

Where we were going seemed to be a city. And it was both like and completely unlike any city I'd ever seen before.

What was similar was that there were a lot of buildings,

streets, and pedestrians. Unlike the geography, the buildings seemed solid. They were rounded, almost like sets of Navaho hogans or Mongolian yurts in various sizes. And there were a lot of them scattered about, many together in large groups, some in smaller groups, a few separate. Couldn't tell if this meant we were at a spaceport or if that's what every building on this moon looked like.

What there wasn't was variety. All the buildings were the same shape, some tiny, some huge, but there was no individuality. There were color differences, but they seemed random, as if that color of metal was what had been there when the building was built so that's what it was made out of, not as if it was an aesthetic choice. In fact, the only aesthetic was conformity: every building had the same doorways—double doors with no doorknobs—no windows that I could spot, and rounded roofs.

We stopped next to the largest of the buildings, and the portion of the land that had transported us here connected us to it, both via the ground and the roof, but also by covering the doorway with what I thought was a tunnel, thereby creating an airlock. I hoped.

There were streets, but they weren't stationary. They moved like our part of the mountain had, because that was apparently how the people of this world traveled.

And what people they were.

CHAPTER 58

"LOOK AT THE PRETTY robots, Mommy!" Jamie exclaimed, as a group of Cradus citizens rode the street nearest to where we'd stopped.

That they were robotic seemed likely. They all gleamed, just like their planet did. Could see exposed wiring in some, none in others. And now we had variety, because there were different kinds—larger, smaller, very humanoid, less humanoid, animalish. Basically, we'd found *Star Wars'* Droid World.

There were males and females, too. At least, I assumed the robots with physical structures that included breasts and wider pelvises were female. Then again, I was prepared to find out that these were just design choices.

"Away team is being formed," Mother said. "Kitty and Gustav, you are requested back at the command deck."

Kissed the kids and handed Charlie to Lizzie. "I'll be back soon. Behave yourselves and no sneaking after us or out onto the planet until we know it's safe."

Wasim nodded gravely. "I will explain the risks to the others."

Lizzie laughed. "He will, I'm sure. He loves doing stuff like that."

Wasim looked a little crestfallen and as if his feelings were hurt, though he was trying to hide it. Lizzie seemed oblivious. Heaved an internal sigh. This was like watching me and Chuckie from our youth, but from the outside, where I got to see how many times I'd hurt Chuckie's feelings without realizing it—or realizing that he'd been in love with me. I didn't for one moment regret marrying Jeff, but I'd seen what Bizarro World Chuckie had been like, and if Lizzie could score with Wasim what Other

Me had with Bizarro World Chuckie, there were far worse ways to be happily married.

"It's tough being the smartest guy in the room, Wasim, but I'm glad you're willing to be helpful. We can't afford anyone to be a maverick right now."

This didn't seem to cheer him up. Heaved another internal sigh. Maybe I needed to have a Mom Talk with Lizzie.

Who finally noted Wasim's expression. She nudged him. "Bet you know more about what's going on than the Martini kids, or any of the rest of the clan. You want to play a trivia game about this while we wait?"

He brightened up. "Certainly, if you'd like to."

She smiled. "I always like doing fun stuff with you, so yeah."

"I will moderate the game," Gadhavi said, presumably offering so that he could assist Wasim in as many ways as possible, most likely in terms of getting game. Gadhavi had a yeoman's job ahead of him, but I found it rather touching that he, like me, cared enough to keep trying. That even someone who'd been the scariest gangster in the Middle East could have a soft spot for a sweet kid who just needed some help to be cool was proof, to me, that pretty much anyone could be redeemed if they wanted to be. "You go do your jobs."

"Include Hacker International. We need to be sure they're occupied, possibly more than the kids."

"None will leave while on my watch," Gadhavi said.

Thusly reassured by our resident grizzly, Drax and I left our gigantic posse in the observation lounge, though Mossy came along with us. Hoped we weren't going to be at the command deck too long, since we were there to choose the away team.

Happily, there wasn't a lot of argument. It was a given that Jeff and I needed to make the trek along with Team Tinman and, of course, our guinea pig, aka Wruck. As discussed earlier, the plan had been confirmed—Wruck would go first and, if he was able to handle the suits Fathade had, then the Kristie-Bot would give it a try and so on.

Chuckie and Reader were with us, too, though Tim was staying on the command deck with the remainder of Airborne, just in case we all got into trouble. Drax and Mossy were approved to go as well, since that gave us five different races represented. Tito insisted on coming in case we needed medical and, miraculously, Mother agreed.

We all went to the airlock with Wruck. While on the way, Drax, Mossy, and I shared what we'd seen from the observation lounge, in case those at command had missed it. They'd seen most of it, but hadn't spotted the people.

"Living robots?" Jeff asked. "That seems . . . far-fetched, and I say that knowing that we have, essentially, living robots with us right now."

"I get why it seems like that," Joe said. "This was done to us, we weren't born this way."

Resisted the urge to put on Lady Gaga but, as always, it took effort.

Randy shrugged. "It's a big galaxy, Jeff. I can believe it. I mean, our brains are basically organic circuits. And I mean everyone's, not just Joe's and mine."

"It's not that much of a leap, honestly," Reader added. "We have trace metals in us."

"This is true," Drax agreed. "Procreation is, at its core, merely the passing along of DNA. All it takes is the right situation for a mass of wiring or a lump of metal to have the correct electrical charge to create life. After that, the evolution begins and, with it, sentience."

"Which is a simplified explanation," Chuckie said, looking both interested and excited, "but not wrong at all. Our world is mostly water and we're mostly water—that's not a coincidence. This world is mostly metal and so its people are mostly metal. It makes sense."

Jeff nodded. "I suppose it does."

Knew when Chuckie was gearing up for a fun scientific discussion, and also knew without asking that the others were probably willing to go all in on it, Jeff included. I was not. "It might, but I vote for us meeting these people and finding out how they came to be directly from the animatronic horse's mouths. If, you know, any of us can survive in their atmosphere."

Wruck chuckled. "Kitty has a point."

"Spoilsport," Chuckie said to me with a grin.

"Guilty as charged. Let's meet their folks and you can talk to their scientific head AI or whomever. I'd like to get us through the initial 'hello' phase, though."

"That's what I'm here for," Wruck said.

"You're sure you can adapt fast enough?" I asked him.

"I am." He smiled at me. "It will be fine."

"We're sure this isn't an ambush?" Mossy asked me quietly.

"Nothing in life's certain other than death, taxes, and that our enemies will always be crazed megalomaniacs. But it seems on the up and up."

We reached the airlock, which was a very large room—all of us could have fit inside it with plenty of room to spare. Grabbed Wruck and hugged him before he went in, just in case. He hugged me and patted my back. "It will be fine." Then he went through the door.

This worked pretty much like in the movies—he was in the chamber, we closed and locked the big door that had a window in it large enough for us to watch everything, he hit a button, the room did its thing, three different doors or barriers slid open—one to the right, one to the left, and one going up—then the doors opposite ours opened, and Wruck stepped through.

He altered instantly into a metal man. At least, he looked shiny now where he hadn't before. He took one more step and waited.

"We can't close the outer door or open this one until he's farther," Drax said worriedly.

"I think he's waiting for someone."

"He might be," Chuckie said. "Fathade did say she'd meet us here."

"Oh, Fathade's definitely a female? I wasn't sure."

"Honestly, I wasn't sure, either. So I asked. She is a female. They have male, female, nonbinary, multiple, asexual, and shifting genders. It's fascinating."

"Remember that we're on a mission and we can't stay here for you to get a Ph.D. in Comparative Robotic Studies."

"Geez, you take the fun out of everything. Jeff, man, I'm sorry she's such a downer on this trip."

Jeff laughed as he put his arm around me and patted Chuckie on the back. "Not to worry, Chuck. You can spend all the time you want learning about these people—if they're open to it—at least until we figure out where Kreaving is."

"Someone's coming," Reader said. "Look sharp. If we're going to have issues, we'll have them here."

Several metal people arrived. They were mostly silvery, but they all had gold and copper in there somewhere, too. They were also varied in final shapes. One was like C-3PO—mostly metal but with wires connecting the stomach area to the upper torso and hips—two were fully humanoid, one looked very much like a collection of filigree and wires while still clearly being a complete person, and the fifth was a metal skeleton a lot like the *Terminator*.

Their eyes and teeth and hair, for those who had it, were also metal. The metal in their eyes looked more liquid than the metal on their bodies but basically they looked like there wasn't anything nonmetallic in any part of them.

However, they didn't look fake or mechanical. They looked very real and very alive.

The humanoid one that was clearly female bowed to Wruck. He bowed back. They spoke—as near as I could tell, introductions were being made. Took a wild one and assumed the female humanoid one was Fathade.

The metal skeleton one produced a round ball of what looked like gold from somewhere—dude was not wearing clothing so it wasn't like he had a pocket. Assumed male based on skeletal structure, but was willing to be unsurprised if its gender was different.

Wruck took the golden ball, they spoke some more, then Fathade and her group backed up, and Wruck hit the button to close the airlock door.

Drax hit the intercom button. "John, are you alright?"

"Yes." Wruck turned to us. "They gave me what they call a Moon Suit. They've had a few visitors in the past—the distant past now—and they created something that allowed those visitors to survive and enjoy their world. I'm going to test it and be sure it doesn't harm me. After that, we'll test it on Kristie, then John Butler, Cameron, Joe, and Randy. If we're all okay, then we'll test on a hybrid, an A-C, and then a human."

"That's a lot of testing. I'm not complaining about it, but why?"

Wruck shrugged. "Because what this is supposed to do is cover the wearer in breathable metal. The metal will filter out whatever is toxic to the wearer and alter it into what isn't. So, for us, it will give us oxygen. Also, the suits protect against Spehidon's radiation."

"Just from a small ball of metal?" Jeff asked suspiciously.

"I think it's gold and I can also believe it." I could. But then, I knew Algar personally. And others.

"It may be gold," Jeff said, "but I'm still having an issue with belief."

Shrugged. "When I was in Bizarro World, the Alfred there had created something very similar. It was about a million times better than Kevlar, as malleable as any fabric, totally breathable, and a little bit covered you from head to toe. I could even put some on a cat." Took a moment to miss Stripes. I was definitely asking Mother to make a set of three-way mirrors for me sooner as opposed to later. "And on my purse."

"Oh, well, on your purse," Reader said. "Well, that sells it for me."

"Careful, James, you're close enough for me to kick."

He flashed the cover boy smile. "Not that you ever would."

"True . . . true . . ."

"Can you two do me a favor and not try to make me jealous right now?" Jeff asked. "At least not until we've seen if this miracle stuff works."

"Oh, I suppose," Reader said. "By the way, I'm the human who'll be doing the test. And, Jeff, before you say a word, you are *not* the A-C who will be doing the test, and that's final."

"Well, we have to either use Paul or Abigail to do the hybrid test," I pointed out. "Because you're high if you think any of us are going to let one of the kids do it."

"Let's get through John and the rest of us," the Kristie-Bot said. "Then we can fret about who is or isn't getting to risk themselves."

"Oh, sure, go be logical. However, one more thing before you use that, John."

"What?" Wruck asked.

"What about our eyes, nostrils, and mouths, let alone our internal organs? What I can see of theirs are all metallic and I'm willing to bet that their internal organs are as well. I doubt very much that we can swallow this metal safely, and while you said the metal was breathable, I still object to any of us being blinded. In Bizarro World, Alfred had goggles and we were on Earth, so breathing wasn't an issue. Here, I'm not as convinced."

"Fathade said they've used these on other oxygen breathers," Chuckie said calmly.

"Our ears are cavities, too," Reader countered. "And while I know you questioned her, Chuck, and I'm also tentatively willing to believe they mean us no harm, I'm kind of with Kitty on all of this. Will this work and is it even worth the risk to find out?"

Wruck smiled. "I asked about all of that."

"And?" Jeff asked.

In reply, Wruck placed the ball of metal against his chest. Results, as happened so often, were immediate.

CHAPTER 59

THE METAL SLID OVER WRUCK. It went under his clothes and on top of them, too, as if it was far more liquid than solid, doing its best to cover every part of anything touching him.

It was his face and head I was most worried about. The metal went over him, into his mouth, nose, and ears, and over his eyes.

"Tito, if this goes badly, how are you as an ENT?"

"I do my continuing education at Dulce, Kitty. I'm trained in, literally, everything by now and in things almost no human doctors are. I'm good, and ready, if something goes wrong. Plus, Claudia and Lorraine are on board, so if I need help, two of the best backups are here."

Heard Randy talking softly to someone. Looked over my shoulder. He was on his phone. Had a feeling he was already calling in our medical backup, just in case.

Sure enough, the girls arrived just as the metal finished attaching to every hair on Wruck's head. Joe and Randy quietly caught their wives up on what had transpired while the rest of us waited for Wruck to writhe or scream in agony or drop down dead.

None of those things happened. Instead, he nodded to us and hit the button to open the airlock again.

Did the usual wait. As the door opened he looked over his shoulder. "I'm fine. I'm going to test the atmosphere and how well this works." Then he stepped out to be greeted by Fathade and the others. They all walked off.

"This is going to take forever," the Kristie-Bot groaned.

"Can't argue with your assessment. Then again, I don't want to discover that the magic metal doesn't work as advertised. Call me a worrywart." We all leaned against an available wall and hung out, idly chatting. "What were the kids doing when you left?" I asked Lorraine.

"Playing a trivia game. It was getting intense."

Claudia nodded. "Wasim really knows his stuff. Most of the adults were playing, too."

"The hackers especially," Lorraine added. "It was fun, everyone was into it."

Something nudged at me. "Were Christopher and Amy into it, too?"

"Yeah, all of us," Claudia said.

"No one was whining about having to wait, or being bored, or wanting to get onto the planet?"

Both girls shook their heads. "Why are you asking this?" Lorraine hugged me. "Everyone's fine. The kids are in great hands. Malcolm and Benjamin are both there. You know they aren't going to let the kids slip off."

"And Mister Gadhavi's on guard," Claudia added.

Algar was also there and Jamie had ACE inside of her. And neither entity was sending me a warning signal. Unless, of course, the feeling that something was wrong was the warning signal. So that could be from ACE or it could just be that I was worried about Wruck and transferring it to the kids. Not definitive.

There was an easy way to tell if Algar was trying to tell me something. Dug into my purse and opened my music. Foreigner's "Girl On The Moon" was queued up.

"Crap." Took off at hyperspeed. I'd been a sprinter and hurdler when I ran track, and I was definitely going as fast as possible right now.

Jeff caught up to me. "What's wrong?"

"I think Jamie's already on the damn moon."

"How? I haven't gotten anything from her. Or Charlie. Or Lizzie, either."

"She can block emotions from you, Jeff. She's done it before, usually to protect you, when we're in a big battle situation. But right now . . ."

"Right now she's bored and there's this magical place right in front of her. Got it."

We reached the observation lounge. Sure enough, though Lizzie and Charlie were both here, Jamie wasn't. And no one seemed to notice—not Siler, not Buchanan, and not Gadhavi.

Was about to start screaming my head off when I saw Algar.

He wasn't joining in with the game that had everyone entranced, he was still staring out the window. Ran over to him. "Ard Ri Al, have you seen my daughter?"

He turned to me. "Indeed I have, lassie. She's got your little laddie. She's a wonderful big sister."

"She is, yes, but I mean Jamie, not Lizzie."

"Ah, yes. I've seen her, too."

"Where is she?" Jeff growled.

Algar smiled. "Showing that she's her mother's daughter." He nodded out the window.

We both turned and looked. There was Jamie, a golden version of her, at least, holding Wruck's hand and skipping down the street. They were with Fathade and the others and Jamie was being introduced, at least as far as I could tell.

"How?" Jeff asked. "How did she get out of the ship, let alone get the suit?"

"No idea, Jeff, but she moved herself from New Mexico to D.C. to save us and Christopher from a crashing Z'porrah spaceship before she was six months old. That she could do this at six years shouldn't surprise either one of us."

"It should not, no," Algar said. "So, the question is—do you wait, or do you join her?"

Looked right at him. "Pardon us for wanting to be sure this planet was safe."

He shrugged. "Caution is good. Boldness is good, too. Especially when meeting a new race. You were bold while the ship was flying, lassie. Why be timid now?"

"Not wanting to get radiation poisoning, for starters."

"Ah, but the amazing race you see before you seems confident they can protect you."

"People have been wrong before," Jeff said.

Algar nodded. "They have, indeed. However, your princess is doing the job the king and queen should be."

"Oh, blah, blah, blah. Good rulers ensure that their subjects aren't exposed to danger for no good reason."

"True enough," Algar said. "The Anciannas has done the main test. Your princess has done the other."

"We won't know if she's gotten radiation poisoning until it's too late," Jeff said, sounding ready to break through the glass.

Algar sighed. "Laddie, really. You worry far too much."

"Yeah? Then, tell me, Ard Ri Al, how do we score the special suits? Fathade didn't leave any extras."

"Didn't she?" Algar asked, looking amazingly innocent.

"Oh my god, fine. We'll go see if she did. Thanks for the assist." Grabbed Jeff's hand and started back, once again at a run.

"What's going on?" he asked me. "I mean with the Ard Ri?"

"He's a jerk. But he tends to be right." We got back to the airlock. "Gustav, close the outer door. That's an order."

"But John is not back," he said, sounding confused.

"Dude, just do it before Jeff loses it, okay?"

"She's not kidding," Jeff growled.

Drax clearly didn't understand what was going on, but he did as requested. As the outer doors, which opened out, closed, they pushed a bunch of the metal balls inside the airlock. Whether they were from Fathade's group or Algar I neither knew nor cared. The inner doors closed and the airlock did its other thing, whatever that was. All I knew was that it took time, and my little girl was wandering around this moon potentially killing herself.

Jeff grunted. "I wonder how he knew."

"Lucky guess is my guess," I lied. "Or else he saw them carrying more than one in or whatever. Maybe Jamie told him, since he was the only one aware she was gone. Who knows? Who cares? We just need to get in there and then out there."

"Excuse me, what?" Reader asked, sounding ready to give a safety lecture and tell us we weren't going anywhere.

"Stow it, James. Jamie's out there already, with Wruck. We're going out, period. Pull rank later, it's *our* daughter."

"And *my* goddaughter." Reader was fully in Commander Mode. "I won't stop you, but I *am* going with you."

"There's enough for all of us it looks like," Claudia said. "Let's all just go."

"I agree," Chuckie said.

"Dude, why are you so gung ho about all this? I mean it—you're normally far more cautious and James is normally far more willing to go for it. It's like were on the Role Reversal Moon or something."

He shrugged. "I just think that, based on their past experiences, these people know what they're doing. They shut themselves off because of a couple of bad encounters in recent times—well, recent for them, older for us, they're a very long-lived race—but they used to have visitors from other worlds, and they were all able to be here safely."

"Airlock is ready," Drax said.

"Into the breach," Tito added. "And yes, I'm going, as her doctor. And because I'm with Chuck on this one."

"Let's rock and roll," was my contribution as I ran in and grabbed a golden ball.

"Whatever," the Kristie-Bot said. "All I know is that your daughter's totally amazing. I can't wait for the *Code Name: First Daughter* spinoff series."

"Be careful, Kristie, or I'm going to ensure we leave you on this moon."

CHAPTER 60

FORTUNATELY, I'd experienced something like this in Bizarro World, so the feeling of this metal stuff going all over me wasn't too bad. It coated my purse, but as a separate thing from me somehow, so I could move it around and even take it off. Hoped that it was coating any Poofs that happened to be On Board, too, but didn't stop to look—the Poofs were from the Black Hole Universe and therefore probably immune to whatever. Jamie wasn't.

A part of me figured Jeff and I were just overreacting. ACE hadn't screamed a warning, Algar had seemed beyond calm and amused, and Chuckie clearly already felt things were safe. Wruck must have, too, since he hadn't grabbed Jamie and run her back to the ship.

But we were still parents and, until I could verify that there was nothing threatening my child, I was going to do whatever I needed to in order to ensure that nothing could or would hurt her, including things she might do to herself.

Stiffened as the metal got to my face, but it really wasn't all that bad. Managed not to panic as it went into my mouth, nostrils, and ears. Could feel it coat the inside of my nostrils, my mouth, teeth, and tongue, but it didn't go down my throat—instead it created a kind of filter at the back of my mouth just behind my tongue. It was weird but I tried swallowing saliva—no issues. So I could both make saliva and swallow it.

The coating on my eyes was different. It didn't hurt or blind me, even though I could feel it contour all around my eyelids and such. But it hooked onto my eyelashes, creating a bubble. If you closed your eyes, there was a little extra line of gold on your lashes—verified this by looking at Jeff. Open your eyes and the gold covered your eyeballs just like goggles, goggles that couldn't slip.

"This is . . . odd," Jeff said, as I did a fast check to see if I could open my purse—I could and things were coated and I saw no Poofs. "But not terrible."

Noted that, even all golden, he was still amazingly handsome. Good to know my libido was doing its best to keep me calm.

"It's like magic," the Kristie-Bot said.

"Any advanced science always is," Chuckie replied. "And yes, this appears to be scientific, or natural, based on how this world operates."

"Is everyone covered?" Jeff asked. "We need to get to Jamie and Wruck."

Everyone was, so Drax opened the airlock. Seemed to take forever before the outer doors opened, but they finally did. Jeff grabbed my hand and we ran down the newly formed hallway between our ship and the big building. His hand didn't feel normal, but it didn't feel bad, either. If I thought of this as a metallic bodysuit, it felt almost normal.

"If she's alright, do we punish her?" Jeff asked as we ran along.

"Not sure, honestly. We're not clanging, do you notice?"

"Yes. I have no idea why not. I'm a lot more focused on Jamie's safety right now, baby."

"I know. Me too. I just noticed the lack of noise. Maybe what's in our ears is blocking the sound?"

"I can hear you perfectly, so I doubt it."

We reached the end of the corridor. The filigree-over-wires person was waiting there. "I am Serion. I did not realize that you would all be coming out so quickly—John Wruck did not give us that indication." The voice was midrange, could be male or female. Around here, went with it not mattering. Then again, maybe it mattered very much. Decided I had bigger things to stress over.

"Hi, Serion, I'm Kitty, this is Jeff. Sorry we surprised you, but I think our daughter is with Fathade." I hoped, anyway.

"She was supposed to wait," Jeff added, "but hasn't and we're a little worried about her."

"Ah, young ones. Come with me." Serion turned and led us to what looked like a solid wall. Serion waved a hand and the wall parted, as if it was the doorway to the Red Sea.

"That is a neat trick." Was relieved to discover that the golden goggles acted like sunglasses. I didn't even have to squint against the sun's reflection on the moon.

Serion smiled at me. "It's just how our world works."

Even though Jeff and I were ready to go at hyperspeed, calmer heads prevailed, since we had no idea if we *could* go that fast here and we also had no idea if hyperspeed would make Serion sick. So, while we hustled off to find Jamie, Serion got introduced to the others. Chuckie point-blank asked Serion what pronoun to use. Serion identified as nonbinary, but said that for our language, it would be fine to go with him. Or her. Whichever we preferred, since Serion had no preference.

Decided I'd go with she, since I found Serion's filigree quite pretty. Serion was flattered by my reasoning, so I had that going for me, which was nice. Since Serion appeared to like it, the others went with she as well.

Thusly pronounced up, we reached the others. Jamie was on Wruck's shoulder looking around and apparently having the time of her sparkly gold life. She saw us coming and beamed, both literally and figuratively.

"Mommy! Daddy! The Cradi are so nice and isn't Cradus just the prettiest place you've *ever* seen? I can't wait to show Charlie, Lizzie, Wasim, and the other kids around!"

Jeff sighed. "Okay, can't be mad at her, can I?" he asked me quietly.

"No, not really. I think we need to have a talk with her, but in private."

Wruck lifted Jamie off his shoulder and handed her to Jeff. "I don't know how she got out here, but her Moon Suit is on properly."

"It's not your fault, John," Jeff said. He gave Jamie a stern look. "You know you should have waited, Jamie-Kat."

She hugged him. "I'm sorry, Daddy. But we were hurting their feelings. And scaring them just a little." She dropped her voice. "They're still worried that we didn't come here to be friends. And they're so nice, I didn't want them to be afraid any longer."

Jeff and I looked at each other. "Oh?" Jeff asked. "I didn't feel anything like that."

"It's harder for you to feel here, I think," Jamie replied. "But it's not for me and Fairy Godfather ACE."

Realized that ACE had likely given me the unsettled feeling

and Algar the musical cue to get us out here faster. Took Jamie from Jeff and gave her a hug and kiss. It felt weird but not in a bad way to kiss her with the Moon Suits on. "You scared us, Jamie. You know that you promised to stay with the others."

"I know. But I had to. It was the right thing to do."

Hugged her again. "We'll talk about it later. Right now, why don't you introduce us to everyone?"

"Okay!" Jamie squirmed out of my arms and trotted over to who I was thinking of as Fathade. "This is Fathade." Scored one for the guessing win column, go me. "She's one of their leaders!" Jamie turned to her, put her palms together like she was going to pray, but put them forward, as you would if you were going to shake hands. "Fathade, these are my parents, King Jeffrey and Queen Katherine."

So Wasim and Gadhavi hadn't been wrong. Or else Jamie had felt that they were right. But, either way, Fathade seemed very pleased by our titles. She took Jamie's hands in both of hers. "We are pleased to meet them, Princess Jamie."

Went to her and offered the paws in the same way Jamie had, because I was really clear that our child was giving us the Hint For The Parentally Slow Of Wit.

Fathade took my hands in hers, just as she had with Jamie. "It is an honor to meet you, Queen Katherine of Earth."

"It's an honor to meet you, Fathade, Leader of Cradus." Well, I had nothing else to go with since I wasn't sure what title she actually had. "I prefer that my friends call me Kitty, I'm one of the people you were talking to when we were in space."

Fathade smiled. "I guessed."

Laughed. "Good. This is my husband, King Jeffrey."

Jeff did the handclasp thing and he and Fathade did the formal intro. "I prefer Jeff," he said when they were done. He nodded to Chuckie. "This is Charles, the other person you were speaking with."

Chuckie did the intro thing, and so it went down the line. This took what seemed like forever. Was starting to come around to the idea of being really glad that Jamie had jump-started this whole exchange.

In addition to Serion and Fathade we met the C-3PO person, who was named Sciea, identified as having shifting gender, preferred the male pronoun, and was Serion's sibling, Feoren, who was the male humanoid, emphatically took the male pronouns, and was mated with Fathade, and the Terminator, who was Cavus, identified as asexual, and preferred being referred to by name only.

We also were told that they called their sun Crion and that they'd been around for many millennia. They knew of the Anciannas and the Z'porrah, which was why they'd been relieved that Wruck was with us. They were on the side of the Anciannas, but preferred noninvolvement.

Tito carried an OVS—an Organic Validation Sensor, created due to the plethora of androids we'd discovered once we'd been moved to D.C.—with him at all times. It verified who was and wasn't human or A-C, as well as what percentage organic someone was. Had no idea how it was managing to work on this world and with us all covered in metal, but he felt confident that none of us were being poisoned by radiation.

"Now," Jeff said pleasantly, once all the intros and verification of us not being poisoned were concluded, "why don't you folks tell us why you allowed us to land on your world?"

"You wanted to," Fathade said.

It was interesting. I'd already known she wasn't good at lying. But none of them were. They were all looking at their feet, around, anywhere but directly at Jeff. So, they might be mostly metal and wiring, but they were definitely people.

Coughed. "Pull the other one, it has bells on."

"Excuse me?" Cavus said. "I don't understand you."

"So few ever do. Look, you guys were doing everything in your power to scare us into going away. We didn't scare. You still wanted us gone. Right up until you determined that we were on a rescue mission of some kind. Then, out of the blue, you wanted us to land. It doesn't take genius to guess that you need help with something."

The five of them shuffled their feet and tried to look casual. Chuckie laughed. "I wonder if they have A-C blood in them somewhere."

"Right? It's so cute."

Reader chuckled. "True enough. Folks, we're on a schedule. At least, we think we are. If we can help you, we'd be happy to do so. If we can't, we need to determine where the people are who *do* desperately need our help and get to them. So, please stop stalling—the clock's ticking."

They still didn't look like they wanted to answer.

Jeff sighed. "Why are you hesitating? We're asking you what you need. Now isn't the time to be coy."

Still nada. Whatever this was, they were as scared of it as they were of us.

Thought about what Fathade had warned us about when we were landing, and also about Lizzie's comment about it. "What's the orange stuff, besides not native to your planet, and why is it dangerous?"

The five of them gaped at me. "How . . . how did you know?" Fathade asked finally.

Shrugged. "I'm a really good guesser."

CHAPTER 61

"WE DON'T KNOW WHAT IT IS," Fathade said. "Other than deadly."

"It's choking out our world," Sciea said. "Wherever it goes it thrives. We don't know how it's doing this or how it got here."

"So it's not the reason you're trying to keep visitors out?" Chuckie asked.

"No, but it's another reason for others to avoid our planet," Cavus said. "Something hit our world. It didn't come from Spehidon or Crion, but it was like a wave in space. Soon after, this pestilence appeared."

"Think it's the same neutron wave that affected Wheatles Kreaving and the solar system he and his ship landed on?" I asked Wruck.

"It's possible. How long ago did this event occur?" he asked the Cradi.

"Recently," Feoren replied. "A few of our months, no more."

Wruck shook his head. "It can't be from the same event. Well, I shouldn't say that. It could be. We have no idea where we really are. Or where Kreaving was when his ship was hit."

"We have star charts," Serion said. "Would you like to see them?"

"We would, but first, can we get a sample of the orange stuff?" Tito asked.

"We have examined it, so we have samples," Cavus said. "But it is deadly to the touch."

"Fantastic," Jeff muttered.

"Is it dangerous to look at? And by that I mean, can we see it safely or does it have spores that are deadly if breathed in?" Hey, I'd paid attention in school. Often.

"We have some in our lab." Feoren indicated one of the buildings nearby. "But are you asking to see the growing scourge?"

"Yes. I'd like to take a look at the Orange Scourge." Hey, I *was* the Giver of Names.

"Sooner would be better than later," Jeff said. "Since we have to find that other solar system and we have little to go on. Is it far from here?"

"Sadly, no," Fathade said. "The Orange Scourge as Kitty has called it has taken over a quarter of our world. Some is quite close by."

The street we were standing on moved, taking us with it. Again it was like a smooth roller coaster with no dips and was, admittedly, a fun way to travel. We zoomed along, passing Cradi along the way, all of whom stared at us, though some waved back when Jamie waved at them. The rest of us started waving, too, since it seemed friendlier. By the time we reached our destination, my arm was tired.

"How large is your population?" Chuckie asked.

"Several hundred thousand," Serion replied. "We maintain our population so that we don't use up our world. As one of us returns to the bosom of Cradus another is born. Not all of us choose to reproduce, but we are able to control when we do so."

"Do you control the gender choice of the child?" Chuckie was definitely in Academic Mode. It was nice to see him excited about something that didn't have to do with people trying to destroy us.

"Oh no," Serion said. "That is the child's choice, once they are old enough to decide. Until then, they can and do play with their internal and external makeup, becoming what they choose, not what their parents or our society chooses for them."

"What about war, fighting, attempts to take power?" Chuckie asked.

Serion shook her head. "We have none of those. It is not . . . logical or right to fight amongst ourselves. We are all one, truly, with Cradus, Spehidon, and Crion. Why would we fight? We can achieve whatever we want in terms of science or art and all are encouraged to do so. Our world is beautiful, full of everything we need, and, until the Orange Scourge appeared, abundant. We have no reasons to be discontented, so we are not."

"So, this is a utopia." Chuckie sounded thoughtful.

"Seems like it. What are you thinking, Secret Agent Man? I can see the wheels turning, even through the Moon Suits."

"Nazez was also a utopia. So was Tropea, before Grumpy and Dopey arrived."

"So? It's nice to visit places that aren't fighting amongst themselves. It's a relief to know that worlds like this exist."

He nodded slowly. "It is. However, this is, technically, the third utopia we've visited on this trip. And we've only made two stops."

"Oh. Huh. Hadn't realized that, but you're totally right. Which seems like far too much of a coinkydink and we don't believe in those."

"Exactly." He was going to say more but we arrived.

Sure enough, there was a ton of orange, pretty much as far as the golden eye could see. But it also looked familiar. Extremely familiar. Like I'd seen this stuff all my life familiar. Even the color, though I was used to the color being something else. "Are those a form of squash? Or carrots? Or carrot-squash?"

"What is squash?" Fathade asked. "Or carrots?"

"Something edible on Earth."

"We cannot eat this," Fathade said. "It is deadly, to us and to our world."

"It's choking any part of the world it touches," Sciea added.

"Can I touch it?" Tito and I asked in unison.

"Why would you want to?" Fathade asked.

"Because I'm betting that we both have the same idea. Tito?"

"I think it's a form of squash, yes, though I agree the color is more in line with carrots."

"Me too. Based on the vines and leaves and such, I think it's an orange squash of some kind, and those things grow like weeds. My dad planted a single zucchini plant when I was little. Supposedly it couldn't grow in Pueblo Caliente's soil and weather. Ha. It not only grew, it flourished. At first, it was zucchini for the nearest neighbors, then the neighborhood, then a mile radius, until everyone said they'd never speak to us again if we gave them one more freaking zucchini. Then we gave baskets to the homeless shelters until we got the same response. Then my parents had to pay people to come take that stuff out before it overtook our house, since it had taken over the entire yard and the dogs literally had nowhere to go to do their business."

Tito nodded. "This looks organic—for our world. But it's not organic for this one. However, if it *is* a type of squash, that means that we can figure out how to get rid of it."

"We cannot risk toxins," Fathade said. "We are one with our world, so any toxins in our world will go into us. We have only managed to keep the Orange Scourge at bay. But soon it will infect us, too."

"Will it hurt the Moon Suits if we touch it?" Didn't want to wreck these things or give myself radiation poisoning just because I felt sure the plants weren't dangerous to me.

"We assume yes," Cavus said. "Use this tool to gather then." Cavus handed me what looked like the things people used to pick up trash without bending over—a long set of pincers. How Cavus produced this I had no idea—as with the ball of Moon Suit that Cavus had given to Wruck, it appeared basically out of nowhere.

Took the tool and grabbed the nearest squash vine, which had about ten squash on it. It took some tugging, but I was able to unearth it.

"Those are roots," Tito said. "And they're long. We need to confirm what this is immediately."

"What are roots?" Fathade asked, sounding freaked out.

"Um, I saw what looked like trees and deer and birds on our way down the mountain. Don't the trees have roots?"

"Nothing like these," Fathade pointed to the squash vine. "The trees are part of the surface of Cradus, they don't go into the core."

"Jeff, you and the others stay here. Chuckie, ask every single question you've got. Tito and I are going back to the ship. We'll be back as soon as we know what's going on."

Jeff opened his mouth, presumably to argue. Put up the paw. He closed his mouth. Wow, the One True FLOTUS Power worked even while in the Moon Suits. "We're fine, you're fine, this moon is not fine. We'll be fast." Grabbed Tito's hand and took off.

"Not that I'm arguing," he said as I tested whether hyperspeed could work here and, happily, discovered that it could, "but why are we racing? I think there's time."

"Maybe, but I have an idea. I just need you to be sure that this stuff is not deadly to anyone on board our ship."

The street managed to match my speed and we returned quickly, this time on a fast roller coaster that took a couple of dips so that we could get where we were going faster. And I might have wanted to see if we could do it and it if was as fun as I'd thought it would be. We could and it was.

The street dropped us off right where we'd come out of the tunnel—the opening Serion had created was still there, so we went through it and ran into the airlock.

Fortunately, Tito had been paying attention, because he did all the door closing stuff. "How do you think we get these suits off?" he asked as he hit the airlock's normalization mechanism.

"Well, in Bizarro World you just sort of peeled."

"Wait until the airlock's ready, just in case."

While waiting, considered where to start the peeling process. Had no good idea. Once Tito gave me the go-ahead tried at the neck, the top of the head, and the wrists. Didn't work. Considered the only part of the suit that seemed like it moved, closed my eyes, and gently grabbed at the extra material that was there.

Success. Was able to peel it over the top of my head, and once I had done this, the rest rolled down easily. Tito imitated me and we were soon standing there with a ball of gold in each of our hands.

"We can't let anyone get to this planet," he said. "They'll destroy it in a month or less."

"Agree with you a thousand percent. Now, you get to your lab or whatever and verify this stuff's toxicity to us and the others on board."

"What are you going to be doing?" he asked as we exited the airlock.

"Me? I need to go have a confab with some of our passengers."

CHAPTER 62

"THIS COULD BE YOUR craziest idea yet," Reader said. "And I say that with the full knowledge of all your other crazy ideas."

"What's our mantra, James? I believe it's that my crazy tends to work a lot better than everyone else's sanity."

"Can't argue that, girlfriend. Cannot argue with that."

Tito had confirmed that whatever form of intergalactic squash had landed on Cradus, it wasn't deadly. Well, he'd confirmed that it didn't appear to be deadly to those of us not from Cradus. There were elements in the squash that he couldn't identify, but none of them triggered the very sensitive multirace and multiplanet tox-screen that Drax had installed into Mother.

I'd found our volunteer in terms of testing whether or not this stuff was going to kill someone. He'd been very willing to volunteer, which was nice.

Thanks to Mother—though I really suspected it was thanks to Algar—our phones still worked to contact each other even on a moon made of all metal, so I'd called some of the others back, mostly so that Tito and I wouldn't have to do the Moon Suit Dance until we knew if my plan was going to work.

So Reader had come back along with Joe and Randy. Fathade had insisted on coming with them. We'd been really worried about her being in our ship because it might hurt her, but she felt that she could adapt. So far, she seemed fine, which was a very good thing. She'd also brought along some extra Moon Suits, per my request.

Tito had the Test Squash laid out on a small platform that was under a clear safety dome. Picked up SuperBun and gave him a hug. "You're a brave rabbit."

SuperBun admitted that he was. He was also a hungry bunny, as were the rest of his people—Mother's food wasn't as satisfying as they'd expected.

Figured this was because of the Nazez black water. That it had altered the rabbits in some way seemed likely. That it worked as a healing medicine had been proven. Hoped that they still had whatever positive properties inside them. Maybe they'd never lose them—Hixxx hadn't seemed to think they would, after all.

Tito raised the safety dome, I put SuperBun down on the platform, Tito lowered the safety dome.

SuperBun sniffed the squash. It smelled like food.

"We're standing by with all the antivenom and such that we can think of."

SuperBun appreciated our preparedness. He sniffed the squash again. Then took a nibble. Then another. So far, it was delicious and not upsetting his tummy.

He ate the whole thing. Then we waited.

"How long, do you think?" Joe asked.

"I know some mushroom poisons can take hours to affect whoever ingested them," Randy added.

"Those people aren't having all their vitals monitored," Tito said. "We'll know in another few minutes."

They were a few long minutes, but ultimately Tito declared SuperBun safe. SuperBun requested another squash, just to be sure. Went and got it for him, using my bare hands. They remained unscathed, as did SuperBun, who ate the second orange squash as fast as he'd eaten the first.

"Okay, so I'm fine from touching it and SuperBun loves this stuff. We have, like, a thousand rabbits on board."

More, SuperBun shared. And many of them were pregnant.

"Okay, we have a tonnage of bunnies here and soon to be here. This could be the easiest problem solve we've ever had. While we can try to harvest everything, it would be faster to let them loose and have them go chow down. But I'm not sure if they can do that, even if they can get a Moon Suit on."

"They might," Tito said thoughtfully. "I'm looking at Super-Bun's internal organs. They're . . . stronger than a normal rabbit's should be. At least as far as I know. As I keep on saying, I'm not a vet."

"Sounds like you need to stop being a slacker and get trained in veterinary medicine. We have enough animals and no vet on staff. So, because I'm a thrifty FLOTUS, I'd prefer our White House Doctor also be the White House Vet."

"Can't wait," Tito muttered.

"Great! Make it so. Get the rest of the White House medical staff trained, too."

"Oh, yes, right away." Tito, too, had a sarcasm knob. "The moment I can talk to them, that's absolutely the first thing I'm going to say."

"Speaking of which, Mother, were you able to send the message Stryker wanted?"

"Yes. Though I am not certain that a reply can reach us where we are. This system is blocked."

"We have protective holograms, yes," Fathade admitted, as if we hadn't flown through them already.

"Let's get back to the matter at hand," Reader said briskly. "Can we put a Moon Suit on SuperBun and have it have a chance of working? If it works, can he ingest food through it and evacuate as well?"

"Gosh, no wonder you're the Head of Field. You think of everything."

"You weren't the one who got the complaints about the rabbit poop, girlfriend."

SuperBun apologized. The Poofs and Ginger had explained the concept of litter boxes and the rabbits were now all clear about where to go to clear out.

"The suits should enable that, yes," Fathade said.

"Wow, really? You mean we could eat and drink and go to the bathroom in the suits? Wouldn't that mean they get really, um, dirty?"

"No. The metal adjusts as needed."

"I don't think we want to eat anything from or on the planet," Tito said. "Even if we can, it's likely dangerous if we do. I suggest all meals be on the *Distant Voyager*."

"What about drinks and snacks?"

"Why would you care about that?"

"Really? We have a ship full of bored people on it, and kids need snacks, and everyone needs water."

"We have no water on our world," Fathade said. "We have rubidium and mercury. Those are as water to us."

"That settles it," Tito said, before I could ask Fathade to give me a refresher course in chemistry and share what rubidium was.

"No one eats or drinks on the moon. Period. People needing drinks and snacks can just come back to the ship or stay in it."

Fathade cocked her head. "Oh, wait a moment. I am connecting with Feoren." We waited a couple of seconds, then she nodded briskly. "Charles and Jeff have already had this discussion with the others. Serion may have the solution. We can create buildings that will shield you as the Moon Suits do. In those rooms you could remove the suits and eat and drink safely."

"Like, a hundred percent safe? Jamie's not the only small child with us, let alone everyone else on board. None of us want radiation poisoning."

"This is true," Mother said. "However, I have spoken with the others at Jeff's request and I believe we can indeed create a safe room for those who leave the ship. I will ensure that rooms for evacuation are included in the creation."

"Mother, you amaze me."

"This form of creation is similar to what I do to create food and other needful things."

"No, not about that."

"The communication is simple for me, based on the fact that you have all worn the helmets and you have all lived inside the ship for long enough. Plus I have provided comm links."

"Nope, not that, either, awesome though all that is. You've already mastered sarcasm. I'm impressed about that."

"I live to serve."

"See? Drax really does great work. How long to make the safe house or room or whatever?"

"We are already done," Mother said. "This world is most . . . accommodating."

Fathade nodded. "Cradus serves those who live upon it and we serve it in turn."

"Hope this doesn't end up with us being fed to a monster in the core of the world or something," Reader said quietly to me.

Fathade heard him and she giggled. "We have no monsters, and the core of our moon is more metals. We have no religion—Jeff asked and Charles had to explain the concept. We are not in need of believing in a supernatural overseer."

"Works for me. Do we want to do the SuperBun planet test now? Or just let everyone else experience the world?"

"Can we do both?" Fathade asked. "I know you are in a hurry and, frankly, so are we. The sooner the Orange Scourge is gone, the better. And if it turns out that the rabbits cannot save us, then the sooner we know that, the better as well. We have been formulating ideas for how to survive in space."

"You're doing okay in the *Distant Voyager*. Maybe you're all adaptable enough to do it."

She shook her head. "As long as we are close to Cradus, Spehidon, and Crion, all that we need we can achieve. But the farther we go from our world, the less . . . alive we are. Many years ago this was tested. Those who traveled off world were returned to us dead. We could not even rejoin their dead bodies with Cradus. We are limited to our world. But if the Orange Scourge cannot be stopped, or we cannot figure out how to take enough of Cradus with us if we must evacuate, then we may be facing extinction."

"Not gonna let that happen, so let's rock and roll. Do you somehow have enough Moon Suits for about a hundred people, several for various other animals, and enough for a massive amount of rabbits?"

She nodded. "We have a full storeroom of them, just in case. We don't waste things, and they were created long ago, when we used to welcome visitors."

"About that," Reader said, "it really seems like you're afraid of something."

"Many things," Fathade said sadly. "But mostly that others will come and try to steal our world from us." She still sounded sad but now looked angry. "Our world is filled with what others consider precious metals and resources. But it is our home and the only place where we can survive."

"I saw a lake of something pale and sort of a silvery purple that I couldn't identify—was that rubidium?"

She nodded. "It was. We also have rivers of gold and copper, mountains of silver and pewter, beaches of platinum, oceans of mercury."

"I can understand why you're trying to keep people away," Reader said.

Joe nodded. "Not just Earth values these things."

"Then let's stop jawing," Randy said, "and listen to Kitty. It's time to roll."

CHAPTER 63

WE TRIED A MOON Suit on SuperBun. It worked on him just as it had on the rest of us. While we did so, he spoke with the other rabbits. All of them were willing to give the suits a go.

Naturally, as soon as the rabbits started heading for us, the others on board noticed. Donned my Recap Girl cape and explained what was going on.

Was somewhat surprised that everyone wanted to try on a Moon Suit and give the world a go. Was less surprised when Gadhavi explained that they'd found another observation lounge, this one that gave them a view of everything that the ship could "see." So, they'd been watching Jeff, Jamie, and the others interact with the Cradi and, naturally, if it was safe for them, everyone else wanted in on the fun.

Christopher was the closest thing to a holdout, but only because he wanted the full explanation for how his children would be safe. Once he'd gotten that from Tito and Fathade, he was also all in on gearing up.

Realized that Team Tinman hadn't exaggerated—the boredom levels had clearly been high. Maybe we'd hit this world just in time, for them and us.

To speed things up, anyone who could walk on their own took at least two rabbits with them as passengers. This included Ginger, Bruno, and Lola, all of whom were all about being able to go out with everyone else and see things, as well as protect everyone from the so-far nonexistent threats Cradus might have for us.

Shocking me to my core, though, was that Algar was also coming along. "You're going Full Metal Jacket, my Ard Ri?" I asked him as Reader parceled out rabbits to various carriers.

"Of course I am, lassie. This is a beautiful place. I want to visit just like everyone else does."

"Um, okay." Maybe he was doing it for cover, though he really had no need.

"The weasels are coming, too," he added, as he put Moon Suits on them as well. Then he handed me their carrier. "Would you take them out for me, lassie?"

Wanted to say no, but reminded myself that this would be a stupid thing do to. Instead I took the Royal Hatbox in one hand, put SuperBun on my shoulder and Peter in my purse, and headed off. Did check to see if I had Poofs On Board. I did not. Maybe they needed the Moon Suits here and that was why Algar was in one.

"Should I put protection onto the Poofs?" I asked casually.

"Oh, I doubt it," Algar said. "This seems like a very peaceful place. They're probably getting a bit of a rest."

Now wasn't the time and we weren't in the place to ask him what the hell he meant. Instead, just went through the airlock with the last group of us. Serion was waiting at the exit from the tunnel.

"There you are," she said pleasantly. "I have gathered the star charts for the galaxy."

"That's great, thank you." Heard squeals of joy from the kids as the street started moving them. There were some squeals from the adults, too. Hacker International weren't on the street—they were too busy trotting over to any Cradus native and asking them excited questions.

She nodded. "We thank you for doing what you can to help us. Not many would."

"I'd argue that mindset, but I can't—your world is filled with too much that the rest of us consider precious. If you had diamonds and other precious gems it would be even worse."

"Oh, we do," she said. "They surround the core of the moon. We have them inside of us, too—they allow our circuitry to run, our minds to think."

"Wow." Told her about the various robots, cyborgs, and androids we had on Earth, including the ones that had originally used diamonds in the brains. "We have to find a better way to protect you guys from unwanted visitors than what you currently have."

"Why so? It's already worked several times."

"It didn't work with us. For all we know, those who you think it worked on are coming back with reinforcements. Maybe it worked and they're not. But statistically you're not going to be ignored forever. Let me get some of us together and ponder the situation."

We caught up with the others at the edge of the Orange Scourge. Everyone had been waiting for SuperBun, so I put him down with a snuggle. "You be careful."

He promised that he would, then he hopped over to the edge and sniffed. This still smelled edible. He started eating. He could successfully chew and swallow in the Moon Suit.

I put Peter down, also with a snuggle. "You be careful, too."

Peter also said he would, then hopped over to join SuperBun. All the many rabbits tried the Orange Scourge. All declared it delicious. No one had an issue eating in their Moon Suit. Several shared that they had no problem pooping, either. They tucked in with gusto. Soon the Orange Scourge was littered with golden rabbits and what looked like normal rabbit pellets, like some bizarre Easter pageant.

The least weasels squeaked at me. They liked what Mother had provided—they got Poof Chow, apparently—but wanted a change.

Put the Royal Hatbox down with a sigh. "You guys had better all come back when you're called. I don't want the Ard Ri freaking out about losing you." Opened the Hatbox and let them scurry out.

They squeaked thanks at me, then raced over to where Peter and SuperBun were and began eating. They didn't look like they were convulsing or anything, so allowed them to continue. Left the Hatbox there, too, just in case.

"How often do they eat?" Serion asked.

"I think at least twice a day at dawn and dusk. Under normal circumstances." Which these were not. "Could I see how far the Orange Scourge extends?"

"Of course." Serion and I were lifted by the ground. Said ground went out of its way to avoid what was truly a vast field of squash. From this perspective, it kind of looked like the Orange Scourge was giving the moon a bad comb-over. Though there was a lot to comb over, so to speak.

"This reminds me of the scene in *Horton Hears A Who* when the evil black-bottomed eagle drops Horton's special clover into a giant field of clover."

"I don't know what you mean," Serion said politely.

"So few ever do." Was really glad I hadn't made a comb-over comment. Saw what kind of looked like water if it was made out of mercury, so assumed this was their ocean. "Does the Orange Scourge grow in the ocean?"

From what I was seeing, it was avoiding it. Turned around to look in other directions. There were patches of orange dotted about—as if the moon had lost most of its hair though some was valiantly hanging on—but we were definitely near the largest patch.

"No, thankfully, it does not, nor in any lakes of rubidium. And it does not seem to affect them, either, for which we are grateful."

We returned to the others. Noted that the rabbits weren't eating the squash stems. Did my best to bring up information from my animal sciences classes from so long ago now. As I remembered, they were less thrilled with stems and anything dry, which might have been why they weren't enjoying Mother's offerings.

The least weasels, on the other hand, were eating the stems. So there was that, for whatever it was worth.

"They seem very hungry," Serion said hopefully. "Does that mean they will clear out the Orange Scourge quickly?"

"No bet." Having seen just how much there was to eat, my real answer was that I doubted it, but that seemed counterproductive to say aloud. Realized we weren't leaving until the rabbits finished, though. Meaning we needed to do a calculation. Meaning Chuckie was up.

Conveniently, he was with Jeff and Jamie. Wruck, Butler, Maurer, and the Kristie-Bot were all in conversation with Feoren and Cavus.

Went to Chuckie and explained the dilemma. He nodded. "I already did the calculations. We're here at least a week."

"I looked at the full expanse, and that was just for the stuff in this area, and I think you're underestimating."

"Should we leave the rabbits and go to Kreaving, then come back?" Jeff asked. "We have no idea how long that system has."

"Only if we know where we're going," Stryker said, coming up behind us. "This place is fantastic! But once the game was over, we were working with Mother to see if we could narrow down the distress call's location."

"When did the game end?"

"Once the Ard Ri told us he saw you guys all outside in Moon Suits." Stryker sounded reproachful. "You just love hogging all the cool stuff."

"That's me, Eddy, all the way. So, what's the good word on finding Kreaving?"

"Terrible. We think we have the general sector of the galaxy identified. But it's a huge area with a lot of stars within it. Mother thinks we could spend weeks searching without a better way to narrow things down."

"We can't just give up," Jeff said.

"We aren't," Stryker said. "It's just going to take time."

"Wasn't my plan, either, Jeff. Serion has their star charts. I say we spend the time here, letting the bunnies do their good eating work, while others figure out where we really need to go. That has to be a better use of time than us just flying around randomly, hoping and shouting Kreaving's name through our hailing channels."

"It makes sense," Jeff admitted. "And the rabbits are going to need more than a day."

"Sounds good," Stryker said. "I've always wanted to be an astrogator."

"A what? I see no gators here." Wondered how Alliflash and Gigantagator were doing for a moment. Hopefully well.

"An astrogator is someone who does astrogation, navigation in space," Chuckie explained.

"Oh. That word sounds totally made up."

"All words are made up, Kitty," Stryker pointed out a tad smugly.

"Blah, blah, blah. Just get all of Hacker International to astrogate or whatever. Chuckie, you're probably going to need to help them."

He grinned. "Not you?"

"Oh, I could, but I have another issue. We need to figure out where the spores or seeds or whatever came from, because while the rabbits can clear this out—we hope—if we leave and Cradus is hit again, it's just going to be the same old déjà vu."

"I agree," Jeff said. "I just have no idea how."

"Happily, I do."

Jeff groaned. "I'm going to hate this, aren't I?"

"Probably. I think it's time for the crew of the *Distant Voyager* to break up."

CHAPTER 64

AMAZINGLY ENOUGH, there weren't a lot of arguments about my idea to have the sports car section of the ship—the one made for exploration and fast exits—take a little trip around this small solar system. Drax felt it was sound, Fathade insisted they could easily get the sports car section of the *Distant Voyager* up high enough for takeoff, and we had more than enough volunteers. And no one was tired, that secret two-day nap having given everyone plenty of rest and energy.

One who wanted to go was Fathade. "If you go to take this risk for us, one of us should go with you," she insisted.

"You just told me how your guys died trying this before," I pointed out.

"And," Jeff said nicely, "That means not just no, but hell no."

"However, the plan is to remain within range of and close to Crion. That means that I should be fine, and if I'm not, I can be brought back quickly."

"She has a point, Jeff," I pointed out. "And you know that James won't let her be harmed."

Because we didn't want to risk having to leave and no one being able to fly the saucer section—which could fly without the sports car portion—it was decided that all of Airborne would stay on Cradus.

Reader had pulled rank and put his foot down, so he was captaining the sports car. Wruck and Drax insisted on joining him. Interestingly enough, Hochberg also insisted on going, just in case. "I'm the Vice President, and I'm military. It's me or Hammy."

Hamlin shrugged. "I'd suggest both of us, Jeff."

"I'm not going to concede authority," Reader said.

Hamlin laughed. "Son, that's not my plan. But I'm Air Force, meaning I can actually fly. I realize that Mister Drax makes ships that can almost fly themselves. But, just in case, you need backup."

"I can agree with that," Jeff said. "But James is in charge." Both Hochberg and Hamlin nodded.

"So, with Fathade, that makes six. Do we need more than that for the away team?" Kind of felt like we did, but didn't want to be a worrywart.

"I'd like Mister Buchanan," Hamlin said. "I realize he's your guardian, Kitty, but, honestly, this is the safest place I've seen in a long time, and we could use his observation skills."

"I agree," Jeff said, giving Buchanan the hairy eyeball.

Buchanan rolled his eyes. "God forbid I do my job, Mister Executive Chief."

"Saving these people matters to Kitty, therefore, it's part of your job." Jeff seemed quite bristly. Maybe he'd forgotten that Buchanan and Adriana were an item.

"Send the boys, too." Everyone looked at me.

"Who?" Hochberg asked. "Some of the children?"

"Dudes, seriously? No. Len and Kyle. They're both smart, observant, and they work well with Malcolm. Plus, they're young and Len has fantastic reflexes. They've both learned to think like me. Take them. Or Mister Joel Oliver. Or all three. But I want someone who absolutely can think like me along, and since Tim's assigned to the saucer and I'm actually going to spend some time being a mother, that leaves Len, Kyle, and MJO."

"All three," Buchanan and Reader said in unison.

"See? Now that wasn't so hard, was it?"

"A crew of nine should be sufficient," Drax said.

"Pity," Camilla said from behind me, "because it's going to be ten. I'm going. I'm with Hammy—this planet is incredibly peaceful and the Moon Suits and rabbits are handling the only threats to our people and the Cradi. So, I'm going, too."

"Agreed," Jeff said quickly.

Drax nodded. "Ten is preferable."

"Super and duper. Let's get everyone rolling."

Preparations were quickly made—Mother had ported a version of herself to the sports car, so everyone would be okay that way. Good-byes were said, the crew got into the lower section, and the spectacle began.

The ship's separation was interesting in that it was normally supposed to happen only in space. But Cradus made it easy, by raising the ship up to the top of the highest mountain again, supporting both sections while separation happened, then lowering the saucer back to where it had been while lifting the sports car section higher. During all of this the *Distant Voyager* sparkled like it was part of Cradus and always had been. The sports car took off in what looked like a shower of fireworks but was just the turbothruster exhaust sparkling against Cradus' atmosphere and Crion's light.

We watched until they went far enough that we couldn't see them anymore, not even gleaming against Spehidon. The gas giant was huge in the sky—larger than our moon or sun ever looked from Earth. It was beautiful, with bands in all the shades of red, yellow, gold, and orange. Really wondered if the Orange Scourge spores weren't from the planet somehow, despite Fathade and her people thinking otherwise. Oh well, that was Reader and his team's job.

Could have looked at Spehidon for a long time, but we had other things to do.

Chuckie, Hacker International, and Brian went to work with Serion, Sciea, and Cavus on the star charts. Jeff insisted on joining them, though I wasn't sure why. Mother provided comm links for all of them so they could include her in all discussions, since this work was taking place in the building dedicated to this kind of research.

The rest of us, however, were now on vacation.

And what a vacation it was.

Feoren was our guide. He took us all over the city, named Pheo, which was considered their spaceport. Though, really, due to how the moon worked, anywhere was a spaceport for Cradus.

This was fun, in the sense that we got to see something different and riding on the streets literally never got old. But it wasn't as much fun as it could be, since all the buildings looked alike. This was just how the Cradi liked it, though—they saw no reason to use anything but the most efficient form of housing, so to speak, and they had no interest in architecture at all. Who would, when you could architect your world into anything you wanted?

"Can we see the deer?" Lizzie asked. "The ones we saw on the mountain?"

"Of course," Feoren said.

For this, we didn't use a street. Feoren gathered some land

under us and we zipped off that way. There was some concern about someone falling off the side, confirmed when Sidney Valentino, who was leaping around to impress Lizzie, lost his balance.

Thought he was going over for sure, but the metal under us expanded out and up, caught him, and placed him back on his feet. Then it created a three-foot wall around all of us, presumably under the correct impression that we were clumsy, foolhardy idiots.

Thusly protected, and little kids held in arms, we continued on to the forest.

It was even more beautiful in person. The wall lowered and we stepped off the platform, which instantly blended in with the rest of the topography, which was very like a typical mountain region on Earth, only all metal. But the metals were different—soft, malleable, and pretty. There were metal leaves on the ground that felt like soft silver, and metal dirt like iron filings. The kids all picked up and played with these, saying they felt like leaves and dirt did at home. They felt like dirt and leaves to me, too. Moon Suits were definitely the way to go.

"It smells a lot like pine," Lizzie said. "But the leaves look more like oaks."

"Different worlds, different things."

"I'm amazed metal can have a scent," Wasim said.

"As Kitty said, every world has something different and special," Mossy said. "I've visited many worlds and they all surprise you."

"I expected this world to smell like a foundry," Gadhavi agreed, as he took Charlie from me and put him on his shoulders, while Siler did the same and lifted Jamie up onto his. The kids grabbed the tree branches nearest to them. One came off in Jamie's hand.

"Oh! I'm so sorry! I didn't mean to hurt it," she said to Feoren, looking ready to cry.

He smiled and took the branch from her. "No pain caused and no harm done. See?" He put the branch against its tree. The branch flowed into the tree and reappeared by Jamie's head. Then it tickled her. She squealed with joy.

This, of course, meant that all the other kids had to do the same. Some of the adults, too. Lots of laughter, lots of fun. Some of the kids climbed the trees. Chance Maurer fell off, and the tree caught him.

"This is like the safest world in the galaxy," I said to Feoren, while the other little kids all fell out of trees now while the young adults watched on and pretended to be too old to do this.

"It is safe, yes. We see no reason to have injuries—repairs take time and cause pain."

Chuckie's comments about this being a utopia nudged at me. "Was it always like this? Did you have strife in the past?"

"No, no strife. Our history is quite complete and we live for long periods. We have never had strife here—strife makes no logical sense if things are good, and they are. Well, I misstate. Among ourselves? No strife. Issues created by visitors? There we have had strife, and worse."

"Who came by that you liked? I mean, you made the Moon Suits for a reason."

"In the olden days, the Anciannas would visit, though those visits stopped long before John Wruck was born. The Z'porrah visited, too—it was they who we created the Moon Suits for. The Anciannas can shift safely, but the Z'porrah cannot. Then, their war started. We maintained noninvolvement and they left us alone. I believe they forgot about us."

"How? I mean that seriously. I can't imagine Earth 'forgetting' about a world like this, especially a world this rich in useful things."

He shook his head. "I don't know. None of us do. But the visits stopped, and we went on with our lives. We had the occasional visitor, normally a ship that was lost or in need of repair that had stranded near our solar space. We would always help them."

"Until? I mean, we know there's an until."

Feoren nodded. "Until some came with the idea of taking our world for their own. They were easily repelled, because they could not survive in our atmosphere and we did not give them Moon Suits. After that, we made the decision to scare off travelers, as opposed to letting them die on our world."

Decided it was time to Megalomaniac Girl Up. "These others who came to claim your world, were they called the Superiors?"

He nodded. "So they told us."

"And I've got Mephistopheles Bingo."

CHAPTER 65

THAT WE WERE ON the Fix What Mephs Ruined And Algar Allowed Tour was now confirmed. Not that I'd had any doubt, but still, it was always nice to be right.

"Excuse me?" Feoren said.

"Nothing. But it explains a lot." Wondered how I could get a message to Reader about this. Closed my eyes and concentrated on SuperBun.

Who was taking a breather from chowing down on the best food he and the other bunnies had ever had and so was available. He agreed to give it a try.

Threw leaves with Charlie—which consisted of me picking them up and him making them fly around us—and played tic-tac-toe in the dirt with Jamie to while away the wait time.

SuperBun came back on my mental airwaves. He'd reached Reader and given him the news. Reader was on it and had advised the others. Also, the least weasels were behaving themselves, still eating stems as well as squash, and not trying to eat any of the rabbits.

Remembered that least weasels were carnivores and asked SuperBun about this. Apparently, these least weasels also liked the squash. A lot. Decided not to complain about it.

This was all I could do about anything, so focused back on the kids. Heard Rachel Lewis say she was hungry, so asked Feoren if we could go back for a meal. He agreed, and I sent word to Jeff and the other astrogators that we were going to eat and to meet us at the safe room.

This time, the ground wrapped around us very like we were actually on a roller coaster—with metal forming around each person in a protective manner—and we raced down the mountain at a breakneck pace. This was fun and exhilarating, and all the young adults asked to do it again.

"After we eat," Denise said, marshaling the kids as was her skill.

We went to the safe room created for us—it had cafeteria-style tables and chairs, bathrooms—all pewter—and food and drink waiting for us, supposedly courtesy of Mother. Felt that this was courtesy of the King of the Elves, but chose not to say anything. Jamie and Charlie ran for Jeff, who was already there, Patrick ran for Brian, Jennifer raced for Hacker International, Nathalie walked with grace to Chuckie, and everyone else hurried to grab seats. Rachel was clearly not the only one who had been hungry.

This room was inside one of the smaller buildings. "There is oxygen in here provided via your ship," Feoren said, as he and I stood in the doorway he'd created. "And it's fully shielded. Wait two minutes for the signal, then you can remove the Moon Suits safely. When you're ready to leave, put your Moon Suits back on, then ask us to open the door—we will be monitoring all of you, just in case."

Gave him a hug. "Thank you."

"Where would you like to go after you eat?"

"It depends on the time of day, I think. We're all jumbled, and have no idea what time it is here."

"We don't worry about time," Feoren said. "We have much time in light, and then much time in dark. Right now, we are on the light side of Cradus. Let me access what you consider a day." He cocked his head, just as Fathade had done when she was connecting to their collective or whatever. "Ah. We have ten days of light and then ten days of dark. We are in the middle of the light days here. This meal for you would be, I think, dinner."

"What do you do when it goes to dark?"

"Some stay and enjoy the darkness. Others move to the other side of the moon. Our buildings are blocked from Crion's light, so we can sleep as needed. And we can see in the dark." His eyes glowed for a moment. "Though I would not recommend any of you go to the dark side."

Resisted making a dark side joke because I knew he wouldn't get it. "Is the world dangerous in the dark?"

"No, just less appealing for most of us. We have no lights for you, though—we don't need them so we have not created them, and back in the past, the Anciannas and Z'porrah had no real interest in the dark side, since they could look at it during its time in the light. I'm sure we could create lights for you, if being on the dark side was important for you, but creating heat would be more difficult, and I cannot guarantee that the Moon Suits would allow you to adapt to the cold the darkness brings—they have not really been tested in that way."

"Oh, it's no big. I was just wondering why most of you didn't stay where you were when the moon orbits."

He shrugged. "We can move, so we do. As you have seen, we can move our buildings with us. This is done all over Cradus. Other than the area where the Orange Scourge has taken . . . root, is that right?"

"Yes, taken root would be the right term. Was that area inhabited before?"

"It was, which is how we know that the Orange Scourge is deadly to us. And our world."

"And yet, it's thriving here . . ."

Because Feoren didn't know me, he didn't ask what I was thinking. Instead he nodded. "Yes, which is our dilemma. I will leave you to relax. Call for me when you're ready."

Went inside and Feoren closed the door behind me. Suggested that we only remove the parts of the Moon Suits covering our heads, and everyone agreed.

Algar was here with the Royal Hatbox, meaning he'd collected the least weasels since I'd talked to SuperBun. He hadn't gone with us to the forest, but I only realized that now. Figured no one else had noticed either way, other than maybe Gower and White. Had no idea what his game was, just that it was a long one and one he expected me to win for him, somehow. Always the way. Literally, as I was fast finding out on this trip.

We ate, drank, and rested. While we did so—and Jeff talked with Christopher, Gower, White, and his brothers-in-law, TCC and Jonathan Price, about how this world was the perfect example of life as we didn't know it but was still amazingly familiar, and I chatted with Amy and Jeff's sisters, Sylvia and Marianne, about how the rest of the Martini clan was missing all this amazing stuff that was almost too good to be true—let my mind work on the Orange Scourge Issue.

Came up with some ideas, but couldn't put them into action until Reader's team was back. So, thought about why Naomi had brought us here. The why of our arrival was obvious—we needed to see what this world was doing to protect itself so we'd feel protective of them. Achievement unlocked.

But why bring the people she'd had Jamie bring? So few of them made sense—Jeff's Cabinet in particular, the Valentino and Price families in the other particular. There had to be a reason. But damned if I could figure out what it was. Maybe it had to do with things on Earth. Meaning I'd find out when we got back. Bottom line—I'd know why they were along when I had to and likely not a moment before.

Back to this situation, then. Clearly, Naomi wanted this world saved, and I couldn't blame her. Also clearly, these people had been, if not truly harmed, at least menaced by Mephistopheles' people. Figured that at least one of the several plans I'd come up with would probably solve the Orange Scourge problem. Figured also that we'd come up with a good way to protect Cradus, since they knew where in the galaxy they were and we could call in help from one or more of our allies.

But there was a pattern, the Utopia Pattern. We now had two solar systems we planned to put under our protection. From what Kreaving had said, was willing to bet that the system his ship had stranded in was also going to somehow be utopian, or at least peaceful. He hadn't been afraid of the locals and, greater firepower or not, if there were enough angry people with spears and rocks, you and your spaceship could be toast.

Maybe the pattern was simple—that utopian worlds were at risk from less than ideal ones. But that seemed too simplistic. Maybe I just didn't have enough intel yet. Three utopian worlds, yes, but Tropea was destroyed and we'd only made two stops. Perhaps the answer lay with the system Kreaving was in. If we could find it.

So, no answers for any of my questions. I was batting a thousand on thinking failure.

Stopped the Debbie Downer mindset. We'd find it. Period. Not just to keep Mother from potentially slagging, but because I refused to believe we'd be too late. Maybe we'd cut it close, but we'd get there and we'd save them. Somehow.

Could have pondered Mephistopheles' message about what was in that system's sun, but didn't have the oomph. Meaning my next steps were clear—right now, I had to continue vacationing.

Realized I wasn't used to it anymore. Back in the day, Jeff

and I would escape to Cabo as often as we could manage. Once we'd been sent to D.C., though, those times were fewer and farther between, and once Jeff had become the President our vacations were nonexistent. Due to how our first trip to Camp David had been, thanks to Operation Madhouse, none of us wanted to go back there, and we'd managed not to return.

During a pause in both conversations, leaned over to Jeff. "You're done helping Chuckie, Mister Amateur Astrogator. Your family needs your attention."

"Why? Is something wrong?"

"Yeah. Our kids haven't seen their father relax in, for Charlie, his entire lifetime. Jamie probably can't remember the last time you weren't stressed out of your mind. Lizzie's only known us through stress and strife. It's time to take the vacation we haven't had that all the kids have been asking for. Whether it's a day or a week, until we know where we're going next, you're on Fun Dad Duty."

Jeff grinned. "Okay. Chuck was doing his best not to ask me why I'd insisted on helping." His smile faded. "And we're no closer to figuring out where to go anyway."

"Then we'll relax. I want the guys each taking time to relax, too, Chuckie and Brian especially. This is their only vacation time, too."

"I agree," Amy said. "Not that you asked. But I think we all need the break this amazing world has offered to us. Oh, and I know what I want to do after dinner. Well, twenty minutes after, at least."

"What's that?" Jeff asked.

Amy winked at me. "I want to go swimming in the ocean made of mercury."

CHAPTER 66

TURNED OUT THAT SWIMMING in the oceans of mercury was something the Cradi did for fun. And the Moon Suits would allow us to do so safely, too.

Being from or around Earth, all of us wanted to be in bathing suits, not our clothes, to do this excursion. The Moon Suits would protect us either way, but everyone was weirded out thinking about going to the beach in, say, a business suit, so we all changed in the *Distant Voyager*. We were able to go barefoot due to the Moon Suits, too.

It surprised me that Horn was interested in the swimming idea—he had burns over seventy-five percent of his body due to the horrific multicar crash a drunk driver had caused decades ago that he'd been involved in. He'd lost his family but he'd pulled every person out of their cars, most of which were burning. He was the only reason anyone had survived, and he was a true hero, but he understandably wasn't excited about the idea of sharing his exposed body. In all the time I'd known him, I'd never seen him in anything but long-sleeved shirts and slacks.

However, the Moon Suit allowed him to do this. He'd put the Moon Suit on in his room, but that was his only concession. And in it, he looked like everyone else, really—golden. He was in board shorts, but otherwise, this was the most undressed I'd ever seen him. He seemed bashful about it, but Elaine was talking and walking with him, and no one commented about anything. It was nice to see Horn getting to do this normal thing for, I had to figure, the first time in public since the accident.

Horn wasn't the only one who'd prepped in his room, though. We were all becoming quite adept at getting the Moon Suits on and off, even the littler kids. Wondered if suggesting that the

Cradi turn their world into a vacation planet would be met with derision, horror, or excitement. Figured I'd get two out of the three, so kept my mouth shut.

Thusly bathing suited up according to whichever custom and style each person followed, we did the airlock thing and headed off to the beach. I'd insisted that Chuckie and Brian join us. Hacker International had given me looks that said that they wanted, nay *needed* to keep on working on the star charts, so I let them off the bathing suit hook. I knew when to do someone a solid.

Going swimming here worked just like it did on Earth—you held your breath underwater and, if you wanted to open your eyes, you wore goggles. The goggles we were all given were equipped with the first clear thing I'd seen on the planet—the eyepieces were crystal. The crystal was ground in a way that made the goggles work just like any glasses or goggles from Earth would—the view was distorted a bit when you were under, not as bad when you weren't. And they fit over the eye protection of the Moon Suits perfectly, not that I'd had a doubt.

The Moon Suits would protect against anyone accidentally taking in a mouthful of mercury or rubidium, so the risks of drowning were less, and the risk of someone getting splashed and inhaling the stuff was slim to none.

Since Wruck was off exploring the solar area, the Kristie-Bot did the first test. She had no issues holding her breath and keeping her mouth shut, or seeing under the mercury, and Tito declared her fine.

Impressing me to my core, the next people to dive in were some of Jeff's Cabinet—Jordan Harris, the Secretary of the Treasury, Scott Davis, the Secretary of the Interior, and Jack Gibson, the Secretary of Veteran Affairs. These three all went under, and stayed under for a few long seconds.

Gibson surfaced first. "It works. I can see perfectly. It's amazing! And so buoyant, too! You have to try it!" The other two surfaced and chimed in on the awesomeness. So, after they came out, Tito wanded them, and they were declared still fully human and not poisoned in any way, the rest of us joined in.

There was no way in the world we were letting Charlie go underwater—he hadn't mastered swimming yet—but Jamie and Lizzie were both good swimmers. Jeff stayed in the shallows with Charlie, Christopher, Amy, Becky, and JR, while I went with the girls and the other kids, all of whom were able to swim.

Mrs. Maurer was with us, of course, as were her son and her grandchildren. It was really neat to see their little family having a fun, normal time together. The Maurers had been through a lot, and this vacation was as necessary for them as it was for us.

As Jamie and Lizzie pulled me under so I could look at the creatures in the mercury with us, realized that I was thinking of everything here as normal. Didn't know whether that showed my great ability to adapt, or whether Cradus was just so nice and relaxing that I'd come to accept it as perfectly safe and fun. As a tiny octopus-type creature with seven tentacles wrapped gently around my wrist, then let go when I tickled the top of its head, decided I didn't care.

Chose instead to enjoy the feeling of bouncing while under the mercury. Swimming in water was really going to be a let-down after this.

Schools of silver and black fish that looked a bit like trout, a bit like salmon, and a lot like aliens—seeing as they had sixteen fins each—swam by. There were what looked like forms of sea-weed and coral that grew at the edge of the shallows and went as far as I could see into the depths, the seaweed golden, the coral copper. More septopi came to play with us, as tiny fish that looked like silvery baby bass swam into the shallows, to tickle the toes of those there.

How we could see through viscous liquid or submerge in such a dense substance I didn't know. Maybe it was the Moon Suits. Maybe it was the goggles. Maybe it was magic. Maybe I didn't care. Cradus was, basically, da bomb and I was hella grateful for it.

The older kids started to have swimming races, though they listened to Feoren and didn't go out past where they had the Cradi version of lifeguards stationed. They had no dangerous deep dwelling predators, but Feoren saw no reason to take chances, and all the adults agreed that precaution was a good way to go.

Lizzie went to race with the other older kids, while Jamie and I floated on our backs holding hands and looking at Spehidon.

"It's so pretty here, isn't it, Mommy?"

"It is. I'm glad we came."

"Me too. I wish we could stay."

"But then we wouldn't see your grandparents and all our other friends and family again, Jamie-Kat."

"Oh, I know. It's not a *real* wish, Mommy, just a fun time wish. Auntie Mimi knows that."

Managed not to stiffen or react. "Oh yeah?"

"Yeah. She says that what we want and what we need aren't the same thing."

"She's very right. Um, does she grant your real wishes?"

"Only when people need help. Fairy Godfather ACE says that otherwise it's des-pot-ic."

"He's not wrong."

"He doesn't let us help nearly as much as I think we should." Said in the disapproving tone you'd use to share that a teenager was constantly having to be nagged to do their chores—punishment might be needed, but it would have to suit the level of the crime.

Cleared my throat. "You do realize that Fairy Godfather ACE is much older and far more experienced than you, right?"

"Oh, yes, Mommy, I know. Auntie Mimi says the same. And I would never do something to hurt Fairy Godfather ACE, cither. But sometimes it's hard to not help."

"Oh, I know that feeling, sweetie, I really do. Is that why you disobeyed and came out without permission earlier?"

"Oh, no. Fairy Godfather ACE approved that, Mommy. I don't disobey him very much. Hardly ever at all. I don't want to make him, you, Daddy, or Auntie Mimi disappointed in me."

Squeezed her hand. "We're never disappointed in you, Jamie-Kat. Ever. You're the best little girl any parents could ever have." Looked at Jamie out of the corner of my eye, which was possible in these goggles—she seemed quite pleased. Good. Considered what to say next. "How often do you talk to Auntie Mimi?"

"Oh, once in a while. Don't worry, I won't tell Uncle Chuckie, Uncle Paul, or Auntie Abby. I understand why it would make them feel bad to know that Auntie Mimi isn't talking to them."

Whatever story Naomi had to give Jamie to keep her from sharing this news was A-okay with me. "That makes sense."

"Oooh, look at Spehidon, Mommy. It's twinkling!"

It was, looking like sparkly orange confetti was coming from the planet, which was presumably some reflection from the sun. But it was beautiful to watch and we stopped talking about stressful things and just enjoyed floating on an ocean of mercury on the other side of the galaxy from where we'd started.

Finally, though, it was declared time to try and get some sleep. There was much good-natured complaining about this, but no one seemed peevish or on the verge of a tantrum. The utopian atmosphere seemed to be rubbing off on everyone.

Swimming, sunning, so to speak, splashing, and floating became a twice-daily pastime. We got up and ate, then everyone went to the platinum beach that felt like sand. We made platinum castles, swam with the septopi, played beach volleyball once that concept was explained to Feoren and the right equipment was created, rowed around on boats made of silver filigree with copper paddles, and generally acted like the happiest bunch of tourists anyone could hope to meet.

Lunch was followed by different trips each day. One day we went to the forest areas, other days we toured the rest of the light side of the moon—different towns that all looked alike, different people of all interesting kinds, ever-shifting landscapes that never got boring—and we always checked on the rabbits, who were making steady progress on the Orange Scourge. They all looked a bit bigger to me, but not fatter, every day. Decided not to worry about it.

Dinner led to the second beach excursion of the day, where we all did more of the same as we'd done after breakfast. Then it was bedtime for everyone, with Mother allowing us natural sleep. Jeff and I got to have a lot of great sex, too, because once the kids were asleep they were *out* for at least eight hours, which made this a fantastic vacation in my opinion. The only bummer was that we weren't able to do it in the mercury ocean, but you couldn't have everything. Jeff managed to make up for this by figuring out how to do it in the Moon Suits, so that was a very sexy memory we'd have that was just ours, too.

We even got Hacker International to join us for a few hours each day, with them alternating the excursions so they could experience all of them, too. Chuckie felt that the mental breaks were important for them, and by the second day, they weren't whining about said breaks at all.

Adam and the Kristie-Bot spent their time having fun and bemoaning that they'd run out of video on the first day on the moon, since they hadn't had the extra memory on them when the *Distant Voyager* took off. Dion quietly took pictures, without rubbing it in, since his camera was digital and he'd brought a ton of spare memory cards with him. Jenkins was interviewing every single Cradi who was willing to talk to him, which was pretty much all of them. So the Press Corps was having fun, too. Presumed Oliver was having fun being part of the away team, so didn't feel sorry for him, though had a feeling Adam and the Kristie-Bot were both jealous that they hadn't gotten to go.

The fourth day's midday excursion was to the rubidium lake. This wasn't treated as a place to swim, but more like a great mud bath with medicinal advantages. The Cradi waded in up to their necks and relaxed, chatting about various things. We were safe to do so as well, though most of us just went up to knees or waists. Other than the young adults, all of whom went up to their necks, presumably because Sidney dared everyone to do it.

The rubidium was warm and comforting, making this seem like a trip to a fancy spa. It seeped into the Moon Suits, but that was what it was supposed to do. We couldn't feel the rubidium on our skin, but it seemed to revive the Suits. It certainly revived the Cradi, all of whom were more sprightly when they got out of the rubidium lake than when they'd gone in.

Considered how pleasant and benign this moon was, especially for how different it was from what we were used to. Earth was abundant, so were most of the other planets our various friends, allies, frenemies, and enemies came from. But Cradus was even more giving, in that sense. It was hard to come up with another world that altered itself in whatever way its people and guests wanted.

Something about that thought made my brain nudge, but couldn't figure out why.

We were just leaving the lake when Louise Valentino, the eldest young adult here, looked up and pointed, interrupting my musing. "Look!"

We all did, in time to see what looked like sports car section heading for us. We took the fast ground roller coaster back to the *Distant Voyager* and were in time to watch it rise up to join with the saucer. This wasn't a quick process, but it was pretty and interesting to watch, and as the two sections came together, everyone cheered. We were definitely in the vacation spirit. Hoped we didn't make the away team feel bad for missing out.

Once the complete ship was back down again, we waited for said away team. Didn't have to wait long. They all came out with bathing suits on under their Moon Suits. "Mother said that we might as well relax while we debrief you guys," Tim said with a grin.

"Good," Jeff said, "but it's dinnertime first, though."

"We won't say no," Kyle replied. "We're starving."

"Didn't you eat on the trip?" I asked.

"We did," Drax said, as Fathade and Feoren ran to each other, hugged, and kissed. "But we chose to not eat these past few hours and just focus on getting back as quickly as possible."

"We found something," Len said to me quietly. "We need to discuss it, and soon. Over food seems best."

"What's the status on finding Kreaving's location?" Reader asked as we headed off.

"Nada," Stryker said. "We've narrowed more, but we've still got too much space to cover. We haven't been able to pinpoint a system yet, though we think we may have found his home planet."

"Well, it's something," Tim said. "Not what we need, but something."

Camilla took my arm, nodded to the others, and held me back. Jeff stayed back as well. "What is it?" I asked her once the others were farther ahead. "We all need to go into the safe room at the same time."

"They can wait a minute," she said briskly. "This news can't. None of us are actually starving, that's just the story to get us all into the safe room together ASAP without a Cradi nearby. Fathade was powered down when we discovered this, and we haven't told her about it yet—we felt it was safer for her if we shared the news when she was back on the moon, just in case. She was okay in space, but like an asthmatic fighting an attack— she had to labor to breathe."

"So, that means this news is hella stressful then, right?"

"Oh, definitely right. You know how the Cradi think that the Orange Scourge came from somewhere other than their system?"

"Yes," Jeff said.

Camilla heaved a sigh. "They're wrong. The spores are absolutely coming from Spehidon."

CHAPTER 67

WE CAUGHT UP TO THE OTHERS. Fathade and Feoren said they'd meet us after we ate, so as per usual we had no Cradi in the safe room with us.

Had Amy, Denise, and Lizzie handle Jamie and Charlie, since we needed an immediate meeting and none of us wanted the kids involved. We point-blank told the civilian adults that they were also to keep the rest of the kids fed and with them. No one argued—the expressions on the away team's faces now that there were no Cradi around didn't welcome complaints.

In addition to the nine of our people who'd gone on the excursion, we had all the rest of the usual suspects, Jeff's Cabinet, my available staff—since I valued both Vance and Mrs. Maurer's input—and Hacker International. In other words, the usual vast number that was the reason we'd had to create the Large Situation Room in the White House.

Fortunately, the room could accommodate. We sat as close to each other as possible, though, so everyone could hear without anyone having to shout.

"Len spotted it," Reader said, "Kyle convinced Fathade to power down and kept her distracted when she powered back up, and MJO was able to use his camera's zoom to get some good shots, so good call on those three, Kitty."

"I'm supposedly still the Head of Recruitment for Centaurion Division for a reason. But what did you guys find?"

"May I?" Oliver asked. Reader nodded. "We cruised the general solar area. This system is relatively isolated but we feel that we're likely in the Norma Arm of the galaxy."

"That tracks with their star charts," Chuckie said.

"It's always wise to verify," Wruck said. "Just in case."

"No argument." Chuckie nodded to Oliver. "Go on, please."

"Based on Crion's position in the galaxy, Mister Wruck was able to determine that it's indeed likely that a neutron wave from the star Mephistopheles destroyed hit Spehidon right before the Orange Scourge appeared."

"So that tracks with what Fathade told us," I said. "But it didn't hit this world like it did Kreaving's ship."

Oliver nodded. "This is a moon. That the wave affected the *Eknara* as it did may have had some to do with where they were exploring, because they couldn't move to avoid its direct path. The moon and planet have no ability to maneuver in that way, and they're both large enough to not be affected like the *Eknara* was. If Cradus was on the opposite side of Spehidon from where the neutron wave hit, then it could have felt far fewer effects as well."

"Okay, but Camilla said that the spores are from Spehidon. How?"

"The neutron wave likely affected Spehidon in some way. However, I captured pictures of the spores being ejected from the planet."

"In all directions?" Jeff asked.

Oliver shook his head. "Only toward the moon."

"You're sure that it wasn't just random?" Chuckie asked.

"Yes. The spores expelled toward the moon—it's moved since we left, and the location from which the spores came changed as well, to match the moon's location."

"How often?" Chuckie asked.

"Every other day," Reader said. "Len spotted it the moment we were closer to the planet. Believe me, it took a lot to keep Fathade from realizing this."

"I know a lot about Cradus' history now," Kyle said. "She's a great teacher, so there's that."

"If they've got part of a Superior in them, does that mean that the spores, the Orange Scourge, or whatever's in Spehidon are sentient?" Or evil, which seemed possible, considering what it was doing to the moon.

"Doubtful," Oliver said. "Not impossible, but it's unlikely."

"John?" Jeff turned to Wruck. "What do you think?"

"I think that we're going to have to figure out how to evacuate this moon."

Hochberg and Hamlin both nodded. "We agree with John,"

Hochberg said. "The *Distant Voyager* may be able to accommodate them in some way to keep them alive until we can find another world they can thrive on."

"Leaving them here is going to be akin to murder," Hamlin added. "Fathade was very clear about what the Orange Scourge does to them."

"So, we're going to evacuate an entire race and just give up on their home world?" Jeff sounded upset, not that I could blame him.

"No," I said. "We're not."

This got me the group's attention. "How so?" Tim asked.

"I have several ideas, after wandering this moon for the past few days." My brain nudged again. There was something about Cradus that was bothering me. "Kyle, have a question for you before I make any suggestions, though."

"Shoot."

"Did Fathade mention how they manipulate Cradus to do whatever they want?"

He looked thoughtful. "No, not really. She indicated that it was all via telepathy, not that she came out and said that, though."

My brain shared that I'd read about things like this before.

"Okay." Considered options. Considered something else. Dug into my purse, pulled out my phone, and opened my music up. Steely Dan's "King of the World" was queued up. Nice to always have Algar on my wavelength. "Look, I need to go talk to the rabbits. So, let's eat, because I can't leave the room until everyone's Moon Suits are back on."

"That's it?" Jeff asked. "You have ideas and the first one is to eat?"

"You've known me how long?"

"Good point."

"I'm all for eating," Reader said. "I know what tends to happen when Kitty says she knows what to do, and I prefer to roll on a full stomach."

We ate quickly, with those of us who'd stayed on the moon telling the away team all about our vacation so far. "I don't want to lose this world," Jeff said when we were done. "It's too special to give up on."

"And we will not. I want everyone to go swimming—the mercury ocean is not to be missed. Everyone other than Richard and Paul, that is. I'd like them with me."

Looked like a lot of people wanted to argue or ask me what I was up to. Put up the paw and was rewarded to see all those people grimace and stay quiet.

"I want to do this so that I don't insult or terrify our hosts and don't get people's hopes up with unworkable ideas. And I want Richard and Paul with me for reasons I don't plan to share yet."

"Fine," Jeff sighed. "Why ask why?"

"That's the spirit!"

We got everyone's Moon Suits on. No one delayed—everyone really loved going to the beach here.

Normally we sort of shouted and somehow a Cradi heard us and came to let us out. Wanted to test a theory, but had to do it quickly. "Jeff," I said quietly, "don't call up just yet." He nodded and I went to the area where Feoren always opened the door. "We'd like to leave," said pleasantly but also softly, "please and thank you." The opening appeared. There were no Cradi nearby.

Everyone filed out. Kissed Jeff and the kids, snagged White and Gower, and headed off toward the Orange Scourge.

"May we know what you're thinking now, Missus Martini?" White asked.

"And why you only want the two of us?" Gower added. "I was looking forward to swimming with my husband, you know."

"James will still be there when we're done, Paul, I promise. As for why you two, it's because I have a theory that I need to test, and the two of you are the only ones who won't instantly tell me I'm crazy."

"This should be good," Gower said. "I'll bite—what's your theory?"

Made sure no one else was around. We were close to where the rabbits were, and the Cradi did their best to avoid this area, so we were good.

"I think we have a real-life Man in the Moon."

CHAPTER 68

TO THEIR CREDIT, neither White nor Gower gave in to the urge to say I was crazy.

"Come again?" Gower asked finally.

"I think the moon is a benevolent, sentient being."

"Why do you think this?" White asked.

"Well, for starters, because it's been done in the comics. In *Green Lantern Corps*, the planet Mogo is both sentient and a Green Lantern."

"Kitty, just because it's in the comics doesn't make it real," Gower said patiently.

"Yeah? I point to Superman and the Flash as merely two examples of my daily real life."

"She has a point, Paul. What else, though, besides the fact that your favorite form of nonbedroom entertainment says that it's possible?"

"Look at you, managing to get the snark in no matter what. You're an artist, Mister White, I've always said so. And the what else is that this moon does whatever its residents want, presumably within limits. They have no crime, they have no predators, they have no worries. Or, at least, they didn't until the Orange Scourge arrived."

"So, what do you plan to do?" Gower asked. "Talk to it?"

"I do, as a matter of fact. And before either one of you tries to scoff, let's all remember that the three of us know someone personally who can merely snap his fingers and make reality whatever he wants."

"An excellent point," White said. "Why is he with us, do you know?"

"Know? No. Suspect? Yes. We're fixing other people's terrible mistakes and he needs us to do it."

"Why can we talk about him so easily?" Gower asked.

"I think we're being allowed to, honestly. Or else Cradus is messing with him, which I kind of doubt."

Called to SuperBun in my mind. He hopped over to us. Picked him up. He was definitely bigger.

"You've grown. Are you feeling alright?"

He was. But he agreed that he and the others were larger. He felt that the delicious squash was the reason.

"Me too. I think there's a very big mind here. I don't know how to connect with it. I'm wondering if you do."

SuperBun considered and suggested we all sit. Which we did, cross-legged on the ground, SuperBun snuggled in my lap. Then he concentrated.

It took a while, but suddenly I felt a surge, similar to when I spoke with ACE, but different—stronger and somehow older, if a feeling could be old—surrounding me. It felt huge but gentle. Cradus?

I am Cradus.

I'm Kitty, and Richard and Paul are with me. SuperBun is connecting us. I'm sorry if we're disturbing you.

You are not. Are you enjoying your time here?

Very much so.

We all are, White said. Very much.

We appreciate your hospitality, Gower added.

Good. You are the first to speak to me in a very long time. Do the people who live here realize that you are here?

No. Could feel the smile in his thoughts. They are wonderful, are they not? So special, so kind, so peaceful. They do not need to know that I am here—they need no gods.

They are indeed wonderful, and that's what they told me, too. But they're in danger.

How so?

The plant that's taken root on your surface—it's deadly to them.

Ah. It itches.

Couldn't help it, giggled in my mind. I imagine it would. Does it hurt you, though? The people living here seem to think it's harming you.

It is not. It is . . . adding something to me, but it is not a dangerous thing.

Adding what?

Adding a different kind of life.

Um, is it sentient life? Because if it is, the rabbits—
SuperBun's people—are eating it, and they enjoy it very
much, but they'll stop if they're eating something sentient.

No, it is not sentient. Not all life is.

True enough. Was relieved that we hadn't done the wrong
thing while trying to do the right one. The planet, Spehidon, is
sending more spores to you on a very regular basis.

She is playful.

She. Because, of course she.

Um . . . do you mean that in a general sense, as in you
refer to Spehidon as female and, say Crion as male, or do
you mean that specifically, as in Spehidon is also a sentient
world?

Our sun is not sentient, which disappoints us both. Spehidon is sentient as I am. But she is lonely. None have chosen to live within her.

It's hard for most life to survive inside a gas giant, White
said.

Most of us can't survive in the radiation, Gower added. It's
why we need the Moon Suits to spend time with you. Your
people can, though. They are amazing.

They are. But they would not be comfortable on Spehidon. She needs those who are more spirit, as she is.

We know of races like that, actually. The Vrierst were living
on Jupiter now, after all.

Could you have them visit her? He sounded hopeful. It
would mean so much to her.

We can try. In the meantime, can you ask her to stop, um,
spitting at you?

I could, but it would make her sad. She is trying to be
helpful.

By sending something that is harming your people?

She thinks she is sending something needful to me.

Is it? White asked.

I don't know. It is unlike me in almost all ways. Just as all
of you are unlike my people in almost all ways. But that
doesn't mean it is bad.

No, it doesn't, Gower said. But we are more alike than you
realize. He put his hand onto the ground. See for yourself. Look
at what we are under the Moon Suits.

The ground swirled up around Gower's hand and forearm. You are mostly something that does not exist here.

Water, White said. Just as your people are mostly metal. But look beyond that.

Stroked SuperBun while we waited.

I can see the similarities, yes. The dirt retracted from Gower's arm and went around SuperBun's middle. He is no longer mostly water. He is becoming a part of me and a part of Spehidon, too. As well as a part of somewhere else.

Uh oh. Presumed the somewhere else was Nazez, but the rabbits had been able to leave.

Um, does that mean I should have the rabbits stop eating the squash?

SuperBun said that the rabbits could help. Some could stay on Cradus.

I agree, Cradus said. You are welcome to make a home here. I will provide whatever I can for you.

That doesn't keep the rest of you or your people safe, I pointed out. Not if Spehidon keeps on sending spores to you. Even with a hundred thousand rabbits, she's sending more than they can eat.

Oh, she has to, though. If the rabbits are to stay.

Why is that?

Cradus chuckled. Because what they excrete kills the plant.

Let that sit on the mental air for a moment. Um, are you saying that the rabbit's, ah, evacuation is killing the very thing they're eating? And is therefore able to keep the Orange Scourge from taking over at least your surface if not the rest of you?

Yes.

Wow. This has to have been the easiest save we've ever had. Poop for the win, I guess.

CHAPTER 69

SUPERBUN WAS HAPPY TO help and keep his people pooping all they could. Could tell he was shocked but also found this as hilarious as I did.

So if they are to stay, then Spehidon's gift is a good one. Cradus sounded like he wanted my agreement, not in a demanding way, but in a hopeful one. Got the distinct impression he didn't want to hurt Spehidon's feelings, not out of fear but out of love and kindness.

I suppose it is. Tell me, has she been sentient as long as you have?

Yes. We have been sentient for as long as we have been created.

Did she tell you how she got these spores to send to you?

She did. Something sailed through space and entered her. She found some of it distasteful and discarded it. But some was good and she kept that.

Huh. So it didn't harm her?

No. It gave me the spores to send to me, which now have given me new people to love and entertain. It is a good gift.

Yes, it is, White said.

But it still risks your other people. My idea was to ask you to create an island that has the Orange Scourge and, now, the rabbits on it, because the Orange Scourge doesn't grow in the mercury or rubidium for some reason and it also doesn't affect them negatively. Would that work? I don't want the rabbits to be cut off from the others, but until a way can be found to protect the Cradi from the Orange Scourge, I don't see how they can live right next door, so to speak.

Your suggestion is a good one. I will make an island for

the Orange Scourge, as you call it, and the rabbits that are staying with me. I will make it large enough for the rabbits to live well and prosper and deep enough that the roots will have room to grow. Spehidon will send her spores to the island only from now on. Should the rabbits want to visit the rest of the world, I will ensure that they can. They will not be cut off.

Will they need water? It's something we from Earth and many other planets need to survive.

SuperBun felt the Orange Scourge was giving them all the water they needed somehow.

It should be impossible for a planet without water to have a plant growing on it that requires and provides water. I'm just mentioning that.

Spehidon has ice within her, and she says that it is in the spores.

Realized what was happening. Spehidon was terraforming Cradus. Wasn't sure if that was in the moon's best interests. Wasn't sure that it wasn't, either. Felt a migraine wanting to show up. Then felt it whisked away and as if someone was petting my brain in a very soothing manner. Cradus was truly a loving entity. Pity we hadn't known him when Chuckie was having twelve migraines a day.

Why does the Orange Scourge hurt your people? Does Spehidon know? I know she's not sending the spores to hurt them. At least, I hoped.

No, she is not. She does not know why, either. But she would not harm me or my people any more than we would harm her.

Gower jerked. You said that there is ice in the spores, because they're part of Spehidon?

Yes.

Maybe that's why the Cradi can't touch it without pain or damage—the water, or the radiation, maybe both, Gower suggested. Are you sure that the Orange Scourge can't hurt you, yourself?

I am, but what you say is most interesting. Spehidon and I have not considered that. She is our planet, we have assumed that nothing she could do could harm any who live upon me.

Maybe before she was hit with that neutron wave that was true. But I agree with Paul—it doesn't seem true now.

That means we will have to determine how to ensure that my people can adapt to the Orange Scourge and whatever else Spehidon wants to send to us.

Take it slowly, White suggested. Rapid change can be very hard on people and the Cradi are afraid of the Orange Scourge, rightly from what they've shown us.

So much so that they are wondering if they would need to evacuate, I added.

That would make me and Spehidon terribly sad.

It would make them sad, too, and then it would kill them. They need to be near you in order to survive. It's been tested.

Then we will work to ensure that my people are able to adapt to this new gift from Spehidon. They are more than capable of it, as long as, as you suggest, we move slowly.

SuperBun mentioned that those rabbits remaining on Cradus would like to be able to take off the Moon Suits.

As long as they won't be hurt by Spehidon's radiation or the gravity you and she create, I added quickly.

There is no worry. The Moon Suits are a part of you now.

All of us? Didn't really want to have to wear these when we left Cradus.

No, just the rabbits. The Orange Scourge is helping them to bond with me and Spehidon.

SuperBun was worried and wanted to know if they could ever leave now, because some of the bunnies wanted to stay with me.

Yes. I can show you how to make the suits hide.

Hide? You mean take them off or internalize them?

Both. They will be able to do what my people do—live upon me freely and with no fear.

Rabbits were often afraid, SuperBun said. They would enjoy not having to fear.

But the Cradi don't use the Moon Suits and, in fact, can't survive too far away from you. And I think only those of us with opposable thumbs can get the suits on and off of the rabbits.

This is true, but my people are of me. The rabbits are not and they were special before they got here. They can adapt to anything.

The black water. Wondered if I'd regret not making all of us drink some of that or end up hella relieved that we hadn't. Ah. The rabbits were taken from Earth to a planet far away and that planet gave them some special abilities.

They can become invincible.

Can they protect you from strangers?

Maybe. But Spehidon does that already.

Pondered this. I mean, we were here, so she wasn't doing that great a job. Oh. Did she create the illusions that entered our ship when we arrived?

She did. She is very protective of us. We are alone and have no others like ourselves to talk to.

Yes, sentient planets and moons are rare.

It's a large galaxy, White said. We may find others like you.

Or you may not. Spehidon and I are happy together. She would just like people, as I have people. It is her only wish.

A wish. James had said, rightly, that needs were important where wants were not, and Jamie had told me that Naomi had said that needful wishes were granted. And this sounded needful—giving a sentient planet people to care for. Maybe she'd stop sending spores to Cradus, too. Maybe not. It was hard to guess—this moon and planet had an interesting relationship.

We'll find people for Spehidon. But she needs to stop the illusion. It doesn't work right. We will help figure out a better way to protect all of you.

Keep it until we return, Gower said. Just in case.

But you are still here. I am happy for you to stay if you choose.

We have to help some others, far away from here. Then, once we've helped them, we will come back and take care of protecting you and finding people for Spehidon.

Can I help you find these others?

Only if you know where the spaceship *Eknara* recently crashed.

I do not know that. I am sorry.

It's okay. We have to do things for ourselves. It's part of what makes us people—that we do and think for ourselves, versus allowing others to do and think for us.

So the rabbits are . . . people?

As I see people, yes. I'm a human, Richard is an A-C, Paul is a hybrid, Fathade is a Cradi, and SuperBun is a rabbit. But we're all highly sentient, able to think of more than the basic necessities of life, and a part of societies in the greater cosmos so, to me, that makes us all people.

Do you consider me a . . . people?

A person, that's the singular of people, and yes, I do. Spehidon, too.

You are different.

So I'm told.

I will give you a gift.

Getting to relax on your surface and enjoy what you offer has been a gift already.

Thank you, but I will give you another gift. A gift of myself, a part of me you can carry with you.

White nudged me, but I already knew what to say. That is a wonderful gift. I am honored and I will accept it with much joy.

The ground in front of me rose up and formed into a large ball of gray metal. This is part of me and carries my essence inside of it.

Thank you. I will guard it carefully.

No need, though I appreciate the sentiment. It cannot be harmed or destroyed.

Really?

Really. Even if the metal disappears, my essence will still be there.

Wow. Who knew that a moon could be so philosophical?

Another ball appeared next to the metal one, this one swirling colors of red, yellow, and orange yet mostly insubstantial. It encircled then entered the metal ball. This is a gift from Spehidon. It is her essence as well. She gifts it to you for your willingness to try to find people for her. And, as with my essence, hers cannot be destroyed.

Thank you both. The ball of metal flowed into my hand and reformed as a ball. It divided into several balls, then reformed as one. Wow again.

Cradus chuckled. You have seen this already, more than this really, and this small thing amazes you?

It does. It's a part of you both, sitting in my hand. You and Spehidon are both amazing.

We are pleased you find us so. Now what will you do?

Figure out where the other people are who need help, go to them, and help them.

You leave us so soon? Cradus sounded sad, which was sweet.

We'll be here until we can determine where we need to go. But I would love to visit again, if we could.

You and your people who have come to visit me are always welcome here. Should you need to leave your home and find a new one, you will always have a place with me. As will any you choose to bring with you.

We'd gotten that offer from Hixxx, too. Nice to know we were winning friends and influencing people on this trip. That is a generous offer, and we appreciate it very much.

We appreciate your efforts to help, both us and others. Spehidon and I will enjoy you while you are here and miss you when you are gone.

And we will do the same.

Felt a warmth in my mind, very similar to how ACE hugged me, and then it was gone. But I still had the ball of metal that was also part of Cradus and Spehidon. And that was the best souvenir a girl like me could hope to score.

CHAPTER 70

WE ALL LOOKED AT EACH OTHER. "Well, that was rem- iniscent," Gower said. "It's been a long time since I've had someone that deep in my mind."

"Do you miss ACE?"

He smiled. "Every day. But I think he's better in Jamie."

"Another friend made, Missus Martini. I'm happy to see that you're keeping your record intact."

"Doing my best, Mister White. So, how do we tell the others what we just did?"

"Straight out," Gower said. "This isn't . . . the other guy."

"Nightcrawler calls him the DJ."

Both men stared at me. "Benjamin knows of . . . the DJ?" White asked, sounding shocked.

"Um, sorta? He's figured out that someone's helping me, he's guessed that you two know who it is, but beyond that, he's not 'there' yet. The DJ appears to be enjoying the challenge. And, yeah, Nightcrawler's the first person in, I think, ever, to get this far on his own. The DJ seems impressed and amused, not ready to smite."

"Well, that's good, I guess," Gower said. He stood up and helped White up, then me. Kept a hold of SuperBun. "So, who's staying on Cradus?" he asked the rabbit.

The pregnant females and their mates, which made up about five hundred of SuperBun's people. He was pleased that they'd reached person status with us.

Snuggled him. "You're awesome. Of course you're at people status, I told you that on Nazez and I meant it. Hope those who are already attached to the rabbits that are staying on Cradus find other bunnies to attach to."

SuperBun felt that this would not be a problem.

Kissed the top of his head, then let him down. He hopped off to share the good word about what was coming.

"Nice to hear the rabbits without you having to interpret," Gower said. "Think that'll last?"

"No bet, but I think the Nazez black water has to be as guarded as Cradus. Possibly more so." The men nodded, and the three of us headed back. "We can't let the Cradi know. They have no gods and Cradus approves of that."

"I agree," White said. "My advice would be to 'suggest' your island idea and that some of the rabbits will remain, and allow them to believe it's they who are creating the island, not Cradus himself."

Considered this. "It's a good idea. Shouldn't we just, maybe, tell everyone that?"

Both men stopped walking. "You want to lie to the others about this?" Gower sounded shocked out of his mind.

White, on the other hand, was clearly considering the pros and cons. "I understand Missus Martini's thought process on this."

"Making you the Army of One as always, Mister White."

He chuckled. "Well, others 'get you' as well. However, you won't be able to explain the gift you received, and while the Cradi may not care—or may care very greatly—that you're taking part of their planet with you, our people will not stop asking about it until you share the why and the how."

"Good points as always. But speaking of that, let's put it away in a safe place." Placed it carefully in my purse, which I had refused to not have with me regardless of where we were or what we were doing because I was experienced by now and, peaceful world or not, not having my purse along was really tempting the cosmos a bit too much. It made the purse heavier, but in the Moon Suit, I barely noticed.

Did notice the envelope that I'd shoved in there while I was still in the White House. Probably needed to take a gander at whatever it was that Algar had given me. And I hadn't asked Serene what she'd dropped into my purse when we were on Nazez, either, nor had I looked for it. Well, I'd empty out my purse when I had a little downtime, but right now, I was still on vacation.

We rejoined the others and Gower did indeed get to swim with Reader. We spoke quietly with those who just had to know

where we'd gone and why, but not everyone cared, which was
fine with me. Those who did care were both shocked and kind
of thrilled to know we were in a sentient solar system—those
who were comics geeks such as myself in particular—and
everyone agreed not sharing this with the Cradi was Job One and
not sharing it with anyone with us who didn't care until we were
off the moon was Job Two.

Had a talk with Team Tinman, all of whom were interested in
Cradus as a world and fascinated and excited in him as a sentient
being. They spent some time communing with Cradus, and he
didn't seem to mind. No one spoke with Spehidon, though. Per
what Butler told me, her mind was too vast and could harm ours,
so Cradus did the go-between, just as he'd done when White,
Gower, SuperBun, and I were chatting with them.

Suggested my brilliant idea of creating Orange Island to the
Cradi and they thought it was a great plan. They were very grateful that so many rabbits were staying and promised to ensure
that the rabbits could leave Orange Island whenever they wanted
or needed to. Chose to drop the Scourge part of the name, since
it was now a place my bunnies were hanging out and they were
not scourge-worthy.

Once that was accomplished, we slipped right back into Cradus Vacation Routine, with swims to Orange Island added in for
those with the stamina. With Wruck, Drax, and Fathade back,
Team Astrogator—which still made me think of Alliflash and
Gigantagator in spacesuits—was stronger, and they continued
to make progress on narrowing down our likely area to find
Kreaving.

On the third day after the chat with Cradus, just as we were
coming back from the morning's time at the beach, we got the
good word. Time to start saying good-bye.

Mother wanted to do some last-minute fiddling with herself
and her programs with some of the Cradi assisting—in no small
part to prevent anyone else from taking her over again—and
Drax and Hacker International assured us that she wasn't trying
to HAL it up, so we took advantage of our last few hours on this
world. I put in a personal request to Mother and Fathade, which
they said they felt they could do, so that was nice.

Feoren took all of us on one more tour of the light side of
Cradus and, as a treat, let us see a tiny bit of the dark side. It was
indeed much colder and it was hard to see, but it was still neat
to see waterfalls of rubidium and mercury flowing over lead

mountains and going into a series of lakes and lagoons that surrounded golden islands with platinum beaches. None of this had
been visible when we were coming in to land. Was kind of sad
that we weren't going to be here long enough to see everything
on the other half of Cradus, but duty called.

"I want to come back again," Jamie said, as we all went one
last time to the beach, so that those who'd solved the Star Map
Mystery would be able to have a last swim, too. The older kids
swam out to Orange Island to give the rabbits the heads-up that
we were getting ready to go.

Charlie nodded enthusiastically. "I like it here." Then he
smiled. "But we'll like it other places, too."

"Have you been talking to Ixtha in your sleep, my little
man?"

"Yes, Mommy. She was scared we weren't coming. But I told
her we had to make stops along the way. She understands."

"Good."

Beach time wasn't too long—once the older kids were back
from Orange Island, we packed up. Then we went to get the
rabbits that were traveling on with us.

Feoren made a bridge of silver from the beach to the island.
Several hundred rabbits hopped over, SuperBun and Peter in the
lead. Noted that all the rabbits that had attached to people on the
Distant Voyager were traveling on with us, which was nice, and
they all ran to "their person" which was nicer. Picked up Super-
Bun and Peter and gave them snuggles.

I wasn't the only one with multiple rabbits, either. Lizzie, for
example, had five rabbits she was carrying back to the ship.

Chose not to complain or make a joke—she hadn't been allowed pets until she'd moved in with us, first because her parents were those Russian spies and then because her adoptive
father was an assassin. Pets slowed you down. Proved by the fact
that Lizzie wasn't moving too quickly, so she wouldn't drop a
bunny.

Jeff heaved the sigh of a man who knows he'll never stop
living in a zoo, picked up Charlie, who had his bunny clutched
in his hands, went to Lizzie, and took two of the rabbits from
her. "Let's not drop them, Moon Suits or no Moon Suits."

She smiled at him. "Thanks."

Handed Peter to Jamie so I'd have a free hand to hold hers
with. She snuggled Peter. "Thank you for sharing Peter with me,
Mommy."

"Oh, I imagine we'll have plenty of bunnies to share, sweetie." Not that I planned to share SuperBun.

Who nuzzled me. He didn't plan to be shared, either.

Out of all of us, and unsurprisingly, Team Tinman didn't want to leave the most. Offered to let them stay. Joe and Randy opted out because of their families, and Maurer did the same. "This is a wonderful place," Maurer said. "But without my mother and children, it would hold no joy for me."

"Ditto, and you know it," Randy said. Joe nodded.

"Hey, I had to ask. I mean, some of the rabbits are staying, so it was only fair to ask you guys. Kristie?"

"Oh, I love this world and adore Cradus himself. But I'm not missing the *Code Name: First Lady* premiere for anything."

"Seriously?" Joe asked. "You love it here and it's a place where you fit."

She shrugged. "I fit everywhere, it's how I moved up the ranks as a reporter. Don't get me wrong—I want to come back. I just don't want to live here. My home is Earth, the galaxy is my playground."

Made the gag face and the gag sound. She laughed and punched me in the arm, but gently. Realized with a form of horror that we were friends. Oh well, I had weirder friends and friends who had started out far more antagonistically to me than the Kristie-Bot, after all.

"John?" I asked Butler, who'd been quiet and looked contemplative.

"No," he said slowly. "This place is wonderful but . . . it's not where I fit." He smiled at me. "I need to help and protect. I do that with you. I'm happy with things as they are."

"Good to know you're all coming with us. I'd have missed you if you'd said you were staying, even Kristie. Sorta."

She snorted. "You can't get rid of us that easily."

Team Tinman sorted out, now it was time for the tearful good-byes. The only saving grace was that, after the first excursion, the rest of our animals had had zero interest in Cradus and had remained in the *Distant Voyager* lounging around and whining at us whenever we came in to sleep at night. But it saved some time now. Not that much, though, since we had a hundred people and several hundred rabbits all saying good-bye to every Cradi we'd ever met.

Went as quickly as it could. It was really hard to say good-bye, though, in no small part because it had been so relaxing here. The Cradi gave us gifts—containers of each of the elements of their world, copies of their star maps, some Orange Scourge for the rabbits, although this was put into a lead container, and little works of metal art, including replicas of each of those we'd spent the most time with, like our own set of amazing metal action figures.

The nicest thing for me was that I didn't feel guilty about having the ball of Cradus and Spehidon in our rooms, since the Cradi had given us some of their world anyway.

Mother had a cargo hold, so we were able to put all the gifts inside of that and have the hold do the airlocking stuff without any of us inside, which saved us a good hour at least. Then we went down the tunnel one last time.

Last hugs for Fathade, Feoren, Sciea, Serion, and Cavus. Into the airlock in groups so that the rabbits could get inside, too. As per Cradus' promise, they didn't need to remove their Moon Suits. As the air changed, the rabbits changed, too, and went back to their normal colors and fluffy fur.

We went into the airlock in the last group. "Thank you for the best family vacation we've ever had," I said as I hugged the five of them one more time.

"Thank you for saving us and for the gift of your companions," Fathade replied. "You have renewed our faith in others in the galaxy."

"Oh, don't be too trusting. There are a lot of bad people out there. There are a lot of good ones, too. We will be back, and I know Chuckie gave you guys a long sign-countersign procedure to follow to verify if someone's really representing us, right?"

"Yes. Charles was quite clear."

"Good. Follow that. We'll be back and we'll figure out how to really put protection onto this system so no one can come in and decide they want your world and just take it from you."

"We await your return with great joy," Fathade said formally. She extended her hands to me palms together.

By now, I knew what to do. Took her hands in mine. "You will always be in our hearts. And, should you need us, we will come."

CHAPTER 71

JEFF, JAMIE, CHARLIE, AND LIZZIE all did the same formal good-bye with Fathade. Then we got into the airlock and closed the door. We waved at them through the outer window and they waved back.

We took off our Moon Suits and added our now round, gold balls of personal protection to the large pile. Then we went back inside Mother.

Did the airlock thing one more time. Cavus gathered up the Moon Suits and handed them off to the others. He took one, though, waved it at us, and put it back. The Cradi waved one last time, and left.

We closed the airlock and I went to retrieve the Moon Suit. "Wow, I can't believe they gave us one of these to keep."

"They gave it to you, Mommy," Jamie said. "So that you can always come back."

"But there are a hundred of us here, and five in our immediate family alone."

"It's sym-bol-ic."

"Gotcha." Tucked the Moon Suit into my purse and then we headed for stations.

Well, first we headed for the observation lounge, so that everyone could take one last look. We stayed there as the moon lifted us up to the top of the highest mountain, letting us see this beautiful world one last time: the metal deer frolicked, the metal birds flew by, and the earth shifted and reformed itself to accommodate us.

But the trip up didn't take all that long, and now that we were high enough up it was time to get ready to leave for real, and that meant crash couches, not the observation lounge, unfortunately, because we were going to hit escape velocity and, per Hughes, had to hit it strong due to the gravitational pull from Spehidon and Cradus both.

Got the kids and noncommand crew all strapped in. Got the backup command crew strapped in as well, despite their whining. Did three different headcounts to ensure that we hadn't actually left someone on the planet—no need to do Home Alone: Cradus, after all.

Reassured that everyone was present and accounted for, including all animals, it was time to go back to work.

Tim, Hughes, Walker, Tito, Jeff, and I trooped to the command deck. "Mother, any chance you'll let Joe, Randy, and Jerry have our seats?" I asked when I arrived.

"No. The command crew stays as is."

"Figures," Jeff said, but good-naturedly.

"We have the right coordinates, we're sure?" Tim asked as we all sat, strapped in, and put the helmets on.

"Yes. There are three solar systems in the area we now feel the distress call came from. We will warp to the nearest one, examine it, and then determine if we have found our goal or move on."

"Lather, rinse, repeat, gotcha."

Mother fired up her engines, or whatever she actually did to get moving, and we lifted off. Fast. Far faster than we had on Earth.

"Why are we moving so fast?" Tim asked, clearly reading my mind.

"Cradus gave us a push," she shared. "It should be enough for us to reach escape velocity easily."

Wondered for a moment if Mother knew that Cradus and Spehidon were sentient. Realized now wasn't the time to ask.

"I do," she said, but as far as I could tell, only in my headset. "We spoke at length."

Wondered what they'd talked about, and why Mother wasn't saying this stuff aloud, since everyone on the command deck knew.

"We spoke of many things. Their goals are the same as mine—to protect the life in their charge. Spehidon wants people, as I know you know. I promised to look for those who might live with her in our travels. And I'm not sharing this with the others because they are focused on flying and they already fear me too much."

Mentioned mentally that Mother reading my mind could indeed be construed as scary.

"Only because you have the helmet on and you're thinking *at* me. I understand the programming changes that were made. Privacy is important. Safety is, too. I am doing my best to walk that fine line."

"Get ready," Hughes said, breaking up my tête-à-tête with Mother.

"Ready as I'll ever be," Tim said.

Hughes and Walker tossed out instructions that pertained more to Tim, Tito, and Jeff than they did to me. However, did get one key order. "Kitty," Walker said, "be sure that you keep hailing frequencies open. We want to be able to spot the distress call just in case there are any errors in our flight plan."

"Um . . ." By now I should have remembered which stupid button did what, but a nice vacation on Cradus had pretty much wiped that information from my memory banks. Besides, the button display was starting to remind me of a maze—and I sucked at mazes.

Happily, a button flashed. Thanked Mother mentally as I pushed it down. Then Tim hit the gas and holding a button down seemed like the hardest thing I'd ever done.

Hughes hadn't been kidding—the pressure on us as we left this little system was intense. Kind of hoped Mother had put the others to sleep but didn't want to take the focus to ask.

However, the pressure didn't last all that long. Well, the bad pressure. We still had the warp jump pressure to go. Could not wait. "Can we make sure everyone's okay from that?" I asked as the guys started doing whatever to get us ready for warp.

"They are fine," Mother said.

"You put them under, didn't you?" Jeff asked.

"I did, yes. It is much safer for them, the children especially."

"Then thank you," Jeff said. "Because that was really unpleasant."

"It won't be like that for most planets," Hughes said. "Cradus and Spehidon just have very strong gravities, particularly because they're so close to each other."

"Get ready," Tito said. "I think we're all set for the warp jump."

"It's weird to have you guys actually doing the work."

Tim snorted. "Tell me about it. I think I was happier when Mother was doing everything."

"I am not in Protection Mode right now," Mother said. "Do you wish me to move to that, Commander?"

Tim looked at Hughes, who shook his head. "As long as we're confident that you don't have more hidden bombs on you, Mother, no, I think we stick with this part of the plan." Tim looked at me. "*Are* we sure?"

"We are," Mother answered. "I ran even more extensive tests and also received some assistance from the planet and moon."

"The Cradi were really great about helping," I said quickly, lest the others realize that Mother had been chatting with Cradus and Spehidon.

"Sentient planets and moons are also nice," Tito said dryly. "We all know, Kitty."

"Oh, blah, blah, blah. Didn't want you guys freaking out at Mother for something."

"We like to save the freaking out for danger situations," Walker said.

"Because it saves time," Hughes added. "And we have no more of it. Tim, I think we're ready. Stations report. Navigation ready."

"Weapons ready," Jeff said.

"Systems and Engineering ready," Tito said.

"Exterior and interior scanning ready," Walker said.

"Um, I've got the button pushed down." This earned me far too many snide looks. "Sorry to spoil the mood. Communications ready."

"Command ready," Tim said. "Let's rock and roll."

Everyone other than me pushed buttons. As stated, I was already on top of things. Felt what was now becoming a kind of normal feeling—the pressure of the jump to warp.

Could tell we weren't going as far as we had prior because the pressures stopped after a pretty short time. "We are in stable warp," Mother announced.

"Great, can I stop holding the button down?"

"You never needed to hold it past two seconds," she replied. "That amount of time puts the button onto hold until pressed again."

"Thanks for mentioning this, oh, before we did two fun jumps."

"You didn't ask."

"Did I say I liked that you'd learned sarcasm already? Because if I did, I was an idiot."

"Mother," Hughes said, "the proper response is 'sorry, not sorry' but I've said it for you, so I've got your back."

"Thank you, Matt," Mother said. "I was also told to say that you're my favorite."

"I did that, bro," Walker said, "because I've got *your* back. Of course, we know that I'm Mother's favorite."

"Actually, I think Tito wins that one," Tim said.

Tito grinned. "I can't argue that Mother has good taste."

"Oh, don't worry, baby," Jeff said. "I'm sure Mother still likes you a lot."

"Everyone's a comedian today." At least my arm could rest now. Not that it mattered—our hailing frequencies might have been opened, but no one was trying to get through anyway.

"Should there be this little chatter out here?" Jeff asked after a while.

"Per my data banks, yes, if there are no ships or planets in need," Mother said. "We can't pick up regular chatter while in warp. It's emergency and distress hails only."

We all agreed this made sense, even though we'd have liked to eavesdrop on whoever we were zooming past. But you couldn't have everything.

A few more minutes, then Mother felt we could wander and wake up the passengers, meaning she wasn't planning to have us all sleep through this leg of the journey. Tim and I refrained from making snide sleeping comments because we were still keeping that between us and Team Tinman. Wondered who would make the connection to the fact that the time to Cradus from Kreaving and the time from Cradus to Kreaving were not going to match at all, and hoped no one would, though I didn't bet on it. Even if the trip was completely uneventful, we had two days' worth of warp to get back to the area we felt Kreaving was in.

But we were all in pretty good spirits. For once, we kind of knew where we were going and it was our own decision, meaning we had a lot less stress and angst. Mother broke down and allowed us to leave the command deck, seeing as most of us could get back in about two seconds or less. Butler and the Kristie-Bot offered to stay on the command deck just in case and, even though they still weren't officially allowed to fly the *Distant Voyager*, Mother allowed this, too, so she wouldn't have to go into Protection Mode. Tim did have her move to Autopilot Mode, however, just in case.

The hailing channel remained open and Mother could patch

it through to wherever we were on the ship as well as coordinate internal communications, so we were essentially free to do whatever until we came out of warp.

While we didn't have the same activities as we'd had on Cradus, we decided we'd try to keep to a similar schedule. And, since we'd left Cradus just before dinnertime, we all had dinner together.

After that, we turned in early, so to speak. Jeff and I were tired enough that we only had sex a few times before sleeping, too. That was us—sacrificing for the cause.

Everyone slept well, at least per the group breakfast chatter. Afterward, and in keeping with the idea that we were still "on vacation" until we arrived at the solar systems we were hoping contained Kreaving and the *Eknara* somewhere, it was time to do something interesting, fun, or relaxing.

So, Drax gave tours of the ship—teaching everyone where things were, what did what, and so on. Did my best to pay attention, but it all sort of ran together in a few minutes. Besides, I was a lot more interested in what we were planning to do after lunch. Because after lunch, it was time to study the stars.

Chuckie, Brian, Drax, Mossy, and Hacker International had combined all the galaxy maps we had in our possession with what Mother had in her data banks into one big map so that we had the most accurate view, at least so far as we knew. We had every identified star system and celestial body marked—and since we now knew about a lot of inhabited systems, Mossy and Drax knew even more of them, and I actually had a list of every planet and system in the Galactic Council on my phone, the map was quite well covered.

Drax had put in several movie theaters for crew entertainment—because of course he had—and Mother was able to superimpose this combined map of what was known of our galaxy onto a screen. The little kids were interested, the older ones were fascinated, and the adults were all clear that this information was vital to our safety and survival, so we had a fully attentive audience.

The map put into clear perspective how far we'd gone already. Really damned far was the general statement on that.

We were headed toward what, due to map placement, we were calling the underside of the Milky Way's halo area. Compared to those who'd come to us during Operation Immigration—who were still, for the size of the galaxy, "in our neighborhood"—we

were going farther than anyone other than the Z'porrah and Anciannas traveled on a regular basis.

The Cradi maps had added a lot of information on the outer
parts of the galaxy, as well as halo areas. But we still had, easily,
thousands of stars and other bodies on the maps identified not
by their "real names" but by what those who'd made the maps
called them.

Because of where Cradus and Spehidon were and where we
felt Kreaving was, there weren't a lot of systems we were passing, relatively speaking, at least as far as we knew, because we
were curving through the bottom of the halo.

"We had to figure that, wherever they are, they're remote,"
Chuckie said after we'd done the in-depth viewing, educational
updates, and the younger kids, Jamie and Charlie included, had
been put to bed. "Because if they weren't remote, someone other
than us should have heard them by now."

"Presuming they haven't already been rescued," Drax added.

"They haven't." Everyone looked at me. Heaved a sigh.
"Really? Gang, this is our goodwill trip around the galaxy. I'm
sure there are other systems in need but, as near as I can tell, wherever we're going, either planned or unplanned, we're going there
to save the day in a big way. We're acting like the Shantanu and
all the other races that go out to do their version of the Red Cross,
only we're going to the remote planets that aren't on the main
maps. Whatever Powers That Be who are affecting us clearly have
their reasons, and those reasons appear to all be the same—save
the obscure cheerleaders, save the worlds. So to speak."

Raj, Len, and Kyle all chuckled. Heard many of Jeff's Cabinet and relatives whisper to each other that they didn't understand me. Heard Christopher whisper back that few ever did.
Haters. Amy rammed her elbow into Christopher's ribs while
Vance snarled in a whisper that the First Lady should always be
respected. Felt better.

"I agree," Wruck said, interrupting all the whispering and
proving that at least more than a handful understood me. "This
is similar to what we and the Z'porrah did thousands of years
ago. The Anciannas still do this, only not as often as we used to."

"A big ol' war with your former BFFs tends to reduce the
focus on the do-gooding, yeah. So, my point is that we cannot
and should not assume that Wheatles and his folks have been
rescued. We're all they have and that means we need to ensure
that we're bringing our A game."

Chuckie nodded and pointed to the area we were heading for. "While there's always a margin of error, we feel pretty confident that we're going to find the system the *Eknara* is stranded in within this area. There are known pulsars within a reasonable distance, too, and at least two black nebulas that the Cradi had mapped, which are the only other solid clues we got from Kreaving."

"Any other good news?" White asked, sounding as if he didn't expect any, which, once again, proved why he was the best Field agent we had, even if he'd never officially been Field.

Chuckie nodded. "If any one of these suns goes nova, then they won't affect the others."

"*That's* the good news?" Jeff asked, sounding just this side of pissed.

"It's about all we've got, yeah." Chuckie shrugged. "You know how it goes."

"I do," Tim said. "Let me guess what the bad news is. What if one of them becomes a black hole?"

"Then we're all in trouble," Chuckie said. "As per usual."

"Check, so the sun that's in Wheatles' system is going to become a black hole." Got the looks again. "Really? Okay, I mean, some of you haven't rolled with me in this kind of situation before, so I guess I can buy you looking confused." And not understanding me. "But the rest of you? Name a time when our luck runs any other way than the worst possible option. I'll wait. Oh, and before you offer this one up, Cradus was the exception that proves the rule, not the norm in any way, shape, or form."

There was a lot of silence in the theater. Jeff heaved a sigh and ran his hand through his hair. "You're right. We need to assume the worst."

"And then do everything to ensure it doesn't happen."

Gower chuckled and got all the looks. He smiled at me. "In other words, routine."

CHAPTER 72

AFTER MORE DISCUSSION AND map gazing, we called it a night and headed for bed. Walked out next to Serene but it wasn't until we all were almost back in our rooms that I remembered something I'd forgotten.

Grabbed Serene before she walked on. "Hey, do you need whatever it was you slipped to me when we were on Nanez?"

She looked blank for a moment. "Oh! You know, I forgot all about that."

"Me, too. I haven't even looked for it."

She laughed. "It's okay. I'm just glad we didn't need it. And no, you can hang onto it."

"What is it, exactly?"

She motioned and I opened up my purse. Jeff and Brian exchanged the "why me?" look and both headed into their respective rooms. Whatever, I didn't want them for this anyway.

We rummaged around in there—noted that the envelope I'd gotten from the hamper in the White House wasn't in here. Couldn't figure out where it had gone, doubted I'd lost a manila envelope, particularly that one. Maybe it was in my rooms. Or maybe the Poofs had been peckish and decided to try out wood pulp.

Just as I decided to fret about this later, Serene came up with a small sphere that looked a lot like a whiffle ball and also like something we'd had used against us. "Gotcha."

"Is that a Poof Trap?"

"Similar, yes. But it's under our control and it's not something the Poofs can't get out of—I've already tested it. However, they're the only animals of ours that can escape. This can expand to cover something as large as a chocho."

"Wow. Doesn't look possible but I'll trust you on it." Serene was, after all, our weapons and miniaturization expert. "How does it work?"

"You need to trigger it," she pointed to a very small button that I'd never have noticed if she hadn't pointed it out, "then touch it to whatever you want it to surround. That can be done via any method, as long as the portable cage touches something small enough for it to contain."

"How can it tell? It's not sentient, is it?" We had sentient metals in the galaxy and, as our trip to Cradus had proved, some of those metals were high up on the mental evolutionary chain. Just didn't want to be wandering around with some in my purse, in case the kids got into said purse. Of course, I'd carried some of Cradus and Spehidon around for a bit, and even when Jeff put things high out of reach, that meant nothing to Charlie.

"No, it's got a surface to weight ratio built into it. Do you want all the scientific details?"

"God no. I just want to be sure it won't try to cage Charlie."

"It could. So don't trigger it and put it against him."

"Um . . ."

She laughed again. "Kitty, it's safe. It only cages its capture, it doesn't harm them." She looked around. One of Lizzie's rabbits was in the doorway. Serene picked it up, triggered the trap, put it against the bunny, and voila, the sphere spread out in the blink of an eye and said bunny was caged.

The rabbit looked at me, eyes wide, asking if it was time to freak out or not. "It's not." Took the cage from Serene, hit the button, the cage retracted into its former sphere. Nuzzled the bunny. "Your lesson? Don't wander off." Handed him to Lizzie, who had come to look for him, accompanied by her other rabbits and the least weasels. "Your rabbit."

She clutched the bunny to her. "Geez. He was just checking to see where you were."

"Right here, testing rabbit traps."

Lizzie looked horrified. "Why do we have rabbit traps?"

"In case we need to hunt them."

She looked more horrified, and ready to ask Siler to take her and all the rabbits back to her School For Gifted Minors in Portugal.

Heaved a sigh. "Geez right back. I'm kidding. Serene was showing me one of her gadgets and it helped to have a test subject. Your rabbit volunteered."

"Sure he did," Lizzie muttered, as she went back into our rooms, cooing to the rabbit about how terrible parental units were and how mothers thought they were funny when they weren't, the rest of the rabbits and the least weasels following behind.

Noted that the least weasels seemed more like medium weasels now, which might be why they were hanging out in our rooms—not enough room in the Royal Hatbox these days. Good to know they were bonding with the bunnies, too.

"It's nice to see that your mother's parenting style is being carried on," Serene said. "Brian says he still has nightmares about being caught by Angela doing anything she didn't like."

"Which, many times, was merely breathing. Mom likes to keep everyone on their toes." Missed my parents. Managed not to say so—Serene's childhood and mine had been very dissimilar and there was no need to rub that in.

She nudged me. "It's okay. Your parents were and are wonderful. You should never feel awkward about that, even though some of us had parents that were less than stellar." She smiled. "Besides, once I met you, I got the family I'd always wanted."

Gave her a hug. "And what a family it is." Realized we were now fully alone in the hallway. "You know, I have a question that, since it's just us, I feel safe in asking."

She raised her eyebrow. "Is it about our sex life?"

Snorted a laugh. "No, and you knew it wasn't going to be."

She grinned. "True. I just like to joke around with you."

"Because you can, because you know I know what the others don't, or don't really recognize. But that's why I want to ask you this. Why do you think the Valentino and Price families are with us for this trip?"

"And not Jeff's other sisters' families, or other extended families on any side?"

"Yeah. I mean, besides the obvious 'we like them and they aren't traitors' reason."

"Especially since the younger kids from those families still don't appear to be tainted. And ignoring all the things we've already been over?"

"Yeah, because they aren't relevant to my question, really. I don't want the 'conspiracy' reason, so to speak. I want what you think, why you, specifically, think they're with us. You, like me, are an outsider who's come into this family. You, unlike me, pay a lot of attention."

Serene chuckled, then looked up at the ceiling. I'd seen

Chuckie do this a lot—it was the universal "smart person thinking hard" position. She looked back at me after about thirty seconds. "Possibly to make a point."

"What would that point be?"

"The good family members get to go on the fun vacation. The bad ones have to stay home."

Pondered this. "It's potentially valid, if we ignore the cool family members left behind."

"If I remove any conspiracy or threat ideas, I don't think it's a message to the kids or the grandparents," Serene said. "I think it's a message to Jeff's other sisters and brothers-in-law."

"Well, they're on Earth right now, doing who knows what?"

She nodded. "They are. And when we all get back, who will be lauded for having gone into space? And not just into space, but all around the galaxy? For the kids, sure, it's a huge thing. But for Sylvia, Clarence, Marianne, and Jonathan, it's something that sets them apart from the others. They came with Jeff on this journey. They have the risk, sure, but they also get all the glory of the trip."

"Glory? Really?"

Serene chuckled again. "You don't think of this as glory. You think of this as work, as us doing what's right, what's needed, and what's necessary. But most people don't think like that."

"I suppose." I'd been told often enough that I didn't think like everyone else, after all.

"Trust me. Right now, while no one knows what's happening to us? Right now, everyone's happy they're not with us. But the moment we're back, alive and well, with fantastic stories to tell of new worlds discovered and new alien friends made? The 'coolness' of working with our enemies will seem that much less cool."

"Or they'll be even more bitter and extra dedicated to hurting us in any way they can."

"That's always the risk. However, Jonathan was borderline when you first came into the family. He wasn't a traitor—yet. But he was definitely eyeing it, since his elder brothers-in-law were so gung ho about the purity of the race and all that. And before you argue, Chuck, Camilla, and I have the proof. But once you showed favoritism toward Marianne and Kimberly? He flipped and has been loyal to this side of the family ever since."

"Huh. Go me, I guess. I didn't show favoritism. Marianne was just the only sister who actually talked to me, instead of at me, when I first met the clan. And Kimmie's a total doll. Who wouldn't show her favoritism?"

"Again, that's your mindset. It's not everyone's. And it doesn't matter, in that sense. Jonathan stayed on the side of what we all feel is right, because of your relationship with his wife and eldest daughter. Think about it. The Price and Valentino families—all of them other than Stephanie—are on this trip with you. If that doesn't say 'favoritism,' I don't know what does."

"But we didn't choose them intentionally."

"Maybe not. But that's how it's going to be spun, once we're home. Presuming we arrive safe and sound and with everyone in tow."

"Which we had damned well better. But okay, so they're along, in your opinion, to say 'nanner nanner' to Jeff's other sisters and brothers-in-law?"

"His sisters for sure. They are going to be green with envy when we get back. And if they're mad enough at their husbands for being left out . . ."

"Gotcha. And, yeah, I guess that makes sense. If you or I are mad at Brian or Jeff, they're going to do something about it, if only to shut us up."

"Exactly. So, anyway, that's my theory, for what it's worth. Now, the key is that we save the day and get home safely."

"Look at you, always focused on the work."

Serene grinned. "It's a dirty job, but someone has to do it."

CHAPTER 73

SERENE AND I HUGGED then went into our rooms. "Everything okay?" Jeff asked when I got into our bedroom.

"Yep, just needed to go over some things with Serene."

"Yeah, I picked that up," he said dryly. "Being an empath and all."

"Do you think the kids are doing okay? We have a lot of empaths along, as well as imageers, and who knows what all the hybrid kids really are. None seem quite as talented as Jamie and Charlie, but that could just be because they're doing their best to fly under the radar." Or Jamie and ACE were ensuring that, which was what my money was on.

"Yeah, they're fine. Christopher and I put blocks into all of them, remember? They can all function with or without their talents. They're fine." He pulled me to him. "Why the sudden worry?"

"Oh, I was just talking family stuff with Serene." Leaned my head against his chest. "I'm pretty sure we're going to arrive sometime tomorrow."

He hugged me. "Then let's get some sleep so we're ready for whatever we're facing."

"Sounds good to me."

We made sure Lizzie was asleep, then we had sex, just to be sure I'd be able to sleep and all that, because Jeff was a great husband that way. We wrapped around each other and Jeff fell asleep immediately.

I didn't, but that was okay. I was comfortable and it occurred to me that now was a great time to check in with ACE, since I knew Jamie was fast asleep.

ACE, are you there?

Yes, Kitty, ACE is here.

I just wanted to see if you're okay. Are Sandy and the others keeping to their promise?

Yes, they are. ACE is free to do what ACE feels is right, within the greater rules that exist.

Rules you can tell me about?

No, ACE cannot tell Kitty about those things, though ACE would like to. Just as there are other things ACE would like to tell Kitty about but cannot.

Things that are going to happen soon?

And later. There are things that ACE will have to do, but now, thanks to Kitty, ACE can do them without fear.

I'm glad. Should I be prepared for these things?

As much as Kitty can be.

Am I prepared for these things?

As much as Kitty ever is. But, ACE is not worried. Kitty always thinks right.

Good to know I remain consistent. Does this mean that you don't have to stay inside of Jamie?

Yes, but ACE and Jamie have discussed it. ACE will stay with Jamie. It is the best way to protect Jamie and also to protect ACE. ACE has a job to do with Jamie, and that is to keep Jamie safe and from becoming—

A despot. Yeah, she told me. And I can't argue about that, at all. I just want to be sure it's your choice and that you don't want to go back to Paul, or go off without a body.

No, ACE is happy where ACE is. ACE will never desert Kitty, or Jamie, or Paul. Or any of the others. All are ACE's penguins. But ACE has to do what is best, and what is best right now is for ACE to stay with Jamie.

Then if you're happy, I'm happy, and I'll never desert you, either, ACE, regardless of who you are or aren't residing inside.

Felt the warmth in my mind that was how ACE hugged me, then it was gone. Heaved a sigh, snuggled my face in between Jeff's pecs, and fell asleep.

Woke up to the pleasant sound of Mother's wakeup alarm. Did the usual morning routine, but as we were finishing breakfast, we got the announcement.

"Command crew to the deck, all other crew and passengers to crash couches. We will be leaving warp in fifteen minutes."

"Or less, if this goes anything like last time," Joe said.

"Hope it goes more smoothly," Randy replied. "Not that that would be hard."

"Let's hurry up," Jeff said, as I put my purse over my neck and picked Charlie up. "Just in case."

We zipped everyone into their seats, ensured the animals were safe, and headed to our positions. Once we were all strapped in and Butler and the Kristie-Bot had trotted off to the safety of the crash couches—needing only to have been flung around once to see the wisdom of being strapped in—I sent a hail.

"Calling the *Eknara*. *Eknara*, can you hear me?"

Nada. Oh well, it was worth a try.

"Leaving warp in five . . ." Mother said. "Four . . . three . . ."

We all winced, prepared for something bad to happen.

"Two . . . one."

On the count of one the pressure started again. It was very brief, however. Nice to know that the pressure was far less coming out of warp than going in. Something to look forward to, should we ever get to have another normal departure and arrival.

The pressure stopped and, as it did, we no longer saw the blur of nothing out the windshield. We saw a star in the distance and a lot of planets nearby, but only nearby in that space sense—we were far from the one that was closest to us.

"We are near the farthest planet from this sun," Mother said. "As a precaution."

"Smart choice. So, how do we tell if this sun is having problems?"

"Scanning," Mother said. "But we may need to verify if the *Eknara* is on one of these planets, in case my sensors don't pick up the solar disturbance properly."

"Can the others get out of the crash couches and maybe go to the Observation Lounge?" Hey, if it was me in the couch, I'd want to see this if I could.

"Yes."

With minimal assistance from Mother, I made the announcement for everyone to head to the Observation Lounge. I was determined the least necessary on the command deck, so I was able to zip out, make sure everyone was doing as requested, and get my kids harnessed in and strategically placed next to Gadhavi, Siler, and Buchanan. Then headed back to the command deck. Surprising no one, Chuckie, Reader, Joe, Randy, Jerry, Drax, and Mossy came with me.

Strapped back in while the extra guys took up positions near the windshield, which was now doubling as our live-action movie screen, and we all looked at this new system—none of the three we were going to had names that any of us knew of.

There were seven planets. Because this was a Drax Industrial vessel, we were able to get what was down there beamed up to our screen. The planet Mother had chosen first was uninhabited and had no spacecraft crashed on it, either.

But the second one looked typical for an early industrialized society—there were buildings and such, farmlands, lakes, rivers, and oceans. "Looks a lot like Earth," Tito said.

"This resembles Tur somewhat, too," Mossy said.

Then we got a glimpse of what looked like a native, from the back. "Um . . . is that a person? Like a human person?"

"It looks humanoid," Drax said.

We zoomed in however we did that—Walker appeared to have control of this—and got a good look. We stared. We were silent. So, most likely, was the person we were looking at.

"Um . . . is that a mime?"

"It *looks* like a mime," Reader replied.

"Surely not," Chuckie said, sounding like he hoped he was right but thought Reader and I probably were. "I mean, maybe that's just their coloration."

"They're mime-colored, then, because I see more of them. And they aren't talking."

Sure enough, there were a lot of different sized and shaped people, different skin colors, but all with white paint on their faces, black paint on top of the white paint giving them expressions, so to speak, with bright red lips, wearing black and white striped garments with white gloves.

None of them were moving their mouths in terms of speaking. They were making kissy faces and such, but no gum flapping was in evidence. They were all doing things with their hands, though—some clearly communicating, some just doing the classics of walking against the wind and being trapped inside a box.

"Mother, tour this whole planet, please and thank you. I mean, maybe we're just seeing the Mime Village or something."

"Something, I'll give you that," Jerry said.

We did a thorough fly-around. Everyone—man, woman, and child—were mimes. And they were all miming. The animals we could see were also mimes, at least, their coloration said they were.

"I think they're born that way," Tito said. "As in, they aren't wearing paint, that's just how they look."

"God help us all," was my contribution. Dug into my purse and pulled out my iPod. Algar was on the case—I had an Anything But Clowns! playlist queued up.

"Oh, mimes aren't so bad," Jeff said.

"I'm ignoring you, Jeff."

Might not have been able to figure out how to make all the buttons work, but it was clear where the docking station was—Drax truly thought of everything. Plugged my iPod in.

"I don't see what's wrong with them," Jeff insisted. "Mimes are fun and funny and can be poignant, too."

"We may have to get a divorce."

"Titanic Clown" by Pop Will Eat Itself came onto our airwaves. It wasn't my husband declaring mimes evil, but it helped me relax a little.

"That's uncalled for," Jeff said quietly.

"She doesn't like clowns, Jeff," Chuckie said. "She's not alone. Quite a lot of people suffer from coulrophobia, the unnatural fear of clowns."

"Sorry, Jeff, and I was kidding." Kind of. "But your acceptance of mimes really makes me wonder about you. Chuckie, it's not an unnatural fear, it's a smart one. Mother, other than the fact that this is the Planet of Mimes, they all seem okay. Let's check the next nearest."

"Unless you have something definitive on the sun," Tim said.

"Nothing yet," Mother replied.

"Figures," Reader said with a sigh. "And yeah, I'm with Kitty—not a huge fan of clowns, either. Though I can handle mimes."

"You're a better man than I am, Gunga Din."

We zipped to the next planet. This ship really did zip along. Which made the realization of how far we were traveling via warp all the more awe-inspiring and scary at the same time.

We circled the next planet. "This is worse than the last," Chuckie said, as the music changed to "Harlequin" by Killing Joke. "Are those harlequins?"

"Of course they are. At least, it sure looks like it to me." Plus, the music was definitely a confirmation as far as I was concerned. This planet's inhabitants were all in the multicolored geometric designs I associated with a harlequin, some in what looked like tights, some in more baggy outfits, all wearing the funky, many-pointed hats with balls on the end. "Why aren't they with the mimes? Pardon me—why are they here at all?"

"Again, nothing wrong with them," Jeff said. "They're pretty."

"Pretty weird. Jeff, it's a *planet* of harlequins."

"And, as with the mimes, I think these are naturally forming," Tito said. "I believe what we'd call their hats are actually part of their heads. And what looks like clothes is, I think, feather or fur or just skin, but it looks attached."

Controlled a shudder, but it took effort. Chuckie wasn't wrong—right after snakes, I found clowns, and all their clown-like offshoots, just this side of terrifying. "I hope someone's comforting all the kids."

"Mimes and harlequins are nice," Jeff insisted.

"Are any of them noticing us?" Reader asked while I contemplated this horrible viewpoint of my husband's while really considering that divorce idea.

"Not that I can tell," Walker said.

"They aren't reacting as such," Tito added. "I think we're far enough away that they can't see us without a telescope."

"We are not stopping, even if they showed us a giant welcome mat. Mother, anything on the sun?"

"No, I'm sorry. Stars by their nature have quite a lot going on inside of them. It's difficult to determine if this one is acting normally or not."

"On to the next planet then," Tim said. "And have you noticed—so far, these planets all seem Earthlike."

"They're all close enough to this sun," Chuckie said. "They might be breathing oxygen."

"I say again that we are not going to swing down there to find out."

"Relax, baby," Jeff said. "I'm sure the next planet will be normal for us."

We reached said planet and Jeff's cheery prediction was dashed just that fast. "Oh, my God, it's like the planet of Red Skelton down there." My music changed to "Tears of a Clown" by the English Beat.

"Who?" Jeff wasn't the only one asking that.

"Really? My family was the only one that watched variety shows while they were still around?"

Tito chuckled. "No, I know who you're talking about, Kitty. And, yeah, it does look like a planet full of tramp clowns."

"We called them the sad-face clowns, but whatever. And

some of these look like rodeo clowns, which is, I guess, their form of racial variety. This is, officially, the weirdest solar system in existence."

Chuckie was busy explaining who Red Skelton was and why people our age knew about him—mostly because our parents and grandparents had loved the guy—and also why his tramp clown shtick had been popular. I was glad he was sharing, because I was far too busy trying to tell myself that this was just a big planet of sweet old men who sometimes dressed up as tramps and other times pretended to be seagulls, versus a planet of danger. Of all the clown types, I could handle the tramp clowns the best, though that wasn't really saying a lot. I'd been okay with the occasional mime, back in the day, but now, after seeing a planet full of them, I doubted I'd want to hang out with any in the near or distant future.

As with the last two, the planet seemed Earthlike and Tito felt that what we were seeing was natural, not face paint or any form of costuming.

What we also hadn't seen was a wreck of any kind of spacecraft, nor had we seen anything that indicated they were spacefaring. Whatever they were doing on these planets, it wasn't related to space.

Scan of this planet done, we headed to the next one. This one was like a harlequin offshoot, but with a lot of acrobatics involved. Everyone was in colorful garb, tumbling, juggling, bopping each other on the head. So, when "The Jester" by Sum 41 came on, it didn't surprise me all that much. I didn't even comment—mostly because I was too busy wondering if we had any Valium on board. We just confirmed the usual—Earthlike, they were just born this way—and moved on.

The music changed to "The Clown" by Elefant before we were near enough to the planet to see who was on it. Took this as a warning, though, and steeled myself.

Which was a good thing. Because this planet was by far the worst. Because this planet was filled with what I knew were called Auguste clowns. As in, it was the planet Bozo came from. Or, rather, as we got a closer look, where the *Killer Klowns from Outer Space* came from.

They all had the weird, bushy hair that only grew on the upper sides of their heads and came in every color not known to man. They had round, red noses with no nostrils. Overly arched eyebrows. Giant feet in bizarre shoes or boots. Big hands in white, Mickey Mouse gloves. Ginormous, red, exaggerated mouths with what looked like carnivore teeth, not herbivore or omnivore. And they were all, to a person, bone white, the kind of white that makes snow look dull and dingy.

"Tito," I said carefully, "do you think those are also naturally built this way?"

"I do."

"Gotcha. Um, I don't care if this is the system in danger. They can all turn to dust as far as I'm concerned. And Jeff? If you say one positive thing about whatever's down there, I will honestly never speak to you again."

"Ah, no," he said slowly. "They look a little terrifying to me, too. The others didn't. But these do. These look . . . predatory."

"They also have spaceflight," Chuckie said, voice tight. "Or at least the means to fire weapons into space." Sure enough, we were looking at something that reminded me a lot of Cape Canaveral.

A face came onto our screen. Realized that we had hailing frequencies opened and that meant that we could be contacted without our having to accept the call, so to speak. The music changed at the same time, "The Joker" by the Steve Miller Band.

The face staring at us looked almost exactly like the Joker from Batman. Well, the Joker on his worst day and with Bozo's hair. Only this face was creepier, the eyes crazier, and the expression far more feral than the Joker ever had been.

He was speaking, snarling, really. Our universal translator wasn't catching on quickly, either. Decided I didn't care. Slammed my fist onto the external communications button. The face on the screen disappeared.

"Mother," Tim said, before I could speak, "get us out of here. Right now. Top speed. Forget the last planet, just get us away from this solar system as fast as possible. And that's an order."

We zoomed away, past the last planet, and into the blackness of space. The total nothing was a relief.

"Are they after us?" Tim asked.

"Not as far as our sensors indicate," Walker said.

"The universal translator has found the right code for translation," Mother said. "Would you like me to play what was said?"

"Honestly? 'Like' is the wrong word. But yeah, we should probably hear it, in case they were asking for help or being nice or something." And maybe they were like Hixxx—terrifying in the extreme when first encountered and yet great once you got to meet them as individuals, as people. Turned my music off so we wouldn't miss anything.

A guttural voice came on. "We see you. Leave our solar system or die. If you come back, we will destroy you. We will find you in your sleep and murder you in your dreams. We will find you wherever you run, we will catch you, slay you, and eat your flesh. We will destroy you utterly. Leave us and never return."

CHAPTER 74

WE WERE ALL SILENT for a good, long minute.

"No one else heard that, right?" Jeff asked finally.

"Correct," Mother said. "I only played it for the command deck."

"Thank God," Reader said under his breath.

"So, they really are the *Killer Klowns from Outer Space*," I managed. "And another 'ridiculous' movie is shown to be a documentary. I hope the kids aren't too terrified by what they saw." I mean, I was terrified, so why wouldn't the kids be?

"I'll be right back," Jeff said. "Joe, take over."

They switched places and Jeff hypersped out of the room.

Jerry cleared his throat. "I'm now with Kitty on the coulrophobia. In a big way."

"How in the hell did something like that evolve?" Hughes asked.

"In a galaxy as vast as ours, in a universe that's even vaster?" Chuckie shrugged. "Anything's possible. By the way, Kitty, don't panic about the whole 'find you in your sleep' thing. That's just a weaker opponent trying to scare off a stronger one. Like a chihuahua telling a pit bull that the chihuahua can take the bigger dog. It can't, but if it barks hard enough, the bigger dog may buy the threats, or just decide the fight isn't worth it."

"Um, dude, did you hear the same words I did and see the same face I saw? Because that guy wasn't joking."

"I did and I'm sure he's their spokesman for those reasons. However, the threats were just that—threats. They didn't say something like 'we'll shoot your spaceship down with our impressive missiles' or 'we have superior firepower' or anything along those lines. They went for the boogeyman approach, and that's done when you don't actually have a real form of offense and probably not a lot of defense, either."

"Chuck's right," Jeff said, as he returned. "I wasn't worried about what the kids were seeing. I was worried about what they might be feeling. Because I felt something, when that message came through."

My throat tightened. What if Jamie had felt the Insane Joker's emotions? I was a terrible mother, because this hadn't occurred to me until now.

Jeff came over and kissed my cheek, hard to do with me in the helmet but he managed. "Baby, it's fine. The kids did pick something up, and it was the same thing I did—fear. The people on the one planet where they saw us were terrified of us. So, Chuck's right—that display was to scare us away. It's just like what the Cradi have set up around their system. Not really effective, but the best they can do."

"Well, it was effective for *me*. That system can dust as far as I'm concerned."

"No," Drax said slowly. "They are frightening because they are similar enough to humans that they're familiar, but different enough to be off-putting. That doesn't make them evil."

"That's pretty much the reasoning for why coulrophobia exists," Chuckie said. "And Drax is right. We have this system marked now. We can send in a team who have no coulrophobia to make first contact—it doesn't have to be us."

"The Vrierst are extremely accepting," Mossy said. "Ensure some are on that mission, along with some Turleens, and we should be fine. I could go down there right now, if needed. I don't find them any odder than any other race I've encountered."

"Maybe send some Juggalos. They might love this system." Someone should. Wasn't me.

While no one supported my Juggalos idea, the others started making noises about doing meet and greets. Steeled myself.

"No," Tim said, before I could freak out. "I'm the Commander and that system isn't in danger. They've threatened us, and while Chuck is probably right, there's always a chance that this is a rare time when he isn't. We have a mission, and it doesn't involve getting to know the Clown Consortium."

"Love that name."

Tim grinned. "Good to know, Shealla. Mother, let's get to the next system and check it out, sooner as opposed to later."

"We will arrive in fifteen of our minutes."

While we waited, I opened our hailing channel again and Mother insisted that Jeff take his position again. Joe grumbled but gave it up. While this was going on, wondered again why Mother was insisting on us keeping our initial assignments. Then again, if I'd been on Weapons, I'd have probably sent nukes into the Clown Consortium solar system, and Jeff wasn't thrown until the last planet and, even then, wasn't ready to push any buttons down. And he wouldn't have even if Tim or I had ordered it, unless he'd felt that the threat was real and one we couldn't escape from. So maybe that was why.

Was hella relieved that Tim had voted for focusing on the mission, versus facing our fears. I'd faced the giant sea serpents and that was, for the moment, more than enough for me to get my Bravery Badge. If the Clown Consortium joined the Galactic Council, they'd have a representative. I'd focus on getting to know and like him or her, or it, in case they were more like the Cradi, then branch out. Possibly I wouldn't be afraid of these people then. Possibly.

But right now, any vacation glow I'd had was fully gone, so I was willing to call it a day in terms of my singing "Kumbaya" with scary aliens. At least until we reached the next system.

Which we did soon enough. And which was, all things considered, very interesting.

The system had eleven planets, most of them within the Goldilocks range of being close enough to their sun to be habitable, and habitable for humans. But there was no life in this system. At all.

We zoomed around each of the planets, but there was nothing and no one. Just a pretty set of beautiful worlds, hanging out with no one on them.

"I can't even identify insects," Walker said as we finished the fastest recon ever. "There's plant life, somehow, and plant life without insects seems impossible, but these planets have everything other than life as we'd know it."

"Could the plants be the higher life-forms?" Hey, we'd met two different kinds of tree people. Maybe there were rhododendron people and fern people. If we could have naturally born harlequins, why not sentient rosebushes?

"I'm not feeling anything," Jeff said. "I'm focused and concentrating, and there's nothing I'm getting."

"Kitty," Tito said, "see if you can feel any animal life."

Did my best. "Nada. I mean, I haven't really tried with

insects other than those on Beta Eight, so maybe there are earth-
worms I'm not connecting with or something, but otherwise, I
get nothing."

"I find nothing in their sun to be different from the sun in the
Clown Consortium system," Mother said. "I am concerned,
however, that I will not be able to determine what is or is not
wrong with the sun where the *Eknara* is."

"We'll worry about that when we get there, Mother," Jeff said
reassuringly.

"Then we mark this system and move on," Tim said. "This
means that the third one is where Kreaving is. And if he isn't
there, then we're going to have to expand our search."

"Twenty minutes to the next system," Mother said, as we
headed off into the black.

"You know, I have a question. Why aren't we picking anything up on our hailing channels? We heard Wheatles for a good
amount of time when we picked his signal up before, and we
were likely much farther away than we have been since coming
out of warp. The Insane Joker could connect and threaten us, but
we haven't heard boo from Wheatles."

"Maybe they've stopped broadcasting," Jerry suggested.

"There's probably a bad reason for why if that's the case,"
Joe said.

Refused to believe we'd be too late. "Maybe the *Eknara* ran
out of power."

"It's possible," Hughes said. "They've been stranded a while
and the ship was damaged."

"Though emergency beacons last the longest," Walker added.

"But we never found out how long they'd been stranded,"
Randy pointed out.

Reader nodded. "And if it's been a lot longer than we've
known about, then, yeah, they could be out of power to use even
hailing frequencies."

"We'll find out when we get there," Jeff said firmly.

We were all quiet for a couple of minutes. "The kids are
okay?" I asked Jeff. "And everyone else?"

"Yeah. Those with no fear of clowns wanted to visit. Those
who are like you wanted to get away. Otherwise, no issues. Are
you okay?"

"Yeah, now that we're far enough away for me to think ratio-
nally."

"You do that?" Reader asked, as he came over and squeezed my shoulder gently.

"Occasionally."

Mossy joined us. "I think we want to get both of those solar systems investigated sooner as opposed to later. We should be in a position to contact the Galactic Council easily, just based on where we are."

"I don't agree," Drax said. My part of the command area was getting crowded. "If we were actually close enough, someone would have already rescued the *Eknara*. No one has, because we haven't seen any activity nor have we picked up any passing chatter. Believe me, at the Core there is constant chatter—we have to mute it out, not leave channels open. Alpha Centauri and Solaris give off a tremendous amount of chatter, too, and they did so even before anyone on Earth was spacefaring."

"Yeah, per my wife, radio waves travel," Tito said. "They knew about us on Beta Twelve before they ever came to visit."

True enough, I'd been told that during Operation Invasion and had never seen evidence to the contrary. "And yet, we are hearing zero right now."

"Makes sense in regard to the uninhabited system," Chuckie said. "But not with the Clown Consortium. They could contact us, so they have the means to broadcast and pick up signals."

"And yet they haven't done anything to help the *Eknara*, so either they didn't hear it or they can't actually help."

"Maybe they're muffled somehow?" Jerry suggested. "I mean, that sounds insane when I say it aloud, but then I remind myself that Kitty says crazy stuff all the time and she's right more often than she's wrong."

"What could muffle two solar systems?" Jeff asked.

"Three if we count the uninhabited one," Tim added.

"Something," Chuckie said. "That's the best we have right now. The bigger issue is the one Mossy brought up—do we try to protect these systems, and the others we've been to so far, right now or do we wait?"

"We have so many systems that need protection right now. I don't know that the Council has enough people to assign. Plus, I want to be sure they're protected, not exploited."

"I think we also want to be sure that the Z'porrah don't find them," Mossy said.

"We have to focus on what we can do right now," Reader

countered firmly. "And that's finding the *Eknara* and saving that solar system."

"Arriving at the third system," Mother said. "Once again, coming in by the planet farthest from the sun."

"Great," Tim said. "Start scanning the sun as soon as you can, Mother."

"I have begun. And, we are in the right place."

"You've found the *Eknara*?" Maybe it was on this nearest planet.

"No. I have found an extremely unstable sun."

CHAPTER 75

"YOU'RE SURE?" Chuckie asked.

"Yes," Mother replied. "Now that I have examined two stable ones, as well as the suns for Nazez and Cradus, along with researching the data I have on our own sun, I can feel confident that I am correct."

"Super. How long do we have?"

"Not long. Hours, most likely, days if we're fortunate. This star is definitely showing signs of the beginnings of a black hole."

We all looked at each other. "Well, Kitty called that one," Jerry said.

"Do we have enough room in the *Distant Voyager* to evacuate the planets?" Jeff asked Drax.

Who shook his head. "*A* planet, perhaps. But if they're fully populated, it's unlikely we could put everyone in here. We could have taken the mime and harlequin populations, for example, but no others."

"Wheatles said the planets were teeming with life, and that seven were inhabited." Some stuff I could remember when it mattered. There was something else I needed to remember about this sun, though, but it wasn't coming out of my memory banks.

"We need to find where the *Eknara* is," Chuckie said.

"Make it so," Tim confirmed.

We circled this world quickly. No signs of intelligent life. Mother shared that there were ten planets. We headed to number nine. No signs of life there, either. So, it was off to number eight for us. Because we were so fast, none of this took too long. Fortunately, we weren't so fast that we couldn't see things.

"I've spotted what looks like spaceship wreckage," Walker said. "It's on this planet, the one we're now nearest to."

"Call it number eight," I said. "Mother, log the farthest one as ten, the next as nine, this one as eight, and so on."

"Agreed."

"Kitty," Jerry said, "I don't hear any chatter, but do a hail, just in case."

"Gotcha. Mission control, this is the *Distant Voyager* requesting permission to land." We waited. "Nothing."

"Not a surprise, they're bronze age, per Kreaving, remember," Chuckie said. "And if the *Eknara* has indeed run out of power, then they can't reply, either."

"Let's get down there," Tim said briskly. "We can at least get the crew of the *Eknara* to safety."

"Check. Mother, do we need to strap everyone into crash couches?"

"No. They are harnessed and should be fine, though those here who aren't strapped in should do so."

Everyone just grabbed onto one of the chairs and hooked their arm through a strap. Didn't have to tell our team twice. "Saving the more advanced crew is not enough," Jeff said. "We need to save everyone."

"I'm open to ideas," Tim replied. "But so far all we have is angst, not answers."

The guys started doing that thing where everyone's talking and everyone's basically saying the same things, only absolutely no positive forward motion is being achieved because no new ideas are being offered. I'd done plenty of meetings like this, both before I'd joined Centaurion and after. Hated all of them, because they achieved nothing other than making everyone upset with each other.

There was a lull as we lowered into the planet's atmosphere. A little turbulence, but no more than any normal airplane flight. "We have to save the sun, that's the only option."

"How, is the question," Tim pointed out. Accurately.

My music turned on before the guys could go back to Not Really Brainstorming. "Dream A Little Dream Of Me" by Mama Cass Elliot. My brain nudged. I'd had a dream, and I'd been told things, about this situation.

"Do we really need a soundtrack?" Jeff asked. He didn't seem to have realized that I hadn't touched my iPod.

"I do. It's part of my process. And it keeps me calm. I can put in my earbuds if it's an issue for everyone."

The guys grumbled good-naturedly but no one really complained. "I like the music," Tim said finally. "So, as Commander, Kitty gets to listen to whatever she wants."

"Tim's my favorite. So, what do we know about this sun? We know that something hit into it, per Wheatles." And per Mephistopheles, too. The music changed to "Famous Monsters" by Saliva. "And Wheatles said that whatever hit it came via that neutron wave . . ."

"What?" Jeff asked. "I know what it means when you just trail off."

"I think we need Wruck here, right away."

"I'll get him," Mossy said. "I can go the fastest of those here who are not controlling the ship." He flew off.

"Why do you want John up here?" Jeff asked.

"Because I need to ask questions and he's likely the only one who can answer."

"Circle the planet before we land," Tim said. "Just in case."

We did as requested, verifying what Walker had seen and also that there didn't appear to be anyone waiting to attack us in some way.

"Mother," I asked as we circled, "how close can we get to the sun safely? And, more importantly, can you tell what's inside it?"

"Currently we could get as close as what we will be calling Planet Two, which is, as far as my sensors show, the last inhabited planet. Planet One is very close to the sun, but it would be dangerous for us to land there, and it is likely too close for us to be even if we remain in space. As for what I see inside, it's different from what was inside the other stars. I need to crossreference before I can make confident statements."

Mossy and Wruck returned as we came back to the crash site of what we could confirm was the *Eknara*. Decided not to pressure Mother for the internal star organs at this precise time.

Mossy had filled Wruck in, such as he could. "John," I asked as we started to lower, "could a parasite, a Superior's soul, join with a sun and survive?"

He stared at me. "It's never been done."

"Wasn't asking if precedent had been set. Was asking if it was possible."

"I don't know. I'd have to think that it wouldn't survive the heat."

"And yet they've survived flying through space and slamming into unwilling hosts? I think they're a lot heartier than you want to give them credit for."

"Perhaps." Wruck didn't sound convinced.

"What if it was Mephistopheles? Could he have managed it?"

Wruck looked thoughtful. "I suppose if the Superior were powerful enough, such as Mephistopheles was, then yes, it would be in the realm of possibility."

The music changed to "Antichrist Superstar" by Marilyn Manson and that meant I was pretty sure I was right.

"So, here's this hour's Megalomaniac Girl proclamation, everyone. What's slammed into this sun is a parasite, and it's likely a really strong one, probably one of Mephistopheles' favorite pals." Mephs had said as much in my dream, after all. "And that means that, despite the odds, this particular parasite is going to successfully bond with this star. Meaning that the most powerful superbeing in existence is trying to form in front of us."

There was that silence you get when everyone is so horrified by what they've heard that they can't speak for a few seconds. But the guys recovered.

"What?" Jeff asked weakly. "How could that be?"

"Look, as per always, I don't make the plans, I just have to figure out what they are and foil them. In this case, it's not a plan so much as it's just the freaking way our luck goes. And this makes sense, if you consider that the neutron wave has been carrying this parasite forward."

Tim nodded. "I can see it. In that sense, it's a good thing the *Eknara* was hit."

"I agree." I did. It, like everything else, made too much sense to be wrong. And I knew things the others didn't, particularly that we were on the Fix Mephs' Big Errors For Algar Tour.

"How so?" Mossy asked.

But Chuckie was with us. "If the *Eknara* wasn't hit and stranded here, who would know what was going on? No one. These three solar systems are close to each other, but they're extremely remote from anywhere else. More importantly, only one planet in all three systems is even close to spaceflight. They can't call for help or warn anyone. Without the *Eknara* crash-landing here, *we're* not here to try to stop it."

"If we can," Hughes pointed out.

"We can," Jerry said confidently. He grinned at me. "Our Fearless Leader is here and she's on the case."

"I feel the love," Tim said. "But if we're talking a being who can harness the power of a sun, then said being can engulf the planets, too."

"And those two other suns and their planets." Knew how the Superiors worked. Just like all the other bad guys worked—get as much as you can, regardless of who you harm along the way. "So, we're trying to save at least three systems."

"No," Jeff said. "If we take your hypothesis as correct, then we're trying to save the entire galaxy. Again."

CHAPTER 76

READER NODDED. "I'm sure Jeff's right. Because if we have a sentient star that's being controlled by someone as powerful and evil as Mephistopheles was, then they aren't going to stop at three systems."

"And the more they consume, the stronger they get," Mossy said. "Just like a black hole."

"And since Mother sees the beginning of a black hole, that totally fits." Managed not to say that black holes sucked—didn't want to hurt Algar's feelings and also didn't feel like getting punned at for the rest of the landing.

"Prepare for final landing," Hughes announced. "The gravitational pull doesn't seem as strong as it was on Cradus—this is a more Earthlike gravity, so we should be fine to take off, even if we're fully loaded."

The landing was, for our crew, the most complicated one we'd done yet, seeing as this planet wasn't forming a landing pad for us. Fortunately, Drax had accounted for this and there were support pillars that came out of the bottom of various parts of the ship—the ones for the saucer section being longer than those for the sport car section in order to keep our "head up"— or else we'd have to land tipped forward. All the landing pillars were high enough to keep our thrusters off the ground, too. The tricky part was lowering the ship while also lowering the support pillars, but everyone who'd flown planes said it was similar to normal landing gear.

So, we managed, me by providing the soundtrack, everyone else by doing something to get us down. We got to listen to "Landing on London" by 3 Doors Down and "Pillar of Davidson" by Live, which I felt was helpful, though actively chose not to ask anyone else's opinion.

Once we were down, Mother did a scan. "Air is breathable for all on board. You should be able to exit via the main gang-plank, not an airlock. Temperature is similar to the Northern United States and lower regions of Canada."

"So, chilly, but not terrible," Tito said. "Whoever's going out should dress accordingly."

"I suggest we put on Drax's nifty body armor."

Drax nodded. "I agree. It will ensure that you don't feel extreme temperatures. The suits are made to keep the wearers safe in all situations."

Those of us strapped in got unstrapped, I grabbed my iPod and dropped it back into my purse, and we all headed for the Observation Lounge via the Hyperspeed Daisy Chain.

"As before, no one is to get off," Jeff said as everyone was getting out of their harnesses. "And that particularly means you, Jamie. We may not be staying here very long, and we want everyone inside and accounted for."

"No one's coming to look at us," Jamie said, sounding disappointed.

Checked the window. Looked like we were in a large basin that was part of a rocky area. There were trees that reminded me of Beta Eight, seeing as their leaves were red. So were the leaves and branches of scrub bushes that were nearby. The area was various shades of red, similar to how it was in Sedona, Arizona, only more so.

Didn't spot a lot of animal life, but that might not mean anything—the ship was huge, and normally something gigantic landing in your home tended to make animals run and even insects cautious. Plus I didn't see any water nearby, so maybe that was why we had no animals.

Realized Jamie was right, though—saw nothing that would be considered a person, unless the rocks were sentient. Put nothing past the galaxy, but Kreaving hadn't indicated that they were on a planet where the people were made of granite, so chose to figure that the people, like the animals and insects, were hiding.

"Maybe they're afraid of a ship as big as ours, Jamie-Kat. I'm sure we'll meet them soon enough." Gave her and Charlie quick hugs and kisses. "You two need to behave. Everyone needs to stay in, just like Daddy said." Gave Lizzie a hug as well. "You, too, please and thank you."

"Oh, fine," Lizzie said with the requisite dramatic sigh. "We'll behave."

Received similar assurances from everyone else. Didn't buy them all that much. Decided to ensure that Jeff's order would happen, and assigned the flyboys to guard the nest, so to speak. Thought about it, and put Rahmi and Rhee on guard duty, too. Then really considered and put Kevin, Buchanan, Siler, Butler, and Maurer on this duty as well. Not that I'd felt that it was anyone's fault other than Jamie, ACE, and Algar's for her early expedition on Cradus, but it never hurt to show that we meant business.

Kevin, being my mom's right hand in the P.T.C.U. and therefore the most used to this kind of situation, immediately ordered everyone into the crash couch room, both because it would be easier to keep everyone in and because if things went wrong, none of the kids needed to see it and we'd be ready in case we needed to make a hasty exit.

Whining about everyone wanting to see what was going on ensued and was promptly ignored, mostly because the rest of us agreed with Kevin's decision. And of course, this meant I got a lot of whining from those assigned to ensure that our civilians stayed on the ship, but we all managed to find the will to go on. Christopher stayed behind to ensure that all heads were counted and everyone was where they were supposed to be.

The rest of us on the away team then headed to the armory and got into the body armor. I was fine with this, since the Elves continued to deliver and I was in jeans, a KT Tunstall *Eye To The Telescope* t-shirt, an Aerosmith hoodie—because I had standards to maintain—and my Converse.

"Do we take weapons?" Tim asked.

"I don't recommend it," White replied.

"Take smaller ones that can be concealed," Chuckie said. "Just in case."

"If you insist, Charles," White said. "But I'm sure we could manage without them."

"I insist," Chuckie said with a smile. "Because I don't trust anyone out there. Yet."

Dropped some smaller guns and some cool sheathed knives in my purse because who was I to argue with the Smartest Guy in the Armory? Grabbed a few grenades, too, 'cause why not?

Didn't appear to have Poofs on Board. Chose not to worry about it and added another grenade.

"Chuck's right," Christopher said as he joined us. "Dad, why are you always so foolhardy?"

"Because it doesn't do well to come to the people you're trying to help waving big guns in their faces," I replied. "Richard knows what he's doing, don't you, Mister White?"

"As you do, Missus Martini. Plus, you'll be there, son, all ready to protect me and whisk me and the others to safety."

Patted my purse. "And I'll make sure, as always, that you're totally safe, Mister White."

"The love in the armory's great," Reader said, as several of the others snorted about my keeping White safe comment. "But I'm still not thrilled that anyone other than Alpha Team is going out there."

"Wheatles talked to me and to Chuckie. He needs to meet us. Trust me on this one."

Received a shot of the cover boy grin. "Always, girlfriend. Always."

"You want me and Mahin with you in case something goes wrong," Abigail said. "And that's not a question, but a statement."

Mahin nodded. "That's earth of some kind out there, so I can move it."

"I've got my own explosive miniatures with me," Serene said. "Just in case." Pretty much everyone put their hands out to get some. Didn't even have to put back the extra grenade to fit them into my purse.

"Nice to see we're armed for bear," Reader said with a sigh. "Not that I think we're wrong to be prepared."

"Then why are the princesses not going again?" Tim asked.

"Because we want everyone staying in the ship and we need muscle to ensure they follow orders," Jeff said. "Since we have limited time, and most of what we're going to be doing on is planet is going to be saying hello, then throwing people into the *Distant Voyager* and flying away as fast as we can, the fewer of our untrained personnel out there the better." He sounded down and angry.

"Way to focus on the positives there, Jeff," Tim said.

Nudged against him. "What's wrong? I know you want to save everyone. I do, too. So does everyone else. And I'm not counting us out yet. Why are you?"

He hugged me to him. Even with the body suits on I could feel his hearts pounding. "I'm just worried."

"We all are."

"Yeah, but I'm worried about more than the rest of you. If we can't fix this sun—and, so far, none of us have the faintest idea of what to do—then we're about to feel millions or billions of people die. That's hard on empaths, and what this ship does not have are isolation chambers."

"Oh. Good point." It was, and what Jeff was worried about was, frankly, frightening. The blowback of all that death and destruction on a regular person would be bad enough. On an empath, it could kill them.

It had killed Christopher's mother, Terry, in Bizarro World. Alfred had told me she'd died in his arms because of White and all the others being annihilated. And those were far fewer numbers than we were talking for a fully populated solar system. This event could kill Jeff, Jamie, Kimmie, and who knew how many of the other kids?

Everyone else's expressions shared that they hadn't thought of this either. We were currently Team Stressed Out.

Jeff ran his hand through his hair. "I didn't mean to upset everyone. Look, stop worrying about this specifically. Let me handle that worry, okay?"

"If you insist," Reader said. "But we'll be prepared to run, more than we normally are, because, ultimately, our people have to come first."

Jeff nodded. Didn't feel any better or think that he did, either. He hugged me again. "It's fine, baby. You just focus on being you and figuring out what the hell we're going to do."

"I'll do my best, Jeff."

"She'll manage," Lorraine said loyally.

Claudia nodded. "She always does."

"Any way I can convince you to stay on the ship?" Reader asked Gower.

"None," Gower replied, as he checked his armor. "You're getting all of Alpha Team, both current and former, and you should be happy about that."

We headed to the elevators because the gangplank was at the bottom of the saucer section, just aft of the front of the sports car's nose. This time the ride was uneventful.

Wruck was going with us but, as always, he didn't feel the

need for body armor. Drax and Mossy were with him, waiting for us at the gangplank. Excuse me, the Debarking Area.

The Debarking Area was big, and it had an even bigger window where we could look out and, therefore, where those still on the ship could observe in case of issues. Drax was there to man the gangplank and Mossy was there as backup, because he didn't feel that it was wise to hit a bronze-age society with someone who looked so different.

Couldn't argue with his caution. Not that we had any idea of what anyone looked like, because by the time the rest of this away team arrived at the Debarking Area, there was still no one visible.

"This bodes. Sorry, but I just have to say it. Wheatles knew we were coming back for them. Why aren't they here?"

"Many possible reasons," Chuckie replied. "Some good, some bad."

"They're dead," Christopher offered, clearly choosing Team Bad Reasons. "The natives stopped being friendly and captured them. Someone else heard them, came by, and captured or killed them."

"Gosh, Sammy Sunshine, we've got it. Any good reasons you can think of?"

"They're waiting to see just who we are," Reader said. "They have no idea who's inside this ship since they no longer have communications. They can't read our alphabet, so they have no idea that the words on our ship say *Distant Voyager*. Kreaving has gotten everyone to hide or play dead or whatever, in case whoever's inside this ship is an enemy, not a helper."

"I prefer James' reasons, in case you weren't sure, Christopher. So, I guess it's down the gangplank and calling yoo-hoo."

This was the first time we were using it, and it was kind of thrilling. The gangplank, like the rest of the ship, had those pretty gold tones that meant it sparkled in the sun. It slid out as if it was unrolling from underneath—one golden plank at a time. This took less time than I'd have thought, considering how high up we were—Drax Industrial efficiency at its finest.

We got into formation. Since we were coming in a peace-keeping capacity, and since we had no visible weapons, we were in a relaxed formation that ensured an A-C was near to a human, just in case. The size of the gangplank meant that we could easily go out three at a time. Frankly, we could go out five at a time, but Reader insisted we have fewer easy targets, just in case.

So, Wruck led the way, then came Serene flanked by Reader and Tim, then me, Jeff, and Chuckie. Next came White, Gower, and Christopher, then Abigail, Mahin, Lorraine, and Claudia brought up the rear. No one came to greet us.

"Now what?" Christopher asked, as Jeff indicated that Drax should raise the gangplank.

We watched it rise back up because it was cool. From this vantage point I could see that I was right—the gangplank rolled up, then slid into its compartment.

Once it was up I waved to Drax and Mossy, then shrugged. "Now we find out where everyone is."

CHAPTER 77

"WE SHOULD HAVE BROUGHT Butler or Maurer," Jeff said. "I think they have navigation built in now."

Pulled my phone out of my purse. "Conveniently . . ." Put my earbuds in and pulled up my music. Not that I was going to listen to it at this moment. But why make it harder on myself? Dialed Butler's number.

"Kitty, are you alright?"

"We are. No one's here and we want to go look for people, but we just realized we don't have navigation with us. Should you come meet us?"

"I don't know that I would be any help. While Cameron and I both do have navigation, these planets are not what we're programmed for." Heard someone talking. "Cameron says that he can't determine where north is, which means that our navigation systems are not working here for whatever reason."

"What's he say?" Christopher asked.

"We're as good to go as he and Cameron are. Okay, thanks, John, we'll possibly be in touch. Or back with people. Or not. It's all a mystery right now."

"I'll ask Gustav and Mother what we can do. I believe we can tap into her navigation, but I don't want to risk causing her any issues."

"Definitely no issues for Mother. We may have to make an extremely hasty exit. Let's not mess with Mother at all unless we have to." We hung up.

"What now?" Jeff asked. "I'm not wild about us splitting up."

"We could just radiate out from the ship," Chuckie said. "Like we were doing on Nazez."

"That didn't work so well," Tim said.

"It worked like it was supposed to," I pointed out.

"There's a very real possibility that if these people are hiding, they're armed in some way and will attack us first and ask who we might be later," White pointed out.

"Well, we have to do something," Abigail said. "Because just standing around isn't going to cut it."

"I could try to raise the dirt where we can't see," Mahin suggested.

"No," Reader said firmly. "No wasting of anyone's talents or energy reserves right now."

My music turned on, presumably because Algar was running out of patience. "Shout" by Tears for Fears was the current selection and that gave me an idea. "Why don't we do what we'd do if it was the kids hiding?"

"What's that?" Christopher asked.

Cleared my throat and cupped my hands to my mouth. "Wheatles! Wheatles Kreaving! Wheatles Kreaving from the planet Ignotforsta and part of the crew of the stranded ship *Eknara*! It's the crew from the *Distant Voyager*, here to rescue you! Come out, come out, wherever you are!"

"You've got to be kidding me," Christopher muttered as I turned and shouted this in a variety of directions.

Managed not to smirk or make a snarky comment as a body stepped partially out from behind an outcropping of rocks. Looked humanoid but he was far enough away and sheltered enough by the rocks that I wasn't able to make out a lot of definition. "Which of you are those I was speaking with?" Sounded like Kreaving.

"It's me, Kitty."

"I don't know any Kitty."

"We never told him our names," Chuckie said. He grabbed my hand. "The rest of you stay here, and Jeff, I mean you in particular. It was the two of us," he shouted to Kreaving as we stepped forward. "I'm Charles Reynolds, she's Kitty Katt-Martini. We're all here to help you."

Kreaving stayed where he was. "Prove it's you."

We looked at each other. "How the hell does he expect us to do that?" Chuckie asked me.

"I may have it." Time to go with the crazy. "Wheatles, if you actually want us to get you off this stupid rock, stop playing coy and get out here. Time is literally running out, because you're not wrong—whatever hit the sun is going to do its business all over this solar system sooner as opposed to later."

"It's her," he shouted to someone. "Weapons down."

"Well, James called that right," Chuckie said.

"So did you, not that I want to shoot these people."

Wheatles walked toward us, followed by a lot of people who were various colors and sizes, just like humans, most with hair on their heads and some without, but who didn't look that much like humans. What they looked like were literally apes—as in gorillas, chimps, and so forth—with no fur. Wearing nice space jumpsuits, carrying space helmets, and looking, to a person, freaked out.

They had the bigger heads—which probably indicated nice, big brains and my likely having to arrange Dazzler Singles Trips to their planet—the thicker limbs, body structures, and digits that apes had over humans. Unlike cartoon ape people, they were wearing shoes, so couldn't compare their toes to ours, but took it on faith that they looked like an ape's more than a human's.

"It's a crazy old galaxy, isn't it?" Chuckie asked me, clearly trying not to laugh. "I think they get to win on the name. You may have to come up with something else for our species."

"Maybe they'll let us keep on sharing it."

Wheatles reached us—he was gorilla in structure and, taking a look at his expression, bearing, and coloring, figured him for the silverback, likely the Commander, and someone I was never calling Wheaties unless we became *very* close friends or he seriously pissed me off—and he shook his head. "I thought you said you were Naked Apes. Did we misunderstand?"

"Nope. You're just far more like true Naked Apes than we are."

"Our evolution branched away from pure simian," Chuckie said quickly. "So we don't have the same body strength I'd assume you have and our body structure is slightly different, but only slightly. Otherwise, we're probably very similar."

Kreaving nodded. Then he put his right fist up to his left pec. "Commander Wheatles Kreaving of the *Eknara* from the planet of Ignotforsta, officially requesting rescue from the *Distant Voyager* of Earth."

Chuckie nudged me as my music changed to "Killer Queen" by Queen. Time to do what I was pretty sure Wasim and Gadhavi would strongly suggest in this situation as well as what Algar obviously wanted.

I bowed to him. "We are Queen Katherine, Regent of Earth in the Solaris system for the Annocusal Royal Family of Alpha Four of the Alpha Centauri system, First Lady of the United States of America on Earth, Earth's representative to the Galactic Council, and Communications Officer for the *Distant Voyager*, and we welcome the crew of the *Eknara* and will offer them safe haven and passage."

Kreaving gaped. Then he did the down on one knee thing and bent his head. All the rest of his crew followed suit.

"Nicely done," Chuckie said to me. "You even remembered the royal 'we.' I'm so proud."

"Thank Wasim and Mister Gadhavi." And the King of the Elves and DJs. "Um, can I please ask them to stand up now?"

Chuckie laughed. "Yes. Commander Kreaving, please rise. The Queen is extremely informal and prefers to be called Kitty, by the way."

They did as requested. "Are you her consort?" Kreaving asked Chuckie respectfully.

Who managed to only snort a little bit of a laugh. "Ah, no. A moment." He turned around and motioned to Jeff, who came over at hyperspeed, which caused the Ignotforstans to jump. "King Jeffrey, Regent of Earth in the Solaris system for the Annocusal Royal Family of Alpha Four of the Alpha Centauri system, President of the United States of America, and Chief Weapons Officer of the *Distant Voyager*, I present Commander Wheatles Kreaving of the ship *Eknara* from the planet Ignotforsta."

"Please don't bow again," Jeff said quickly as Kreaving and crew started to bend.

"The king is also extremely informal," Chuckie said, as Kreaving and his people straightened right back up, "and prefers to be called Jeff."

"Thank you for coming to us, your highnesses," Kreaving said.

"We would have been here sooner but we had a heck of time figuring out where in the galaxy you were. This system is hella remote."

Kreaving blinked. "Ah . . ."

Winked at him. "Chuckie *did* say that we were extremely informal, dude. Get with the program here. The greeting is to level the playing field, so to speak, or unlevel it, or whatever works, basically. As of now, though, we're all just people, trying to save ourselves and as many others as we can."

"True enough, but please call me Charles or Chuck," Chuckie said. "She's the only one who gets to use that familiar of a nickname for me."

Kreaving nodded. "Understood. Can you really get us out of here?"

"Your crew, absolutely. The rest? That's the problem." Pointed to the *Distant Voyager*. "Our ship is huge, and clearly bigger than yours, because we saw the wreckage, but despite its size, it's not able to evacuate all this system. We might be able to get everyone on this planet off. Maybe."

Kreaving shook his head. "They won't go. Our shuttle was still intact—though it has a limited warp capacity, it can only hold six so it's not viable to get us all out of here. But its long-range capacity is such that we were able to send a team to the other planets. While all of them were welcoming, which was somewhat surprising, none of them want to leave."

Jeff groaned. "And, just like that, it's worse."

Chuckie squinted at the sun. "I'm able to see that the sun is flaring in an odd way. Can't they?"

"Yes," Kreaving said. "They feel it portends good things."

"It doesn't. That sun's going to become a black hole, and then it's going to become something much, much worse." Looked around. "Is this your entire crew?"

"Yes, we've chosen to stay together in case help arrived."

"Any locals hanging with you? Anyone who might actually not want to trust the portends and instead listen to the clearly more scientifically advanced visitors?"

"We crashed on this planet," Kreaving said wryly. "Therefore, we're not really impressing the locals."

"Will we?" Jeff asked. "Our ship is impressive."

"It is," Kreaving agreed. "However, no one on any of these planets is scared. They all want to wait it out."

Something about this was bothering me. The hundred percent thing. No group had a hundred percent who all wanted to do the same thing, ever. Sure, less advanced cultures might have more people willing to listen to the leader or high priest or whomever, but even then, there were always rebels. Even the A-Cs had rebels, few and far between though they were. I was married to one, after all.

My music changed to "Another State of Mind" by Social Distortion and it dawned on me. "Someone's controlling them. It would make sense. Whoever is in the sun wants all that he or she can get. Keep the people, get more of their essences or whatever it is the Superiors want or need to survive."

"The Superiors?" Kreaving shook his head. "Their star exploded hundreds of years ago."

"Oh, well, as to that . . . have *we* got a story for *you.*"

Jeff nodded. "We do. Let's tell it inside the *Distant Voyager.*"

CHAPTER 78

WE GOT THE CREW of the *Eknara* on board. They were traveling with fewer people than we were—who wasn't?—but they still had twenty-five, all crew or scientific personnel. We also had the intact shuttle moved into our cargo hold, just in case, as well as anything salvageable from the remains of the *Eknara*, their scientific and surveying equipment in particular. Having A-Cs along, Christopher especially, meant this went quickly.

The *Eknara* had a ship's doctor, but Tito did medical examinations on all of them in our medical bay just in case. Possibly also because he was thrilled to finally get to actually do the job he loved. Everyone pronounced healthy though slightly dehydrated, we got them all water, then did tight quarters assignments, just in case we could convince others to get on board, so they didn't take up all that many rooms.

I'd broken down and turned off my music when we'd gotten on board, though I'd kept my earbuds in despite a couple of meaningful looks from Jeff. I was ready to turn the music back on the moment things got stressful, which I expected at any time.

We let our people out of the Nonessential Personnel Station, aka the jail, per Lizzie. Then we all went to the mess hall, so the Ignotforstans could have a meal and we could all talk comfortably. We ate, too, just to be sociable.

Because the *Eknara* was a science vessel, everyone on board was trained in astrophysics and all related subjects. Meaning they were having a great time talking to Brian, Chuckie, Drax, Mossy, Mother, all our Dazzlers on Board including those who identified as housewives, and Hacker International, while the rest of us smiled politely and shut our ears off. Or perhaps that was just me.

Happily, while the Ignotforstans had never heard of humans, A-Cs, or Turleens, they didn't seem too thrown by any of us. They knew of the Vata, but the races had never met. They'd had no interaction with the Anciannas or Z'porrah. Found all of this interesting since I'd thought the Anciannas and Z'porrah had meddled everywhere in the galaxy, and that the Galactic Council had identified every ally or enemy possible. Clearly this wasn't the case, since we'd only run into essentially "undiscovered" or forgotten systems on this trip.

The *Eknara* hadn't been carrying any children, which was a huge disappointment to our kids. However, their ship's doctor, Setah Momac, who resembled a taller chimp, and the ship's navigator, Bremelos Merplon, who was representing orangutans, were enamored of children, so they were making up for the lack of new age-appropriate playmates by letting all the kids hang off of them and answering all of their questions, even the impertinent ones.

They were a couple, found out almost immediately via the first impertinent question, which came from my daughter. They were not yet married, which was the second impertinent question, which came from my ward. Truly, I was Mother of the Year.

Thankfully, had to switch tables to do the intelligence briefings, so I could stop contemplating my parenting failures for a bit. We spent some important time bringing Kreaving and his command crew up to date on what was going on, including that we'd been flung around the galaxy by the Powers That Be and, therefore, had no real idea of where we were going and so forth.

We also shared Modern Superior History and described what parasites did and why I thought that we had a parasite in the sun. After the requisite questioning of my methods, and the subsequent listing of all the times Megalomaniac Girl had been right, they stopped arguing. Save worlds, solar systems, and galaxies enough, and apparently some people can be convinced that you might be competent.

Grentix Wheekus, the *Eknara*'s science officer, who was on the gorilla side of the Ignotforsta house, had been on the shuttle team, and she described the people and the inhabited planets. The planets were similar—mostly rocky with water, animal, and plant life, but each one had a predominant color. The planet we were on was red, but the others were blue, green, saffron, orange, brown, and purple. Resisted making a Beta Eight comment, but it took effort.

We were dealing with races that were humanoid and similar to each other—no one had taken the time to do DNA samples because of the situation, but the natives on each planet looked like the natives on the other planets. Plant and animal life was similar, too. The only real difference the Eknara's away team has seen between one world from the others was that all the living things on any particular world matched their world's hue in terms of skin color and hair, and that included the plants and animals.

The natives looked a lot like we did, as in like humans. They were smaller than us by a lot, though—Tito and the flyboys, who were the shortest guys with us, were taller than any of the males they'd seen, and I would be an Amazon for the females. Well, a lot like us other than the color thing and one other key factor—their skin was flaky, but not as if it were dry because it didn't fall off. Grentix described it as almost as if their skin was a form of feathers, or heading that way.

Population estimates were a good million plus per planet, and there were people scattered all over each planet, not all clumped together, which presented us with the disheartening truth that we had no normal means to save the majority of these populations.

But the real bottom line came all too soon. "We could take these people by force, but they don't want to leave," Kreaving said. "If we aren't willing to force them, there's nothing we can do other than desert them for our own safety, because none of us have anything that we can use to stop this sun's fast descent into a black hole."

My music turned on. "Evil Is Alive And Well" by Jakob Dylan. Really didn't think Algar meant that Kreaving or his people were the evil ones. "Look, we can't just run away. This won't stop here. If whoever's inside this sun succeeds—and, trust me, they will—then we are looking at a galaxy-ending event. *The* galaxy-ending event, really."

"Someone that powerful could end the universe," Chuckie added.

"Chuck's right and I agree with Kitty," Reader said. "There has to be something we can try, something we haven't thought of or can cobble together."

Grentix shook her head. "We need a way to shoot something

that will destroy this parasite or superbeing or whatever it is or is becoming without also destroying the star itself. We have nothing like that and, even if we did, no way to get it into the star without it burning up well before it reaches the target."

"The shooting the ship might be able to do," Drax said. "We need to figure out the what first, or the how doesn't matter."

While the others brainstormed ideas for what to toss at the sun, I tried to come up with some crazy plan. Nada. Knew we were all thinking about this wrong, but couldn't say why.

My music changed to "Too Fast for a U-Turn" by Lit. Stopped fretting and focused on the song, because it seemed totally out of left field. So, what was Algar trying to tell me or make me think?

Well, if I thought about the song's title and related it to our trip, we'd been going too fast to stop and help this system earlier. But that had been because Naomi had wanted us on Cradus first.

But why? This situation seemed far more dire.

Got distracted by Christopher suggesting we treat this like we did the other superbeings, Mephistopheles in particular. Heard that get shot down, since we didn't have any self-contained nukes laced with alcohol on hand. Though I kind of figured I could get one out of my purse if I asked nicely enough.

Was about to chime in and support Christopher's idea, when a new song came on. "Dear Enemy" by The Exies.

Considered this message from Algar. Had to be about Mephistopheles, and not just because Christopher had just mentioned him. So, thought about Mephs. He'd probably given me a clue somewhere in my dream. Not the obvious clues or answers, but a hidden one.

Got distracted again by Serene saying she felt she could create whatever explosives we might need, and everyone discussing how blowing up the star was just as bad as it turning into a black hole.

While Serene patiently explained that she wanted to create something that would target the parasite, specifically, realized that I desperately needed to talk aloud. And there was no one around who could hear what I needed to say.

Was tempted to grab Algar but, since he was in the mess hall with us, couldn't come up with a smooth way to get him alone that wouldn't seem just too odd to everyone and probably identify Algar as the DJ for Siler. But I needed to run my mouth with someone who could answer and also add in.

My music changed again, to Barbra Streisand's version of "Life On Mars," and I considered what Algar was suggesting. Well, why not? Per Mephistopheles, he, like me, was on a Fix Everyone Else's Mess life journey, too.

Got up and went over to Wruck. "John," I said quietly, "I need the Martian Manhunter. Can I speak with you in private?"

He nodded and got up. Everyone was really into the brainstorming— since Brian was suggesting creating a probe with the remains of the *Eknara* and A-C hyperspeed—though we got a couple questioning looks. "Want to try something," I said to those so looking, "and only have John witness it if it's a stupid idea. Be back shortly."

We headed out and I headed us for the good ol' supply closet. Interestingly, my music stopped playing once Babs was done doing a great cover of a Bowie classic. We didn't speak until we were inside.

"What's going on?" Wruck asked me.

"I need to talk to someone. Well, really, I need to talk *at* someone, but have that someone add in. And what I need to talk about can't be shared with the others. Any of the others."

He cocked his head. "I'm intrigued. And I promise not to share whatever it is we talk about with anyone else, not even Benjamin and Malcolm."

"Great! Because I want to talk to you about all the dead people who talk to me."

CHAPTER 79

WRUCK STARED AT ME for a moment, then sat down on some boxes. "Alright, I'm now *officially* intrigued."

"Super. Um, where to start . . . people visit me in my dreams a lot. And not via the DreamScape which I only discovered existed at the beginning of our latest Foray O' Fun."

"All dead people?"

"Oh, no, just ones I know. And, in one particular case, killed."

"Who would that be?"

"Mephistopheles."

Wruck looked thoughtful. "Interesting. Why him?"

"Because he likes me. Seriously. And, honestly, by now, I kind of like him." Gave Wruck a brief history of the Heartwarming Me and Mephs Story Coming to a Hallmark Channel Near You. "So, I know there were clues in what he told me, clues specifically for this situation, but I don't know what they were."

"Alright. But you said 'people.' Is there someone else?"

"Yes, only she's not dead. Well, not really dead. Dead as far as everyone is concerned but not. Unless that made sense."

"Somewhat. I know the history. Of the women who've died that you were close to, I would have to guess that it would be one of the Gower women."

"Yes. Naomi. Gladys visits me in my dreams. Occasionally. Mephs is, realistically, my most reliable dream interrupter."

"Paul and Abigail's sister is not dead? Does Charles realize his wife is alive?"

"No, thank God, he does not, and this is one of the big 'tell no one' things I was referring to. Besides, as I'm about to explain, she's dead to *us* for reasons."

Wruck nodded. "I won't say anything to anyone. But, explain what you mean."

Heaved a sigh and described what had happened during Operation Infiltration. "So, she's a superconsciousness now. And I'm really sure she was at the controls when we were sent from the Eagle Nebula to Cradus."

"She's not the only powerful force working with or through you, is she?"

"No. We have ACE. We have Sandy. There are others." Managed not to say that Wruck was rooming with one of them. "But I'm pretty damned positive that Naomi was at the controls when we went from Nazez to Cradus. And I'm positive she sent us on an erratic path so we'd go past this system, solely so we'd pick up the *Eknara*'s distress call."

"Then why did we go to Cradus first?"

"See, now, that's why I need you. Because, while that *is* the question of the hour, I don't know. The situation there was, for the Cradi, dire, but it's nothing compared to what's going on here. And yet, Naomi sent us to Cradus first *and* didn't give us any help in figuring out how to get back."

"Which was why we got to know the Cradi so well."

My brain nudged. It was there, it was right there, but I wasn't able to grasp it. "Right," I said slowly. "So, the question is—why was it important for us to go to Cradus first? And stay a lot longer than we're probably going to in this system?"

"Because of what we learned there?" Wruck suggested.

"Possibly. Probably." My brain nudged harder. "Maybe because of what we . . . got there?"

"Well, realistically, they got more than we did. We left them almost half of our rabbit population. Though they did give us some nice metals."

Jerked. "They did. But I got something more. I got a part of Cradus and Spehidon. Specifically, something with both their essences inside it."

"How would that help in this situation?" Wruck asked.

"John, currently, I have no freaking idea. That's not the way this game is played, but I appreciate your trying. So, okay, let's just assume that my present from Cradus and Spehidon is going to help. But we still have to get whatever into the star to take out the whomever in there. Wish we knew more about them."

"Does who's in there matter?"

Pondered this. "I'm Shealla, Giver of Names . . ."

Wruck was quiet for a few moments. "And?" he asked gently.

"And everything had a name. And what doesn't have a name needs one. Names matter. The name is the thing and the name affects the thing. The parasites are Superior soul vessels or whatever, but they contain the entire essence and, from what I've gleaned, ancestral memories, of the Superior they'd originally been."

"Yes, that's true."

Thought back. It had been a long time since Operation Fugly, after all. "I think . . . I think Mephistopheles named himself. The other in-control superbeings, those were 'imaginatively' named by Centaurion Division. But I think Mephs told them his name in some way."

"You're sure?"

"No, not really. But I think he influenced the naming choice, let's put it that way. He, like you, chose a name he felt was fitting."

"Why does this matter?"

"Again, don't know, just know that it does. Just like I knew I had to give the other PPB net we were fighting a name during Operation Invasion, to put her on the same footing as ACE. But Lilith is, therefore, taken. Not that we know that the Superior in there is male or female."

"PPB net?"

"Um . . . Physic-Psycho Barrier. I think that's the correct term. I've done my best not to worry about it because the abbreviation is so much easier. It's what ACE was but, due to being freed, is not anymore. Lilith isn't one anymore, either. We scattered her to the galaxy."

"And, again, does it matter?"

"It might."

We were quiet for a few moments. "Do you think this Lilith is inside the sun?" he asked.

"Ooh, good one. But no. Because I think Mephs would have insinuated that in some way, and he didn't. At all." Thought about Mephs' warning. "He was talking about his own people. John, do you have any idea who Mephistopheles would have considered his right-hand man? Or woman. Or whoever he might have considered one of his top lieutenants, either worse or better than he was?"

"You mean someone whose counsel he would have wanted?"

"Yeah, like his Chuckie or Christopher. Or his Goebbels or Mengele."

Wruck shook his head. "I might have known at one time, but it happened so long ago. Let me see if I can come up with anything."

My music turned on and I was treated to "My Goddess" by The Exies. Considered if this was Algar telling me that the being in the sun was female. Then considered how I might be able to confirm.

Sent a text to Tim. Got a snarky reply back. Sent the same request with more stern language and some nasty words. Waited. The reply came. Verified certain words and got confirmation. Always nice when the Megalomaniac Girl Skills were fired up.

"Interesting. Okay, John, I had Tim ask the Ignotforstans if the natives referred to the sun in any way, if they thought the sun was a real person or people or whatever."

"What was the response?"

"They feel that the sun is a mother goddess who is manifesting to give them an uplifted life."

We exchanged the "oh, really?" look. "They used the word 'uplifted'?" he asked.

"Yes, Tim said he verified that."

"And we're sure that it wasn't a Z'porrah who came to them?"

"Lemme check." Sent another text to Tim, who replied quickly. "Nope, he already asked. They don't know who the mother-goddess is—she spoke to them in their hearts, per what they told Grentix and the rest who were on the shuttle's away team verified it. Same words on every planet."

"The Superiors had no gods. They considered themselves gods once the uplift happened."

My music changed to "Mama I'm Strange" by Melissa Ethridge. Considered this. "You know . . . when we were fighting them, way back when during Operation Fugly, I saw absolutely no reproductive organs on any of the in-control superbeings. I assumed that they reproduced via parasitic infection. But, when we were talking during my dream, Mephistopheles insinuated that he was born. In fact, I asked if he'd been born and he said 'just like you were' and tapped me on the nose."

"I'm not going to ask about the last part. But yes, the Superiors could reproduce. Similar to those from Beta Twelve, via a form of cloning where the DNA from each was combined to create a new life."

"That's kind of how we all do it, but I assume you mean in a lab, versus bumping uglies. Not that I actually think human and A-C genitalia are ugly."

"Let's not go there."

"Wow. Everyone's a freaking critic. Fine, fine. So, anyway, would Mephistopheles consider his mother his right-hand person or an advisor or similar?"

Wruck looked thoughtful. "Since joining with you I've spent some time researching human history. Your father has been very helpful in that regard."

"Yeah, Dad lives for the teaching, even if he's somehow still on sabbatical from ASU."

Wruck chuckled. "It's amazing how the father-in-law of the most powerful man on Earth can get concessions."

"You make it sound so dirty."

He grinned. "I'm proud. At any rate, in many cultures, especially ones from your biblical times, the most powerful woman in a kingdom was not the queen, since she could be and often was, ah, replaced."

"You mean killed."

"Or divorced. Even then it was a viable option. But since most of Earth is so patriarchal, the king has the most power in most cases. And therefore the most powerful woman would be the Queen Mother."

"Huh. Interesting take." My music changed to "The Last Of The Real Ones" by Fall Out Boy. Hoped this meant that whoever was in the sun was the last really dangerous Superior.

Wruck looked like he was trying not to laugh. "I'll point to your own mother as the obvious example."

"But I'm one of those disposable queens you were talking about."

"Not in this situation. But your mother holds great sway with both you and Jeff. Far more than his mother does."

"Well, that's true. Mom's been in covert and clandestine ops for, like, ever. Lucinda makes the best brownies in the galaxy. Different skills."

"You're proving my point. If you're looking for a female who was likely to influence Mephistopheles, then I believe we could count his mother."

"And if we take his 'just like you were' statement to its fullest, we'd add 'born of woman' and that definitely says Mama Mephs is in this sun. But why would he want me to stop her?"

"Does he really? Could he be fooling you?"

Considered this. Wasn't the first time I had, after all. "No. He's sincere. The Powers That Be that allow him access to me are on our side. I rarely get visitations from our true enemies. I mean, it's happened, but nothing like with Mephistopheles. After all this time, I'm willing to take him at his word, because, frankly, every time he's visited me in my dreams, he's helped me, always greatly."

Wruck nodded. "That's fine. I just wanted to be sure you were sure. In that case, the answer to your question of why he'd want to stop his mother was already given to you by him—he has the perspective of true death and the realization that he will watch until it all ends or he figures out how to help you fix it. He's trying to help you fix it."

"Me over his mother? He didn't make it sound like he hated the person he was talking about. He was warning me about them, but it wasn't with distaste."

"You can love someone who you realize is evil or wrong, you know," Wruck said gently. "If Jamie did something terrible, you would still love her because she's your daughter."

"True enough, and I sincerely hope that wasn't you giving me a warning or some creepy foreshadowing."

He laughed. "No. She's a wonderful little girl and I sense no evil in her. ACE is a help in that way, of course. I used her merely as an example."

"Okey dokey. So, let's say it's Mama Mephs in there. She's been the queen mother to the most powerful Superior there was. Maybe she agreed with his decision to destroy their sun. Maybe he tried to send her into it to do what she's doing with this sun only it didn't work. Maybe he sent her into their sun because she'd disagreed with him. But she's been in space for hundreds of years and, instead of landing in a mammal—and I want to point out that she was near an entire ship full of them when the neutron wave hit the *Eknara*—she went for a sun. So, the next question is—how did she manage to get inside it without being incinerated?"

"I have no idea. But I believe another question is just as important. How is she able to speak to and influence every living native on these planets? She's turned people who should be terrified of what they can see happening to their sun into docile sheep."

"Did the Superiors have the same tele-talents that the A-Cs have?"

"No. The A-Cs are particularly strong in those, just as those you've told us about on Beta Eight who are far stronger in teletalents than the norm out there. There are many races with teletalents, but statistically they're a minute percentage of the whole of the known galactic worlds."

"Does that mean you don't think that Mama Mephs is telepathic?"

"No, it means that we don't know where her telepathy would come from. Perhaps she was just lucky."

"So, she was like Ronald Yates, a sport—someone who deviated or varied abruptly from type."

"Possibly. Or she's had time to learn somehow while sailing through the galaxy."

"And she just somehow hits a star? Should I be worrying about coinkydinks?"

Wruck shook his head. "The space between galactic bodies is vast. That so many Superiors have managed to reach planets is amazing. And I know you feel that Mephistopheles was calling to them once he joined with Ronald Yates, but even so, it's amazing."

Jerked. "Wait. You just said it. Mephs was calling them. I mean, we've always assumed that's what it was. Frankly, we thought it was Yates doing it, but he was never really as in control of the pairing as he'd thought. That means they have telepathy and it's freaking strong, because Mephs was calling to his people thousands and tens of thousands of light-years away *and* they were able to alter their courses somehow and reach Earth."

"How do we counter that?"

Didn't have to think too long on this one and, for once, didn't really need the musical cue of Tom Petty's "A Mind With a Heart of Its Own," though, as always, tunes were enjoyable. "We ask a wascally wabbit for help."

CHAPTER 80

WE DECIDED THAT WE could leave the closet and do the rest of this in my rooms. We headed off at hyperspeed and joined the majority of the animals lounging around in my suite. Interestingly enough, Bellie was here, too, but MJO was presumably still in the mess hall with everyone else.

Bellie greeted me like my long-lost bestie. "Floaty! Floaty! Floaty!" She flew into my arms and started nuzzling. Yeah, say what you will about Operation Fundraiser, it had really bonded me with this bird.

Stroked her head and gave her a gentle scritchy-scratch between her wings. "Good to see you, too, Bellie. And who would like to explain to Kitty how Bellie got in here?"

Bruno birded up and shared that Bellie had been lonely and the Poofs had done her a solid and brought her over. Chose to be magnanimous and not complain about this.

Handed Bellie off to Wruck, who she proceeded to coo at. Yeah, African greys were supposed to be one-person birds, but Bellie's viewpoint was that whoever the top man in the room was, he was hers. And so were all the other men. That she'd taken to me probably had a lot to do with her deep and abiding love for Jeff more than anything else.

Found SuperBun and gave him a snuggle, then sat with him on the couch while Wruck and Bellie took the armchair. Most of the other animals gathered 'round, too. Well, it wasn't like they were going to tell anyone other than me what was going on, not even the rabbits, because I swore them to secrecy first. R.E.M.'s "Animal" came on, which I took to mean that Algar agreed that the animals were trustworthy and might be helpful.

Animal spit swears and pinky oaths given, it was time to get down to business. "SuperBun, we have a situation and we need your insights." Explained the current dilemma in detail and was quite pleased that Wruck didn't do one single thing to make me feel crazy for talking about this with a rabbit. He even added in as necessary. As confidants and brainstorming partners went, he was top-notch. "So, we think that we have a hugely powerful telepath in that sun and we're wondering if you can scope her out in any way."

SuperBun shared that he'd give it a shot. He closed his eyes, leaned against me, and concentrated.

Knew this could take him some time, so chatted quietly with the others while SuperBun did his Most Powerful Psychic Rabbit In The Galaxy thing and Lifehouse sang "Into the Sun" because Algar sometimes enjoyed being really obvious.

"Any ideas for what to send into the sun to get rid of the parasitic Superior superbeing and ideas for how to get whatever in there without destroying our weapon or the sun itself are absolutely welcomed at this time."

Once again, Wruck expressed no derision for my asking the animals for ideas. "Please remember that whatever is sent has to travel more quickly than the blink of an eye or runs the very real risk of being disintegrated before reaching its target."

The animals shared that they had nothing just yet, but they'd noodle on it, so to speak. Shared this with Wruck who, once again, took it in stride.

"You know, John, you might be the only adult aside from me who doesn't think what we're doing right now is crazy."

"Oh, it is crazy. However, I've learned that your form of crazy works very well. And the thinking in the other room wasn't getting us anywhere. Appealing to those who haven't heard all the ideas already—both the good ones and the bad— seems wise, honestly. Plus, I'm sure that a few of the others would think this was a sound option, as well."

"Possibly Richard, and he's probably about it. Everyone else is supportive because they kind of have to be."

Wruck chuckled. "Everyone loves the animals. They're full members of the team."

The animals sent a lot of love Wruck's way. Other than SuperBun, who was still concentrating.

Finally, though, as My Chemical Romance sang "Mama," SuperBun's eyes opened. He shook himself in a way that was adorable. Then he heaved a huge bunny sigh.

"What did you get?" I asked him.

He'd gotten that there was indeed a very strong, sentient presence in the star. Female, based on her thoughts. She was distracted with the joining of her essence to the star, which was the only reason she hadn't exerted power on the crews of the *Eknara* and *Distant Voyager*. And, in that sense, we didn't matter. The moment she was one with the star she was going to engulf all the planets and life on them. She was gleefully looking forward to this.

"Can we stop her without destroying the star?"

Possibly, was SuperBun's take on it. But it would take something powerful enough to hold the star together while expelling the parasitic telepath. Or something nonexplosive.

"We can call her Mama Mephs or the Anti-Mother. You guys pick."

"Why Anti-Mother?" Wruck asked.

"Because Galactus is a dude and Galactusa sounds dumb. Plus, Galactus is, like, my least favorite comics villain of, possibly, all time, and while that sounds like a great moniker to assign, I just don't have the love for it. Besides, Mama Mephs is basically the opposite of Mother. Mother wants to protect everyone. Anti-Mother wants to destroy them. And, for a comics comparison, the Anti-Monitor, while a lot like Galactus, is far cooler."

"I like it," Mother said. "I was not eavesdropping, but you said my name and I thought you needed assistance."

"No worries. Have the others come up with any good ideas in our absence?"

"Sadly, no. They are all quite filled with despair."

"Glad we left," I said to Wruck.

Who nodded. "Mother, could you ensure that everyone stays there? We're possibly making progress and I don't believe we need input from anyone beyond those in the room with us."

"Certainly, John. Would you like me to continue to listen or not?"

We looked at each other. "Up to you," Wruck said.

"Um . . . you know what? Sure."

"As you wish. I will not intrude unless you ask for me, the others come up with something helpful, or I feel that my input will assist."

We gave our attention back to the animals. "SuperBun, did you get any feel for how long we have until Anti-Mother is going to be unstoppable?"

Not long, but long enough. However, SuperBun felt compelled to point out that we had no good ideas for what to send into the star nor how to get there safely.

My music changed to "Walkin' on the Sun" by Smash Mouth. Considered this clue. "Are there people who can walk on or go into stars who we could appeal to for help?" I asked Wruck.

His turn to jerk. "There are. Any superconsciousness of enough power could do it. And I could alter myself into a form most likely to survive the star's heat—there are some very rare beings who can enter a star."

"I can't pop up the numbers, but as far as I've ever heard, stars are like the definition of hottest things in the universe."

"They are, but that doesn't mean that beings can't survive inside of them."

"Oh, just like in the Narnia books."

"If you say so. We have a Superior joining with a star—clearly survival is possible, at least for a few."

"So we need a superconsciousness to help. Does it make me a bad person that I don't want ACE to do this?"

"No, it does not," Wruck said. "ACE resides in your daughter. You not wanting to risk ACE or Jamie shows good maternal instinct."

"I don't know if Sandy is close enough. We don't know who's hanging out in the dark nebula that the *Eknara* was near so there's no guess if they'll help us or not. Naomi's not allowed to manifest as far as I know. Who does that leave us with?"

"Me."

Only the person who said this wasn't Wruck.

CHAPTER 81

WRUCK'S EYES OPENED WIDE and he stared at some-one who was on my left, but just outside of my peripheral vision. My music changed to "Faith in Each Other" by INXS.

Turned to see who was speaking. They were somewhat form-less, a collection of sparkling motes, like a living version of the Pantone Matching System. I'd only seen something like this once.

"Lilith?"

The motes spun. "Yes. It is . . . good to see you again, Kitty."

"Um, really?"

"Really."

"I, um, killed you. Sort of."

"No. You saved me. You and Jareen and the others. You gave me to the galaxy and I was able to become much more than I ever could have been prior. I understand why ACE chose to stay as they originally made us. But I am grateful for the new life you gave me."

"I'm glad it worked out. Um, why are you here?"

"I was called. I have seen what is inside this sun. An evil the likes of which I could never have achieved in my former exis-tence. It must be stopped. This is my galaxy, just as it's yours, and I must assist you or we will all be destroyed."

"Wow, it's like totally Old Home Week. But glad to have you on the team. What are your thoughts about getting into the sun?"

"I could manage it," Lilith said slowly. "But I believe it would destroy me. However, I am willing to sacrifice if that is what's needed."

"Can't express how much I don't want people on our side dying if it's at all possible. Besides, if you're destroyed getting us in, how do we get out?"

"Us?" Wruck asked.

"Dude, I'm going, too. I'll wrap up in as many sets of Drax body armor as possible and you can do whatever to shield me, but someone has to actually stop the Anti-Mother. Getting to her is just the first part. Stopping her? My first job with Centaurion Division was as a parasitic superbeing exterminator. I've trained for this."

Poofikins jumped onto my lap and mewed. This seemed like a very dangerous plan. No kidding.

"Well, I don't want to die. I don't want anyone else to, either, though. But, if it comes down to it, this falls under the heading of My Job." I'd had that confirmed by Mephs, after all. Was able to be gung ho because I wasn't allowing myself to feel any fear. Which was hard, but so far I was managing. My music changed to "Champion" by Fall Out Boy. The chorus was, "If I can live through this, I can do anything." Really hoped that was going to be true.

SuperBun shared that he had to go, too. He felt he had a chance to win if he could go head-to-head with the Anti-Mother telepathically. But he knew he had to be close to her to do it.

Harlie and Jamie's Poof Mous-Mous joined Poofikins on my lap. The Poofs were having a discussion, and it was one they weren't allowing me to understand.

The discussion didn't take long. Mous-Mous purred at me, then hacked something up. In any other animal this would have been gross. But the Poofs, being Black Hole Universe Animals, were able to ingest almost anything and, if it was something they weren't actually eating, cough it back up later.

And what Mous-Mous hacked up was worth its weight in whatever precious stones or metal you wanted to name.

There was a Z'porrah power cube sitting in my lap.

The power cubes allowed the user to move anywhere they could think of. If you could see it in your mind's eye, you could go there. And you traveled in a moment. They were hugely powerful and had been used against us for years. We'd scrounged a few and used them against our enemies, too.

But they were too powerful to just leave in anyone's possession—the Mastermind had used one successfully for far too long, after all. The Poofs had collected all of those we knew about and many we hadn't and had given them to Algar, who kept them in the "water reclamation facility" under the Dulce Science Center where he lived. Was sure that this was some sort of pocket universe or similar, but had never asked outright.

Basically, she who had a Z'porrah power cube had the means to go anywhere. Even to the center of a star. She also might have the means to get out again, which was the very definition of win-win.

"This is how we get there, all of us, in the blink of an eye." Hugged the Poofs. "You guys are the best." Mous-Mous mewed at me. "*And* it's all set up for Kitty, no fiddling needed? You are the best Poofs ever!" Received much Poof love in return.

My music changed to "Get on the Ball" by No Doubt. Right, I'd forgotten something. Got up and went to where I'd put the ball that was Cradus and Spehidon. "And we also have this." Explained what it was to Lilith.

The motes reached out and caressed the ball. "Yes, I can feel them in there. I agree that this should be brought with us. And I have an idea. But it will require you to trust me."

"Shoot."

"If I enter you, you will become stronger and I will be able to ensure we both last longer inside the star."

"What happens after?"

"You birth me. Unlike ACE, I do not wish to be limited. I will not try to remain or bend you to my will. I give you my word."

"Tell me who called you to come help us."

The motes touched me and I could see Naomi's face in my mind. She blew me a kiss.

"Good enough for me."

"We will join just before we make the attempt," Lilith said. "I would prefer to . . . stay as we both are for as long as possible."

"Are you afraid I'll try to keep you?"

She was quiet for a long moment. "No. I know you. You have honor. And you would not keep any against their will. You offered to birth ACE and would have done it if ACE had agreed. You have offered this to ACE many times. I trust you."

"Good. I give you *my* word that I'll birth you as soon as it's safe for us to do so, once we've either won or lost against the Anti-Mother."

"If we lose, I will not allow you to birth me," Lilith said. "If we lose, I will be all that could keep you alive."

"Thank you." It was weird to be working with another former enemy in this way, but apparently this trip was all about the Fate of the Galaxy making me have the strangest bedfellows yet.

Wruck went to the armories to gather all the body armor he could find. While he did that, I dumped my purse out to see what

I might have that could be helpful. "I have a lot of firepower, but the ones I'd bet work the best are Serene's."

"Explosives may cause the star damage," Lilith pointed out.

"True enough." The trap Serene had made rolled against my thigh as "Supercollider" by Fountains of Wayne came onto my airwaves. Picked it up. "You know . . ."

"What is that?" Lilith asked.

Explained what the trap did. "I wonder if this would work on a parasite."

"It's not solid."

"No, it's not." Looked at Lilith. "Um, do you trust me?"

"Yes. Why?"

Triggered the trap and tossed it at her. The trap expanded, went around her, snapped shut, and went back to its original size. Caught it before it hit the ground. I'd guessed right—"as big as a chocho" indicated mass, not merely size. Lilith looked bigger than Wilbur, but mass-wise she could contract down to something with far less weight and take up far less space.

"Can you get out of that?" Lilith didn't answer, but she also didn't stream out through the many openings. "Gonna take that as a 'no.' Hang on, going to hit the release button."

Hit said button and Lilith streamed out of the trap. "I would have appreciated a warning first. That was somewhat frightening."

"Sorry, I just figured it would be faster to see if it could hold you than fret about whether it would work on a parasite or not. This appears to be able to do the trick. We want to capture the parasite so that we don't have to destroy it inside the sun and thereby risk the star itself."

Wruck returned, laden with body armor balls in a giant sack, like the Anciannas version of Santa. There was far too much Fake Santa going on during this trip. "I cleared out all the armories. Hopefully no one will need body armor any time soon."

"Also hopefully Mother can create more."

"I can," Mother confirmed.

"Awesome."

"But it takes some time, so what you have is all that you can use right now."

"Figures and no problem, I'm sure we'll be good." That was a total lie, but leaders were supposed to be all about the positives. "I think we should all wear these, including SuperBun. Let's see how many we can get on each and still be able to move."

"I also found similar armor but designed with face masks with breathing apparatus," Wruck said, pulling these out of his bag of goodies. "They work like the body armor and we should bc able to layer these as well."

"It *is* Christmas!"

Wruck put on a face mask. Still looked like him. "Feels natural enough."

"I can see all of you but can't see the breathing apparatus."

"The entire mask is a filtration system."

"God, Drax is really an artist, isn't he?"

"He is. I never took my armor off," Wruck said, as he put on another set. He flexed. "Normal movement is not impaired so far." He reached for another ball, then stopped and looked at me. "We're going right now, aren't we? Without telling anyone, without saying good-bye."

"We are. If I tell the others what we're doing they'll stop us. If I so much as look at Jeff or the kids I'm not going to be able to go. Because this is pretty much the definition of a suicide mission. But we all know it's the only way."

"I believe that it is," Lilith said. "Otherwise, I would not have been called."

Wruck nodded. "I agree with your mindset. I, too, would have . . . issues seeing the others and not being convinced to try another way."

"Based on the population estimates for this system," Mother said, "and adding the system Kitty has named the Clown Consortium—since the assumption is that it will be engulfed quickly—there are well over two billion lives hanging in the balance right now. Not to mention the fate of the entire galaxy."

"Which is Mother's way of saying there is no other way. Because if there were, she'd be telling us what it is. She's made to protect; the Anti-Mother is her opposite. And the good of the many outweigh the good of the few."

Wruck nodded. "Let's do this."

CHAPTER 82

AS SUPERBUN LET HIS now-internalized Cradi Moon Suit show, my music changed to "Metal Heart" by Garbage and I realized I'd forgotten something else—I'd been given a Moon Suit as a gift.

Went and got said Moon Suit. I already had body armor on and, just before I put the Moon Suit on over it, a thought occurred. "Lilith, I know you wanted to wait, but what if I get all this armor on and you can't join with me?"

"It's unlikely, but I understand the concern. And the time waste if that concern turns out to be reality is not in our best interests. Please be ready."

Made sure I was standing with my feet flat and about shoulder width apart, which was a good thing. Lilith entered me and it was a shock, exhilarating and mind expanding.

I'd felt this before, when ACE had entered me, so long ago now. But with Lilith it was different. ACE had seen the Alpha Centauri and Solaris systems and he'd shown all that to me. Lilith had seen the entire galaxy by now, and seeing that in my mind, all in a few brief seconds, was pretty much the definition of mind-blowing. I never had and I never needed to use drugs— my life ensured that I got all the weird, out-of-body experiences naturally that anyone could hope to have.

Noted something as Lilith calmed down and settled in my mind. It was a little thing, and not relevant to the current situation. Decided I'd ask about it once we found out if I was asking on the living plane or the one where everyone seemed to go when they died.

It is good that you had me join you now, Lilith said in my

head. Entering was slightly impaired by the armor. This is good—it gives us more of a chance of survival.

Great. Just, please, in the immortal words of Han Solo, never tell me the odds.

Realized I needed to do something first. Took off my body armor and ensured that my earbuds were tightly in my ear canals and my phone was in the back pocket of my jeans. Put my first set of body armor back on, put on a face mask—as Wruck had said, it felt fine and definitely more normal than the Moon Suit had the first time—then got into said Moon Suit. It was still weird, but I could breathe and see, though everything looked golden now. Phone wasn't affected, and the song was now "According to Plan" by Augustana so clearly Algar approved. "Wish we had one of these for you, John."

"I can actually create a Moon Suit while also adapting into a star surfer."

"Yay, you're amazing, and is that what the beings who go into the stars are called?"

"As you'd understand it, yes. They are few. They perform some kind of service for the star and the star powers them in return—a symbiotic relationship, at least as far as we know. Most stars don't have a star surfer."

"So, the star surfers are kind of like those little birds that clean hippo teeth? Only it's just a few lucky hippos who get to have said little birds?"

He chuckled. "Yes, I suppose so."

"How do you know them?"

"My wife and I ran across one once, long before I ever came to Earth. So long ago that I'd forgotten about the experience." He looked sad.

"It hurts to remember your wife?" I asked gently.

"Sometimes. But she would agree with what we're doing. And laugh at me for forgetting about the star surfer." He smiled. "It was one of our better shared memories. But it was truly long ago—we were still what you'd call newlyweds."

"What happened?"

"It's a short story, really. When we met the star surfer, she was dying, stranded too far from a proper sun. We were able to help her find another before it was too late."

"How could you forget something like that?"

He shrugged. "I've lived a long time and have done many

things. Some memories are stronger than others, some need to be nudged out, some are gone forever. Fortunately, I did meet the star surfer and this memory was nudged out, or else I would have no way of knowing what to change into."

"She could go into a star and also be with you and not, I don't know, burn you guys up?"

"The star surfers aren't made of flame. They're made of what, for want of a better term, I think you'd call flame retardant."

"It's a freaking awesome galaxy, isn't it?"

"It is. Which is why we're doing this—so it continues to be so."

Wruck and I put on layer after layer of body armor and face masks, continuing to make chitchat about anything other than what we were about to do, while DJ Algar spun a lot of sun songs like Lit's "A Place in the Sun," Two Door Cinema Club's "Sun," Everlast's "Blinded By The Sun"—which meant I asked the Poofs to do us a solid and get us the darkest sunglasses possible, they delivered, and we put them on at around Layer Twenty—Primal Scream's "Deep Hit of Morning Sun," and Elton John's "Don't Let the Sun Go Down on Me."

After about thirty layers, movement started to become impaired. At layer thirty-five and the soundtrack choice of Fountain of Wayne's "Number 45 Sunblock" we both felt we were at maximum while still being able to move decently.

Put a bunch of armor and face masks on SuperBun and, once he said he was pretty much having to work hard to move his ears, we stopped. Then it was time to cover my purse—it was holding the trap, so it had to be hella protected, too.

We discussed whether or not we wanted to bring any of the metals the Cradi had given us along. None of us could come up with a good idea of what they'd do—other than melt, and that quickly—while inside the sun, so we voted no, and only kept the sphere from Cradus and Spehidon.

Realized we had no idea what the natives called this star.

Does it matter? Lilith asked.

It does to me.

Ah, yes. You are Shealla for a reason. You named me, and you were right—it mattered.

My music changed to "Be My Yoko Ono" by the Barenaked Ladies.

"Um, could the star be called Yoko or Ono?"

"Why not?" Wruck asked.

SuperBun said he could hear the name the natives thought and it sounded right.

"Yoko Sun it is, then."

SuperBun corrected. Yoko Ono, both names, as in, this was the Yoko Ono System.

"So many jokes to be made, so little time. Really, sometimes life's not fair, is it?"

CHAPTER 83

FINALLY, WE WERE READY TO GO. And at that moment I realized that we were all insane and going to die. I'd never see my husband, my children, my family, or my friends again. I wouldn't be able to fix the rest of Mephistopheles' errors, and Wruck wouldn't be able to fix those the Anciannas and Z'porrah had made. We were just being idiots.

We needed to find someone else to do this. Someone more powerful, more experienced, someone who wouldn't die in less than a second by going into the center of a sun. Maybe search out a star surfer and see what they had going. Sure, that would probably take too long, but at least we'd still be alive.

Started to hyperventilate and was about to call this entire insane expedition off, when I heard a voice in my head. "Even when you have lost faith in yourself, I will always have faith in you." Mephistopheles had said that to me. And I knew he'd meant it.

I have faith in you as well, Lilith said. Or I would not be risking all. You think right, Kitty. Never forget that.

My music changed to Sting's "If I Ever Lose My Faith in You," his song about never losing faith in love and the existence of God. Algar had faith in me, too. And while the temptation to ask why Algar didn't just snap his fingers right now and save us all was strong, I shoved it aside. It was a dirty job, and we were the team who had to do it. Period.

Took a deep breath and let it out slowly. Made sure that all my stuff and Serene's trap were in my well-protected purse and put it over my neck, picked up SuperBun and cuddled him to my breast with one hand, ensured I had the power cube tightly held in my other, and nodded to Wruck. "Okay, Suicide Squad, let's do this thing." Hey, the Suicide Squad, despite getting the worst missions, usually came back with all members intact. I was good with that.

Wruck shifted into something that seemed to be more like Lilith than anything else—he was glittering in a way that looked white-hot and seemed almost insubstantial. But as he wrapped himself around me, could tell there was substance there and he didn't feel hot. He felt insulated. And I could see through him, meaning I wasn't obstructed. It was as if I was wearing a Wruck Suit.

"Ready," Wruck said from all around me.

"SuperBun, it's up to you now. Concentrate on the Anti-Mother. We need to land as close to her as possible, since we have no idea how long we'll last at the core of Yoko Ono."

Even in this tense a situation, knowing the sun was called Yoko Ono gave me a great deal of humorous satisfaction. It's the little things you treasure.

As SuperBun shared the target in our minds, my music changed to "Superunknown" by Soundgarden, and I triggered the power cube.

We were inside the sun in less than the blink of an eye. The core of the sun was surrounded by a large parasite—it was clear that the Anti-Mother was trying to engulf the core. She was also trying to burrow into the core at the same time. There was a black circle in the middle of the core. It was small, but I could see it clearly. This appeared to be what Anti-Mother was trying to reach, so it didn't take genius to realize that if she did, this was how Yoko Ono would become a black hole.

But the core was fighting back. Had no idea if stars could actually be sentient, but this one at least had a survival instinct of some kind.

It was warm but not hot. Felt a layer of armor burn away and it felt a little warmer. Meaning there was no time to dillydally. "SuperBun, do your thing. Hey, Anti-Mother! Your son says that you're a disappointment. Yoko Ono, hang on, babe, and keep on fighting, we're here to help!"

As an opening gambit, these lines weren't my greatest ever. The consolation was that no one who heard them was likely going to share them with anyone else, seeing as we were all going to be dead sooner as opposed to later. Felt another layer burn off. Wasn't sure if the layers were burning off of just Wruck or off of Wruck and me both, but actively hoped I'd never have to find out for sure unless or until we were back with the others, fully alive and unscathed.

But, lame opening lines or not, felt a surge of hope from Yoko Ono via SuperBun, and the parasite turned its attention to me, for just a moment.

Lilith went into action. Suddenly I wasn't just seeing the core of the sun and the parasite surrounding it—I was *seeing* them, the individual atoms and the way they were moving, how they created a real thing, how there were two different things here, how the parasite's atoms were attacking the core's atoms, how the core's atoms were fighting back, how the core's atoms were losing and being engulfed by the parasite's.

Then saw the subatomic particles. Really wished Chuckie was with us, if only for someone else to rely on with the deeply scientific stuff. However, he wasn't, so it was time to pull up my Big Girl Panties and represent.

"Go away, insignificant creatures," Anti-Mother said.

"Make us." I was basically managing schoolyard-level stuff. Which meant I should have been ignored. My music changed to "Small Talk and Pride" by Olivia Newton-John. Took this to mean that Algar approved of the Schoolyard Taunting Method and that I should keep it up.

And I wasn't ignored. Schoolyard Taunting Method for the win. "You dare speak to me in that way?" The Anti-Mother sounded pissed. Interesting.

"I do. I'm insolent, me. Whatcha gonna do about it?" Another layer burned away and I was warmer. Didn't think about it. Well, as much as I could.

"I will destroy you."

"Blah, blah, blah. You're a relic, an insignificant backup singer in a band that was over centuries ago. Your power was never your own, and it's not your own now. You're trying to steal power, which is the only way your kind ever gets it, because you're not actually powerful in your own right."

Felt SuperBun communicating with Yoko Ono in a way similar to how I did with ACE or, now, Lilith—as if he were inside Yoko Ono's head, or whatever the equivalent was for a star. Also felt him starting to worm his way into the Anti-Mother's mind, through a back door. He could do this because I was distracting the Anti-Mother enough that she wasn't paying attention to any of the others.

The Anti-Mother's subatomic particles were zooming at a

high rate and while most of them were still around Yoko Ono, a portion were pulled away, heading for me. "I will engulf you first."

Another layer gone. "Sure you will. I mean, you'll try. I get why you want to, of course. Because I'm more powerful than you."

SuperBun needs us to coordinate something very carefully, Lilith said. Once enough of the Anti-Mother is pulled away from Yoko Ono, we have to throw SuperBun and the sphere from Cradus and Spehidon, accurately, at the core. Aim for the black spot.

Wanted to whine and say no. But felt SuperBun's resoluteness and determination that this was the right way. Couldn't ask him to be less than he was, and he was a hero. This was what heroes did. My music changing to "My Hero" by the Foo Fighters was also something of a confirmation. Got it.

Love for me radiated from SuperBun. Sent the same right back to him.

Fortunately, SuperBun was in my throwing hand already. Unfortunately, my hands were kind of full and dropping the Z'porrah power cube was *not* an option. Therefore, how I was going to get the sphere was another story. One I'd worry about once I had a clear shot.

Another layer burned away. Be prepared, Lilith said. I am matching our frequencies to that of the star itself. It will feel odd to you, but it will keep us all alive longer. John is around you and, due to his abilities, I can alter him as well.

If the surge when Lilith had entered me was mind-blowing, this change was so much more that I felt like I was the entire galaxy or that the entire galaxy was contained within me or both. I was one with Yoko Ono, saw how the fusion worked to power the star, understood how the black spot at the core could be triggered and how it could be kept dormant, saw the heat going to the planets, saw every single thing on each planet, down to their subatomic particles, and yet it was all instantly comprehensible. No wonder the Superconsciousness Society had rules.

Saw all the other stars in the galaxy, all the billions of them. Yoko Ono was one of the rarest—a sentient star. But her powers were weak—no star surfer had visited her in a long time to give her an exchange of powers—and that was why the Anti-Mother had targeted her. Yoko Ono needed help to become all that she could be.

"In this form . . . I can see . . . what Yoko Ono needs," Wruck said. "And I believe we can give it to her. When I'm in a form I can do what the form is capable of doing."

SuperBun said that he was definitely part of that help and that this was, realistically, what he'd been created to do. And because I was holding him, Lilith had been able to make his atoms match Yoko Ono's as well. He saw what she needed also. And she needed all of us in different ways.

Figured physical action was going to be what I was bringing to the table, and knew I could pull the Anti-Mother away from Yoko Ono if I could get her to move just a bit more.

The layers of body armor were still burning off, but it didn't matter, because we were one with the star. It couldn't hurt us because that would be harming itself. The only way we'd be hurt was if the Anti-Mother succeeded. And we were not going to allow that to happen.

My music changed to "Mr. Shuck and Jive" by Art Garfunkel. Realized that time was going slower for us or faster for us or just running differently than normal, because I was hearing the full songs being played but time didn't seem to be passing along with the songs. Or something. Chose not to try to figure it out but instead to take the hint.

"You're ugly and you dressed your son funny."

"What?" the Anti-Mother roared as she moved more of herself toward me. "You dare insult me? You who are nothing more than an insignificant worm? You dare insult my son? He who was the greatest leader this galaxy has ever known?"

Was more than amazed that this level of taunting was having such an effect. However, the Anti-Mother had been alone in space for a really long time and no one had probably ever spoken to her like this when she was alive. Maybe it was the novelty of the approach that was getting to her. Or the lameness.

Then again, if faded memory served, I hadn't been much more scintillating when dealing with the living Mephistopheles. Maybe the Schoolyard Taunting Method was just my best go-to option. However, since my motto was "Whatever Works," I was good with how things were going, particularly since we were not turning to dust at this moment.

"You're the epitome of insignificant, lady. No one even remembers who you are and no one cares, either."

"They will care. I will show them, then bring my son to me! He who conquered all!"

"You mean he who destroyed your star and billions of people

in a fit of pique? We're talking about the same guy, right? Mephistopheles, Lord of the Fuglies, who is totally disappointed in his Mommy Dearest right now."

"As if *you* would know?"

"He told me so. Personally."

"As if he would deign to speak with the likes of you?"

"Oh, he more than deigns. We hang. We're kind of BFFs in a really weird way. And he's not happy that you're still on this pathetic kill 'em all kick, destined to ensure that you fail and die in a less than spectacular way. Then we won't mourn you at all. Just in case you weren't sure. And by 'we' I include Mephistopheles."

"I will enjoy destroying you." The Anti-Mother was getting seriously pissed—could tell by the way her particles were moving. We were close to where I'd have a clear shot to hit Yoko Ono. There was nothing for it. Had to put the Z'porrah power cube in my purse and pull the sphere out.

Looked at the cube as I did so. For the first time, saw every aspect of the cube and comprehended it all. How to work it, what it could do, how to change it to do whatever I needed, and more were burned into my mind. Figuratively, at least at this moment. Didn't want to think about later moments.

Felt Wruck sending some kind of essence toward Yoko Ono. Followed the trail of it, too, because even telepathic thoughts and similar things had subatomic particles. Who knew? I hadn't, but accepted it as reality since that's what my reality was now. All this was great, too, because it gave me a trajectory to follow.

Put SuperBun on my shoulder while I carefully placed the cube in my purse and pulled out the sphere. Saw Cradus and Spehidon, their essences, what they really were. They were both beautiful, different from people just as Yoko Ono was, special in ways that were hard for a human brain to describe and something a superconsciousness brain took for granted. And they were both ready to do whatever they needed to in order to assist.

All of this had taken less than a second, because being joined to Lilith and the star as we currently were meant I was moving far faster than warp speed. But the music sounded normal. Time was weird in this situation and I needed to stop worrying about it. All my focus needed to be on the key situation.

"You can't destroy anything. You're nothing but a parasite. And an ugly one at that."

That did it. Taunts that wouldn't affect anyone over the age of sixteen were working on her like a charm. Chose not to complain—I was all about the universe actually doing me a solid.

The Anti-Mother moved toward me. Despite being very much like jellyfish blobs, parasites moved fast when they wanted to, and she did. She also moved enough of herself away from Yoko Ono that I now had a very wide strike zone to aim for.

But I was one with the star, the galaxy, the universe, and that meant I was faster. Went into a windup and tossed the sphere of Cradus and Spehidon at Yoko Ono. Direct hit. Wruck's trajectory of power had been quite the assist. Go team.

Grabbed SuperBun off of my shoulder, kissed the top of his head through what was left of our armor, went into another windup, and tossed him as well. Another direct hit. I was "on fire" so to speak. Maybe I should talk to the Diamondbacks whenever we got home. That was me, focused on the potential for survival.

"Prepare to be utterly destroyed," the Anti-Mother snarled.

Moved into a fighting stance, Metallica's "Fight Fire with Fire" on my airwaves, then said what I'd said often in these circumstances.

"Yeah? Bring it."

CHAPTER 84

THE ANTI-MOTHER LUNGED TOWARD ME. Part of her was still around Yoko Ono but the rest was stretched out, reaching for me.

But I'd been hoping for this and therefore prepared. "John," I said quietly, "let go of me . . . now!"

He did as ordered and I leaped forward and grabbed her.

If we'd been on Earth, this would have meant I had icky parasite all over me and was likely to become a superbeing. But here, with my ability to see as Lilith saw, could spot what to grab, how to move, to actually hold onto the parasite and keep it contained. And I had enough body armor left that I couldn't really feel her. Drax Industrial totally for the win.

As we started wrestling, realized for the first time that we weren't standing on anything. This might have thrown me, but when Lilith and I had met, I'd been fighting against her vessel, Uma, aka Bitch Leader, in what had been a weird, invisible sphere where up and down had no real meaning. Meaning I'd had a fight to the death like this before, nothing to get freaked out about.

And we *were* wrestling. It was a good thing that I'd been a jock in school, because while track and field was my sport, I'd had an interest in all the others, too. I'd had friends on the wrestling team, and Mom and Chuckie both had pushed for me to learn how to escape from wrestling holds well before I started taking kung fu, so wrestling with a slippery parasite wasn't all that weird. At least on the Kitty Weird Scale, at any rate.

Since I wasn't the goal, the Anti-Mother also wasn't trying to join with me, which was a huge positive. Maybe she couldn't because of the body armor or just had no interest. She *was* trying to smother me, to cover me up and engulf me. Could see her atoms rearranging to disintegrate me in some way, and saw that they'd be able to do it, if I couldn't figure out how to win, or at least how to keep her off balance.

The Anti-Mother was a much larger parasite than I was used to, so she had a real shot at this. She was the size of a beach towel, and I was used to parasites being no bigger than a medium-sized watermelon, if that big. And a beach towel could wrap up a smaller human, and I was a smaller human.

But the beach towel comparison gave me an idea. Grabbed her top two corners, so to speak, and started rolling them like you did with a towel when you were going to make a rat's tail and snap someone with it. Did this at hyperspeed, made even faster by the fact that with Lilith inside me I was at warp speed already.

The Anti-Mother hadn't been expecting this tactic, and she struggled to keep her equilibrium. Saw her start to lose her grip on Yoko Ono, as Wruck, now not having to hold onto me, went closer to the core, doing something that I couldn't risk focusing on.

Didn't see SuperBun, but I felt him in my mind. With Lilith and Wruck's help, he was doing what the Anti-Mother wanted to do—he was joining with Yoko Ono while keeping this knowledge from Anti-Mother. Took a moment to be impressed. Then had to immediately kick Anti-Mother in what I hoped was a tender spot, since her bottom half got around my legs.

This went on for what might have been ages, might have been seconds, but music indicated was less than five minutes. Chose not to care about how time was or wasn't passing here. Had to keep on fighting, distracting, making the Anti-Mother focus on only me.

"Now!" Wruck shouted, as my music changed to "Throw It Away" by Joe Jackson. Wrenched at the Anti-Mother with all my strength and she pulled away from the core.

Let go of her, reached into my purse, grabbed the cage, triggered it, and did what I was being told—threw it away, at the parasite.

Results were, happily, immediate.

The cage expanded, went around the parasite, snapped shut, and went small. As I'd done with Lilith, dove to make sure I caught it before it fell into the star or into space or whatever. As my hand closed around it, Wruck wrapped around me.

Time to go, Lilith said. We only have moments.

Dropped the cage into my purse and grabbed the Z'porrah power cube. Had to have a destination and needed to think of it in less than a split second, as I felt our body armor burn away much faster now. Had to be careful, though, and pick the right place, or else we'd end up dead or far away from the others.

Closed my eyes and thought of the one place that always meant I was safe.

CHAPTER 85

"OOOF!" JEFF SAID, as we landed in his arms. "What the hell?"

Opened my eyes. We were back, in the *Distant Voyager*, in the mess hall. Well, three of us were back. "Check the sun!"

"Why do you weigh so much more than normal?" Jeff asked as he put me down carefully. The song ended and another one didn't start up. Clearly we were back and, hopefully, back to normal. Well, as normal as we ever got.

"Because John is with me." Noted that Denise and the younger kids weren't in evidence, but all the older kids were here.

Wruck unwrapped and went back to his standard form for hanging around with all of us. Jeff wasn't the only one staring.

"Why are you both in Moon Suits?" Christopher asked.

"Long story. Look, someone, anyone, check the sun. Right now."

Jeff's eyes narrowed. "What did you two just do?" He jerked. "And what the hell is inside of you, Kitty?"

"Lilith."

At this name, everyone who'd been involved with Operation Invasion gasped and most of them went for weapons.

Put up the paw. They all stopped. Even in this situation the One True FLOTUS Power still worked. "Lilith is on our side."

"She'd force you to say that," Reader said.

Looked at Wruck. "Your turn."

He went into Anciannas form, full wingspan out impressively. "Check the sun!" he thundered.

Had to give it to human and A-C hindbrains. When a being that looks like an angel says to jump, every human and A-C asks how high. Apparently this worked on the Ignotforstans, too, because they, like the others, were racing to give us sun specs. Or they were running out of the room in terror. Really, it could go either way.

Started peeling off the remaining layers of body armor and face masks. "Gustav, let me be the first to say that you are a designer of the highest order, and you are not allowed to take a contract from anyone other than the United States, specifically Centaurion Division. Amazing stuff. We, ha, burned through more than a few of them, but the body armor is fantastic. The face masks are, ha, stellar, too."

"Baby, are you alright?" Jeff asked, sounding incredibly worried. "What are you talking about?"

We were not gone as long for them as it seems to us, Lilith said. As you noted, time is different in the center of a star. And yes, before you ask, any star, not just one at risk of becoming a black hole. Which Yoko Ono will now not become.

"Oh. Gotcha. Um, Mother, you want to tell everyone what just happened? I assume that you, at least, were monitoring."

"Yes, Kitty, I was. Well done."

"What do you mean by that?" Jeff asked suspiciously.

"Kitty and John, assisted by Lilith, took SuperBun into the sun."

"Well, that was succinct and to the point, Mother. Perhaps not nearly as impressively told as it could be, though."

"What did you do with SuperBun?" Lizzie asked, sounding anguished.

Had all the armor and the Moon Suit off now, so went to her and hugged her. "I let him be the hero he always was and wanted to be."

Stop being upset, a voice that was kind of like SuperBun's and kind of not said in my mind. Saw everyone else's expressions—this voice was speaking in everyone's mind. We did what we had to do.

"SuperBun? Yoko Ono?"

"Why are you asking about the woman who broke up the Beatles?" Christopher asked.

"Absolutely zero awareness of popular culture but that pseudofact you know? Yoko was just in the wrong place at the right time. However, now isn't the time. No, the star of this system is called Yoko Ono by the inhabitants."

This earned the appropriate stunned silence, though I could

see Reader and Tim desperately trying not to crack up. Raj sidled over to Christopher and started telling him about the Yoko Situation. He was talking softly and at hyperspeed, but with Lilith inside me I could hear him and the speed of the words didn't make me sick.

Not anymore. We aren't SuperBun or Yoko Ono now. We're combined, something like the way that Dopey and Grumpy combined. Better, I think. Whole. Complete.

Got into my purse and pulled the trap out. The Anti-Mother was definitely still in there. "Um, does SuperStar work as a name for you?" Heard Lilith chuckle in my mind.

Yes. We like it.

"Great. SuperStar, do I put this into a vat of pure grain alcohol or do I do something else with the Anti-Mother?"

"What in God's name is going on?" Jeff asked Wruck quietly. "Is the sun's degradation affecting everyone's minds?"

"Hang on a moment, SuperStar." Turned to Jeff. "Geez. Okay, here's the fast recap. No one had any good ideas, I had one, talked to John about it, we decided to go for it, Lilith came to help because she's not evil anymore and we needed a superconsciousness as part of the team. We went into the sun, Lilith and I fought the Anti-Mother parasite while John helped SuperBun join with Yoko Ono, I trapped the Anti-Mother in this cage that looks like a whiffle ball that Serene created, we're back without SuperBun because he's now part of the new sun called SuperStar, the day is saved, the end. And I want to know if I'm destroying the Anti-Mother or not. I'm asking SuperStar what to do because I'm not sure if I should trust my decisions regarding a parasite of this magnitude."

Everyone, to a person, other than Wruck, gaped at me.

Heard a chuckle in my head. It will be easier to just give you all the knowledge.

"Easier isn't necessarily better. Just sharing that because it's in the Superconsciousness Society Handbook, I think. I could try telling it with more details."

Saw everyone other than Wruck jerk, blink, gasp, and relax. Then they all stared at us. Clearly SuperStar had decided that Superconsciousness Rules didn't apply today.

"You went into a star?" Jeff asked. Could tell he wasn't sure if he should be thrilled, freaking out, hugging me, or bellowing.

"We did. And, ta-da, we're back. Unscathed, too. And they say miracles don't happen. Moon Suits and Drax Industrial

Battle Armor are a great combination. Having Lilith inside me also raised our survival chances astronomically. And John knowing how to turn into a star surfer was a happy bonus. Oh, and having the most powerful rabbit telepath in the galaxy was also one for the win column."

"You could have died," Lizzie said quietly.

"I know. Frankly, we expected to die. It's why we're kind of giddy right now."

"Then why did you go?"

Stroked her head. "The good of the many outweigh the good of the few. I know you know that. Besides, my husband and our three children were among those who were in danger."

She looked at me in a way I hadn't seen before. Realized that she looked proud. "Yeah, that's true." She hugged me. "I'm glad you made it back . . . Mom."

Hugged her back tightly and enjoyed the moment. "Me too."

"Paul," Jeff said, as Lizzie and I stopped hugging, "what do you think we should do with the parasite?"

Gower shook his head. "I understand why Kitty's asking SuperStar for counsel. In this case, I honestly can only think that we destroy the parasite. I'm not sure that's the right answer, though."

"Serene, is there a way to lock this trap so the Anti-Mother can't get out? Kind of like they did in *Ghostbusters* only without the easy release that can be orchestrated by an insufferable busybody at the worst possible time?"

"You're so lucky Raj made all of us watch every movie you like," Serene said with a laugh. "I have an idea." She zipped off and was right back, with several other traps. She triggered one and had it encircle the trap I was holding, then she locked it. She did the same with the rest of the traps.

Was left holding a larger whiffle ball. "Um, this is sort of like Russian nesting dolls. It doesn't take much to open these—one turbulent patch and we have a seriously pissed off parasite on the loose inside the ship."

"Oh, I know," Serene said calmly. "I can put more traps on, but they could all be opened. However, this is a good stopgap for now. Once we decide what we're doing with the parasite, I'll put this into something that can't be easily opened. Or you'll put it into a vat of grain alcohol."

That decision has to be yours, SuperStar said. The Anti-Mother is evil, yes, but without her, this system would never have been saved. Because Yoko Ono was dying, but as SuperStar, we will live for a very long time.

"So, from evil comes good," White said. "It's fitting."

"What happens now?" Kreaving asked, before any of my family or friends could say anything else.

Now, SuperStar said, we're moving.

"Um, excuse me?"

I'm taking this system to Spehidon and Cradus. We will become a binary system and Spehidon will have people.

"You can do that?"

Yes. Solar systems move all the time. Some move more than others. Some are drawn into other systems. This happens with galaxies, too. We're powerful enough to move of our own accord and we know where we're going—part of Cradus and Spehidon resides inside of us now. We belong together.

"But the native people live on top of planets. They aren't the kind that can live within a gas giant."

Right now, no, they aren't. But they are evolving. What was taken to be feathers is the beginning of their transition into more ethereal forms. They will become beautiful birdlike creatures who will need what Spehidon can offer them, because as they evolve they are draining their planets and, once fully evolved, will have no planets left.

Lilith showed me the atomic makeup of the natives. They were definitely changing and, since she was inside of me, could tell that they were evolving in a way that would indeed make them more like the Vrierst than like any of us. "Won't that take a long time, though?"

Maybe. But time is different for suns, planets, and moons. Spehidon and Cradus are overjoyed that we are coming to join them.

"You've talked to them?"

Yes. For my mind now they are not all that far away. And, as I said, they are a part of us.

"Wow. Um, can we head off before you move the entire neighborhood? We have that other stop we need to make, if you remember."

I remember. We will wait until you leave. And, as Cradus and Spehidon told you, you will always have a home with us, if you choose it or need it.

Sniffled. "My little bunny's all grown up."

SuperStar laughed. Yes, I suppose I am. Or just born. It depends on your perspective.

"Everything does." Heaved a sigh. "I'm going to miss snuggling you."

That's why you have Peter. We'll always have Nazez and Yoko Ono.

"We will, won't we?" Blinked my eyes a lot. Probably they were just watering because they'd gotten dry from being inside the sun.

CHAPTER 86

THE POSITIVES OF SUPERSTAR having given everyone the knowledge of what happened was that Wruck and I didn't need to spend time with explanations and, more importantly, arguments. The fact that we had to make a fast getaway now didn't hurt, either.

The decision was made to get the crew of the *Eknara* home first, then figure out where the hell Ixtha was. Decided I had things to do that required privacy, so bowed out of the discussion and the determination of where Ignotforsta was in comparison to where we were.

Went to our rooms. Thankfully, no one was there. Looked just like we'd left it what was really only a short time ago, though it felt like weeks. "You want out now?" I asked Lilith.

It's probably wise. Will the others try to use a trap on me?

"I won't allow it. They saw you help, I think we're good."

You should sit or lie down.

"Don't worry, I remember." Lay down on the bed. "Are you zooming off the moment you're out or are you sticking around?"

That depends.

"Just in case you take off, then, first off, can you tell us where Ignotforsta is and/or the fastest path to get there? And secondly, when you first entered me and I saw everything, I thought I saw a solar system that was floating outside of the galaxy, all by itself."

I can and you did.

"*Will* you help us get the right coordinates for Ignotforsta? And what's up with that system?"

I will remain and tell you about it when you wake up.

"Promise?"

Yes.

"Holding you to it." Then I relaxed and closed my eyes.

Felt Lilith leaving me, filtering herself out of my mind and body. It felt like a loss but also exhilarating at the same time. It was a lot to take, though, and I was lying down because the normal reaction to birthing a superconsciousness or a demigod was to do what I did—pass out.

As before, when I'd transferred ACE from Brian to me and then from me to Gower, saw things. These things were different, though.

Saw the solar system I'd spotted and asked Lilith about. One big sun with what looked like only two viable planets, though there were a lot of moons and dwarf planets present. The two big planets were separated by an impressive asteroid belt. One planet was blue and green and looked a lot like Earth only at least four times bigger. The other was red and orange and resembled Mars, only it looked very much alive.

This system was floating away from the Milky Way, out there in the blackness between galaxies, the No Man's Land of Space. It looked lost and lonely.

"You did well."

Looked around. Once again I was sitting next to Mephistopheles.

"Yeah? Thanks. You telling me you had faith in me really mattered. Thank you for that."

"Of course. And it was and remains true. I was touched that you told my mother we were Best Friends Forever."

"I'm just hella relieved I managed to scratch that clue out."

He smiled at me. As usual, creepy and sweet at the same time. "I knew you would."

"What do we do with her?"

"I find it interesting that all of you are struggling with the decision."

"Dude, it's one thing when you're in the middle of the life-or-death fight. It's another when you've captured your enemy."

"My mother would counsel killing a captured enemy."

"Which is why we're thinking about it. I honestly don't know what to do. It's why I'm asking you for *your* counsel about it."

"As SuperStar said, that decision remains yours. The humane choice is sometimes hard to determine."

That definitely felt like a statement preggers with hidden meaning. "Is keeping her in a cage more humane than killing her? I mean, we can't let her go. She didn't come across as redeemable."

"And yet you just worked with someone you would have said was irredeemable a few years ago."

"I guess, though ACE told us Lilith was scattered and one with the galaxy, which is different from letting loose a powerful parasite bent on total galactic domination."

"This is true."

Groaned. "You're not helping."

"You always need less help than you think you do."

"Yeah? I'm pretty sure that I need more help than you all want to tell me I do." Was certain, for example, that my Suicide Squad had had a lot of help from a source that liked to pretend he wasn't getting involved.

"I believe you all have a saying—God helps those who help themselves."

"Yeah, we do."

"Then you had to take action or God would not have helped."

"Is *that* the story being passed around in Powers That Be Land? Impressive spin."

"As you like to say, whatever works."

"We have two more stops that I know of. One to drop Wheatles and his crew off on their home planet, and the other to find Ixtha. Any chance you can give me clues for what we'll be facing when we get there?"

"A hero's welcome."

Sighed. "I meant when we got to Ixtha, not when we dropped off Wheatles and Company."

Mephs patted the top of my head. "Keep on thinking right. And remember—I will always have faith in you. You have survived the nonsurvivable. Now, you can do anything." And with that, he was gone.

Opened my eyes. All the colors of the Pantone Matching System were floating around me. "Are you alright?" Lilith asked worriedly. "You were passed out for longer than I'd have expected."

"Fine, just having my usual weird dream experience." Considered the dream. "Do you know about the DreamScape?"

"Yes. Were you in that?"

"Unsure. So, if you promise you're sticking around to tell me about that lost solar system, we should probably help the others get the coordinates for Ignotforsta so that we can get those folks home."

"I can do that without you. While waiting for you to wake up,

Mother confirmed that they no longer see me as a threat. And you should probably rest longer."

"Okay." Yawned. "Wow. Yeah, I guess this all took a lot out of me."

Lilith laughed. "I took myself out of you, and that is tiring for the vessel. You rest, I'll be back shortly." She sparkled off.

Tried to go back to sleep. Nada. Probably because I wanted confirmation or denial. Got up and headed for the supply closet. Closed the door tightly behind me. "I know that, despite everything, someone had to be helping us."

Algar appeared. "Why would you say that? You prepared impressively. And you had a superconsciousness assisting. What else could you have needed?"

"We were inside a freaking sun. I have to figure that we only survived that because someone snapped their fingers and made us invulnerable."

"Oh, I doubt it. I'm sure it's possible, but that seems rather far-fetched."

Considered things. "Or else someone planted a memory of an event that Wruck never actually experienced."

"That seems possible," Algar said noncommittally. "Or it was as he said, buried and needing to be nudged out."

"Someone might have given Lilith the suggestion to match frequencies with Yoko Ono, too. Maybe SuperBun got some tips, as well. Bottom line, I don't think we went in there without protection."

"Perhaps you did," Algar said. "Wouldn't that be impressive?"

"Impressively unlikely."

He shrugged. "Star surfers are real. That's not their real name, at least, not the name they call themselves, but they exist. And they do just as John Wruck said—they go into stars. Sentient stars only, though."

"How is it there are sentient suns, planets, and moons?"

"It's a fascinating galaxy. Most of them are."

Gave up. "Thanks for making that memory a positive one for John."

"Well, whoever did it, I'm sure they saw no reason to cause pain."

"Yeah, about that. What do we do with the Anti-Mother?"

"There are worse things than death."

"Yeah. She's in a prison like they want to put you in, isn't she?"

"Oh no. Hers is far more humane. But it's still a cage."

"So we should kill her?"

"That's up to you."

"Ugh. Why will no one tell us the right thing to do?"

Algar patted my knee. "Why would we do that, when the person who thinks right is right here?" Then he snapped his fingers and was gone.

"I wasn't done. Why did you give me, then take away, a large manila envelope?"

No reply, but an envelope appeared where Algar had been sitting. Picked it up. Looked like "the" envelope, seeing as it had the same marks from being inside my purse that the other had.

Heaved a sigh and pulled out the contents.

"Holy crap."

CHAPTER 87

ONCE AGAIN FREAKING WITH no one to talk to about the information I was sitting on. Well, staring at. Same difference. And I needed help interpreting why I had this information, too, and what, exactly, said info was trying to tell me.

Decided that I needed to get this envelope back into my purse pronto, though. Used hyperspeed to get back to our rooms, which were happily still void of anyone else. Shoved the envelope into my purse, then tried to figure out what to do.

"Kitty," Mother said, "we are preparing for takeoff."

"Um, is there any way in the galaxy that you'll let Jerry handle my position for this part of the trip?"

"Are you still tired from birthing Lilith?" Mother asked solicitously.

Lied like the human I was. "Yes. Really tired. I'm worried about my reflexes. And things."

"Then, in this case, yes. You will need to recover by the time we've identified where Ixtha is, however."

"Promise I'll be fine by then."

"You may have time." Mother sounded worried. "I still cannot reproduce the coordinates."

"No worries, I have some ideas." Did I ever. No clue if those ideas were any good, of course, but hope liked to spring eternal.

"Good. Please strap in, just in case. All beds have the ability to become crash couches."

"Gotcha and will do. You can sign off in here, by the way, I don't need monitoring."

"As you wish."

"Thanks, I'll call if I need you."

The intercom went dead. Hadn't been paying attention

during the trip to see if I could actually tell when the com system was off, so just took it on faith that the reprogramming Hacker International had done was working.

There was no way I was lying down. Not because I wanted to be tossed around the room if things were bad, but because I was only going to have a short time before someone came looking for me.

On the plus side, this was going to give me an opportunity to do what I'd been lax about doing for too long.

Went over to the thing that had been created for me on Cradus—a really amazing standing three-way mirror. Spent some time doing little adjustments while I sat exactly in the middle of the mirrors. Even if it didn't work, this was the most beautiful three-way mirror in existence, made of silver with gold filigree, pewter trim, copper backing, and mercury mirrors. Had no idea how the mercury was held in place, but it rippled if I touched it.

Finally got the mirrors into place and used the lovely lead locking mechanisms I'd asked for to hold it as I wanted. Just in time—felt the ship beginning takeoff.

Jumped onto the bed and was able to get under the automatic restraints at the last moment. Good thing, too, since this takeoff was more like the one we'd had leaving Earth and I was definitely being pressed deep into the mattress.

However, because it was a planned takeoff, versus Mother's Snatch and Grab Special, the pressure didn't last too long. As soon as I could tell we were in space, I triggered the restraint release and got back to my business. And I had a lot of business to get back to. Of which the contents of the Super-Secret Envelope were a part, but not all, that I had to take care of.

Sat down cross-legged in the middle of the mirrors again and stared at myself. Only, not really. Per how the Jamie in Bizarro World had taught me, if you focused just right, you could see the multiverse out of the corners of your eyes.

Took me a little bit, since I was kind of out of practice, but finally, as Mother did a general "we're in space but not going to warp" announcement, I saw them.

The multiverse spread out and the worlds started to flash past. Since my time in Bizarro World I'd gotten good at using this system and now knew how to make the Universe Wheel spin faster or slower, and even how to make it stop and hone in on a specific world.

The key was to never turn your head. You turned to look, you lost them all. Find them via peripheral vision, remain unfocused straight ahead, and then you'd "see" the world you were doing a deep dive on in front of you. It stayed as long as you didn't focus straight ahead, which was a learned skill, but one that I'd managed to master quickly.

My first stop was always Bizarro World. Sometimes I saw Jamie at the mirrors, but, these days, usually not, and today was no exception. Which made me happy. Searched for her and Other Me in this universe. Found them with Chuckie, Charlie, Max, and a little brother whose name I didn't know. They were at their home in Australia celebrating something, with pretty much all the good people I'd met while I was there. Jamie had Stripes draped around her shoulders and I noted that there were a lot of Poofs in evidence, too. It was a nice scene, and meant I could stop worrying about that universe for a while.

Started flipping through the universes again. Most of them were a lot like mine and Bizarro World—pretty normal, all things considered. There were a few that were really out there where Jamie and I didn't exist—like the Dinosaur World that indicated the Z'porrah had won that round on Earth, and what I called Genocide World, where Hitler and his kind had all been victorious throughout the ages, which was the most depressing world out of the entire multiverse.

There were some that looked really cool where we did exist, though, including one that had a lot of blimps and such and seemed far more technologically advanced than ours, one where technology didn't seem apparent at all and was almost like all the descriptions of fairyland, one where the railroads were still king and cars didn't exist but horses remained in high use that I thought of as Westworld, only hopefully without all the animatronics and killings, and one that was incredibly futuristic, as if we'd gotten jetpacks and flying cars way back when they were promised to us the first time.

The Universe Wheel spun quickly, but felt there were more universes now than there had been in the past. Per how universes supposedly split off, that made sense. But even so, because of the mirrors, could see them all in a second or two and comprehend what I needed to.

Normally centered my search on Jamie, because in every world she was in, so was I. But I needed to look at everything, so I pulled back and, as the Wheel spun again, looked at the solar system, then the solar neighborhood, then the galaxy.

And spotted something. There was a dark mass in the majority of them. And it boded.

Focused in on it in random universes and the mass was always the same—it resembled a hazy wolf or dragon head, some kind of predatory thing. Not all that large, but large enough—it was hard to get a fix on its actual size because I was seeing it floating in space. This one was floating outside of Earth's atmosphere.

Flipped through the Wheel again, now only looking for the black mass. Found it almost everywhere—though, interestingly enough, it was absent from the Dinosaur and Genocide Worlds—but it was never in the same place. It always gave me a bad feeling, though, whenever I looked at it. Though, admittedly, not as bad as the feelings looking at Genocide World gave me. That place looked like the worst place imaginable to be hanging out. Sincerely hoped I'd never end up going there.

Tried to drill down on it but couldn't manage it. Whether I didn't have the skill, the black mass didn't want me to see it, or some other reason, just couldn't do it. Wondered if I should try harder to see what this was and gave it a shot. Still nada. And I was likely running out of time, so had to focus on the things that mattered right now.

So, gave up on the black mass and did one more run through the Wheel to see if I could spot any world—well, really, any Jamie and/or Whatever Version of Moi world—that might be desperately in need of my services. And to get the feeling of dread that seeing that black mass gave me just once more for fun.

Noted that the world with all the blimps and such really seemed like a steampunk world, which was cool, and also noted that there seemed to be a giant space war of some kind going on, but didn't get any signs that I was needed.

Fairyland seemed cool, and my family was doing something that looked like a ceremony to the Earth or similar, but, again, didn't seem to need me.

Westworld looked interesting, and there was a lot of action of various kinds, but my family lived on a huge ranch with a lot of security, so while it might still be the Old West there or whatever, we looked safe.

The futuristic world seemed utopian, and I really wondered if that was the goal for us on this trip—to see how utopian societies worked and emulate them. But my gut, and life experience, said that utopia only worked until the first nasty dude with a gun showed up to take over. Either way, nothing other than serenity seemed to be going on there.

The downside to the mirrors was that you couldn't see what was going on in your own world too often, so I couldn't tell if the black mass was here, too.

Took a few moments to enjoy the various worlds where my family life was clearly idyllic. I was married to Chuckie or Reader in the majority of these worlds, but not all.

Noted who Chuckie was married to in the worlds where it wasn't me and was happy to see it was the same person every time. Clearly it was a small world for some of us. Though not for Reader, who had an array of different partners if he wasn't married to me. Being the most gorgeous human around had its benefits.

There was one world I spotted where I was apparently married to Buchanan. Decided to never mention that to Jeff or Adriana. Still had a few where I was married to guys I didn't know. The ones where I was married to gals I still didn't know seemed just as happy as those where I was married to guys. I was apparently a great spouse regardless of who lucked into marrying me.

Self-congratulation time over, had to try to do the other necessary thing. Find Naomi.

"Are you there?" I asked softly, as I let the Wheel spin on and didn't focus on any world specifically. "I need to talk to someone who understands."

Nothing, not that I'd expected it. Hoped for it, yes, but expected, never.

"I'm sure you know, but the Cradi, the crew of the *Eknara*, and the Yoko Ono solar system are all going to be fine. Thank you for helping us help them."

Nada.

Heaved a sigh. "I'm sitting on vital information that I have no way of explaining to the others. I'm not even sure if I'm looking at this stuff right, but it appears to be a set of galaxy maps that are very different from the ones we have, seeing as they all look like photographs. In some of them, there's a solar system that's floating outside the galaxy itself, but it's not in all of them. I spotted this same solar system when Lilith went inside of me. I have no idea if it matters or not, but it sort of seems like it must. And I'm not sure what the maps are trying to tell me but it's clear that, whatever it is, it's vital."

Still nothing.

"And we lost the coordinates to get to Ixtha. I realize that you wanted us to handle everything we've just done, and I have no complaint or argument about that, but everyone feels we need to get to Ixtha, and we don't know how."

Was expecting the lack of response I got this time.

"And I don't know what to do with the Anti-Mother. Dropping her into a vat of grain alcohol, though satisfying, seems wrong. But I don't know how to ensure that someone doesn't accidentally release her."

Saw an image of Cradus. Interesting. Well, the Anti-Mother was, realistically, the biggest threat to the entire ship, crew, and galaxy, so Naomi responding to this request of mine made sense. Not that anyone else had been remotely interested in helping. Of course, the clue—since I seriously doubted that Naomi was suggesting we make another stop at Cradus—had come after I'd said that killing the Anti-Mother felt wrong, though. Maybe that was why she'd superconsciousnessed up and actually handed out said clue. So, had to figure out what she meant.

The obvious reared its head and waved at me. Better slow than never, that was my motto.

"Oh. Duh, and thank you. I cannot tell you how much I appreciate your giving me an actual idea for what to do. I doubt it'll kill her, but it should contain her successfully and safely, and that's what we need."

The image of Cradus disappeared. In its place was the face of a beautiful Dazzler with ebony skin, kind eyes, and a lovely smile. Naomi.

"We still miss you so much. Everyone's managing, though. Abigail and Jerry seem solid, just like Paul and James. Your parents are hanging in. Chuckie's doing well with Nathalie, and I assume you approve or I'd know about it."

Naomi laughed, not that I heard a sound, and nodded.

"Good. Things seem reasonably calm in the multiverse, so I assume that all the action's happening here, like always."

She bobbed her head to the side, as if to indicate that, yes, it was business as usual here, but that didn't mean that it was all calm in the multiverse.

"I'll be ready, like always, if you need me elsewhere. Um, a question? Why are so many people with us? I mean like Jeff's Cabinet and the families. I think I get why on the Valentinos and Prices, but the Cabinet's reasons for being with us elude me."

She laughed again and I saw a picture of something that

looked like a lot of pomp and circumstance that featured the politicians and Jeff's sisters and their families. Everyone looked happy to be there, but I had no idea where "there" was or what was going on.

Naomi looked pleased, though, as if she'd given me all the info I needed and expected that I'd clearly made the leap. Decided not to disabuse her of that notion. "Super and duper I suppose. Um, another request? We need to find Ixtha and we have no idea of where she is. Plus, it looks like that solar system that's drifting in the black is probably in dire need, too."

Naomi gave me a look I was familiar with. I hadn't seen it from her often, and I surely hadn't seen it from her in a long time, but I still recognized it. It was her "Duh" look.

Before I could ask or say anything else, though, there was a knock on the door. Naomi blew me a kiss and disappeared and I was merely looking at my reflection. The Universe Wheel was gone.

Heaved a sigh, got up, and went to the door. To find the possibly last person I wanted to see at this particular moment.

Chuckie.

CHAPTER 88

"H EY," CHUCKIE SAID. "Are you okay? You look funny." He cocked his head at me. "Actually, you look guilty." Dang. Chuckie always knew when I was lying.

"Um, why are you here?"

He raised his eyebrow. "Because Jeff wanted you checked on and, normally, I'd be one of your preferred options."

"You still are." Well, normally. Just not when I'd been talking to his beloved dead wife.

His eyes narrowed. "Are we fighting and I don't know about it?"

"Oh, for God's sake." Pulled him into the room. "No, we are not secret fighting."

"Huh." He looked around and went into my bedroom.

"Seriously? Did Jeff think I was having an affair and you're the one he sent to check to see if someone's hiding under the bed?"

"No." He came back out. "Stop looking guilty. I get it."

"You do?" Had no idea what he was getting.

"You wanted to check the Universe Wheel and you didn't want to be bawled out for not focusing on the issues at hand."

It was rare when Chuckie jumped to both the wrong and the right conclusion at the same time, but was grateful it had happened now. "Yeah. I just . . . I haven't checked as often as I'd promised the Jamie from Bizarro World I would, and since they made this for me on Cradus, it was about time I used it."

"And birthing a superconsciousness can take a lot out of a girl, at least so I've heard." He grinned at me. "Relax, Kitty. I'm not here to narc on you. Jeff was just worried and, frankly, so were James and I, so I came to check on you. Everyone else is still on the command deck, hoping to get to fly the ship. I don't care about that, and Wheatles is there to help with any issues as we get to his part of the Milky Way, so I figured I'd check on you and run an idea I had by you at the same time."

Sat on the couch. "Shoot."

"What if we put the trap that has the Anti-Mother into some of the metal we got from the Cradi? That could keep it safe in transit and, hopefully, fully contained."

"Dude, sometimes we're so in sync it's scary. I came up with that one just now, too." Oh, sure, with help, but still, I'd managed to get there. And I wasn't the Top Genius Man, either.

"Great. If you're up to it, I'd like to do that now. The longer that thing is able to be easily opened, the longer we have something far worse than a live nuke on board."

"No argument from me." Slung my purse over my neck and we headed for the cargo hold.

It was several decks down from where we were and chose not to use hyperspeed because that would help me keep the fiction that I was exhausted going.

"So, what did you see?" Chuckie asked me as we walked to the elevator.

"Things look quiet, particularly in Bizarro World. They're all good there."

"Good. I'm sure all the other worlds where we are matter, too, but we haven't met anyone from them, so it's harder to care."

"Yeah." As we got into the elevator, considered telling Chuckie about the black mass I'd seen, but since I had no idea what it was or what, if anything, to do about it, decided there was no reason to worry someone else about it. Instead, described the future world, since I knew he'd like hearing about that one.

"Who are you married to in that world?" he asked as we got out. "And how many kids?"

"You scored the big win in Futuristic World and we have just a tonnage of kids, which kind of surprised me, since you'd think that in a world that sleek and high-tech there would be some moratorium on how many kids every family could have."

"Maybe there's enough abundance that it's possible," he suggested. "Or we've colonized the solar system. Or we got special dispensation."

"Any of those could happen, or something else entirely. It's hard for me to gather a lot of nuance."

He laughed. "I'm sure. I can understand why Jamie in the other world wanted to just watch the mirrors all day. It must be fascinating."

"In a way. I'm usually too busy to take a lot of time with it and I'm looking for dangerous stuff happening to or around me and Jamie, so for me it's kind of like work versus fun."

We reached the cargo hold and went in. It had the gifts from the Cradi and the *Eknara*'s shuttle and yet still looked fairly empty.

"I think we can move the Orange Scourge," Chuckie said. We went to the lead container. Being made of lead, it was hard to open. Luckily I was enhanced, because it took both of us.

There was a lot of Orange Scourge in here. "Have we not been giving this to the rabbits and least weasels?"

"I have no idea. Mother?"

"Yes, Charles?"

"What's the situation with the Orange Scourge here?"

"SuperBun requested that we not give it to the animals until we were on the way to Ixtha."

Chuckie and I looked at each other. "Now, why would he have asked that?" I asked.

"You said SuperBun, not SuperStar," Chuckie said. "Does that mean this request happened before that merging?"

"Yes, Charles. SuperBun requested that after we first left Cradus."

"Why didn't you mention it?"

"Because it did not appear to be a dangerous request. Was my interpretation wrong?"

"No, not at all that we can tell. Can we get this into wherever you store foodstuffs, though? Chuckie and I want to use the lead container to hold the Anti-Mother."

"That is a good plan," Mother said. "I will ask the young adults to help you move the produce."

"Where are all the kids, anyway?" Mother of the Year here had forgotten to check on her younger children, or keep track of her older one.

"In the Observation Lounge, enjoying the sights and spending time with the majority of the Ignotforstans while they still can. Since we are not traveling at warp speed, there are things to see, and since we're in their part of the galaxy now, the Ignotforstans are educating the children about the various celestial bodies we are passing."

"Super. Should we really pull the older kids away from that, then?"

"They can use the responsibility." The com turned off.

"Wow, you named her right," Chuckie said.

"Go team."

We unloaded the Orange Scourge from the container. We just finished getting the last of it out when those young adults appeared. Lizzie, Wasim, Clinton Kramer, Louise, Sidney, Claire, and Anthony Valentino. Realized something.

"Um, Mother?"

"Yes, Kitty?"

"When we first took off, you said that we have a dozen young adults on board."

"Yes."

"Um, I count seven, not twelve. So, who were the other five you were referring to?"

"I included Chase Maurer, Raymond Lewis, Kimberly Price, Cassidy Maurer, and Rachel Lewis in my first count. Having observed them and their interactions with the others, I have reprogrammed myself to consider them neither young adults nor children."

"Well, Chase *is* thirteen and Raymond and Kimmie are both almost twelve, but they're still children to us. And they're kind of far away from Anthony, who is our youngest young adult."

Clinton laughed. "Mav's going to be upset if he ever finds out that he didn't make the presumed young adult cut. Especially when Rachel did."

Lizzie grimaced. "No one tell Maverick about this. That's an order."

"Oh, yes, boss," Sidney said with a grin.

Claire sniffed. "Lizzie's not wrong and you know it. Mav's feelings will be hurt."

"I wasn't saying we weren't going to follow orders," Sidney said, grin still going strong. "Now, Anthony, he might not listen to Lizzie. But I'm always faithful."

Anthony gave his brother a dirty look. "As if I don't listen?"

"Everyone's awesome," Lizzie said, shooting Wasim a "why me?" look. Wasim winked at her, but as soon as she turned away he looked sad. The kids kept on ribbing each other about listening to Lizzie or not, though Louise, as the eldest, remained above it. Mostly.

"My God," Chuckie murmured to me as he watched them, Wasim in particular. "It's like reliving high school."

Nudged against him. "Yeah. There are times I think I can never apologize to you enough."

He nudged me back. "It's okay. You're still my best friend, and that still means the world to me. And it honestly helps to know that, in other worlds, we're together. In this one, things are different. And that's okay, because I wouldn't trade the short time I had with Naomi for anything. Nor would I trade what Nathalie and I have, either."

"That's good, 'cause I hadn't really noticed before, but guess who you're married to in, literally, every world where you're not married to me?"

He stared at me. "Really?"

"Scout's honor. So, you're with the 'other woman' you're supposed to be with. Don't screw it up."

He laughed. "Not me. Not her, either." He looked at Wasim again. "I hope it works out the way it's supposed to."

"Not one way or the other?"

"Nope. I can extrapolate how different our world would be if you'd married me instead of Jeff. And our world is a lot better because you joined Centaurion Division. So, how it *should* be is fine with me."

We loaded the young adults up with Orange Scourge. "Keep it somewhere safe and clean," I told Lizzie, "but figure we're going to be breaking it out for the bunnies and least weasels sooner as opposed to later."

"Got it, Mom," Lizzie said, in her Patented Teenager Exasperated With Adults Voice. This time it didn't really bother me, because she'd called me Mom in front of the others and no one had reacted in any weird or even slightly surprised way. "We're not babies." She rolled her eyes at me with a laugh, then sashayed off, the others following behind.

"You've done well," Chuckie said when they were out of the hold. "And, for a kid you didn't actually birth, my God is she like you."

"Yeah, she is." Felt ridiculously proud.

Chuckie laughed softly. "Now you know how your mother feels."

"What do you mean?"

He shrugged. "I've known Angela as long as I've known you, but for most of that time, in a very different way than you or the rest of your friends did. She was always proud of you, but once you joined Centaurion? She was just bursting with pride. It's nice for parents to see the best parts of themselves reflected in their children."

"Yeah?" Felt even better and missed Mom like crazy.

"Yeah. Let's get the Anti-Mother contained. I'll call you SuperMom if you want."

Snorted. "No, trust me, that moniker is not going to fly." Looked into the container. "It's hella roomy in here, isn't it?"

"It is, and I know what you're thinking and I'm thinking the same thing—we can't just leave the trap loose in here. The lid's heavy but it's not *that* heavy."

"We can fill it. I think the mercury will be the easiest to get into this. But will it kill the Anti-Mother?"

He rubbed the back of his neck. "Maybe is the best I have for you. But if it's her or us, you know my vote, and it's the same as everyone's on board."

"True enough. Just hope we're strong enough to lift the container ourselves."

"Me, too. But if not, we'll just call the young adults back to help."

"Oh, man, dude, let's definitely be strong enough."

CHAPTER 89

FORTUNATELY, strong enough we were. But first we shoved it next to the lead container. "I have no idea if I should stress to Charlie that he leave this alone or never mention it in the hopes that he isn't aware that it's here."

Chuckie nodded as we took the lid of the mercury container off—it was a lot easier to lift than the other had been. "I just want to say that, despite him being named for me, I was never this much work as a kid."

Snorted again. "Yeah? Talk to your mother about that. I think she'd view having a child genius to raise differently than you do. And I say that with full confidence."

He eyed the containers. "You know, I think the mercury vat will fit inside the lead container. Which, while it will be heavy, will still be a lot easier than pouring. And, when did my mother whine to you about me?"

Did some hand measurements. Unsurprisingly, Chuckie was right. "All the time, dude. Usually when I was in trouble with my parents. I think to prove to me that every kid gets in trouble. Your mom's great that way."

"She is." He put the lid back on the mercury container. "Remember to lift with your thighs."

"Trust me, I remember." We hefted the mercury. Heavier than the lead but we managed without calling The Young Mouthy Adults back. "Have they met Nathalie?"

"Yeah, they have."

"Good. Um, sorry to ask this at this time, and please don't drop your side of this heavy, dangerous object, but when are you popping the question?"

He sighed. "I was planning to do it right after the *Distant Voy-*

ager launched. Now? Who knows." We got the mercury container into the lead one. Perfect fit, with room on top to lock the lead lid.

"Do you have the ring on you?" Pulled the Anti-Mother Trap out of my purse.

"I do, as a matter of fact. I carried it with me in case something happened during Jeff's speech or the tour of the ship that would make proposing then more romantic."

Dropped the trap into the mercury. "I think you should propose as soon as possible."

"Why so? Is there someone macking on my girl that I'm missing?" The trap floated for a minute, then started to submerge.

"Not that I've seen. But you're on a space aged vacation and, in terms of romance, it probably doesn't get any better than this."

"Maybe. If we can figure out where we're going after Ignotforsta, maybe. Otherwise, I'll be too busy staring at star charts to be romantic."

The trap was finally covered by mercury. We put the mercury lid on and locked it down, then did the same with the lead one. Then we shoved the lead container into a dark corner of the hold. Dug through my purse for a marker, found one, and put all the usual warnings all over the container, including a skull and crossbones that Chuckie said was some of my best artwork.

Through all this, tried to figure out how to show him what I'd gotten in that envelope without having to explain how I'd gotten it and from whom. If Lilith weren't continuing on with us, could have said they were from her, but that lie would be caught out immediately since she was going to hang out. And we needed her, so her staying was a good thing.

We headed out of the cargo hold. "Where to now?" Chuckie asked.

"Observation Lounge or command deck, I guess. You pick."

"You want to see the kids or figure out what we're doing?"

"Ugh. Both. But if the kids are 'in school' with Denise, leaving them alone is probably the wisest course of Bad Mommy action."

"You're not a bad mother," Chuckie said gently. "You're a working mother who has an incredibly demanding set of jobs that affect, literally, the fate of the entire world and, as we're learning, the entire galaxy. Cut yourself some slack. Little kids would like their parents with them twenty-four-seven but that doesn't mean it's possible. Do the best you can, like your mother did, and it'll all work out."

Hugged him as we reached the elevators. "Thanks, I needed that."

"So, command deck it is," he said as we got in and headed back up. "That'll be an exercise in calm stress. And yes, everyone's stressed because we don't know where we're heading after Ignotforsta and yes, Jeff has his blocks up."

Needed to show Chuckie what I had. And needed to be able to not say how I'd gotten it. As we rode up, occurred to me that he was the one who'd always said that the best lies told as much of the truth as possible. "Actually . . . we need to go to a supply closet."

"Excuse me?" We stepped out and I headed us for the Closet of Secrecy.

Didn't say anything until we were inside. "Okay, look. I found something in my purse, and I don't know who gave it to me." My only lie. I *assumed* that Algar had given it to me, but I didn't *know*. I'd indeed found the envelope in my purse. And elsewhere. But finding it in my purse wasn't a lie at all. "My guess would be one of the Superconsciousness Society, but I don't think it's from ACE or Lilith because I think they'd have told me, versus being sneaky." Was sure it wasn't from ACE or Lilith, but couldn't *know* that it wasn't from, say, Sandy.

"Okay," Chuckie said slowly. "So, what is it? And why are we in here?"

"We're in here because Mother can't monitor us in here. I don't think we need to hide this from her, but until you and I go over what I have, I don't want to share with anyone else."

"The secrecy is fun. Fine." He sat on the same boxes Wruck and Algar had used as chairs. Fitting. "What were you given?"

Pulled the envelope out of my purse and handed it to him. Did not congratulate myself on my lying to my best and oldest friend. In no small part because I didn't want to so congratulate and then have him figure out I was lying. I knew how the cosmos loved its little jokes.

Chuckie examined the envelope. "Looks like it's been in your purse for a while."

"It has. I really only just now had time to take a look at what was inside."

"We've had downtime, but I know you, and I know what you and Jeff were doing when the kids were asleep, so I get why you haven't looked at this until now. So, let's see what's in here." He pulled the contents out and took a look. And whistled. "Wow."

"Yeah. So, when I was first joined with Lilith, I saw the entire galaxy in a glance. My limited experience says that when a superconsciousness joins with you, you, the vessel, see all they know of. When it was ACE I saw Alpha Centauri and Solaris. But Lilith has been all over."

"So, you saw this?" He waved the first map at me.

"No." Showed him the one on the bottom of the stack. "I saw *this*. And this," pointed to the solar system in the black between galaxies, "in particular."

He nodded but didn't speak, so I didn't, either. He thumbed through the stack of pictures. There were a hell of a lot of them.

Got bored, because Chuckie thought silently and I didn't. "I wonder if it's like animation or something, like one of those flipbooks where you see the stills of Peter Pan but when you flip the pictures he's now flying."

He jerked and looked up at me. "I hadn't thought of that." He took the stack in one hand and did the fast flip through with his thumb. He did this from every side. "Good call, Kitty. I think I know what these are."

"A space flipbook?"

"In a way. I think they're a series of pictures that show the progression of the galaxy over time. Over a *lot* of time."

He handed the stack to me and indicated I should do the flip. So I did.

"Wow. So, somewhere, a long time ago, this solar system started to, what, move? And now it's moved out of the galaxy?"

"Yes, I think that's part of what we're being shown. But it's more than that." He got up, leaned over my shoulder, and turned the stack ninety degrees. "Flip just the first quarter."

Did so. "Huh. We're looking at a different solar system here."

"Yes, we are, but I think for a reason." He turned the stack again. "Flip the first third now."

"Oh. Wow. So, if I'm interpreting right, this system is the first one. Something happened—it looks like the star exploded—and then, suddenly, we're focused on this other system."

"Right." He flipped the book ninety degrees once more. "Flip from here."

"Huh. So, something happened again, not in this new system but near it, and it knocked them, what, out of galactic orbit?"

"Exactly. I knew you paid attention in more than our animal sciences classes."

"Tell no one, that remains our little secret."

He chuckled. "I know. But I do love it when you hit Stryker and the others with higher thought they persist in thinking you're incapable of. But you having protective coloration is more important."

Turned the stack once more without prompting, and flipped it again, this time trying to see as much of each page as possible. "So, do we take the leap and assume that we care about the people in these solar systems, versus the systems themselves?"

"Yes, absolutely. We've been on a rescue mission. Yes, we've had to save planets and a sun, but the real focus has been saving the people, the sentient beings."

Went back to the first page and stared at it. "How old is this image, do you think?"

"Old. I can't calculate it without a computer of Mother's level or higher, the hackers, Drax, and probably your pal Tyson."

"Who is probably green with envy that we're on this trip."

"No, he's probably frantically working to figure out how to get us home. Once we're back? Then he'll be envious."

"Good point." Resisted the desire to keep our "probably" one-upmanship going, though it took effort. "So . . . I guess the question is, why do we care about this system? Not the one that's moved out of the galaxy. I mean, that looks dangerous in the extreme, like 'Here Be Dragons' should be written in huge letters next to it. I'm talking about the first system. Why, specifically, are we being shown this? And don't say progression. We could have started from when the newer system moved and gotten the clue that leaving your galaxy is probably dangerous."

Chuckie was about to speak when the door opened and Jeff looked in. "What in the hell are you two doing in here?" He didn't sound happy.

CHAPTER 90

"UM ... THIS PROBABLY** looks bad but it isn't."

Jeff rolled his eyes. "Why me? Baby, I may have my blocks up, but I can feel you and Chuck easily. Neither one of you is hiding an illicit affair from me. We're going to be coming up on Ignotforsta sooner as opposed to later, though, and I think you two should be on the command deck, not playing cards."

"How soon?" Chuckie asked.

"An hour or two, give or take."

"Plenty of time." Chuckie pulled Jeff into the room and closed the door. He then explained the pictures, meaning I didn't have to lie again, because Chuckie was the one stating things as fact. I loved it when a plan came together.

We then had Jeff do the flipbook thing, and reach the same conclusions we had. "Okay," he said when he was fully caught up, "I'm assuming we have to save this escaping solar system because of course we do. Why are you two still stressing?"

"I want to know why we care about the first system."

Jeff examined it again. "Chuck, this is showing the star exploding, you're sure?"

"Yes."

"Huh. Baby, I wonder . . ."

We waited. He was wondering silently. Was I truly the only one who thought aloud? "Wonder what, Jeff?"

"If this is where the Mykali came from."

We'd met the Mykali during Operation Immigration. We called them *Glaucus atlanticus* and thought they were a form of sea slug, but that was because only Turleens and those with Dr. Doolittle powers could talk to them. They were tiny blue and white creatures with bodies that resembled a gecko but with six rounded and spiny limbs or fins, depending on who you talked to.

"The Mykali had been on an abundant world, a very old world, that had run out of water. At least, that's what they told us."

"Suns going supernova get larger and hotter and dry up the water on the planets closer to them," Chuckie said. "And this explosion is definitely a supernova."

We all stared at the first picture. "So, this is where the Mykali come from?" I asked.

"That's my only guess," Jeff said. "Their race is millions of years old on Earth, and they aren't *from* Earth."

"I think it's a good guess," Chuckie said.

"But the Mykali were sent out in meteoric spaceships. Would there have been enough time to do that, with a sun going supernova?"

"Sure." Chuckie rubbed the back of his neck. "There are signs when a sun is going to start that progression. If you were scientifically advanced enough—and anyone who could send the Mykali through space as they did were definitely advanced enough—then you'd know and could plan."

"So . . . what?" Jeff asked. "I don't know what we do with this information."

Chuckie shook his head. "There has to be a reason these were given to Kitty. A significant reason. One that matters to us and why we're on this trip in the first place."

"Well, we're on this trip because of Ixtha." Jerked. Naomi had certainly indicated that I was being an idiot. "Ixtha's in that system that's floating away from our galaxy."

Both men nodded. "I can accept that leap," Chuckie said.

"Kitty's rarely wrong when she makes these guesses," Jeff said, rather proudly, which made me feel quite good.

"So, we have our heading after we drop Wheatles and his crew off, then."

Chuckie nodded. "We do. We should be able to easily determine where we are in relation to where this system is, even if the galaxy has rotated a bit since this picture was taken."

My bet was that the galaxy hadn't rotated any more than it had in the time since we'd left Earth, if that, but kept that bet to myself.

"Great and one big problem solved. But we still need to figure out what the issue is with this first system and why we care about it. It's gone, just like the Mykali told us. And I don't think any of us felt we needed confirmation that they were telling the truth."

Jeff studied the first picture again. "Chuck, I know you said you can't tell for sure without a supercomputer and some of the others, but what's your best guess for how old the galaxy is in this first picture?"

"Ancient. Early days of the galaxy ancient. You can tell—most of the nebulas we know about aren't here, far fewer pulsars, fewer black holes, among other things."

Felt like I knew what was going on, but couldn't verbalize it or even come up with the right concept, as if the answer was there, but just out of reach.

Really wished I had my earbuds in. Decided I could do the next best thing. Pulled my phone out and queued up my music. The Cosmic Thing playlist was up, and I hadn't created it, which wasn't that much of a surprise. It was a short playlist. Clearly I was supposed to catch on quickly. Hoped I was as smart as Algar thought I was.

"What are you doing?" Jeff asked.

"Trying to figure out what's going on. Just gimme a mo, Jeff."

Took a look at the song list. Billy Idol's "Cradle of Love" was the first song up. Looked at the next songs—"The Beginning" by Lifehouse, then the Backstreet Boys' "The Answer to Our Life," followed by Tears for Fears' "Sowing the Seeds of Love." The last song was "Feels Like The First Time" by Foreigner.

It was there, right there. But Jeff jerked. "Raj needs us."

And just like that, it was gone. Sighed, but there was nothing for it. Hopefully the idea would come back to me. I could listen to the songs later, and maybe that would spark it. But right now, duty appeared to be calling.

Chuckie took the pictures from Jeff, put them back into the envelope, and handed them to me. "Keep them in your purse and on you. We'll deal with this once we get the Ignotforstans home safely."

Shoved them into my purse just as a knock came on the door and Raj stuck his head in. "There you three are. Thankfully I ran into the Ard Ri and he said that you liked to meet in this closet. I'll ask why later. We have a situation."

"Of course we do," Jeff said with a sigh. "What's up?"

"We have issues of state we need to deal with," Raj said. "I'd prefer that you hear this directly, as opposed to being translated through me."

We followed Raj to what turned out to be a conference room. Filled with Jeff's Cabinet members, Gower, White, Drax, and, interestingly enough, Gadhavi.

"What's going on?" Chuckie asked, eyes narrowed, as the three of us sat down.

Hochberg rolled his eyes. "Really, son? We may be on some bizarre road trip instead of relaxing at Camp David, but things still need to be handled, unplanned vacation or no."

"Like what?" I asked.

"Like where we're going from here," Hamlin said.

"To save Ixtha and her people from whatever galaxy-ending situation they're in." Everyone stared at me. "Really? You guys haven't noticed that we're on a galaxywide rescue mission?"

"We've noticed," Ernesto Iriarte, the Secretary of Labor, said, sarcasm knob at five and rising.

"We just don't know why we're here," Julie Cruz, the Secretary of Health and Human Services added. "Other than that we were all in the wrong place at the wrong time." Gibson, Davis, and Harris all nodded. They rarely backed Cruz under normal circumstances, but she appeared to be speaking for everyone.

Well, almost everyone. "Stop complaining," Horn said mildly, but with a lot of authority. He'd been the head of the FBI's Alien Affairs Division and had been a good friend and ally when he was in that position. Horn was now the Secretary of Homeland Security and doing a good job with expanding that position to cover all of the Solaris system.

Horn wasn't someone who scared easily. He wasn't scared now, but I had a feeling that a lot of the Cabinet members *were* scared, and that Horn found that somewhat unacceptable. A sentiment I kind of agreed with.

"We aren't, Vander," Carlos Garcia, Jeff's Attorney General said. "But we need to take the time to get a handle on what it is we're trying to do out here."

"And how we're going to handle the Ignotforstans," Elaine added.

"What do you mean, handle?" Jeff asked. "We're taking them home. What's to handle?"

"Other than everything?" Gibson said. "How about handling their expectations?"

"What expectations?" Jeff asked. "They expect to get home safely. We're handling it."

Gadhavi rolled his eyes. "This is how you brief your President? You attack him out of nowhere with no facts, no information, just random demands? You bicker amongst yourselves but with no purpose? It's amazing you've held things together so well, King Jeffrey."

"Oh, if Mister Gadhavi is tossing around royal titles, it means we're missing something, Jeff." Gadhavi smiled and winked at me, not that I'd been worried about being wrong.

Drax nodded. "You are. The Ignotforstans are from a rather isolationist solar system. All the planets in the Apata system know of Vatusus and some other key core systems because of radio waves. But they've stayed away due to what they call caution."

"And I call fear," Gadhavi said. "Fear that is not without reason."

"Fear often keeps you alive," Alvin Wong, the Secretary of Agriculture, said.

"Alvin's not wrong," Gower agreed.

"Why are you and Richard here, Paul?" Chuckie asked. "You don't normally join Jeff's Cabinet meetings."

"Miz Freeman and Mister Moskowitz asked us to join," White said, smiling at the two of them. Jessica Freeman was the Secretary of Housing and Urban Development and Murray Moskowitz was the Secretary of Energy. "Separately," he added, which made sense, since I'd never seen these two as buddies.

"They're here to help convince Jeff to do whatever it is that everyone wants us to do, Chuckie. Which either means that Paul and Richard are in agreement, or Paul and Richard are tired of staring out the window into space and wanted to have the entertainment a Cabinet Meeting in Space provides."

"My money is on both, Queen Katherine," Gadhavi said. "Prince Gustav, please get to the point."

"Agreed. Mister Gadhavi and I have spent time with the Ignotforstans—they remain very impressed by royal titles. And I may have mentioned that Mister Gadhavi is an influential person on Earth."

"Why did you so mention, Gustav?"

Gadhavi sighed. "Because you're both so focused on saving the galaxy that you're not aware that we are heading into a political situation with great ramifications."

"The Apatan system is quite cohesive," Raj explained. "For example, once they found out that there was life on the other planets, even though each planet had a different name for it, they all got together and gave their sun the new name of Apata, which each planet agreed to. They work together to care for their solar system. The *Eknara* was only manned by Ignotforstans, but that was due to the danger of the mission—the Ignotforstans are considered the most daring in the system. The Apatans are fully capable of joining the greater galactic community. But they're afraid to. They don't want to be conquered. And that definitely includes the Ignotforstans."

"Can't blame them," Jeff said dryly. "Most people don't want to be. So are you saying we need to protect this system, too? Because if you are, at the rate we're going, we're not going to have anyone to protect Solaris or Alpha Centauri."

"And that could be the greater plan," Hamlin said. "We've been taking it on faith that whoever's pulling our strings wants us to save the galaxy."

"They do," I said firmly. "On this, I'm certain. And I don't want to spend any time arguing about it, and that's a freaking Queen Katherine order. I'm the one who gets to have all the special times with the various Powers That Be. Until they choose to basically screw up your life on a regular basis, my opinion is the one that counts."

"We agree," Nathalie said quickly. "This is not a meeting to complain about what we've been doing. Or will do."

"Sure seems like it," Chuckie said mildly. But I knew him and he was pissed, though not at Nathalie, just the situation.

"It's not," Raj said, Troubadour Tones set to Soothe. "We just haven't gotten to the point yet." He looked at Drax.

"I apologize. The point is that this stop is not like all the others."

"How so?" Jeff asked.

Drax sighed. "As Raj said, the system is very cohesive."

"Think Alpha Centauri but no friction," Gower added.

Drax nodded. "And the entire system plans to honor us for saving the crew of the *Eknara*. And that celebration will take days, if not weeks."

"So we say thanks but we're on a schedule and move on," Jeff said.

Gadhavi shook his head violently. "That will ensure that this system will be offended. Deeply offended. Do you know what happens when you deeply offend someone?"

I knew. "They join your enemies the first chance they get." The room nodded. "Great. Look, we know where we need to go. Now's as good a time as any to tell you guys." Pulled the envelope out of my purse, took out the last picture, and put it in the center of the conference table. "We're going here." Pointed to the solar system that was outside of the galaxy.

Everyone took a minute to look at the picture while Chuckie did the explanation for why we had this in the first place. Once the picture had made the rounds, and I'd watched various faces drain of color, it came back to me and I put it back in the envelope and said envelope back in my purse.

Took a moment to do a quick check of my phone. Sure enough, had a different playlist up—Apatan Nights. Algar was hilarious. As were the song choices, at least the first one—"Stay Down Here Where You Belong" by Tiny Tim. Followed by "If You Wanna Stay" by Bidwell, "Split Screen Sadness" by John Mayer, "Divide" by Disturbed, and "Separate Lives" by Phil Collins. Felt that I had the key idea. Which was good, because there were no more songs.

"The coordinates for where we were originally headed have been lost," Davis said once I gave the table my full attention again. "Maybe that means we don't need to go there after all."

"We do," I said. "Trust me, we do. But, I have an idea of how we fix this." And the best part of that idea was that I was just about a hundred percent sure I'd figured out what Naomi had been trying to tell me.

CHAPTER 91

"IT HAS TO BE VOLUNTARY," Chuckie said when I was done sharing the brilliance that was my interpretation of Algar's and Naomi's clues.

"Oh, I know. Because it's just as dangerous to leave our people in this system as it is to take them outside of the galaxy."

"Those staying have a better chance of getting back to Earth than those going," Gibson said. "Just like in any war situation."

"Most aren't going to be willing to stay," Raj said. He smiled at the shocked looks. "We've survived several life-or-death situations already and we haven't lost anyone. Those who wanted new pets got them. Everyone had pretty souvenirs from Cradus."

"Raj is correct," White said. "And while you could order them to stay, I don't recommend it."

"The kids will never agree, so don't bother to try," I said. "Frankly, we can't leave all the Cabinet, either."

"I'm going with you," Horn said calmly.

"I as well," Nathalie said.

"Me too," Elaine chimed in.

Shook my head. "Elaine, I think it's important that you and Fritzy stay here." Which was too bad. I'd have liked Elaine to come with us. But since we were in the Meeting Of Grownups, had to act like one and choose what was best, versus fun.

She looked shocked and disappointed. "Why?"

Jeff chuckled. "Because you're the Secretary of State and you're going to be negotiating bringing the Apata system into the fold. Our fold, specifically."

"Exactly. Fritzy's the Vice President and I'm sure we can spin that to show how vitally important he is. Frankly, Vander, it might be good for you to stay, too. Homeland Security is going to matter to these people." Another bummer, because I'd have liked Horn with us, too.

Horn and Elaine both grimaced. "I hate it when you make sense," Horn said.

"I know, and it's so rare, too."

Horn snorted. "Don't try to play me, Kitty. I've known you too long."

"I think I need to stay as well," Raj said regretfully.

"I agree." Leaving the Super Troubadour with the politicians was probably going to be a good thing, and that meant we had the Number Two in the A-C CIA on site as well.

"So, you want the rest of us to go with you?" Harris asked, trying really hard not to sound or look nervous and not totally succeeding. Most of the Cabinet looked like they were trying to be calm and cool and also were praying really hard that Jeff was going to say no.

"No," Jeff said. "Kitty, who do you want?"

"Hammy and Nathalie." Nathalie had already been gung ho, but it was nice to see that Hamlin appeared pleased versus freaked out. Not that I'd expected any less from him.

"And?" Chuckie asked.

"And that's it. I mean, unless you're asking if I want you to stay, Secret Agent Man, and the answer is not just no but hell no. You're coming with us. Gustav, it's up to you and Mister Gadhavi to decide what you two want to do."

"If you feel confident that the ship can function without Prince Gustav, I strongly suggest he remain," Gadhavi said. "Again, royalty means much to these people."

"The ship has been tested and repaired," Drax said, "and as long as Mossy and the hackers are with you, you should be fine without me for this portion. Plus, should something, ah, delay your return, I can ask my father for assistance in returning those of us who remain behind to Earth."

"Makes sense—you're the one most likely to get help fast." Including if we needed someone to come rescue us, which was always a possibility. "Wasim stays with me, though."

"I agree," Gadhavi said. "And that means I stay with you. And before you say anything, yes, his bodyguard is excellent. However, one man is not enough."

Chose not to point out that we had a lot more than one person watching out for Wasim. Gadhavi coming along was not going to be a bad thing.

"I recommend that we leave Mister Jenkins as well," White said.

"Not MJO or Dion? Or Adam and Kristie?"

"Mister Joel Oliver will not miss the opportunity to go where we're going," White said. "Dion will likely want to take the rarest photographs in the galaxy. Kristie will be better utilized with us, and Adam as well. Mister Jenkins, on the other hand, is quite good with people, and it will ensure that we have someone immortalizing the events."

"Oh, gotcha. Bruce is the Royal Scribe who will take notes about the ceremony and such so that all will know of it sort of thing?" And it would leave someone we could trust keeping an eye on the politicians, too.

White nodded. "Anyone else you want to remain?"

"Camilla." Said by me, Jeff, and Chuckie in unison.

"Agreed." White sighed. "You need to offer this to the others, Jeffrey. But be prepared for them to say no."

Considered this. "I have an idea how to get at least some of them staying. They're part of the Royal Family, meaning they're representing you to this new solar system."

"It's worth a shot," Jeff said. "But you just said that the kids won't want to be left behind."

"I meant our three. The others won't want to be left, either, but I think if we spin it right, they'll be willing."

Raj nodded. "I can do that and I'm sure I can convince Sylvia, Jonathan, and Marianne. Clarence will do whatever Kitty asks. However, the children are excited about visiting Ixtha—we all spoke with her in the DreamScape and everyone learned the language, including those we're now leaving behind."

"That's okay. If everything goes according to plan, they'll get to meet Ixtha and see her world."

"The goal is to bring that system back into the galaxy in some way?" Moskowitz asked.

"Yes," Jeff said. "I assume that's why they're calling us."

"Could be for another reason," Gower said. "But it's a good working hypothesis."

We decided that there was no time like the present to share what we wanted to do, so we headed off en masse. Happily, everyone other than the command crew were in the Observation Lounge, so Raj was able to explain things one time, once Drax, White, and Gower got the Ignotforstans out of the room on the pretext of going over the different worlds with them.

I also got the opportunity to be a mother for a couple of minutes. Jeff was holding Charlie, I had Jamie and Lizzie. While Raj was talking, made sure I quietly told the girls what was going on from my viewpoint, so they didn't create arguments.

There were, of course, the expected protests from the others. But we quelled them fairly easily by sharing that we expected to bring Ixtha to them. Plus, the Cabinet members who were staying all stressed that this was a mission of vital importance to the nation and solar systems.

Dion asked to remain with Jenkins. The opportunity to take rare pictures was overridden by his desire not to die. Couldn't blame him. Besides, he was getting along really well with the Ignotforstans, so that just meant he was going to do double duty as a diplomat.

After some discussion, the agreement was that family groups would not be split up. If one was staying, all were staying, and vice versa.

"I want to stress that the Valentino and Price kids are all talented, and that means you guys need to be paying attention and being careful. You're going to have to be functioning at a higher level than normal, especially you older kids."

Who all looked thrilled with the authority. Kimmie did, too. "We'll do a good job, Aunt Kitty," she said. "We promise."

"I know you will. Take direction from Raj, you guys. Don't go off on your own on commando missions. Remember—you're all representing the Royal Family. If Wasim wouldn't do it, you don't do it."

"We'll all follow that rule, Aunt Kitty," Louise said. "I'll make sure of it." The other kids all nodded, even JP Junior and Miriam, who I expected to not be allowed out of their parents' sight, based on Jonathan and Marianne's expressions.

I'd insisted that the Maurer family and the Kramer kids stay as well. This meant we'd lose one of our androids, but that meant that those staying in the Apata system would have an android with them, and who knew if they'd need one or not. Mrs. Maurer seemed relieved and Clinton seemed pleased. Yeah, I'd figured he'd want to stay wherever Louise was.

Tried to get Christopher to stay, but he and Amy were having none of it. Couldn't complain. Had a strong feeling we were going to need the hybrid kids, and we always needed the Flash. And Amy always came through. Plus White was coming with us, so we weren't breaking up that family.

Didn't even suggest that the Dwyer, Weisman, Muir, and Billings families stay behind—we needed all the flyboys, with Drax gone Brian's expertise was even more vital, whether Mother allowed him to fly the ship or not, and I wanted the girls with us anyway. Irving was the only one who looked disappointed.

Abigail sidled over to me. "I'm going to advise the command crew of what's going on so the guys know. Any objection?"

"None, just make sure you don't share this in front of any of the Real Naked Apes."

She grinned. "Got it." She zipped off.

The hardest decision was the Lewis family. We all wanted Kevin with us, but most of the kids were staying behind, meaning that Denise was going to be more helpful there. It was Sylvia who made the decision. "The youngest children are the ones who are going on. To me, that means you need Denise with you, on the *Distant Voyager*, not staying behind with the rest of us."

"My sister has a good point," Jeff said, as Raymond and Rachel high-fived each other. Sylvia beamed. Yeah, his sisters thought Jeff walked on water.

"As the father of the youngest ones, I'm in agreement, too, so thank you, Sylvia," Christopher said. She beamed at him as well. Not a surprise—Christopher was also a water-walker to the Martini women.

"What about me?" Vance asked as Abigail returned and gave me the "all good" sign.

"You stay with Jeff and Kitty," Raj said. "Because I'm staying on-planet." Vance didn't complain, possibly because MJO was going on.

"Tim wants me to stay on-planet," Alicia said. "And I haven't asked him, I just know."

"What do *you* want to do?" Vance asked her.

"I want to go."

Vance nodded. "Then you're going. I'll keep an eye on you if he's busy Commandering."

She grinned. "Thanks."

"I can help anyone with spin, if and as needed," Jenkins said. "So, if you're not sure what to say and Raj isn't nearby, find me."

"What Bruce said." Hey, wanted to be sure we spun our spin correctly, and the Tastemaker was great with spin.

Jeff looked up. "I think we're close to the system. The Ignotforstans just all got excited at the same time."

"That means it's showtime, folks," Raj said. "Remember—we're staying because it's an honor and because we all have jobs to do."

"Dirty jobs," Sidney said, rather proudly.

"Done dirt cheap," Lizzie added with a grin.

"And," Claire said, "we're just the team to do them."

CHAPTER 92

"COMMAND DECK PERSONNEL,** please return to stations," Mother intoned over the com. "All others, please strap in. Landing should be smooth, so if you wish to remain in the Observation Lounge, you should be safe to do so."

We got the kids strapped in, then Jeff, Chuckie, Drax, and I headed for the command deck doing the hyperspeed daisy chain. Mother didn't demand that Jeff and I switch with Reader and Jerry, and none of us asked about it, either.

We were in time to see Kreaving's solar system come into view. The only Ignotforstans here were Kreaving and Grentix. Had no idea where the others were, but figured by now White and Gower had taken them back to the Observation Lounge.

Wruck was here as well, as was Lilith. Wruck was staring out the window. "It's a lovely system."

"Looks a lot like Alpha Centauri," Chuckie said once we'd gotten close enough to the window to see things. "Three suns, two far larger than the third, almost twenty planets."

"They're not orbiting like those in the Alpha Centauri system, though," Reader said. "We've already asked."

"We've radioed ahead," Jerry shared. "They know we're coming and we should get to do an actual docking at an actual space station this time."

"Not on-planet?"

"Nope," Hughes said. "They have a nice space station that's conveniently located for all their spacefaring planets, which is about half of the system."

"So, Wheatles, you guys are flying around doing interesting things. You have enough spaceflight that your system has a space station. How is it that you didn't know about the Galactic

Council and so forth?" Sure, he'd talked about this with Drax and Gadhavi, but he hadn't done so with me.

Kreaving shrugged. "Per all the maps, our system is near the edge of the galaxy."

"Much farther out from the core than we are," Tim added.

"We haven't ventured too far from our own neighborhood," Kreaving said. "We've paid attention for centuries to what's outside of our area—radio waves do carry."

"So we've been told. A lot. But okay, why no real interaction?"

"Because we haven't felt confident enough to try to reach the core. And we were leery about reaching out to others. From what we can tell, there's some kind of war going on out there, many of them, but one that's bigger than the others. Our system is at peace, and we all want to stay that way."

"They're not isolationist," Reader said, in a way that told me he'd definitely talked with Abigail and knew the current party line. "Just cautious. Which, based on what we know, is wise."

Grentix nodded. "While we know of many, you're the first more advanced civilization we've met."

"I don't know that we're more advanced," Jeff said. "Just more traveled. In some ways."

"I'm still shocked that the Anciannas and Z'porrah left you guys alone, honestly. That, to me, seems hard to believe, based on experience." Very hard to believe, isolationist system or no.

"They probably weren't left alone by my people," Wruck said. "Shape-shifters can blend in." He changed to look just like he was Wheatles or Grentix's cousin. Then he shifted back. "Presumably they're far enough away from the core that the Z'porrah don't care. Yet."

"Yet is the key word, yeah." Wondered if I should mention us wanting to protect this system or not. "But we're allies now, so if you need us, we'll come."

"And we're grateful for that," Kreaving said.

"This system may be being ignored simply because the Z'porrah are being more cautious," Lilith said. "They have lost more and more battles, and their Federation of Planets is starting to question their goals and methods."

"Hey, did anyone else catch that the Z'porrah's group name is the same as the good guys in *Star Trek*?"

"We did," Tito said. "The rest of us just chose not to mention it."

"Haters."

"Trying to bring in new systems that the Anciannas have already claimed is not wise at this moment," Lilith continues, "because the Anciannas can call on Earth for backup."

"Gosh, we've gone from insolent, loser backwater to major player pretty fast."

Everyone looked at me. "Yeah," Walker said, sarcasm knob at ten and rising. "I wonder why the hell that is, Kitty. Wouldn't be because of you or anything."

"Um, it's a team effort."

"It is," Reader agreed. "But we know who's at the top of our enemies' hit lists, and that's you, girlfriend."

"I'll preen later. Right now, let's check out this cool space station. Wheatles or Grentix, which one of you wants to do the running commentary?" Hoped it would be Kreaving—he had the best voice of those from the *Eknara*.

"I will," Kreaving said. He proceeded to tell us all about the station, which planets in their system had worked to build it, how they'd brought along the other planets in the system, and how the ones that weren't spaceworthy yet were on their way. The inhabitants of their system were all humanoids that seemed to have evolved from animals similar to those on Earth. Tim had had Mother show Wheatles and Grentix our known allies, starting with Earth and the Alpha Centauri system.

Kreaving had had their system's information uploaded to Mother, so we could see what the folks on their various planets looked like. While none in this system were exactly like those we knew best, they were all similar.

"I wonder if interspecies breeding would take," Tito mused, more to himself than the rest of us.

"Why would you wonder that?" Grentix asked.

"A-Cs and humans breed well," he replied. "Your canine-based people look shaggy and more muscular than the Canus Majorians, but the overall structure looks familiar. Same with the feline-based race versus the Feliniads. There are other similarities, including those between you and us."

"I think we might be rushing the Apatan's acceptance," Jeff said. "As in, Tito, stop freaking them out."

Wheatles shook his head. "It's a shocking suggestion to us because it's not something we've ever considered."

"No one's fallen in love with someone from another planet?" Surely humans couldn't be the only ones.

"Not that we know of," Grentix said. She grinned. "But we'll make a note that humans will mate with anything."

This got a tension-reducing laugh, and Wheatles went back to his Space Station Tour Monologue.

The space station was impressive. Per Drax, not as big as those in some of the busier solar systems and those that were scattered around the galaxy for emergencies, but still, it could dock a dozen ships of any size at one time.

It looked like a giant, spiky, spinning top with a long spindle at the bottom. And it was spinning slowly to help the gravity generators or some such. Kreaving was happily using a lot of scientific and engineering speak and my ears politely shared that they were bored and wanted to either just listen to Kreaving's voice without having to try to comprehend the words or to hear music. Probably a good thing I was on the command deck and not being the worst example ever for the kids.

Knew better than to put my earbuds in at this time, however. It would be rude to the Ignotforstans and there was no desperate need. At least, I hoped.

The docking took a while and, interestingly enough, was the most complex of any landing we'd done so far. Made the comment that apparently parallel parking was hard for many to master—even though I, personally, happened to be great at it—and received a lot of "shut ups" from the guys, either via expressions or out loud, depending on the guy.

Of course, the real issue was that our ship was a lot bigger than any ship in the Apatan system, so getting our main airlock to line up with the corresponding airlock on the space station wasn't as easy as it would have been for the *Eknara*.

After some serious complaining on the part of the guys at the controls, Mother did Tito a solid and allowed Randy to take his place. Tim and Reader, however, were stuck, which was obviously a huge disappointment to Joe, since he was hovering behind Reader, ready to offer suggestions at any given second. To his credit, Reader didn't complain about this. Much.

Hughes remained cool as a cucumber, and, despite us having to veer off and try again a couple of times, we managed in the end, and without anyone getting flung around.

Once docking was complete, though, the next part of Mission: Split Up went into action.

Kreaving did his fist-to-pec salute. "As the official representative for Apata on the *Distant Voyager*, I would like to formally invite King Jeffrey and Queen Katherine to be our guests for the Festival of Thanks being prepared in your honor."

I was standing closest to Kreaving, so I did the bow. "We are honored by your invitation. However, the king and I are required to go on to the next planet that needs our assistance. With your permission, however, we would like to ask that we have some of the Royal Family and many of our retainers of highest importance remain to participate in our stead." The Washington Wife class continued to pay dividends in the strangest of places.

Kreaving looked a little disappointed. "You can't remain?"

"No. But we can return, once we are victorious. And, since we will be leaving over a third of our crew with you, many of them close blood relatives, you can be assured that we will return."

"The Festival takes many days," Grentix said. "If your next mission completes quickly enough, the Festival may still be going."

"See?" Smiled at Kreaving. "It will all work out. But we have to go—we gave our word that we would be coming to help, and Jeff and I don't go back on our word."

Kreaving nodded slowly. "You promised me you would find us and save us, and you did. I cannot ask or expect you to not do the same for others, regardless of our protocols."

"We're leaving my closest advisors, and the next people in line to protect our world if something happens to me and Kitty," Jeff said. "They can speak for us."

Kreaving grinned. "Based on my short experience with you, while they may indeed speak for you, I'm quite clear that no one else speaks for Kitty."

"I knew I liked you."

CHAPTER 93

OF COURSE, there was some pomp and circumstance we
had to get through at the space station, though not nearly
what was coming for those of our crew who were sticking around.

We had the full Festival described to us and it made any exceptional Earth religious holiday or sporting event victory celebration look pathetic by comparison. Even if our trip to Ixtha
lasted longer than our stay on Cradus, the chances that this Festival would still be going on when we got back were hella high.

The folks we were leaving at the station were all introduced
as vital to the running of our planet and solar systems, including
Alpha Centauri, in part to make everyone sound even more impressive and in other part because Jeff and I were the Regents so
it was kind of true.

Planetary leaders had come to the station to meet us, so by
the time all the intros were done and our explanation for why the
rest of us were leaving so fast was given, a few hours had passed.

Those of us traveling on began saying our good-byes, giving
last minute instructions to those staying behind, and getting
back on the ship. Christopher spent a lot of time running around
and making sure everyone was where they were supposed to be,
while Chuckie, Brian, Mossy, and Hacker International spent a
lot of time asking Drax every question about the ship they could
possibly come up with.

While this was going on, Kreaving and Grentix pulled me
and Jeff aside. "Is it impertinent or insulting if we request to go
with you?" Kreaving asked.

Jeff looked around. "What, all of you?"

Grentix laughed. "No, just the two of us. The others want to
stay home—some to ensure that your family and retainers are

well cared for, some because we spent much time thinking we might never see our homes again."

"So why do you two want to come, then?" Jeff asked.

"We're scientists and explorers," Kreaving said. "And we heard that you were going to leave the galaxy." He sounded excited, versus scared. A nice change from most of the Cabinet.

"We think we are, yeah," I said. "And that means it's a dangerous mission. We'd leave more of our crew here if we thought we could get away with it. And we don't mean that your system wouldn't be welcoming. Those going with us *want* to go."

"We do, too," Grentix said. "Very much. Wheatles and I are disappointed that our mission was disrupted, but the results were amazing. The idea that you're leaving the galaxy is overwhelming. We truly want to be a part of it."

"And you could use more scientists with you," Kreaving added. "You're very, ah, light in that regard."

"Sold," Jeff said. "Because you're right. And you're both well trained and, frankly, good company. We'll be happy to have you. Will coming with us cause any issues, though?"

"No, it will smooth them over," Grentix replied. "Now we will be a part of your continuing mission and that means we will return with glory for Apata."

Refrained from making a *Star Trek* reference because why bother when no one I was talking to would get it? Of all the old TV shows that Jeff was addicted to, he wasn't excited about watching any of the science fiction ones, probably because he, like the rest of the A-Cs, wasn't into documentaries. "And it indicates we aren't trying to get rid of people we don't like, too, I'd imagine."

Kreaving grinned. "Yes."

"We might not come back." Hey, had to point this out. Truth in Advertising and all that jazz. "I mean, not by choice."

They both nodded. "We understand that risk," Kreaving said. "We almost didn't return. It's a risk we all understand. Grentix and I are willing to take that risk because the reward is worthwhile."

"Super and duper, how long do you need to be ready?"

"We're ready now," Grentix said. "We had supplies on the space station."

"We've replaced what we needed, added some things in, and so forth." Kreaving indicated two rectangular things on wheels that looked a lot like rolling suitcases made for Real Naked Apes if I was any judge, and I was. "We can leave right now."

"Then let's do this thing."

Two Real Naked Apes back and ready for action on board, we got the rest of our flock settled in and accounted for. Miraculously, everyone was where they were supposed to be. It was easy for Christopher to verify since everyone who wasn't assigned to the command deck was in the Observation Lounge, getting ready to watch us take off.

I assigned Kreaving and Grentix to the command deck because I'd seen enough *Star Trek* to know that you wanted your Science Officers close at hand so they could share pithy info at just the right time.

Drax had done a long commune with Mother and somehow convinced her that, with him not being on the ship, she needed to break down and let Brian fly her. For whatever reason, she acquiesced. Per Mossy, easily. Decided that as the Many Mysteries of Mother went, this one could be deciphered later.

Brian had insisted on being on the command deck, and he'd actually won the argument with Mother about who was going to be the Commander for this part of the mission. Well, sort of. Tim was still the Top Man as far as Mother was concerned, but Brian was going to be allowed to sit in the Commander's seat. It was a small victory, but we took it.

Tito was also allowed to be relieved of duty, though not allowed to leave the command deck. Jeff and I, however, were required to sit our butts in our assigned seats and do our Mother-assigned jobs, thank you very much. Ignored Kreaving and Grentix asking those not at posts why we were all allowing our AI to order us around, but the sarcasm from the guys' replies was at least a twelve on the one-to-ten scale.

Brian, Hughes, Walker, me, Jeff, and Randy were at the controls, with Tim, Joe, Tito, Jerry, Chuckie, and Reader assigned as our respective backups.

Drax, being the genius designer he was, had added on standing restraints for those doing backup as well as those just hanging out on the command deck. This had only taken him a short time while we were docked thanks to some supplies from the space station and having Dazzlers On Duty do the speedy lifting.

So, everyone strapped in. In addition to the twelve of us

flying or backing up flying the ship and our two Real Naked Apes, Mossy and Wruck were here strapped in as well. Lilith was with us, too, but she needed no harness.

Managed not to mention that this was a crowded command deck, because I didn't want Mother to demand that the others head for the crash couches and I just knew she would if I complained in any way.

Might have been the hardest landing, so to speak, but the departure was by far the easiest we'd ever had. Some probably due to the fact that Brian was finally getting to do his job, but mostly because we were floating in space and therefore had no escape velocity to worry about.

Once we were well away from the space station and I'd said our good-byes to Apata Mission Control, Chuckie had me pull out the picture of our final destination. Really hoped that my thinking of it that way wasn't going to mean we were trying to escape inevitable death in a bad movie sort of thing. Actively chose not to say this aloud.

The picture was studied and Mother overlaid our known maps. After some discussion, it was determined that, galactically speaking, we weren't all that far away, and it would be much safer if we went around the galactic perimeter, versus trying to get through the more crowded center.

"It's definitely on its way to Andromeda," Chuckie said finally. "Not that they have a prayer of getting there before their sun dies."

"*Is* their sun dying?"

"Hard to tell from this picture, Kitty, but the space between galaxies makes the actual galaxies look tiny. Even the youngest star would be likely to burn out before a solar system floating through space were to reach the next galaxy. And, based on what we've looked at, this system's sun is not young."

"Two billion years from now, give or take, they'll hit Andromeda, or get smashed between Andromeda and the Milky Way, because our two galaxies are heading for each other," Grentix said. "So, it's very safe to say that this system will not survive the journey."

"I have a question sure to be unpopular," Brian said. "But why are we bothering?"

This got the room's attention. "Excuse me?" Jeff asked.

"I want to know why we're doing this," Brian repeated. "Trying to get to this particular solar system."

"Um, because we were asked to help?"

"Yeah, I get that, Kitty. But we've had a lot of people ask for help over the course of time, and by 'we' I mean the United States. We don't help everyone."

"Because it's impossible to," Reader pointed out.

"My point," Brian agreed. "This is looking impossible. We already know we can't evacuate all the inhabitants, unless we're looking at the least populated system in the galaxy."

"Brian's not wrong," Chuckie said. "It's a dangerous proposition."

"Thanks, Chuck. Kitty, it's dangerous even before I mention that we have to be going even faster than normal to escape the galaxy's gravitational pull."

"We have to try," Jeff said calmly. "They need us."

"We think they need us," Brian countered. "We have zero proof that they do. We don't know that this is Ixtha's system. I agree, Kitty's guesses are normally correct. But if she's wrong, this is going to be a much more dangerous situation than we've ever been in, and I say this knowing that most of you on this deck were all superbeing exterminators before. But I'm the only trained astronaut here, and I'm telling you, this is the most dangerous thing you've ever suggested."

"As dangerous as going into a sun?" I asked.

"Maybe," Brian said. "Maybe more so. This could be some elaborate trap. Or we could die merely trying to get there. Or trying to get back."

"Elaborate traps are our enemies' go-to move," Reader said. "And Brian could have a point. Though we face death all the time and we're kind of used to it."

"You all talked to Ixtha in the DreamScape," I pointed out.

"We did," Brian said. "But you, Jeff, Tito, and Tim didn't. Maybe that's why Mother kept you awake—so you wouldn't be fooled."

"I talked to Ixtha before all this started." And, more importantly, I'd talked to Algar, ACE, Sandy, and Naomi. And everyone seemed very certain that this solar system mattered a hell of a lot. Galaxy Ending Event was the phrase most tossed about by the Powers That Be. Meaning we had to do whatever we could think of, crazy, dangerous, or not, to get to Ixtha and save her day in some way.

Though, reality did nudge in and mention that while I *thought* this was Ixtha's system, I hadn't bothered to try to reach Ixtha to find out for sure. But I *was* sure, and that had normally been enough.

"And you dismissed her," Reader said. "You told us. I think Brian's concerns need to be addressed now, before we risk everyone on what could be a trap or just a suicide mission. We owe it to ourselves and to the solar systems waiting for us to come back."

"Well, short of my taking a nap, how would you like me to prove that we're headed to the right place?"

"I could put you into sleep," Mother said. "Right here, if necessary."

That caused us all to stop bickering. "Would that be safe?" Jeff asked.

"Absolutely," Mother said.

"No," Tim said calmly.

"What?" Jeff asked.

"I said no." Hadn't remembered that Tim had a Commander Voice, but he did and it was on Full right now. "I'm the Commander of this mission, isn't that correct, Mother?"

"Yes, Tim, it is. Your word is the final word on the ship."

"Good. Then, as Commander, I'm telling you, Brian, that we're doing what Kitty wants. Period."

"Without confirmation?" Brian asked.

"Correct. The only confirmation we need is that Kitty thinks this is what we need to do. You haven't worked with her like I have. She may be wrong, but if she is, then she'll still be right and this system is going to need us. That's our job, in case you weren't clear—to save people. It always has been. And, as far as I can tell, it always will be. So, we go, and we go now."

Everyone was quiet for a few moments. "It's always a good feeling when you see someone really grow up and into the role they were always meant to have," Tito said. "I'm with Tim. We do what Kitty wants."

"Thanks, Tito," Tim said in his regular tone. "And unless you want me to relieve you of duty, Brian," he added, Commander Voice back on Full, "you'll get us underway immediately."

Brian nodded. "Yes, sir, Commander." Though he still looked worried, he had zero irony in his tone.

"My Megalomaniac Lad's all grown up."

Tim made eye contact with me—hard to do with me in a helmet, but he managed it—and winked. "Team Maverick forever."

As I laughed, heard Lilith in my mind. This is why Mother

made Tim the Commander. For this one decision. Because she knew that, no matter what, Tim would always back you.

Not that I mind him having the authority, but why not just make me the Commander, then?

Because you need to be on Communications. You are who makes the connections, the person who creates the allegiances, and you do it with your words as well as your actions.

Okay, I guess I see it. So, why Jeff on Weapons?

He's the one who will fire if necessary, but *only* if necessary, and he'll wait until the last moment to fire. If anyone else had been at the controls when you arrived at Cradus, that system would be at war with us now.

Huh. And Tito?

The man who never panics? The man who saved a life before he was even out of medical school, when the A-Cs couldn't? There is no situation that Tito feels he cannot overcome — rightly. Every command crew needs someone who will never look at a situation as anything other than something to be solved.

Chuckie's backup because he's the smartest guy on the ship?

And one of the bravest, yes. James is backup for the same reasons. The others are all qualified, all brave, and all loyal to you.

So Brian's the only holdout?

She laughed. Brian's relationship with you is different than all the others'. He will always see you as his first real girlfriend before he sees you as anything else. And that leads to exactly what just happened. There is nothing wrong with him questioning your authority or assumptions, but, in this case, time is more of the essence than any of you can comprehend. We have very little time before, no matter what we do, that system will be lost to the blackness between galaxies forever.

Just in case Bri's right to be worried, could you verify if the system we're headed for is the right one? I haven't confirmed anything other than that I just *know* we have to go there.

It's as dangerous for me to leave the galaxy as it is for you. I'm willing to leave with you, but not alone. You would have difficulty finding me and bringing me back if things went wrong.

Then we go together. I refuse to ask you to risk more than the rest of us. I'm still hella grateful that you showed up when you did and are still with us.

This is the thing that sets you apart, makes you who you are, and gives those who are more powerful than you reason to respect and even fear you. That you will never ask anyone else to risk more than you yourself do. And that you care, about everyone, even those who are or were once your enemies.

"So, we're back to risking our lives?" Mossy asked, bringing me out of my head and back into the current situation. Realized that my conversation with Lilith had taken far less time than it had felt like. "I just want to be sure."

"Yes. We're going with my gut, my feminine intuition, and whatever else we want to call it. Full speed ahead to get out of the galaxy. Sort of thing."

"One suicide mission coming up," Reader said ruefully. "I have to be honest—there was a part of me hoping that Brian would win the argument."

"Look, I get it. It's dangerous. You guys can stop whining, though. Lilith, John, and I went into the middle of a freaking *sun*. With a rabbit. Let's talk danger and suicide missions, shall we?"

"I still don't know how you managed that," Brian said.

Had a thought and dug into my purse. Sure enough, the Z'porrah power cube was still there. And the knowledge of how to work it—how to *really* work it—was still inside my brain parts. "Wow. Have *I* got an idea for all of *you*."

CHAPTER 94

"I CAN'T BELIEVE WE'RE DOING THIS," Jeff said.

"This is riskiest for Lilith," I pointed out. Jerry had taken my place and I was enjoying not having the helmet on. My purse was over my neck, so I was prepared for anything.

"No," Chuckie countered, "we're all at risk in a big way. But this does seem safer. Somehow."

My idea was simple—use the power cube to move the *Distant Voyager* to Ixtha. But in order to do that, whoever was touching the cube had to be touching everything and everyone in the ship.

So Lilith had expanded herself to cover the entire ship and everyone in it, like the biggest Cradi Moon Suit imaginable.

"If this doesn't work, you're going to be floating in space, Kitty," Brian said, sounding as worried as the rest of the guys looked.

"And I can think of this ship and this exact spot in less time than it takes to blink, let alone try to breathe, or freeze to death, so I'm good."

"If this works," Kreaving said, "it solves the biggest issues we have—getting out of and back into the galaxy. And if it doesn't, hopefully we lose nothing."

"Remember that the ship will be moving if you have to get back fast," Reader said.

"Dudes, the Earth is moving all the time when we use these cubes. The Z'porrah freaking move their fleets with these puppies. We will be fine. *Fine*."

"I'm not worried," Wruck said calmly. "As Kitty said earlier, this seems less terrifying than going to the center of a sun. If

you'd prefer that only Kitty, Lilith, and I go, we'll all understand."

"Hilarious," Jeff growled. "No, we're all going."

"Good to know." Pulled out my phone and earbuds. Earbuds
into my ears, phone into my back pocket. Hit play on my music.
"Alright" by Lit came on. Good—Algar approved of my plan.

"Really?" Jeff asked.

"You want me calm or you want me freaked out? I wore this
setup into the star, okay?"

"Yes, and it was totally the bravest thing ever and only you,
John, Lilith, and a rabbit did it," Chuckie said. "And we're going
to be hearing about it for the rest of our lives."

There was a moment of stunned silence on the deck that I
tried to draw out and couldn't—the Inner Hyena appreciated
Chuckie's sense of humor too much.

Once I started laughing my butt off, everyone else did, too.
"Thanks, dude, we all needed that." Chuckie grinned at me.
"And, for the last time, Jeff in particular, everyone has their pro-
cess. This is mine. When a mission fails because I'm listening
to music? Then I'll stop. Until that time, however, if I'm going,
I'm going with tunes."

"I'm ready," Lilith said. It sounded like I was hearing it in my
mind and through my ears at the same time. Could tell that
everyone else was hearing it the same way.

"That's freaky but cool. So, everyone, let's do this thing."

I stared at the picture of the system. We were in a spaceship
so I didn't need to know anything about any of the planets, other
than that I wanted to be somewhere outside of them. Also
wanted to avoid their gigantic asteroid belt, because landing in
that would not be healthy for the *Distant Voyager* or her crew.

Manipulated the cube to account for a full ship and crew. The
Z'porrah didn't need a Lilith because they had one of these in
each of their ships, tied to their navigation systems. For those of
us using them in this fashion, however, the Lilith Approach was
going to be necessary, or at least the safest option.

The music changed to "Ready, Steady, Go" by Meices,
meaning it was time.

Focused on the space around the big blue planet, then chose
a spot that seemed clear in the space around it. Took the proverbial deep breath and triggered the cube.

Traveling by cube was always the way to go.

Felt the movement, probably because of our leaving the galaxy or due to our using the Lilith Method, though it was gentle and nothing like using a gate, more like a gentle tug moving us from one place to another. However, I was still inside the ship and so was everyone else. And we were in a solar system that looked very much like the picture. Only a lot bigger.

The sun was huge and red. The blue planet was easily four times larger than Earth, and I was prepared for someone to share that it was larger even than that. We were far enough away from the blue planet that we could make out the asteroid belt—which up close was even bigger than the picture had shown—and the slightly smaller but still huge red planet. The moons and dwarf planets were all present and accounted for, too, and then some. This solar system was littered with asteroids of all shapes and sizes. It was like some giant solar beanbag chair made of rocks instead of tiny beans had exploded.

The guys at the controls instantly started doing things that I was happily able to ignore. "Shields on full," Brian said. "Weapons loaded, just in case. Scan the system."

"Do I start hailing?" Jerry asked.

"Kitty?" Brian asked. "That's your area."

"Um, you know . . . I have no idea, really. But I'd think Lilith could condense now."

"Belay that," Hughes said sharply. "We have projectiles coming at us from the red planet."

"Of course we do," Brian muttered.

"I heard that. Do we want me to use the cube and skedaddle out of here, or are you going to try evasive maneuvers?"

"Doing that now, Kitty," Hughes said, sarcasm knob at six, easy. "Thanks for the tip."

"Everyone's a critic."

"This seems incredibly fast for someone to be firing at us," Chuckie said. "We literally just appeared. Even the fastest computer reactions would take longer than this."

Realized I hadn't asked a question that I should have back when we first got dragged into this trip. "You know, for a ship as advanced as this one, why don't we have cloaking?"

"We do," Brian said. He hit some buttons. "And I've engaged it. It's top-of-the-line, too. We hide our heat signature, ambient noise, and an array of other things I know you don't want me to list. The only time they'll see us is if they accidentally hit us."

"Better late than never. Just sayin'. So, will the rockets miss us now?"

"Yes, because I think they're not actually firing at *us*," Walker said. "I'm tracking the trajectory and I'm pretty sure they're firing at the blue planet, but the rockets are being sent over, versus through, the asteroid belt."

"Meaning, cloaked or not, we're still in the way," Tim said. "Let's get out of the way. Unless we can't move for some reason."

"No, we have full power," Brian said, as the ship took a sharp right turn and I remembered there was a harness with my name on it. "We just needed to be sure we weren't going to slam into one of the many dwarf planets, moons, or stray asteroids."

"Is that the excuse for the cloaking, too, Bri?"

"No. We haven't needed it until now, and I haven't been active, really, until now."

"Those sound like my kind of excuses, so I'll buy them." Got to said harness and got strapped in just in time, before we had to zoom upward. "Guys, seriously, I want Lilith to disengage. If we take a hit, the ship has shields but she doesn't."

"Agreed," Jeff said. "Tim?"

"I agree as well."

Felt Lilith retract. She sparkled near me. "Thank you. That was . . . taxing. The blue planet is not returning fire."

"Anything else you can tell us? I mean, if you're allowed to."

"I am not actually a part of what you call the Superconsciousness Society. I'm more of a . . . let me find the term that you'll understand . . . got it. Free agent. I'm a free agent."

"I'm gonna take a mo to enjoy this fact. I'm sure the joy will be gone soon, but for now, yahoo!"

"The system is at war," Lilith shared. "The red planet feels that those on the blue planet have wronged them in some terrible way. The reasons for this are lost to time, but the belief is still there."

"Just like any good religion," Chuckie said.

"Yes." Lilith paused, presumably because we'd moved to safety and were able to watch the rocket land.

"Those look like mushroom clouds," Tito said.

"Fantastic. We only have one Moon Suit." Me and you, together again? I asked Lilith in my mind.

Yes, regardless of what plans get made.

"They might not be nuclear," Chuckie said. "They came from far enough away that the impact alone could create what we just saw."

"Nice of Ixtha to mention a solar system war," Reader said, sarcasm knob at eight and rising.

"Well, she did tell me she was looking for the Warrior Queen. I guess we should have taken that leap."

"Possibly before we took this one," Brian said.

"Bri, seriously, stop being a Donald Downer. We're here now, we're going to handle things." Somehow. "Jerry, are you getting any kind of chatter?"

"None. And considering that one planet is attacking the other, there should be some."

"Maybe we're not on the right channel," Joe suggested.

"I'm scanning the entire solar space," Jerry replied. "There is zero chatter. You can feel free to try to do better."

"I would, but that's Kitty's job," Joe said. "And I wouldn't want to overstep."

"The blue planet has no external communications," Lilith said. "They've been destroyed. The red planet knows we're here—they did see us before we cloaked—and have gone to silent running."

"Or playing possum," I suggested.

"Possibly more than you realize," Lilith replied. "The blue planet has no clear idea why the red planet hates them. That world is filled with fear. The red world is filled with rage. There are other emotions, but those are the predominant ones."

"Jeff . . ."

"I have my blocks up, baby, stop worrying. Not my first war zone. And the other empaths on board have their blocks up, too, kids included. I've had the kids keeping their blocks up since we got things sort of under control at the start of this adventure."

"No more projectiles are being fired," Randy said. "Chip and I are both scanning and I see nothing leaving either planet."

"Correct," Walker said. "So, no idea if we should hail and make ourselves officially known, or try to sneak down to one of the many choices."

My music changed to "Round and Round" by Aerosmith. Considered what Algar was trying to tell me. "Maybe we should cruise the system first. Just in case."

"Good idea," Grentix said. "There could be life on the dwarf planets and moons."

"There is not," Lilith said in a way that made me pretty sure she knew why there was no life, too. "But we should indeed look."

We did the fast cruise around thing that would have made the Mercury, Gemini, and Apollo astronauts green with envy.

"This system is strange," Brian said as we completed our first circle around and were starting our second. "The dwarf planets are scattered far from the sun, and you'd think at least some of them would be closer to it. And it makes no sense that they'd still have moons—you'd think the moons would get pulled into the red planet's gravity."

"This system was traveling through the galaxy," Chuckie said. "The planets are huge, the sun huger. Maybe its gravitational pull stole the dwarfs from other systems."

"We need to take a closer look at the smaller objects," Walker said, voice tight. "Because I don't think we're seeing what we *think* we're seeing."

We flew closer and Walker and Randy did whatever they did in order to put objects onto our viewing screen and magnify them.

"You know, I realize that most celestial objects aren't truly round like a ball or a marble, like the pictures in textbooks," Tito said slowly, "but these don't look like moons so much as . . ."

"Shrapnel," Wruck said. "These aren't dwarf planets or moons. They're debris."

"Correct," Lilith said. "This system used to have more planets, none of which were dwarf planets, and no moons. The asteroid belt consists of the remains of the smaller planets in the system. The debris outside of the red planet's orbit is from the larger planets."

"Nice of you to share," Jeff said, keeping his sarcasm knob only at around three.

"Despite how it seems to you, accessing entire planets to find information takes time," Lilith replied. "And you all determined this without me anyway. I'm along to help, not do it all for you."

"We did," Jeff admitted. "And you're right."

"It's as if a billion souls cried out in terror and were suddenly silenced," Tim said.

"I feel something terrible has happened." Hey, Ixtha kind of considered me Obi-Wan; this dialogue was fitting.

"Let's not head for that small moon, then," Reader added.

"Is now the time, you guys?" Brian asked.

"It's always the time, Bri. And that's no moon."

"Enough with the *Star Wars* jokes," Chuckie said mildly. "We need to focus."

"Can we determine how long ago this was done?" Kreaving asked.

"Within the last hundred years," Lilith replied. "At least as far as I can discern."

My music changed to "Get the Girl! Kill the Baddies!" by Pop Will Eat Itself. "I think we need to get down there. Probably to both planets." Since I had to figure the girl was on the blue one and the baddies were on the red one. Knew where I was headed, therefore.

"How?" Brian asked. "We don't know if we can land safely on either planet, or if the red one will try to blast us out of space should we decloak or if they can see through our cloaking somehow. We don't know if we can take off, either."

"So, we stay in orbit and take a shuttle down. We did that on Nazez."

"Nazez wasn't being shot at by the neighboring planet," Reader pointed out. "Nor was it doing the shooting. Not that I'm saying that the shuttle idea is out. But it's not the same situation."

"True enough. And we're going to have to take two shuttles— one team going to the blue planet to find Ixtha, the other going to red one to find whoever's in charge and get them to stop."

"Are you sure we should go for the blue planet?" Joe asked. "Maybe we want to side with the aggressor in this case."

"So as to not be blown up," Randy added.

"We want to side with Ixtha. At least, I think we do."

"Why do you think Ixtha's on the blue planet?" Hughes asked.

"I guess because it looks more like Earth. And I don't think that she'd have been asking for the Warrior Queen if she was on the side with all the weapons."

"At the risk of getting told to shut up, I don't think we want to drag a warring system back into the galaxy," Mossy said. "It's not like we need anyone else fighting."

My music changed to "Red Red Sun" by INXS. "I think their sun is old, isn't it? That means it's going to go supernova or something in the near future, universe-wise. And that means, warring or not, they're all going to die if we leave them here."

"The galaxy needs what supernovas create, too," Kreaving said. "It's how star factories are formed."

"You mean nebulas?"

Grentix nodded. "Yes. If we can get this system back so that when the star explodes it doesn't affect other systems, it would be a good thing for the galaxy."

Everyone other than Lilith and the Real Naked Apes heaved a resigned sigh. We sounded like a giant tire deflating. "Kitty doesn't need to say it," Reader said. "We have to do this thing, because the Superconsciousness Society expects us to."

"Orbiting the planet or hiding out near the biggest piece of a former planet and away teams using shuttles it is," Tim said. "Can't wait to see who volunteers."

CHAPTER 95

I COULD HAVE JUST USED the Z'porrah power cube to get us down and then over, only I had no idea what spot to aim for, and without a destination in mind, you could end up nowhere or in the middle of a wall or worse. Plus, once down, we all needed to be able to escape, and that wasn't going to work with just one cube because everyone would have to be touching me and we were going to have to split up. It was use shuttles or give up and leave.

We didn't have to hide the ship, though we still kept it cloaked, because Lilith could determine that if we were up high enough, the red planet's projectiles couldn't aim accurately to reach us, because we were so much smaller than the targets they were used to hitting. That wasn't going to be the case for the shuttles, though they did have cloaking of a sort, but they were maneuverable enough that the assumption was we could avoid missiles fairly easily.

Because we were going to be in two teams, the ship was hovering above the asteroid belt and as near to the middle of the distance between the planets as possible. Their orbits weren't that far off from each other—they weren't aligned with the sun or each other, but they were close enough that one shuttle wouldn't have to go that much farther than the other.

Once we got out of range of the red planet and the majority of the asteroids, Tim insisted that the flyboys and Brian remain at the controls and, under the circumstances, no one argued. Tim pointedly put Hughes in charge, not Brian, who was smart enough not to complain about this. "I wouldn't leave you guys here, you know," Brian said, sounding kind of hurt.

Patted his shoulder. "We know, but you've seen the least

amount of action with us. We're considering this a war zone, and that means you keep military at the controls."

Brian somewhat appeased, shields were verified as set to full and staying that way, then Mossy trotted off to get Hacker International so they could all do what they could to ensure that the shuttles would also be shielded, more from fear of stray asteroid hits than the weapons.

Mother verified that we could survive on both planets. The blue one was definitely Earthlike and she expected no issues. The red one also had a breathable atmosphere. "It should be a colder planet, based on where it is, but it's quite hot," Mother said, sounding as worried as an AI could within the programming limitations. "For those from desert climates, you should be fine. Others should prepare to feel very hot if you have to go there."

"Meaning the A-Cs should be going to the red planet," Jeff said, clearly anticipating the next discussions to come.

"Um . . . no. You don't get to own the heat, my big man. Some of us are from Hell's Orientation Area, thank you very much. But thanks for the lead-in for the determination of who's going where."

Because we were going to be in two teams, Jeff and I had to first have the fight about whether or not we were going together or separately.

Finally won on the idea of separately by explaining that those who had the most experience working together needed to stay together, meaning I was going with White and Jeff was going with Christopher. Plus, king on one team, queen on the other seemed wise. Jeff only gave in because Lilith said she was going to be with me.

This part of the plan grudgingly agreed to, then had to have the fight for who was going to red and blue. Won that one by Chuckie pointing out that the person with the best record against the baddies was me, not Jeff.

With my husband hugely unhappy but resigned to merely muttering about how his uncle was constantly rating higher in his wife's esteem, how sidelining the guy who used to run the entire Field to the presumed safe planet was the rest of us being petty, how his closest friends weren't being supportive, and how he knew his wife needed his backup more than she ever wanted to admit, we then divvied up the rest of those who were conscripted to go, ensuring that we had those with hyperspeed on both teams.

Through all of this, the Cosmic Thing playlist was on constant repeat. Algar wanted me to know something, but I just wasn't getting it. However, I liked all the songs, so that was good.

Two teams of twelve finally settled—which was double what the *Star Trek* gang took along, because that was us, always doing it up big—meant it was time get the other members of the Away Team who weren't on the command deck, so we headed to the Observation Lounge. While we were explaining what we were doing and who was going where and why those who weren't named were going nowhere, my children in particular, I gave the kids hugs, starting with Charlie and Wasim and ending with Jamie.

"Be careful, Mommy," Jamie said seriously. "Daddy won't be with you and you won't be with him." She looked worried.

"I will be sweetie. Daddy and I are always careful. And we can get to each other fast." Well, I could get to Jeff fast via the power cube or with Lilith's help, and that counted, right?

She shook her head. "That's not what I mean." She lowered her voice. "I think he's crazy."

"Who, Daddy?"

"No. The Sheep Man. I think he's mean and crazy and he won't like you, Mommy."

Didn't have time for the full deciphering of whatever my little girl was talking about. Gave her another hug. "I'll handle him, Jamie-Kat, don't you worry."

Hugged Lizzie again as I stood up. "Try to make sure no one's telling Jamie weird stories," I said quietly. "I think she's believing them. Especially whatever about some sheep dude."

"No one's been doing that," Lizzie said softly, sounding confused. "We've totes been looking at the planets and Wasim has been talking about why red suns are old. No one's mentioned sheep."

"Huh. Well, okay. I guess." Wondered just what had scared Jamie and why a sheep was now the focal point. Something Mother of the Year was going to have to figure out in my copious spare time.

Adam pulled me aside. "Is there a reason you're sidelining me, Kitty? I'm a former athlete and a former Army Ranger, and you're letting Kristie go."

"Kristie's a cyborg, you're a regular human dude, impressive Army experience I didn't know about or not. I'm not taking Mister Gadhavi, either, or Tito, and, trust me, those men can handle themselves in a fight. I'm not taking the princesses who, let's be honest, can probably take on an entire planet by themselves. I want people up here who can come in and save us if we need it. If I take all my tough guys, who's left?"

He brightened up. "Should I have us ready, just in case?"

"Sure, why not?" Hey, that none of us had thought of this was just Adam showing he was an important member of the team. "I want you, Tito, Mister Gadhavi, Naveed, Rahmi, Rhee, Jeremy, Jennifer, Mister Joel Oliver, and Hammy all primed and ready. You'll all want to have body armor and weapons. Don't get into them now, but be standing ready to get equipped fast. Maybe we come back and you'll have just waited around. But, based on experience, we're going to need you, somewhere along the line."

"Who do you want leading that team? I'm willing, but I'm also the least experienced."

"See, this is why I like you. You're always willing and you check your ego at the door. You're in charge. You had the idea, you have the background, and the princesses have a lot more respect for any man who's been in the military." Sure, it had taken me years of work with them, but they *had* learned to respect some men. "Let me know if anyone gives you any trouble about this, and rely on Tito if the princesses get uppity."

Adam grinned. "You got it, Chief." He hustled off to get his team together.

Emergency Backup Team chosen and prepping, the two official away teams headed for the armory, because if I wanted Adam and his team in armor carrying big guns, I wanted that for the rest of us even more so.

First, however, made a pit stop.

Went to the bathroom so Lilith could join with me before I suited up. For whatever reason, I didn't want to tell the others she was going to be inside me, though couldn't have said why. It was less shocking this time, mostly because I was prepared for it. Got a lot of information about where we were, but it went in fast. Figured I'd ponder what Lilith had learned when we had a moment of dullness. Waited until she'd settled into the back of my mind, where she wouldn't be intruding on my conscious thinking unless necessary, then joined the others.

Happily, Mother had been able to create more suits, so we weren't out. Some of the suits Wruck and I had used were still available, though no one took those. Chickens.

Jeff's team was him and Christopher, Reader and Gower,

Claudia and Lorraine, Wheatles and Grentix, Tim and Serene, and Butler and the Kristie-Bot—who was totally jazzed about being on the show.

Pulled my team together as we were doing all this, the Cosmic Thing playlist still going strong, as a way for Algar to remind me that I still wasn't getting something he thought was hella obvious. "I want us agreeing that no one goes off alone. Everyone has an assigned partner, and they don't leave that partner. I'm with Richard, Malcolm and Nightcrawler are a team, Len and Kyle, John and Mossy, Abby and Mahin, and Chuckie and Kevin. I'm not wild about the fact that we have teams that have no A-Cs, so I want all of us staying as close together as we can because, let's be real—we want to be able to grab our teammates and run at hyperspeed if things go wrong."

"You mean when," Siler said, "not if."

"Potato, potahto."

"Let's call the whole thing off," Buchanan said, sounding like he meant it.

"Can't do it, and you know it."

"I do, Missus Executive Chief. I do. I'm just not happy about it. On the other hand, I'm almost ready to faint that you actually chose to take your security team with you, versus making us go off with Mister Executive Chief."

"He's got all of Alpha Team, both former and current, other than me and Richard. He's good."

"Like everyone else who's been sidelined for most of this trip," Kevin said with a smile that showed off his awesome teeth, "I'm glad to be coming along."

Kevin was highly competent and someone who was great in danger situations. Having worked with him a lot, I'd demanded he be on my team. That Kevin had bags and bags of charisma had nothing to do with it.

"Hey, I wanted the hot guys with charisma with me, what can I say?" Well, okay, not *much* to do with it.

He laughed. "The flattery will get you everywhere."

"Should the rest of us also be flattered?" Siler asked.

"Absolutely. I choose my team based on looks. And the girls are hotties, too."

Abigail and Mahin laughed as Chuckie snorted. "Just don't say that where Jeff can hear you."

"Too late," Jeff said, coming up behind me. "Nice to know you're swinging back to thinking humans are hotter than A-Cs."

Turned around and hugged him. "Only hotter than some A-Cs."

He shook his head. "I know, not hotter than my Uncle Richard."

"Hey, girls like the Silver Fox look."

"This is why we fight to be on Missus Martini's team, Jeffrey," White said. "We enjoy the compliments."

"And somehow," Jeff said, "people wonder why I still get jealous."

CHAPTER 96

JEFF PULLED ME A little away from the others. "Baby, I'm agreeing to this because we all know our time is tight. But I'm not happy about it. I don't want us to have gone through all we have only to orphan our children here. Lizzie shouldn't lose more parents, nor should she have to become a surrogate mother. Jamie and Charlie shouldn't lose us. None of the kids should lose their parents, not over this."

"Jeff, I know you're worried. But I know in my gut that this solar system is vital for some reason. I can't come up with that reason—yet. But I know we'll figure it out. And the moment we do, I can also say that we'll all be glad we're here, doing what we're doing."

He hugged me tightly. "I'll trust you on that, baby. Mostly because honesty forces me to admit that you're rarely wrong in these cases." He put his finger under my chin and tilted my head up. "Just promise me . . . you're coming back alive, well, and whole."

"Only if you promise me the same thing. Because while I have a lot of hotness on my team, I've been spoiled and I'm kind of used to being with the hottest, smartest, sexiest, bravest guy, so you'd better be planning to not get hurt or killed, too."

He gave me a slow smile, then bent and kissed me deeply, though not for too long. Well, long enough for me to be ready to go off and do the dirty deed despite all that we had going on, but considering Jeff was the God of Kissing, it didn't take much to get me primed and ready.

"I promise," he said as he ended our kiss. "Because you always give me the best reasons to keep living for."

We pulled apart and I made sure that Lorraine, Claudia, and

Serene all had adrenaline for Jeff, just in case. Claudia and Lorraine were carrying med kits and Serene had an emergency pack on her.

"You don't have any medics on your team," Claudia said, sounding worried. "Should you take Tito along after all?"

"Nah. We'll be good. Our Martian Manhunter has a med kit, and so does Abby. And I have my purse."

"Well, then nothing to worry about," Lorraine said, sarcasm knob heading for the higher numbers.

"Geez, you guys. Lighten up. We're going to get down there, figure out what's going on, and save the day. In that order."

Thusly encouraged, or not, we headed for the shuttle bay, Wruck bringing body armor and weapons for Mossy, who was still there.

He and Hacker International were finishing up. "You should be good as long as you don't hit anything larger than a baseball," Stryker said. "We have extra patch kits in each shuttle, too."

"Get a third shuttle ready in the same way in case our backup team needs to come help either planet. In fact, get two shuttles ready, in case that team has to divide and come to both planets." Hey, I was confident, not insanely optimistic.

"Will do. The cloaking isn't great, but it's better than nothing. The shuttles have a way to go reflective, based on Earth military camouflage, so you'll be hard to spot unless you're against a backdrop that shows the perspective is off, or similar. You didn't use it on Nazez, but we strongly suggest you activate it here."

"Will do."

"Good. I need your phone for a couple of minutes, though. And take out your earbuds, you're not going to need them."

"Why?" Took out my earbuds and handed the phone to him.

Stryker rolled his eyes as he fiddled with the phone and I reluctantly put my earbuds away. "We've set up a communications system so that you guys can all be on a super version of Bluetooth and therefore able to talk to us and each other. We've done it before, if you remember."

"Not in space."

"No, but since Mother can boost all the signals and we're on our own system, we should be good. We've been working on it during any downtime. Everyone else is getting a single earpiece, but we know you, and Big George convinced the rest of us that it would be easier to just make yours work for your phone as well."

"So I can listen to music and take calls?"

"So you can listen to music and connect to the ship which will then connect you to your team and the other team, as needed. No calls, you're all going to be using these." He handed me my phone, two earpieces, and an oval pin made of what looked like pewter. "Attach the pin to your chest. It's your communicator."

"Just like in *Star Trek*?"

"Different design, but yeah. Learn from and imitate the best is our motto."

"Cannot argue." Pinned the pin over my heart. "Hope they can't shoot well."

"The disk is made from metals from Cradus. We tested—the metal repels bullets."

"Cool!"

"But not laser shots. So try not to get hit."

"Thanks for that." The earpieces were small and inserted into the ear canal. Could still hear just fine, too. "Nothing over the ear?"

"Too easily spotted, too easily broken."

"No cord?"

"None. Welcome to nineteen-ninety-nine."

"Smartass." Turned my music back on. Picked up right where we'd left off, on the umpteenth repeat of the Cosmic Thing playlist, currently featuring the Backstreet Boys desperately trying to get me to make the connection about "The Answer to Our Life" and not succeeding at all. "Wow, the sound is great, really clear."

"We should be set up so that only you hear the music. When no one's talking, you'll hear music in both ears. When someone's communicating, then music in the left, Jerry or whoever you're talking to in the right. These are the opposite of noise-cancelling, too, so you should be able to hear external sounds as long as you don't have your music blasting."

"Choosing not to resent that last statement. What if we need to be silent and the other team doesn't know? The best way to ruin a mission is to have someone on the other line going 'yoo-hoo' or similar."

Stryker turned around to Ravi. "You owe me twenty bucks. Told you she'd ask how to turn the calls off or mute them." Ravi grimaced and Stryker turned back to me. "Two ways. First off, you tap your communicator to reach Jerry, then he connects you to who you're trying to reach. You tap the communicator again to turn it off. If you can't reach the communicator for some reason, or you need to turn off the earpiece and Jerry's not able to get to you as fast as you'd like, press your finger against your tragus and hold for a long second."

"I beg your pardon?"

He rolled his eyes again and touched the part of the ear that was kind of pointy and you could make lay over the ear canal a little.

"Wow. I learn something new every single day. Had no idea that had an official name."

"It does, and it's how you turn a live call off, or back on, without hitting your communicator. It'll work to alert Jerry that there's an issue if you turn it on and off too often, too, so don't play with it."

"You guys are amazing and I'm going to ignore you suggesting that I'm a little kid who can't stop touching the new toy. Make sure the backup team has this stuff, too."

"Thanks, just a warning, and no kidding about prepping the backup team. Thank God you're here, we'd have never come up with that one on our own."

"Careful, Eddy. I'm not against kicking you in the shins. Or hitting you in the tragus."

"The more things change, the more they stay the same, Kitty."

Stryker went off to give others this fab new tech and I headed for my team's shuttle. Jeff's team had Butler, Reader, and Tim, who all got to fight for who was going to fly the shuttle. Knew Butler was going to win that one—he and Maurer had already proved that androids made great shuttle pilots.

My team had me, Buchanan, and Len to fight about who was going to do the flying. So. I was sort of surprised to see Wruck in the pilot's seat. He chuckled at my expression. "You do remember where we were the first time you and I ever really talked."

"Yeah, in a helicopter you were flying. Works for me, but I'm snagging the seat next to you. I want to see the view from straight ahead, not just by looking through the moon roof that is cool but now makes me wonder if we have a metal cover for it."

"That's fine on your seating, but only because you have hyperspeed. Windshields can take asteroid hits, too, you know. And yes, the shuttles have metal covers for the moon roof and windshield." He pushed a button and a metal lid slid over the moon roof. "They weren't used when we were visiting Nazez because that system didn't have the debris this one does. The windows, like the hull, can take a lot of hits before they crack."

"Thanks for reassuring me and taking all the fun out of it at the same time. You got your snazzy earpiece?" Could see the communicator on his clothes.

"I did. I got to confirm that we can't hear your music."

"Everyone's a hater these days."

The rest of my team filtered into the shuttle. My right earpiece beeped softly. "James wants to confirm that I can connect everyone," Jerry said in my ear. "So, I'm going to be doing that while you all travel down to the planet. It's going to be boring and annoying, but necessary, so don't whine."

"Check. Wait. Do I have to hit my communicator for you to hear that?"

"No, not if I'm contacting you. You tap it to contact me, though, and then you tap it again when you're turning it off. I can do both from here, for all of you."

Heard Reader in my ear. "Testing, testing. Sound off if you hear me. This is James."

While Jerry started the communications tests, we took off. Jeff's team went first, with ours following right after. As with our other shuttle voyage, took the time to look back at the ship. Saw nothing. Good to know our cloaking was spot on. Figured the kids were watching us and sent love at them. Sent some love at Jeff, too, just 'cause.

This was different from Nazez in a lot of ways, though the uncertainty was similar. "Think we have to find and stop an evil megalomaniac here?"

"Does a duck swim?" Len asked. "Does a bear poop in the woods?"

"A simple 'yes' would have sufficed."

"Where's the fun in that?" Kyle asked.

"Good point."

CHAPTER 97

WE HAD TO MANEUVER around asteroids more and more the closer we got to the planet. However, the communications testing was distracting enough that I didn't have a lot of time to worry. Wruck and Butler were both great pilots, though, and neither shuttle took any asteroid hits.

The Blue Team reached their planet's atmosphere first. "James is live to all of you," Jerry said in our ears.

"This planet is a lot like Earth," Reader said. "Mostly oceans, several large landmasses, some big islands. We're orbiting to find the most populated area or what might be a spaceport."

Things went quiet and we continued on toward the red planet.

Any idea where Ixtha is? I asked Lilith in my mind.

No. I have been searching for her, but haven't found her yet. She may be in some kind of shielded area.

Shields work on superconsciousnesses?

Sometimes. It depends on what the shield is made of.

"All cities seemed bombed out," Reader said a few minutes later. "No signs of spaceports or similar."

"That was fast for a planet that size," Chuckie said.

"The shuttles can go at supersonic speeds when inside a planet's atmosphere," Wruck said.

"Really glad Kitty got Drax onto our side," Chuckie said.

"Really hope we don't find out they have one like him on this planet," Buchanan countered.

"We've found a safe place to set down," Reader said. "Near what looks like an older city. Jeff says he gets a different emotion from this area than the rest of the world. And before Kitty worries, his blocks are back up and he doesn't need adrenaline."

"Abby?"

"My blocks are up, Kitty," Abigail said. "No worries."

"Starting descent to the red planet," Wruck said.

Buchanan advised Jerry. "Missus Executive Chief, they want us to do the same commentary that Reader did. You're in the shotgun seat, so it falls to you."

Tapped my communicator. "Jerry?"

"I'm here. Putting you live to the Blue Team, Red Leader."

"Thanks, Mission Control. Okay, this planet is not like Earth. At least, I hope not. The red is everywhere."

We got lower and started the supersonic speed Wruck had talked about. "Going fast around this puppy, and while there are cities of a sort, this place looks a lot more like Darkseid's home world of Apokolipse. And I mean, it really looks like it. Lots of active volcanoes, lava, even the water is red. Not as technological as Apokolipse, but it sure looks like they're trying."

"James is explaining what you mean to most of his team," Jerry said. "But the rest of us are with you, Red Leader."

"Good. This place looks horrible. I could understand why you'd want to leave it, but not why you'd want to destroy your most viable options for where to go next. So I'm running with the idea that whoever's in charge is really like Darkseid which means likely evil. I'll be thrilled to find out differently, but that's our working hypothesis. The heat is clearly coming from all the volcanoes, and they are volcanoes versus fire pits, for those keeping comics score at home."

We kept on circling. "Not a lot of what we'd call cities but possibly that's due to available resources—everything appears to be made from the rock, earth, and lava. The colors are red, orange, and yellow, and all minglings of such. Maybe they're shooting at the blue planet because they're afraid of it—there is nothing in the blue, green, or purple ranges here, nor is there any white."

"What about mining?" Jerry asked. "Do you see anything?"

"Not really. No spaceport here, either. Many rocket silos, though, all aboveground, at least the ones we can see. No idea who creates rockets to blow up other planets in their system but doesn't try to make a spaceship, but we're about to land and try to meet them. And before anyone says something, of course we're going to be careful. However, this is the planet that has communications and the weapons, so my assumption is that we're going to land and be taken to their leader sooner as opposed to later."

"Red Team, Blue Team has not been approached and sees no sign of life," Jerry said. "They're splitting up to search the area."

"Roger that. I'll stop our sightseeing commentary." Noted that my music was still on the Cosmic Thing playlist. Still had no idea what I was supposed to figure out. I'd been close the first time I'd seen the list of songs, but now I had nothing.

We found a spot that seemed safe to land—no volcanic activity, no buildings, no people, no animals, just a lot of red dirt and what could be charitably called scrub plants. This area made the desolate parts of Beta Eight look like amazing places to live. We set down, Wruck verified that we could all breathe here, and we got out.

Happily, the song changed, finally, to something new. "The Worst Day Ever" by Simple Plan. Couldn't argue that being on this planet was probably going to qualify as the worst day and hoped the song didn't indicate our failure. Felt fairly confident it didn't, since I figured Algar knew what I was planning and agreed with it—it was a simple plan, after all.

"No one around," Buchanan said. "That seems suspicious."

"Maybe our cloaking worked," Mahin suggested.

"Never assume things are going our way, Mahin. Trust me on that one. And Malcolm, on Nazez we had rabbits. So I'm expecting anything here."

"I agree," Kevin said. "Oh, and Kitty, I want to know what your plan is. The real plan, not whatever you told Jeff and James you were planning on doing."

"I can't believe I demanded you be on my team."

"Uh huh. Spill it."

"Fine. I expect to be captured, hopefully as soon as possible. This is a big planet and we're going to need to get to the Head Megalomaniac fast because we don't have time to sway the hearts and minds of the citizens. Per Lilith, we're on as fast a timeline here as we were at every other stop."

"Figures," Buchanan muttered.

"Why so serious, Malcolm?"

"No reason. Do you want all of us captured?"

"So glad you asked. No, I do not. I want Richard and myself captured."

"Who else?" Kevin asked.

"No one. Who will come rescue us from wherever we get imprisoned if I let all of you guys get captured?"

"I hate this plan," Buchanan said, almost cheerfully. "But it's totally you, so I know you're not lying. How soon do you want to split up?"

"What do we all think?"

"We're in the middle of nowhere," Abigail said. "And I don't feel anyone other than us." She cocked her head. "But I feel angry." She bent down and picked up some of the earth. "Interesting. The dirt makes me angry. I think this planet may be poisoned in some way."

"Perhaps due to all the volcanic activity?" White suggested.

"Maybe." Abigail didn't sound convinced. "I'll monitor along the way."

"So we go together for at least a little ways," Wruck said as he closed the shuttle doors and we headed off.

"Everyone remember where we parked." Missed Tim, but Chuckie laughed at this, so all remained okay in my world.

"Let's hope we can get back to it, all of us," Siler said.

"And those who aren't playing the roles of sheep to slaughter should plan to remain close enough to grab each other and run," White added.

We'd landed on a hill with a flat top that was surrounded by much larger hills with no signs of anyone on them, so we had to walk down toward what seemed like a lot of nothing on a slight incline. Saw no real roads, certainly no paving, no buildings, no fences. It was weird—the world was advanced enough if they were firing missiles, but they showed no real signs of advanced civilization otherwise.

We walked for a good fifteen minutes—during which time Algar went back to the Cosmic Thing playlist, possibly because he now hated me—and saw pretty much nothing other than rolling red hills of dirt.

Finally, my music changed again, which was again a welcome relief. Not the song choice, though, since it was "Danger" by Third Eye Blind. "Everyone get ready, just in case," I said softly as I looked around to see what had sparked this song.

White was looking in the opposite direction than I was. "I believe that I see what look like farm animals in the distance."

We all turned to check it out. Sure enough, if sheep could be orange, there were orange sheep. "Wow, Mister White, that sheep to slaughter reference was spot on. Should we investigate?"

"Sure, we can be the aliens that approach a farmer on his isolated farm," Chuckie said.

"So, you're saying that those theories are sound?"

"We parked where there was space to land and leave our shuttle in part because no one was around. I think if you're doing an exploratory mission, you don't land in New York City."

"You know we've been on Earth longer than you've been alive, Charles," White said.

"I do. I also know that others came by, and I'm not even talking about John's people or the Z'porrah."

"Let's cut the chatter," Kevin said. "Just in case."

"I don't see anything other than sheep," Len said. "Why are you worried?"

Couldn't say the real reason I'd mentioned danger. But I had a reason that worked. "Because it's weird that no one's come to meet us."

"We didn't hail," Kyle said.

"Plus, we were camouflaged," Abigail added.

"And Lilith said they were playing possum. Speaking of which, are those giant opossums in the field with the sheep? Giant reddish opossums?" Which could be a great name for a band. Though Giant Orange Opossums had a better ring.

"Sure looks like it," Kevin said. "Though this is still chatter, in case you all weren't sure."

"Hilarious." The animals weren't doing much, just standing or lying there. All their backs were to us, so we couldn't see any faces. "Think they're dead? Maybe something killed off the inhabitants and the rockets are launching automatically?"

"I give up," Kevin said with a sigh. "Please, talk away."

"You know this is how she rolls," Len said.

"All the time," Kyle added.

"Why do we need to be stealth right now?" I asked.

Right on cue, we found out why.

CHAPTER 98

THE SHEEP AND OPOSSUMS all stood up on their hind legs and turned around. To a one they were holding weapons that looked like some kind of gun, only a gun made for those without opposable thumbs.

Stopped looking at the weapons and checked out their faces. They weren't the faces I was expecting.

They were still animal, yes. But they resembled Earth sheep and possums like gargoyles resembled Michelangelo's David. Sure, there were similarities, but you'd never mistake a gargoyle for David's close relative.

They fit this world, though. They all had big, crazy eyes, extra-large tusks protruding from their mouths and, on the male sheep, seriously deadly-looking horns. Not to be left out, the possums all had long claws. Their front hooves and paws were more evolved, almost handlike, which explained how they could hold the weapons. Their back ones were more footlike, which made sense for them being able to stand upright.

Couldn't tell if the sheep's wool was naturally a burnt orange color or if it was from them lying in the dirt, but the opossums' fur was definitely a rather pretty strawberry blonde. That was me, Ms. Diplomacy, always finding something to compliment.

The sheep were all about my height, the opossums were shorter, though they were all probably taller than Algar. Really hoped they didn't have hyperspeed.

"You are our prisoners," one of the sheep said as my music changed to "Simple Rules" by Massive Attack. Realized the Universal Translator wasn't how I was understanding these words—this was one of the languages we'd learned in our sleep.

Wondered if Ixtha was actually on this planet, but decided to listen to Kevin and stop chattering. At least, about that.

Decided instead to stick with my plan, since that was my take on the song cue. "Take us to your leader." Wished Tim or Reader were on my team to enjoy this one, since not even Chuckie snickered behind me.

"What are you two doing here?" the sheep asked. "Brandishing weapons?"

Risked a hopeful look around. Only White and I were standing here. Took the leap that Siler had gone chameleon and grabbed the others or Abigail had grabbed everyone and used hyperspeed. Or both. Hoped it was both.

"Looking for your leader," White replied as he slung his large laser gun onto his back. Did the same, because that seemed the most diplomatic, and nonthreatening, way to handle this situation at the moment.

"Why would you think we would know the Mad Lord Johpunnt, may the sun continue to love his reflection?" the sheep asked. Wondered if this was the crazy sheep man Jamie had warned me about, or if I was going to meet him later, or if it was just a coincidence I was trained to never believe in.

The music changed to "I'll Talk My Way Out of It" by Stuttering John. Took this to mean Algar wanted me to run my yap. Never a problem. "Excuse me, who?"

"Mad Lord Johpunnt, may the sun continue to love his reflection. He is the leader of our world."

"Um, where we come from, 'mad' means insane."

"Oh." The sheep nodded as if this cleared everything up. "Here it means 'enraged.' Mad Lord Johpunnt, may the sun continue to love his reflection, is filled with righteous rage."

"Gotcha. We'd still like to meet with him, regardless of the sun's views about his reflection."

"Why?" the opossum next to the sheep asked.

"Because we're visiting from another solar system and we want to talk to the leader. Is he the only leader on the world, or just one of many?" It was a damned big world, and, after all, on Earth the leader depended on where you landed, particularly since Jeff didn't push the whole King Regent thing. Frankly, as Algar's cover story proved, we had a lot of little kingdoms scattered all over a much smaller surface.

"We have only one ruler, and Mad Lord Johpunnt, may the

sun continue to love his reflection, rules the entire world by right and by might."

"Super. By the way, what are your names?"

They both looked surprised. "Why would our names matter to you?"

"Because it's considered polite and normal to refer to people by their names."

They still seemed thrown by this request. "On our world, we share names," White said.

"We also have no idea what planet this is, or what your sun is called."

The sheep lurched back into some semblance of authority. "I am called Roanach, you stand on the mighty world of Helix Rime, and our noble sun is called Helix Prime."

"I am called Clorence," the possum added quickly. Noted he was a little cross-eyed. Decided not to mention it.

"We have a friend named Clarence," I said conversationally.

"But I am Clorence," the possum said.

"Yes. The names are similar. I was making small talk or polite conversation."

"Why?" Roanach asked.

"Because you two aren't taking us to Mad Lord Johpunnt and we assume that there is a reason you're delaying," White said.

The song was now "Keep This Train a Rollin'" by The Doobie Brothers. Presumably we needed to continue this fun chat. "Maybe they aren't authorized," I said to White, in a stage whisper. "They're kind of out in the middle of nowhere."

White nodded. "Perhaps we chose the wrong landing spot." He was using the stage whisper, too. I loved working with White.

"We are part of the Outer Guard," Roanach said, sounding slightly offended. "We are authorized for much."

We turned back to Roanach and Clorence. "Sorry," I said sweetly. "It just doesn't seem like it. And I have to ask—if there's only one leader and, therefore, one would assume, only one kingdom, what is it you're all guarding against?"

They all gaped at me. "Enemies," Clorence said finally.

"Enemies within your own kingdom?" White asked.

"No," Roanach said strongly. "All are loyal to the Mad Lord Johpunnt, may the sun continue to love his reflection."

"So, back to the original question then. If you're not fighting amongst yourselves, and there is only one ruler in all the world, what are you all guarding against?" Really wondered if they actually knew about other parts of the world or not.

"We have been a unified world for thousands of years," Clorence said. Identified him as smarter than Roanach, which currently appeared to be a low bar. "We have no strife amongst ourselves. We serve Mad Lord Johpunnt, may the sun continue to love his reflection, as our forebears served those Lords who came before him."

"We guard against enemies," Roanach said as if he'd just figured something out. "Enemies like you, who appear out of nowhere."

Obviously these two were not going to grasp the nuances of our issues with their job descriptions. "Okey dokey. Well then, we're not enemies, we're visitors. And we need to meet with Mad Lord Johpunnt. Could you direct us to someone who could take us to him?"

"Why do you want to see Mad Lord Johpunnt, may the sun continue to love his reflection?" Clorence asked.

"Because we have information he will want."

Some of the other sheep and possums had gathered 'round. Roanach noticed. "If you truly have information Mad Lord Johpunnt, may the sun continue to love his reflection, would want, why did you arrive in secret?"

"We didn't," White said politely. "We couldn't determine where to land, so we chose a spot that seemed uninhabited where our ship wouldn't harm anything on your planet."

"By the way, sorry, but I just have to ask—are you required to say 'may the sun continue to love his reflection' every time you use the dude's name, or is it just actually part of his full name?"

"Why would you think that was required?" Clorence asked.

"Because you say it every time," White said. "For instance, while I could introduce my companion as Queen Katherine the brave and beautiful, I don't have to say that every time I speak her name."

"Though it does have quite the ring to it, Mister White."

"I'll make a note, My Queen."

"You're a queen?" Roanach asked suspiciously.

"As hard as that might be to believe, yes. And yet I'm still nowhere closer to getting to have a meeting with Mad Lord Johpunnt and his reflection."

The rest of the sheep and possums seemed far more convinced than Roanach and Clorence, and both of them noticed.

"Perhaps the Mad Lord frowns upon those who bring visiting dignitaries to meet him," White said to me in the stage whisper. "Maybe we were misinformed and the Mad Lord is not actually the most powerful person in this solar system."

"Mad Lord Johpunnt, may the sun continue to love his reflection, is the most powerful person in the galaxy!" Roanach said.

"Um, well, see . . . gosh, how to say this . . . not so much anymore." My music changed to "Danger Danger" by Hello Hollywood.

So wasn't that surprised to hear a step behind us. Sounded like a heavy something with an even heavier hoof. "Bring them to Our Lord," a very deep voice said. "He will want to meet them before we kill them for their insolence."

White and I both turned around. To see a very big, impressive bull who was on his hind legs. Though his hide was black, he had the same big, crazy eyes, scary giant horns, large tusks, footlike rear hooves, and handlike front hooves as the others. He wasn't carrying a weapon in his hands, but he had weapons strapped to his back. Wasn't sure but they looked edged versus projectile and, like him, they were huge.

Speaking of huge, the people on this world didn't seem to have chosen to wear clothes. With the sheep and the possums it wasn't that big a deal. On bulls, however, this one in particular, it was kind of a weird form of advertising.

"Wow. You've never met a cow who didn't want to get frisky, have you?"

The bull blinked. "Excuse me?"

"Where we come from we cover our impressive, ah, members," White said. "Out of politeness to others."

The bull snorted, which was the most impressive snort I'd ever heard or seen. Steam literally came out of his nostrils. "We have no need for false modesty on Helix Rime."

"Nothing to be modest about on you, dude, trust me."

"This is Queen Katherine and Mister White, Telzor," Clorence said. "My Queen, this is Telzor, the Captain of the Guard for Mad Lord Johpunnt, may the sun continue to love his reflection."

Telzor raised his forehoof, and it was clear he intended to smash Clorence for something, whether introducing us politely, giving us his name, or most likely, referring to me as My Queen. Clorence wasn't an ally, but he also wasn't doing anything wrong, at least as far as I was concerned, and decided that my opinion was the one that counted.

Moved at hyperspeed, grabbed Clorence, and got him behind me and White before Telzor's swing could hit him.

The bull looked shocked as his strike whiffed impressively. "What did you do?"

"Prevented you from hurting someone whose only crime was to try to introduce the people who want to meet your leader to you. Unless I read you wrong and you were going to give him a high five, not smash his head in."

"He was going to smash my head in," Clorence whispered. "I overstepped."

Noted that Roanach and the other sheep and possums were sidling behind me and White. Had no idea if this meant that they were going to attack us from behind or if they were hoping that they wouldn't get hit by Telzor. Possibly both.

White noticed and he turned so that his back was to Telzor. So, we were as ready as we were going to be.

Telzor's eyes narrowed. "Just because you're a female, don't think that I consider you anything other than an enemy."

Time to fight, Lilith said. I'd forgotten she was there. Be ready.

"I'm always ready." Moved into a fighting stance. "Telzor? Feel free to bring it, you big, nasty bully."

"You would fight me here, now?" Telzor asked.

My music changed to "Little Queen" by Heart. It was always nice when Algar and I were in sync.

"I would. Because Mister White and, therefore, Clorence, only gave you part of my introduction. I'll give you the rest—I'm Kitty, the Warrior Queen."

Results, as so often happened, were immediate.

CHAPTER 99

TELZOR ROARED AND ATTACKED, but without drawing a weapon. He went for my head.

To be nice, I didn't grab my gun and shoot him dead. Instead, I went into scissor splits, put my hands together in a double fist, and slammed them right up into his gigantic balls, using all my enhanced strength and hyperspeed. Lilith gave me an impressive assist here, too. We were a good team. Besides, under the circumstances, it was literally impossible to miss.

Heard gasps from the sheep and opossums as Telzor's roar changed to a scream of agony, then a squeak, as his hooves left the ground. Yeah, it had been a *good* hit. I brought my right leg around and spun on my butt, then leaped to my feet in a move worthy of Jet Li. Prayed White had seen it.

Telzor landed flat on his face. I went to his head and slammed my foot onto it. "I am the Warrior Queen," I bellowed. "And I demand an audience with Mad Lord Johpunnt or I will deal with every person on this planet as I've just dealt with this one!"

"You haven't killed him," Roanach said in the way one does when a superior has missed a key step and the underling doesn't want to get killed for mentioning or not mentioning it. Noted that all the Outer Guard who were male—which was most of them—were all in a commiserating protective crouch around their groins. The few females looked like they'd just learned a new move. That was me, taking feminism to the stars.

"No, I haven't." Looked at the ridiculously huge swords this guy was carrying and decided I'd ruin the show if I tried to lift one of those, enhanced and with Lilith inside me or not. "We show mercy where I come from. Once." Shoved my foot on Telzor's head again. "And only once. If you ever disrespect me or my people again, I will end you in a way that ensures you die in agony."

Telzor managed a high-pitched moan of pain.

"I'll take that as an apology. And it if wasn't, understand that the next time I'm not going to hit them, I'm going to rip them off."

"We eat your kind where we come from," White said in a cheerful, conversational tone. "You might want to remember that, as well. My Queen, shall we? Clearly we need to work harder to find this Mad Lord. Or else he fears you, as I suspected."

"Mad Lord Johpunnt, may the sun continue to love his reflection, fears no one," Telzor managed to squeak out.

"Oh yeah? Then why are will still waiting to meet him?"

Clorence cleared his throat. "We need Telzor to take you to Mad Lord Johpunnt, may the sun—"

Put up the paw. Clorence shut up. The One True FLOTUS Power worked everywhere! "Unless you are required by law or the threat of death to say the rest of that phrase about his reflection, stop it. We got it, the Mad Lord and the sun have a 'thing' and everyone's really proud of it."

"It's not a 'thing,' " Roanach said. "It shows our love and respect."

"Work under the assumption that we figure you love and respect the dude and that we neither want nor need to hear the thing about the sun ever again. Or at least not until you do the official introductions."

The sheep and opossums seemed unsure. Time for more of my kind of diplomacy.

"You know, I can and do kick people right in their special parts as hard as I hit them."

"Maybe harder," White said in that Helpful Retainer way.

"True. Maybe harder. Does anyone want to find out?"

Every head shook violently to indicate that no, they did not. Even the females.

"Then let's get this show rolling." Looked down. Telzor was still wrapped around his own personal pain. "You all need to pick Telzor up and carry him to wherever it is we're going."

"The capital is far from here," Clorence said.

"So, is Telzor only the Captain of the Guard for the Outer Guard, then?"

"No," Roanach said. "He is the Captain for Mad Lord Johpunnt, may—" He caught me glaring. ". . . ah, yes. For the Mad Lord."

"He can be taught. Then that means that Telzor came from the capital, and pretty quickly, all things considered. Meaning Telzor has the means to travel fast. Take us, and him, to those means. And chop-chop, time's a wasting."

Sheep and opossums other than Roanach and Clorence lifted Telzor. It took twenty of them, and they were struggling with it. They dropped him a couple of times. Did my best not to enjoy this. Failed.

"Where do you think the others are?" I asked White softly while the Outer Guard continued to drag, drop, and carry Telzor and we followed. Roanach was leading and Clorence was hanging close to us.

"No idea, but I assume they're enjoying watching you work."

"I hope they're taking notes, then."

We reached a large vehicle that looked like a flatbed truck as visualized by the *Star Wars* gang. No tires, it floated above the ground. The Outer Guard managed to toss Telzor face down onto the flatbed. Even though he took up a considerable portion of the bed, there was plenty of room for more cargo.

Checked out what I was going to consider the cab of this vehicle until told otherwise. It was a lot like the front of most trucks—a bench seat, a steering mechanism created for someone with hoof-hands, pedals for hoof-feet, and space behind the back of the bench seat, presumably to store their version of jumper cables or similar. There was an opening in the back of the cab that, on Earth, would be for a window. This was just open. Chose not to care about why at this precise time.

The cab was roomy, clearly made for Telzor's bulk and height. Eyed the others. No one other than White was going to be tall enough to drive this puppy unless I made them tag team it, and that just seemed like more than they were going to be able to emotionally handle. And we didn't want to crash this vehicle, so White driving was out.

My music changed to "Mr. Cab Driver" by Lenny Kravitz. The clue seemed clear.

Looked around. "I would like my Royal Driver to appear, please."

Had expected Len, but it was Buchanan who appeared out of nowhere. Could have been that he let go of Siler. Could have been that he just wanted us to see him now. Buchanan had Dr. Strange powers, and if he didn't want you to see him, you didn't.

The sheep and opossums gasped even louder than they had

when I'd smashed Telzor's tenders. Interesting. They didn't have hyperspeed, presumably only the bulls had extra strength, and they didn't have anyone who could go invisible or just appear out of nowhere.

"My Queen," Buchanan said with a bow. "You called?"

"I did, Doctor Strange. We need to drive this puppy to wherever the capital is. And I would prefer that you do this, versus Mister White."

Buchanan nodded—you didn't need to tell any human working with the A-Cs why we didn't want an A-C at the controls of things like this. If it wasn't A-C made, their reflexes were too good and they'd destroy the machine—I'd experienced this firsthand during Operation Fugly, and some lessons I learned immediately.

Buchanan examined Telzor. "He looks ready to get up. You want me to make him dead?"

"Only if he becomes a problem."

Buchanan put his face near Telzor's. "I think he *wants* to become a problem." Buchanan had a really crazy mad look in his eyes. "And I prefer to remove problems before they bother my queen."

Telzor growled. "She made her point. I will allow her to meet Mad Lord Johpunnt. He will deal with all of you."

Buchanan nodded. "Gotcha." Then he slammed his elbow right between Telzor's eyes.

"Um, is he dead?"

"No," Buchanan said. "He's just unconscious, which is how we want him." He removed the two giant swords Telzor had on his back and put them behind the seat in the cab. He did the same with the gun he had strapped on his back, and indicated he wanted mine, which I handed over. Both of those went behind the seat. "Let's go."

"First, Roanach and Clorence, we have no idea where we're going. Do you?"

They both nodded. "We will show you the way," Roanach said.

"Great, then get on next to Telzor and stick your heads through the opening when you need to give us directions." Looked around as I said this, hoping the rest of my team would catch the clue. "We're about to head off. It's been nice meeting all of you," I said to the sheep and opossums. Who continued to stare at me in a form of shock.

My music changed to "Drive Away" by The All-American Rejects. Chose to take the hint. Got in next to Buchanan, who was already in the driver's seat, White got in next to me with his gun at the ready, the living embodiment of riding shotgun, and we took off, Roanach and Clorence sticking their heads in on either side of mine.

"Cozy," White said.

"Speak English," Buchanan said, in English. "Think about it, we're all speaking the native tongue, but we have a language they won't understand."

"Wow, you're right." Had to actively shift my brain to talk the language I'd been raised in. "That sleep teaching stuff really works."

"Did the others get onto the truck?" White asked.

"Hope so," Buchanan said. "That was our plan even before Missus Executive Chief asked me to appear. We considered taking the shuttle and following you in that, and they may have done so, but I have no idea now."

"Have you heard anything from the others?" I asked.

"Not yet, no. Give everyone some time. What I do know is that Abby felt angry when the sheep and possums first turned around. But once we ran off and came back using Siler's blend, she didn't feel angry anymore. She doesn't know why yet, but it's something for us to keep in mind."

We drove along, Roanach or Clorence giving directions as needed, Algar flipping me back to the Cosmic "Kitty's Not Getting It" Thing playlist. There were no roads at all. Probably because you didn't need them if your vehicles floated. Or else there were too many volcanic eruptions to bother. We passed two in the near distance in the time it took to travel along to what really appeared to be nowhere.

There were farms, though, or what looked like farming. "Is that Orange Scourge, do you think?" I asked as we passed groves of a bright orange substance that looked familiar.

"Possibly," White said. "They have to eat something."

"The rabbits and least weasels said it was delicious, too."

"This system has been traveling," Buchanan added. "Could mean that the spores got sent out somehow and just finally hit Cradus."

"True enough." We subsided back into silence. Saw a lot of sheep and opossums. Could tell that the females were doing most of the farming, based on the number of smaller sheep and opossums that were hanging about. All of them had wool or fur the same colors as the world.

"Why do they all have tusks, do you think?" White asked in English.

"Bulls have horns and possums come equipped with them," I pointed out. "Sometimes the possum tusks are small, but I've seen some with big ones."

"But while sheep can have horns, they do not have tusks. And if they're growing crops, then they don't need tusks to kill their food. While a mating ritual is possible, I would, based on what we've seen so far, find it unlikely."

"No idea," Buchanan said. "Though I'm sure we're going to find out just like I'm sure it's going to be a reason we all find horrific. This world is the definition of horrible."

However, what we weren't seeing were things that looked like towns, let alone a capital. Nor was there any industry that could produce rockets. Frankly, there was no industry at all, though did spot some crops that looked like cabbages or lettuces or similar that were all burnt yellow in color.

"You're not just trying to take us to some prison, are you?" I asked Clorence. Twice. Once I did it in English, he looked blank, and I shifted my mind back to the native tongue.

"No. We told you—the Outer Guard stays far from the capital."

"Why?" White asked, not having any language shifting issues.

"We need to guard the farmlands. We have many enemies."

This again. "Do you? Because what we saw when we came into this system was a lot of planetary rubble floating in space and your planet shooting bombs at the only other planet left in this system."

"We have been oppressed since time began," Roanach said, sounding like he was quoting scripture, which, for this place, he might well be. "We are fighting against our oppressors."

A thought occurred. "Did you have enemies when your people first arrived on this planet?"

"Yes," Clorence said. "The dangers were many and our forebears had to fight to survive and create an existence on this world. The strong survived, as they always do."

"How many enemies have you all, personally, had to tangle with, before we showed up?" Buchanan asked.

Roanach and Clorence were both quiet.

"I'm going to go out on a limb and bet that the answer is 'none.' Isn't that right, Clorence?"

He sighed. "Yes, it is. The Outer Guard is not blessed with the same levels of opposition as the other Guards are."

"You know what we're going to find, right?" Buchanan asked in English. "There is no 'opposition,' not any more. There was once, and that's probably why they all evolved tusks. But that opposition has died or been stamped out and they *could* be living peacefully, but they aren't. Meaning, there's only this Mad Lord and he's got these people under his control and that's how he keeps the control."

"Just like Darkseid. Only Darkseid has powers, and I'm not getting the feeling that anyone on this planet does. The few things we've done have amazed and terrified them. That sort of screams backwater to me."

"Never assume that the ones put on the worst duties are indicative of the others," White said.

"Telzor's supposedly the Captain of the Guard. He had no defense for hyperspeed and, let's face it, he's now our prisoner. He didn't recognize that we were carrying laser guns, or guns of any kind. I'm not impressed yet."

"Other than by his package," Buchanan said dryly. "Yes, we were all staying close by and heard everything."

"Cool! So everyone saw my awesome Johnny Cage in *Mortal Kombat* moves?"

"Yes, we did. Anyway, everyone's impressed. And happy you like us."

There was a soft beep and I now had Billy Idol singing "Cradle of Love" in one ear, while in the other ear I had Jerry. "My Warrior Queen, your King would like a word with you."

CHAPTER 100

"HEY JERRY. Um, were you eavesdropping?"

"Chuck called ages ago to tell me to monitor via Richard, so I did. I have the ability to share with the command crew. We all enjoyed the show earlier."

"You can see us?" We rounded a gentle curve to see more crops—these looked like alfalfa or something similar, though it was, like everything else, fitting this color scheme and coming up a light red. These fields were being tended to by a lot of cows, accompanied by calves and some rather spindly-looking bulls. These bulls were not going to cause Telzor any self-esteem issues. The bulls and male calves all had black hides, the cows and female calves had reddish hides.

"Yeah, the hackers figured out how to properly enhance Mother's ability to drill down visually. Great moves. We're all impressed."

"Yeah? Did you know where I learned those moves?"

"Watching Johnny Cage in *Mortal Kombat*."

"Got it in one!" As with the other farms, there were sheep and opossums on guard duty. Unlike the others, we were passing much closer by these farmlands. Wondered if we were going to have issues, but Roanach or Clorence waved to them, depending, and the guards waved back. Had the feeling that Roanach and Clorence were showing off that they were on one of these vehicles in positions of, if not authority, at least not disgrace.

"I never had a doubt. Oh, and those who bet against me have to pay up—I told them that's where you got the idea."

"Steal from the best, that's our motto."

"True enough. Love your new ride, too. And, from what we can see, the sheep and possum aren't lying to you—you're heading for something that sort of looks important, at least compared to what you've been traveling through. Now, here's Jeff."

"Baby, I hear you've been using your own special form of diplomacy."

"Could have let a giant bull clobber me. Chose to clobber him."

"That's my girl."

"Always, Jeff. What's up? I'm in the middle of, hopefully, getting to see the top man around here. One of these days, at any rate."

Because this thing could float and Roanach was one with the idea of the straightest line possible, we were heading over what appeared to be a dig site. This was the first evidence of activity besides farming we'd seen.

"We can't find anyone on the surface, and we've searched the entire world by now."

"I'd ask how but I assume that the 'we' means Christopher."

"Yes. He and Butler used the shuttle to search the rest of the landmasses while we dug around here. I feel people, so we assume they're underground, probably because of the bombings. There's a lot of destruction."

"Did they have cities? Does it look highly civilized?" We were over the giant hole now. And large rabbits were working on it, doing the digging. They looked about the same size as the sheep, had orangey fur, and the few that looked up at us had the same crazy eyes as the rest of this world's residents. They had the adapted front paws, though their rear paws were still pretty rabbitlike. Their claws were long and sharp, sharper even than the possums', and while they didn't have tusks, their teeth were impressively large and looked sharp, too. No one would want to cuddle one of these, other than another one of these.

"Yeah, it does. Very civilized. I think this was another utopian planet—I don't see any means to fight back, we haven't found weapons or anything we think could be weapons."

"So, not like where we are. The weapons we've seen so far are edged, clubs, and some kinds of things that look like guns made for hoof-hands. Haven't seen so much as a crossbow, let alone any other kinds of projectile weapons, and no one's fired those guns, thankfully, so they may not work like we think they do."

"So a lot more than we're seeing here."

"Noted." None of the rabbits waved to us and Roanach and Clorence didn't wave, either. The guards around this dig were all rabbits, too and, for the first time, something other than a bull looked threatening in a real way. "Anything else going on?"

"Not really. If I didn't feel others besides those in our away team, I'd honestly say this world was deserted."

"Are you going to search for the people? Lilith said she thought they might be shielded in some way." Couldn't make out what the rabbits were digging for. However, the dirt they were digging up was being formed into a hill by other rabbits. Wondered if the other hills we'd passed had been formed like this, too. But there had been no evidence of digs, and for this hole they were too far into the earth to make the idea that this was going to be another area where crops were grown make sense.

I believe they are all underground, Lilith said in my head. At least half of this population is underground and harder for me to spot. I assume it's the same on the other planet. I was able to sense them here when we went over this hole.

"Yes, but first we're investigating without interference."

"Wise. I'm assuming a human suggested that."

"Actually, I did." Jeff's sarcasm knob was only at about a five. "If you can believe it."

"I'm so proud! Search underground, Lilith thinks that's where we're going to find the majority of the populations. And all this is great, but I have to ask—why are you calling? Not that it's not great to hear the melodious sounds of your voice, but this feels very non-urgent."

"I'm calling because of what we just found and triggered."

"Okay, I'll bite—is it a doomsday device and we only have a few minutes to defuse it? If so, never cut the red wire."

"No. It's nothing like that. We found what looks like a giant meteorite."

"Is that what the red planet is using to bomb the blue one?"

"No. We saw evidence of their bombs. Nasty, but not this. But based on what Wheatles and Grentix think, this is likely the same kind of thing that sent the Mykali to Earth."

It was there, right there. Focused on the playlist again. Had "Sowing the Seeds of Love" by Tears for Fears playing now. "Seeds . . ."

"What do you mean?"

"Not sure yet. You said you triggered it. Does that mean it's going to explode or open?"

"Open."

"Careful, that's one way you can become Hawkman and then you'll be mated forever with whatever girl's standing there."

"Huh?"

"Ask James. Just be careful."

"We are. Hang on." Heard talking in the background. "Okay, it's fully opened now and the Ignotforstans are examining what's inside."

"I'm so glad the Real Naked Apes wanted to come along."

"Don't call them that, but yeah, me too."

"I think they'll like it. Grentix has a great sense of humor, and Wheatles is pretty cool."

"Thanks for the assessment of our newest allies. Hang on." Heard more voices in the background. They sounded excited. "Huh. Wheatles and Grentix aren't sure, but they think that what's inside is some kind of recording device. We're going to try to figure out how to make it work."

"Good luck with that. You're sure it's not a bomb?"

"Pretty sure. And we have hyperspeed and are prepared to run if we need to. And—and this may shock you—I've been doing work like this far longer than I've known you."

"Blah, blah, blah. Okay, great, then call me back when you have more." My music changed to "Red Door Blues" by Indigo Swing. "I need to concentrate."

"You don't want to listen in?" Jeff sounded shocked.

"Oh, I do. Only, we're finally coming to what I think is the capital and I'm going to have to be fully focused."

"Okay. Love you, baby."

"Love you, too. Be careful."

"You, too."

"Always."

"Never," Jeff said dryly, "that I've ever seen."

"Everyone's a critic." Tapped my communicator and the call went dead. Just in time. No need for Jeff to hear what was about to go on.

We'd been told to make a sharp right around another hill and found the capital. And there was a whole line of bulls with swords and pikes waiting to greet us.

CHAPTER 101

THIS PLACE RESEMBLED A fort from the Old West a lot more than a city. In places like Arizona and New Mexico, wood was scarce, so most forts didn't really have barriers, just people on guard. This place was quite similar. Unsurprisingly— hadn't seen anything that looked like a tree anywhere.

There were people and buildings, of course. The buildings weren't that impressive. They seemed more like mud huts than anything else. Had no idea what kind of industry this world had, but whatever it was, it wasn't high tech. Other than, you know, them launching rockets at the other planets in their system. Maybe that was their industry. Maybe it was hidden somewhere. Maybe I'd find out.

There were various people on the streets, all of them matching one of the four types we'd already seen. Hadn't spotted anything that flew, and if there were insect people, they weren't in evidence.

"Where are we?" I asked Clorence.

"The capital city."

Managed not to say "duh" really loudly, but it took effort. "Um, really? What's this magnificent place called?"

"It *is* magnificent, isn't it?" he replied, with absolutely zero irony. "We are in Luhgremn."

"What?" He said the name again. Forced him to spell it. Realized I would think of this place as Loogie if I wasn't really careful. "Luhgremn. Got it."

Most of this city is underground, Lilith said in my head. I believe we are also going to find the source of the rage here. Abigail is not wrong, but something here definitely is.

"How do you want to handle this?" Buchanan asked in English as one of the bulls approached.

"Asking them to put on loincloths is out, Malcolm," White said. "Sadly."

"They're into being natural or nudists or however you want to think of them. Anyway, the handling is going to depend on Telzor."

The bull came up to the side of the cab. Buchanan did his best not to look at the giant phallus flopping around basically in his face, but was pretty sure it was taking superhuman effort. Managed to control the Inner Hyena, but it took almost the same level of effort.

"What's going on here?" the bull asked as he bent down and gave Buchanan something of a break.

Shocking me to my core, Roanach answered. "We are bringing the visiting aliens, Queen Katherine and her retainers, to meet Mad Lord Johpunnt, may the sun continue to love his reflection."

The bull looked at the flatbed. "What happened to the Captain of the Guard?"

Decided the truth was the way to go. "He pissed me off."

Telzor groaned and sat up. "This is the Warrior Queen. She is not from our world. And she is vicious and violent." We hadn't seen anyone who looked human, so sharing that we weren't from around here, after Roanach had said we were aliens, seemed like overkill, but perhaps Telzor was just trying to regain a modicum of authority.

"Ah," the other bull said. He nodded to all the other bulls. They separated so we could keep going. "You will take them to our Mad Lord?"

"I will," Telzor replied.

Noted that the bulls didn't need to say the crap about the sun. Not that this was a total surprise. This place was definitely the inspiration for Apokolipse. Wondered what the Mad Lord was going to look like, other than naked with his junk flapping about. Figured he had to be a bull—they were the biggest creatures I'd seen here, and they had the nastiest horns and the biggest hooves. And other things.

We started off again. Telzor pushed Roanach and Clorence out of the way, shoved his head in between mine and Buchanan's, and started giving directions.

"Oh, my dear God. Dude. Do they have breath mints on this planet?"

"I don't know what you mean," Telzor said. "But I assume it's an insult."

"Only to your breath. I'm still very complimentary about your manhood, especially since I've just seen other examples. You're the Top Bull for a reason." Buchanan and White both tried to pretend they hadn't heard this.

Looked around as my music changed to "Smoke and Mirrors" by Symphony X. Saw no smoke, saw no mirrors, so figured Algar was telling me that things might not be as crappy as I was seeing. Or else we were heading into a trap. Possibly both.

"Telzor, what is it that you do on Helix Rime?" I asked, as we weaved between huts and the people moved out of our way. As with the way here, there weren't roads so much as places that you could float over. Had to say this—the planet required less upkeep than a lot out there.

"What do you mean? I told you, I'm the Captain of the Guard."

"Yeah, not what I meant. I mean, what do you do, create, enjoy? I mean, everyone's gotta eat, and I've seen farms. But there have to be things to do other than farm and guard things. And dig holes."

Telzor rolled a giant eye at me. "You saw digging?"

"Yeah. On the way here. The long, boring way here. Seriously, what industry does this planet have?"

"You ask many questions."

"I do. I'm interested in why you don't want to give me any answers."

"I'm curious as to how Telzor found us so quickly," White said.

Telzor snorted. "It's my job to know when things are not what they should be."

"So, you saw us land?" I asked.

Telzor didn't answer.

"I'm pretty sure this thing can go a lot faster than I've been going," Buchanan said in English. "I figured we needed to see what was around us and I didn't want to lose anyone if they're still on the back."

"It's a long blend for Nightcrawler if they are."

"He's been practicing," Buchanan said with a grin. "But if you're trying to figure out how our friend here got to us so fast, this is probably the way. Based on how lightly I've been pressing the pedal and by what I think are numbers indicating speed, we're nowhere close to as fast as this can go. Figure they saw us land or saw us exit the shuttle somehow and sent the big guy out to stomp us into the ground."

"I'd brag about not letting that happen, but I know how our luck rolls, so I'll keep that one to myself."

"I'm impressed with your self-control," White said.

"Stop here," Telzor said, before I could get in another rejoinder. We stopped. Looked around. Wasn't much to see. Other than a big hole that looked to be an easy fifty feet in diameter, and a very large capstan that looked like it needed at least eight bulls to move. The whole area was guarded by bulls and rabbits.

Telzor got off the truck bed. Roanach and Clorence did, too. The three of us followed suit, Buchanan taking the time to take our and Telzor's weapons out from behind the seat. He put his gun back on, tossed mine to me, gave one of the swords to White, and kept one for himself. Decided this was smart thinking.

Telzor looked like he wanted to demand his weapons back, but then he looked at me and changed his mind. So he'd heard and understood my threat about ripping them off. Good.

However, he didn't seem clear that what we were wearing on our backs were weapons. Possibly because we hadn't used them in that way—we'd already put our weapons away by the time he'd joined our party, and they looked nothing like the weapons this world had. Decided this was us being stealthy and hoped it wouldn't blow up in our faces in some embarrassing way later.

Telzor went to the side of the hole and waited. Went with him, though all of us stood far enough away that he couldn't shove us in easily, Roanach and Clorence, too. My music changed to "Demons" by Imagine Dragons. Not the most comforting of song choices, but at least it wasn't the Cosmic "So Close Yet Still So Far" Thing playlist for the moment.

The source of the rage is nearby and underground, Lilith said. Be cautious.

Looked down. Saw nothing. "I wonder if it's going to be like on Nazez. Where we're going down into an illusion."

"This is no illusion," Telzor said as he nodded to one of the rabbits standing around the hole. It pointed to the bulls, and sixteen of them went to the capstan and started turning it. This required a great deal of effort on the bulls' part.

Hadn't meant to speak the native language, nor had I realized I'd done so. Oh well, my, as always, bad.

"What is this place?" Buchanan asked.

"The entry to the palace of Mad Lord Johpunnt," Telzor said. "May the sun continue to love his reflection."

Chose not to mention that he hadn't used the sun phrase until now.

A platform rose up. It was metal and had intricate designs depicting a solar system, but not the one we were in, at least, not as far as I could tell. The system shown reminded me of the one we'd seen in the picture sets—the first solar system, the one whose sun had gone supernova, the one we felt the Mykali had come from.

"That's a beautiful design," I said to Telzor.

He nodded. "It is."

"Is this the design on every platform, or do they change?"

"This is the approved design."

Telzor stepped on the Approved Design and the rest of us did, too. Telzor indicated that he wanted some of the rabbits to join us, which they did. Had no idea where the rest of our away team was, but there was enough room that they could all be on this thing and no one would know. Once we were on, Telzor nodded to the rabbit in charge of the capstan. It had the bulls start turning in the opposite direction. We started down.

This platform went faster than the one on Nazez had, possibly because it was being run by real people. Looked around for signs of illusion, but saw nothing. We went down with dirt all around us until we were about as deep as I'd seen the rabbits digging in that other hole. Then we left the dirt, though we could still see the sky above us. But what we were in now wasn't dirt.

We were in a city, a real city. Just a totally underground one.

Actively made sure I was speaking English. "This looks a lot like how Tolkien described the underground dwarf cities."

"Complete with very active mines," Buchanan said, nodding his head toward one.

"And volcanoes," White added as he looked around. "I have no idea how they're harnessing them, but these volcanoes look as active as the ones we saw erupting."

Noted that Roanach and Clorence looked awed. Switched back to their native tongue. "This city is amazing. It must have taken decades to build."

"More than a thousand years," Telzor said. "And this city is more than ten thousand years old. We reap the benefits of those from Helix Rime who have come before us."

"Wow. It's lasted that long? That's amazing."

"We survive and endure on Helix Rime." This also sounded like a scripture quote.

"Brilliant architecture, too." It was. Somehow the pillars were holding up not only the earth but a crisscross of metal latticework that was both beautiful and efficient—many things hung from the lattice, including what looked like homes, work areas, and mining offices.

This reminded me much more of Haven—Fancy's underground network of cities protecting her and her people—than it did of the factory on Nazez. This place definitely felt real. Unlike Haven, though, I was really sure that people, not Algar, had built it. What people was the question—the architecture I was seeing sort of screamed the need for opposable thumbs. Though, who knew, maybe I was selling those with hooves and claws short. After all, they were driving, farming, and wielding weapons. Why not create a gigantic underground city, too?

Had to figure the smoke and mirrors clue related to the top of the world versus what lay underneath. From the outside, this planet only looked like Apokolipse. From the inside, however, it looked very functional, civilized in a certain Industrial Age way, and quite bustling.

Spotted a machine that looked more futuristic than anything else anywhere on this planet. Saw a variety of rabbits going to it, getting something out of it, and eating.

Eat nothing from that machine, Lilith said urgently. It is the source.

Of evil? I think it's some kind of food replicator.

It is not food as they're growing aboveground. That is the food of rage.

Noted that there were giant telescopes, or things that certainly looked like telescopes, on platforms that raised and lowered just like the one we were on. So they were definitely able to look at what they were shooting.

Are those the telescopes of rage? I asked Lilith.

"We've found the industry," White said in English, which I was starting to think of as Our Secret Tongue, before Lilith could reply. "They're building the rockets here, as well as other machines."

Looked for the machines. There were vehicles like the one

we'd driven in on rolling off of an assembly line. There were also things that looked suspiciously like parts of a rocket, but not the bomb kind. These were bigger and likely for spacecraft.

"Have your people ever traveled to other stars?" I asked Telzor.

"Not for a long time."

"Why not?"

"We had . . . things that had to be done first. The Mad Lord Johpunnt, may the sun continue to love his reflection, will share what he feels is best with you."

"Gotcha." We were still a good ways from the bottom, but that was because the pillars were so very high—twenty stories if they were one, and potentially more—when the song ended and we went right back to the Cosmic Thing playlist, this time with Lifehouse crooning "The Beginning."

My phone beeped right after. "Kitty," Jerry said softly, "I'm going to connect you to Tim. We know you're going underground and I assume you don't want to be caught talking to no one, and we really don't want you losing your communicator and earpiece. Tim won because we think he's the best at deciphering all your clues, particularly in situations like this, so you should be good. Oh, and some of your team is in the shuttle, hovering over the hole you just went into. The rest are with you in there, using stealth and Siler's skills. Everyone's listening in, but only Tim can talk to you."

"Um hum," I said softly. Telzor seemed not to notice.

"Hey, Kitty," Tim said, "we found more information. We can't translate it—it's not in any language the Universal Translator knows, Wheatles and Grentix don't recognize it, and it's not one of the languages Ixtha taught to us in our sleep."

"Wow, this trip down is boring except for looking at all the cool underground architecture, which is amazing and impressive, like something out of Tolkien." Didn't speak in English, because I had to figure that was going to make Telzor suspicious at this juncture. Wondered who was in the shuttle and who was, presumably, on the huge platform with us. Wished Jerry had told me, but I'd just have to roll with the surprises.

"Yeah, yeah," Tim said. "I know that was a dull preamble. But you needed to know it, because we think whatever we found is important. It's definitely from the first solar system, the one whose star went supernova. We were able to use some equipment the Ignotforstans brought with them and carbon-date it.

Close to what everyone thinks is the beginning of the galaxy, maybe even the universe."

The beginning. Just like the song playing.

"Chuck says we can't be sure without Wruck's input, though," Tim continued, "but the hackers are checking."

So Chuckie was, presumably, in the shuttle, and Wruck was, presumably, on the platform. Wondered if Wruck was disguised. Possibly as Telzor. Really hoped that wasn't the case. Though he could be Roanach or Clorence. Or Buchanan. Or one of the extra rabbits. Or else Siler was on the longest blend of his life. Perfect time for it.

"Telzor, this deep underground, how is it that we can all breathe?"

He seemed shocked by this question. "It's complex."

"Do I need to table this?" Tim asked. "You sound like you're in trouble. Like always."

"I'm sure it is. But I'm also sure it's fascinating."

It appeared I'd found Telzor's hobby. He started talking about how the air was pumped in, and White, being the quick study that he always was, asked questions and kept Telzor rolling.

Thankfully, Tim picked up that I wanted him to keep on going, too. "Gotcha. Like the stalling technique. Try not to let your eyes glaze over, though."

Telzor paused for breath. "Can you tell me about why there aren't more people than the ones I've seen? Races, I mean. I've only seen sheep, opossums, rabbits, and cattle. We have more races on our planets, which is why I'm asking. From little jellyfish ones all the way up to huge elephants, and more besides."

Telzor shook his head. "That is for our Mad Lord Johpunnt to share."

"I'm very interested in how you keep the temperatures so moderate," White said, not missing a beat. Wondered if he and Buchanan were on the call, too. Kind of hoped so. "Particularly with all the active volcanoes."

We'd hit another one of Telzor's interests. He started yabbering away about airflows and such.

"Got it," Tim said. "We'll deal with your concern first—Mother's scanned where you are and you're not in some weird fake world—what you're seeing should be real. The animals scan as the sizes you're seeing, based on where you're all looking when you talk to them and what the others described to us when they ran away at the start of your interaction with the natives."

"Hmmm." Ensured I looked fascinated. Telzor seemed to buy it.

"We're certain that the planet that sent this meteor spaceship—because that's what Wheatles is certain the meteor actually is, a spaceship—is the same one that sent the Mykali to Earth. And—"

Tim stopped talking. And I didn't hear voices on the other end.

CHAPTER 102

HAD NO IDEA WHAT TO DO. Really wanted to panic, but now was the definition of not the right time. "I'm amazed that we're not witnessing eruptions, though." Went with lame, because it was all I was up to.

"I just explained that," Telzor said.

"Sorry, it's just a lot to take in and it's so interesting. And I'm kind of afraid of being blown up, call me a silly worrywart."

"The Queen enjoys this kind of thing but she has, ah, people for it back on our home worlds," White said.

"Ah," Telzor replied knowingly. "I will explain again." He started talking, this time more slowly. Actively chose not to be offended, mostly because me acting stupid was currently the best cover I had for this weird call.

"Sorry," Tim said, sounding excited. "We saw movement and I had to be quiet just in case we were being attacked. We're not. Everyone's fine and, great news—Ixtha's found us!"

"Really?" I said to something Telzor said, doing my best to sound fascinated. Again, Telzor seemed to buy it, if me getting a kindly look and more Explanations For The Slow Of Wit were indicators.

"Yeah! They were underground, just like we'd suspected. But Christopher moved so fast, they couldn't make contact with him and Butler on any of the other landmasses."

Heard more voices in the background, but had no way to make a comment—Telzor was in full explanation mode.

Tim returned. "Ixtha says we were hard to find because we chose to land in what they consider the ancient dead city. What we've been digging through hasn't been touched for thousands of their years, possibly longer. And she's not sure that anyone ever found the room we're in, which is where the meteor space-ship is. A-Cs for the win, and Real Naked Apes are pretty great, too. By the way, they love that nickname you gave them. And, get this—Ixtha's not alone. There are lions. And tigers. And bears."

"Oh my."

Telzor took this as my being hella impressed by volcano containment and carried on.

"Knew you'd enjoy that. Literally there's every animal we've ever seen. And I mean ever. Christopher's done a fast run through—every animal we know of, at least its original, unadulterated form, is represented, including animals that are extinct. But no crossbreeds, so nothing like Labradoodles, though I see more than one dog. And there are humans, too. Ixtha's one, or at least looks like us, at least as much as the A-Cs do."

"Huh."

Telzor took this as my not quite getting the explanation of how they had to dig deep into the planet to find water, not only to drink but to power things like the volcano containment and airflow. So he explained again.

"It's like *Zootopia* here. They can all speak, and they're all walking upright and wearing clothes."

"You are *so* lucky." Whoops. That one slipped out by accident.

However, Telzor seemed pleased by my enthusiasm for their finding vast springs underground. He continued on with his explanation.

"We heard," Tim snickered. "Better all of you than all of us is the Blue Team's reaction to the nudist colony you landed on. Anyway, it's not just creatures from our planet. We can see examples of everything. There's a bird that looks like it could be where both Peregrines and peacocks come from, for example. Beings from all the other planets we know, but, as with ours, nothing that's a hybrid created by humans or A-Cs . . . what?" Heard voices in the background. "Oh, yeah, good point, no Apatan hybrids, either. Christopher's found things none of us recognize, too. He says the only things he can't find are Poofs."

Which made sense. Poofs weren't from this galaxy. My brain nudged, hard.

"Oh," Tim went on, "James says to tell you that they do have sheep, opossums, rabbits, cows and bulls here—all dressed. All what we'd call normal sized, too."

My brain nudged again. Ran through the songs on the Cosmic Thing playlist. I'd heard them so much that I had their titles and order memorized so I didn't need to look at my phone.

"Ixtha's explaining things as best she can," Tim continued. "Their society is definitely utopian. No violence, they don't eat each other, they have some kind of replicator things that allow them to make whatever it is their internal systems need to survive. Hang on, some of the team are going to check those out. Huh, most of the team. Sorry, that means I'll be doing handshakes and stuff for a couple minutes, so as to keep these people at ease, and that's an order from your husband."

"Uh huh," said to a particularly boring bit of information about airflow systems. The Blue Team was definitely scoring the far more interesting information share. It was also nice that Tim seemed to feel that I had all the time in the world. Chose to believe he felt that this meant I had the situation in hand, not that he was just so excited that he was forgetting that the Red Team wasn't in *Zootopia* but were still hanging out in Apokolipse.

Wished I could share that there was a replicator here that Lilith was afraid of, but couldn't come up with how to do that in this situation.

Telzor had covered all of volcanic containment and airflow issues, and White and I had gotten him onto how the platforms worked and how they chose where to dig one and why before Tim finally stopped shaking paws and patting backs and returned to our call.

"Okay, the others are back. Jeff says to tell you that their civilization has gone up and down in terms of technological knowhow. This current regime is more, ah, mystic than scientific. The food replicators are ancient—Wheatles and Grentix feel that they are easily as old as what we found inside the meteor spaceship. But they run perfectly. Wheatles feels strongly that they were created by an extremely advanced race and set up to run indefinitely somehow. We're afraid to fiddle with them, just in case. Jeff says that, based on what you two learned from Wruck when you met the Mykali, these weren't created by either the Z'porrah or the Anciannas, so the prevailing theory is that they were created by the same people who sent the meteors."

"Interesting." Telzor looked gratified that I gave their reasons for choosing where to dig a big thumbs-up.

"Oooh!" Tim sounded really excited. "Grentix says that, thanks to Serene's help, she's pretty sure that she's found a way to break the code on the recording. And Wheatles says that he's about ninety-nine-point-nine percent certain that he's found a DNA listing. It's long, like thousands of codes, maybe more."

Cradle indeed. Well, Algar had to work with what he and I both had, in that sense.

"Ha, great," Tim said. "Butler's running these codes through his systems, it's even faster than sending them up to the hackers. One is definitely the code for a form of chimp DNA. He says that the important thing for you to focus on is that he feels that everyone here, like the rest of us, have adapted to the planets we live on. The DNA he's reading from the list Wheatles found seems purer than our DNA now. I have no idea what he means by that, though. Claudia and Lorraine are working on it while Serene and Grentix work on getting the recording to work."

Was pretty sure that I knew what that DNA list meant, and had a good bet I was going to come up with what the girls did. Because everything had finally clicked into place and, besides, genetics were my jam. Meaning I knew why this solar system mattered, more than all the other ones combined.

"Telzor, do you have films here, movies? It's a form of entertainment. Moving pictures, some are animated."

He seemed shocked by this total subject change, not that I could blame him. "Ah, no, we don't."

"Pity. I would have loved to have shared a favorite of mine with you, called *Titan A.E.*"

"Holy crap," Tim said. "You really think so?"

We reached the ground. "What I think is that it's time for me to go meet Mad Lord Johpunnt and find out why he's got such a hankering for the ultraviolence."

Right on cue, my music changed to "Top Jimmy" by Van Halen and I heard it in both ears. Either Tim had hung up or, more likely, Algar had ended the call for me. Managed to control the Inner Hyena, but it took effort. Checked out the bulls. Nope, didn't help. The Inner Hyena was really ready to roar.

Forced my mind back onto the platform and its Approved Design. Because it was part of all of this, too, in its own way. Managed to get back into the serious mindset of being about to meet the top man of this world.

Telzor stepped off the platform while Buchanan and White helped me off. Wisely. No reason for me to trip and fall flat on my face at this particular juncture. Roanach and Clorence hurried off after us.

The rabbits leaped off the platform and formed what might have been an honor guard around me, White, and Buchanan, but what I figured was more of a security setup guaranteed to not allow us to make a fast exit. The bulls went behind them, basically forming a wall. Yeah, Telzor might have been being nice on the long platform ride, but now we were all back to business. On the plus side, it reduced my desire to laugh, so there was that.

He led us down a long hallway. "I'm getting Nazez flashbacks again," I said quietly to White and Buchanan in English.

"That's why I'm here," Buchanan said calmly.

Took us a while—Algar had time to change the song to Lifehouse's "Smoke & Mirrors," which didn't tell me if I should feel that I was being fooled or needed to do the fooling, particularly since I'd been told by Tim that what we were seeing was real—but we finally arrived at two huge doors. Two of the bulls trotted up from behind us and opened them. Looked like they were straining to do so. Really wished I had more A-Cs with me all of a sudden.

Straightened up and did my best to look regal as we followed Telzor through the doorway, Roanach and Clorence scurrying along behind us, my music changing to "Get The Picture" by Kool Moe Dee.

The interior was interesting. This room had the intricate latticework all along the ceiling, too, and had many things hanging from it. In addition to what I was pretty sure was Johpunnt's living quarters—the largest house-thing I'd seen so far—large, bottomless metal cages hung from the lattice, too. How often they were used these days was up for debate, but what they existed for wasn't. They were on a pulley system, and it didn't take genius to guess that they were used to capture prisoners.

The walls were covered in tapestries, and, based on my musical clue, focused on them. All of them were orangey with some yellow, black, and red in there. Didn't want to verify, but was pretty sure that these were made out of the fur, wool, and hides of the planet's residents, hopefully collected after said residents had died of old age, though I wasn't willing to bet on it. Those cages might have multiple uses.

The tapestries told a story, as tapestries everywhere were apparently meant to do. A world that looked perfect, and a sun exploding in the distance. What looked a lot like what I thought a meteor spaceship would look like sailing through the heavens.

Several meteor spaceships landing on a fiery red planet. Lots of sheep, some cows and bulls, opossums, and rabbits staggering out of the crashed spaceships, along with a few other animals, all smaller rodents. Said animals on their knees, appealing to a sun that was bright yellow; this tapestry had what looked like that food replicator off to the side. Horrible monsters that looked a lot like the sandworms from *Dune* only bright orange and with a lot more teeth attacking and the animals fighting back. The four races that were still here crying over the bodies of the smaller rodents. Another few tapestries showing various lamentations or sandworm attacks, and in many of them the food replicator was represented.

Then the story changed. The next tapestry showed a sheep standing on top of a sandworm, clearly victorious. He had a splash of bright orange wool on his chest. Then a tapestry showing the animals shoving the sandworm's body into the food replicator. The next tapestries showed either a sheep, a bull, or a rabbit leading—and each of them had a swath of bright orange somewhere on them, usually on the back or sternum, but one of the rabbits had a bright orange cottontail. No possums led, or if they did, they didn't score a tapestry. In many of these they were feeding sandworms to the replicator in what looked like a religious ceremony. Then we had the digging and building tapestries. Followed by the making machines that worked tapestries, and the creation of telescopes and more advanced weapons.

Finally, we came to the tapestries that dealt with things outside the solar system. There were a couple showing the system leaving the galaxy. Then one that showed the system as we'd seen it in the earlier pictures—with intact planets and moons. And then a tapestry devoted to each of the other planets' destruction. The last tapestry wasn't finished, and while it was shown in black, it was clear that the planet being destroyed was the blue one.

There was also a throne, but no one was sitting on it. The throne sat on a dais raised a good twenty feet in the air, and light shone down from above to bathe the throne in sunlight. Presumably this was where the sun and the person who sat in that throne did their reflection thing.

Someone was on the dais, but they were in shadow, clearly for the effect. "Who comes from the stars to visit me?" The speaker seemed to feel he was commanding, but his voice was nasal and nowhere near as deep as Telzor's.

"Mad Lord Johpunnt," Telzor said respectfully, "may the sun continue to love your reflection, I present Kitty, the Warrior Queen."

"Gaze upon your lord and ruler," Johpunnt said. "And tremble."

CHAPTER 103

MY MUSIC CHANGED TO "Black Sheep" by Saliva as the Mad Lord stepped dramatically into the light.

Well, he was successful because I was trembling. But from trying to keep the Inner Hyena inside, not from fear. This was the hardest Inner Hyena test yet, even though I'd looked at the tapestries, and Jamie and Algar both had warned me.

It wasn't a bull on the dais. It was a sheep. Not much of a sheep, either. Roanach was more impressive. But this sheep was different from the others—most of his wool was black, other than the wool on his head, which was the same color as the Orange Scourge.

Additionally, and unlike the other sheep, who hadn't done much with their look, his wool was combed out and stylishly done, or at least I presumed he thought it was stylish. The wool on his body was quite fluffy, at least what there was of it—had a feeling he was dealing with whatever sheep called early male pattern baldness. On his head, what there was of it was sort of swoopy, as if he was trying to go for a Young Elvis look but only achieving a Not Enough Pomade look.

To top it all off, he had really wimpy horns. It was if they'd stopped growing when he was a lamb or something. Roanach didn't have the greatest horns, but he was King of the Rack in comparison to Johpunnt.

"The Warrior Queen has arrived," Mad Lord Johpunnt said imperiously. "The prophecies will now come true."

"What prophecies are those?" I asked. Compared him to the tapestry pictures of the other leaders. Either they'd been far better specimens or the artists had made sure they looked impressive. Gave it even odds for either.

Mad Lord Johpunnt looked directly at me for the first time. If I'd thought the rest of the people on this world had crazy eyes, that was only because I hadn't seen his. He was the definition of eyes staring into the crazy void. Jamie had actually undersold this dude.

"The prophecies say," Johpunnt said in a tone that said he was preparing a really great evil cackle, "that when the Warrior Queen comes, I shall kill her and then we will rule the universe." On cue, he cackled. I'd heard better. "So," he added in a totally normal tone, "prepare to die. Oh, and Telzor, be sure that everyone with her dies, too. Oh, I'm sorry. That will include you, as well."

"My Mad Lord?" Telzor asked, sounding a little surprised.

"You lost to her. Pathetically. You failed me. So, you get to die, too, along with those two pathetic traitors who chose to befriend her instead of just killing her where she stood."

Telzor's shoulders slumped and he bowed his head. "As you command."

Heard a whimper behind me. Reached back and stroked Clorence and Roanach's heads. "That's it?" I asked, as Buchanan and White both shifted into fighting stances, hefting Telzor's swords like they'd trained with them. "No chitchat about our different planets, no interest in why I'm here, no explanation of your rightful place among galactic leaders, just nice to meet you, so long?"

"Yes," Johpunnt said. "You exist only to be defeated by my warriors so that we can ascend to the next levels. And I care nothing for the galaxy. We are about to rule the universe."

The rabbits, not the bulls, surrounded us. The bulls were just blocking the exits, but the rabbits looked ready to leap. And ready to rend and tear. The rabbits looked quite eager to fight. Realized they were the shock troops of this world. Not great for us.

My music changed to "Red Carpet Grave" by Marilyn Manson and Tim Skold. Took the hint that if I didn't start doing what I did best—keep the bad guy monologuing until I could formulate the way to win—we were all dead. "Um, you know, as to that, are you aware that your solar system has left its galaxy of origin?" I mean, the tapestries seemed clear, but maybe he never looked at them.

"Of course I am." Johpunnt shrugged. "We are going to rule the universe."

"No. Your sun is going to die and you're going to die with it."

He chuckled. "So naïve. No, we will live forever."

"Sure you will. Also, seriously, how can the prophecy work if it's your rabbits killing me, instead of you doing it yourself?"

"What?" Johpunnt seemed a little thrown by this question. Good.

"I mean, I get it, I'm supposed to be here and get defeated. But if your rabbits are the ones who defeat me, doesn't that mean they're the ones who should lead or ascend or whatever, not you? I mean, you're just standing there imperiously, not doing anything. They'll be doing the real work and the real defeating. Why should you get to rule when they're doing all the heavy lifting?"

"Because I am Mad Lord Johpunnt! And their honor is to serve me!"

"Just like Darkseid," I said as an aside to White. "Couldn't care less about his people."

"Most despots are like that," White replied. "The problem is that they tend to have so many minions willing to die for a cause that doesn't serve their interests in any way and for a leader who doesn't care about them."

"Well, until the despot is killed." Did the entwined-fingers arms-over-the-head stretch. "And that's what I'm here to do, I guess, since reason doesn't seem to be on the table."

"Some people only respect strength," Buchanan said.

"True dat. You guys ready?" Noted more rabbits coming in. They were massing in groups, but didn't expect that to last long. "I think the Mad Lord has called in more troops, just in case. Because he's a coward." Ensured my voice carried.

"You accuse *me* of cowardice?" Johpunnt seemed offended. Good again.

"Yeah, I do. You don't have the balls to fight. At least Telzor tried. Sure, he failed, but he gave it a shot. You're too afraid of me to come down off that dais and fight me like a sheep. Or do you go by sheeple?" Wasn't sure how sheep fought, actually, but that didn't matter at this precise time.

"Sheeple has a ring to it," Roanach whispered to Clorence. Chose not to share that it was a derogatory term on Earth. Why spoil the moment?

"I am the *leader*," Johpunnt snarled. "And I go by the title of Mad Lord!"

"Blah, blah, leader, blah, blah, mad lord. Well, that's right, at least. You're totally bonkers."

"I am the one who rules all and leads all of Helix Rime!"

"That means you should *lead*, you insignificant pompous ass. It doesn't mean you hide behind everyone else shouting orders and screaming for your entitlements. You lead by example, by doing the best for your people. You're doing the worst for them now. Your system isn't going to survive too much longer, and instead of figuring out how to find a new star, you're just happy floating in the black between galaxies, pretending everything's fine when it's all going to hell in a really big handbasket."

"That was tried!" Johpunnt said. "And they doomed us!"

"Excuse me?"

"In the old, old days, the star of our ancestors was dying. They said they would save everyone, send us to a paradise. But *we* were sent *here*! To hell!" He shook his head and started pacing. "For so long, our ancestors waited. Waited for the others to find us, to bring us to the promised land. And then, then somewhere along the way, we realized that no one was coming!"

Had to offer the sane option, just because it was required, not that I thought he'd respond to it. "Perhaps they just didn't know where you were."

"They knew! They sent us here on purpose! Once we realized that, then we spent so long, too long, thinking we were to blame, that we had done something wrong, something to deserve the punishment of this place. Then we realized." He stopped pacing, spun, and looked at me and I realized who he reminded me of— Farley Pecker, the head of the Church of Hate and Intolerance. This was a sermon, of sorts, and he was the preacher. And he definitely believed.

"That you just needed to figure out how to get into space to find the rest of your people?"

"No! We realized that we were the chosen ones! Chosen to become stronger, better. Chosen to rule. Chosen to destroy those who had the easy lives. And from that moment, we knew only one thing—the joy of revenge. We will have our revenge! We will destroy everyone and then rule the universe as is our birthright!"

"You know, I'm losing you. If you destroy everyone, what is there to rule?"

Johpunnt blinked. "What?"

"It's not an exact science, desperately sending out meteor spaceships. Planets move. Asteroids and other space crap knock your ships off orbit. Maybe you don't land where you were supposed to. Maybe you land far from where you were supposed to go, maybe you land close. Maybe some of your spaceships get destroyed. And that doesn't indicate evil intent."

"No, what do you mean about ruling?"

"I mean that all that doesn't mean that you get to go on some insane rampage just because your spaceship didn't hit a nicer location. And I still fail to see how destroying all the other locations works in your favor. If there's nowhere else to go, why bother?"

Johpunnt gaped at me. "To . . . to rule the universe."

"But you said you want to destroy all of it. So, how does that work? You're the king of nothing?" On cue, Algar shared "The King of Nothing" by Seals and Crofts. "Look at this planet! It looks unlivable, but your people are surviving and thriving here. And instead of doing what you can to make that better, you're only focused on some ancient vendetta and bizarre form of rulership that leaves everything devastated."

"Our rage is everything," Johpunnt said. "Our rage is all that matters."

"Sheep crap it is. Caring for your people is what matters. Not destroying everything. Making things better is what the leader is supposed to do, not make them worse."

"I am the chosen leader of my people," Johpunnt said. "When the Lord finally loses his fight with life, a new one is chosen. I was marked as a child as the future leader." He indicated the wool on his head. "And I have ruled Helix Rime well for all the years that I have been the Lord!"

"Um, how long *is* that, exactly?"

"I have—what?" He seemed confused.

"I'll speak more slowly. How long have you been the sheeple in charge? I'm sure your time doesn't correspond with mine, but since we're speaking the same language, I assume I'll manage to do the math. So, how long?"

"Five hundred years."

"Wow. You all must live a hella long time."

White cleared his throat. "Their view of what years are is far quicker than ours, My Queen. In our terms, it would be just over forty-one months."

"So not even three and a half of our years? Wow, he's in his first term as President for our world. And doing as crappy a job with it as I've ever seen."

"You have insulted me for the last time," Johpunnt said. "All of you, prepare for my order to kill them!"

The rabbits all squatted, presumably in preparation to leap onto us the moment Johpunnt gave the word. But before they could do anything there was a scream. A bird's scream. Several of them, actually. And I knew the voices.

Peregrines appeared out of nowhere. Only, not nowhere. They'd been in Len, Kyle, Abigail, Siler, and Kevin's arms and, as they flew out of said arms, the people appeared. Presumed this meant that Mossy and Mahin had stayed in the shuttle with Chuckie.

Bruno was shrieking in Peregrine, and what he was saying was that any rabbits that thought they were going to leap onto me and the others had another think coming.

But that wasn't all. "Look!" Clorence shouted. Looked around and realized that Clorence was looking behind us. Turned to see one of our shuttles swoop in—well, the hole was more than big enough to let it in, as were the doors to the throne room, and the cavern was ginormous. The camouflage had obviously worked well enough on the way in because I didn't see a ton of Johpunnt's troops coming in.

The shuttle didn't land but, as my music changed to "Here Comes The Hammer" by MC Hammer, the door opened and Adam, Rahmi, Rhee, Tito, Naveed Jeremy, Jennifer, MJO, and Gadhavi all jumped out and landed around us. Figured Hamlin was flying the shuttle with Bellie as copilot. Go Backup Auxiliary Team. They all had weapons ready, though only the princesses had weapons that our enemies seemed to recognize as such.

But that wasn't all they had. Because more were coming out of the shuttle. Rabbits, our rabbits, twenty of them if there was one, and the least weasels. Only they weren't small. All of them were at least as big as Algar, maybe bigger, the weasels in particular.

"So, I see the least weasels have become the most weasels. Go team. And Orange Scourge, I presume." Figured that this was how the animals on this planet had managed to survive and grow larger, too.

"Did you know," Tito said conversationally, "that a pack of least weasels can take down a full-grown sheep? On our world, that is. I mean, here, on this one, with the size they are, I'm pretty sure just one weasel could take one sheep. Maybe more."

"Nice!" Turned back to Johpunnt. "This, in our world, is what we call a Mexican Standoff. No one can advance or retreat without losing position or safety. So, Johpunnt, before you give the order to attack, I'd like to give you a chance to reconsider your position."

"There is nothing to reconsider. You have never faced enemies such as my troops. They will rend all of you and then we will feast on your flesh."

"You're herbivores," I felt compelled to point out.

"Only when we have no meat to devour," Johpunnt said.

Looked at Telzor out of the corner of my eye. He looked kind of sick to his stomach. "Telzor," I asked quietly, "is that true?"

"In the past we have been . . . required . . . to eat the remains of our enemies. It is not something most of us relish doing, but it is required."

"By whom?"

"By our laws, the laws given to us in the distant past."

"Yeah, about that. It's not the distant past anymore. I think it's time for you guys to come into the current future."

"I don't see how that will happen," Telzor said, somewhat sadly.

"One question. How do your laws of succession work? As in, should one of us manage to kill the Mad Lord there, will we automatically be in the middle of a gigantic war, or will we rule this world?"

"It depends on who would dare to kill the Mad Lord. Normally the next chosen would rule, but we have not had such a birth yet."

Meaning no one else had the Neon Orange Birthmark. Oh well, that could make things easier.

Considered how best to handle this. Well, I *was* the Warrior Queen, but that didn't mean that I was required to fight fair. Superman and the Flash were on the blue planet, Batman probably would approve, and I was only Wonder Woman on Bizarro World. Here, in my universe, I was Wolverine With Boobs. And Wolverine was very willing to cheat if it meant saving the lives of a lot of innocents and grunts who were just forced to be doing their distasteful jobs.

My music changed to Panic! At the Disco's "Crazy=Genius." Nice to see that Algar agreed with my plan.

"Rahmi, Rhee, two things."

"Yes, My Warrior Queen?" Rahmi asked eagerly, sounding like she'd been waiting forever to address me this way and was overjoyed that the time had finally come.

"One, is that if things go as they usually do, figure you're going to really be having a great time."

"What is two, My Warrior Queen?" Rhee asked, sounding even more eager and thrilled about using this title for me than her older sister. Well, their mother *was* the queen of her world.

"Two is that if things go as I'm hoping they do, I'm sorry."

Flipped my gun into my arms, aimed, and fired.

CHAPTER 104

DIRECT HIT. I was good with this thing. Shot again, several times, just in case. Hit my target every time.

Cages fell and slammed onto the ground. All the rabbit shock troops, other than the few around us, were trapped and it looked like no one had gotten smooshed, either.

Didn't wait for the reactions. Instead I ran and did a flip into the air. Lilith gave me an assist and I sailed onto the dais to land perfectly in front of the throne. There were a hell of a lot of gasps from the audience, from my team included. Had no time to be impressed myself but planned to revel in the moment later.

Stood eye to eye with Johpunnt. He was less impressive up close. Put the point of my gun to his chest. "Surrender."

"Never. You will have to kill me."

"Dude, you seem to think that someone named the Warrior Queen has trouble killing people. I find that funny. Almost as funny as your hairdo." My team snickered.

Kept the gun on him but turned to the audience. Had a great vantage point in that I could probably hit every one of the scary rabbits the cages didn't get from up here before they could attack. But that would send the wrong message, particularly since I saw a lot of sheep, possums, and cows crowding in through the doorway to see what was going on. The rabbits in the cages were trying to lift them. Figured they might succeed.

"You don't have a lot of time," I shared with the room. "Your sun is dying and your solar system is in the Deep Black where, soon, no one will ever find you again. We came to help you."

"She lies!" Johpunnt shouted. "They came to conquer us."

"Hardly. Why would we want to? This planet isn't exactly the garden spot of the galaxy."

"They want what all our enemies want," Johpunnt said. "Our destruction!"

My music changed to "Blue Wonderful" by Elton John. Hoped I was interpreting the clue right. "The planet you're trying to blow up is more than willing to welcome you, but you've never asked them for help, you've just attacked them without provocation."

"They are our enemies! They live in beauty while we were condemned to horror." Realized Johpunnt really believed this. It was unlikely I was going to get through to him. But I still had to try.

"They aren't anyone's enemies. They're peaceful and, as an aside, they don't eat each other, even after a big battle or whatever your nauseating custom is. You could be like them. But your leader wants destruction. We'd prefer peace. But understand— I'm called the Warrior Queen for a reason. Think on that, before you choose your next actions."

Too many here have believed too long, Lilith said in my head. If the leader does not choose peace, then neither will they.

Turned back to Johpunnt. "Look, you can die for some ancient cause. Or you can live and save your people." Took my gun off his chest and slung it onto my back. "You see what I'm choosing—peace between us."

He produced a large knife from somewhere. "I will not be the one dying, and we will never choose your way!" Then he lunged at me.

Didn't bother to move. I was in a bodysuit that only Ginger's claws had been able to penetrate. Did the simplest of blocks and knocked the knife out of his hand. It skittered away. "That's your plan? Your whole plan? You're sure?"

My music changed to "Blitzkrieg Bop" by The Ramones, so I had a guess that this wasn't over.

"No," Johpunnt cackled. I'd still heard better. "*They* are my plan!" He pointed. Sure enough, some of the rabbits in the cages had gotten out. They sprang toward my people, and the fight I'd hoped to avoid started.

The Peregrines and princesses engaged first. The Peregrines had claws easily as sharp as the rabbits did, and they could fly away—and this world had no birds, so the rabbits had never dealt with something with wings that could go much higher than they could jump.

The Peregrines could also grab a rabbit, fly up high, and drop it. Which they did. Right over the princesses' heads. It was like a violent form of baseball, where the pitcher ensured the batters never missed and the balls were ripped, sliced, and diced.

The bulls creating the "back wall" broke ranks and ran to lift the cages off of the other rabbit troops while those who'd been in the doorway scattered. Possibly because a battalion of sheep were trotting in.

Which was too bad for the sheep, because the Most Weasels called dibs on them. Winced and turned away as sheep started screaming—in terror. It was going to be a bloodbath. Because even though Helix Rime was barbaric, it was still far more civilized than the Animal Kingdom. And sheep weren't really meant to be violent, even those who'd evolved impressive tusks and horns. Plus, they weren't fast, and the Most Weasels were moving like they had hyperspeed. Perhaps they did.

Of course, some of the attacking rabbits made it through the Peregrines and princesses. Telzor wrenched his sword out of Buchanan's hands but didn't attack our team with it. Instead, he was swinging it against the rabbits, effectively. Roanach and Clorence were also using their weapons against the rabbits, though not that well. Len and Kyle took pity on them and put themselves between Roanach and Clorence and the attacking rabbits.

My rabbits were going two on one with the attacking rabbits and winning. Their claws were sharp, so were their teeth, and they were repulsed by what these rabbits were like. They felt like a human fighting a zombie would—the enemy was so warped from the norm that the horror had to be destroyed. My rabbits were definitely fighting with the extra oomph this kind of revulsion gave you.

The bulls charged, but on their back legs only, not on all fours and leading with their best weapons. Instead, they left themselves wide open for those with lasers to shoot them. It was easier than shooting fish in a barrel. Sure, it took a lot of shots, but no bulls got close to anyone on my team.

It was sad. It was obvious that this world hadn't had a real enemy for at least a generation. They were just a bunch of people all dressed up, or undressed up, rather, with no one to fight. They hadn't fought each other, hadn't practiced, they'd just been guarding nothing and being mean to whoever Johpunnt didn't like today. They weren't organized—none of the rabbits were fighting as a team, the bulls weren't going back-to-back like the princesses and most of my team were, no one was moving in any way that could be called evasive, the sheep that weren't dead were running away screaming.

And that's when the Auxiliary Backup Team's secret weapon appeared.

Ginger leaped out of the shuttle, caterwaul set to eleven, all claws out on all paws. For the first time, these people were seeing a real predator, one that considered them all food, and food it enjoyed hunting, toying with, killing, and devouring. Ginger's snarl hit most of the fighters right in the same place a tiger's growl hit a human—in the soft bits.

She landed on the dais in front of me and roared. Had no idea ocellars could do that, but Ginger had the chops. And what she was saying in cat was that she was also the Warrior Queen.

Every Helix Rime denizen froze, in terror. And my team didn't hit anyone who wasn't moving.

All this had happened quickly—The Ramones were still singing. Turned to Johpunnt who, like me, had been watching, not fighting. "Surrender. Stop this needless bloodshed. Too many of your people have died already. Show that you're actually a good leader, and surrender, so they get to live."

"Never," he snarled. He raised the knife again. Okay, so maybe I'd been watching and he'd been scrambling for his knife. Minor detail.

He lunged, and this time, I merely stepped aside. He tripped over Ginger, and went tumbling down. He landed with a mighty splat and big gasps from the crowd. Sure enough, he'd landed on his knife.

"And nasty little men like you always get their comeuppance," I said to his dead body. Picked Ginger up and gave her a snuggle. Received a smug and happy purr in return. Looked up at the crowd. "People of Helix Rime, you have a choice. You stop fighting and you get to live. You keep on fighting and we'll make the rest of you as dead as we've already made your friends and relations and as dead as your so-called leader has made himself."

"Are you saying that the Mad Lord killed himself?" Telzor shouted quickly. He sounded hopeful.

Made eye contact. He was an animal. More humanoid than animal, as we'd all just proved, but still, animal. Concentrated. Got a feeling of why he'd asked.

"Yes, that's what I'm saying."

Telzor smiled at me. Then he turned around. "Brothers and sisters, the Mad Lord Johpunnt has committed the ultimate crime! It is forbidden for our leader to willingly leave this life before his time, before the next leader has been born. That means that the Mad Lord's rules are now considered evil and wrong. And *that* means that we must surrender to the Warrior Queen." Telzor turned back to me, dropped his weapon on the ground, and knelt down, head bowed.

Those who were holding weapons dropped them. Then they all did what Telzor had, crazy rabbits, too. Even the ones who were wounded. Wanted to tell them to stand up, but knew that was the wrong move. Didn't want to rule these people. Just wanted to save them, from themselves and from the situation their leaders had allowed them to end up in.

My music changed to "Kings and Queens" by Aerosmith. Time to remember that I had a job, and a reputation, to maintain here.

"My first ruling—stop bombing anyone, ever, anywhere, immediately. If bombs are set to go off, someone had better make damn sure they abort those rockets. Now."

Several sheep and rabbits ran off. Some of my rabbits went after them, so they could report what was being done.

"My second ruling—you will cease all the 'guarding.' I want all the weapons you have brought here."

"We can assist with that, My Queen," Abigail said with a grin.

Thought about it. "Huh. Mahin's already doing that with Chuckie, isn't she?"

"And Mossy." Abigail shrugged. "There's so much dirt on this planet . . ."

"Yeah, Mahin's having an earth-bending field day, got it. Well then, all A-Cs, please collect all the available weapons in the cavern. If it's a ridiculous task, though, just let me know, don't waste the effort. Other than Mister White, whose counsel I want to have right at hand."

"Of course, My Queen," White said with a twinkle. He looked around. "I suggest we tend to the wounded and bury the dead."

"Yeah, that's important. Only not nearly as important as getting these people evacuated to a solar system that's not drifting in the Deep Black. Telzor, what's the spaceship situation? We saw that you're building some."

"Our rockets are not made for travel," Telzor replied. "And our spaceship is not ready. The Mad Lord was more interested in the rockets."

"I'll bet. Does anyone have a population estimate for this planet and the other one?"

"It's called Helix Noblora," Jerry said in my ear. "And while we *might* be able to stuff everyone from Helix Rime into the *Distant Voyager*, it would be tight, and we don't have a good count for how many are underground there. It goes without saying that we don't have enough room for those on Helix Noblora, with or without Helix Rime's residents."

"So, find another way," Tim said.

"Um, are we on a group call?"

"Has your team stopped fighting?" Jeff asked, sounding mildly annoyed.

"Geez, yes. It's not like we wanted to. Who's in charge over on Helix Noblora?"

"No one," Reader said with a sigh. "Everyone. There's a council. It's gigantic—anyone who wants to be on it can be, meaning most of them feel that they're council members. And there are a *lot* of residents on this planet. They get nothing done, as you'd imagine. However, at least they aren't spending all their time trying to destroy everyone else."

My rabbits connected mentally with me and shared that all the rockets had been turned off and that the sheep and rabbits they'd followed were telling everyone that they now reported to the Warrior Queen. They suggested I send off some emissaries to do this topside and to assist with continuing to do so in the caverns.

Heaved a sigh. "Look, can we get off the phone and meet up in person? Because it's going to take me a little bit for my crazy to come up with something genius and, until then, I have a lot of newly loyal subjects to patch up, bury, bawl out, and reassure."

"So," Jeff said, "routine."

CHAPTER 105

SINCE MY RABBITS HAD requested it, and it made sense, had Telzor handle sending out the good word of my newly appointed reign to the rest of the world. He assigned people to do this, but he stayed with me. Was fine with that.

We had a lot of dead and injured, and this world, shockingly, wasn't well equipped in the patching up department. So Reader flew a shuttle over with reinforcements. But he went back to Helix Noblora because we already had two shuttles here and could handle the extra bodies, and without him, they had no shuttle there.

Would have liked to have gone to Helix Noblora with him, but it was clear that I needed to stick around, because the people on Helix Rime were very used to having someone telling them what to do.

Lorraine and Claudia were here to help Tito with the doctoring, Gower was here to help me and White get the natives into a less bloodthirsty mindset, and Christopher was here to help with the weapons pickup, since Abigail and the Barones had come back with the news that the caverns ran all through the world.

Abigail had also come back with information. "I couldn't tell you this earlier, because I was so angry I had to use all my focus not to go berserk. But once the rabbit shock troops were killed and Johpunnt died, the rage subsided."

"That's interesting."

"Isn't it? So I investigated when you sent me off. The food from that replicator is only given to those in the capital city and to those who the Mad Lord feels have earned the privilege. The rest of the planet is fed by the farms."

"Lilith said the replicator was evil."

"I think it is. I think it's broken, or tainted. This world is tainted, in that sense, but nothing like as much as right here."

"While you're at everything else we need to dismantle that replicator, then."

Abigail grinned. "On it, boss."

Would have loved it if Jeff had come to Helix Rime, but with us taking most of the A-Cs over here, he had to stay there. Instead, the Kristie-Bot had managed to finagle a seat on the interplanetary shuttle. She was sitting with me and Ginger on the dais while everyone else went about the tasks I'd set them to.

"*Code Name: Warrior Queen* sounds like a great title," she said.

"Kristie, so help me God . . ."

She laughed. "I just wanted you to chill out a little."

"Wish I could. We have an entire solar system to save and I don't know how."

My music had been off since I'd asked for the rest and repair break. But it came on now, "Astronaut" by Simple Plan. It was about floating away alone. Like this system. Needed to figure out what to do, and fast.

"Why don't we just ask Gustav's father for help and have him send enough ships to evacuate?" she suggested. "I mean, we made it out of the galaxy safely, why not them?"

"They don't have what I have. And getting out is, frighteningly enough, easier than getting back in. Besides, this system matters. All of it. Not just the people."

"I know Grentix was talking about how the galaxy needs what the supernova will create. But it's a big galaxy. What's one system lost?"

"It's not just 'one system' at all. It's more than that."

"How so?"

Sighed. "This system is the Cradle of Life."

"Isn't that in Africa?"

"For Earth? Yes. I'd imagine that's where most of the meteor spaceships hit. Probably when all the continents were one big landmass. The meteor spaceships may be what broke up the big landmass into the continents. That would be my guess, anyway."

The Kristie-Bot shook her head. "Sorry, you need to explain that."

My music changed to "Alien" by Lifehouse. Had no idea

what Algar was going for. "It's like this—the system, the original one whose star blew up so many tens of millions of years ago, that was the system that sent out the meteor spaceships."

"Right. And one hit Earth, with the Mykali in it."

"Yes, more than one. But I think there were two types of meteor spaceships sent out. In *Titan A.E.*, the Earth is under attack. They send space shuttles off the planet, filled with people. Some make it, some don't. But they also sent the Titan, a different kind of spaceship, one that has the DNA for all of life on Earth. So it can create a new Earth." Good old Planet Bob.

"I haven't seen it, but okay."

"It's a good movie. And I think whoever wrote it got the idea from an ancestral memory about how to escape and have your species, all of them, survive when your sun is going to die or your planet is going to be blown up."

"I totally do not follow you."

"That system was the original Cradle of Life. Eden, if a Biblical reference is easier. It was for me when I first joined this business we call keeping the galaxy together. So, Eden is where life, all life, forms, for the first time. It's just the right place for it, for whatever reason." My music changed to "Aliens Exist" by blink-182. Still had no idea what Algar was going for, other than possibly a reminder that there were other worlds with people on them. But I had the answer for that.

"Okay. So?"

"So, the people there became very advanced, and they realized that their star wasn't going to last. So they created ships that would send their people away. But not just their people. Ships can get destroyed or lost, right? So, in addition to their people, they sent out their DNA. My bet is that they sent the DNA first, just in case. If it didn't make it, oh well, they haven't lost their living people."

"Wait . . . so you think they, what, seeded the galaxy?"

"Yeah, I do. I think that, based on what you guys all saw on Helix Noblora and what I've seen here pictorially, that's what happened. Sending vials of DNA in a spaceship is a lot safer than sending a living person. And everything's represented on Helix Noblora."

"Well, the shape-shifters aren't," the Kristie-Bot pointed out.

"True enough. Because the DNA, when it landed, landed on a different planet. Many different planets. And, if the meteor spaceship opened right, it seeded that world. And the DNA

adapted to that world. To all the worlds. It probably didn't take
everywhere, probably some of the DNA was more adaptable
than another type depending on the world, but it took in a lot of
places. Some places, like Earth, it all took. Some places, like
Cradus, only some survived. And all the DNA that survived
adapted to its world."

"What about the ships that didn't make it?"

"If a meteor spaceship was, say, hit by a real meteor or comet
or whatever, if the DNA got into or onto that, then it landed
wherever that body landed. And presumably did the same thing."
My music changed to "My Alien" by Simple Plan. Unless Algar
was trying to tell me that Jeff needed me, was still coming up
very short in the figuring out the clues department. Seemed to
be my theme for this portion of the intergalactic road trip.

"Okay, I understand why that first system was so important.
But why does *this* system matter?"

"Because of what, or rather who, is here. One of their first
attempts at sending living people was the Mykali. They sent
them across the galaxy to a planet that had a lot of water, which
the Mykali need. But it was a long way away and their sun
wasn't getting any younger or less unstable. So they had to
hurry up. I figure they found a system that was closer. Maybe it
moved and that made it more desirable, maybe they'd just
missed it, maybe it wasn't quite as good as Earth but would do
in a pinch."

"So they, what? Tossed everyone in spaceships, aimed them
this way, and hoped for the best?"

"Yeah. They'd seeded the galaxy already, so they knew their
races and way of life would go on. And most of those spaceships
made it. And they had the pure DNA added into their spaceships, too, Just in case."

The Kristie-Bot looked around, specifically at the tapestries.
"But not all the spaceships made it to the world they'd aimed
for."

"Right. Not all. Some landed on other planets. Some probably fell short or went too far. Most landed on Helix Noblora.
And some landed here. I'd assume that once this world discovered they weren't alone, they reached out to the other planets.
Either they were ignored, the messages never arrived, or the
people on the other planets weren't interested in helping for
whatever reason."

"Ixtha said that they consider this world to be evil. Her

people have been afraid of this world for as long as their history shows. They think it's where bad people go when they die."

"Makes sense. They think they're on New Eden and that makes this Hell World. Fitting. Wrong, but fitting. I mean, they had to have had contact somewhere along the line—they both call the sun Helix Prime, right?"

"Ixtha does, yes."

"So that means they had to have agreed on the name, long ago."

"Maybe it was agreed to before they left," she suggested. "That would be why they both call their planets Helix Whatever, too, right? Or maybe their original sun was called Helix."

"Right and either theory makes sense." Heaved a big sigh. "But that's why this all matters. This system contains the descendants of the original Cradle of Life for, most likely, our entire galaxy. Losing it to the Deep Black not only seems wrong, but I'm willing to bet that it'll be dangerous for our galaxy, too. Galaxy-ending, most likely, for whatever reason."

"No more DNA that's in the stars and the planets and all of us would be my guess," the Kristie-Bot said. "Or no replenishment of the DNA or something like that. Or maybe a galaxy dies if it loses its Cradle of Life."

"You don't think I'm crazy?" Lee Press-On And The Nails were now singing "Hidden" for me. Had a feeling Algar thought I was crazy, but in the wrong way right now.

"Like a fox. No. I'm a cyborg. We've gone all over the galaxy and are now floating outside of it. Nothing you're saying sounds crazy. But, unfortunately, nothing you've said is a plan for how to get this back into the Milky Way, though I'm now with the cause a hundred percent."

"So are the rest of us," Jerry said in my ear. Kristie's too, if her jumping a little was any indication. "I was going to ask you something when I heard you two discussing what's going on and decided not to interrupt. It sounded important, so I broadcast it to the others."

"Glad I didn't say anything about my sex life."

"Oh, we all know all about *that*," Jerry said with a laugh. "But we all also agree with your assessment, the team still on Helix Noblora in particular. Because they did break the code and what you described is pretty much what they've just gotten translated via Butler and Mother."

Kristie punched me gently on the arm. "Look at you, right again!" Realized I'd started thinking of her as Kristie, not as the Kristie-Bot. Yeah, she'd moved into the Friend Zone. And I'd correctly figured out how life in our galaxy had come about. It was a trip filled with stranger and stranger things.

CHAPTER 106

"ALL THAT'S NICE,** but we're still no closer to figuring out what to do." My music changed to "Inside You" by Pop Will Eat Itself. Well, that was a duh. At least I thought I had this clue right. "Lilith, any ideas?"

Not really, and yes, I am sharing this with everyone's minds, or all those on the call, at any rate. I could do some, but I cannot do all. To do this requires great power. Moving the ship with a Z'porrah power cube was one thing. I cannot contain the entire solar system. And there is a matter of rotation. The speed we will need to achieve to reenter the galaxy is great. I cannot do it alone.

But you could if Fairy Godfather ACE helped.

Jamie?

Yes, Mommy. Fairy Godfather ACE and I are just talking to you and Lilith, not the others. Not even Daddy, because we think it will upset Daddy to talk to him like this right now.

Oh, right you are, sweetie. But I can't ask Fairy Godfather ACE to risk it any more than I can ask Lilith to risk it. And, as your mother, I have to say that you are not allowed to risk yourself in this way.

It is not a risk. This was ACE. ACE will not allow Jamie to risk. ACE will leave Jamie, as Lilith will have to leave Kitty, in order to assist.

Doesn't that increase the risk for both of you?

It does, Lilith said. But it lessens the risk for you and your daughter.

I can do it, Mommy, Jamie said stubbornly.

I'm sure you can, Jamie-Kat, but you're a little girl and that's asking a lot of you. Of course, she hadn't had ACE inside her when she'd time-warped from New Mexico to D.C. to save me, Jeff, and Christopher by holding a Z'porrah spaceship in the air and lowering it safely.

Stop selling your daughter short, Lilith said, right on cue.

Look, I'm her mother. I'm supposed to protect her, not the other way around.

The other kids want to help, too, Jamie said. Charlie has a good idea.

Perfect. Now my toddler son wanted to get in on the action. Jeff was going to flip out. Um, what idea is that?

Charlie says that he can lift the sun.

God forbid that he actually could. That's not what we need, sweetie. We need to move the solar system back to where it was, not move it around where it is.

We know. Jamie sounded exasperated. Clearly I was missing her point. But Missus Denise says that when we all work together all the tasks are easier. We've been practicing, even Becky and JR.

Fantastic. Now I'd have Jeff and Christopher freaking out. Probably the other parents, too. I mean, I wanted to freak out, but had to control it. Oh? Um, good for all of you!

Mommy, you don't have to worry. We know what to do. And we know we can't do it alone. Fairy Godfather ACE says that what we want to do is be like Auntie Abby and Auntie Mimi were, and how Auntie Abby and Auntie Mahin are, only more so.

"SuperStar could move an entire solar system," Tim said before I could mention that those women were full-grown adults and one of them was technically dead. Realized that the chat in my head was going a lot faster than I'd have figured. That had happened earlier, too. Presumed it was because Lilith was inside of me.

"But we don't have anyone like that with us now. Our rabbits and the Most Weasels have telepathy thanks to the Nazez water and the Orange Scourge, but none are as powerful as SuperBun was." My music changed to "Metal Heart" by Garbage. "We can't ask SuperStar or Cradus to help with this—it puts them at too much risk." The volume on my music turned up for a few seconds, then lowered. Algar really wanted me to pay attention.

"The only ones who've gone into a sun and survived are Kitty, Wruck, Lilith, and SuperBun," Chuckie said. "I'm saying that before Kitty feels the need to remind us."

"Oh, blah, blah, blah, dude. Besides you're not quite right. The Anti-Mother went in and came out, too. Oh. Oh my God." Thought about Algar's current musical cues. Part of the chorus from "Hidden" was "everyone jump like the gators do," and using alligators had been considered totally insane. And yet, they'd helped us save the day during Operation Drug Addict. But that had only happened because I'd gone with the crazy.

"No," Jeff said strongly. "You cannot be thinking what I know you're thinking."

"I'm thinking that I need to do the craziest thing I can think of, and that's talk to the Anti-Mother, yes."

"It's better to let this system float into the Deep Black and die than release that monster," Christopher said. "You know that, Kitty. Why are you even considering this?"

My music changed again, to "Faith" by George Michael. Mephistopheles had repeated that he'd always have faith in me the last time we'd talked. Maybe I needed to live up to that faith. "I need to get up to the *Distant Voyager*."

Everyone started arguing. The call shut off for me, though I could tell that it was still on for Kristie. I stood up. Kristie tapped her communicator and stood up, too. "You turned the call off, too?"

Nodded. "I have to at least try. Maybe I can get through to the Anti-Mother in some way. I was able to connect with her son, after all."

"I'm in." She shrugged at the shocked look I was giving her. "They all want to argue, but none of them have any ideas. This sounds crazy. But crazy is *Code Name: First Lady*'s specialty."

Looked around. We were going to have to steal a shuttle, and that was not going to sit well with anyone. There is another way, Lilith said. Take hold of the cyborg.

Grabbed Kristie's hand and felt something go around us, just like I had when ACE had taken us to Alpha Four during Operation Invasion. Felt the gentle tug and we sailed from the throne room of Helix Rime through space into the cargo hold of the *Distant Voyager* as if we were ghosts. There was something different about the system, but didn't have time to figure out what it was.

"Wow," Kristie said when we landed. "That was amazing."

"Yeah, traveling via superconsciousness is the best way to go. Z'porrah power cubes are faster, but you get to see the sights with superconsciousness in the driver's seat. Help me with this." Went to the lead container and moved it out of the corner where Chuckie and I had shoved it.

"Now what?" Kristie asked.

"No idea, honestly. I'm going to try to reach the Anti-Mother telepathically. If I can." She wasn't an animal, it was going to be tricky.

Heard a sigh in my mind. I'm right here, Lilith said. I can tell you're not used to this kind of combination. Hang on. Waited a few moments. My music changed to "Inside of Me" by 3 Doors Down. The Anti-Mother and Cradus will speak to you now.

Cradus?

I am here, Kitty. It is good to talk with you again.

Wow. I hadn't realized your essence went with everything from your planet. Um, I had to use your present to save the other solar system.

I know. Spehidon and I are overjoyed that our gift was so useful for you so soon, and that by giving the gift of ourselves, you were able to save the system that is soon to join with us.

So, you can connect with yourself even if a part of you is separated?

I can. Spehidon can, too. We both agree that what you want to do is the right thing.

Um, great. So, the reason for my speaking to you is who we have imprisoned inside of, um, you, I guess.

You named me The Anti-Mother, she said. And I, too, am here, Kitty.

Had no idea how to start, so just gave up and started wherever. Um, do you like that name?

Well, it was fitting.

Was. Do you mean it's not fitting anymore?

I have had . . . time to . . . think.

To think about what?

As you'd understand it, my sins.

You've had less than a week.

In your time, yes. The Anti-Mother chuckled. Have you not realized that mind time goes much faster than time out of mind? The music changed to "Time Out of Mind" by Steely Dan because Algar enjoyed DJing a lot. Noted that the music seemed to be keeping up with time as I'd think of it, but was pretty sure that, when this was over, Kristie wouldn't be asking me why I'd spent fifteen minutes staring at a metal container.

Yes, I've started to pick that up. So, what did you decide about your sins?

That I now understand why you and my son became . . . friends. There is more to this life, this existence, than domination. Life should be preserved and encouraged.

I'm sorry to seem incredulous, but that's a hell of a change of heart.

Cradus has been . . . helping me. There was something in the way she said it, the tonal or mental inflection.

Oh my God, are you two like an item or something now?

In a way. The Anti-Mother sounded happily embarrassed, as if, if she was a person, she'd be blushing and looking over coyly at Cradus.

Yes, Cradus said, sounding pleased. As you would be able to understand it. We have spent every moment together since you submerged the trap inside of me. And in that time, we have come to an understanding.

Cradus taught me about his people. And about what he and Spehidon know is out there. And about you. He showed me another way. A way that, I believe, is a better way than I have ever known before.

Um, I hate to ask this, but what does Spehidon think of this, ah, relationship?

She is pleased, Cradus said. We are eagerly waiting for SuperStar. To have another sentient star join us is a source of great joy. The Anti-Mother is a powerful consciousness. To have her with us is also a source of joy, now that she has come to understand how we see our worlds and galaxy.

"Me, Myself & I" by L7 came on. So, um, does that mean that you're all sort of one, even though you're all also separate.

Yes, in a way. Cradus sounded like Olga normally did when I'd figured out something—a kindergarten teacher pleased with a prized pupil.

So, you guys want me to believe that the Anti-Mother has become a force for good now? And I should believe that this isn't some sort of trick and the moment I let her out, she'll turn evil again?

You can't really 'let me out,' the Anti-Mother said. I need to remain inside of Cradus now. We have combined and the trap is dissolved.

Better and better. Focused on the good side—I wouldn't have to stick my hand in mercury or get into the Moon Suit right now. If I can't take you out, how do I get you into the sun?

You send us in just as happened before. The star's heat can melt Cradus, but if we're going fast enough we will still hit the surface. As long as we do that, we can join with the sun.

Then what happens? The supernova we're all dreading?

No. We will have the power to move the sun.

Really hated what I was thinking now. Because I was thinking about Charlie.

CHAPTER 107

H E FEELS HE CAN lift the sun, Lilith said, obviously reading my deeper thoughts. Lifting this container into the sun will seem easy.

He's a little boy, practically still a baby. Just because he thinks he can do something doesn't mean he can.

He's your child. He, like your daughter, is exceptional. And the other exceptional children will help him. And each other.

Why are you okay with this? Why is ACE?

Because we understand two things you do not. This is the only way, and your children are going to do what they think is right, with or without your permission. Wouldn't it be better if their mother was helping them, rather than working against them?

Argh. All that makes sense. However, their father is not going to be so easily convinced.

You may be surprised.

Someone nudged me as my music changed to "Children in Bloom" by the Counting Crows. Had that right. "We are not alone," Kristie said.

Turned around. Sure enough, Jeff was here, along with Jamie and Charlie. "How did you get here so fast?"

He shook his head. "Our children wanted a family powwow." He cleared his throat. "So Jamie and ACE brought me over like Lilith brought you and Kristie."

"Well, that saves time, I guess. Where's Lizzie, then?" I asked Jamie.

"She's getting the other kids ready," Jamie said calmly. "We'll talk to their mommies and daddies, too, but not yet." Presumed they wanted to get me and Jeff on board first, which made sense. The kids were many things, but dumb was not one of them.

"Okay, so, what are we talking about?" I mean, I knew, but why not be polite?

"If Daddy is a king, and you are a queen, Mommy, then that makes Lizzie and me princesses and Charlie a prince. And princesses and princes are supposed to do what's right for their kingdoms. That's what Auntie Rahmi and Auntie Rhee always say."

"They do, that's true. But they're grown up."

"They were protecting their people when they were little," Jamie said. They were Amazons, I was certain Jamie wasn't making this up but had been told about it by the princesses. Probably many more times than once.

"But—" Jeff started.

Put up the paw. He stopped. "Let her finish, Jeff."

Jamie beamed at me. "Thank you, Mommy." She turned to Jeff. "Just because we're little doesn't mean we can't do things. If we don't help, then you can't win, and if you don't win, then everything dies."

"Well, just this solar system," Jeff said. He winced. "Not that this is what we want."

"And all the people in it," I felt compelled to add. "Which currently includes us."

"Not just here," Jamie said. "Everything will die. Sooner than it should, I mean."

Strongly doubted Denise was teaching death and dying courses to the kids, and knew they weren't in Sidwell's curriculum until higher grades. There was no way in hell that ACE or Lilith had been handing out this kind of information to Jamie. Naomi, on the other hand, might have, and Algar was a definite possibility. But regardless of the source, one thing was accurate. "She's right, Jeff. Every Power That Be has been telling me this, in one way or another. We have to do whatever we can to save this system."

"But that was you, me, the others. Not the kids."

"The kids are on this trip for a reason. Everyone is on this trip for a reason. Every person has a role. Some of those roles aren't clear. Some are more important than others. But everyone has their part in all of this. Our kids included. You and Christopher had to grow up at ten. At least this is our children's choice, not a choice forced upon them."

Speaking of people whose roles I wasn't clear on, Vance and

Alicia came in. Both were wearing communicators. Hacker International was having a field day making us into the crew of the *Enterprise*.

"There you are," Vance said. "The bridge got a panicked call that you, Jeff, and Kristie were missing. Alicia and I got assigned to the least likely places you'd be hiding."

"Score one for us," Alicia said.

Vance tapped his communicator. "Found them, they're fine. They'll be back soon, I'm sure. Just tell everyone to carry on with whatever while the King and Queen are having a meeting of state."

"He's good," Jeff said to me.

Alicia cocked her head. "What are we interrupting?"

What the hell. Gave them the fast Recap Girl Update. When I was done, both of them looked impressed but not worried. "So, since you guys are here, you want to add in your thoughts?"

Alicia didn't answer. She came over and knelt next to Charlie. "I think it's time we tell them. They need to know. It will help, I promise."

"I guess," Charlie said truculently.

Alicia put her arm around him. "A few days before Jeff's speech I was driving to work. I was stopped at a light, the light turned green, I looked, no one coming. So I started across the intersection. Out of nowhere, an SUV careened down the street at a very high speed, heading right for me. It was going to T-bone me, on my side. And I had nowhere to go, it was all happening too fast for me to brake or floor it or anything else."

She hugged Charlie. "But then that SUV flew up and over my car, while my car and I got moved into a safe parking place a block away. The SUV crashed into a pole, but no one in the car was hurt. The driver was drunk, at eight in the morning, so when the police heard him say that his car was flying, they didn't believe him."

"That doesn't mean it was Charlie," Jeff said hopefully.

Alicia and I exchanged the "men" look. "Right before the cars moved, I heard someone say, 'Don't worry, Auntie Alicia, I got you,' and then the accident that probably would have killed me was miraculously avoided. I talked to Charlie about it once we were up here in space, privately. He begged me not to tell anyone." Her expression went hard. "Because he was afraid that he'd get in trouble. For saving my life."

Knelt down and hugged Charlie, Alicia, and Jamie as my

music changed to "Help The Children" by MC Hammer. "I'm so proud of you guys. Your sister told you what was happening, didn't she?"

"I did," Jamie admitted.

"Good. Protectors gotta protect. It's our thing. Your father understands that, even if he doesn't want to admit it."

"Jeff," Alicia said, looking up at him, "your son is already a Field agent. You just haven't acknowledged it."

Jeff heaved a sigh, knelt down, and joined the group hug. "You're right. And . . . I can't ask anyone to be less than they are. My children especially."

"The love in the room is great, isn't it?" Vance said to Kristie. "Think it's going to save the day or are we just singing kum-baya?"

"I think *Code Name: First Children* is going to be a great spinoff series, that's what I think."

"Kristie . . ."

"Heh. Gotcha. Again. Man, are you easy to bait."

"You're hilarious." We stopped hugging and everyone stood up. Well, now I knew why Alicia was with us. Vance's turn to man up and prove why he'd been dragged along. "Vance, do you have anything to add, suggest, or say regarding what's going on?"

He shrugged. "I was your enemy once. So were a lot of people. Kristie blackmailed you to get on the team."

"Hey," she said.

"Oh, it's true, we're all past it, and stop acting shocked that we all remember. Anyway, Vance, go on."

"I just think that you've got a good track record for turning people who were against you to your side. Guy and I always say that anyone who bets against you is an idiot. You'll always find a way to win. I think you've found the way—you're just afraid to trust that Cradus has the same ability you do, and afraid to go with what you know you have to do, because it's your kids that will be involved."

"But they've been involved before," Kristie said. "A lot."

"They have," Jeff said with a sigh.

"By the way," Vance said, "have you looked at the solar system recently?"

"How recently?"

"I haven't, really," Jeff said. "I was pulled here quickly and I didn't really pay attention to anything much other than the fact that ACE was taking me somewhere."

"Well, it's boring waiting while everyone else is doing something," Vance said. "By now, Denise is out of ideas for what to do to keep the children from their own form of mutiny. So she's asked the rest of the adults who have nothing to do for ideas. I suggested that the kids work on puzzles. Mother made some. They completed them fast, enjoyed it, and wanted more. So," he shrugged, "the kids worked on the next puzzles they could find."

"Link up," Jeff said. We all did and he raced us to the Observation Lounge and my music changed to "Where Do the Children Play?" by Cat Stevens. "What the hell?"

One of the inner planets had been put back together.

We stared at it for a long moment. "Vance, thank you. I now know why you came along. And I know what to do. But first, a question. What's holding the planet together? Puzzles interlock. Blown-up planets probably don't."

"The other kids," Jamie said. "It's not hard once Charlie moved everything and Wasim explained how gravity works."

"Is that draining energy we're going to need?"

"No, Mommy," Jamie said patiently. "It's not hard because things are floating."

"Super. Does that mean that we can put something inside that puzzle?"

"Sure. It'll be fun."

"Great. Then I have our plan. Jeff, you're in charge of calming down the other parents. Vance, you help him with that. Alicia, can you stay with the kids? I'd like to have as many adults who can help without interfering improperly with them."

"You got it. Amy's already on board, I think, and I'm sure Denise will be. Doreen and Irving might be an issue."

"Irving's in," Doreen said from behind us. "I gave him no choice. And Kitty, by now it should go without saying, but I get why I have to say it. Bottom line—whatever the situation is, I'm helping you."

"That's awesome." Looked at her expression. "You know something you're not telling."

She grinned. "I was listening outside the doorway earlier and heard that you were trying to figure out why certain people were brought along on this trip. And I know why I'm here." She patted her stomach. "I'm carrying a conduit."

CHAPTER 108

"A S ALWAYS," JEFF SAID, once we had everyone advised and had handled any arguments or whining, "I hate this plan."

Shocking no one, Christopher was the last to approve the plan and he only did because Amy and Doreen both snarled at him. Becky had apparently already been working on her mother telepathically, and all the adults who'd been with Vance had witnessed the kids doing their Space Puzzle, so most of them took less convincing than those who'd been on the planets.

"Good. Then it's likely to work. And I don't know why you're whining—you're actually not going to be in life-threatening danger for this one."

"Yes, that's such a comfort." Jeff's sarcasm knob was definitely turned to eleven.

My plan was multifaceted, but a good part of it relied on Mahin and Abigail being able to bind the planet puzzle together so that it could actually hit the sun. So it wasn't just the kids I was risking. Go me. Of course, I was risking, too, as were others. It was the highest-stakes game imaginable, really.

"How sure are you?" Jeff asked. Did not need him doubting me right now.

"A Matter of Trust" by Billy Joel came on my airwaves. "Do you trust me?"

Jeff sighed and hugged me. "Yes, I do. And no one has any better ideas. And we all know we're just about out of time."

We'd left several of our people on the planets—Tim, Reader, Wheatles, and Grentix were still on Helix Noblora and Adam, Kevin, Hamlin, MJO, Naveed, Len, Kyle, and Gadhavi were still on Helix Rime. We needed all the A-Cs, so we had to leave the humans, but they were all armed and felt that the situation was more than under control. We'd been advised that Len and Kyle were bonding with Telzor, which was nice, MJO was making Roanach and Clorence feel happily important, and Kevin, Adam, and the others had everything else well in hand. Besides, they still had the Peregrines, our Super Rabbits, the Most Weasels, Bellie, and Ginger hanging out—no one on Helix Rime was going to give them any trouble.

Those who I needed for the Plan were back on the *Distant Voyager* in the Observation Lounge, so we had a clear view of the system.

Jamie had Doreen sit on the floor so the kids could sit in a circle around her. "Dianne says that she wants you to be sure that you spell her name with two Ns, Auntie Doreen," Jamie said as she led Doreen to her spot. My music changed to "Roxanne" by the Police.

"Huh. Dianne, not Roxanne?"

Jamie smiled at me and went to Alicia. "Auntie Alicia needs to sit back-to-back with Auntie Doreen."

So that was how the kids had known Alicia was in danger. Laughed softly. "Alicia, does Tim know?"

Alicia grinned as she sat down. "Not yet. I haven't had time to tell him. I was going to do it after Jeff's speech and then, well, it didn't seem right to share it on Cradus—because we both know Tim would have freaked out and not let me do anything—and we haven't had any time otherwise."

"Yeah, there were a lot of 'do it after Jeff's speech' plans going around. I guess you don't have to struggle with the name."

"Nope. I like it. Besides, it's Tim's grandmother's name."

Decided that Jamie had earned being in charge of this part of the Plan. "Jamie-Kat, you get everyone situated. I need to talk to Uncle Chuckie for a second." She beamed at me and proudly started moving people into position. Went to Chuckie and pulled him aside. "Do it now," I said quietly.

"Do what now?" He looked legitimately confused.

"Propose. Take Nathalie somewhere on this ship and ask her to marry you. Now. Before we know if we're going to live or die or succeed or fail."

"Kitty, it's not the right time."

Rolled my eyes. "Ten extra seconds of boldness and we'd have been married since that Vegas trip. You were bold enough to ask Naomi to marry you before the world ended. Be bold now. Trust me. This is the right girl. Just . . . don't make her wait to *know* she's the right girl any longer."

"I thought you wanted me here, doing important things."

"I do. Don't take the time to have sex or anything. Just propose and then get back here. Or would you rather go into the center of a sun?"

He laughed. "You're right. This, especially compared to that, is not a scary thing at all."

He sauntered over to where Nathalie was, spoke to her quietly, took her elbow, and led her out of the room.

Trotted back to what I was seriously now thinking of as the Summoning Circle. Jamie had placed everyone where she wanted them so that everyone would have equal access to the two pregnant women. As had happened during Operation Assassination, when Doreen was pregnant with Ezra, figured the kids were accessing those in utero to create some kind of Hybrid Super Kids Powers Activation. Also figured that if I asked Jamie how this was being achieved the answer would make every adult more than uncomfortable, so kept my yap shut.

Each kid was in an adult's lap, so Sean was with Claudia, Ross with Lorraine, Ezra with Irving, Patrick with Serene, and Becky with Amy. Because I needed his father and he was the youngest, JR was in Doreen's lap. Jamie was in Lizzie's lap.

Lizzie wasn't the only nonhybrid involved, either. Raymond was in Denise's lap and Rachel was, interestingly enough, in Alicia's. Wondered, not for the first time, if Kevin and Denise had A-C blood in them, or if they were just so damned charismatic that it was its own superpower. Still had no bet either way.

Charlie was in Jeff's lap, situated so that he had a clear view of the window. We'd arranged the other adults so that his view wouldn't be blocked.

Abigail and Mahin were stationed at the window. Gower, White, Jeremy, Jennifer, Siler, Rahmi, and Rhee were standing by, when, not if, the girls needed to get energy and power from them. Tito was on hand just in case, and I'd assigned Buchanan to be on guard in this room, versus following me. Under the circumstances, he hadn't argued about it. Much.

"Remember, I'll tell Uncle Jerry to give the signal. Don't start until he tells you to, because that could cause a lot of problems."

"We promise, Mommy," Jamie said cheerfully. The kids all looked excited and the adults all looked worried and/or grim. So, as I'd expected.

My music changed to "God Give Me Strength" by Elvis Costello. Which was Algar's way of telling me to step on it. Took Jamie's hand in mine. Are you sure you can leave her safely?

ACE is sure, Kitty. Jamie will be fine. Jamie is strong and the other children will ensure that Jamie does not fall asleep as others do when ACE or Lilith leave them.

Then let's do this thing.

ACE left Jamie and filtered into me. Having both ACE and Lilith inside of me was beyond anything I'd experienced before, but it wouldn't last for long. Welcome back, ACE.

Jamie leaned against Lizzie, who kissed her head. "It's all okay, Mommy," Jamie said. "You do your part and I'll do mine."

Bent and kissed her head. "That's my big little girl." Kissed Lizzie's head, too. "And my bigger big girl." Jeff and Charlie were next to the girls, so I kissed Charlie's head. "Be safe, my little man." Kissed Jeff on the lips. "And my big man."

"Meddler." He didn't say it like it was a bad thing.

"You disapprove?"

"Hell no. I was going to have that talk with him, you just beat me to it." He took my hand in his. "Promise me that you'll be safe."

"I promise that I'll do my best, Jeff. That's all I can promise."

He squeezed my hand. "And that's always been enough. See you on the other side, baby."

On to the next stage of my setup, before I delayed any longer. "Great. My team, with me, please." Headed out, with Christopher, Kristie, Butler, Mossy, and Wruck.

We went to the cargo hold. Christopher, Butler, and Kristie made sure that everything other than the vat with the Anti-Mother in it was tightly tied down. Wruck shifted into a form that was hella strong and moved the container next to the part of the ship that would open and lower when the hold was opened.

Put my hand on the vat. You're sure?

Yes, the Anti-Mother said. But, I do have one request.

What?

I'd like a different name. A name that *you* like, that means something good, and something good to you.

Had no idea what name to pick. My music changed to "Lucinda" by The Knack. It was fitting. How about Lucinda? That's my mother-in-law's name. She's lovely, makes the best brownies in the galaxy, and loves her entire extended family and all their friends. And she and I started out as antagonists but now we love each other. A lot.

I love it! Thank you. We will not disappoint you or betray your trust.

And I won't betray yours, either. Had to say it, now, before we were all committed. You know, if this doesn't work, or doesn't work as we're all hoping, the sun will go supernova and you'll die.

No. I will live in everything. That is what Cradus showed me—how I can be more than I ever imagined, no matter what happens next. And this is why your enemies become your friends—you warned me before you knew if I could be trusted. Because you care.

I do. Time to stop stalling. Good luck and let's go save the solar system and thereby save the galaxy.

Nodded to the others, but before we rolled, Chuckie and Nathalie arrived. Nathalie was glowing and she had a very large diamond on her left ring finger. Chuckie was very good at determining what kind of ring each woman actually wanted.

They didn't need to say anything. I already knew, and it was easy for the others to guess. Hugs and kisses all around. "You're sure this will work?" Chuckie asked me.

"Dude, I'm as sure of this plan as I am of all the others."

"So, no," Christopher said.

Chuckie shook his head. "See you on the other side." He took Nathalie's hand and they headed off, presumably for their posts in the Observation Lounge, Nathalie to assist Tito if needed, Chuckie to advise as needed.

"Ready?" I asked the others. They all nodded.

Christopher reached his hand to me and I took his in mine. ACE flowed from me to him. Felt a little loss, but not the energy drain, because Lilith was still inside of me.

Christopher's eyes were opened wide. "Wow. This is . . . amazing."

"You have to return him to Jamie when this is done. Unless ACE wants to be free, like Lilith."

"ACE does not," Christopher said, in a voice that wasn't his, indicating that ACE had control of the mind and body. "ACE will never leave Jamie, or Kitty. ACE loves ACE's home. How can ACE protect if ACE leaves?"

"Just want you to know that you always can, if you want to. We don't want you to go, either, so we're all on the same page there."

"That was freaky," Christopher said. "Hey, no palsy."

"Maybe you're better at it than Paul was."

Christopher laughed. "I think it's that ACE is better at it, honestly."

"Let's hope. Okay, gang, group hug."

We hugged and a part of ACE and Lilith went into the others. Everyone had Christopher's reaction, even Butler and Kristie.

Once the Sharing of the Superconsciousnesses was over, Wruck shifted into a star surfer. "Ready." We'd discussed it and he felt that, while he could double Christopher, star surfers were the fastest beings out there, so that was his choice for the Plan.

Mossy flew onto my shoulder. "I'll shift once the hatch opens." Per my talk with him, Turleens did this sort of thing for fun, and with the turbo boost of having a bit of ACE and Lilith inside him, Mossy had no worries.

Kristie and Butler had also felt more than capable, in no small part because we were all still in Drax body armor and face masks. At least my team was eager and confident. My music changed to "Built for Speed" by American Hi-Fi. Algar also had no concerns, so that was good.

Kristie hit her communicator. "Jerry, connect me and John Butler to Kitty, Christopher, John Wruck, and Mossy."

"Will do," Jerry said in my ear. "Godspeed, everyone. And I mean that in all the ways it can be taken."

"Remember that the perspective of how the galaxy is spinning depends on where we are in relation to it," Butler said. "And that might change once we get this system closer."

"If we do it right, it won't matter." That was my prevailing theory, anyway. "Remember, we have to encircle the system from six different directions. Stay aware of where the others are—having to deviate from your path will slow us down and I'm sure I don't need to explain why hitting into each other will be the definition of Worst Save Ever."

"What's life without risk?" Kristie asked with a grin. "If you feel like you're slowing down, Kitty, just let me know. We can discuss all the *Code Name: First Lady* sequels I'm thinking of suggesting to Jürgen."

"You're hilarious." Took the requisite deep breath and let it out slowly. "Jerry, give us the countdown, and remember to open our door, please, and thank you."

"Will do, Commander. Your favorite flyboy lives to serve."

CHAPTER 109

JERRY STARTED AT TEN. We all moved to stand near the container with Space Lucinda in it. We were in position on the eight count. Giving us what felt like a hell of a lot of time to wait. We chose our paths in the next six seconds, which sort of seemed like six minutes, possibly hours.

"Two," Jerry finally said. "And . . . one." The hatch opened and my music changed to "Into the Great Wide Open" by Tom Petty & the Heartbreakers. True enough—we were all sucked out, the heavy lead container included.

The container zoomed off, so knew Charlie was doing his thing. The rest of us scattered and started running, which we could do because of ACE and Lilith.

Christopher had the longest path—he was going around the system in an oval that meant he was above and below the elliptic plane. Mossy had the elliptic plane of the intact planets. My path was around the middle and was, therefore, the shortest. Butler and Kristie were crisscrossing along the diagonals, so to speak. Basically, the five of us were trying to look like a super atom, the humor of which was not lost on me. And Wruck was circling the sun, creating what we hoped was a vortex that would pull Space Lucinda into the center of Helix. So he was the nucleus. Doing it all for science!

Actually, we were doing it all in order to create enough momentum for the sun to be able to reverse course and head back toward the galaxy, while not leaving any of its satellites behind. And once we achieved that, then the hard stuff would start. We were being helped greatly by ACE and Lilith and, I suspected, even more greatly by Algar. God helped those who helped themselves, presumably so that he could pretend it wasn't him doing it.

Charlie, meanwhile was moving the lead container into the center of the Puzzle Planet and, the moment he did so, the other kids were helping move the pieces back together while Abigail and Mahin were gathering space dust, asteroids, and tiny parts of exploded planets to create a "whole" orb.

Because they were inside of the six of us, ACE and Lilith were covering the entire solar system in a spinning form of Tupperware. Or perhaps that was just how I was thinking of it.

Got into the groove quickly because there was nothing like having the Superconsciousness Boost. Because of that, even as we started to go faster and faster, getting up to well beyond Ludicrous Speed, we could still see each other and the things in the solar system.

Could also see the Milky Way. It looked far away. A lot farther than it had looked on the picture. Scary far. Stopped looking at it. Steering was going to fall to Space Lucinda and Wruck, with a likely assist from Charlie, at least if I knew my son at all.

Concentrated on running as fast as possible and focused on the Puzzle Planet, not the Milky Way. The Puzzle Planet was well on its way to Helix. So far, so good.

You must go faster, Lilith said. All of you. Stop watching everything else and focus on your paths.

Tried to put on more speed. I was a sprinter. This was a sprint. Sure, a long-distance sprint, but a sprint nonetheless. Felt like I was going my fastest.

Kitty, you must find more speed. The others are now at the speed they need to be. You aren't, and if you don't speed up, the chances of you colliding with the others is high.

Had no idea where I was going to get more reserves of speed. My music changed to "A Question of Lust" by Depeche Mode. Not what I'd have expected. But I focused on the lyrics. This was a love song, about a how a couple survived challenges, how they stayed together. If I didn't do my part, my family wasn't going to be together ever again.

Stopped trying to go faster to save the galaxy and just ran for the joy of running, for the love of my family and friends, and for the chance to have sex with Jeff again.

There, Lilith said. You're perfect. Be prepared—the planet has been captured in the orbit John Wruck has created.

I could keep this speed going now, so I did, while DJ Algar spun "Born to Run" by Bruce Springsteen, "Run Baby Run" by Garbage, and "Fox on the Run" by Sweet. I watched the Puzzle Planet start spinning around the sun, faster and faster, until it was a blur. Then it was gone.

What happened?

Don't slow, Lilith warned. What we wanted to happen has happened. The planet protected the container just long enough.

Made sure I kept on running at the same speed I had been. But I still watched Helix. So I saw the sun flare then contract. Um . . .

Lucinda is containing the sun's thermonuclear reaction. Be ready. In a moment we will be moving and you will need to continue running.

The sun looked less red. Not a lot less, but it no longer seemed at the end of its line. Felt the pull, as the sun started to move. The music changed to "You Spin Me Round (Like a Record)" by Dead or Alive and I knew we were ready.

A lattice of light went around the system. Which made it look like an oval Z'porrah power cube. And the six of us running were the ones who were going to trigger it.

We had to be in the right positions to trigger, so we had to keep running until we were all set at the right place and the right time, which was going to take precision. Thankfully, we had ACE and Lilith along to ensure that we could be precise.

Because of the sun's movement combined with those of us running and whatever it was the kids were doing, the solar system started to tip as if it was rolling. Which was what we wanted.

Now, Lilith said, as my music changed to Van Halen's "Jump" and we all jumped on her cue. Saw the power oval trigger.

Heard ACE and Space Lucinda give directions to the others, tiny course adjustments to account for the system itself starting to tumble through space. Because I was covering the middle, I had no corrections to make, just the onus to keep on running as fast as I could. My music changed to "I'll Tumble 4 Ya" by Culture Club. Fitting.

Figured that the music and time weren't necessarily going in a linear fashion. Wasn't sure how long it took the Flash to run around an entire solar system, but had to figure it was more than a second. Then again, even with Lilith inside of me, could barely spot Christopher as anything but a blur.

"We're moving toward the galaxy," Butler said. Was hella impressed that he could talk while doing this. I certainly wasn't planning to try running my yap. "And we're on our side, so to speak, which could be good or bad."

Risked one syllable. "Why?"

"Because we're going to hit the galactic disk straight on, with our solar disk slicing into it."

"Do I slow?" Christopher asked.

No, Lilith said. All of you need to go faster.

Algar did me a solid and put on "Toys in the Attic" by Aerosmith. Found the will to run faster with my boys in my ears. When the next song came on and was "Uncle Salty," had the happy realization that I was getting the entire *Toys in the Attic* album, which was my favorite.

So, running along and rocking out, we tumbled toward what was either going to be a miraculous save or a really big crash.

Ready, Lilith said finally, as "You See Me Crying" was ending. Impact in five . . . four . . . three . . . two . . . My music changed to "Time for You to Go" by Sum 41. One.

And we hit.

The impact was hard to describe—it was what I figured a bubble would feel like when it hit a surface. The bubble is floating along, then it slams into something and breaks apart, but the thing it hit doesn't even notice.

We weren't breaking apart, but was pretty sure that was only because the six of us were doing our running thing and Charlie and the other kids were helping keep us steady while Lilith and ACE kept things together.

But once the initial impact was over, we continued to tumble, through the perimeter and back inside the safety of the galaxy. Felt another pull—the core's pull on our sun.

We're inside, Lilith said, sounding hella relieved. You cannot slow yet. We need to ensure that we are not at the edges of the galaxy.

We need to ensure that we are not too near any other systems, as well, Space Lucinda said. I will not be able to contain Helix for too long. And when this system dies, we don't want to take others with us.

We ran on, still tumbling, moving closer to the core and the safety that represented. But not too close. Algar treated me to a lot of songs about home, including but not limited to "On the Way Home" by John Mayer, "Home" by Daughtry, "Ass Back

Home" by Gym Class Heroes, and "Baby Come Home" by American Hi-Fi. But when we got to "Finally Found a Home" by Huey Lewis & the News, knew we were close.

Begin slowing, Lilith said. Gradually, this is just as important as speed was before.

Slowed down listening to Aerosmith's "Sunny Side of Love" while checking to make sure that all the parts of the solar system had come with us. Well, the most important parts, anyway—I wasn't going to stress about the asteroids and such. But Helix, Helix Noblora, Helix Rime, and the *Distant Voyager* were all accounted for.

More Aerosmith, more slowing. As "I Don't Want to Miss a Thing" was finishing, Lilith told us all to run to the ship. Wruck swooped over and gathered us up, which I appreciated.

We flew into the cargo hold. "Jerry, time to close the door."

There was silence. Looked at the others, doing my best not to panic. They all looked as freaked out as I felt.

The cargo doors closed. "Jerry?" Kristie asked. "Jerry, are you there?"

Still silence.

"Um, Mother?"

Nothing.

"Did we do all this and lose everyone?" Mossy asked, sounding freaked out.

Tried not to lose it. This was supposed to save everyone. "Are people still on the planets?"

"Sorry!" Jerry's voice came through. "The move caused the ship some distress. We're all fine, so are those on the planets— they all went underground, where it was much easier to handle the move. We had a few issues, and communications was damaged, which is why I wasn't answering. It just took Mother a little time to fix."

"Thanks for the heart attacks."

"You're sure the speed didn't affect those on the planets or the ship?" Wruck asked.

"You're asking that now?" Kristie said, sounding a little outraged. Couldn't really blame her.

Lilith and ACE were protecting, ACE said. All penguins were protected.

Yes, Lilith agreed. That's one of the reasons we went into the six of you—the barrier you created kept those inside it safe.

My music changed. To "God Is a DJ" by Pink. Started to laugh. "Let's just get up to the Observation Lounge and make sure," I suggested. So we did.

Happily and to all our relief, everyone seemed okay. Most of the kids were sleeping. Jamie, Rachel, and Raymond were still awake, though they looked tired.

The adults also looked pretty spent. Abigail and Mahin were sitting with their backs against a wall, as were all the others who'd been there for energy assistance.

Anyone not sleeping got hugged by all of us and vice versa. Some kissing was involved, too, at least between Christopher and Amy and me and Jeff.

"Stop looking worried," Tito said after we'd all finished being relieved that everyone was alive and okay. "Everyone's exhausted, but that's all. How are the six of you?"

We all looked at each other. "I feel fine," I admitted. The others chimed in with the same. "That's going to end once ACE and Lilith leave us, though."

It would be best if ACE and I stay inside of all of you for a while. We will withdraw from one of you at a time, but not just yet. We also need to recover and you will all be less exhausted if we wait.

"Works for me. I'd love to spend time sleeping and celebrating, but we have two planets to evacuate somehow. Space Lucinda said that she can't control Helix's degeneration for too long."

"Excuse me," Jeff said. "Space who?"

Explained how I'd give the Anti-Mother a new name and why.

"Only my girl."

"Hey, I named a new solar system after your mother. Well, an old new one. And while it won't last forever, it's still an honor."

"And that's exactly how I'm going to spin it, baby, believe me."

"We have a communication coming from the Apata system," Mother said.

"Put it through to the whole ship, please, Mother," I said.

"Hi, everyone, it's Raj. I wanted to be the first to congratulate you on doing the impossible."

"Thanks, Raj. Two populated planets, lots of planetary debris, and one older sun back where they belong. At least sort of. Mission accomplished. If we can evacuate two large, heavily populated planets before the old sun goes bye-bye."

"I've been doing more than just shaking hands and eating interesting new cuisine, as have the others. What matters most to the current situation is that Gustav has spoken to his father while we were being political. Vatusus advised Galactic Council allies in the general area of what you were doing, so you've been monitored. Everyone is impressed. Extremely impressed. Earth's cachet just rose immeasurably."

"That's why we did it," Jeff said, sarcasm knob at eleven and threatening to go to twelve. "For the accolades."

Raj laughed. "You'll appreciate them because they're how you're going to evacuate the planets. Now that you're relatively stationary, Vatusus is sending ships. They need a destination for the refugees, but they can evacuate without issue."

Jeff groaned. "We have to find them homes, too, don't we? Solaris is full up, so is Alpha Centauri."

"Stop stressing. I know where they're going."

"Where?" Raj asked.

"The Goldilocks system by the Clown Consortium system. Those planets are all Earthlike and all uninhabited. And I claimed them for Solaris, and the people from Helix Noblora and Helix Rime are now considered Earth citizens and wherever they live Earth territories."

"That will fly with the Council," Raj said. "Vatusus expects ships to you within a few hours."

"Perfect. We'll start getting the natives ready for evacuation. It may take some time, though."

"You're the heroes of the galaxy right now," Raj said. "Take all the time you'll need."

Jeff caught my eye and smiled. "I plan to."

I laughed. "I'm glad you're always laser focused on the priorities."

CHAPTER 110

EVERYONE ON THE PLANETS was truly okay, which was a relief. The evacuations went more smoothly than any of us had expected. They took longer than anyone wanted, too. But smooth and slow was better than chaotic and fast, at least in this instance.

We disintegrated the Helix Rime food replicator, but not before we got confirmation that feeding the planet's dead sandworm monsters to it had created the planet's rage virus.

We'd lucked out in one way—all those who were irreparably mutated from eating the replicator's food were all dead, killed in our battle or by each other when imprisoned after. ACE and Lilith both felt that, with the replicator and the truly mutated gone, we were okay allowing Helix Rime to disintegrate into the galaxy along with the rest of the system when Helix and Space Lucinda finally went supernova. And the rest of that population was decreed healed or healing.

ACE and Lilith drained out of each of us during this time. ACE went back to Jamie, Lilith went back to being free, though she stuck around with us.

I finally got to meet Ixtha. She was cool and, I was happy to note, a lot like me, though our frames of reference were very different. Jamie and Charlie were overjoyed to get to see her, and she spent a lot of time with all the kids, making them all happy and giving them something to lord over the others when we got back to the Apata system.

Settling refugees wasn't something that was going to be completed in a weekend, though. Alpha Four had been contacted and they were sending ships, too, with supplies for a new colony. After all, if they were Solaris territories, that made them part of the Annocusal Empire. That was us, expanding Alexander's holdings everywhere we went.

Kevin and Adam volunteered to take charge of refugee resettlement. Hamlin insisted on going, too, and ultimately, we sent Len, Kyle, Mossy, Wruck, Jeremy, and Butler as well. The Vata guaranteed that our people would be returned to us, either at Apata, Vatusus, Alpha Four, or Earth, depending on where the rest of us were when the resettlement was completed. Lilith chose to go with them, which felt right and meant that they'd have great help.

They'd also have the rabbits of ours that had gone giant and the Most Weasels. Those animals had decided that they were needed to keep the Helix Rime people in line. Couldn't argue because I knew they were right. On the plus side, not all the rabbits had chowed down on the Orange Scourge, per Peter because SuperBun had given them instructions before he'd become SuperStar. Worked for me, because we still had all our personal rabbits. And the Most Weasels had obviously been brought along by Algar to do exactly what they'd done and were planning to do, so no arguments from me there.

The rest of us, including Denise, Raymond, and Rachel, went back to the Apata system. Ship docking went much more smoothly with Brian and the flyboys at the controls. Now that the Helix system was back in the galaxy, Mother didn't care who was driving.

Grentix and Kreaving were treated like returning heroes, deservedly. So were the rest of us. Apata had gone from isolationist to pro-Galactic Council in the time we'd been gone, in no small part due to who we'd left in the system. Jeff's family had really stepped up and so had our politicians. It was definitely a Go Team experience.

We'd made it down to Ignotforsta, which was a lot like the Earth, only less paved, but we were only there a day when Chuckie got a communication from Councilor Leonidas of Alpha Four.

"Leonidas thinks that we need to send some people to Alpha Four," he told me and Jeff.

"Is something wrong?" Jeff asked.

"Not really. But other systems are getting lots of face time and they aren't. It's totally political. He doesn't want me to come, for example. But he does want you and Kitty, Jeff. And the kids. And Richard and Paul. I think there's a religious festival going on and Alexander wants to include the Exonerates. Honestly, that's a huge thing. I think you guys need to go."

"We can't leave right now," Jeff protested. "The Apatans will be offended."

"Leonidas doesn't want everyone. Just a handful."

"We can take the sports car." Both men looked at me. Shrugged. "I can fly it, and if you want to freak out about that, then ask James to come, too. I mean, if Paul's going, James is going to want to go anyway. We'll take them, us, the kids, Nightcrawler, and Richard. You know, we can take the Ard Ri, too. That's an extra royal." And that way I'd know exactly where Algar was.

"Who else?" Chuckie asked. "I think you need a couple more to make it look good."

"How about MJO and Kristie? That way they get press coming with us."

Chuckie nodded. "That's a group of a dozen. I think that works. I'll let Leonidas know you're coming. You guys are going to have to leave in the morning, though."

"No rest for the wicked, the weary, or the just plain done with it all, we know."

Gathered our impromptu Impress Alpha Four team together. The only one protesting wasn't on the guest list. Buchanan was basically having kittens that he wasn't going. Finally got him calmed down a little by explaining that the Role of the Guy Who Haunted My Every Step would be played by Siler for this short trip, but he was still pissed.

Jeff finally lost patience. "Look, not only can the rest of us protect her, but she can protect herself. You're the best, no argument. However, you're going to serve everyone better by staying here and ensuring that we haven't offended these people irrevocably by doing this side trip. And, I'll pull rank if I have to. Don't make me have to. Or make me ask the Ignotforstans to imprison you until we leave."

"Fine," Buchanan said, clearly angry and somewhat disgusted. "God forbid I do my job."

"Malcolm, we still have most of the leadership of the United States in this system. We will feel a lot better if we know you're doing your thing here, taking care of business, and ensuring that we don't come back to a war zone. But none of that matters as much as this—nothing can happen to Wasim. I want you to guard that kid as if he were me. And I promise to tell my mom that it's all Jeff's fault if something goes wrong."

Buchanan managed a grin. "Fine. I'll hold you to that, Missus Executive Chief. And I'll watch Gadhavi, too. We don't want him hurt or worse, either."

"That's my Doctor Strange."

Happily, Algar gave us no trouble about going. Neither did anyone else. Christopher protested that his father was leaving, but he was still tired from running around a solar system and ACE leaving him, so he didn't argue all that much.

MJO and Kristie were jazzed about being on the team. Bellie was excited, too, which, of course, was the most important thing. Bruno and Lola were also coming along, as were Ginger, Wilbur, and our family's rabbits. Our Poofs shared that they wouldn't miss this for anything. So we were covered, animals-wise.

We moved our stuff from our rooms in the saucer section into rooms in the sports car section. Then we said our good-byes again, with assurances that we'd be back quickly. Since we'd already gone and come back in the time promised, the Apatans seemed cool with our leaving. Kings and queens were great, but your own guys having done the impossible was even better.

The sports car flew a little differently than the saucer. Reader and I got to sit next to each other, like we were in a human-created ship. There were seats behind us, so after Jeff got the kids strapped in, in the back row of course, Lizzie between Jamie and Charlie, he sat behind Reader. Algar was in the seat behind but between us, and White was behind me. Siler, Gower, MJO, and Kristie were in the row behind them, in front of the kids.

Mother activated the version of herself she'd already ported to the sports car, which I immediately named Mini-Mother. "Have a safe trip," Mother said. "I will monitor you, just in case."

"Thanks, Mother," Reader said. "Mini-Mother, are you ready?"

"I am." Mini-Mother sounded a lot like Mother, which was to be expected.

We separated from the saucer. It was easy because we were in space. Space stations were where it was at.

"I don't want to go to warp just yet," Reader said as we flew away from the space station. "I'd like Kitty to get comfortable with the controls first."

"Works for me."

We spent some time with Reader talking me through various

differences between this ship and an Earth airplane, as well as this from what I was used to with the saucer section. Since I was mostly used to pushing buttons, this was helpful.

We'd been zipping along for a couple of hours when I noticed something out of the windshield. "Do you guys see that dark mass off in the distance?"

The others looked. "I believe I do, Missus Martini," White said. "It looks something like a giant wobbly wolf's head."

My stomach clenched. "Yeah, it does."

"And I think it's heading right for us," Reader said, voice tight.

Heard a sound—someone snapping their fingers. And the mass was gone.

Or we were.

Instead of the blackness of space and the light of a few nearby solar systems, we weren't alone now. There were ships, lots of them, all around us. But they looked nothing like ships we were used to.

Most were made of bronze, some of bronze and gold. There was steel, but not as much as you'd expect. Many of these ships had different blimpy shapes or were modeled like a sailing ship. Some looked vaguely familiar—was fairly sure I saw a bronze version of a Vrierst Manta Ray, only I could see hinges, periscopes, and more on it.

We all stared.

"Where the hell are we?" Reader asked finally.

"We appear to be exactly where we were, galactically speaking," Mini-Mother said. "The solar systems are where they were, nothing has changed. Other than that we are now surrounded by ships where none were before."

"Ships that don't exist in our universe," Reader pointed out.

"How is that possible?" Jeff asked.

"I have no idea," I lied, as I realized that I recognized the ship directly in front of us—I'd seen it in the three-way mirrors. "But I can say this—we're definitely not in Kansas anymore."

Read on for a sneak preview of
the seventeenth novel in the *Alien* series
from Gini Koch:

ALIENS LIKE US

"AH," Jeff said slowly, "are those ships all turning toward us?"

"Yes," White replied. "And unless I'm mistaken, they're readying to fire."

"You're not mistaken," Reader said, voice tight. "Ready to take evasive maneuvers."

Well, there was certainly no time like the present for me to do what I'd trained for during Operation Interstellar. Really hoped that the universal translator was up to snuff and that Mini-Mother was going to help, versus hinder.

"I need hailing channels open," I said calmly. The button flashed. "Mini-Mother, you rock." Pushed the button down. "This is the crew of the satellite ship of the *Distant Voyager* from Earth in the Solaris system. We have no idea what's going on, but we didn't mean to intrude on what's either a party or a fight. We'll just be going now, so you can, um, relax your trigger fingers."

Silence from the other side. "Let go of the button," Mini-Mother said. "I will keep communications open and put any responses on view if able."

Tried not to worry about this. My kids were with us—had no idea what we might see and I really didn't want them terrorized by someone threatening us. This moment's example of closing the barn door after all the animals had fled.

"You're who from where and which ship, exactly?" a male voice asked. A really familiar voice. One I'd known since the first day of ninth grade.

"Chuckie? Is that you?" My Chuckie was still in the Apata system, hanging out with people who looked a lot like those of us from Earth and Alpha Centauri, only more heavily animal than we were.

Heard a lot of background noise, as if whoever was on the other line wasn't alone and I'd freaked them out in a real way.

"Identify," the guy I was really prepared to swear was Chuckie said.

Heaved a sigh. Time to pull out the gun I was pretty sure I had to use. "I'm Katherine Katt-Martini from Earth. On my Earth I'm also the First Lady of the United States and the Queen Regent of Earth for the Annocusal Royal Family. I have no idea what or who I am here, other than from Earth, though my guess is that I know you, since I'm betting you're Charles Reynolds, also of Earth."

Heard more background noise and was really sure that guns were cocking. "What do you mean, 'your' Earth?"

"Dude, I'd think it was self-evident for people flying around in really cool spaceships that look literally nothing like our really cool spaceship. We live in a multiverse. In my universe, we don't have spaceships like this. In my universe, we don't have a war going on in this exact spot in the blackness of space between solar systems."

"We don't have anything called the United States," Chuckie replied. "But you're right—my name is Charles Reynolds. However, we're at war with the Annocusal Royal Family, so that means you're our enemy."

"How is this helping?" Jeff asked urgently.

Looked at him over my shoulder and gave him the "shut up" glare. "No, it doesn't. Dude, use that big brain of yours. We're from *a different universe*. In our universe, the Annocusal Royal Family are good guys. Spoken modestly, God love me, in no small part due to my interference and assistance, along with the interference and assistance of all the adults in this ship with me."

"Adults? Do you have children on board?" Chuckie's voice sounded tight.

"We do. Your godson, for one. Because, in my world, you're my oldest friend and one of my two best guy friends. My version of you stayed behind at a solar system we've just befriended but my other best guy friend is with us. He's named James Reader. No idea if he's also on board whatever ship you're on, but I'm willing to bet that he is."

I'd seen this world in the three-way mirrors that had been created for me on the sentient metal moon Cradus so that I could have it on the ship with me and check on the various universes like I'd promised my daughter from another universe I would.

I'd learned how to use them during my first universe switch, when I'd gone to Bizarro World.

While the others with me, other than Algar, probably had no idea where we were, I did—we were in the Steampunk Universe. And I knew there was a version of me here, because I'd seen her, and Chuckie, Reader, and, most importantly, Jamie.

"You sound like spies," Chuckie said, though I heard the uncertainty. "This isn't a battle, it's a planning meeting. And it would be the best place for spies to sneak in."

"Stupid spies, sure. Dude, if we were spying on you, we sure as hell wouldn't have chosen this way to show up on your metaphorical doorsteps."

"Maybe. Maybe this is your gambit—that you come to us with some bizarre story so we trust you."

"I get the concern, but we're not trying to Trojan Horse you guys. We didn't actually plan to be here, it just happened. When this kind of crap perpetrates itself on me, that usually means that wherever I'm going needs my special form of crazy to save the day."

"I don't follow you."

"So few ever do. Look, my daughter, Jamie, is also on board the ship with us. Why don't you do everyone a solid and go find your Jamie and ask her if we're enemies or not."

"A what? What do you mean by a solid?"

"Wow. Learning each other's slang is going to be the issue, isn't it? A solid means a favor. In our world. As in, do all of us one and get Jamie, pronto if not sooner."

Silence.

"Baby, seriously, what are you doing?" Jeff asked quietly.

"We're clear that we've changed universes now," Gower added. "Because we're not stupid."

"So, totes don't feel obligated to explain it," Lizzie said from the cheap seats. "Even Charlie and the pets are clear on the sitch."

"Geez, everyone's a critic. I've seen this world before. I exist here, so do Chuckie, James, and Jamie. I have no idea who else is here or isn't, but if we're talking to who I'm prepared to swear is Charles Reynolds, then his version of Jamie is there, somewhere." Because I'd seen her, on a ship like the one that was moving toward us. It was the only ship that reminded me of the *Distant Voyager*. In fact, it reminded me of the *Distant Voyager* very much, only the *Distant Voyager* was still brand-spanking new and this ship looked ancient. Lovingly cared for, but still, old as dirt.

Looked down at Algar, who contrived to look innocent. Yeah, I wasn't buying it. He'd been here before, of that I was certain.

The viewscreen went live and sure enough, there were people I recognized. They weren't dressed anything like us, but they were us, or at least some of us.

Jamie was in front of Chuckie, who was standing next to this world's version of Reader. Both men were in leather pants and boots and brown shirts that were sort of like button-downs and sort of not.

Chuckie had on what looked like a leather lab coat with about a zillion pockets, all full of something, that just about hid the gunbelt and laser pistol. He had interesting goggles with a ton of lenses and levers shoved up onto his forehead and what looked like a porkpie hat on the back of his head. He was also wearing black gloves.

Reader was in a leather duster that had its pockets and guns on the inside and he, too, was wearing gloves. He had a cowboy hat on, albeit not a ten-gallon one. As with anything and everything else and any and every other universe, Reader looked ready for the runway.

That they also looked ready for a version of the Wild West while hanging out in space was a conundrum I'd ask about once we weren't wondering if they and the rest of the fleet of ships around us were going to try to blast us to smithereens.

This world's Jamie was in high boots and what looked like a leather romper, with a big bow on the top of her head, just like Minnie Mouse, only pink, not red with white polka dots. So some things were universal—in any universe, Jamie loved the color pink. She, too, was wearing gloves, which I could see because she waved at us. "I'm so glad you finally got here."

My Jamie shoved into my lap. Chose not to ask how she'd gotten unstrapped and away from everyone else—all twelve of us in here were pretty focused on the situation at hand, and the animals were never going to tell Jamie not to do something unless it was dangerous for her health and safety.

"I'm glad we're here, too," my Jamie said. "Can you make Mommy calm down and stop getting ready to shoot us?" Knew without asking that she didn't mean me.

Steampunk Jamie nodded. "I'm trying." She looked up at Chuckie. "Daddy, you need to make Mommy calm down."

"I can hear them, too, sweetheart," Chuckie said. He picked her up and hugged her. "I'll do what I can." He handed her to Reader.

Who hugged her and kissed her head. He looked at us suspiciously. "Charles may be willing to believe you, but I'm not."

"Yet," Steampunk Jamie said. "But, Daddy, I promise, they're here to help us."

"Daddy?" Jeff said. "She just called Chuck daddy."

Chuckie returned with this world's version of me. She was dressed in leather pants, had two ray guns strapped to her hips, and was wearing a rather jaunty bowler hat that had goggles on it that were grandiose but still couldn't hold a candle to the ones Chuckie was sporting. She had on a shirt with a leather corset over it, knee-high boots, and a sword strapped to her back. Like the others, she was wearing gloves.

Chuckie's arm was already around her waist and they joined Jamie and the guy I was now going to think of as James, just to make it easier on my brain. She put her other arm around his waist as she gave her Jamie a kiss.

"Wow, girlfriend," Reader said. "You look badass in Steampunk-wear."

"Thanks, I think. You, as always, look ready for your photoshoot. So, Cosmic Moi, am I right in thinking that you solved the issue of which of your best guy friends to marry by marrying both of them?"

Cosmic Moi grinned. "We aren't as uptight as our several-greats-grandparents were."

Heard Jeff muttering behind us. Reader laughed softly. "Jeff, in our universe I'm gay and Chuck's in love with Nathalie. Chill out."

Looked at Jeff over my shoulder. He didn't seem appeased. "What our James said, to infinity, Jeff." Turned back to the screen. "So, do you guys recognize anyone else on our ship? It's just the twelve of us and our animal companions, and you should be able to see all of us."

"Why are we being so chatty?" Siler asked from the back.

"Because they're us, and they're not our enemies any more than we're theirs."

"That's not quite true," Cosmic Moi said, voice tight. "I see one of our enemies—our biggest enemy, to be frank—sitting behind James."

We all looked at Jeff. Who looked as confused as the rest of us likely felt. "What? What the hell? How am I an enemy of these people?"

"Because," Cosmic Moi said, voice like ice, "you're King Jeffrey of Alpha Four and what's been forced to become the Annocusal Royal Empire, and the one who made an alliance with the Z'porrah and betrayed the entire Consortium of Aligned Systems. You're considered Galactic Enemy Number One and we are just thrilled to pieces that we're going to be the ones who get to kill you, you vicious, murdering scum."

Gini Koch used to live in Hell's Orientation Area (aka Phoenix, Arizona) and now lives in Hotlanta (aka Atlanta, Georgia) because any kind of heat is better than any kind of cold. She works her butt off (sadly, not literally) by day and writes by night with the rest of the beautiful people. She lives with her awesome husband, four dogs (aka The Canine Death Squad), and two cats (aka The Killer Kitties). She has one very wonderful and spoiled daughter, who will still tell you she's not as spoiled as the pets (and she'd be right).

When she's not writing, Gini spends her time cracking wise, staring at pictures of good looking leading men for "inspiration", teaching her pets to "bring it", and driving her husband insane asking, "Have I told you about this story idea yet?" She listens to every kind of music 24/7 (from Lifehouse to Pitbull and everything in between, particularly Aerosmith and Smash Mouth) and is a proud comics geek-girl willing to discuss at any time why Wolverine is the best superhero ever (even if Deadpool does get all the best lines).

You can reach Gini via her website (www.ginikoch.com), email (gini@ginikoch.com), Facebook (facebook.com/Gini.Koch), Facebook Fan Page: Hairspray & Rock 'n' Roll (facebook.com /GiniKochAuthor), Pinterest page (pinterest.com/ginikoch), Twitter (@GiniKoch), or her Official Fan Site, the Alien Collective Virtual HQ (thealiencollectivevirtualhq.blogspot.com/).

Gini Koch
The Alien *Novels*

"Told with clever wit and non-stop pacing.... Blends diplomacy, action, and sense of humor into a memorable reading experience."   —*Kirkus*

"Amusing and interesting...a hilarious romp in the vein of *Men in Black* or *Ghostbusters*."   —*VOYA*

To Order Call: 1-800-788-6262
www.dawbooks.com

Celia Jerome
The Willow Tate *Novels*

"Readers will love the first Willow Tate book. Willow is funny, brave and open to possibilities most people would not have even considered as she meets her perfect foil in Thaddeus Grant, a British agent assigned to look over the strange occurrences following Willow like a shadow. Together they make a wonderful pair and readers will love their unconventional courtship."   —*RT Book Review*

TROLLS IN THE HAMPTONS
978-0-7564-0630-1

NIGHT MARES IN THE HAMPTONS
978-0-7564-0663-9

FIRE WORKS IN THE HAMPTONS
978-0-7564-0688-2

LIFE GUARDS IN THE HAMPTONS
978-0-7564-0725-4

SAND WITCHES IN THE HAMPTONS
978-0-7564-0767-4

To Order Call: 1-800-788-6262
www.dawbooks.com

Lisanne Norman

The *Sholan Alliance* Series

"This is fun escapist fare, entertaining..."   —*Locus*

"Will hold you spellbound."
—*Romantic Times*

To Order Call: 1-800-788-6262
www.dawbooks.com

Jacey Bedford
The Psi-Tech Novels

"Space opera isn't dead; instead, delightfully, it has grown up."　　—Jaine Fenn,
author of *Principles of Angels*

"A well-defined and intriguing tale set in the not-too-distant future.... Everything is undeniably creative and colorful, from the technology to foreign planets to the human (and humanoid) characters."
—*RT Book Reviews*

"Bedford mixes romance and intrigue in this promising debut.... Readers who crave high adventure and tense plots will enjoy this voyage into the future."
—*Publishers Weekly*

Empire of Dust
978-0-7564-1016-2

Crossways
978-0-7564-1017-9

Nimbus
978-0-7564-1189-3

To Order Call: 1-800-788-6262
www.dawbooks.com

Jim C. Hines

Janitors of the Post-Apocalypse

Terminal Alliance
978-0-7564-1274-6

and coming in 2019
Terminal Uprising
978-0-7564-1277-7

To Order Call: 1-800-788-6262
www.dawbooks.com